"Pa⋯   it
be ⋯   l-
cen⋯   s
betᵥ⋯   d
Fra⋯   c
of l⋯

"Th⋯   ,
mu⋯
crin⋯   ₃
thro⋯   ᵈ
inte⋯   -
men⋯   y
beh⋯   ₁
194⋯   ₁
whic⋯   t
mon⋯

"*The*⋯   ₁
kind⋯
veye⋯   ₃
also⋯
the s⋯
zer ⋯

"This book is in fact the story of three men who loved dogs: the young narrator, the cold-blooded assassin with his pedigree canines and Trotsky himself. It is this insight into their characters, this glimpse of tenderness within, which redeems the leading personages from being mere historical ciphers, and Padura bestows the novelist's gift of turning them into living human beings for whom one can feel pity and fear. When this novel was published in Spanish five years ago, it received literary acclaim across Europe and rightly so, for it is a monumental work." *Independent*

"As such, like fellow novelist Pedro Juan Gutiérrez, Padura writes along the razor's edge. In his detective novels, he cagily navigated a quasi-permissible space, but in *The Man Who Loved Dogs* he finally lets it rip. Although Fidel Castro is never mentioned by name, his creation – the Cuban revolution – is rendered here as a crumbling tropical gulag. It is a calculated risk by Padura, a keen student of Cuban chess, and one based on the fact that there is a wider opening today than ever before on the island since the revolution. Moreover, as Cuba's greatest living writer and one who is inching toward the pantheon occupied by Gabriel García Márquez and Mario Vargas Llosa, Padura may well now be untouchable." **Washington Post**

"Leonardo Padura, known for his detective novels, has made his entrance to the Latin American Modernist canon by writing a Russian novel. Its Russian quality comes not only from its length and the fact that it returns constantly to Moscow, but from its Tolstoyan passion for historical trifles and Dostoyevskyan pleasure in examining the moral life of its characters... *The Man Who Loved Dogs* tells the story of the exile of Leon Trotsky, who was assassinated by Ramon Mercader in Mexico on August 20, 1940." **New York Times**

Other Bitter Lemon Press books
by Leonardo Padura

Havana Red
Havana Black
Havana Blue
Havana Gold
Havana Fever

THE MAN WHO LOVED DOGS

Leonardo Padura

Translated from
the Spanish by Anna Kushner

BITTER LEMON PRESS
LONDON

BITTER LEMON PRESS

First published in the United Kingdom in 2014 by
Bitter Lemon Press, 37 Arundel Gardens, London W11 2LW

www.bitterlemonpress.com

First published in Spanish as *El hombre que amaba a los perros*
by Tusquets Editores, S.A., Barcelona, 2009

Bitter Lemon Press gratefully acknowledges the financial
assistance of the Arts Council of England

A CIP record for this book is available
from the British Library

Paperback ISBN 978-1908524-447
Hardback ISBN 978-1908524-102
eBook ISBN 978-1908524-119

Printed and bound by
TJ International, Padstow, Cornwall

Supported using public funding by
ARTS COUNCIL
ENGLAND
LOTTERY FUNDED

Thirty years later, still, for Lucía

This happened when only the dead were smiling
Glad to have found their resting place at last . . .
—ANNA AKHMATOVA, *Requiem*

Life . . . is wider than history.
—GREGORIO MARAÑON,
Tiberio: Historia de un resentimiento

London, August 22, 1940 (TASS)—London radio has today announced: "In a Mexico City hospital, Leon Trotsky died as a result of a fractured skull sustained in an attack perpetrated the previous day by a person in his innermost circle."

LEANDRO SÁNCHEZ SALAZAR: Wasn't he suspicious?

DETAINEE: No.

L.S.S.: Didn't you think that he was a defenseless old man and that you were acting with cowardice?

D: I wasn't thinking anything.

L.S.S.: You were walking over from where he fed the rabbits, what were you talking about?

D: I don't remember if I was talking or not.

L.S.S.: He didn't see when you took out the ice axe?

D: No.

L.S.S.: Immediately after you stabbed him, what did the gentleman do?

D: He jumped as if he had gone mad, he screamed like a madman, the sound of that scream is something I will remember for the rest of my life.

L.S.S.: Tell me what he did, let's see.

D: A . . . a . . . a . . . ah . . . ! But he was very loud.

(From Mexico City's chief of secret police Colonel Leandro Sánchez Salazar's interrogation of Jacques Mornard Vandendreschs, or Frank Jacson, the presumed killer of Leon Trotsky, the night of Friday, August 23, and the early hours of Saturday, August 24, 1940.)

PART ONE

1

Havana, 2004

"Rest in peace" were the pastor's last words.

If that well-worn phrase, so shamelessly dramatic in the mouth of that figure, had ever held any meaning, it was at that exact moment, as the grave diggers nonchalantly lowered Ana's coffin into the open grave. The certainty that life can be the worst hell, and that the remains of fear and pain were disappearing forever with that descent, overcame me with paltry relief. I wondered if I wasn't in some way envious of my wife's final passage toward silence, since being dead, totally and truly dead, for some can be the closest thing to a blessing from that God with whom Ana tried to involve me, without much success, in the last years of her difficult life.

As soon as the grave diggers finished moving over the stone and placed the wreaths of flowers our friends had brought on the grave, I turned and walked away, resolved to escape the hands patting my shoulder and the habitual expressions of condolence that we always feel obliged to offer. Because at that moment every other word in the world is superfluous: only the pastor's well-worn formula had meaning and I didn't want to lose it. *Rest* and *peace*: what Ana had finally attained and what I also asked for.

When I sat down inside the Pontiac to await Daniel's arrival, I knew that I was about to pass out, and I was sure that if my friend didn't remove me from the cemetery, I would have been unable to find the way back to my life. The September sun was burning the top of the car, but I didn't feel up to moving to any other place. With what little strength I had left, I closed my eyes to control the vertigo of loss and fatigue while I felt the acidic sweat running down over my eyelids and cheeks, springing from my armpits, neck, arms. It was soaking my back scorched by the vinyl seat until it turned into a warm current that flowed down my legs in search of the cistern of my shoes. I wondered if that foul sweat and my deep exhaustion were not the prelude to my molecular disintegration, or at least the heart attack that would kill me in the next few minutes. It seemed to me that either could be an easy, even desirable solution, although frankly unfair: I didn't have the right to force my friends to bear two funerals in three days.

"Are you ill, Iván?" Dany's question, through the window, surprised me. "Holy shit, look at how much you're sweating . . ."

"I want to leave . . . But I don't know how, dammit . . ."

"We're leaving, my friend, don't worry. Wait a minute, let me give a few pesos to the grave diggers," he said, my friend's words transmitting a patent sense of life and reality that seemed strange to me, decidedly remote.

Once again I closed my eyes and remained motionless, sweating, until the car was set in motion. Only once the air coming through the window began to calm me down did I dare to raise my eyelids. Before leaving the cemetery, I was able to see the last row of tombs and mausoleums, eaten away by the sun, weather, and oblivion, as dead as their inhabitants, and—with or without any reason for doing so at that moment—I again asked myself why, amid so many possibilities, some faraway scientists had chosen my name specifically to baptize the ninth tropical storm of that season.

Although at this point in my life I've learned—or rather have been taught, and not in a very nice way—not to believe in chance, the coincidences were too many that led the meteorologists to decide, many months ahead of time, that they would call that storm "Ivan"—a masculine name starting with the ninth letter of the alphabet, in Spanish, that had never been used before for that purpose. The fetus of what would become Ivan was spawned by the meeting of ominous clouds in the vicinity of Cape

Verde, but it wasn't until a few days later, already baptized and converted into a hurricane with all of its properties, that it would rear its head in the Caribbean to place us in its ravenous sight . . . You'll see why I think that I have reasons enough to believe that only twisted fate could have determined that that particular cyclone, one of history's fiercest, would carry my name, just when another hurricane was closing in on my existence.

Even though it had been quite a long time—perhaps too long—since Ana and I had known that her end was decreed, the many years during which we dragged her illnesses had accustomed us to living with them. But the news that her osteoporosis—probably caused by the vitamin-deficient polyneuritis unleashed in the most difficult years of the crisis in the 1990s—had developed into bone cancer, had made us face the evidence of an end that was near, and given me the macabre proof that only a perverse fate could be responsible for burdening my wife specifically with that illness.

From the beginning of the year, Ana's decline had accelerated, although it was in the middle of July, three months after the definitive diagnosis, that her final agony began. Although Gisela, Ana's sister, came frequently to help me, I practically had to stop working to take care of my wife; and if we survived those months, it was thanks to the support of friends like Dany, Anselmo, or Frank the doctor, who frequently came through our small apartment in the neighborhood of Lawton to drop off some supplies drawn from the wretched harvests that, for their own subsistence, they managed to obtain in the most devious ways. More than once, Dany offered to come help me with Ana, but I rejected his overtures, since pain and misery are among the few things that, when shared, always multiply.

The scene we lived between the cracked walls of our apartment was as depressing as can be imagined, although the worst thing, under the circumstances, was the strange power with which Ana's broken body clung to life, even against its owner's will.

In the early days of September, when Hurricane Ivan, having reached its full potential, had just crossed the Atlantic and was nearing the island of Grenada, Ana had an unexpected period of lucidity and an unforeseen relief to her pain. As it had been her decision not to go to the hospital, a neighboring nurse and our friend Frank had taken over the task of providing her with intravenous fluids and the dose of morphine that kept

5

her in a startling lethargy. Upon seeing that reaction, Frank warned me that this was the denouement and recommended that I give the patient only those foods that she asked for, not insisting on the intravenous fluids and, as long as she wasn't complaining of pain, stopping all drugs to thus give her some final days of intelligence. Then, as if her life had returned to normal, an Ana with various broken bones and very open eyes became interested again in the world around her. With the television and radio on, she fixed her attention in an obsessive way on the path of the hurricane that had initiated its deathly dance devastating the island of Grenada, where it had left more than twenty dead. On many occasions throughout those days, my wife lectured me on the hurricane's characteristics, one of the strongest in meteorological history, and attributed its elevated powers to the climate change the planet was undergoing, a mutation of nature that could do away with the human species if the necessary measures were not taken, she told me, completely convinced. That my dying wife was thinking of everyone else's future only added to the pain I was already suffering.

While the storm neared Jamaica with the obvious intention of later penetrating eastern Cuba, Ana developed a sort of meteorological excitement capable of keeping her on constant alert, a tension she escaped only when sleep conquered her for two or three hours. All of her expectations were related to Ivan's doings, with the number of dead it left in its path—one in Trinidad, five in Venezuela, another in Colombia, five more in Dominica, fifteen in Jamaica, she added, counting on her crooked fingers—and, above all, the calculations of what it would destroy if it penetrated Cuba through any of the points marked as possible trajectories deduced by the specialists. Ana experienced a kind of cosmic communication at the point of the symbiotic confluence of two bodies that know they are destined to consume themselves in the span of a few days, and I began to speculate whether the illness and the drugs had not made her crazy. I also thought that if the hurricane didn't come through soon and Ana didn't calm down, I would be the one who ended up going crazy.

The most critical period—for Ana and, logically, for each of the island's inhabitants—occurred when Ivan, with sustained winds of approximately 150 miles per hour, began to pass over the seas to the south of Cuba. The hurricane was moving with a lazy arrogance, as if it were perversely choosing the point at which it would inevitably turn north and break the country in two, leaving an enormous wake of ruins and death. With bated breath and her senses clinging to the radio and the color television that a neighbor had lent us, a Bible near one hand and our dog Truco beneath the other, Ana cried, laughed, cursed, and prayed with a strength that was not her own. For more than forty-eight hours she remained in that state, watching Ivan's careful approach as if her thoughts and prayers were indispensable to keeping the hurricane as far away as possible from the island, blocking it in that almost incredible westward path from which it couldn't resolve to deviate to the north and flatten the country, as all historic, atmospheric, and planetary logic predicted.

The night of September 12, when information from satellites and radars and the unanimous opinion of meteorologists around the world were certain that Ivan would chart a course for the north and that with its battering gusts, gigantic waves, and rain squalls, it would rejoice in the final destruction of Havana, Ana asked me to remove from the wall of our room the dark, corroded wooden cross that twenty-seven years before the sea had given me—the driftwood cross—and place it at the foot of the bed. Then she begged me to make her a very hot hot chocolate and some toast with butter. If what was supposed to happen happened, that would be her last supper, because the battered ceiling of our apartment would not withstand the force of the hurricane, and she, it goes without saying, refused to move from there. After drinking the hot chocolate and nibbling a piece of toast, Ana asked me to lay the driftwood cross next to her and began to pray with her eyes fixed on the ceiling and on the wooden beams guaranteeing its balance and, perhaps, with her imagination devoted to playing out the images of the apocalypse lying in wait for the city.

The morning of September 14, the meteorologists announced a miracle: Ivan had turned toward the north at last, but it had done so so far to the west of the designated zone that it barely brushed the westernmost point of the island without causing any major damage. Apparently the hurricane had felt remorse for the many calamities piling up, and had steered away from us, convinced that its passing through our country would have been an excess of bad fate. Worn out by so much praying, with her stomach ravaged by lack of food, but satisfied by what she considered to be a personal victory, Ana fell asleep after hearing confirmation of that cosmic whim, and in the grimace that had become habitual on her lips there was something very much like a smile. Ana's breathing, strained for so many days, was relaxed again and, along with her fingers caressing Truco's wiry hair, was the only sign in the next two days that she was still alive.

On September 16, practically at nightfall, while the hurricane started to disintegrate on U.S. soil and to lose the already diminished force of its winds, Ana stopped caressing our dog and, a few minutes later, stopped breathing. She was at last resting, I'd like to think, in eternal peace.

In due time you will understand why this story, which is not the story of my life (although it also is), begins as it does. And although you still don't know who I am or have any idea what I'm going to tell you, perhaps you will have understood something: Ana was a very important person to me. So much so that, to a large degree, it is because of her that this story exists—in black and white, I mean.

Ana crossed my path at one of those all so frequent times during which I was teetering on the edge of a precipice. The glorious Soviet Union had started its death rattle, and the lightning bolts of the crisis that would devastate the whole country in the 1990s were beginning to come down on us. It was predictable that one of the first consequences of the national debacle had been the closing, due to a lack of paper, ink, and electricity, of the veterinary medicine magazine where for ages I had worked as a proofreader. Just like dozens of press workers, from typesetters to editors, I had ended up in an artisans' workshop where we were supposed to devote ourselves, for an indefinite period of time, to making macramé crafts and polished seed decorations that, everyone knew, no one would be able to or dare to buy. Three days into this new and useless destiny, without even having the decency to quit, I fled from that honeycomb of enraged and frustrated bees and, thanks to my friends the veterinarians whose texts I have reviewed so many times or even rewritten, I was able to start working shortly after as a sort of ubiquitous helper in the likewise poverty-stricken clinic of the University of Havana's School of Veterinary Medicine.

Sometimes I am so overly suspicious that I come to wonder if that whole series of global, national, and personal decisions (they were even talking about "the end of history," just when we had begun to have an idea about what the history of the twentieth century was) had as its only objective that I be the one who received, at the end of a rainy afternoon, the desperate and dripping young woman who, carrying a shaggy poodle in her arms, appeared at the clinic and begged me to save her dog, which was afflicted with an intestinal blockage. Since it was after four o'clock and the doctors had already left, I explained to the girl (she and the dog were trembling from the cold and, observing them, I felt my voice falter) that we couldn't do anything. Then I saw her break into tears: her dog was dying, she said to me; the two veterinarians who had seen him didn't have anesthesia to operate on him; and since there weren't any buses in the city, she had come walking in the rain with her dog in her arms, and I *had* to do something, for the love of God. Something? I still ask myself how it's possible that I dared to, or if in reality I was already wanting to dare to; but after explaining to the girl that I was not a veterinarian and asking her to write her petition on a piece of paper and sign it, thus freeing me of all responsibility, the dying Tato became my first surgical patient. If the God invoked by the girl had ever decided to protect a dog, it had to be that afternoon, since the operation—about which I had read so much and seen carried out more than once—was a success in practice.

Depending on how you look at it, Ana was the woman that I most needed or who was least advisable for me at that moment: fifteen years younger than me, too undemanding in the way of material things, horrible and wasteful as a cook, a passionate dog lover, and gifted with a strange sense of reality that made her go from the most eccentric ideas to the firmest and most rational decisions. From the beginning of our relationship she had the ability to make me feel like I had been looking for her for many, many years. That's why I didn't find it strange when, a few weeks into the calm and very satisfactory sexual relationship that began the first day I went to the house where Ana lived with a friend to give Tato an IV, the girl threw her belongings into two backpacks and, with her ration book, a box of books, and her nearly recovered poodle, moved into my damp and already peeling apartment in Lawton.

Besieged by hunger, blackouts, the devaluation of our salaries, and a transportation standstill—amid many other evils—Ana and I lived through a period of ecstasy. Our respective scrawniness, accentuated by the long trips we made on the Chinese bicycles that our workplaces had sold us, turned us into almost ethereal beings, a new species of mutants capable, nonetheless, of dedicating our remaining energies to making

9

love, to talking for hours, and to reading like fiends—for Ana, poetry; for me, a return to novels after a long time without them. But they were also unreal years, lived in a dark and sluggish country, always hot, that was falling apart day by day without quite falling into the troglodytic primitiveness that threatened us. And they were years in which not even the most devastating scarcity was able to stamp out the joy that living together brought Ana and me, like the shipwrecked who tie themselves to one another to either jointly save themselves or perish together.

Apart from the hunger and the material shortcomings of all kinds that besieged us—although between us we considered them outside us and inevitable, and thus foreign to us—the only sadly personal episodes we experienced at that time were the revelation of the vitamin-deficient polyneuritis that Ana began to suffer from and, later on, the death of Tato at the age of sixteen. The loss of the poodle affected my wife so much that, a couple of weeks later, I tried to alleviate the situation by picking up a stray pup infected with mange, whom Ana immediately started to call "Truco" due to his ability to hide, and whom she fed with rations taken from our paltry survivors' diet.

Ana and I had achieved a level of such rapport that, one night, under a blackout, with ill-contained hunger, unease, and heat (how was it possible that it was always so damned hot and that even the moon seemed to shed less light than before?)—as if I were just carrying out a natural need—I began to tell her the story of the meetings that, fourteen years before, I had had with that character whom I had always called, from the very day I met him, "the man who loved dogs." Until that night on which, almost without prologue and as an outburst, I decided to tell Ana that story, I had never revealed to anyone the subject of my conversations with that man and, less still, my delayed, repressed, and often forgotten desire to write the story he had confided in me. So that she would have a better idea of how I'd been affected by the proximity to that figure and the dreadful story of hate, betrayal, and death that he'd given me, I even gave her some notes to read that many years before, from the ignorance I wallowed in at the time, and almost against my own will, I had not been able to keep myself from writing. She had barely finished reading them when Ana stared at me until the weight of her black eyes—those eyes that would always look like the most living thing of her body—began to berate me and she finally said, with appalling conviction, that she didn't understand how it was possible that I, especially I, had not written a book about that story that God had put in my path. And looking into her eyes—those same eyes now being eaten by worms—I gave her the answer that had slipped away from me so many times, but the only one that, because it was Ana, I could give her:

"Fear kept me from writing it."

2

The icy mist swallowed the outline of the last huts, and the caravan again plunged into that distressing whiteness, so limitless, without anything to rest your gaze on. It was at that moment that Lev Davidovich was able to understand why the inhabitants of that rough corner of the world have insisted, since the dawn of time, on worshipping stones.

The six days that the police and the exiles had spent traveling from Alma-Ata to Frunze, through Kyrgyzstan's icy steppe, enveloped by an absolute whiteness in which any notion of time and distance was lost, had served to reveal the futility of all human pride and the exact dimension of its cosmic insignificance in the face of the essential power of the eternal. The waves of snow coming down from the sky, in which all trace of the sun had vanished and that threatened to devour everything that dared to challenge its devastating persistence, proved to be an indomitable force which no man could stand up to; it was then that the apparition of a tree, the outline of the mountain, the frozen gully of a river, or a simple rock in the middle of the steppe, turned into something so noteworthy as to become an object of veneration. The natives of those remote deserts have glorified stones, because they assure in their capacity for resistance, that there is a force, enclosed forever inside of them, like the fruit of an eternal will. A few months earlier, while already in the midst of his deportation, Lev Davidovich had read that the sage known as Ibn Battuta, and farther east by the name of Shams ad-Dina, was the one who revealed to his people that the act of kissing a sacred stone results in a comforting spiritual pleasure, since upon doing so the lips experience a sweetness so deep that it leads to the desire to keep kissing it until the end of time. For that reason, wherever there is a sacred stone, it is forbidden to wage battles or kill enemies, as the pureness of hope must be preserved. The visceral wisdom inspiring that doctrine seemed so lucid that Lev Davidovich asked himself if the revolution really had any right to disrupt an ancestral order, perfect in its own way and impossible for a European mind affected by rational and cultural prejudices to gauge. But the political activists sent from Moscow were already in those lands, focused on turning the nomadic tribes into collective farm workers, their mountain goats into state livestock, and in showing Turkmens, Kazakhs, Uzbeks, and Kyrgyzstanis that their atavistic custom of worshipping stones or trees in the steppe was a deplorable anti-Marxist attitude that they should renounce in the name of progress of a humanity capable of understanding that, at the end of the day, a stone is only a stone and that you don't feel anything besides simple physical contact when cold and exhaustion have eaten up all human will, and in the middle of frozen desert, a man armed with only his faith finds a piece of stone and takes it to his lips.

A week before, Lev Davidovich had seen how they wrested away from him the last few stones that still allowed him to orient himself on the turbulent political map of his country. He would later write that that morning he'd awoken petrified and overwhelmed by a bad premonition. Convinced that he was not just shaking because of the cold, he had tried to control his spasms and had managed to make out the tattered chair-turned-night-table in the shadows. He had felt around until he found his glasses, the shakes making him fail twice at placing the metallic stems over his ears. In the milky light of the winter dawn, he had finally managed to spy on the wall the almanac adorned with the image of some statues of young people from the Leninist Komsomol that had been sent to him from Moscow a few days before without his knowing who sent it, since the envelope and the possible letter from the sender had disappeared, like all of his correspondence in recent months. Only at that moment, as the numbered evidence of the calendar and the rough wall it hung from brought him back to his reality, did he have the certainty that he had woken up with that anxiety due to having lost the notion of where he was and when he was waking. For that reason he felt a palpable relief upon discovering that it was January 20, 1929, and he was in Alma-Ata, lying on a squeaking cot, and that at his side was his wife, Natalia Sedova.

Taking care not to move the straw mattress, he sat up. He immediately felt the pressure of Maya's snout on his knees: his dog greeted him, and he rubbed her ears, in which he found warmth and a comforting sense of reality. Dressed in a rawhide cloak and a scarf around his neck, he emptied his bladder in the toilet and moved to the room that was simultaneously kitchen and dining room, already lit by two gas lamps and heated by the stove on which rested the samovar, prepared by his personal jailer. In the mornings he had always preferred coffee, but he had already resigned himself to accept what was assigned to him by Alma-Ata's miserly bureaucrats and its secret police guards. Seated at the table close by the stove, he began taking a few sips of that strong tea, too green for his liking, from a china cup while he caressed Maya's head, without suspecting that he would soon receive the most perfidious confirmation that his life and even his death had ceased to belong to him.

Exactly one year before, he had been confined to Alma-Ata, at the limit of Asian Russia, closer to the Chinese border than to the last station of any Russian railway. In reality, ever since he, his wife, and their son Liova had stepped out of the snow-covered truck in which they had covered the final stretch of their road to a malicious deportation, Lev Davidovich had begun to wait for death. He was convinced that if by a miracle he survived malaria and dysentery, the order to eliminate him was going to come sooner or later ("If he dies so far away, by the time people find out about it, he will already be well buried," his enemies thought, without a doubt). But while they waited for that to happen, his adversaries had decided to make the most of their time and devoted themselves to annihilating him from history and memory, which had also become the party's property. The publication of his books, just when he had reached the twenty-first volume, had been halted, and an operation was being carried out to remove copies from bookstores and libraries; at the same time, his name, slandered at first and then discredited, began to be erased from historical accounts, tributes, newspaper articles, even from photographs, until they made him feel how he was turning into an absolute nothing, a black hole in the memory of the people. For that reason, Lev Davidovich thought that if anything had saved his life until then, it was fear of the schism that the decision to eliminate him could cause, if there was indeed something still capable of altering the consciousness of a country deformed by fear, slogans, and lies. But one year of enforced silence, accumulating low blows without any chance to reciprocate, seeing how the remains of the opposition he had led were dismantled, convinced him that his disappearance was becoming more necessary every day for the macabre decline toward despotism of the great proletarian revolution.

That year of 1928 had been, he didn't even doubt it, the worst of his life, even though he had lived through many other terrible times confined in Czarist jails or wandering penniless and with little hope through half of Europe. But during each disheartening circumstance, he had been sustained by the conviction that all sacrifices were necessary when aspiring to the greater good of the revolution. Why should he fight now, if the revolution had already been in power for ten years? The answer was becoming clearer to him every day: to remove it from the perverse abyss of a reaction that was intent on killing human civilization's greatest ideals. But how? That was still the great question, and the possible responses crossed his mind, in a chaos of contradictions with the capacity to paralyze him in the midst of his strange struggle as a marginalized Communist against other Communists who had stolen the revolution.

With censored and even falsified information he had followed the miserable start of a process of ideological destabilization, of the confusion of political positions that had been undefined until recently, through which Stalin and his minions stripped him of his words and ideas, by the malevolent procedure of appropriating the same programs through which he had been harassed to the point of being thrown out of the party.

At that moment of deep thought, he heard the door to the house open with a creak of frozen wood and saw the soldier Dreitser enter, dragging in a cloud of cold air. The new head of the GPU watch group tended to demonstrate his power by entering the house without deigning to knock at that door which had been stripped of locks. Covered by a hat with ear flaps and a leather cloak, the policeman had begun to shake off the snow without daring to look at him, because he knew that he was the bearer of an order that only one man in the entire territory of the Soviet Union was capable of devising and, furthermore, of carrying out.

15

Three weeks earlier, Dreitser had arrived as a sort of black messenger from the Kremlin, bearing new restrictions and the ultimatum that if Trotsky didn't halt his oppositionist campaign amid the colonies of deportees, he would be completely isolated from political life. What campaign, since it had been months since he could send or receive correspondence? And what new isolation was he being threatened with if not death? To make his control more evident, the agent had decreed a prohibition on Lev Davidovich and his son Lev Sedov going out to hunt, knowing that with those snowfalls it was impossible to hunt. Nevertheless, he confiscated shotguns and cartridges in order to demonstrate his will and his power.

When he managed to free himself of the snow layered on his coat, Dreitser approached the samovar to serve himself tea. By the motion of the wind, Lev Davidovich had deduced that it must be less than thirty degrees below zero outside and that the empire of interminable snow, with the exception of some redeeming stones, was the only thing that existed on that damned steppe. Following his first sip of tea, Dreitser had at last spoken and, with his Siberian bear accent, told him that he had a letter that came from Moscow. It wasn't difficult for him to imagine that a letter capable of passing postal control could only bring the worst news, and this was confirmed by the fact that for the first time Dreitser had addressed him without calling him "*Comrade* Trotsky," the last title he'd kept in his turbulent decline from the heights of power to the solitude of banishment.

Ever since receiving the news of the death of his daughter Nina from tuberculosis in July, Lev Davidovich had lived with the fear that other family misfortunes would occur, a by-product of regular life or, as he feared more with each passing day, of hate. Zina, his other daughter from his first marriage, had had a nervous breakdown, and her husband Plato Volkov was, like other oppositionists, already in a work camp in the Arctic Circle. Fortunately, his son Liova was with them, and the young Seriozha, the *Homo apoliticus* of the family, remained a stranger to partisan struggles.

Natalia Sedova's voice, saying good morning while simultaneously cursing the cold, reached him at that moment. He waited for her to enter, met with joy by Maya, and felt his heart shrink: Would he be capable of transmitting fatal news to Natasha about the fate of her beloved Seriozha? With a mug in her hands she had sat down in the chair and he watched her. *She's still a beautiful woman*, he thought, according to what he would write later. Then he told her that they had correspondence from Moscow and the woman also became tense.

Dreitser had left his mug next to the stove to rummage in his pockets in search of his pack of unbearable Turkmeni cigarettes and, as if taking advantage of the act, stuck his hand in the interior compartment of his cloak, from which he removed the yellow envelope. For a second it seemed that he had the intention of opening it, but he chose to place the packet on the table. Trying to hide his anxiety, Lev Davidovich looked at Natalia, then at the stampless envelope where his name was imprinted, and threw the cold tea in the corner. He handed the mug to Dreitser, who was forced to take it and return to the samovar to refill it. Although he had always had a flair for the theatrical, he understood that he was wasting his histrionics before that reduced audience, and without waiting for the tea he opened the envelope. It contained one sheet, typewritten, with the GPU seal and was undated. After replacing his glasses, he spent less than one minute reading it but remained silent, this time without any dramatic gestures: surprise at the incredible had left him speechless. Citizen Lev Davidovich Trotsky should leave the country within a period of twenty-four hours. His expulsion, without a specific destination, had been decided by virtue of the recently created Article 58/10, useful for everything, although in his case, according to the letter, he was accused of "carrying out counterrevolutionary campaigns in order to organize a clandestine party hostile to the Soviets . . ." Still silent, he passed the note to his wife.

Natalia Sedova, her hands atop the rough wooden table, looked at him, petrified by the severity of the decision that, rather than condemning them to freeze to death in some corner of the country, forced them to take the road to an exile that appeared like a dark cloud. Twenty-three years of a life together, sharing pains and successes, failures and glories, allowed Lev Davidovich to read the woman's thoughts through her blue eyes. Exiled, the leader who had moved the country's consciousness in 1905, who had made the uprising of October 1917 a triumph and had created an army in the midst of chaos and saved the revolution in those years of imperialist invasions and civil war? Banished for disagreements over political and economic strategy? she had thought. If it were not so pathetic, that order would have been risible.

As he stood up, he sarcastically asked Dreitser if he had any idea when and where the first congress of his "clandestine party" would take place, but the messenger limited himself to demanding that he confirm the receipt of the communication. In the margin of the order, Lev Davidovich wrote, "The GPU's decree, criminal in substance and illegal in form, has been communicated to me on the date of January 20, 1929." He signed it quickly and pegged the page with a dirty knife. Then he looked at his wife, who was still in shock, and asked her to wake Liova. They would barely have time to gather their papers and books. He walked to the bedroom, followed by Maya, as if impelled by haste, although in reality, Lev Davidovich had fled for fear that the police and his wife would see him cry over the impotence caused by humiliation and lies.

They ate their breakfast in silence and, as always, Lev Davidovich gave Maya some pieces of the soft part of the bread smeared with the rancid butter they were given. Later, Natalia Sedova would confess to him that at that moment, she had seen in his eyes, for the first time since they met, the dark flash of resignation, a frame of mind so removed from his attitude of a year before when, upon trying to deport him from Moscow, it had taken four men to drag him to the train station as he continued to scream and curse the faces of the Grave Diggers of the Revolution.

Followed by his dog, Lev Davidovich returned to the bedroom, where he had already begun to prepare the boxes in which he would place those papers that were all that remained of his belongings, but that were worth as much as or more to him than his life: essays, proclamations, military reports, and peace treaties that changed the fate of the world, but above all, hundreds, thousands of letters signed by Lenin, Plekhanov, Rosa Luxemburg, and so many other Bolsheviks, Mensheviks, revolutionary Socialists among whom he had lived and fought ever since, while still an adolescent, founding the romantic South Russian Workers' Union, with the outlandish idea of overthrowing the Czar.

The certainty of defeat pressed on his chest, as if a horse's hoof were crushing him and asphyxiating him. So he picked up his boot covers and his felt galoshes and took them to the dining room, where Liova was organizing files, and began to put his shoes on, to the young man's surprise, who asked him what he had in mind. Without answering him, he took the scarves hanging behind the door and, followed by his dog, went out into the wind, the snow, and the grayness of the morning. The storm, unleashed two days earlier, did not seem to have any intention of abating; and upon entering it, he felt how his body and his soul sank in the ice, while the air hurt the skin on his face. He took a few steps toward the street from which he could make out the foothills of the Tien Shan mountains, and it was as if he had hugged the white cloud until he melted into it. He whistled, demanding Maya's presence, and was relieved when the dog approached him. Resting his hand on the animal's head, he noticed how the snow began to cover him. If he remained there ten or fifteen minutes, he would turn into a frozen mass and his heart would stop, despite the coats. It could be a good solution, he thought. But if my henchmen won't kill me yet, he told himself, I won't do their work for them. Guided by Maya, he walked the few feet back to the cabin: Lev Davidovich knew that as long as he had life left in him, he still had bullets to shoot as well.

Natalia Sedova, Lev Sedov, and Lev Davidovich had sat down to drink one last tea as they waited for the police escort that would conduct them into exile. In the bedroom, the boxes of papers were ready, following a first sorting out in which they had put aside dozens of books that were considered dispensable. Early in the morning, one of the police picked up the discarded books and had barely taken them out of the cabin when he set fire to them after pouring gasoline on them.

Dreitser arrived around eleven. As usual, he entered without knocking and told them the trip would be postponed. Natalia Sedova, ever concerned with practical matters, asked him why he thought the storm would abate the following day. The head of the guards explained that he had just received the weather report but, above all, he knew because he could smell it in the air. It was then that Dreitser, once again in need of projecting his power, said that Maya the dog could not travel with them.

The Exile's reaction was so violent that it surprised the policeman: Maya was part of his family and was going with him or no one was going. Dreitser reminded him that he wasn't in any position to issue orders or threats, and Lev Davidovich agreed, but he reminded him that he could still do something crazy that would end the guard's career and send him back to Siberia—not to his hometown, but to one of those work camps that his boss in the GPU directed. When he observed the immediate effect of his words, Lev Davidovich understood that that man was under great pressure and decided to finish this game without showing any more cards: How was it possible that a Siberian could ask him to abandon a Russian wolfhound? And he lamented that Dreitser had never seen Maya hunt foxes in the frozen tundra. The policeman, slipping out the door, tried to demonstrate that he still had power: they could take the animal, but they would be responsible for cleaning up her shit.

Dreitser's Siberian sense of smell would be as wrong as the meteorologists' predictions, and the storm under which they left Alma-Ata, far from abating, grew as the bus moved through the steppe. In the afternoon (he knew it was afternoon only because the clocks indicated so), when they reached the village of Koshmanbet, he confirmed that they had spent seven hours to cover twenty miles of flat road under the ice.

The following day, heading over the frozen track, the bus managed to reach the mountain post of Kurdai, but the attempt to use a tractor to move the seven-car caravan in which they would all travel from that point on was useless and inhumane: seven members of the police escort froze to death along with a notable number of horses. Then Dreitser opted for the sleighs on which they would glide for two more days, until Pishpek was in sight, on flat roads again, where they got into cars.

Frunze, with its mosques and aroma of goat fat escaping from the chimneys, seemed like a saving oasis to the deporters and the deported alike. For the first time since leaving Alma-Ata, they were able to bathe and sleep in beds, and be relieved of the foul-smelling coats whose weight practically prevented them from walking. Confirming that in misery every detail is a luxury, Lev Davidovich even had the opportunity to taste a fragrant Turkish coffee, which he drank until he felt his heart speed up.

That night, before they went to bed, the soldier Igor Dreitser sat down to drink coffee with the Trotskys and inform them that his mission at the head of the guards ended there. Many weeks of cohabitation with the sour-faced Siberian had turned him into a habitual presence, so at the moment of his departure Lev Davidovich wished him good luck and reminded him that it didn't matter who the party secretary was. It was all the same if it was Lenin, Stalin, Zinoviev, or him . . . Men like Dreitser worked for the country, not for a leader. After listening to him, Dreitser shook his hand and, surprisingly, told him that, despite the circumstances, it had been an honor for him to know him; but what truly intrigued him was when the agent, practically in a whisper, informed him that, although the order specified that they burn all of the deportee's papers, he had decided only to burn a few books. Lev Davidovich had barely managed to process that strange information when he felt the Siberian pressure of Dreitser's hand on his fingers as the soldier turned around and went out into the darkness and snow.

With the changing of the police team, at the head of which an agent named Bulanov was placed, the deportees held the hope of piercing the veil and finding out the fates assigned to them. However, Bulanov could only inform them that they would take a special train in the Frunze depot, without the order specifying toward where. So much mystery, thought Lev Davidovich, could only be the product of the fear of the improbable but nonetheless dreaded reactions of his decimated followers in Moscow. He also wondered if that entire operation was nothing but an orchestrated pantomime to create confusion and control opinions, a preferred technique of Stalin's, who on various occasions throughout that year had made rumors circulate about his imminent exile, which, though later denied with greater or less emphasis, had served to spread the idea and pave the way for the sentence that the people would only have news of after the fact.

Only during the months prior to the expulsion, while suffering a political defeat that managed to tie his hands, had Lev Davidovich begun to appreciate, seriously and with horror, the magnitude of Stalin's manipulative abilities. Incapable of appreciating the Georgian ex-seminarian's genius for intrigue, his shamelessness in lying and putting together shady deals, Lev Davidovich understood too late that he had underestimated his intelligence, and that Stalin, educated in the catacombs of the clandestine struggle, had learned all the forms of subterranean demolition. He now applied them, for his personal benefit, in search of the same ends for which the Bolshevik Party had used them before: to achieve power. The way in which he disarmed and displaced Lev Davidovich while using the vanity and fears of men who never seemed to have fears or vanities before, the calculated turns of his forces from one extreme to another of the political spectrum, had been a masterwork of manipulation that, to crown the Georgian's victory, had benefited from the unpredictable blindness and pride of his rival.

Beyond orchestrating his expulsion from the party, and now from the country, Stalin's great victory had been to turn Trotsky's voice into the incarnation of the internal enemy of the revolution, of the nation's stability, of the Leninist legacy, and had crushed him with the wall of propaganda that Lev Davidovich himself had contributed to creating, and against which, due to inviolable principles, he could not oppose if it meant risking the permanence of that system. The struggle on which he had to focus from that moment on would be one against men, against a faction, never against the Idea. But how to fight against them if those men had appropriated the Idea and presented themselves to the country and the world like the very incarnation of the proletarian revolution? It was a question he would continue to ponder after his deportation.

The railroad odyssey of their pilgrimage began as soon as they left Frunze. The snow imposed a slow rhythm on the old English locomotive, which pulled four cars. Throughout his years at the head of the Red Army, when he had to cover the geography of a country deep in civil war, Lev Davidovich came to know almost the entire network of the nation's railways. On that special train he had traveled, by his calculations, enough miles to go around the world five and a half times. Because of that, after leaving Frunze, he was able to deduce that they were crossing the Asiatic south of the Soviet Union and that his destination could be none other than the Black Sea, one of the ports of which would serve to get him out of the country. To where? Two days later, after a quick stay at a station lost in the steppe, Bulanov arrived with the news that ended their wait: a telegram sent from Moscow informed him that the Turkish government had agreed to receive him as a guest, on a visa for health problems. Upon hearing the news, the deportee's anxiety felt as frozen solid as if he were traveling naked on top of the train: of all the destinations he had imagined for his exile, Kemal Pasha Ataturk's Turkey had not figured among the realistic possibilities, unless they wanted to put him on the gallows and decorate his neck with a well-oiled piece of rope, given that, since the triumph of the October Revolution, this neighbor to the south had become one of the bases for the White Russian exiles most aggressively against the Soviet regime, and placing him in that country was like dropping a rabbit in a dog pen. That is why he yelled at Bulanov that he didn't want to go to Turkey: he could accept being banished from the country the Kremlin had stolen, but the rest of the world did not belong to it and neither did his fate.

When they stopped in legendary Samarkand, Lev Davidovich saw Bulanov and two officers descend from the command headquarters car and disappear into the mosque-like building that served as a station; perhaps they were following through on the deportee's demands and Moscow would arrange for another visa. On that day the anxious wait for the results of those consultations began, and when it became clear that the process would be delayed, they made the train move forward for over an hour before stopping it on a disused branch line in the middle of the frozen desert. It was then that Natalia Sedova asked Bulanov, while they waited for Moscow's response, to telegraph her son, Sergei Sedov, and Anya, Liova's wife, so that they could get together with them for a few days before leaving the country.

Lev Davidovich would never know if the twelve days during which they remained stranded in that spot in the middle of nowhere were due to the delays in the diplomatic consultations or if it was only because of the most devastating snowstorm he'd ever seen, capable of lowering the thermometers to forty degrees below zero. Covered with all of the coats, hats, and blankets at their disposal, they received Seriozha and Anya, who traveled without the children, who were still too little to be exposed to those temperatures. Beneath the occasional gaze of one of the guards, the family enjoyed eight days of pleasant small talk, fierce games of chess, and reading out loud while Lev Davidovich personally took charge of preparing the coffee brought by Sergei. Despite the skepticism of his audience, every time the guards left them alone, Lev Davidovich's compact optimism was unleashed and he initiated talk of plans to continue the struggle and make his return. At night, when everyone else was sleeping, the deportee curled up into a corner of the car and, listening to the staccato breathing due to the cold epidemic that had run through the convoy, he made the most of his insomnia to write letters of protest directed to the Bolshevik Central Committee and oppositionist struggle programs that, in the end, he decided to keep to himself so as not to compromise Seriozha with any papers that very well could lead him to jail.

The cold was so intense that the locomotive had to turn on its motors from time to time and cover a mile or two just to keep its engines from seizing up. Prevented from going outside by the snow's intensity (Lev Davidovich didn't want to lower himself to asking for permission to see Samarkand, the mythical city that centuries before had reigned over all of Central Asia), they awaited the newspapers only to confirm that the news was always disheartening, since every day there were reports of new detentions of anti-Soviet counterrevolutionaries, as they had baptized the members of the opposition. The powerlessness, boredom, the pain in his joints, the difficult digestion of canned food, drove Lev Davidovich to the edge of desperation.

On the twelfth day, Bulanov offered a summary of the responses:

Germany was not interested in giving him a visa, not even for health reasons; Austria made excuses; Norway demanded countless documents; France brandished a judicial order from 1916 by which he was not allowed to enter the country. England didn't even deign to respond. Only Turkey reiterated its disposition to accept him . . . Lev Davidovich was certain that, because of who he was and for having done what he had, for him the world had turned into a planet to which he lacked a visa.

As they headed toward Odessa, the former commissar of war had time to make a new account of the actions, convictions, and greater and lesser mistakes of his life, and he thought that, even though they had forced him to turn into a pariah, he did not regret what he had done and felt ready to pay the price for his actions and dreams. He was even more firm in those convictions when the train passed through Odessa and he recalled those years that now seemed tremendously remote, when he had entered the city's university and understood that his future lay not in mathematics but rather in the struggle against a tyrannical system; thus had begun his endless career as a revolutionary. In Odessa he had introduced the recently founded South Russian Workers' Union to other clandestine groups, without having a clear idea of their political influence; there he had suffered his first imprisonment, had read Darwin and banished from his young Jewish man's mind, already too heterodox, the idea of the existence of any supreme being; there he had been judged and sentenced for the first time, and the punishment had also been exile. That time the Czarist henchmen had sent him to Siberia for four years, while now his former comrades in arms were deporting him outside of his own country, perhaps for the rest of his days. And there, in Odessa, he met the affable jailer who supplied him with paper and ink. This was the man whose resounding name he had chosen when, having fled Siberia, some comrades gave him a blank passport so that he could embark on his first exile and, in the space reserved for the name, Trotsky wrote the jailer's last name, which had accompanied him ever since.

After going around the city by the coast, the train stopped at a branch line that went all the way to the port's quays. The spectacle that unfolded before the travelers was moving: through the blizzard beating at the windows, they contemplated the extraordinary panorama of the frozen bay, the ships planted in the ice, their spars broken.

Bulanov and some other Cheka agents left the train and boarded a steamship called the *Kalinin*, while other agents introduced themselves in the car to announce that Sergei Sedov and Anya should leave, since the deportees would soon be embarking. The farewell, at the end of so many days of cohabitation within the walls of the train car, was more devastating than they had imagined. Natalia cried while caressing the face of her little Seriozha, and Liova and Anya hugged as if wanting to transmit through their skin the feeling of abandonment into which they were being thrown by that separation without any foreseeable end. To protect himself, he bid farewell briefly, but as he looked into Seriozha's eyes, he had the premonition that it was the last time he would see that young man, so healthy and handsome, who had enough intelligence to spurn politics. He hugged him strongly and kissed him on the lips, to take with him some of his warmth and being. Then he withdrew to a corner, followed by Maya, and struggled to drive out of his mind the words Piatakov said to him, at the end of that dismal Central Committee meeting in 1926, when Stalin, with Bukharin's support, had achieved his expulsion from the Politburo and Lev Davidovich would accuse him in front of the comrades of having turned into the Grave Digger of the Revolution. As he was leaving, the redheaded Piatakov had said to him, with that habit of his of speaking into one's ear, "Why? Why have you done it? . . . He will never forgive you this offense. He will make you pay for it until the third or fourth generation." He asked himself: Was it possible that Stalin's political hate would end up extending to these children who represented not just the best of the revolution but of his life? Would his cruelty one day reach Seriozha who had taught the young Svetlana Stalina how to read and count? And he had to answer himself that hate is an unstoppable illness as he stroked his dog's head and observed for the last time—he felt it deep down inside—the city where thirty years before he had wed himself to the revolution forever.

3

"Yes, tell him yes."

For the rest of his days, Ramón Mercader would remember that, just a few seconds before pronouncing the words destined to change his life, he had discovered the unhealthy density that accompanies silence in the middle of war. For weeks he had lived amid the din of the bombs, the shots and the engines, the shouted orders and the cries of pain, and it all accumulated in his consciousness like the sounds of life; the sudden leaden fall of that heavy silence, capable of causing a helplessness too much like fear, turned into a troubling presence when he understood that, after that precarious silence, the explosion of death could suddenly take him away.

In the years of imprisonment, of doubts and alienation, to which those four words would lead him, many times Ramón persisted in challenging himself to imagine what would have happened with his life had he said no. He would insist on re-creating a parallel existence, an essentially novelistic journey in which he had never ceased to be called Ramón, to be Ramón, to act like Ramón, perhaps far from his country and his memories, like so many men of his generation, but always being Ramón Mercader del Río in body and, above all, in soul.

Caridad had arrived a few hours before, in the company of little Luis.

They had traveled from Barcelona, through Valencia, driving the powerful Ford that was confiscated from some executed aristocrats and which the Catalan communist leaders usually used to get around. The safe conducts, adorned with signatures capable of opening all Republican military controls, had allowed them to reach the side of that rugged mountain of the Sierra de Guadarrama. The temperature, several degrees below zero, had forced them to stay inside the car, covered with blankets and breathing in air polluted by Caridad's cigarettes, which took Luis to the edge of nausea. When Ramón was at last able to make it down to the safety of the mountainside, bothered by what he considered to be one of his mother's many customary interferences in his life, his brother Luis was sleeping in the backseat and Caridad, a cigarette in hand, was pacing around the car, kicking rocks and cursing the cold that made her exhale condensed clouds. As soon as she noticed him, the woman enveloped him with her green stare, colder than a night in the sierra, and Ramón remembered that ever since the day they had met again, over a year ago already, his mother had not given him one of those wet kisses that, when he was a child, she used to deposit at the corner of his mouth so that the sweet taste of saliva, with its lingering taste of aniseed, would drip down his taste buds and cause the overwhelming need to keep it in his mouth for longer than the process of his own secretions would allow.

They had not seen each other for several months, ever since Caridad, convalescing from the wounds she received in Albacete, was commissioned by the party to travel to Mexico to gather material support and moral solidarity for the Republican cause. In that time, the woman had changed. It wasn't that the movement of her left arm was still limited by the lacerations caused by shelling; nor was it because of the recent news of the death of her son Pablo, an adolescent who she herself had forced to go to the front in Madrid, where he'd been crushed by the crawler tracks of an Italian tank. Ramón attributed it to something more visceral that he would discover that night.

"I've been waiting for you for six hours. The sun is about to come out and I can't go much longer without some coffee" was how the woman greeted him, focused on crushing a cigarette under her military boot as she looked at the small, shaggy dog accompanying Ramón.

Cannons roared in the distance and the sound of fighter plane engines was an all-encompassing rumble that descended from the starless sky. Would it snow? Ramón wondered.

"I couldn't drop my rifle and come running," he said. "How are you? How's Luisito?"

"Anxious to see you; that's why I brought him. I'm fine. Where did that dog come from?"

Ramón smiled and looked at the animal, who was sniffing around the Ford's wheels.

"He lives with us in the battalion . . . He's really taken to me. He's handsome, right?" And he bent down. "Churro!" he whispered, and the animal approached him, wagging his tail. Ramón stroked his ears as he picked burrs off of him. He looked up. "Why did you come?"

Caridad looked into his eyes for longer than the young man could bear without averting his gaze, and Ramón stood up.

"They've sent me to ask you something . . ."

"I can't believe it . . . You've come all the way here to ask me a question?" Ramón tried to sound sarcastic.

"Well, yes. The only question that matters: What would you be willing to do to defeat fascism, and for socialism? . . . Don't look at me like that; I'm not kidding. We need to hear you say it."

Ramón smiled joylessly. Why was she asking him this?

"You're acting like a recruiting officer . . . You and who else need it? Is this a party thing?"

"Answer and then I'll explain." Caridad remained serious.

"I don't know, Caridad. Isn't that what I'm doing now? Risking my life, working for the party . . . Keeping those fascist sons of bitches from entering Madrid."

"It's not enough," she said.

"What do you mean it's not enough? Don't make things any harder for me . . ."

"Fighting is easy. So is dying . . . Thousands of people do it . . . Your brother Pablo . . . But would you be willing to give up everything? And when I say everything, I mean everything. Any dreams of your own, any scruples, being yourself . . ."

"I don't understand, Caridad," Ramón said, completely sincere as a sense of alarm grew in his chest. "Are you serious? Can't you be any clearer? I can't spend all night here, either," and he pointed toward the mountain from which he had come.

"I think I'm already speaking very clearly," she said, and took out another cigarette. At the moment in which she lit the match, the sky was

28

illuminated by the flash of an explosion and the back door of the car opened. Young Luis, covered by a blanket, ran toward Ramón, slipping on the frozen ground, and they held each other in an embrace.

"Wow, Luisito, you've become a man."

Luis sniveled without letting go of his brother.

"And you're so thin, man. I can feel your bones."

"It's the fucking war."

"And is that your dog? What's his name?"

"It's Churro . . . He's not mine, but it's as if he were. He showed up one day . . ." Luis whistled and the animal came to his feet. "He's a quick learner and he's so good . . . Do you want to take him?" Ramón caressed his younger brother's messy hair and cleaned his eyes with his thumbs.

Luis looked at his mother, undecided.

"We can't have dogs now," she confirmed, smoking avidly. "Sometimes we don't even have enough to eat ourselves."

"Churro eats anything, almost nothing," Ramón said, and instinctively lifted his shoulders to protect himself when a cannon rumbled in the distance. "A whole family could eat with what you spend on tobacco."

"My cigarettes are not your problem . . . Luis, run along with the dog, I need to speak with Ramón," Caridad ordered, and walked toward an oak tree whose leaves had managed to resist the aggressive winter in the sierra.

Under the tree, Ramón smiled while he watched Luis frolicking with little Churro.

"Are you going to tell me why you came? Who sent you?"

"Kotov. He wants to make you an important proposition," she said and again fixed him under the green glass of her gaze.

"Kotov is in Barcelona?"

"At the moment. He wants to know if you're willing to work with him."

"In the army?"

"No, on more important matters."

"More important than the war?"

"Much more. This war can be won or it can be lost, but . . ."

"What the hell are you saying? We can't lose, Caridad. With what the Soviets are sending us and the people from the International Brigades, we're going to fuck those fascists one by one . . ."

"That would be great, but tell me . . . Do you think we can win a war

29

with the Trotskyists making signals to the fascists in the trenches next to them and with the anarchists taking combat orders to a vote? . . . Kotov wants you to work on truly important things."

"Important like what?"

An explosion shook the mountain, too close to where the three of them were. Instinct pushed Ramón to protect Caridad with his own body and they rolled around on the frozen ground.

"I'm going to go crazy. Don't those bastards sleep?" he said, on his knees, as he shook the dust off one of the sleeves of Caridad's cloak.

She stopped his hand and leaned over to pick up the smoking cigarette. Ramón helped her to stand up.

"Kotov thinks you're a good Communist and that you could be useful in the rear guard."

"Every day there are more Communists in Spain. Ever since the Soviets and their weapons arrived, the people have a different opinion of us."

"Don't believe that, Ramón. People are afraid of us; a lot of them don't like us. This is a country of imbeciles, hypocritical bigots, and born fascists."

Ramón watched as his mother exhaled cigarette smoke almost furiously.

"What does Kotov want me for?"

"I've already told you: something more important than firing a rifle in a trench full of water and shit."

"I can't imagine what he could want from me . . . The fascists are moving forward, and if they take Madrid . . ." Ramón shook his head, when he felt a slight pressure in his chest. "Shit, Caridad, if I didn't know you, I would say that you talked to Kotov to get me away from the front. After what happened to Pablo—"

"But you *do* know me," she cut him off. "Wars are won in many ways; you should know that . . . Ramón, I want to be far away from here before the sun rises. I need an answer."

Did he know her? Ramón looked at her and asked himself what was left of the refined and worldly woman with whom he, his brothers, and his father used to walk on Sunday afternoons through the Plaza de Cataluña in search of fashionable restaurants or the elegant Italian ice cream shop that had recently opened on the Paseo de Gracia: there was nothing left of that woman, he thought. Caridad was now an androgynous being who reeked of deeply embedded nicotine and sweat, talked like a political commissar, and only thought about the party's missions, about the party's politics, about the party's struggles. Lost in his thoughts, the young man did not notice that, after the mortar explosion that had thrown them to the ground, a heavy silence had settled over the sierra as if the world, overcome by exhaustion and pain, had gone to sleep. Ramón, who had spent so much time submerged in the sounds of war, seemed to have lost the ability to listen to silence, and into his mind, already disturbed by the possibility of a return, floated a memory of the seething Barcelona that he had left a few months earlier, and the tempting image of the young woman who'd given his life a deep sense of meaning.

"Have you seen África? Do you know if she's still working with the Soviets?" he asked, shamed by the persistence of a hormonal weakness that he could not shake off.

"You're all talk, Ramón! You're just as soft as your father," Caridad said, taking aim at his vulnerable side. Ramón felt that he could hate his mother, but he had to admit she was right: África was an addiction pursuing him.

"I asked you if she was still in Barcelona."

"Yes, yes . . . She's going around with the advisers. I saw her at La Pedrera a few days ago."

Ramón noticed that Caridad's cigarettes were French, very perfumed, so different from the stinky cigarettes that his battalion mates gave him.

"Give me a cigarette."

"Keep them . . ." She handed him the pack. "Ramón, would you be able to give up that woman?"

He had felt that a question like that was coming and that it would be the most difficult one to answer.

"What is it that Kotov wants?" he persisted, evading the response.

"I've already told you: that you give up everything that we've been told for centuries is important, only to enslave us."

Ramón felt like he was listening to África. It was as if Caridad's words spilled forth from the same Kremlin tower, from the same pages of *Das Kapital* from which África's came. And it was only then that he became conscious of the silence that had been surrounding them for several minutes. Caridad was África, África was Caridad, and the sacrifice of his entire past was demanded of him now as a duty, while that painful and fragile silence rested on his consciousness, feeding the fear that in the next minute his body could be broken by the mortar, the bullet, or the

31

grenade lying in wait and destined to destroy his existence. Ramón understood that he feared the silence more than the perverse rumblings of the war, and he wished to be far from the place. Without knowing that his life hung on those few words, it was then that he said:

"Yes, tell him yes."

Caridad smiled. She took her son's face and, with treacherous precision, planted a long kiss on the corner of his mouth. Ramón felt the woman's saliva mix with his, but he couldn't find the taste of aniseed now, not even of the gin that she'd drunk the last time she kissed him; he only received the sickening sweetness of tobacco and the fermented acidity of her heartburn.

"In a few days, you'll be called to Barcelona. We'll be waiting for you. Your life is going to change, Ramón. A lot," she said, and shook the dirt off of herself. "I'm leaving now. The sun is rising."

As if it were nothing, Ramón spit, turning his head, and lit a cigarette. He walked behind Caridad toward the car, from which Luis emerged with Churro in his arms.

"Let go of the dog and say goodbye to Ramón."

Luis obeyed her and again hugged his brother.

"We'll see each other soon in Barcelona. I'll take you to sign up for the Youth Brigades. You've already turned fourteen, right?"

Luis smiled.

"And will you sign me up for the army? All the Communists have gone to the People's Army . . ."

"Don't rush, Luisillo." Ramón smiled and hugged him tight. Over the kid's head he noticed Caridad's gaze, lost once again. He avoided the unease caused by his mother's eyes and, in the day's first light, made out El Escorial's stony and hostile silhouette.

"Look, Luisito, El Escorial. I'm on the other side, up that slope."

"And is it always this cold?"

"Cold enough to freeze your skin off."

"We're leaving. Get in, Luis," Caridad interrupted her sons, and Luis, after saying goodbye to Ramón with the militiamen's salute, went around the car to get in the passenger seat.

"If you see África, tell her I'll be there soon," Ramón almost whispered.

Caridad opened the car door but stopped and closed it again.

"Ramón, it goes without saying that this conversation should remain a secret. From this moment on, get it into your head that being willing to give up everything is not a slogan, it's a way of life." The young man saw his mother open her military cloak and take out a gleaming Browning. Caridad took a few steps and, without looking at her son, asked, "Are you sure you can do it?"

"Yes," Ramón said just as a bomb explosion illuminated the distant mountainside, and as Caridad, with weapon in hand, placed Churro in her sights and, not giving her son any time to react, shot him in the head. The animal rolled, pushed by the force of the bullet, and its corpse began to freeze in the cold dawn of the Sierra de Guadarrama.

Winters in Sant Feliu de Guíxols had always been misty, prone to storms that came down from the Pyrenees. Summers, by contrast, are a gift of nature. The rock that rises from the sea forms a mountain that opens up there in a cove of coarse sand, and the water tends to be clearer than anywhere else on the coast of Empordà. In the 1920s, only fishermen and some faithless hermits lived in Sant Feliu, the first fugitives from urban life and modernity. But in summer Barcelona's wealthy families, the owners of beach houses and mountain cabins, appeared. The Mercader clan was one of the fortunate ones, thanks to the textile business that had received a second wind during the Great War.

His father's family, related to the local nobility, had accumulated wealth through several generations; like good Catalans, they had been devoted to commerce and industry; Caridad's family were the owners of a castle in San Miguel de Aras, near Santander, and were colonists who returned from Cuba before the disaster of 1898; they had returned with their fortune in ruins, since part of it had been lost with the blacks they had to free when the end of slavery was declared on the island. Although Pau, Ramón's father, was several years older than Caridad, in the boy's eyes they were an enviable couple who shared a passion for horses, like good aristocrats, and just to see them take their horses out to trot, one knew they were excellent riders, she the more talented one.

That summer of 1922 was the first and only one in which the family enjoyed an entire month of sun, beach, and freedom in that cove that their memory would store as the epitome of happiness. Just two years later, when his life began its own winding path, Ramón would learn that his always budget-minded father's decision to exchange the summer visit

33

to the stone castle of San Miguel for the privacy of the rented house on the Empordà coast was rooted not in his children's possible enjoyment but rather in the attempt to bring about the repair of something that was already beginning to be unsalvageable: his relationship with his wife.

It was in Sant Feliu de Guíxols that summer that his parents clung to the vestiges of their married life, and it must have been there that they conceived Luis, born in the spring of the following year. A long time later, Ramón would find out that that act of love must have been like the remains of the wave that breaks on the shore to immediately retreat into unreachable depths. Because something unstoppable had begun to grow inside of Caridad before she had conceived his younger brother: hate, a destructive hate that would always pursue her and that not only would give meaning to her own life but would also change the lives of every one of her sons to the point of devastation.

A few months before, with the latent fear caused by anything that brought him closer with his mother, Ramón had dared to ask her about the red bumps standing out on the extremely white skin of her arms and she had barely responded that she was sick. But soon enough, when the storm was unleashed and the bourgeois house in Sant Gervasi was filled with screaming and fighting, he would know that the marks had been made by the needles she used to inject herself with the heroin that she had become addicted to in a parallel life, one that she led at night, beyond the pleasant walls of the family home.

Many years later, on a Mexican night in August 1940, Ramón would hear from Caridad's lips that it was her respectable, enterprising, and Catholic husband himself who had urged her to take the first step toward the downward spiral from which she would be rescued, after having suffered many humiliations and received an infinite number of blows, by the supreme ideal of the socialist revolution. Pau Mercader, thinking that he would help her overcome the sexual reluctance she had felt ever since they married, had invited her to accompany him to certain exclusive brothels in Barcelona where it was possible to enjoy the sight of the most daring sexual acrobatics through special windows. Here a man and a woman could participate, or two couples, or a man with two women or even three, or two women alone, all experts in erotic positions and fantasies, the men endowed with penises of an exaggerated size, and the women trained to receive natural or artificial objects of disproportionate dimensions in any of their orifices. The results of this experiment met his father's expectations very poorly, since it caused Caridad to reject his sexual demands even more forcefully, although she took a liking to certain spirits served in those mauve-curtained, dimly lit dens, liqueurs that took away her inhibitions and, at the end of the night, allowed her to open her legs almost as a reflex. A while later, in search of those elixirs, she had begun to frequent the city's most select bars, many times without her husband, who was increasingly called away by his absorbing business. But soon Caridad would feel that those places had an excess of that which she wasn't seeking (men willing to inebriate her to throw her in bed) and something, still undefined, was lacking, something capable of motivating her and reconciling her with her own soul.

Then that fine woman, surrounded by luxury and comfort from birth, educated by nuns, an expert rider of Arabian horses, married to that owner of factories who was, by his very nature, removed from the feelings of men who worked for their wealth, removed her jewels and attractive clothing and descended in search of the shadiest corners of the city. She felt another world with her hands when she decided to walk the streets of the Barrio Chino, the darkest plazas of the Raval, the narrow and fetid alleyways near the port. There, as she tasted less sophisticated and more effective alcohol, she discovered a dark humanity, weighed down by frustration and hate, who tended to speak in a language that was new to her about things as tremendous as the need to do away with all religions or to turn the bourgeois, exploitative order—that enemy of man's dignity, that world from which she herself came—upside down. The anarchist fury, of which she had only a vague notion up until that moment, was like a blow that shook every cell in her body.

With her libertarian friends and the underclass from the ports and the red-light district, Caridad had tried heroin, paid for by her generous purse, and found in its iconoclasm a hidden satisfaction that gave life a more attractive flavor. She rediscovered sex, on a different level and with other ingredients, and practiced it in a primitive way whose existence she had never imagined in her sad married life: she enjoyed it with stevedores, sailors, textile workers, streetcar drivers, and professional agitators, for whom she also bought drinks and heroin with her husband's money. It satisfied her to prove that among those rebels one's origins and level of education didn't matter: she was welcomed among them, since she was a companion willing to break the rules and to free herself from the chains of bourgeois society.

Despite the fact that the four children conceived in her womb were already sleeping in her house, it was in the midst of that vertigo of new feelings and recently learned libertarian sermons that Caridad became conscious of the hate eating away at her and she finally turned into an adult woman. She never knew for certain to what point she shared the anarchists' ideas out of conviction or out of rebellion, but after getting mixed up with them, she realized that she was working for her own physical and spiritual liberation. On occasion, she even thought that she was taking delight in her degradation because of the disdain she felt for herself and toward everything her life had been and could continue to be. But whether it was out of conviction or hate, Caridad had gone down that path in a way that, from then on, would always be thus: with a fanatical and uncontainable force. To prove it, or perhaps to prove it to herself, she decided to cross her greatest frontiers and, along with her new comrades, planned her absurd class suicide: first she worked with them to promote strikes in the shops belonging to Pau, whom she had turned into the very incarnation of the bourgeois enemy; later, in her spiral of hate, she began to prepare something more irreversible, and with the group of her companions planned the blowing up of one of the factories that the family had in Badalona.

At barely ten years of age, Ramón had no notion of what was happening underneath the family's surface. Enrolled in one of the city's most expensive schools, he lived carefree, focusing his free time on physical activities, preferring them to the intellectual tasks that had been practiced in his house since birth where, at established hours, they spoke in four languages: French, English, Castilian Spanish, and Catalan. Perhaps something deeply rooted in his character already existed then, since his best friends were not his classmates or his sports rivals but rather his two dogs, gifts from his maternal grandfather when the boy showed proof of a special weakness for those animals. Santiago and Cuba, baptized by his expatriate grandfather with nostalgic names, had come from Cantabria as mere puppies and the relationship that Ramón established with them was intimate. On Sundays, after Mass, and in the afternoons on which he came home early from school, the boy used to go beyond the city limits in the company of his two Labradors, with whom he shared crackers, long runs, and his predilection for silence. He barely saw his parents. Increasingly, Caridad slept all day and went out in the evening to take up her social life, as she called the nocturnal outings from which she returned with new red bumps on her arms. His father, meanwhile, either stayed at his office very late, trying to salvage his business from the collapse caused by his older brother's indolence, or enclosed himself in his rooms without any intention of seeing or talking to anyone. In any event, home life continued to be calm, and the dogs even made it satisfactory.

When the police showed up at the Sant Gervasi house, they had two options for Caridad's fate: jail for being accused of planning attacks against private property, or the insane asylum as a drug addict. Her comrades in arms and debauchery were already behind bars by that time, but Pau's social position and both of their family names had influenced the police's decision. In addition, one of Caridad's brothers, who was a municipal judge in the city, had intervened on her behalf, saying she was a sick woman without any will of her own, manipulated by the diabolical anarchists and syndicalists who were the enemies of order. In an effort to save his own prestige and whatever remained of his bourgeois and Christian marriage, Pau obtained a less radical solution and promised that his wife would no longer frequent the anarchist circles nor take drugs, and he gave his word (and surely some good money) as a guarantee.

Two months later, with the detoxification treatment which Caridad had agreed to undergo completed, the family left for that vacation in Sant Feliu de Guíxols, where they experienced days that came close to happiness and perfect harmony, and Ramón kept them that way in his recollections, where they became his memory's greatest treasure.

As Caridad's womb swelled, the family went on with its peaceful routine of daily living. Pau's business, however, could barely recover in the middle of the crisis brought about by breaking with his dissolute older brother and the workers' mounting demands. Luis, who would be the last of the brothers, was born in 1923, shortly before Primo de Rivera's dictatorship began and in the midst of the truce that Caridad would break a year later: because hate is one of the most difficult illnesses to cure and she had become more addicted to revenge than to heroin.

Caridad would go back to her anarchists' world in a peculiar way. Her brother José, the judge, had confessed that he was experiencing serious financial problems due to some gambling debts that would end his career if they became public knowledge. Caridad promised to help him monetarily in exchange for information: he needed to tell her who the judges would be in the courtrooms where her detained anarchist friends would be tried. With these facts, other colleagues waged an intimidation campaign on the judges, who received letters threatening them with a variety of reprisals if they dared to impose sentences on any libertarian. Pau Mercader quickly discovered the drain on his capital and understood where it was going. With the weakness that always characterized his relationship with Caridad, the man only took measures to ensure that she not have access to great sums and again concentrated on the businesses he was trying to maintain afloat from his new office on Calle Ample.

Upon seeing how her contribution to the cause was being obstructed, Caridad rebelled again: she went back to the brothels, where she drank and took drugs, and to the meetings in which she yelled for an end to the dictatorship, the monarchy, the bourgeois order, and the disintegration of the state and its retrograde institutions. Her brother José planned the most honorable way out with Pau and they managed to have Caridad committed to an insane asylum by a doctor friend.

Fifteen years later, Caridad would describe to Ramón the two months in which she lived in that inferno of cold showers, confinement, injections, brainwashing, and other devastating therapies. That they would try to drive her crazy was something that still enraged her to the point of aggression; and if they didn't achieve it, it was because Caridad had the luck that her anarchist colleagues came to save her from that prison, threatening to bring down Pau's business and even the asylum itself if they didn't set her free. The coercion worked and Pau was forced to bring his wife back; she entered the house in Sant Gervasi only to collect her five children and some suitcases with necessities; where she was going, she didn't know, but she would not again live near her husband or any of their families, upon whom, she swore, she would take revenge until she made them disappear from the face of the earth.

Facing the evidence that nothing was going to stop her, Pau begged her not to take the children. What was she going to do with five kids? How was she going to maintain them? And above all, since when did she love them so much that she couldn't live without them? Perhaps it was another form of revenge against her husband, who professed a distant and silent affection for them, since he didn't know how to be any other way; perhaps she took them in search of some spiritual support; perhaps it was because she already dreamed of making each of them into what they would be in the future. The fact is that, resolved as she was to take her children with her, no pleading made her change her mind.

Everything that would happen from that moment on would take on a sense of novelty and adventure. Ramón, who was already accustomed to Caridad's crises, accepted the move as a passing tempest and only regretted having to leave Cuba and Santiago, but he calmed down when their cook assured him that she would take care of them until he returned.

In the spring of 1925, with her children in tow, Caridad crossed the French border. Although her purpose was to reach Paris, the woman decided to make a stop in the pleasant city of Dax, perhaps because at that moment she felt unsure of herself, as if she needed to redesign the map of her life, or because she had convinced herself that destroying the system and raising five children at the same time can be more complicated than it appears, especially when—one of the paradoxes of life—you don't have enough money.

Shortly after arriving in Dax, Ramón and his siblings, with the exception of Luis the baby, entered a public school and Caridad began to look for political company, which she quickly found, since anarchists and syndicalists were everywhere. To keep herself afloat, she began to sell her jewels, but the rate of expenditure imposed by nights out at taverns, cigarettes, a pinch here or there of heroin, and good meals (only a Communist can be hungrier and have less money than an anarchist, Caridad declared) became unsustainable.

For Ramón, this period was an initiation into an apprenticeship that would begin to redefine him. He had just turned twelve; until then he'd been a boy enrolled in exclusive schools, raised in abundance, and suddenly, from one day to the next, he had fallen, if not into poverty, at least into a world much closer to reality, where coins were counted out for snacks and beds remained unmade if one didn't make them oneself. Small Montse, who was ten, was charged with caring for and feeding Luis, while Pablo had taken on the nuisance of cleaning. Jorge and Ramón, because they were the oldest, were responsible for shopping and, very shortly after, for preparing the meals that would save them from dying of hunger when Caridad didn't come home on time or returned from her political activities drugged. His friends in Dax were the children of poor villagers and Spanish immigrants, with whom he enjoyed going into the nearby woods to collect truffles, guided by pigs. In that period, Ramón also learned to feel the burn of a cold stare on his skin from the small city's young bourgeois citizens.

After asking for reports from Barcelona, the Dax police decided that they did not want Caridad in the area and, without further thought, demanded that the family go on their way. So they had to pack their bags again and go to Toulouse, a much larger city, where she thought she could pass unnoticed. There, both to avoid police repression and because she was convinced that her jewels would not cover much more, Caridad began to work as the hostess of a restaurant, since she had the manners and education for the job. Thanks to the owners of that place, who quickly took to the children, Jorge and Ramón were able to enter the École Hotelière de Toulouse, the former to study to be a chef, Ramón to be a maître d'hôtel, and the stability they regained made them embrace the illusion that they would once again be a normal family.

Caridad had definitely not been born to seat the bourgeoisie at tables and smile at them as she suggested entrées. Full of the fury of total revolution and hate for the system, her life seemed miserable to her, a waste of the energies demanded by the fight for freedom. Although the incident was never clarified, Ramón spent his whole life thinking that the massive poisoning of the restaurants' customers that happened one night could only have been engineered by his mother. Fortunately, no one died, and doubts about the intentionality and, as such, the authorship of the attack were never clarified. But the owners of the business decided to let her go and the commissioner in charge of the case, with reasons enough to suspect Caridad, appeared at their house several days later and demanded that she disappear or he would put her in jail.

Even before the poisoning of the diners, Caridad lived in a stupor and swung like a pendulum from outbursts of enthusiasm or anger to depressive silences into which she fell for days. It was clear that her life, lacking firm ideological support, had lost sense and, when she saw herself deprived of the possibility of the struggle and demolition, she could only see before her a vicious circle of depression, anger, and frustration, with no way out. She then lost control and tried to kill herself by swallowing a handful of tranquilizers.

Jorge and Ramón found her only because they decided to go into her room at night to take her some food. The recollections that Ramón would keep of that moment were always hazy and one could almost think that they had acted on reflex, without stopping to reason. A desperate Ramón dragged her out of the bed, which was covered in excrement and piss. With the help of Jorge, who used a metal prosthetic because of the lingering effects of polio on one of his legs, he managed to drag her to the street. Without noticing her feet scraping over the cobblestones, without feeling the cold or the rain, they managed to take their mother to the avenue and get a taxi to the hospital.

Caridad never spoke of that episode and didn't ever pronounce a word of gratitude for what her sons had done for her. For many years, Ramón would think that her silence was due to the shame caused by the evident weakness into which she had fallen—she, the woman who wanted to change the world. Besides, to add to her humiliation, when she left the hospital, Caridad had to accept that her husband, notified by the kids, would take responsibility for their custody: the only time Ramón saw his mother cry was the day on which she said goodbye to Jorge and him, to go with Pau and her small children to Barcelona.

In the midst of the storm of love and hate in which they lived for so many years, Caridad would never know, since Ramón never gave her the pleasure of confessing it, that in that moment, seeing her as she set off rescued by the very incarnation of what she most disdained, he had ceased to be a child. He was convinced that his mother was right: if one truly wanted to be free, one had to do something to change that filthy world that wounded people's dignity. Very soon, Ramón would also learn that change would only come about if many embraced the same flag and, elbow to elbow, fought for it. The revolution had to be made.

4

"Today's petrified crap . . ." Lev Davidovich threw the newspaper against the wall and left his study. As he went down the stairs, he smelled the scent of goat stew that Natalia was preparing for dinner, and that appetizing aroma seemed obscene. Behind his desk he contemplated the beautiful Sara Weber, who was typing with a speed that at that moment seemed automatic, definitively inhuman. He crossed the door to the barren garden and the Turkish policemen smiled at him, willing to follow him, and he stopped them with a gesture. The men acted like they were following his wishes, but they did not let him out of their sight, since the order they received was too precise: their lives depended on the Exile not losing his.

The beauty of the month of April in Prinkipo barely affected him as he, followed by Maya, went down the dune that ended on the coast. He asked himself: What agony could grip the brain of a sensitive and effusive man like Mayakovsky to make him voluntarily decline the aroma of the stew, the magic of a sunset, under the gaze of feminine charms, to shut himself up in the irreversible silence of death? And he walked along the shore to observe his dog's elegant trot, a gift of nature that also seemed offensively harmonious.

Three years earlier, when they were on the verge of banishing him from Moscow and his good friend Yoffe had shot himself in the hopes that his act would cause a commotion capable of moving the party's conscience and preventing the catastrophic expulsion of Lev Davidovich and his comrades, he had thought that the drama of the act made sense in the political struggle, even though he didn't approve of such an exit. But the news he had recently read had shaken him due to the magnitude of the mental castration enclosed in its message. How far had mediocrity and perversion gone for the poet Vladimir Mayakovsky—Mayakovsky of all people—to decide to evade its tentacles by taking his own life? Today's petrified crap that so alarmed the poet in his final verses, had it overcome him to the point of suicide? The official note drafted in Moscow could not have been more offensive to the memory of the artist who had fought for a new and revolutionary art with the most enthusiasm, the one who had, with the most fervor, handed over to the spirit of a completely new society his poetry laden with screams, chaos, broken harmonies, and triumphant slogans; the one who had most insisted on resisting, on withstanding, the suspicions and pressures with which the bureaucracy besieged the Soviet intelligentsia. The note spoke of a "decadent feeling of personal failure," and since in the rhetoric implanted in the country the word "decadence" was applied to bourgeois art, society, and life, by making the failure "personal," they were reaffirming with calculated cruelty that individual condition that could only exist in the bourgeois artist that, they usually said, every creator always carries within, like original sin, no matter how revolutionary he claims he is. The death of the writer, they clarified, didn't have anything to do with his "social and literary activities," as if it were possible to separate Mayakovsky from actions that were no more and no less than his very way of breathing.

Something all too malignant and repellent had to have been unleashed in Soviet society if its most fervent spokespeople were beginning to shoot bullets into their own hearts, disgusted before the nausea caused by today's petrified crap. That suicide was, as Lev Davidovich knew well, the dramatic confirmation that more turbulent times had begun, that the last embers of the marriage of convenience between the revolution and art had gone out, with the predictable sacrifice of art: times in which a man like Mayakovsky, disciplined even to the point of self-annihilation, could feel the disdain of those in power boring into the back of his head, those for whom poets and poetry were aberrations on whom they could perhaps

43

rely to reaffirm their preeminence and whom they could do without when they didn't need them.

Lev Davidovich recalled that many years before he'd written that history had conquered Tolstoy, but had not broken him. To the end, that genius had been able to maintain his precious gift for moral indignation and thus directed his cry of "I cannot be silent!" against the aristocracy. But Mayakovsky, forcing himself to be a believer, had remained silent and thus ended up broken. He lacked the courage to go into exile when others did so; to stop writing when others broke their pens. He insisted on offering his poetry to political activity and sacrificed his art and his own spirit with that gesture; he pushed himself so much to be an exemplary militant that he had to commit suicide to become a poet again. Mayakovsky's silence was a harbinger of other silences that were as painful or more so, in all certainty, to come in the future: the political intolerance invading society would not rest until it suffocated it. "As they suffocated the poet, they are trying to smother me," the Exile would write, stranded next to the oppressive Sea of Marmara that had been surrounding him for a year already.

To the end of his days, Lev Davidovich would remember his first weeks of Turkish exile as a blind transit through which he had to move, feeling his way against walls in constant motion. The first thing that surprised him was that the GPU agents in charge of overseeing his deportation, in addition to giving him $1,500 that they said they owed him for his work, maintained a pleasant attitude toward him despite the fact that, once they had crossed into Turkish waters, he had sent a message to President Kemal Pasha Ataturk advising him that he was settling in Turkey only because he was forced to do so. Afterward, it was the diplomats from the Soviet legation in Istanbul who were as cordial as they would have only been to a first-class guest sent by their government. Because of that, in the face of so much faked kindness, he was not surprised when the European newspapers, encouraged by the rumors spread by Moscow's ubiquitous men, speculated that perhaps Trotsky had been sent to Turkey by Stalin to foment revolution in the Near East.

Convinced that silence and passivity could be his worst enemies, he decided to take action, and while he insisted on applying for visas from various countries (the president of the German Reichstag had spoken of his country's willingness to offer him a "freedom asylum"), he wrote an essay, published by some Western newspapers, in which he clarified the conditions of his exile, denounced the persecution and the jailing of his followers in the Soviet Union, and declared Stalin, publicly for the first time, the Grave Digger of the Revolution.

The change in attitude of diplomats and policemen was immediate and, curiously, coincided with the arrival of new refusals to house him from Norway and Austria, and with the news of what was happening in Berlin, where Ernst Thälmann and the Communists loyal to Moscow had started an uproar against the renegade's possible acceptance there. Expelled without the least consideration from the Soviet consulate and divested of all protection, the Trotskys had to lodge at a small hotel in Istanbul, where their lives were exposed to the predictable aggressions of their enemies, red and white. Even so, as soon as they arrived, Lev Davidovich sent a telegram to Berlin with which he burned the last ship in which he had entrusted his luck: "I interpret silence as a very disloyal refusal." But he had no sooner sent it off when it seemed insufficient and he reinforced his position with a last message to the Reichstag: "I am very sorry that the possibility is denied to me to study in practice the advantages of the democratic right to asylum."

The dawn of spring surprised them in that dismal hostel of cracked and dirty walls where they were lodging. Although he didn't have the foggiest idea what his next steps could be, Lev Davidovich decided to take advantage of the season and get to know the exultant Istanbul in his spare time. But not even the discovery of an exquisite world that went back to the very origins of civilization could manage to shake him out of the pessimistic lethargy into which he had fallen and which made him feel like a stranger to himself: Lev Davidovich Trotsky needed a sword and a battlefield.

A few weeks later he accepted, without much enthusiasm, his wife and his son's proposal to travel around the Sea of Marmara to the Prinkipo islands. The small volcanic archipelago, an hour and a half from the capital, had been the refuge of dethroned Ottoman princes and the place in which, in 1919, a peace conference to end the Russian civil war had been proposed. Lev Davidovich would use that journey to take his mind off things, sunbathe, and taste the delicate Turkish pastries known as *pochas* and *pides* of which Natalia had become a fan. Two young Trotsky sympathizers whom his friend Alfred Rosmer had sent from France a few days before traveled with them to guarantee a minimum of security.

The small steamboat sailed at nine in the morning. Covered in hats, they occupied the prow and enjoyed the scenery that Istanbul's two halves offered. Lev Davidovich, nonetheless, tried to look beyond the buildings, the pointed churches, the convex mosques; he tried to look for himself in that city in which he did not have a single friend or a trustworthy follower. And he didn't find himself. He felt that, at that exact moment, his exile was beginning—true, complete, without any support. Aside from his family and a very few friends who had reiterated their solidarity, he was a man who was overwhelmingly alone. His only useful allies for a battle like the one he had to initiate (how? where?) were still confined in work camps or had already given in, but all of them remained within the borders of the Soviet Union, and his relationship with them was snuffed out by distance, repression, and fear.

Every time he evoked that seemingly pleasant morning, Lev Davidovich would remember that he had felt the urgent need to press Natalia Sedova's hand in his to feel human warmth close to him, to not suffocate from the anxiety caused by the threatening sensation of loss. But he would also remember that at that moment, he had confirmed his decision that, although he was alone, his duty was to fight. If the revolution for which he had fought was prostituting itself in the dictatorship of a czar dressed up as a Bolshevik, then he would have to rip it out by the roots and replant it, because the world needs true revolutions. That decision, he was well aware, would bring him closer to the death that was pursuing him from the Kremlin's watchtowers. Death, nonetheless, could only be considered an inevitable eventuality: Lev Davidovich had always thought that, since individual sacrifice is often the firewood burned in the pyre of the revolution, the lives of one, ten, one hundred, one thousand men could and even should be devoured if the social tornado demanded it in order to reach its transformative ends. So he laughed when certain newspapers insisted on mentioning his "personal tragedy." What tragedy were they referring to? he would write. In the superhuman process of the revolution, there was no room for personal tragedies. His tragedy, if anything, was knowing that in his struggle he didn't have any fellow believers at hand who'd been forged in the ovens of the revolution, nor the economic means and, less still, a party. But he still had what had always been his best weapon: the pen, the same one that had spread his ideas in the contributions he made to *Iskra* and that, during his first round of exile, had led him to the heart of the struggle on that night in 1901 in which he received the message capable of locating his life as a fighter right in the vortex of history: his pen had been called for at *Iskra*'s headquarters in London, where he was expected by Vladimir Ilyich Ulyanov, already known as Lenin.

With a wave of his hand, Liova commented that the fishermen's village visible on the coast was called Büyükada, and the young man's words brought him back to the reality of an islet covered by pines and dotted with some white buildings. It was then that, tempting fate, he asked if they could disembark there to have lunch: almost without thinking, he added that he liked that place, since it was undoubtedly a calm enough place to write in and had good fishing to test his muscles. Natalia Sedova, who knew him like no one else, watched him and smiled: "What are you thinking, Liovnochek?"

The woman would find out just a week later and be happy: they were going to live in Büyükada, the largest of the islets in the archipelago of exiled princes.

It had not been hard to find the right house to fit their needs and pockets. Built atop a small promontory, about six hundred feet from the dock, its two levels seemed to reach higher and to place historic Propontis at the disposal of its inhabitants. They also appreciated the fact that the building was surrounded by a dense hedge that facilitated security, the responsibility of two policemen sent by the government and some young Frenchmen, fellows of his follower Raymond Molinier. In reality, the villa, the property of an old Turkish Baha'i, was as run-down as its owner, and Natalia Sedova was forced to roll up her sleeves to make it inhabitable. Between all of them—including policemen, watchmen, and even passing journalists—they cleaned, painted, and equipped the furnished spaces that were necessary to eat, sleep, and work. The temporary nature of their settlement in that refuge could be seen in the absence of any objects meant to make it beautiful; there wasn't even a simple rosebush in the garden: "To plant a single seed in this land would be to accept defeat," Lev Davidovich had warned his wife, since he still had his mind focused on the centers of battle to which, sooner or later, he thought he would manage to gain access.

Throughout that first year of exile, the most tiresome task facing those guards charged with the revolutionary's security had been to deal with the journalists intent on getting a scoop, that of welcoming editors from around the world (who had offered contracts for various books and made generous advances capable of alleviating the family's economic difficulties) and verifying that the followers and friends who began to arrive were who they said they were. At the margin of these interferences, life on an island lost to history, inhabited throughout most of the year only by fishermen and sheepherders, seemed so primitive and slow that any outside presence was immediately detected. And although he was a prisoner, Lev Davidovich had felt almost happy for having found that place where a car had never driven and where things were transported as they were twenty-five centuries before, on the back of a donkey.

Barely settled, the Exile began to prepare his counteroffensive and decided that the first necessity was to unite the opposition outside the Soviet Union, although he would soon discover the extent to which Stalin had anticipated this, tasking his peons in the Communist International with converting Trotsky's person and ideas into the specter of the revolution's greatest enemy. As could be expected, there were few European Communists who dared to adopt the "Trotskyist" heresy, especially when it didn't seem to offer any practical advantages and, soon, would lead to immediate excommunication from the party and even from the ranks of revolutionary fighters. Nonetheless, Lev Davidovich insisted, and he unloaded on the shoulders of his son Liova the organization of the oppositionist movement while he focused on working personally with the most noteworthy followers. The rest of the time he would spend writing an autobiography he had begun in Alma-Ata and gathering information for a planned *History of the Russian Revolution*.

Among the visitors he received in those initial months were his old comrades Alfred and Marguerite Rosmer, the ever politically complicated Pierre Naville and Boris Souvarine, and the impulsive Raymond Molinier, who, with the same enthusiasm with which he would embark on a summer excursion, had dragged along his wife, Jeanne, and his brother Henri. But the first to arrive, as could be expected, had been his good friends Maurice and Magdeleine Paz, whom he had not seen since the Trotskys were expelled from France in the middle of the Great War. The couple's arrival, weighed down with French cheeses, brought a breath of happiness wrapped in the certainty of a freedom that allowed them the luxury of welcoming old comrades. Throughout the year of deportation in Alma-Ata, the Pazes had been their representatives in Paris and had traveled to Prinkipo to update their accounts and duties and to reconfirm their unshakable solidarity.

One of the conversations they had with the Pazes would take on a strange dimension a few months later when Stalin broke the sacred blood barrier. It had taken place on an afternoon in early May, when Natalia, Liova, Maurice, Magdeleine, and Lev Davidovich, with Maya the dog running ahead, had gone down to the coast to enjoy the afternoon breeze with a carafe of Greek red wine while the Turkish policemen prepared a seafood-based dinner in the Ottoman fashion, seasoned with spices. Due to his excessive exertions in setting up the villa, Lev Davidovich was suffering from a lumbago attack that barely allowed him to make headway on the many writings he was engaged in. After the first glasses of wine, the Pazes had given free rein to their enthusiasm over the possibility of being able to fight alongside the mythical Lev Trotsky. It pleased them that the Exile who was watching the sunset with them in Prinkipo in 1929 was not the same man to whom they had bid goodbye in Paris in 1916, when he moved with an exalted voice but without a specific role in the clandestine movement on whose success very few were betting. Now they said that he was the Exile, known around the world as Lenin's companion, the leader of the October uprising, the victorious commissar of war and creator of the Red Army, the cheerleader of the Third International, which he had founded with Vladimir Ilyich. Even Maurice, perhaps convinced that his host was in need of encouragement, reminded him that he had been at a height from which it was impossible to descend, from which he was not allowed to withdraw, and he spent his time exalting his historical responsibility, since no Marxist, with perhaps the exception of Lenin, had ever had so much moral authority, as a theorist and as a fighter. And he had concluded: "Your rival is History, not that upstart Stalin who will fall at any moment under the weight of his own ambitions . . ."

The Exile tried to downplay that historic greatness, reminding his interlocutor that, besides his back pain, he had nothing else behind him. The hostility surrounding him was infinite and powerful and his main conflict was with a revolution that he had led to triumph and with a state that he had helped to found: that reality was tying one of his two hands.

Despite praises like these and the proofs of affection that arrived with his correspondence every day, Lev Davidovich knew that those followers did not have the scars that can only be left by real combat. Because of that, he silently entrusted the future of his battle to the deportations of oppositionists that Stalin would undoubtedly order; the tempering of those men forged by repression, torture, and confinement, with their convictions unaltered, would strengthen the movement.

The arrival of summer would break the island's peaceful charm with the noisy and vulgar arrival of businessmen and government employees from Istanbul with the economic means to withdraw to Prinkipo, but not enough to travel to Paris and London. Confined to his house, Lev Davidovich had managed to make a final push in the work in which he reviewed his life, despite not having been able to escape the disappointment he felt as he received news of the orgy of surrenders through which the opposition groups were dragged by their most important leaders. From the recently founded *Bulletin Oppozitsii*, which they started to edit in Paris, and through the messages filtered to the interior of the Soviet Union in the most incredible ways, he focused on warning his comrades that Stalin would try to make them give up their positions with political promises that he would never keep (Lenin used to say that his specialty was breaking promises) and announcements of rectifications that he would not execute, since they implied the acceptance of compromises that the man from the mountains would never recognize. To those who surrendered, he wrote that Stalin would only admit them into Moscow when they showed up on their knees, willing to recognize that Stalin was always right, and never them, he wrote.

That stream of surrenders convinced Lev Davidovich that his war seemed to be lost, at least within the Soviet Union. Stalin's sudden about-face, after appropriating the opposition's economic program and forcing his former rivals to declare themselves supporters of the strategy that was now presented as Stalinist, sealed the political failure that wrote its most regrettable chapter with the surrender of men who, with hands and feet tied, had started to ask themselves why they needed to keep enduring deportations and submitting their family members to the cruelest pressures in order to defend some ideals that, at the end of the day, had already been imposed. The most painful proof of the fall of the opposition had been the announcement that brilliant men like Radek, Smilga, and Preobrazhensky had demonstrated their willingness to reconcile themselves with Stalin's line, declaring that there was nothing reprehensible about it, once the great objectives for which they had fought had been achieved. Especially despicable to him was the attitude of Radek, who had declared himself an enemy of Trotsky's ever since the latter had published articles in the imperialist press. The saddest thing was knowing that, with this surrender, those revolutionaries were falling into the category of the semi-forgiven. Presided over by Zinoviev, these men would live in fear of saying a single word out loud, of having an opinion, and would be forced to slither along, turning their heads to watch their shadows.

The most vivid news about the state of the opposition would come to Büyükada through an unexpected channel. It happened at the beginning of August and its messenger was that ghost from the past called Yakov Blumkin.

Blumkin had sent him a message from Istanbul, begging for a meeting. According to his note, the young man was on his way back from India, where he had carried out a counterintelligence mission, and he wished to see him to reiterate his respect and support. Natalia Sedova, when she found out about Blumkin's desires, had asked her husband not to see him: a meeting with the former terrorist, now a high-ranking GPU officer, could only bring about disgrace. Liova had also expressed his doubts about the usefulness of that meeting, although he'd offered to serve as a mediator in order to keep Blumkin far from the island. But Lev Davidovich thought that they should hear what that man wanted, linked as he was to Lev Davidovich ever since the latter exercised the most dramatic of all his powers: that of letting Blumkin live or sending him to his death.

Twelve years before, when the newly made commissar of war Lev Trotsky had called for him in his office, Blumkin was a callow youth—like a character out of Dostoyevsky—who faced charges that the military tribune would penalize with a death sentence. That young man had been one of two militants in the social-revolutionary party that had tried to kill the German ambassador in Moscow with the intention of discrediting the disputed peace with Germany that the Bolsheviks had signed in Brest-Litovsk at the beginning of 1918. The evening before the trial, after reading some poems written by the young man, Lev Davidovich had asked to meet with him. That night they spoke for hours about Russian and French poetry (they shared an admiration for Baudelaire) and about the irrationality of terrorist methods (if a bomb could solve everything, what was the good of parties, of class struggle?), at the end of which

Blumkin had written a letter in which he regretted his action and promised, if he was forgiven, to serve the revolution on any front to which he was assigned. The influence of the powerful commissar was decisive enough to pardon his life, while the German government was informed by official means that the terrorist had been executed. That day Yakov Blumkin's second life had begun, thanks to Lev Trotsky.

During the civil war, Blumkin had stood out as a counterintelligence agent, something which earned him decorations, promotions, and even militancy in the Bolshevik Party. Considered a traitor by his former comrades, he miraculously escaped two attempts on his life. In the final months of the war, as he recovered from the wounds from the second attempt, he was an adviser to Lev Davidovich, who recommended him to the military academy upon seeing his aptitude. His capacity for espionage missions would lead him to the world of intelligence, and for many years he had shined as one of the stars of the secret service, for whom he still worked despite the fact that everyone, even the GPU's highest leader, knew that, because of his devotion to Trotsky, his political sympathies were with the opposition.

When Liova relayed the details of his meeting with Blumkin (the former terrorist had gone to India, and now to Turkey, to sell some very old Hasidic manuscripts in order to obtain funds for the government), Lev Davidovich was convinced that the secret agent still had the same affection for him as always. And despite all of Natalia Sedova's precautions, he agreed to see him.

When Lev Davidovich saw the unmistakably Jewish face of little Yakov, as he used to call him, his large eyes sparkling with intelligence again, he felt a deep happiness infused with waves of nostalgia. They melted in a hug and Blumkin kissed his host's face and lips many times, only to cry later, as he did on the night in which he had written the saving letter in the office of the powerful commissar of war.

The three visits that Blumkin made to Büyükada in the second week of August were like a reviving breath of air against the discouragement that was overcoming Lev Davidovich. Between evoking the past and news of the present, they laughed, cried, and argued (even about Mayakovsky and the lamentable state of Soviet poetry), and Blumkin, in addition to bringing him up-to-date about the desperate situation for the opposition inside the country, insisted on serving him as a courier during his imminent return to Moscow, since he thought that his work in intelligence had the mission of neutralizing enemies outside of the USSR, but was not incompatible with his oppositionist political ideas.

From the agent's mouth, Lev Davidovich also heard Radek's arguments to dramatize a surrender that, according to the young man, could only be a maneuver to gain time. Blumkin, showing his invincible capacity for loyalty, defended his friend Radek's position, since he also thought that if it was possible to fight from within the party, it was better than doing so outside of it. Lev Davidovich confessed that he no longer trusted the abilities of a party that was led by a man like Stalin and in which Radek was active. But Blumkin was surprised at his pessimism and reminded him that it was he, Lev Trotsky, who could not become weak.

The young man's departure left a void in the Exile that, weeks later, would be replaced by the malignant feeling of indignation caused by infidelities. The catalyst for the mood change had been a letter from the Pazes in which, following colder greetings than usual, the authors went right to the matter without further ado: "Don't put too much stock in the weight of your own name," began that paragraph with the air of an epitaph, which made the revolutionary face the evidence of his political ruin in an alarming way. "For five years, the communist press slandered you to the point that for the masses there is only a vague remembrance of you as the head of the Red Army, as the workers' leader in October. With each passing day, your name means less, and the machinery that has been unleashed will end up devouring you after your name has been devoured." Upon reading it for the third time, he had needed to clean his glasses, rubbing them with the edge of his Russian shirt, as if the lenses were truly responsible for the murky perception of words that sounded painful but true. When he stepped away from the window from where he had observed the garden taken over by weeds and, beyond, the oily shine of the former Propontis, he felt that not even his impermeable optimism nor his faith in the cause could remove him from the invasive feeling of solitude that seized him. How many setbacks had taken place in the span of just a few months so that Maurice and Magdeleine Paz would write him that letter poisoned with truths? How had reality come to insist on exchanging a discourse dedicated to the pride of a colossus for these reflections directed at the humiliation of a forgotten man? . . . The most insulting thing about the letter was the fact that, just one month before, during their second visit to Prinkipo, the Pazes had not dared to confess to him their apprehensions and had left promising to work for the unity of French Trotskyists, amid whom, they had again confirmed, the Exile's prestige and ideas had remained unscathed.

For weeks that letter floated around Lev Davidovich's desk as a testament to what he didn't want to wash his hands of but that he didn't want to take care of either. Motivated by the calm brought by the approach of winter, he had focused on serious work and was immersed in the writing of his *History of the Russian Revolution*. At some point, Natalia Sedova had even told him to answer that letter once and for all and he had made excuses.

Prinkipo's winter temperatures were nothing like the ones they had experienced the year before, in Alma-Ata. Barely covered with an old coat, Lev Davidovich had gotten used to enjoying the arrival of morning in his study as he drank coffee and contemplated how the dawn's light filtered in through a silver veil that made the sea sparkle. That day he was ready to work on his *History of the Russian Revolution*, when Liova entered to pull him out of his deliberations: news had arrived from Moscow. As always, the feeling that something serious could have happened to a loved one wounded the Exile. Liova, as if he couldn't make up his mind to speak, went to sit on the other side of the table so he would be in front of Lev Davidovich, who remained silent, convinced that he was going to hear something terrible. But his son's words overwhelmed him. They had executed Blumkin.

Liova had to relay all of the details: there was no news about the agent because for two months he had been shut up in the depths of the Lubyanka, subject to interrogations by his secret police comrades. According to the Soviet informer, the detention had occurred following a denunciation by Radek, whom Blumkin himself had informed of his meetings with Trotsky. Radek, nonetheless, denied that he had betrayed him, and insisted that the GPU had found out on its own that Blumkin visited Trotsky and returned to the Soviet Union with correspondence for the oppositionists. No one knew the exact date on which he had been executed, Liova said.

Lev Davidovich noticed how a feeling of guilt invaded him. Natalia Sedova had been right: he should have never received the young man, since now it seemed clear that Stalin had made him go through Turkey because he knew Blumkin would try to see him and a meeting would allow him to teach the oppositionists a real lesson. But this time Stalin had gone too far: killing his rivals over political disputes was making the same mistake as the Jacobins and opening the revolution's doors to revenge and fratricidal violence. One of the conditions always demanded by Lenin (who was not very compassionate when politics demanded it of him, he told Liova) was that blood should not run between them. Little Yakov's death had to serve to stir the consciences of all the Communists obeying Stalin. Blumkin could be the Sacco and Vanzetti of their struggle, he told Liova, who stared at him. If the young man had felt compassion for his father for a moment, by then he must have already been reproaching himself.

When Liova left, Lev Davidovich, his eyes fixed on the sea, thought that he would regret for the rest of his life that his emotional weakness had prevented him from recognizing Blumkin's presence in Turkey as the start of a sibylline game of chess organized by Stalin. With that spirit, he took a sheet of blank paper and set about to fulfill an outstanding obligation:

M. and Mme. Paz:
Today I've received news that highlights the pettiness of people like
you, who are nothing more than parlor-room Bolsheviks and for
whom the revolution is a pastime. You, who have not suffered
repression, torture, or winter in the work camps, have the possibility of
giving up the struggle when it doesn't meet your expectations of
success and prominence. But the true revolutionary is born when he
subordinates his personal ambitions to an idea. Revolutionaries can
be educated or ignorant, intelligent or stupid, but they cannot exist
without will, without devotion, without the spirit of sacrifice. And as
those qualities do not exist in you, I am grateful to you for having so
diligently stepped out of the way.
L. D. Trotsky

In that first year of exile, Lev Davidovich had only been able to count defeats and defections: inside the Soviet Union, the opposition had practically disintegrated, without there being any of the expected deportations. Outside the country, his followers were fighting for a piece of power, over being more or less to the left, or simply abandoned the struggle, as the Pazes did, unable to resist Stalinist pressures or because of a lack of a clear prospect for success . . . Perhaps it was for that reason that the news of Mayakovsky's suicide continued to shake him for weeks, during which he had come to feel guilty for having argued with the poet so many times, perhaps providing fodder to the detractors who had popped up all over the country.

The arrival of the first copies of his anxiously awaited autobiography barely gave him any satisfaction amid so many losses. Upon rereading the work, finished a year earlier, he regretted having dedicated so many pages to a self-defense that was beginning to seem futile in the middle of the torrent of adversities that preyed on his friends' lives and dignity; his insistence on contextualizing his disagreements with Lenin throughout twenty years of struggle seemed opportunistic, and above all, he reproached himself for not having the courage to recognize, with helpful or perhaps harmful hindsight, the excesses that he himself had committed in order to defend the revolution and its permanence. Although he would never publicly admit it, for many years already Lev Davidovich had regretted the moments in which, from his position of power, he had allowed force to take over, independent of the goals being pursued. The militarization of the railroad unions he imposed, when the outcome of the civil war depended on the locomotives standing still on the country's tracks, now seemed excessive to him, even when it was upon that measure that the fate of the revolution had rested. He already knew that he would never be able to forgive himself for the attempt to apply the same coercive measures to postwar reconstruction when it became clear that the nation was on the verge of disintegration and it was not possible to persuade disenchanted workers without applying force. On his shoulders lay the responsibility for having removed union leaders, for having erased democracy from workers' organizations, and for contributing to their turning into amorphous bodies that now gladly used Stalinist bureaucrats to cement their hegemony. As part of the power apparatus, he had also contributed to killing the democracy that he now demanded as an oppositionist.

His role in crushing the Kronshtadt naval base rebellion in the ill-fated month of March 1921 was no less shameful to him. That detachment, whose support guaranteed the success of the Bolshevik coup in October 1917, would demand four years later such basic rights as greater freedom for workers, less despotic treatment for the peasants forced to hand over the bulk of their harvests, and, above all, the sacred right to free elections to the Soviet assemblies. The reasoning that the new sailors

of the Baltic fleet were being manipulated by anarchists and counterrevolutionary officers should never have justified the measure that he, as
commissar of war, had applied: the squashing of the revolt and the unleashing of violence that even extended to the execution of hostages. For
him and for Lenin, it had been clear that the punishment was a political
necessity, since even though they knew that the protest had no possibility
of turning into the predicted third revolution, they feared that it would
aggravate to unsustainable limits the chaos in a country besieged by hunger and economic paralysis.

He knew that if in March 1921 the Bolsheviks had allowed free elections, they probably would have lost power. The Marxist theory, which he
and Lenin used to validate all of their decisions, had never considered the
circumstance that once the Communists were in power, they could lose
the support of the workers. For the first time since the October victory,
they should have asked themselves (did we ever ask ourselves? he would
confess to Natalia Sedova) if it was fair to establish socialism against or at
the margin of majority will. The proletarian dictatorship was meant to
eliminate the exploiting classes, but should it also repress the workers?
The dilemma had ended up being dramatic and Manichaean: it was not
possible to allow the expression of the people's will, since this could reverse the process itself. But the abolition of that will would deprive the
Bolshevik government of its basic legitimacy: once the moment arrived
in which the masses ceased to believe, the need arose to make them
believe by force. And so they applied force. In Kronshtadt—as Lev
Davidovich knew so well—the revolution had begun to devour its own
children and he had been bestowed the sad honor of giving the order that
started the banquet.

The harshness with which he had acted (generally backed by Lenin)
could perhaps have been justified in those years. But now, upon reviewing their attitudes, he couldn't stop asking himself whether, if he'd had
the necessary shamelessness and shrewdness to grab power after Lenin's
death, he would not also have turned into a pseudo-communist czar.
Wouldn't he have raised the excuse of the revolution's survival to crush
rivals, as Lenin did in 1918 to outlaw the parties that had fought for the
revolution alongside the Bolsheviks? Would he have been capable of withstanding the democratic relevance of an opposition, of factions within
the party, of a press without censorship?

Lev Davidovich would prove how deeply absorbed his energies were in the avatars of politics when his wife surprised him with the news that Liova wished to leave Prinkipo. The hidden tremors that had been shaking the cement of the Büyükada villa for some months were revealed at that moment, when they had already reached earthquake-like proportions. He then remembered that Natalia Sedova had commented once that it wasn't good for Jeanne Molinier to spend long periods of time with them while Raymond returned to Paris. He had engaged in that conversation on an afternoon in which they had gone on a walk to the impressive structure of the former Prinkipo Palace Hotel, the largest wooden building in all of Europe, and when he heard her, he had sardonically asked what was happening. She smiled while she explained things with her usual pragmatism: what was happening was that wives should be with their husbands and their Liovnochek was getting old and the years had clouded the vision of even a man like him.

Until that moment, the comings and goings of Raymond Molinier had been just one more event in the routine of Büyükada. Gifted with that *énergie Molinièresque* that was so attractive to Lev Davidovich, he had turned into the mainstay of the opposition in Paris. Excited by the possibility of turning Trotskyism into a political force within the French left, Molinier had placed his devotion, his fortune, and his family at the service of the project, and while he fought in Paris to find new followers, his wife, Jeanne, had turned into the intermediary between the secretariat managed by Liova and the Trotskyist sympathizers in Europe. Molinier's energy had touched a sensitive nerve in the experienced revolutionary, and that is why he had decided to put the fate of the French opposition in his hands, ignoring the opinions of other comrades, such as Alfred and Marguerite Rosmer, who discreetly decided to withdraw from the ring.

But it was only now that he found out that, from the first time that Raymond left his wife in Büyükada, Natalia had sensed what was coming: Jeanne was a young woman gifted with a languor that served to contrast her husband's bullishness, and every cell of Liova's body pulsed with his twenty-three years, even when he had given himself over body and soul to the cause. Because of that, while his wife conveyed the news that Jeanne would travel to Paris with the intention of breaking off her relationship with Raymond, and that Liova was planning to go off somewhere else with her, the revolutionary understood how little he had worried about his son's needs, although he immediately thought that the work of so many months—the Pyrrhic and painful benefit extracted from upsets and defections—could go down the tube, dragged by the egotistical impulse of a man and a woman. And that same night, unable to contain himself, he reprimanded Liova for his sentimental affair, unforgivable in a fighter.

Fortunately, Raymond's reaction was deeply French, according to Natalia, and he allowed Jeanne to go live with Liova, who was already planning to move to Germany. Lev Davidovich then understood that he had no alternative but to accept his son's decision: although the young man's spirit of sacrifice was immeasurable, he could not demand that he invest his youth in a lost island. What would hurt him the most, he wrote, would be losing the only man with him on whom he could unload the weight of his frustrations, the only one from whom he could receive sincere criticism, and the only one whom he could trust to never be the one tasked with stabbing him, serving him poisoned coffee, or sending the bullet through his head that, sooner or later, would take his life.

But his concern over Liova's departure was momentarily overshadowed by a little-known event that gave Lev Davidovich a bad premonition: the German elections, carried out on September 14, 1930, had turned Hitler's National Socialist Party into the country's second most popular. The leap had been to 6 million votes from 800,000 in 1928. Perplexed before the strange political irresponsibility of the German Communists, Lev Davidovich read that the Communists were celebrating their own increase from 3 million to 4.5 million votes, and declared that the Hitlerite upturn was the swan song of a petit bourgeois party condemned to failure. Several months earlier, in one of the letters with which he used to bombard the Soviet party's Central Committee, he had already warned them about the dangerous establishment of National Socialism in Germany, which he saw as the bearer of an ideology capable of coalescing all of that "human dust" of a petit bourgeoisie crushed by the crisis and eager for revenge. Since then, he'd begun to insist on the need for a strategic alliance between Communists and Socialists to stop the process that could bring the Hitlerites to power. But the response to his premonitory cry of alarm had been the order from Moscow, channeled through the Comintern, that the German party should abstain from any alliance with Socialists and democrats.

Never more than at that moment had Lev Davidovich felt the weight of his sentence. Shut away on an island lost in time, his ability to act was reduced to writing articles and to an organization of scattered followers, when in reality he should have been in the center of events that, he could feel it in his skin, involved the fate of the German working class, the European revolution, and perhaps of the Soviet Union itself. He knew that it was necessary to mobilize the consciousness of the German left, since it was still feasible to avoid the disaster being drawn over the sky of Berlin. Didn't anyone notice that if his path wasn't closed off, Hitler would come to power and the Communists would be his first victims? What was happening in Moscow? he asked himself. He sensed that something dark was brewing behind the Kremlin's red walls. What he still could not imagine was that very soon he would hear, from the highest towers of the Muscovite fortress, the first howls of a macabre creature capable of terrorizing him.

5

The dense air caressed the skin and the sparkling sea hardly emitted a lulling murmur. There, one could feel how the world, on magical days and moments, gives the deceptive impression of being an affable place, tailor-made to the dreams and strangest desires of man. Memory, imbued with that relaxed atmosphere, managed to become lost, and bitterness and sorrows fell into oblivion.

Seated on the sand with my back leaning against the trunk of a casuarina tree, I lit a cigarette and closed my eyes. There was an hour to go until the sun went down, but, as was becoming a habit in my life, I was in no rush and had no expectations. I practically had none, and practically without the practically. The only thing that interested me at the time was enjoying the gift of twilight's arrival, the fabulous moment at which the sun closes in on the silvery gulf and draws a fiery trail on the surface. In the month of March, with the beach practically deserted, the promise of that vision was the cause for sudden calm within me, the state of closeness to the balance that comforted me and still allowed me to think in the palpable existence of a small happiness tailor-made to my meager ambitions.

Prepared to wait for the sunset in Santa María del Mar, I had taken out the book I was reading from my backpack. It was a volume of short stories by Raymond Chandler, one of the writers at that time, and still today, to whom I was solidly devoted. Getting them from the most unimaginable places, I had managed to make an almost complete collection of Chandler's works out of Cuban, Spanish, and Argentine editions, and besides five of his seven novels I had several short story collections, including the one I was reading that afternoon, called *Killer in the Rain*. It was a Bruguera edition, printed in 1975, and along with the title story it had four others, including one called "The Man Who Loved Dogs." Two hours before, while I was making the journey by bus to the beach, I had started reading the book right at that story, attracted by such a suggestive title that directly touched on my weakness for dogs. Why, amid so many other possibilities, had I decided to take *that* book on *that* day and not a different one? (I had at my house, among the many recently obtained and waiting to be read, *The Long Goodbye*, which would end up being my favorite of Chandler's novels; *Rabbit, Run* by Updike; and *Conversation in the Cathedral* by the already excommunicated Vargas Llosa, that novel that a few weeks later would make me shake with pure envy.) I think I had picked *Killer in the Rain* completely unconscious of what it could mean and simply because it included that story that features a professional killer who feels a strange predilection for dogs. Was everything organized like a game of chess (another one) in which so many people—that individual whom I would name, precisely, "the man who loved dogs" and I, among others—were pieces in a game of coincidence, of life's whims or of the inevitable intersections of fate? Teleology, as they call it now? Don't think I'm exaggerating, that I'm trying to make your hair stand on end, nor that I see cosmic conspiracies in each thing that has happened in my damned life; but if the cold front that had been predicted for that day had not dissolved with a fleeting rain shower, barely altering the thermometers, it's possible that on that March afternoon in 1977 I would not have been in Santa María del Mar, reading a book that, by coincidence, contained a story called "The Man Who Loved Dogs," and with nothing better to do but wait for the sun to set over the gulf. If just one of those circumstances had been altered, I would have probably never had the chance to notice that man who stopped a few yards away from where I was to call out to two magisterial dogs who, just at first sight, dazzled me.

"*Ix! Dax!*" the man yelled.

When I lifted my gaze, I saw the dogs. I closed the book without thinking twice about it in order to devote myself to contemplating those extraordinary animals, the first Russian wolfhounds, the valued borzoi, that I had seen outside the pages of a book or the veterinary magazine for which I worked. In the diffuse light of the spring afternoon, the wolfhounds looked perfect while they ran along the seashore, causing explosions of water with their long, heavy legs. I admired the sheen of their white hair, dotted with dark violet on their spines and their back legs, and the sharpness of their snouts, gifted with jaws—according to canine literature—capable of breaking a wolf's femur.

About sixty feet from them was the silhouette of the man who had called to the dogs. When he began to walk toward where the animals and I were, the first thing I asked myself was who that guy could be to have two seemingly purebred Russian wolfhounds in Cuba in the 1970s. But the animals running and playing shifted my attention again, and with no other motive but curiosity I stood up and walked a few steps toward the shore to better see the borzois, now that the sun was behind me. In that position, I once again heard the man's voice and for the first time I decided to look at him.

The man must have been around seventy years old (I would later find out that he was almost ten years younger), his salt-and-pepper hair was in a buzz cut, and he wore tortoiseshell glasses. He was tall, olive-skinned, mostly thick but also somewhat gawky. He had two leather leashes in his hands and his right hand was covered by a band of white cloth, as if he were protecting a recent wound. I noticed that he was wearing khaki-colored cotton pants, leather sandals, and a wide, colorful shirt: an outfit that immediately revealed his condition as a foreigner in a country of this-is-all-we've-got shirts (striped or checked), run-or-I'll-kick-your-ass or "stinky feet" shoes (Russian boots or plastic moccasins), and sailcloth or polyester pants that would smother your balls in the summer heat.

We came so close to one another that our eyes inevitably met: I smiled at him, and the man, with the pride of the owner of two Russian wolfhounds, also smiled. After calling to the dogs again, he lit a cigarette and I decided to imitate him, to advance another four, five steps to where the presumed foreigner had stopped.

"Your dogs are beautiful."

"Thank you," the man answered. *"Ix! Dax!"* he repeated, and I was still incapable of placing his accent.

"It's the first time I have ever seen borzois." I preferred to look at the animals, now that they were running close to their owner.

"They're the only ones in Cuba," he said, and I thought: He's a Spaniard. But there were some strange inflections in his intonation that made me doubt it.

"They need a lot of exercise, although they have to be careful with the heat."

"Yes, the heat is a problem. That's why I bring them out here."

"I've read that these animals are very strong but at the same time very delicate. They were the dogs to the Russian czars." I wondered if it wouldn't be too daring, but since I had nothing to lose, I made the leap: "Did you bring them from the Soviet Union?"

The man looked toward the sea and dropped his cigarette in the sand.

"Yes, they were given to me in Moscow."

"I'm sorry, but you're not Russian, right?"

The man looked me in the eye and snapped the leashes against the leg of his pants. I deduced that perhaps he hadn't liked being mistaken for a Russian, but I convinced myself that my question did not give the impression of that possibility. Or was he Russian—no, perhaps Georgian or Armenian, by the color of his hair and his skin—and that was why he had that strange intonation and a certain thickness upon pronouncing his words?

At that instant, in the clearing between the casuarinas, I saw a tall, slim black man who, with a towel rolled over his shoulder, observed us without the least reserve, as if he were keeping watch on us. But I turned my gaze when I heard the man in tortoiseshell glasses whispering something in a language I couldn't place, either, as he put the leashes on the dogs. When the man stood up, I noticed that his steps faltered, as if he'd gotten dizzy, and I heard him breathe with some difficulty. But he immediately asked me:

"How is it that you know so much about dogs?"

"I work for a veterinary magazine and, coincidentally, I just reviewed an article about genetics that a Soviet scientist wrote, and he said a lot about borzois and two other European breeds. Besides, I love dogs," I answered in one breath.

For the first time the man smiled. The lack of response regarding his origins, his unusual look, and the fact that he had lived in Moscow—in addition to the presence of that tall, slim black man watching us—suggested the possibility to me that the man with the dogs was a diplomat.

"I would like to read that article."

"I think I could get a copy," I said, not considering that to fulfill that promise (until the magazine came out, which wouldn't be for another couple of months) I would most likely have to type up that article full of strange genetic codes myself.

"I love dogs," the foreigner admitted, using the very verb "to love" in that way in which almost no one ever used it anymore, and in his smile I seemed to glimpse a hidden nostalgia that had nothing to do with what he said next: "Goodbye."

I mumbled a delayed farewell, and I'm not sure if the man, who was already walking away toward where the tall, slim black man was, heard me. The dogs, when they discovered his intent, started running toward the black man, who got on his knees to welcome them and devoted himself to rubbing their bellies with the towel that had been hanging on his shoulders until then. The foreigner got close to them. He veered off, as if he were making a small turn or it was impossible to walk in a straight line, and after saying something to the black man, he got lost among the casuarinas, followed by the two wolfhounds, who were now walking at their owner's pace. The black man, who had turned around for a moment to look at me, placed the towel over his shoulder again and followed them, until he also disappeared amid the trees.

When I looked at the coast again, the sun was already touching the sea on the horizon and drawing a red trail that came to its end, with the waves, just a few yards from my feet. The night of March 19, 1977, was beginning.

When I met the man who loved dogs, it had been just over a year since I had started to work as a proofreader at the veterinary magazine. This fate was the result of my third fall, one of the most drastic in my life.

In 1973, when I graduated from the university with excellent grades and the added prestige of having published a book, I was selected to work as the editor in chief of the local radio station in Baracoa, the lost and remote town (there are no other adjectives to describe it) that was filled with the pride—according to a combination of historical fact and human imagination—of having had the privilege to be the first *villa* that was founded, as well as the first capital of the island recently discovered, by the Spanish conquistadors. The promotion to a position with so much responsibility—as the *compañero* who assisted me at the work placement office, department of recent university graduates, told me—was due to the fact that, in addition to my scholarly achievements, as a young man of my time, I should be willing to go wherever and whenever I was ordered to go, for the necessary amount of time and under whatever conditions, although he decided to omit the fact that, legally, I was obliged to work wherever they sent me due to the stipulations of the call to social service law that all of us recent graduates were meant to fulfill in return for having received our degrees for free. And what the *compañero* also failed to tell me, despite this being the real reason for which someone decided *to select and promote me* to Baracoa, was that they had deemed I needed a "corrective" to bring me down and place me squarely in this world, as the saying goes.

The greatest incentive to get me on the bus that would deposit me in Baracoa twenty-six hours later was thinking about the advantage that kind of exile in a tropical Siberia would provide: if anything was plentiful in the place, it would be time to write. That dream beat inside me like a fetus in its placenta, like a biological need. Around that time, I was already pretty lucidly conscious that the stories in my published book were of a calamitous quality, and if they'd received the coveted standing of finalist in a young writers contest, which included the publication of the volume, it was more due to the issues discussed and my approach to them than to the literary value of my texts. I had written those stories imbued by, more so stunned by, the closed, rugged world lived between the four walls of literature and ideology on the island, devastated by the cascade of defenestrations, ejections, expulsions, and "*parametraciones*" of people who were inconvenient for a variety of reasons carried out in recent years and by the predictable raising of the walls of intolerance and censorship to celestial heights. I was not the only one, or anything close to it, who had acted like the diligent ape Chandler spoke of, and under the romantic conviction that almost all of us had at that time, I had begun to write what, without much room for speculation, *should* be written at that moment in history (of the nation and all of humanity): stories about hardworking sugarcane cutters, brave soldiers defending the homeland, self-denying workers whose conflicts were related to the hindrances of the bourgeois past still affecting their consciousness—machismo, for example; doubts about the application of work methods, to give another example—legacies that, hardworking, brave, and self-denying as they were, they without a doubt found themselves in the midst of overcoming on their ascent toward the moral condition of New Men . . . But sometime later, when I had looked inside myself and made a shy literary attempt to remove myself from that blueprint so as to paint it with different shades, they had slapped me with a ruler so that I would remove my hands.

It now seems strange, almost incomprehensible, to explain that, despite the reality that tried to assault us every day, for many of us that was a period lived in a kind of bubble, in which we kept ourselves (in truth, we were kept) removed from certain fires raging around us, even in our own neighborhoods. I think that one of the reasons that nourished my gullibility (I should say *our* gullibility) was that at the end of the sixties and beginning of the seventies, when I was going to high school and college, I was a die-hard romantic who cut sugarcane to the point of physical exhaustion during that interminable harvest of 1970, who broke his back planting Caturra coffee, underwent devastating military training to better defend the homeland, and joyously attended parades and political gatherings, always convinced, always armed, with that compact militant enthusiasm and that invincible faith that imbued almost all of us in carrying out almost all of the acts of our lives and, especially, in the patient although certain wait for the luminous better future in which the island would flourish, physically and spiritually, like a garden.

I think that in those years we must have been the only members of our generation in the whole of Western student civilization who, for example, never put a joint between their lips and who, despite the heat running through our veins, would belatedly free ourselves from sexual atavism, led by the damned taboo of virginity (there is nothing closer to communist morality than Catholic precepts); in the Spanish Caribbean, we were the only ones who lived without knowing that salsa music was being born or that the Beatles (the Rolling Stones and Mamas and the Papas *too*) were the symbol of rebellion and not of imperialist culture, as we were told so many times; and besides, as should be expected, amid other shortcomings and disinformation, we had been, at the time, the least informed about the extent of the physical and philosophical wounds produced in Prague by tanks that acted as more than threats, about the massacre of students in a Mexican plaza called Tlatelolco, about the historic and human devastation unleashed by our dear Comrade Mao's Cultural Revolution, and about the birth, for people of our age, of another kind of dream, kindled in the streets of Paris and in rock concerts in California.

What we were aware of and very sure of was that only loyalty and

67

more sacrifice was expected of us, obedience and more discipline. Although after the painful failure of the 1970 harvest, we knew that the luminous future was approaching slower than we had thought (I'll never forget the four months that I spent on a sugarcane field, cutting, cutting, cutting, with all my strength and my faith in each blow of the machete, convinced that that heroic enterprise would be decisive for our exit from underdevelopment, as we had been told so many times). In reality, we barely had a notion of how that political-economic disaster, if you'll allow me to call it that, had changed the country's life. The shortcomings that became sharper since then didn't surprise us, since we were already growing accustomed to them; nor did it alarm us that, as a response to the economic failure, ideological demands would become even more evident, since they were already part of our lives as young revolutionaries aspiring to be true Communists, and we understood or wanted to understand them as necessary. That in the midst of all that effervescence we would find out that two of our university professors had been suspended from their jobs for having confessed to their religious beliefs moved us, but we listened in silence and accepted as logical the accusations destined to cement a decision ratified by the party and with the support of the Ministry of Education. Later, that two other professors would end up being definitively turned out due to their "inverted" sexual preferences didn't alarm us too much and, if anything, caused a hormonal shakeup, since who would have said that those two professors were a pair of dykes, especially the dark-haired one, who was pretty hot for being forty.

It had to have been at some point in 1971—the year in which the environment became heated with the express order to hunt down any type of witch that might appear in the distance—when I committed a serious sin of sincerity and innocence in a public way. Everything started when I dared to comment, among my friends, that there were other professors who, thanks to the red ID cards they carried in their pockets, were allowed to keep teaching when everyone knew all too well that they were less capable as educators than the ones who had been removed for being religious; and that there were others, also survivors and holders of this ID, who seemed more like faggots and dykes than the two exterminated professors. I don't remember if I even added that, in my opinion, neither the beliefs of one set nor the sexual inclinations of the other should be considered a problem as long as they didn't try to force them upon their students. A few months later, I would find out that this inopportune comment had become the cause of my first fall, when in my growth as a youth militant I was denied entrance in the youth elite due to not having been capable of overcoming certain ideological problems and for lacking in maturity and the ability to understand the decisions made by responsible *compañeros*. And I accepted the critique and promised to make amends.

Although I didn't know it at the time, those murky gusts of wind were part of a hurricane blowing silently but devastatingly across the island, bringing with them a concept of society and culture adopted from Soviet models. The inclusion of two sessions of weekly classes set aside for reading political speeches and materials, the renewed demands regarding hair length and pants width, and the critique of students whose preferences leaned toward Western and North American culture, had almost symbiotically integrated themselves into the universe we lived in, and we dealt (at least, I dealt) with all of those fundamentalisms without any great conflicts or worries, without having any notion of the quasi-medieval darknesses and desires for lobotomy underpinning them. Almost without questioning anything.

With all of my political and literary ingenuity weighing me down—and a bit of talent, I think—I started writing those stories out of which I made a volume of almost one hundred pages that I sent off to a contest for unpublished writers. Two months later, surprised and happy, I received the notice that I'd been named a finalist, which, in addition, meant the manuscript's publication. That success cleaned my spirit of possible doubts, and for the first and only time in my life—perhaps because I was completely wrong—I felt sure of myself, of my possibilities and ideas: I had proved that I was a writer of my time, and now I only had to work toward cementing the ascent to artistic glory and social utility, as we thought of literature back then (that it seemed more like a damned staircase and not the profession for unhappy masochists that it really is).

Between the demands of my studies and the never-ending extracurricular political-ideological activities (as controlled and valued, perhaps even more so, as the scholastic ones)—in addition to the paralysis caused by the drunkenness I felt as a result of my success and the resulting unexpected popularity and preeminence (I was elected secretary for cultural activities of the student federation in my department) but above all, thanks to the real literature I was reading at that time—for almost two years I didn't write another story that seemed even close to my abilities and ambitions. But by the fourth and final year of my degree, with my book—*Blood and Fire*—already published, I had to stay in bed for three weeks due to a sprained ankle. Then I wrote a story, longer than the ones I tended to write, in which I found a subject and, after that, a tone and way of looking at reality that made me happy and showed me, without my being a genius, how much I was able to surpass myself. Without a doubt, the reflux from the fatalistic tide, but especially those readings that I had pursued with more effort, trying to find the ethical reasons and technical qualities of the greats—Kafka, Hemingway, García Márquez, Cortázar, Faulkner, Rulfo, Carpentier (damn! how far away from them I was)—bore the most timid fruit in that tale in which I relayed the story of a revolutionary fighter who feels afraid and, before becoming an informer, decides to commit suicide. Of course, I couldn't even imagine that I was getting ahead of myself and borrowing from my own future of panic-ridden fears and about something worse: their devastating effects.

At the end of January 1973, when the first-semester exams had barely ended, I drafted the final version of that story and took the typed pages to the same university magazine where a year and a half before one of my stories had been published, endorsed by an editorial introduction that spoke of me as a promise of national, almost international literature because of my realist solutions and socialist artistic vision. They received the new work enthusiastically and told me that surely they'd be able to publish it in the March issue or, at the latest, in April. But I didn't have to wait that long to know how my best story was read and received: one week later, the magazine's director called me for a meeting in his office and there I experienced the second and, I think, most painful fall in my life. I had just entered when the man, in a rage, spit out the question "How dare you turn this in?" "This" referred to the pages of my story that the infuriated director, disgusted I would say, held in his hands there, behind his desk.

To this day, the unnatural effort of remembering what that powerful man, sure of his ability to fill me with fear, said to me is still too painful. No matter that my story repeated itself so many times, with so many other writers, I'm going to summarize it: that story was inopportune, unpublishable, completely inconceivable, almost counterrevolutionary—and hearing that word, as you can imagine, caused a chill. But despite the seriousness of the matter, he, as the magazine's director, and *los compañeros* (all of us knew who they were and what *los compañeros* did), had decided not to take any measures against me, keeping in mind my previous work, my youth, my obvious ideological confusion, and they were all going to act as if that story had never existed, as if it had never come out of my head. But *they* and he hoped that something like that would not happen again and that I would think a little bit more when I wrote, since art is one of the revolution's weapons, he concluded as he folded the sheets, stuck them in a drawer of his desk, and, with overt gestures, locked it with a key that he put in his pocket with the same forcefulness with which he could have swallowed it.

I remember that I left that office burdened with a vague and doughy mixture of feelings (confusion, disquiet, and a lot of fear), but above all, feeling grateful. Yes, very grateful that when I had just four months left to finish my degree, other measures had not been taken against me, and I knew what they could be. Today, besides, I knew exactly what it was to feel FEAR, like that, a fear with a capital *F*, real, invasive, omnipotent, and ubiquitous, much more devastating than the dread of physical pain or the unknown that all of us have experienced at some point. Because that day what really happened was that they fucked me for the rest of my life, since besides feeling grateful and full of fear, I left there deeply convinced that my story should never have been written, which is the worst thing that they can make a writer think.

It's obvious that that episode, in addition to my well-tracked commentary about the expulsions of my professors and my recent interest in writers like Camus and Sartre (Sartre, so beloved on the island until just a few years before and now so damned for having dared to voice some criticism that revealed his morally corrupt petit bourgeois ideology), were on another desk the day on which they decided my professional fate as a recent graduate. The brilliant idea they had was to send me, for a necessary purification under the guise of a reward, to the remote Baracoa, where I arrived in the month of September, under the reign of a humid and suffocating heat as I had never felt before, although with the innocent feeling that there I would manage to mend my literary hopes. What I could still not even conceive of was how abysmal that second fall had been, the irreversible inoculation that I had experienced, and because of that I was still convinced that, despite the slipping of the "inopportune" story, I was prepared to ably write the works that my time and circumstances demanded. And with these I would show, incidentally, how receptive and trustworthy I could be.

The radio station's chief editor was only waiting for my arrival to get away from Baracoa and barely dedicated a week to instructing me on the technical details of my job. At first sight, my responsibility was simple: reviewing the bulletins drafted by two writers and making sure that they were never missing the national news published in the party and its youth arm's newspapers, nor the chronicles by the official journalists and the volunteer correspondents about the innumerable activities that the provinces' institutions generated and, especially, those promoted by the party, the Youth, the unions, and the rest of the organizations in the "regional," as the former and later recovered municipalities were classified. I will never forget my colleague's smile when he shook my hand and gave me the key to his office, the day on which control was officially ceded to me. And it's less likely that I will forget the words he whispered:

"Get ready, friend: you either become a cynic here or they'll turn you to shit . . . Welcome to the real reality."

Its own inhabitants say that hanging over Baracoa is the curse of Pelú, a mad prophet who sentenced it to being the town of never-fulfilled plans. The first thing that they'll tell you upon arriving is that its fame is based on three lies: that it has a river called Miel (Honey) that doesn't sweeten anything, because only water runs through it; having a Yunque (Anvil), which is the mountain on which nobody can forge anything; and having a Farola (street lamp)—the name of the highway that connects the "city" with the rest of the country—that doesn't light up anything.

I knew that Baracoa owed its name to the indigenous chiefdom that existed there when the conquistadors arrived. But very soon I would discover that, four and a half centuries later, it was still a chiefdom, ruled now by the leaders of local organizations. I would also quickly learn that the maxim of "small town, large hell" was never more appropriate than it was there. And to complete my education in real life, in Baracoa I would experience the consequences of my human and intellectual incapacity to deal with caciques and devils every day.

The Radio Ciudad Primada de Cuba Libre station was precisely the medium charged with bringing about a virtual reality even more deceitful than the rivers, mountains, and highways with capricious names, because it was built on plans, promises, goals, and magical numbers that nobody took the care to prove, on constant calls to sacrifice, the watchfulness and discipline with which every one of the local leaders tried to build the staircase for his own ascent—crowned with the prize of getting out of that lost place. My job consisted of receiving phone calls and messages from those figures so that I would look out for their interests, which they always called, of course, the country's and the people's interests. And my only alternative was to accept those conditions and, cynically and obediently, order the two alcoholic and moronic automatons who worked as writers to write about expectations exceeded, commitments accepted with revolutionary enthusiasm, goals achieved with patriotic combativeness, and incredible numbers and sacrifices taken on heroically, in order to give a rhetorical form to a nonexistent reality, based almost always on words and slogans, and very seldom on real plantains, sweet potatoes, and pumpkins. The only alternative was to refuse or, further still, quit and run away, and despite what I thought many times, fear of the consequences (canceling my university degree, for starters) paralyzed me, as it did so many others. That was the real reality that my predecessor had welcomed me to.

But instead of doing that job pragmatically and shamelessly, like so many other people, and filling my free time with reading and literary projects, out of my own fear or incapacity to rebel I saw myself dragged by a whirlwind of activities, meetings, rallies, and gatherings always preceded by an invitation to the "journalist *compañero*" to the eating and drinking fests (who said there are shortages?) organized by the head of the morning and evening edition sectors. With a bit of surprise, I discovered that in that environment, my usual sexual shyness disappeared with the barriers brought down by alcohol, the feeling of escaping from the confinement of that remote place, and the urgency (my own and that of my occasional lovers) to free something within ourselves. I never ate, drank, or screwed so much or with so many women or in such inconceivable places as during those two years, at the end of which I ended up reacting like a cynic capable of lying without any scruples, with gonorrhea that I generously spread around, and—like many of the inhabitants of the area—turned into an alcoholic of the sort who have a drink of *aguardiente* and a cold beer for breakfast to clear up the effects of last night's hangover.

Baracoa, it's time to say it, is one of the island's most beautiful and magical places, and its inhabitants are surprisingly kind and innocent people. Although I have never returned to visit—I am panic-stricken and terrified by the idea of returning there and by thinking that for some reason I wouldn't be able to leave again—I recall, like in a haze, the beauty of its sea, its decadent colonial fortresses, its mountains thick with vegetation, its multiple streams and rivers that could become furious, like the Toa. I recall the friendliness of its people—always willing to welcome outsiders and pariahs looking for a place to lose themselves—and the poverty that besieged the city for almost half a millennium and that was its true curse; a poverty that was still throbbing and was always discussed in the past tense, like something that had been definitively overcome, throughout my two years at the head of the "information center" of the local radio station.

Now it seems clear that only by being drunk, rolling around with the first woman to cross my path (who was also drunk if, like me, she was one of the ones sent to work there for two or three years), and wrapping myself in cynicism was it possible for me to resist that journey through reality. My third fall would take place when, back in Havana, I admitted myself to the addiction treatment center of Calixto García Hospital, after having enjoyed a three-week stay in the adjoining wing, where they admitted me to the trauma clinic. I had arrived there on a stretcher, with fractures and wounds received as the result of a tumultuous fight that, perhaps to free some of the fear stuck deep within me, I had unleashed in the first bar I visited upon returning to Havana.

6

Her parents named her África, like the patron saint of Ceuta, where she had been born, and rarely had a name fit someone so well: because she was vigorous, unfathomable, and wild, like the continent to whom she owed her name. Ever since the day he met her, at a meeting of the Young Communists of Cataluña, Ramón felt absorbed by the young woman's beauty, but above all, it was her rock-solid ideas and her telluric drive that ensnared him: África de las Heras was like an erupting volcano who roared a permanent clamor for revolution. África tended to cite passages by Marx, Engels, and Lenin from memory; she spoke of dear Comrade Stalin as the incarnation of the future on earth and called him with adoration the Guide of the World's Proletariat while she championed the strictest partisan discipline. Besides, she considered dancing and wine to be bourgeois poisons for the spirit; she seemed to have sewn the book of Marxism under her arm and possessed a militant consciousness that overwhelmed Ramón's romantic enthusiasm and constantly put him to the test.

Ramón had returned from France a year before, when he was about to turn twenty. Barely arrived in Barcelona, he had managed, thanks to his training as a maître d'hôtel, to be placed at the Ritz as a kitchen aide, and he never knew if it was because of the ideas that Caridad had transmitted to him or because of his own spirit of rebellion, but he soon approached the local Communists and made his first steps toward his enrollment. The Spain that Ramón had found was simmering, waiting for someone to add fuel for the flames to reach the heavens; it was a country in pain that strived to throw off the burden of the past and the frustrations of the present. The dictator Primo de Rivera had just resigned and the monarchists and the Republicans had unsheathed their swords. The unions, dominated by Socialists and anarchists, had multiplied their power but, in comparison with France, the Communists were still very few and, as could be expected in an almost feudal and horribly Catholic country, were ill regarded and frequently pursued.

Ramón enjoyed that tense environment, in which everyone was expecting something to happen very soon and in the end it happened when the Republican Socialists, with the support of the syndicalists, won the municipal elections of 1931, causing the fall of the monarchy and the proclaiming of the Second Republic. Until the end of his life, Ramón would think that he had returned to his country at the exact moment, at the right age, and with his mind bubbling; it was as if his life and history had been lying in wait for each other, each one weaving its story to set him on the path that would lead him, a few years later, to the Sierra de Guadarrama and, from there, to a commitment with the highest responsibility.

The party strategy at the time was to first consolidate the Republic to later radicalize it, and because of that, young Communists supported at that difficult time the government's feeble measures against the Church's power and landholdings, for the equality of women and men, for workers' rights, and, above all, for the rights of the great Spanish rural masses, backward and wretched. Years later, Ramón smiled upon recalling slogans more full of words than solutions; but for all of those years, even during the war, that had been the country of slogans, and each party, each faction, each group, unfurled theirs wherever they could, at meetings and in newspapers, on walls, on display windows, on streetcars, and even on the coal trucks that ran around the cities.

Ramón rode the tide of those years fully and irresponsibly. More than any real knowledge of communist principles, it was his capacity for obedience and self-sacrifice that allowed him to hold a position of prominence on the board of the Young Communists, and that role pushed him to live intensely. Ramón would always long for those days in which, like never before in the history of Spain, he had loved so much, with so much anxiety, as if there were an orgy of physical and intellectual passions.

It was then that he met África de las Heras, the second woman who would be of crucial and also traumatic importance in his life. She was three years older than he was, dark-haired, intelligent, and very beautiful; she never put cosmetics on her face and she lived every second and every act like a true communist militant. Despite Ramón's already internalized rejection of everything established by the codes of bourgeois morality, he couldn't help falling in love with her. Like any young man with hormones charged with dynamite, he made it his job to be deserving of the girl's attention, and threw himself after her in the most frenetic political maelstrom. When he listened to her reasoning, he assumed the theories professed by that red beauty without a single critique and understood (or said he understood in some cases) the risks awaiting the political struggle in a republic of lesser nobles and bourgeoisie; he reaffirmed the idea that the Trotskyists were the most sybilline enemies of the Communists and that anarchists and syndicalists could only be viewed as disposable fellow travelers on the ascent to the highest purposes, which would be divergent when they, the Communists, were able to promote the true revolution led by a necessary proletarian dictatorship. For the first time Ramón would hear insistent talk of Trotsky the opportunist, exiled in Turkey at that time, as the slyest of enemies, and of his Spanish followers as dangerous infiltrators within the working class. But África's true passion gushed out when she spoke on the political thought and practice of Joseph Stalin, the man who led the Bolshevik revolution to its radiant consolidation. África's devotion was able to infect him with that terrifying hate for Leon Trotsky and worship of Stalin, without Ramón being able to imagine where those passions would lead him.

When Ramón managed to get África to pay attention to his demands, the young man entered a higher phase of dependency. The complete way of making love with which África crushed him—that uninhibited and elemental wisdom capable of driving him crazy—placed him at the woman's mercy and gave him equal measures of pleasure and pain, since in his still palpable petit bourgeois weakness he dreamed that África was his, and when he possessed her, he thought he was the luckiest man on earth. But when he saw that she was slipping through his fingers, he experienced attacks of rage-filled jealousy, even though he tried to strengthen himself by accusing himself of lacking the necessary ideological conviction to break down the barriers of emotion and of lacking the drive to reach the revolutionary heights from which that woman's principles shined, committed as she was only to the cause, wed only to the idea.

África de las Heras would show Ramón that love and family were feelings and circumstances that could bring down the revolutionary: she, for example, had broken with her husband over an overt ideological incompatibility, since he was professing the anarchist-syndicalist creed. Ramón, who already felt the need to free himself from his family ties, barely maintained any relation with his relatives in that time, and since then decided to become stronger and not encourage them. Of Caridad, he received only news that she had been through Paris and now lived in Bordeaux, while he had cut off all contact with his father since, upon returning to Barcelona, he found out through the house's former cook that Don Pau, selling the family mansion to move in over the warehouses of Calle Ample, had given away Ramón's dogs to a peasant he had found in the Sant Gervasi market. Of his siblings, he knew that Montse and little Luis had been taken in by his father, that Jorge had also fallen for the party, and that young Pablo, the only one he saw with any frequency, was active in a Catalan nationalist organization, like their father.

But the breaking with his old affections was not difficult because Ramón, in reality, had eyes that saw only what África brought to light as he followed her around Barcelona brainlessly, begging her between meetings and gatherings to give him a couple of hours of passion, for which his flowering body was always ready.

It was precisely in the spring of 1933 when Ramón understood that, no matter how much he ran, he would never catch up with África unless he made a moral and prodigious leap toward the future. While Ramón, África, Jaume Graells, and the leaders of the Young Communists in Barcelona were working to achieve the growth in the militancy that would allow them to become a force of influence in the decentralized Spanish political panorama, Ramón was called to fulfill his military service and sent for four weeks to a training camp near Lérida. When he returned to Barcelona with his first pass, he challenged himself to carry out the plan he elaborated during that month, always calling up the look África would give him in his imagination: Was it a happy one or mocking one? he tormented himself. They arranged to meet at a café close to the cathedral and, to make a big entrance, he waited for África's arrival using the window of a religious articles shop as a mirror. When he saw her approaching, he controlled his anxiety and let a few more minutes go by. Then he walked toward the café, ready to face the young girl's reaction to his change of appearance: Ramón was wearing the army's dress uniform for corporals designated to lead parades. He qualified thanks to his height (he was more than six feet high, taller than the typical Spaniard of his time) and physical abilities (he was able to bend a copper coin between his fingers). Ramón knew that the dress uniform, which included a silver hat, looked marvelous on him, but above all it made him feel different and gave him the pleasure of knowing he was being looked at. The shine of those stripes had made him think that perhaps he could make a career out of the army, where, he would explain to África (whose knowledge seemed infinite), he would carry out effective work gathering recruits for the party and the future revolution.

When Ramón entered the café, he didn't find her. He thought that she had gone to the bathroom and he went to lean on the bar, where he held back the desire to ask for a drink and opted for chamomile tea. The owner of the café observed him with the admiration that Ramón knew he inspired and served him the tea. When she returned from the lavatory, he stood up with all of his dazzling height. África looked at him with her critical eyes and brought him down with one blow:

"Why did you come all dressed up? Do you like it when people look at you?"

Ramón felt the world falling apart around him and, with difficulty, managed to share his idea of working for the cause from within the reactionary redoubt of the army. The girl only commented that they should consult with their superiors, since it wasn't a personal decision: a militant responds to his committee and discipline and . . .

He understood; that was why he was asking her.

"It could be a good idea," she said, perhaps as a consolation; but without offering any apology, she told Ramón she had to leave for a meeting.

The young man ordered a cognac and, while he drank it, felt like crying. Since África wouldn't be returning, he thought he could allow himself that. You're too soft, Ramón, he told himself. He finished his drink and went out to the street, where a young woman's intense stare raised his devastated self-esteem.

A few months later, at the very moment he was going from obligatory service to an intended profession in the army, Ramón would have his dreams of feeling important and doing a great service for the revolution crushed when his political affiliation was considered an impediment and the army decided to let him go. Then he swore to himself that the military would pay for that affront.

Reformism leads to restoration: only communist power, mercilessly proletarian, can carry out the deep transformations that a country like this, sick with hate and inequality, demands—as África, always adept at formulas, used to repeat. And Ramón would understand the extent to which that young woman had been right when, at the end of that same year, the conservatives rose up with the electoral victory and began an artful dismantling of the Republican political changes with the repeal of social benefit decrees and the start of an agrarian counterreform that would return the lands to the feudal lords and the country to its interminable Middle Ages.

It was the Asturian miners and the Catalan nationalists who in the month of October 1934 reacted against the laws promoted by the dismal Spanish Confederation of the Autonomous Right, and first proclaimed a general strike and, in the end, rose up: the miners clamoring for revolution and the nationalists for a statute of autonomy. The young Communists had been given the order to be prepared to intervene, even in a violent way, if the conditions evolved favorably in Barcelona. But the Catalan project was devastated in one blow and before the popular revolt that they were awaiting could begin. By contrast, the Asturian miners' strike was consolidated and the Young Communists, as part of the communist block, supported the rebels. África and Ramón, disillusioned by the Catalan leaders' lukewarm response, asked to be sent to Asturias, where things were steaming following the drastic abolition of currency and private property and the creation of a proletarian army. As a reactionary ring was already being set against the miners, the party ordered the young Communists to stay in Barcelona, where they would work to procure the weapons that the rebels needed so badly. Ramón, anxious to get to the action, in that meeting dared to criticize that dilatory tactic, and it was África herself who shook him, alarmed by his inability to understand the party's strategic decisions at a time of murky historical circumstances. "The party is always right," she said, "and if you don't understand, it doesn't matter: you have to obey," and she cut the discussion short.

The repression of the miners was brutal and that October Revolution ended up diligently crushed. The casualties—almost 1,400—and the arrested—more than 30,000—convinced Ramón that compassion doesn't exist, nor can it exist, in a class struggle. And he trusted that someday their day would come: at least dogma stipulated that it would be so.

With the Asturian defeat, the Communists were placed on the black list of the most vigorously pursued enemies. Many were among those imprisoned for their participation in the Asturias events or simply because of their militancy and, as had happened in prerevolutionary Russia, recalled África, so conscious of history, so dialectic, the rest had had to go down into the catacombs, to work from there and wait for the moment (called "revolutionary situation") to deal a blow to the system.

It was in these circumstances that the Young Communists' leaders received the mission of creating clandestine cells in the city's neighborhoods and factories. África went to work in Gràcia and Ramón went into El Raval and La Barceloneta, where he also organized literacy classes. With the goal of making the political work more efficient and of preparing members for future conflicts, Ramón organized a cell with Jaume Graells, Joan Brufau, and other comrades that would present itself as the Peña Artística y Recreativa, and they gave it the least suspicious name they could find: "Miguel de Cervantes." The Joaquín Costa bar, at the end of Calle Guifré, turned into the meeting place. They went two and three nights a week, many times with África, who developed her skills as an agitator there, with a vehemence that left Ramón ever more entranced by the young woman's passion and faith in the fate of a humanity without exploiters or exploited. Everything worked according to plan for several months, until they made the mistake of becoming too complacent and were surprised when the police burst in, carrying off seventeen of them (África managed to escape by leaping over a wall difficult for even a man to scale), accusing them of conspiring against the republic to subvert order and institute an atheist and communist dictatorship.

If Ramón had still needed any reasons to convince himself that the whole pantomime of a democratic republic was just a façade and that the system needed to be pulled out by the roots, the eight months he spent in jail in Valencia ended up deepening his convictions. It wasn't that the accusations hurled at them were false: it was true that they were conspiring to subvert order, but it was also assumed that they had the right to that option in a republic that, according to what was preached, existed in a supposedly democratic country since 1931.

Spain's prisons were overflowing with prisoners, perversely mixing common prisoners with political ones, although the detained Communists were so great in number that the cell blocks turned into forums where they discussed the party's projections, the dangerous ascent of fascism in Germany and Italy, the USSR's economic successes, and the principles of class struggle. The unexpected directive from Moscow, that an alliance be established between the Communists and the leftist parties (except for Trotskyist opportunists) to throw themselves into the fight for power together, even made its way into prison, and Ramón accepted the order without daring to question that radical strategic change. For him, the real punishment of his prison stay was that África did not visit him during all those months or even send a letter, a breath of hope.

The elections of February 1936, won by the new political front of Socialists, Communists, and anarchists, returned power to the left and, immediately, the freedom of those detained for their activism or participation in the 1934 revolts. After eight months of prison, when Ramón stepped out onto the street, he was no longer an impulsive young romantic: he had turned into a man of faith, a terrifying enemy of everything that could block the path to freedom and the proletarian dictatorship. To that goal, he would dedicate every breath of his life, he thought: even if I have to pay the highest of prices for it.

Like many of his prisonmates, Ramón went directly from Valencia to Madrid, where the Popular Front parties had organized a great rally to celebrate victory and the formation of a new government. In the capital, they found that festive and nervous air that reigned over Spain until the start of the war. The wineskins leaped from the sidewalks to the trucks of the recently released, the women tossed flowers at them, and cries of "Long live liberty" and "Death to the monarchy, to the bourgeois, to the landholders, and to the Church" competed. The revolution could be smelled in the air.

In the meeting, Ramón heard General Secretary José Díaz's speech and for the first time saw an exalted and dramatic woman who looked like a rally herself: Dolores Ibárruri, whom the world would know as La Pasionaria (Passion Flower). To his great pleasure, in the midst of that combative crowd, he felt the longed-for arms grab on to his neck, from

82

which came the perfume of violets that he had not ceased dreaming of during his imprisonment. With every cell of his body, Ramón enjoyed the sound of the voice of the woman for whom, like the world revolution, he was willing to give everything; but upon seeing her, he thought that miracles might exist, for África was a confirmation. In those months, she had become more beautiful, she was rounder and firmer, as if a beneficent cloak, capable of transforming her, had fallen over her face. A few minutes later, when they escaped the crowd inflamed by songs and wine, he would know that something moving really had taken hold of the woman's body—something that had been distant from his life until that moment: a month and a half before, África had given birth to a girl. Ramón's daughter.

Ramón Mercader would think, almost until the idea wore out, that in his life, so full of tremendous convulsions, one of the greatest and most instructive things that shook him from head to toe was receiving that news. África told him that she hadn't gone to see him in prison or brought him up to speed on her pregnancy so as not to weaken him with feelings that were unnecessary for a revolutionary. Besides, she had preferred to deal with her pregnancy alone, since—from the moment she discovered it and was advised not to abort due to how far along she was, she had decided that the baby would not interfere with the greatest purpose of their lives: the revolutionary struggle. Because of that, as her due date approached, she had gone to Málaga, where her parents lived, and there had the girl, whom she had named Lenina de las Heras, to immediately hand her over to her grandparents and return to Barcelona to fight for the Popular Front's electoral victory, as the party's committee had ordered her. Her decision to keep the girl far away was irrevocable and nothing would change it: she was only fulfilling her duty to be honest by informing him of what had happened.

A cloud of passionate feelings crowded Ramón's head. To the surprise of learning he was a father was added África's determination of keeping with her ideals. Although it all ended up being too overwhelming to digest in one piece, he was surprised to feel a sharp gratefulness toward the woman he loved so much and who showed him her political stature with a drastic and liberating action. Nonetheless, in the deepest recesses of his consciousness, he felt a sliver of curiosity about what the girl he had fathered was like, what it would be like to have her close and raise her. Didn't África feel the same? Ramón knew that the needs of the struggle would soon erase that blip, and he thought, with more conviction: África is right, family can be a burden to a revolutionary. As they crossed the Plaza de Callao, he believed that much without knowing precisely why.

África opened the door to a café on Gran Vía and, upon entering, the light from the street prevented Ramón from seeing the inside of the place, one of those old bars in Madrid with the walls done over in dark wood. África, as if guided by an interior light, walked to the back, skirting tables and chairs with that confidence so like her. He tried to follow her, leaning on the backs of the chairs, when he made out the silhouette of a woman, according to her hair, in the back, a tall, strong woman, he realized as he got closer. The shadow approached him, and before Ramón had identified her, he felt a tremor run through him when the woman kissed him, so close to the edge of his lips as to leave the unmistakable taste of aniseed in his mouth.

7

Kharalambos moved the rudder slightly and, under the afternoon sun, the boat entered the golden river over a sea that the young fisherman had learned to navigate with his father, his father with his grandfather—just as his grandfather had with his great-grandfather—in an accumulation of knowledge that went back, perhaps, to the days in which Alexander's armies passed through those waters with the fury and glory of the great king of the Macedonians. More than once, observing Kharalambos's seafaring expertise, Lev Davidovich had asked himself if the time had come for him to carry out an act of utmost wisdom and throw off all of his defenses to give himself the chance to breathe, for the first time in his adult life, the simple air that nourished the fisherman's blood, far from the maelstroms of his epoch.

Four years of exile, five of being marginalized, dozens of deaths and deceptions, revolutions betrayed and ferocious repressions, Lev Davidovich added them up and had to admit that there were few reasons for hope. The cosmopolitan man, the protagonist of the struggle, the leader of the multitudes, had begun to grow old at fifty-two: he had never imagined that the corner of the world in which he was living would one day cause him to feel that perhaps he had that which is called a home. And still less that, for a moment, he would wish to give everything up and throw his weapons into the sea.

It had been a year since he had seen Liova leave by the route that Kharalambos now navigated. With a mix of concern and relief, he had accepted the young man's decision to live his own life, far from his father's shadow. The receipt of a scholarship to continue studying math and physics at Berlin's Technische Hochschule had facilitated the paperwork, and Lev Davidovich had decided to make the most of the situation of the young man being transferred to a privileged position, where he would serve as his eyes and voice while he remained immobile in Turkey.

As the date of his departure drew near, Lev Davidovich had evoked, too frequently, the memory of those cold mornings in the tormented Paris of 1915, when Liova had been initiated into political work at just barely eight years of age. They then lived on rue Oudry, close to the place d'Italie, and he spent his nights writing antiwar articles for the *Nashe Slovo*. In the morning, on the way to school, with young Seriozha by the hand, Liova was in charge of handing over the recently written pages to the print shop. Only with the certainty of separation could Lev Davidovich understand the immense space that Liova occupied in his heart and regretted the outbursts of anger in which, so unfairly, he had accused him of laziness and political immaturity. As happened to him two years before when he separated from Seriozha, after his departure he was seized by the same disastrous feeling that perhaps he would never again see his beloved Liova, but he managed to dispel that feeling through the most realistic inversion of equations: if they didn't see each other again, it wouldn't be because Liova would miss their next meeting. The absent one would surely be Lev Davidovich himself, who with each passing day was feeling older and attacked by rivals who wished for his absolute silence.

But the young man's departure was not Lev Davidovich's greatest concern during those weeks. With his best foot forward, although full of fears over his inability to deal with domestic problems, he also had to prepare himself for the announced arrival of Zina, his oldest daughter, who had finally obtained a Soviet permit to travel abroad with the purpose of undergoing treatment for her advanced tuberculosis.

In the letters that she sent from Leningrad, Alexandra Sokolovskaya, Zina's mother, had kept him up-to-date on the girl's physical and mental deterioration in recent years, above all as she devoted herself to taking care of her sister Nina at the same time that, due to her activism in the opposition, she experienced political repression that had culminated in the deportation of her husband, Plato Volkov, and with her own expulsion from the party and the loss of her job as an economist. Zina would experience the personal touch of pettiness, however, when her exit permit from Soviet territory excluded her little daughter, Olga, who would become a political hostage. With the sentence imposed on an innocent girl, Lev Davidovich would once again see proof of what Piatakov had assured him of years before: Stalin would take revenge on him, treacherously, until the third or fourth generation.

Zina arrived on a sunny morning in January 1931 with young Seva at her side. Natalia, Liova, Jeanne, the secretaries, the bodyguards, the Turkish police, and even Maya followed Lev Davidovich to the dock to welcome them. Each of their moods was as festive as the circumstances allowed and was rewarded by the smile of a thin woman, exultant and expansive, and by the scrutinizing look of a boy, intensely blond, who had rejected the attention of grandparents and uncles to bestow his favoritism on Maya the dog.

Despite her calamitous state of health, Zina immediately proved that she was the daughter of Lev Davidovich and the indefatigable Alexandra Sokolovskaya, who in the clandestine meetings of Nikolaiev had placed in the hands of the young fighter the first Marxist pamphlets he would read in his life. With wheezing breath and besieged by nocturnal fevers, the young woman arrived demanding a role in the political work, willing to show her abilities and her passion. Conscious that she needed medical attention more than additional responsibilities, her father had assigned her the lightest task, although overwhelming in and of itself, of organizing his correspondence, while he charged Natalia with accompanying her to Istanbul, where the doctors started to work with her.

With the letters that Liova began to send him from Berlin, the old fighter managed to get a better sense of the inexorable disaster at the door of the German Communists. Again and again he asked himself how Moscow was displaying such political clumsiness. You didn't have to be a genius to notice the significance of the rise of Nazism that, without taking power, had already begun a violent offensive, backed by attack forces that in just two months had grown from 100,000 to 400,000 members. The facts revealed that it could not be due to political blindness: the suicidal strategy of the German Communists must have a reason, beyond the explicit guidelines dictated by the masters in Moscow, he thought and wrote.

Some words pronounced in the heart of the Soviet Union revealed a truth that alarmed him. In a hunger-stricken Moscow, where shoes and bread were a luxury, in which dozens of men and women were detained every night without fiscal orders so that they could be sent to Siberian camps, Stalin proclaimed that the country had reached socialism. Socialism? Only then did Lev Davidovich manage to see a ray of light in the darkness: that had to be the origin of the suspicious apathy, the absurd triumphalism that tied the hands of the German Communists, preventing them from any alliance with the country's forces on the left and center. He was terrified when he understood the real reason behind all of those surprising attitudes was that Stalin, to achieve the concentration of power, could not rely on the ghosts of the possible aggressions of French imperialism or Japanese militarism, but rather needed an enemy like Hitler to cement, with the threat of Nazism, his own ascent. Although Lev Davidovich had always been opposed to the possibility of founding another party, out of respect for Lenin's ideas and out of the concrete fear of what the schism could cause, the proof of the betrayal that Stalin was carrying out, whose consequences would be devastating for Germany and dangerous even in the Soviet Union itself, had begun to stir doubts in his mind.

Luckily, the presence of little Seva mitigated his fears. Lev Davidovich established a close relationship very different from the one he, so absorbed in the struggle, had had with his own children. The grandson had managed to appropriate the few hours of free time that his grandfather could give him, and between them they had started the habit of going down to the beach every afternoon, where Seva ran with Maya and, whenever the affable Kharalambos allowed it, boarded the fisherman's boat and navigated out to the cliffs. The affection he felt for the boy lessened his political concerns, and on many occasions he was surprised by a great peace, which allowed him to feel like a grandfather who was beginning to grow old; and for the first time in thirty years he managed to free himself from the urgencies of the struggle. Seva and Maya's races, the conversations with Kharalambos about the art of fishing, the rides around the Sea of Marmara, would soon become pleasant images that he would cling to in the even more difficult moments that awaited him.

One predawn morning in that first summer he spent with Seva, Lev Davidovich would save his life and that of his family thanks to the insomnia of which he'd always been a victim. Lying on his bed, he let one of those weary nights go by while he listened to nocturnal sounds and thought of his son Sergei. That same morning he had received a letter in which Seriozha assured them that his life in Moscow was following a normal course; he spoke of his recent marriage and of his progress in his scientific studies. Although the young man maintained his aversion to politics, his father's intuition told him that that distance could not last much longer and that any day now politics would show up at his door. Because of that, after discussing it with Natalia, he had decided not to put off the proposal any longer that Seriozha begin the procedures that would allow him to travel to Berlin to be reunited with his brother. Wrapped up in those deliberations, it had taken him a while to notice Maya's restlessness; the dog had approached the bed various times, and he had even heard her sniveling. Suddenly a sense of alarm had made him regain his lucidity: the smell of burning wood was unmistakable, and without another thought he had awoken Natalia and run to the room where Seva had been sleeping with the young secretaries ever since his mother had moved to Istanbul to be operated on.

The fire had started on the wall outside the room he used as his office, and Lev Davidovich immediately understood the saboteur's intention: his papers. While the Turkish policemen, awakened from their slumber, threw buckets of water over the fire that was spreading to the living room, he had left Seva and Maya in Natalia's care and, with the help of his secretaries, the bodyguards, and the recently arrived Rudolf Klement, he had started moving the papers that represented his memories and most of his life. Amid the smoke and the water being thrown, they had managed to remove the manuscript folders, the files, and many of the books before the ceiling of that part of the villa gave a groan prior to falling.

In those predawn hours, among boxes of papers and books thrown on the floor, Natalia and Lev Davidovich had watched the fire do its work while he caressed the ears of the shaking Maya. Although the work of improvised firemen had prevented the total destruction of the villa, at sunrise they saw that it was left in such a state that it would have to be entirely rebuilt to again be inhabitable. While the rest of them removed the objects and clothing that had been saved, he devoted himself to gathering dozens of books, water-damaged but perhaps salvageable, and to regretting the loss of other volumes and documents (the photos of the revolution! he would always lament) consumed by the fire.

Rudolf Klement, the young German who had traveled to take over for Liova in the secretary's office, found a house that offered some security, in the Anglo-American residential suburb of Kadıköy, in the outskirts of Istanbul. The residence, in reality, ended up being too small for the family, the secretaries, the bodyguards and the police (four of them since the fire), but above all too small to live with Zina, who—recovered from a surgery that would soon reveal itself to be a complete failure—had begun to demand, with unhealthy vehemence, greater responsibility in the political work.

Several strange events would mark the months that they lived between the oppressive walls of the house in Kadıköy. The first was the possibility, very soon cut short by the joint work of fascists and Communists, that he would travel to Berlin to give some lectures. That predictable setback was a painful disappointment for him: he had again felt on his back the price he had to pay for his past actions and the insuperable weight of a confinement that made him think of that which Napoleon suffered. Do they fear me so much? he had written, exasperated by the invulnerability of the siege that confined him to Turkey and removed him from any possibility of direct participation.

Then there was another attempted fire. Fortunately, this one reached only the backyard shed, and investigators deemed it an accident upon finding the remains of a box of matches Seva had played with on the heating boiler.

The third event, more intriguing and at the same time revealing, happened when they were visited by a high-ranking Turkish domestic security officer charged with informing them that the country's police had detained a group of Russian émigrés who were preparing an attempt against his life. The leader of the plot had turned out to be former general Turkul, one of the White Guard leaders that the Red Army defeated during the civil war. According to the officer, the conspiracy had been dismantled and he could remain calm, under the hospitality of the Honorable Kemal Pasha Ataturk.

As soon as they said goodbye to the officer, Lev Davidovich commented to Natalia that the framework of the story was shaky. The danger that the Russian émigrés stationed in Turkey would commit violent acts against his person had always been latent. But nothing had happened in over two years, which proved that the White Russians did not deem it a priority or understood that attacking him when he was considered a personal guest of the implacable Kemal Ataturk was a challenge that could only prejudice them.

The worst experience of that time, however, were the tensions caused by Zina's instability: she was more demanding every day regarding the participation in partisan jobs, but her behavior oscillated between enthusiasm and depression. Although he insisted, in the kindest ways, she had refused to submit herself to psychoanalytic treatment, since, she repeated, she didn't feel like unearthing all the filth she had accumulated within her. Her disorder had reached a critical point when the failure of her operation was discovered, since the Turkish surgeons had invaded her remaining healthy lung. Fearful for Zina's life or of a direct confrontation with her, Lev Davidovich ordered Liova to make the necessary arrangements for the woman to travel to Berlin and be seen there by specialists capable of mending her body and her spirit.

Once Zina's reservations had been overcome, the woman left for Berlin, leaving her father feeling a mixture of relief and a cutting feeling of guilt. Lev Davidovich had promised her that, as soon as she recovered a bit, she would begin to work with Liova and they would send Seva to her. Meanwhile, for his own stability, the young boy would stay in Turkey, although his grandfather knew that behind the decision to keep the boy was a dose of selfishness: Seva had turned into his best medicine against exhaustion and pessimism.

Zinushka had left in the company of Abraham Sobolevicius, Senin the Giant, one of Lev Davidovich's collaborators based in Berlin, who, coincidentally, had spent a few days at the house in Kadıköy. For the last two years, Senin and his younger brother had turned into his most active correspondents in Germany, but since Liova had been placed at the head of the German followers, relations with the Sobolevicius brothers had undergone a period of tensions, and he attributed it to the preeminence he had given his son in the terrain where the brothers had reigned. The strangest thing in the changed attitude from those comrades was the more or less direct rejection of certain guidelines destined to unmask the irresponsible Stalinist policies regarding the German situation. The resistance of the Sobolevicius brothers, precisely because it came from men who were so experienced, worried Lev Davidovich.

Just a few days after Zina's departure, information filtered in from Moscow to illuminate like a flash of lightning the darkness in which the Exile had spent two years. The source of the information was trustworthy: it came from Comrade V.V., whose existence only Liova and he were aware of, since his role within the GPU made him especially vulnerable and useful. V.V. warned in a report that he had heard just an echo of a comment about the Sobolevicius brothers carrying out espionage work for the GPU within Trotsky's closest circle. But placed in its precise context that comment gave form to the riddle of the brothers' strange attitude.

The discovery of the true nature of the agents—who disappeared as soon as Lev Davidovich made their real affiliation public—plunged him into deep concern. The fact that he had trusted those men to the point of having handed over his daughter to them—of having let them sleep in his house, play with Seva, speak privately with Natasha and with him—warned him of the fragility of any possible system of protection and made evident the dominion Stalin had over his life: for now, the Grave Digger was satisfied with knowing what he was doing and what he was thinking, but what about tomorrow? He was convinced that the fires and the presumed conspiracy of former general Turkul had only been distraction maneuvers in an attack that had barely begun and whose denouement would require neither spectacular actions nor the conspiracies of old White Russian enemies. The final shot would come from a hand, trained by Stalin himself and capable of passing through all the filters of suspicion, until it became the closest thing to a friendly hand. The actions of the Sobolevicius brothers showed him, nonetheless, that his life still seemed necessary for the general secretary to rise to the most absolute of powers. Terrified before the evidence that clarified the reasons for which he'd been allowed to go into exile instead of being killed on the steppes of Alma-Ata, he understood that, while he was alive, he would be the incarnation of the counterrevolution, his image would stain all demands for internal political change, his voice would sound like the perversion of any voice that clamored for a minimum level of truth and justice. Lev

Trotsky would be the measure of justifying all repression, the basis for all the explosions of critics and inconvenient people, a side of the enemy coin of the world Communists: the piece that, to be perfect, would soon have the image of Adolf Hitler on its reverse side.

When the reconstruction work on the Büyükada villa was completed, Lev Davidovich demanded to return. Throughout the nine months he lived in Istanbul, the vertigo of transience and the feeling of finding himself at the edge of a cliff never left his spirit, and he had not even managed to progress as he had hoped on the writing of *History of the Russian Revolution*. For that reason, he trusted that the return to what he now considered his house would allow him to concentrate on what was truly important.

Kharalambos and other villagers were waiting for them on the dock. The Trotskys appreciated a welcome that included a basket of fish, oysters, and fresh seafood; bags of dried fruit tied with goat cheese and plates of the sweets they called apricots; and, as a special treat, a clay pot with a selection of *pochas* and *pides* lying inside, needing only to be placed in boiling olive oil to deliver to the palate a Mediterranean voluptuousness so different from the simple tastes of Russian and Ukrainian recipes.

Very soon the Exile regained his work rhythm and dedicated ten and even twelve hours a day to writing the *History* and to the preparation of two articles for the *Bulletin*. At the end of the day, with the exhaustion that tended to cause bothersome tearing in his eyes, he called to Seva and, preceded by Maya, they went down to the coast to see the sunset. There he told his grandson stories about the Jews of Yanovska; he told him about his mother, Zinushka, recovering in Berlin; and he taught him, supported by the intelligence of the patient Maya, to communicate with dogs and to interpret their language of attitudes.

Just three weeks later, Lev Davidovich would receive the sword cut unleashed from Moscow as the clearest warning that the war against him would not stop and that he would never be allowed the slightest hint of peace. A perplexed Liova was the one who transmitted the news to him: beginning on February 20, 1932, Lev Trotsky and the members of his family who found themselves outside the territory of the Soviet Union ceased to be citizens of the country and lost all constitutional rights and the protection of the state. The crime committed by the former party member—he was no longer mentioned as a leader—had been participation in counterrevolutionary actions, by virtue of which he was considered an enemy of the people, undeserving of holding the nationality of the world's first proletarian state. The decree from the Central Committee's executive presidium, published in *Pravda*, the Communist Party's mouthpiece, included in the recently enacted sentence of revocation of citizenship, thirty other exiles, also enemies of the people, who in their time had been distinguished Menshevik figures.

As he read that malicious communiqué—which, with calculated malevolence, mixed him with former exiles who he himself and Lenin had invited to emigrate in 1921—he closely examined the details and sought the hidden objective in a measure that he himself had inaugurated in Soviet history. Without a doubt, Stalin's prime intention was that of turning him into an outlaw, without a state behind him, totally at the mercy of his enemies, among whom you could now count the very Soviet people. But behind it was the logical consequence of turning his supporters within the country from political oppositionists to collaborators with a "foreign" agent and, as such, accusable of the crime of treason, the most feared in days of patriotic and nationalistic fervor.

Before the abyss he and his family were staring at, Lev Davidovich regretted as never before the lack of realism and the excess of trust that had blinded him for years, to the point of allowing, before his very eyes, the birth and growth of that malignant tumor clinging to the Kremlin's walls called Joseph Stalin. A man like him, who had always valued his own ability to understand the human soul, men's needs and weaknesses, and had prided himself on having the ability to move consciousnesses and the masses—how had he not noticed the fateful air around that dark being? For years, Stalin had been so insignificant that, as much as Lev Davidovich searched his brain, he never managed to visualize what must have been their first meeting, in London in 1907. Then he was the Trotsky that had behind him the dramatic participation in the 1905 revolution, when he came to be the president of Petrograd's Soviet; the orator and journalist capable of convincing Lenin or of confronting him and calling him a dictator in the making, a Russian Robespierre. He was a high-ranking, spoiled, and hated revolutionary who would have looked without any great interest at the recently arrived Georgian, uncultured and without history, with his pockmarked face. By contrast, he could recall him at that fleeting meeting in Vienna, during the year of 1913, when somebody introduced him formally, without deeming it necessary to tell the man from the mountains who Trotsky was, since no Russian revolutionary could help but recognize him. Lev Davidovich still remembered on that occasion Stalin had barely held out his hand before turning back to his cup of tea, like a malnourished animal—whom he would only manage to fix in his memory because of that cornered and yellow stare, coming out of small eyes that, like those of a lizard lying in wait (yes, that was the detail!)—didn't blink. How could he not have noticed that a man with that reptilian stare was a highly dangerous being?

During the vertigo of 1917, on very few occasions Stalin had passed in front of him, like a furtive shadow, and Lev Davidovich had never given him a thought. Later, when he at last stopped to think of him, he discovered that the Georgian had always repelled him because of those qualities that must have been his strength: his essential meanness, his psychological crudity, and that cynicism of the petit bourgeois whom Marxism had freed from many prejudices but without managing to substitute them with a well-assimilated ideological system. Before each one of the attempted approaches carried out by Stalin, he had instinctively stepped back and had unwittingly provided the distance for resentment; but he had not understood the error of his calculation until years later. "The main quality that distinguishes Stalin," Bukharin had said to him one day, "is laziness; the second, limitless envy of everyone who knows or could know more than he does. He has even undermined Lenin."

Lev Davidovich would come to have the conviction that his greatest mistake had been not fighting at the moment in which it was already clear that a struggle for power had begun and he had in his hands the crushing victory represented by Lenin's letters reprimanding Stalin for his brutal handling of the "nationalities question" and the "Testament" in which Vladimir Ilyich asked that the Georgian be removed as party secretary. But at that moment he had thought that Stalin was not a considerable rival and that launching a campaign against the man from the mountains would be viewed as a personal battle to take over Lenin's position (as it would have been manipulated by Stalin's followers within the party), and Lev Davidovich was not able to think about that possibility without feeling ashamed. Later he would understand that even with the support of Lenin's will and opinions, he had lost that battle a long time before: beneath his feet a well-laid-out conspiracy had been organized, and Stalin—with Zinoviev and Kamenev's complicity and Bukharin's cowardly support—had disarmed him without his noticing; his fall was already a reality that needed only to be consolidated. The worst, nonetheless, was knowing that his defeat did not signify only *his* defeat but that of an entire project—and not because he saw his access to power impeded but because he had also facilitated Stalin's ascent and, with it, the annihilation of the social dream that the unstoppable Georgian was carrying out.

Lev Davidovich needed several days to begin to ponder the response demanded by that decree. Knowing that he was going to be assaulted by enormous and immoral propaganda resources, capable of lying before the eyes of the world without the slightest shame, he debated between drafting a measured communiqué, focused on the illegality of the sentence, and a frontal attack directed against the dictator. But what occupied his mind most vehemently was whether the time had not come to resign from a struggle for the reform of the party and the Soviet state that was becoming all the more unviable: whether the hour had not arrived to throw himself into the void and proclaim the need for a new party capable of recovering the truth of the revolution.

The echoes of the decree would soon begin to penetrate the atmosphere of his private life. Zina, also affected by the punishment, sent him a desperate message from Berlin: How would she now meet with her daughter again, who was still in Leningrad? And she demanded Seva's presence, since she wanted to live with at least one of her children. Never before that moment had Lev Davidovich felt the burden of family.

A message brought from Moscow by friendly hands arrived at Prinkipo to confirm for Lev Davidovich the magnitude of the disaster that was being forged in his old country. The remittent was Ivan Smirnov, the old Bolshevik he was united with in an intimate friendship, and who had been one of the staunch oppositionists in the summer of 1929. Smirnov had quickly understood that, even though he had been assigned an official position, his fate had been marked by having confronted Stalin under the renegade Trotsky's banner. Sensing the counteroffensive his old comrade would undertake, Smirnov had decided to run the risk of sending him a report about the proportions of the economic and political devastation ravaging the USSR and that, nonetheless, offered very little hope for the victory of any opposition, at least in the short term.

To justify his capitulation, Smirnov commented that in 1929 the economic about-face unleashed by Stalin seemed a logical and even moderate process that followed the ideas almost step-by-step about industrialization and the collectivization of land that until then had been the program and simultaneously the mark of an opposition accused of being the enemy of the peasants and fanatics of industrial development. However, the crushing of the faction led by Bukharin and the surrenders of the last Trotskyist oppositionists had left Stalin without adversaries and allowed him to turn the war against the enriched peasants in a storm of collectivizing violence that had succeeded in paralyzing Soviet agriculture: first the large landholders, then the medium and small landholders later, upon seeing their wealth threatened by expropriations that included even the hens and guard dogs, had opted for a silent sabotage, and an orgy of animal sacrifices resulted that filled the countryside with foul-smelling bones and the steam of boiling oil, and that finished off half the nation's livestock. As could be expected, they also began to devour the wheat and all other grains, without stopping at the seeds meant to guarantee the coming harvest, which was only planted and tended to when the peasants were placed at the end of the barrel of a rifle. The neglect was aggravated with the transfer of entire villages and towns from the Ukraine and the Caucasus to the forests and mines of Siberia, from where the government planned to extract the wealth the land had ceased to produce. The predictable result had been a startling famine that ravaged the country from 1930 with no end in sight. In the Ukraine, there was talk of millions of people dead from starvation, and it was even said that there had been acts of cannibalism. In the cities, the people fell over themselves for potatoes in the black market, paying exorbitant amounts of rubles so devalued that many could only engage in commerce through barter. How many lives paid the price of that "attack" on socialism was something that could never be known, and Smirnov was of the opinion that the nation's agriculture would not recover in the next fifty years.

No less devastating, Smirnov said, was the way that Stalin had insisted on erasing those elements of memory that didn't meet with his version of Soviet history, dedicated to promoting his preeminence. A few months before, Riazanov, the director of the Marx-Engels Institute, and Yaroslavsky, the author of the most widely circulated *History of the Bolshevik Revolution*, had been expelled under the charge of not sufficiently rescuing the Leninist legacy. The real reason was that Riazanov could not prove that Stalin had made any contribution to Marxist theory, and that Yaraslavsky's *History*, already sufficiently altered, could not totally glorify Stalin, since the events of the revolution were too recent and too many of its main characters were still living.

Stalin's violent egotism, his former comrade commented, had taken even more painful paths due to their irreversible and catastrophic effects. With the "Great Change," the idea had arisen to convert Moscow into the new socialist city; and Stalin placed himself at the head of the project that had started with the transformation of the Kremlin, within whose walls the monasteries of the Miracles and of the Ascension, built in 1358 and 1389, and the magnificent Nicholas Palace, a work from the time of Catherine II, were demolished. Outside of the Kremlin, the most regrettable destruction had been that of the Temple of Christ the Savior, the biggest sacred building in the city, 270 feet high, its walls covered with Finnish granite and marble slabs from Altai and Podole, its dome lit up by bronze sheets, its main cross thirty feet high and its four towers, topped by fourteen bells among which that giant one weighing twenty-four tons stood out, challenging the laws of physics and inspiring the envy of all of Europe's faithful. That temple, blessed in 1883 before 20,000 people inside, had perished only forty-eight years after its consecration, when Stalin decided that the spot occupied by the church was the ideal place, due to its proximity to the Kremlin and Red Square, to raise the Palace of the Soviets. To Smirnov, that decision had seemed the most triumphant proof of Stalin's power to choose not only the political fate of the country but also that of its agriculture, livestock, mining, history, linguistics (he recently discovered that capacity of his), and even its architecture, since, with Christ the Savior demolished, he commented that Red Square would look better without the nuisance of St. Basil's Cathedral. All of this, Smirnov concluded, had occurred under a policy of terror that had shut the mouths of workers and eminent scientists alike—a terror turned not just into fearful obedience but into the apathy of the very people who had led the most spectacular social transformation in human history.

Although his prestige was at an all-time low, Lev Davidovich knew that his Turkish isolation had to end. Perhaps by being somewhere closer to events, his presence might help to prevent greater evils, and for that reason he initiated a new campaign to obtain a visa to any place and under any conditions, and concentrated on France and Norway, since Germany, where his presence would have been the most useful, was ruled out due to the hostility that would rain down upon him from Communists and fascists alike. In fact, his former political comrades were even more aggressive, and in reply to each of the Exile's warnings about the national socialist danger, he received a barrage of insults from Ernst Thälmann, who declared that Trotsky's idea of a communist alliance with the left and center was the most dangerous theory of a bankrupt counter-revolutionary.

Sometime in the fall of 1932, a diffuse light came to break up the darkness when the possibility arose for Lev Davidovich to travel to Denmark for a few days, invited by the social democratic students to participate in a conference commemorating the fifteenth anniversary of the October Revolution. With a joy that he himself knew was frenzied, he immediately went into action. He was hoping that if he passed through France, Norway, or even Denmark, he could perhaps obtain at least transitory asylum that would allow him to regain space for his political work.

The weeks prior to the trip were charged with tension. Between the transit visas that weren't arriving, the increasing restrictions the Danes were imposing on his stay, and the calls for anti-Trotsky protests in France, Belgium, and Germany, a less determined man would have given up on an adventure that began with so many discouraging omens.

On November 14, with a Danish visa that allowed them just eight days, the Trotskys left Istanbul, still moved by the news of the recent and dark suicide of Nadya Alliluyeva, Stalin's young wife. During the nine days it took them to get through Greece, Italy, France, and Belgium, his enemies made the Exile feel that he would have caused less of a commotion if he'd made that journey as the president of a belligerent country or as the leader of a working conspiracy and not as a man who was only accompanied by his past and his condition of exile. To think that his presence could still generate dread among leaders and enemies was, more than proof of adversity, a comforting confirmation that he was still considered someone capable of inciting revolutions.

But three weeks later, enclosed again in Büyükada, Lev Davidovich had to admit that he had only been received with some affability in Mussolini's Italy, where he was allowed to visit Pompeii on the way out, and to spend a day in Venice on the return trip. The rest of his journey had been a succession of police cordons (he was unsure whether they were meant to protect his life or control him), while the days spent in Copenhagen had passed under the tension of Moscow's diplomatic protests and a petition from the Danish prince Aage that he be tried as one of the murderers of the family of the last czar who had been the son of a Danish princess.

Nonetheless, he could not deny that he had deeply enjoyed the occasion to talk about the Russian Revolution before a packed auditorium of more than two thousand people, who made him feel the comforting taste of agitation before the masses, to which he had always been so addicted. Moreover, the reencounter with an extreme climate, with a city of dim lights and pallid nights like those of St. Petersburg, had filled him with nostalgia. For that reason, even knowing the response he would receive, he insisted on presenting medical reports testifying to his state of health and the need for specialized treatment. When it was communicated to him that his request hadn't even been considered by the Danish authorities, Lev Davidovich concluded that if many times he had had doubts about the faithfulness of his friends, he could be sure of the perseverance of his enemies, whichever party or faction they were in.

The return to his island prison, where his papers and books, his grandson Seva and his spoiled Maya were waiting for him, didn't have the friendly scent of a return home but rather the stench of a seemingly endless marginalization. At the quay, there weren't enthusiastic or cursing crowds, no police lines or trembling government workers, as there had been in each place they had passed through in recent days, but just some fishermen friends and the Turkish policemen who often sat down at his table. In Prinkipo, his presence didn't cause any fights, and this fact would make him understand that if his name still generated excitement in Europe, it wasn't due to what he could do but rather what his enemies demanded as payment for his actions: hostility, repression, rejection. Stalin's hate, turned into a *raison d'état*, had put in motion the most powerful marginalization machinery ever directed against a solitary individual. More so, it had become exalted as a universal strategy of a communism controlled from Moscow and even as the editorial policy of dozens of newspapers. For that reason, swallowing the rest of his pride, he had to admit that while in the Kremlin they were determining the moment at which his life would cease to be useful to them, they would keep him trapped in an unbreakable ostracism that would be maintained until they declared the fall of the curtain and the end of the masquerade. And for the first time he dared to think about his life as a tragedy: classic, Greek-style, without the faintest hope of appeal.

The year 1933 arrived with an overwhelming invasion of discouragement. Zina wanted Seva sent to Berlin without any more delays, and, just barely returned from Copenhagen, Lev Davidovich and Natalia had said goodbye to the boy. During the brief meeting they had had as he passed through France, Liova had spoken to them about Zinushka's lamentable state and the medical suggestion that the presence of a son to take care of her could perhaps provide some benefit for her broken spirit. Although Lev Davidovich and Natalia had thought the same thing many times, they had decided to put the boy's mental health before his mother's; but their authority over Seva was limited, and faced with Zinushka's insistence, they had to compromise. The morning they saw him depart, tearful over having to leave his great friend Maya and Kharalambos's children, he and Natalia, trained in farewells and losses, could not help but feel that a piece of their hearts was being taken.

The only way that Lev Davidovich found to combat the void was immersing himself in the rewrites, always obsessive, to which he submitted his *History of the Russian Revolution*, and in the review of materials with the idea of undertaking one of his projects: the history of the civil war, a joint biography of Marx and Engels, a biography of Lenin. Nonetheless, a constant worry kept him alarmed and unfocused, as if he were waiting for something. He never imagined it would arrive in such a cruel way.

The first cable sent by Liova was succinct and devastating: Zinushka had committed suicide in her Berlin apartment and Seva's location was unknown. The paper in hand, Lev Davidovich closed himself in his room. The impossibility of being close to the events was as painful as what had happened, and he couldn't stand to hear or see anybody. Although he'd already been expecting an end like this and his bad premonitions of recent days had been centered on the young woman, more painful was the feeling of guilt that assaulted him. He knew perfectly well that Zinushka's terrible life, and now her death at just thirty years of age, were the fruit of his political passion, of his insistence on leading the salvation of the great masses while he threw the fates of those closest to him onto the fire, sacrificed on the altar of vengeance of a perverted revolution. But what hurt him the most was to think that something could have happened to Seva: the feeling of agony that the boy's fate caused him was revealed as a new reaction in him, and he chalked it up to old age and exhaustion.

At the end of the afternoon, one of the secretaries arrived in the capital bringing a second cable from Liova that gave some hope. He ran his eyes over the text, skipping over the details of the suicide, until he found the certain relief he was looking for. In a letter left by Zinushka, she noted that she had taken Seva to a Frau K., of whom she gave no other details, but Liova and his comrades were already searching all of Berlin. Tied to that hope, he spent the night awake, trying not to look at the clock. He had decided that in the morning he would get on the first ferry to Istanbul, to try to communicate with Liova by telephone. To his sorrow, he recalled the ill-fated lives of his two daughters too many times, and he couldn't get the idea out of his mind that a similar misfortune could also mark the lives of Liova, young Seriozha, Seva. Then he wondered whether the moment had not come to execute the only radical measure able to stop that chain of sacrifices: because perhaps his own death could calm the anxiety for revenge that was directed at his clan, hostages of the limitless confrontation. Many times he looked at the mother-of-pearl revolver that Blumkin had brought him from Delhi. Did a revolutionary have the right to abandon the battlefield? Was the life of his children worth more than the fate of an entire class, more than a redeeming idea? Would he give Stalin that gift? Although he knew the answers, the idea of using the revolver fixed itself in his mind with a force he had not known until that day.

At the dock, shaking with the cold breeze coming from the sea, he saw the morning's first ferry arrive. Among the few passengers traveling at that time and in that season, he made out the figure of his collaborator Rudolf Klement, in whose face he encountered the most encouraging smile and from whose lips he received the most desired news: they had found Seva. For a moment Lev Davidovich was about to give thanks to some god, and he recognized how egotistical he was for the happiness caused by this news. That same afternoon, overcome by tension, he felt how the reserves of energy keeping him afloat were running out and fell on his bed in the throes of a bout of malaria.

A few days later Lev Davidovich received a letter from Alexandra Sokolovskaya, written in Leningrad, where she was at the limit of her ability to resist. As could be expected, it was a letter full of pain and resentment, in which she accused him of having marginalized Zinushka from the political struggle and of having thus pushed her to her death. Without the physical or moral energy to respond to a wounded mother, he chose to accept the blame that was his and to pass on the rest that was not. With the begrudging mental coldness he was capable of, he prepared an open letter to the Bolshevik Party's Central Committee accusing Stalin of Zina's death, a political exile only because she was part of his family, separated from her daughter, her mother, and her husband for the same reason, thrown out of the party and dismissed from her job only out of the most perverse revenge. Revenge, when it involves innocent people, is even more cruel, more criminal, and more treacherous, he said. But, to his pain, Lev Davidovich had to recognize that Joseph Stalin was as guilty of Zinushka's death as the supposed Communists, who, in a surfeit of shamelessness at the recently closed party congress had proclaimed Stalin "Genius of the Revolution" and "Father of the World's Progressive Peoples," while millions of peasants were dying of hunger throughout the country, hundreds of thousands of men and women languished in labor camps and colonies of deportees, millions of people were without shoes, and Soviet policy was offering up the fate of German and European workers to Nazi voraciousness.

The secretaries prepared the copies that would go out to Moscow and to the newspapers, parties, and political groups of Europe the following day. Lev Davidovich was counting on Zina's death resonating as Blumkin's murder hadn't, and having the capacity to generate compassion that his own exile had not generated. But again History came to yell in his ear, and the echo of more thunderous events buried his hopes, for at the time that his letters were leaving Prinkipo, a wave of justified fear was running through Europe and the world: Hitler had proclaimed himself chancellor of Germany and fascist banners were unfurling across the country amid the cheers of millions of Germans. Berlin was the city of a triumphant Hitler, not that of a young communist political exile and suicide.

8

As soon as he arrived, Ramón had the feeling that Barcelona had aged.

The order from the Popular Army's chiefs of staff calling him back to the city had arrived at the camp a week after Caridad's visit to him in the Sierra de Guadarrama. Full of doubts and weighed down with a good dose of shame, Ramón had taken leave of his company members and, his clothing covered with mud, stepped onto the military transport that evacuated the wounded from the front. *No pasarán!* he had yelled to his trench mates, who responded with the same words: *No pasarán!* Ramón Mercader did not imagine it would be the last time he would use that slogan.

Six months before, when he returned to Barcelona with the remains of his military regiment destroyed by Franco's first offensive on Madrid, Ramón had found a city in such a state of political effervescence that, in a few days, he'd already managed to organize a new battalion willing to join the recently created Popular Army. The majority of his surviving comrades joined behind him and dozens of young people from the Columna de Hierro de las Juventudes Socialistas, elated at the possibility of leaving for the Madrid front, where everything seemed to be decided. Faith in victory was the oxygen the city breathed.

For Ramón, in those early days at the start of the conflict, Las Ramblas synthesized the spirit of an exultant Barcelona, drunk with anarchist, communist, and syndicalist dreams. Even when the malignant winds of war and death no longer felt like a viscous presence, hundreds of people ran around dressed in blue workers' overalls, wearing the badges of a variety of recently created militias, all of them wrapped up in the strident revolutionary marches that clamored from the speakers placed on practically every building, from which hung slogans and banners of the parties loyal to the government. To be a worker, activist, militia man, or soldier of the Republic had become a sign of distinction and one could think that the moneyed classes, like his own family, who had adorned the geography of the place for decades, had disappeared from the face of the rejoicing earth where people greeted each other with their fists held high, exchanged slogans, and prepared themselves for sacrifice, convinced that they had to fight for a human dignity that had been only recently discovered by many.

Ramón had partaken in that crazed atmosphere in which no one seemed to have any true notion of the tragedy pursuing them, and had felt elated, more ready to push forward the wheel of history. A few weeks later, at the war's most critical moment, when the lifesaving Soviet decision to provide military help to the Republic had arrived, the news, joyously received, had given support to the party and its militants, who had been abandoned during the early weeks swamped by an anarchist tide enjoying the best summer in its history.

With the support of África, Joan Brufau, and his colleagues at the head of the Juventudes Unificadas, Ramón exploited the increased revolutionary enthusiasm, and together they quickly conducted a hunt for fresh blood. The "Jaume Graells" battalion (poor Jaume, the group's first martyr, fell in the defense of Madrid) hurried to leave for the new military destination they had been assigned, a few miles from the Madrid besieged by the Nationalists. Ramón, who was already considered a veteran and proudly showed the wound from the bullet that had grazed the back of his right hand in the first days of the war, would be its commander until the group joined the Fifth Regiment, and for several days he walked around Barcelona displaying the insignia that filled him with militant fervor.

África used the two weeks of October 1936 that Ramón spent in Barcelona before returning to the front to bring him up to speed on the dark political events that were already beginning to take place beneath the air of enthusiasm and combativeness. The greatest danger facing Republican forces, according to the young woman, was factionalism, which had worsened since the start of the war. Catalan nationalists, syndicalists with an anarchist orientation or socialist affiliation, and renegade Trotskyists like those from the Workers' Party for Marxist Unification (POUM)—at the front of which was that stubborn thorn Andreu Nin (who was even a member of the Generalitat government)—were already opposed to the communist strategy and had put on the table the most transcendental question of the moment: War *with* revolution, or war *with* victory but *without* revolution? Even before the Soviet advisers and directors of the Comintern had arrived in Spain, the Communist Party had digested Moscow's ever-correct policies and shown their position clearly: offering massive and immediate assistance to leftist forces with unity in order to obtain military victory and prevent the entrenchment of a fascism that threw itself behind the rebel military offering it massive and immediate aid. Only after that Republican victory could there be talk of establishing the bases for the social revolution whose very mention, at that moment, frightened the fickle democracies, who didn't need to be frightened, since they ought to be the Republicans' natural allies against the fascists. The POUM activists, with the Trotskyist philosophy of European revolution, and the anarchists, with their libertarian sermons (motivated by them, criminal excesses had already been committed that were as despicable as those of the rebel soldiers), had opposed this strategy from the start. It was erroneous according to them because they advocated for war and, along with it, revolution against the bourgeois system. That difference in principle foreshadowed fiery battles, and the work of the Communists, África said, was as important on the front as in the rear guard, where they had to fight for the validation of a policy demanded by Soviet advisers who had already conditioned their support on there not being any of the ideological breaks that libertarians and Trotskyists insisted on generating.

"Those revisionists love playing at revolution," África had said to him. "If we let them, the only thing they'll achieve is that we're left on our own and lose the war. They have Trotsky's sign on their heads and we're going to have to rip it away from them by fire. Without Soviet assistance, you can't even dream of victory, so now tell me how in the hell we're going to make a revolution? It seems like they've already forgotten 1934."

In the luxurious Hispano-Suiza that she drove around, África had taken him to see the poor neighborhoods and towns close to Barcelona so that Ramón could see the chaos that Trotskyists and anarchists were bringing to the country. Outside Las Ramblas and the city's central areas, a regrettable desolation had settled, with streets blocked by absurd barricades, paralyzed factories, buildings ransacked to the core, and churches and convents turned into charred ruins. África told him about the executions carried out by the anarchists and about how fear of expressing their opinions was growing among workers. The middle class and many business owners had been divested of their goods, and the project to create a military industry was being run by a sea of syndicalist volunteers. A scarcity of products had taken hold in stores and markets. The people were enthusiastic, that was true, but they were also hungry, and in many places bread could only be acquired through long lines and only if they had the coupons distributed by anarchists and syndicalists, who had become the owners of a city in which central and local government were distant references. Although the anarchists were confident that having entered an era of equality was enough to maintain the support of masses who'd been enslaved for centuries, África asked herself how long the enthusiasm and the faith in victory would last.

"This Republic is a brothel and we've got to whip it into line."

Now, in a period of only a few months, with the return of the smell of blood and the roaring from the front where young men like his brother Pablo or his friend Jaume fell daily, Ramón found himself in a tired, more still, disenchanted city, besieged by scarcity and anxious to return to the normality broken by the war and revolutionary dreams. It was as if the people only aspired to live a regular life, sometimes even at the despicable price of surrender. The *franquistas'* devastating attack on Málaga, where the rebel infantry and navy, with the support of Italian aviation and troops, had massacred those escaping from the city, had dented people's faith. Although posters still hung from buildings, from confiscated churches and from the few vehicles that ran through Barcelona, instead of clamoring for unity in victory, they now yelled furiously for the elimination of enemies that a short while before had been considered allies, even brothers. Meanwhile, the bourgeoisie, who'd been forgotten up until a few weeks before, were emerging from their caves again: in the still poorly stocked cafés of Las Ramblas fur coats were seen once again amid the proletarian overalls. In the surviving bars, by contrast, it was the anarchist militia who in their idleness drank what they found, played dominoes, smoked foul-smelling cigarettes, and rolled around with the prostitutes whom a few weeks before they had tried to convert to the proletarian revolution. The effervescence of the previous months was losing its splendor, like the faded letters of the posters that, in these same bars, written by the same men, still recalled the Great Plans: DANCE IS THE BROTHEL'S WAITING ROOM; THE TAVERN WEAKENS CHARACTER; THE BAR DEGENERATES THE SPIRIT: LET'S CLOSE THEM!

On the way to the confiscated palace of his relative the Marquis of Villota, Ramón, conscious that he smelled like the hills and gunpowder, felt pride in knowing he was faithful to his purposes and also anxious to find out what his new fate would be. The underlying reasons for Barcelona's atmospheric change still escaped him, but from that moment he had the notion that concrete—draconian, to be precise—actions were being imposed to restore the broken faith and implant the discipline that had never existed and that the overwhelmed Republic cried for.

While the streetcar went up to the heights of La Bonanova, Ramón remembered the times he and his parents had visited the house of their wealthy and noble relative, the owner of an admirable pack of dogs with whom Ramón spent the visits. That memory seemed remote, almost foreign, as if between those easy days of the past and the difficult hours of the present, many years—perhaps many lives—had traveled through his body, and of the boy Ramón, little more remained than barely a name and fragments of nostalgia. On the high gate of the property, a cardboard sign now hung announcing the location of the headquarters of the Group of Antifascist Women, presided over by Caridad. Although the building could not hide its splendor, the garden had become full of weeds, stripped cars, and starving dogs that Ramón preferred not to look at. Without anyone stopping him, the young man crossed the garden and the palace's porch, with its Italian marble floor stained by mud and grease and a large photo of an illuminated and serious Stalin hanging in the privileged place where, he remembered perfectly, the marquis displayed a dark still life by Zurbarán. When they informed him that Comrade Caridad was in the back garden, Ramón, who knew his way through the house, searched for the exit from the library and saw a small table under the cypress tree where Caridad and the solid and ruddy Kotov were talking, smiling.

Ramón had met the Soviet man through his mother, when he had just arrived in Barcelona with the first intelligence advisers and those sent from the Comintern. Before Ramón left for Madrid and Caridad for Albacete, they had had many meetings with Kotov. Ramón had admired the marvelous capacity for analysis of that secret agent with transparent and sharp eyes and a slight limp in his left foot that he was sometimes able to hide. Later, when the fall of Madrid seemed imminent, comments reached the young man about the almost suicidal acts of that Moscow emissary, who, following the path of the first Soviet tanks, had many times placed himself at the head of militias and internationalists, violating the Muscovite order that prohibited advisers from directly participating in the actions of war. He also knew that his mother felt devoted to that man, who was capable, according to her, of reading a five-hundred-page book in one night, of reciting almost all of Pushkin's poetry from memory, and of expressing himself in eight different languages, including Cantonese.

As if she had just seen him that morning, Caridad offered him a seat. Meanwhile, the effusive Kotov welcomed him with a bear hug and offered him a drink of vodka that Ramón rejected. The cold March air did not seem to have any effect on the Soviet, who was dressed in only a crude wool shirt with a multicolored handkerchief tied at his neck; Caridad, by contrast, was covered in blankets.

"How did you leave things in Madrid?" Kotov wanted to know, and Ramón tried to explain to him what could be known or speculated, from a trench twenty miles from the city, about the situation of the interminable battle for the capital, although he expressed his conviction that the offensive initiated in Guadalajara would end like the one at Jarama: it would be a new victory over the fascists.

"That's a given," Kotov declared, as if he could predict the future, even of that unpredictable war, and took one of Caridad's cigarettes from the table. He began to smoke without inhaling. "But now we have a more complex battle here in Barcelona," he added, and without further ado he painted for Ramón a picture of the political tensions in the Catalan capital in which the Generalitat at last was trying to be something more than an assembly of councillors whom no one obeyed. There, in Barcelona, more than in Madrid, the path of the war could be decided, he assured him.

Listening to Kotov, Ramón recalled the question that Caridad had asked him a few days before and her insistence on the idea that there could be more important fronts in that war. According to Kotov, President Companys seemed ready to discipline his territory and had ordered the requisition of weapons in the dismantling of anarchist and syndicalist vigilante patrols that effectively controlled Barcelona. For the party, the need to neutralize the different Republican, or falsely Republican, factions had become a task of the first order and because of that they should support Companys's plan. The problem lay in the fact that the communist policy was constantly limited by the hostility of the conciliatory government of the Socialist Largo Caballero, who continued to demonstrate his dislike of them and, what was worse, his inability to direct the war. The panorama became clearer for Ramón when Kotov explained that a group of completely trustworthy militants was going to work for what was presented as an urgent political need: to get rid of those burdens affecting discipline and military will and catalyze the Republican efforts dedicated to unifying the forces. To reach this objective they were going to use all means, from the most aggressive propaganda to the possibility of creating such a crisis that it would lead to a change in the government and allow the replacement of Largo Caballero by a leader capable of obtaining the unity of the forces.

Ramón was beginning to make out the dimensions of the mission he'd been called on to undertake, and he listened to Kotov's reflections about the urgency of initiating the offensive with a purge of the army, where they had to get rid of some of the leaders who were unconditionally loyal to Largo Caballero. Comrade Stalin himself had suggested that they purge the highest levels and designate more capable leaders: in the Málaga disaster, they had behaved like idiots—worse, like traitors and saboteurs. Therefore it was necessary to remove recalcitrant opponents and, at the same time, achieve the preeminence of the Communists within the Republican alliance, in the army as well as in the institutions. Only thus could they achieve necessary cohesion and begin to dream of victory.

"Kid, in this war many things are being decided for the future of the proletariat, for the whole world, and we can't go around like wet rags. We know that Largo and his damn Socialists are organizing a miserable campaign against the Soviets, the Communists, and our political commissars. Or does it seem like a coincidence to you that they are talking more and more about how Mexico is offering the Republic disinterested assistance? Some have even accused us of having taken the reserves of Spanish gold to Moscow as payment for the weapons, when everyone knows that—besides selling the Spanish weapons that nobody would sell them—we're protecting that treasure that could've fallen into the hands of the fascists, which would have been the end of the Republic. It's very clear: at the root there is an alliance between Socialists and Trotskyists to discredit the Soviets. We even suspect that the government is negotiating a pact with the English to carve us out of the game. We would leave as we came in, lamenting the defeat of the Republic, but what about you? You would be the scapegoats and would pay with your blood. Franco is going for everything, with Hitler and Mussolini pushing him on."

Ramón, angered by what he was listening to, observed Caridad, who lit a cigarette, puffed on it a few times, and threw it far away from her.

"I feel terrible. I have angina," the woman said, and leaned over the table. "And the damn tobacco . . . I think Kotov has been clear."

Ramón felt his ideas forming a dark medley in his mind. The list of plots, betrayals, and pettiness enumerated by Kotov was overwhelming for him, and the project of a wide antifascist front, in which he had believed and for which he had fought, seemed to undo itself beneath the weight of that information. But he still couldn't see his place in a decentralized war, in which enemies jumped out from any corner and not just on the battlefield. The adviser stood up and looked him in the eye, forcing him to keep his head held up.

"So that you understand me better: surely you found out that a month ago they withdrew several advisers from the first group that arrived. What you surely don't know is that right now they're in Moscow, they've been tried, and many of them will be executed. Do you want me to tell you who's next on the list?" The adviser lowered his voice and paused dramatically. "The order just came that we send Antonov-Ovseyenko, our consul here in Barcelona, back to Moscow. Antonov," Kotov's voice changed upon repeating the name, "a symbol in and of himself, the Bolshevik who in 1917 assured the taking of the Winter Palace . . . Do you know what it means when he and other former militants are being taken out of the game? Have you read the news about the trials that just took place in Moscow? Well, all of this means that we can't feel pity for anyone, Ramón, not even for ourselves if we commit the slightest error. Republican Spain needs a government capable of guaranteeing military success. That is why we need to move quickly and carefully."

"What are we supposed to do?" Ramón was afraid that he had not exactly understood what was drawing itself in his mind, and he found that he was scared by the revelations he was hearing.

"The party has to take real power, even by force if necessary," Kotov said. "But first we have to clean house."

Ramón dared to look for Caridad's glassy green gaze; she was periodically taking sips from a yellowish liquid served in a cup decorated with the Marquis of Villota's coat of arms.

"Don't stare anymore: it's lemon juice, for the angina . . . ," she said, and added, "África is working with us, in case you didn't know." And Ramón felt a pang. He again looked up at Kotov. And took a step that brought him closer to África.

"What do I have to do?"

"You'll find out when it's time . . ." Kotov smiled and, after circling for a moment, returned to his chair. "What you need to know now is that if you work with us, you will never again be the Ramón Mercader that you once were. And I should also tell you that if you commit any indiscretions, if you weaken during any mission, we will be very ruthless. And you have no idea how ruthless we can be. If you're here and have heard all of this, it's because Caridad has assured us that you are a man who is capable of remaining silent."

"You can trust me. I'm a Communist and a revolutionary and am willing to make any sacrifice for the cause."

"I'm glad." Kotov smiled again. "But I should remind you of something else . . . We're not inviting you to participate in a social club. If you decide to enter, you'll never be able to leave. And never means never. Is that clear? Would you really be willing to fulfill any mission, make any sacrifice, as you say, even things that other men without our convictions could consider immoral and even criminal?"

Ramón felt himself sinking in quicksand. It was as if his blood had fled his body and left him without any warmth. He thought that África had been subject to the same interrogation, and it wasn't difficult to guess what her response had been. The ideas of the revolution, socialism, the great human utopia, for which he had fought suddenly seemed like another one of those romantic slogans pinned on the coal trucks led by mules: words. The truth, the whole truth, was enclosed in a question made by the envoy of the only victorious revolution that, to sustain its ideals, practiced a necessary lack of compassion, even with its most beloved children, and demanded the eventual rejection of any atavism. His ascent to that stratospheric level signified turning into much more than a simple follower of the revolution and the rhetoric of its mottos.

"I'm willing," he said, and suddenly he felt superior.

As he observed the port, where a few ships were anchored, Ramón felt the days of the start of the war becoming so distant that they seemed like flashes from another incarnation, even lived in another body, but above all with another mind.

That afternoon, after taking a shower, Ramón had spoken for a while with little Luis and with a sad-eyed young woman named Lena Imbert, whom he'd gone to bed with once or twice and who had turned into Caridad's assistant. Instead of taking the Ford that his mother offered him, he preferred to walk to the Paseo de Gracia. He needed to wrap his mind around the new condition of his life, but above all, he needed to speak with África and obtain confirmation from her of the electrifying panorama painted by Kotov. In front of the La Pedrera building, several party militiamen were on guard and Ramón's military and political credentials were not enough to permit him entry. Since September, that child of Gaudí's delirium had turned into the general barracks for Soviet intelligence and party leaders in Cataluña and was the city's most protected building. Ramón managed to have one of the militiamen agree to give a note to Comrade África and he sat down to wait on one of the Paseo's benches.

A short while later, he felt hunger pangs and went out in search of one of the port's surviving inns. Later he went to the Church of the Merced and found the very modest building where his father, who he knew was now working as an accountant, was living following the crash of his business. His curiosity fulfilled, he realized that he didn't feel any desire to see the man, since he couldn't even imagine what he would talk about with that bourgeois gentleman so attached to his retrograde Catalanism and who was too soft for his liking. He left Calle Ample and headed for the start of Las Ramblas, where he had designated a meeting place with África.

The night was getting cold, his anxiety to see the young woman was tormenting him, and Ramón took refuge in his thoughts. What had been clear for him until a few months before had now turned into a cloudy darkness full of twists and turns. From the enthusiasm with which he had gone to jail, and that with which he had entered La Barceloneta to teach literacy to the sons of workers, as well as the fury with which he would later hand himself over to the organization of the aborted Popular Olympics, he had immediately gone on to defend the Republic from the military coup. Then anarchists, POUM members, Socialists, and Communists fought together to prevent the victory of the coup. Joining a militia and almost immediately afterward the ranks of the new Republican Army were the steps that he naturally took, with all of his enthusiasm and his faith, convinced that his life only had meaning if he was able to defend with a rifle the ideas in which he believed. But after half a year of war, and before the evidence of the political meanness of the British, the Americans, and, above all, the French Socialists, it was clear that only the Soviets would maintain them and that the Republic depended on that support.

Deep in his thoughts, he was surprised by África's arrival. Since he hadn't expected to see her, he felt an even greater happiness upon hearing her voice and breathing in the young woman's unalterably feminine perfume. Ramón kissed her furiously and forced her to step back so he could get a better look at her: he didn't know if four months of military campaigns amid the stench, cries, blood, and death had influenced his perception, but before him he saw an angel in combat uniform, with her shorn hair giving her a definitively military air.

África had the keys with her to a small apartment in the Barceloneta, and they walked quickly, looking for the alleyways that would make the path to the consummation of their desire shorter. They climbed some dark steps impregnated with the smell of dampness, but when they opened the door, Ramón found a small room dominated by a double bed over which was draped a sheet smelling of soap. With his accumulated anxiety and exhausting feeling of need, Ramón made love to her with an uncontainable fullness and fury. Only when he felt satiated, while he was resting before a new attack, did he dare to start the conversation that he desired as much as the body of the woman whom he would most love in his life.

África told him that their daughter was fine, although she had not had any news of her for a few weeks. She knew that after the bloody taking of Málaga by the Nationalists, her parents had managed to go to a small town in the Alpujarras where some relatives of theirs lived. Besides, África had had so much work in the office of Pedro, the local leader of the Comintern's advisers, that she barely had any time left to think about herself and none at all to worry about Lenina, whom her parents would know how to care for.

"I'm working with the propaganda group," she explained, and detailed the underground work on public opinion that was aimed at overcoming the resistance of those who were opposed to the Soviet presence in the country, starting with Largo Caballero, who with all slyness accepted the weapons but listened to the advisers' counsel with clenched teeth. Increasingly, the Socialists, before the evidence of the party's exponential growth and their growing prestige on the front, were calling them marionettes for Moscow's designs and accusing them of wanting to control the Republic. The attacks by the POUM's Trotskyists were worse, making it their duty to unmask their true reactionary essence.

"I've also been asked to work to get all of those people out of the way," Ramón said, already completely convinced of the need for his new mission, and he told her about his interview with Kotov.

"You know what, Ramón?" she said. "What you've told me could cost you your life."

"You also said yes to them. I know I can trust you."

"You're wrong. You can't trust anyone . . ."

"Don't get paranoid, please."

África smiled and shook her head no.

"Comrade, the only way that everything we do will work is if we do it in silence. Get that into your head, because if you don't, what you're going to get is a bullet. And listen to me now, because I'm risking things with what I'm going to tell you: the Soviets want to help us win the war, but we're the ones who have to win it, and if things don't change, we'll never win. You are going to be part of that change. As such, forget that you have a soul, that you love anyone, and that I even exist."

"That last part is impossible," he said, and tried to smile.

"Well, it's the best thing you could do . . . Ramón, perhaps tonight will be the last time we will see each other for a long time. In a few days I have to leave Barcelona . . . ," she said as she began to dress, and he watched her, feeling his desires freeze. "And don't ask me, because I haven't asked you why or where, either. I'm a soldier and I go wherever they send me."

9

Throughout the spring of 1977, I traveled many times to that beach, and on each occasion, moved by the most innocent curiosity, I sat down under the pines awhile seeking a new encounter, surely improbable, with the owner of the Russian wolfhounds, whom, the same day on which I met him, I had named "the man who loved dogs."

Ever since leaving Baracoa two years before, with the cure to my alcoholism completed, and which kept me radically removed from drinking for fifteen years—when the crisis started and I felt that I could again have a drink of rum or a beer and not go up Jacob's ladder, since I was down that low—I had turned my life around in an important way. Without yet knowing very well what I wanted, and to the surprise of my friends, I had not accepted the placement that was being given me in the information services team of a national radio station, a reward for the work that I was supposed to have carried out in Baracoa, evaluated as excellent. I had begun to trawl in the underworld of the cultural and journalistic sphere, which was still packed with fallen angels who had once been celebrated or controversial writers, journalists, promoters, all defenestrated, perhaps for life, and for a variety of reasons or no reasons at all. That search ended up leading me to the very modest position of proofreader at the *Veterinaria*

Cubana magazine, as its former occupant had died a few weeks before, apparently by his own hand. That work seemed sufficiently obscure, anonymous, far from any possible passions and ambitions, and guaranteed me the two things I needed at that moment: a salary to live on, and peace and a routine to try to recompose my spirits. In due time, I thought, I would try to return to the writing that at that moment I still didn't think was possible.

In reality, I wasn't very clear on the way in which I would carry out the attempt to write again, since we were right in the middle of the year 1975 and nothing on the horizon indicated that anything could change in the conception of politics and literature that, under the deadweight of the most rigid orthodoxy, only produced and promoted works like the one I had written four years before: *"nonflictive"*—as they were later labeled—and complacent, without a hint of social or human tension that was not permeated by the influence of official propaganda. And if there was something I was sure of, it was that that writing no longer had anything to do with the person that I could become. The problem was rooted in the fact that I didn't have a fucking idea of what kind of literature I should and, above all, perhaps I could write—and far less, the what and the how of the person that I wanted to be.

Around that time in which I was making those trips to the beach—by which, I would later learn, I was tempting my fate—my relationship had already begun with Raquelita, the recently graduated dentist who, that same year, would become my wife. We had met on the same beach during the previous summer and for that reason, from the beginning, she was familiar with my desire to participate in the squash games that were played on the courts of Santa María, El Mégano, and Guanabo, especially those that could take place between November and April, when bathing in the sea ceases to be attractive for Cubans, and only the most fanatical make the trip from Havana to the beaches to enjoy some friendly and challenging games.

In that way, each afternoon that I had to go to the print shop to hand in originals or galleys, instead of returning to the magazine's editing room, I went by my godmother's house, where I used to keep my racket, and boarded La Estrella, the mythical route of wobbly Leyland buses that travel between the city and the beaches, until I arrived at the beach of Guanabo.

It was two weeks after our first meeting and following three or four excursions to the beach that, in April already, I again ran into the foreigner with the wolfhounds. The mise-en-scène was very similar to our first encounter: the dogs were running on the sand and, in the distance, their owner followed them with their leashes in his hands and that definitively clumsy gait—drunk, perhaps, I thought that time. That day the man was wearing white pants, a light fabric, and a checked shirt, like a cowboy. I, unlike the first time, remained seated, with the novel I was reading in my hands—I had begun *Rabbit, Run*, that book that Updike never surpassed. After whistling to the dogs, who barely noticed me, I smiled at the man and greeted him with a nod of my head, which he returned by raising his right hand, still covered with a piece of cloth. A few minutes later, to complete the picture, the tall, thin black man made his appearance, again between the casuarinas.

When the man stopped, I stood up and took a few steps toward him, as if it were a completely coincidental meeting.

"How are you?" I asked him, indecisive about which path to take with the possible conversation.

"I've been better," the man said, and smiled with a certain bitterness.

Since I didn't smell alcohol on his breath, I was about to ask him if he was sick, since the way he was walking hinted at some problem with his balance. At that moment I noticed that the sallow color of his skin was accentuated, and I thought that perhaps it was due to some illness, perhaps with his liver, circulatory or respiratory, but I abstained from asking and went the safe route.

"So how old are the dogs?"

"They just turned ten. They're getting old; wolfhounds don't live long."

"And how do they cope with summer here in Cuba?"

"We have air-conditioning at the house . . . ," he began, but stopped, since without a doubt he knew that in Cuba almost no one could afford that luxury. "But they've adapted well. Especially Ix, the female. Dax's character has changed a little bit lately."

"Has he gotten aggressive? Sometimes that happens to borzois."

"Yes, sometimes," the man said, and I was certain that I had gone too far: only a specialist, or someone who was interested in that breed for some reason, could know those details about the behavior of Russian wolfhounds. I then chose to reveal a part of the truth.

"Ever since I saw them the other day," I pointed at the animals, "I was so impressed by them that I looked for more information about them. I'm really taken with your dogs."

The man smiled, less tense, obviously proud.

"A few months ago, they asked me to loan them out for a movie. It tells the story of a rich family that didn't want to leave Cuba after the revolution, and the director felt that Ix and Dax were perfect for those people . . . I had to take them every time they appeared, and the truth is that it was great fun to be at the filming, seeing how a lie is put together that later can look like truth. I have a great desire to see how it all turned out . . ."

The conversation went on for a good while, always with the tall, thin black man observing us from the casuarinas; we talked about movies and books, about the pleasant temperature of spring on the island, about my work and the aristocratic line of the borzois, which, according to the man, were already recorded in a French chronicle from the eleventh century, where it is said that when Anna Yaroslavna, daughter of the Grand Duke of Kiev, arrived in Paris to marry Henry I, she came accompanied by three borzois.

"The Russians say quite proudly that the borzois are the dogs of czars and poets, because Ivan the Terrible, Peter the Great, Nicholas II, Pushkin, and Turgenev had these wolfhounds. But the greatest breeder of borzois was the Grand Duke Nicholas, who ended up with various breederies. After the revolution, borzois almost disappeared, and now are the dogs of the nomenclature, as they say." He made a gesture of pointing up high. "A regular Soviet could not feed these animals, although, in reality, they eat very little for their size. The real problem is that they need a lot of space. If they don't exercise, they feel terrible."

That afternoon the man finally satisfied one of the questions hounding me: he told me he was Spanish and that he had lived in Moscow for many years, since the end of the Spanish Civil War, of course, in which he had fought on the Republican side, also of course. He'd been living in Cuba for three years, above all because his wife, who was Mexican, had never adjusted to the Soviet Union: the cold and the Russian character drove her crazy ("crazier than she already is," he said literally).

When we said goodbye, I also knew that the man was named Jaime López and that he was happy to have seen me again. As on the previous occasion, I saw them walk away, accompanied by the tall, thin black man.

Then, driven by curiosity, I waited a couple of minutes and went out to the highway. In the distance, I saw the man, the black man, and the dogs as they crossed the parking lot's deserted esplanade and approached a white pickup-style Volga, which Ix and Dax entered through the back door. The car, driven by the black man, went out to the highway and moved toward Havana.

Throughout the month of April and during the first weeks of May, López—as the man asked me to call him—and I met on the beach several times, almost always briefly. No matter how much I think about it, I still can't really explain my persistent interest in that figure, who almost never talked about himself and didn't seem too interested in me or in the environment of the country where he now lived, despite the fact that, according to what he told me, his mother had been born in Havana when the island was still a Spanish colony. Nonetheless, when the matter of the dogs and his remote family connection with Cuba were exhausted—and in each meeting they became exhausted more quickly—the conversations could broach issues that gave me a little more information about the reserved "man who loved dogs."

One of the first details that López revealed to me was that in his work he had been assigned a chauffeur (the watchful tall black man who appeared and disappeared amid the casuarinas), not because he was important enough to need it, but rather because he suffered from frequent dizzy spells and he had caused two traffic accidents, luckily minor ones. For the last few months, he told me, he had been undergoing medical tests, increasingly complicated ones; while they had determined that he wasn't suffering from any neurological or auditory affliction that could cause those bouts of vertigo, the fact was that they were increasingly besieging him with greater insistence and intensity. I also came to learn that he had two children: a boy who was more or less my age, who dreamed of studying to be a merchant ship captain, and a girl, seven years younger, and who was the apple of his eye, he said, with his propensity for ready-made phrases. For periods of time, another "almost" son also lived with them, a nephew of his wife's, who had become an orphan when he was very little.

On one occasion in which I asked him what kind of work he did in Cuba to have a new car and the possibility of a chauffeur, Jaime López only told me that he was a ministry adviser and immediately changed the subject. And when I wanted to know where he lived, he was elusive, saying "on the other side of the river," an imprecise direction that no Havana native would have given, since the foul Almendares River had not served as a reference of anything for anyone for years.

With the start of May and rising temperatures, the beach began to receive more visitors, and it became clear that López and his dogs would have to find another place. By then I had lost almost all interest in that impenetrable Spaniard, the son of a Cuban mother about whom he told me nothing ("I don't like to talk about her," he said), who had fought in a war about which he didn't speak ("It hurts me to remember it"), lived in a Moscow about which he had no opinion, and worked and lived in Cuba, in imprecise places marked by a river that had been famous in other times and was currently forgotten. Because of that, when the man who loved dogs disappeared, I didn't miss him, and if it hadn't been for the two borzois that I remembered quite frequently, the image of Jaime López would have perhaps disappeared forever from my mind, like the Almendares River and so many other fond characters and places that started disappearing from Havana's weakened memory.

That summer of 1977 was marked by my ill-fated wedding to Raquelita and, weeks later, the regrettable revelation of my brother William's homosexuality.

My decision to marry Raquelita surprised my friends, especially when they found out that she wasn't pregnant. I was simply run over by a visceral need for company, a desire to further strengthen my personal refuge, and she accepted the proposal because—I would find out a few years later, when she decided to leave me and humiliate me as well—being married greatly facilitated the paperwork a relative of hers, very well-placed (the nomenclature), would take care of to exempt her from social service, so unappealing and ideologically strengthening for the rest of the graduates. The wedding took place in a very unconventional way, since we brought the notary to Raquelita's parents' house, in Altahabana, and despite it having been my friend Dany who introduced me to my imminent wife, for reasons of antiquity I selected as my witness *el negro* Frank, recently arrived from his social service as a doctor in Moa, the mining city, the other Cuban Siberia. The party that followed was in the new spirit of the proletarian poor that had been established, with the beer that was sold to newlyweds for a fixed price and the edible and drinkable contributions of both sets of friends. Once the usual honeymoon in a Havana hotel had been enjoyed, we went to live at my house, in Víbora Park. Although we shared the space with my parents and my brother, William, my wife and I had the privacy of a bedroom with its own bathroom, to which we would soon add, to avoid guaranteed frictions with my mother, a small kitchen, taking part of the roofed terrace.

The calm world that I was trying to build experienced a brutal shakeup just a few weeks after the wedding. The truth is that William's homosexuality had always been, for me and my parents, a reality that we fought even as we refused to see it, and, of course, something that we never talked about. Since he was a boy, William dragged along an underlying femininity that seemed to sink, perhaps disappear, when he entered secondary school. My parents took him to a psychologist and consoled themselves by thinking that, after two years of consultations, he had achieved the miracle of "curing" the kid with an array of injected hormones that had caused the collateral effect of making his cock grow to horselike dimensions. Although in recent years, my relationship with William had become distant, at times prickly, the whole time I suspected that his homosexuality was just latent and would one day raise its head. But I never imagined that upon waking it would turn into a real nightmare that would end up enveloping us all.

Due to the extent of the effect of their nature and fate on this story, I'm urged to make a small commentary about my parents. In reality they were two people who were so normal that it made you feel bad: they were workers, they got along, all they wanted was that William and I would have a good life and go to college, something they had not managed to do. He was a Mason and she Catholic, and they never hid those affiliations in an era in which almost everyone preferred to hide and even renounce these and other petit bourgeois caprices, belonging to a past in the midst of socialist improvement. Ever since I can remember, I recall that my parents tried to instill the conviction, in me as well as in William, that the truth should always be faced, that only work makes man grow, and that, in all situations, the decent behavior of an individual always had the same characteristics (you shall not kill, you shall not steal, you shall not betray, etc.) and, further still, that against those three values (truth, work, and decency) no force in the world could prevail. As you can see, my parents were utterly credulous. Of course, at that time, I didn't precisely formulate or understand that elemental compendium of Masonic-

Christian ethics, nor do I think did my parents. What I'm sure of is that this view of life had a strong influence on my and my brother's consciousness, and that having been educated with those precepts was not very healthy in an age when perhaps the best thing would have been to learn from the cradle the arts of dissimulation or duplicity as a means of promotion or, at least, as a strategy for survival.

William was a brilliant guy. That summer he had finished his first year at the medical school with grades that were as high as they were unusual for that period, the most difficult degree. But just after the start of his second year, in September, my brother and his anatomy professor, with whom he had maintained an intimate relationship since the previous year, were accused of being homosexuals by another professor, in a meeting of the party's leadership in which both teachers were active. Following procedure, a disciplinary commission was put together composed of "all the factors": the party, the Communist Youth, the Union, and the Students' Federation and—despite the lack of proof or even of suspicions that they had practiced their aberrations, as they were called on campus—they were subject to interviews in which the professor emphatically denied any homosexual indiscretion. But William, after having rejected that accusation for weeks with all his vehemence, called on a courage that I didn't know in him and rebelled against an exhausting and repressive cover-up, and said that yes, he was homosexual, and had acted as such from the age of thirteen, actively and passively, although he refused to confess with whom he'd carried out those activities, since that was a private matter and wasn't anyone's business but his. Although it was not possible to relate the sexual inclinations of the accused with their behavior as professor and student, and despite the fact that the output and teaching of each one was noteworthy, the sentence was decided beforehand and the commission of "factors" applied its sentence: the professor would be indefinitely expelled from the party and the national teaching system, while William would be removed from the university for two years and definitively from the study of medicine.

Beyond the university suspension, it was the shame that attacked the moral precepts of Antonio and Sara, my parents, head-on that led them to complete the young man's sentence and to commit what would turn into the most regrettable mistake of their lives: they threw William out of the house, despite my protests (I had always felt pity for my brother), which were not enough to make them see reason. The family that had been united until then began to disintegrate, and the clan's final disgrace began to form itself on the horizon.

I know that the story of William's fall, like many of my own stumblings, may seem exaggerated today, but the truth is that for many years it was common for so many people. At that moment, moved by a feeling of compassion and urged by a Raquelita who was horrified by those manifestations of homophobia and family cruelty, I went out to look for William in all of Havana until I managed to find him . . . at the house of his former professor. Slowly, with all of my caution and patience, I tried to build a different relationship with my brother, and shortly after I would come to replace my primitive feeling of pity with a justified admiration, due to the way in which he was facing his sentence: fighting. It was the complete opposite of what I would have done, of what I had done. William had accepted the expulsion from medical school, but he clamored for the right to continue his university studies, since no rule or law prevented it. Meanwhile, my relationship with my parents deteriorated, and although I continued to live with them, I allowed a wall of tension and resentment to rise in the middle of the house in Víbora Park.

It was at the end of October, in the middle of that family crisis, at the time when the beaches emptied again before the approach of the always light Caribbean fall-winter, that I again met the man who loved dogs. It happened at the same spot as always, at the hour at which evening began to fall, and with the usual succession of characters, including the tall, thin black man. That day I had gone to play squash; I was with Raquelita and did not even think about the possibility of seeing him, although I recognize that I was happy to find him—and even more so his wolfhounds—on the almost deserted beach. The first thing that surprised me upon seeing them was the evidence that the man had lost several pounds, while his breathing had become labored and the color of his skin definitively sick. But I understood that something was not well and I noticed that, seven months after our first contact, his right hand was still bandaged, as if he were covering an incurable ulcer.

After introducing him to my wife (I said *compañera*, as it sounded more modern and appropriate) and asking about his dogs (Dax was experiencing increasingly frequent rages, and a veterinarian had advised López to think about putting him down, something that he had immediately rejected), I relayed the details of our wedding and talked to him about a book that I had been given to edit about the dangers of genetic degeneration in five dog breeds of different origins, and coincidentally one of the breeds under study was the borzoi. Finally, I dared to ask him about his dizzy spells. López looked at me for a few seconds and, for the first time since we had met, suggested that we sit on the sand.

"The doctors still don't know, but I'm more fucked-up every day. I can barely even walk my dogs on the beach anymore, one of the things I like the most in life. I'm in and out of the clinic, they take my blood from all over, they search me inside and out, and they never find a damned thing."

"Then you don't have anything. Nothing serious, at least," Raquelita said with her scientific logic.

He looked at her and I got the impression that he was doing it as if he had discovered a small speaking insect. He almost smiled when he said to her:

"I know that I'm dying. I don't know what, but something is killing me."

"Don't talk like that," I said to him.

"You have to take the bull by the horns," López said, and smiled, looking at the sea. With mechanical gestures, he searched for a cigarette in the pocket of his shirt, which now seemed big on him. He kindly extended the box to Raquelita, but she rejected it with a gesture that was a little brusque.

"Well, for starters, you shouldn't smoke," Raquelita interjected.

"At this stage? You know what the only thing is that alleviates my dizziness? Coffee. I drink liters of coffee. And I smoke."

While the brief October afternoon gave way to darkness, expected at that time of year, the man who loved dogs, with unusual loquacity, confessed that he liked the sea so much because he had been born in Barcelona, on the Mediterranean: the sea, its smell, its color, had become one of his obsessions. If he weren't so fucked-up and if he had the money, he concluded, he would do whatever he could to return to Spain, to Barcelona, because since that son of a bitch Franco had died, almost all the exiles had been able to return. Although I didn't understand exactly whether López could or couldn't return to Spain—if the problem was health, money, or of some other nature—his desolation and his feeling that his death was approaching, far from his place of origin, saddened me.

The man lit another cigarette and, watching Raquelita with a mixture of sarcasm and irony, said:

"The day after tomorrow I leave for Paris . . . I'm going to have some tests done on my lungs."

Raquelita's reaction was immediate and, even more, uncontainable.

"To Paris?" she asked him, and looked at me.

At that time—and still now, for the majority of us—Paris was in another world: it was a universe you could travel to through books, through the films of Truffaut, Godard, and Resnais, and lately, above all, thanks to Cortázar and *Hopscotch*. But that a real-life person would talk about going to Paris in front of us—to the real Paris—sounded as strange and mysterious as Alice's leap through the looking glass.

"Are you going to be there long?" my wife wanted to know, still impressed.

"It depends. No more than two weeks. At this time of year, Paris is horrible: what they say about the beauty of autumn in Paris is all lies. Besides, I don't like Paris."

"You don't like it?" This time I was the one who asked.

"No, I don't like Paris, nor do I like the French," he said, and put his cigarette out in the sand, pushing it almost forcefully. "Well, night already," the man then explained, as if he were just recovering the notion of the time and place he was in at that instant. "Will you help me?" He extended his arm upward.

I stood up and offered him my right hand. López grabbed on to it with his, still bandaged, and I noticed that, for the first time, I had physical contact with that individual. López stood up, but upon letting go of my hand, his feet stumbled, as if the ground had moved, and I sprang to hold him up by his arms. At that moment, I heard the threatening growls of the wolfhounds and remained immobile, but without letting López go. He understood what was happening and spoke to the dogs in Catalan.

"Quiets, quiets!"

As if he had come out of the shadows, without my noticing, the tall, thin black man appeared next to us.

"I'll help you," the black man said, and I slowly let go of the man.

"Thanks, kid," López whispered, and added, looking at Raquelita, "Goodbye, young one, and congratulations," and he almost smiled. Leaning on his chauffeur, he moved away with difficulty through the sand in search of the paved path that ran between the beach's casuarinas.

"What a strange man, Iván," Raquelita then said to me.

"What's strange about him? That he's a foreigner and is sick? That he says Paris is a shit hole?"

"No. There's something dark about him that scares me," she commented, and I couldn't help but smile. Something dark?

10

Lev Davidovich knew that they were plotting something, so he decided to pretend he was asleep. From the rigid bed where he tried to mitigate the pain of the lumbago attack and through the cloudiness of his myopia, he made out Seriozha, who, with careful steps, was entering the rooms of the Kremlin that had been turned into the family apartment after the government moved to Moscow. The boy was carrying what appeared to be a box of sardines in his arms, with the sides bleached by whitewash. A strip of red cloth—Seriozha would confess to him that he had cut a flag, one of the few attainable articles in those times—tried to make a bow to give the package the air of a present. And he could also see, peeking in the door, the complicit faces of Natalia, Liova, Nina, and Zina while small Seriozha walked toward him.

That day Lev Davidovich was turning forty-five and the October Revolution was celebrating its seventh anniversary. His wife and children had decided to give him the best present within their reach, the gift that, they knew well, could best satisfy him. So, when the birthday boy at last sat up, surrounded by his family, he was able to guess what the rattling box of sardines contained. When he managed to release the bow, he lifted the lid and exaggerated his surprise upon seeing the white-and-red-haired ball that raised its head to him.

Since that day in 1924, Maya had won his heart and become his favorite dog. When in the black spring of 1933 he placed her body in the open grave along the wall of Büyükada's cemetery, he couldn't help but recall the moments of happiness given to him by that animal who had become part of his family and whom he had now lost.

For ten days he'd fought to save her life. He made two veterinarians come from the capital. They agreed in their diagnosis: the animal had contracted an incurable infection due to pulmonary bacteria. Despite everything, Lev Davidovich tried to combat the illness with the remedies that Yanovska's old Jews applied to their dogs and that the pastors of Büyükada tended to prescribe for their own. But Maya's light went out, and this created another painful reason for the unhealthy sadness surrounding the Exile. Although he was experiencing another one of his lumbago attacks at that time, he insisted on carrying the body of his beloved borzoi in his arms to where she would be buried. Fearing that once he left Büyükada, the villa's new inhabitants would profane that grave, he had obtained the villagers' approval to bury her along the cemetery wall. Kharalambos dug the hole and his new secretary, Jean van Heijenoort, prepared a small wooden marker. When he placed her in the grave, Lev Davidovich felt that he was letting go of a good part of his life. In keeping with his style of saying goodbye, he threw a fistful of dirt on the Persian sheet that served as a shroud for the corpse and turned around, to take refuge in the more tangible and oppressive solitude of the Büyükada house.

Ever since receiving news of Zina's death and of Hitler's triumphant rise to power, Lev Davidovich had felt the ground under his feet cracking open and had tried to focus his energies on the negotiations taken up again by his French friends, led by his translator Maurice Parijanine and by the Molinier clan, who were pulling strings with the hope that Édouard Daladier's new radical government would grant him asylum.

Although Lev Davidovich was already expecting the ascent of National Socialism in Germany and knew about the pressures silencing the local Communists, he had insisted on warning them that there was still one last option remaining, and they couldn't waste it. The coalition that had brought Hitler to power was too heterogeneous, and the left and the center had to exploit that weakness before the fascist leader consolidated his position. But days had passed without the Communists making even so much as a complaint, as if their fate were not in the balance. He would never forget that the news that the German Reichstag building had burned down on the night of February 27 had reached him while he was writing one of those missives to the German workers. The incomplete and contradictory information summarized at least one alarming certainty: Hitler had announced a state of emergency and the fulfillment of his promise to eradicate Bolshevism in Germany and in the world.

Liova's messages, weighed down with uncertainty before the path of the events, soon brought news that directly affected the Exile of Büyükada. The prohibition of *Bulletin Oppozitsii* and, almost immediately, the confiscation of his works from bookstores and libraries and the public burning of entire boxes of the recently published *History of the Russian Revolution*, was a clear sign that the fascist inquisition had him and his group on their list of enemies. He then decided that it wasn't the time for running risks and ordered Liova to leave Berlin without delay.

Lev Davidovich's indignation exploded when he found out that the executive of the Communist International had issued a shameless declaration of support for the German Communist Party, whose political strategy it qualified as impeccable, while it repeated that the victory of the Nazis was just a transitory situation from which progressive forces would emerge victorious. The most worrying thing was that it was not only the domesticated Germans but also the rest of the parties affiliated with the Comintern who had silently complied with that incriminating document of political suicide with predictable consequences. How could the Communists submit themselves to such a crude manipulation? Wasn't there a drop of responsibility left in those parties that would put them on their guard against a tragedy that threatened their survival and peace in Europe? If they did not at the very least accept the imminence of the danger, he wrote, on the brink of rage, they had to admit that Stalinism had degraded the communist movement to such an incurable degree that trying to reform it was an impossible mission. One of Lev Davidovich's most intense political doubts was settled at that instant: it was time to throw it all on the fire. With the pain produced by rejecting a son who had gone off the path until he turned into an unrecognizable being, he decided that the moment had arrived to break with the International and, perhaps, to create a new one that would oppose fascism with concrete acts and not with propaganda slogans that hid macabre ulterior motives.

Just a week after Maya's death, the anticipated news that Daladier's government was giving him asylum arrived to pull him out of the morass of depression. Although he immediately knew how limited the hospitality being offered him was, he didn't hesitate to accept: according to the visa, he was authorized to reside in one of the departments in the south, on the condition of not ever visiting Paris, and of submitting to the control of the Ministry of the Interior. More than a refugee, he would again be a prisoner, only now in a central corridor and not in a confinement cell. And from there he thought he could act.

The morning on which the retinue of secretaries, bodyguards, fishermen, and police were going down to the dock where their bags were already waiting, Natalia and Lev Davidovich remained for a few minutes in front of what had been their home. They wanted to say goodbye to Prinkipo, where he had finished his autobiography and written the *History of the Russian Revolution*; where he had ceased to be a Soviet and had cried over the death of a daughter; and where, in the midst of the worst abandonment, he had decided that his fight was not finished and that he needed to live—to harass the most ruthless power that one man alone, without resources, who was aging by the day could conceive of confronting. Good Kharalambos, who was silently watching him from the path, must have asked himself if it was true that that lonely man had ever been an explosive leader capable of inspiring the masses to revolution. No one would have said so, he surely concluded, as he saw him close the garden gate and lean over to pick some wildflowers on the ground where four years before he had prohibited the planting of a rosebush. When they came close to him, Kharalambos smiled at them, his eyes watering, and accepted the flowers that the deportee extended to him. Without saying a word, Lev Davidovich raised his eyes to the pines hiding the white walls of the cemetery of the islands of the exiled princes.

Nine days later, without the jubilation they expected, Lev Davidovich, Natalia, and Liova arrived at Les Embruns, the villa that Raymond Molinier had rented in the outskirts of Saint-Palais, in the French Midi. The former commissar of war's entrance into the house had not exactly been dignified: he was trembling with fever, thinking that the pounding in his temples would burst his skull, and felt as if his waist was being broken by a biting and unrelenting pain. Because of that, as soon as he crossed the threshold, he fell on a couch and immediately accepted the aspirins and sleeping pills that Natalia Sedova gave him.

They had barely left Istanbul when he had felt a crisis of lumbago, accompanied by a return of malaria. During the entire crossing, Lev Davidovich had remained in his cabin and even refused to speak with the journalists who were waiting for him in El Pireo, attracted by the rumors of his imminent return to the Soviet Union, after his meeting in France with Stalin's new commissar of foreign affairs. When Marseille came into sight, dozens of journalists, policemen, and protesters opposed to his presence in France were also waiting for them, and his wife had surprised him with the news that Liova and Molinier had come from the port in a ferry to avoid encountering the crowd that could have upset the authorities. Seeing his son again after a tense separation, and hearing him say that in the course of a few days Jeanne would travel from Paris to bring Seva to him, brought him happiness capable of dulling his pains. He then found out that Molinier had prepared everything so that they disembarked in Cassis, from which they traveled in cars to Saint-Palais. But that almost two-hour-long journey on narrow roads had ended up conquering the recently arrived man's physical resistance.

The pills were starting to take effect, when Lev Davidovich heard some voices ripping him away from that kind lethargy. He would confess to Natalia Sedova that at first he thought he was dreaming: in his dream someone was screaming "Fire! Fire!" But he had enough lucidity not to brush away the nightmare returning him to the nights of arson in Büyükada and Kadıköy as insignificant. He managed to open his eyes just as he felt his arm being pulled and saw the terrified expression on Liova's face. Then he knew that reality was greater than the ramblings of his fever, and, leaning on his son, he managed to go out to the garden, above which smoke was floating, and he had the feeling of carrying hell with him. Shit! he thought, and fell on the grass, where he at last found out that the fire (seemingly caused by a train spark that had fallen on the very dry earth) had only affected the hedge and the backyard's wooden shed.

Liova and Molinier were in a rush to speak with Lev Davidovich, as in just one month the founding assembly of the Fourth International planned by the Exile would take place in Paris. However, stopped by Natalia

Sedova, the men had to contain their impatience and give the sick man a few days of peace. Nor could Seva's anxiously awaited arrival be celebrated as it should have been, due to the fevers overtaking him; he asked Natalia to let him talk to the boy, though, since he wanted to see how his spirits were and explain why his beloved Maya was not with them.

When the fever receded a bit, and particularly when the lumbago pains began to decrease, Lev Davidovich put a deaf ear to his wife's prohibitions and held a meeting with Lev Sedov, Raymond Molinier, and his coreligionist Max Shachtman, who had accompanied him from Prinkipo. The Exile knew that he was racing the clock and that the four weeks until the constitutive meeting in Paris were forcing them to be especially efficient, since he sensed that he was playing the most important card of his exile. His main concern was Liova and Molinier's capacity for gatherings, since they would not only be in charge of organizing the meeting but also be his voice, impossible as it was for him to travel to Paris due to the conditions of his asylum. Weighing each of his collaborators' judgments, the old revolutionary listened to their opinions and immediately was sure that the Fourth International was hanging on a precipice, affected by his own contradictions and created at an adverse time, perhaps too quickly. While Liova offered the dismal panorama (fear and doubts in Germany, dispersion and rivalries in France and Belgium, adventurism in the United States), Molinier trusted in the Exile's authority to overcome the doubts of many followers and in the possibility of taking advantage of the rise of fascism to call for unity.

Before returning to Paris, Liova would confess to his mother that, for the second time in his life, he had felt compassion for Lev Davidovich and even asked himself if it was worth continuing to fight. Although his father hadn't given up, the truth was that only his pride, his historic optimism, and his responsibility made him insist on his ideas: at the end of thirty years of revolutionary struggle it was clear, seeing how the world was breaking under the weight of the reaction around him, the totalitarianism, the lies, and the threat of a devastating war, that the man was on his own.

It was precisely that optimism about the future and the laws of history that constituted Lev Davidovich's mainstay throughout the weeks in which, from his sofa, he devoted up to fifteen hours daily to drafting the thesis to be discussed in Paris. His political perception, altered by events of recent years, allowed him to clarify some of his purposes in calling for a new International, to which he hoped to attract the dispersed Trotskyist groups and those unhappy with the Stalinist policy applied in Germany, and also some radical sectors, which were always difficult to discipline. But its great contradiction continued to be the policy the meeting of parties should adopt regarding the Soviet Union: the situation there was different, and for the time being caution was the priority, since the struggle had no reason to attack the basis of the system if it managed to unmask it and, when the time came, dethrone the bureaucratic excrescence.

The work, in any event, would not be easy. Stalin had already ordered the "friends of the USSR" to initiate a campaign destined to get hold of the antifascist monopoly, at least on the verbal level, since, when it came to action, they didn't seem too interested in opposing the necessary enemy that had finally emerged from the German ashes. Stalin's new campaign propagated the myth that the Soviet system was the only possible choice against Hitler and barbarism. While they accused the democracies of being sympathetic to and even having been the cause of fascism, they reduced the ethical and political options to just two: on the one hand terror, made incarnate by fascism; and on the other, hope and the common good, represented by the Communists led by Stalin. The trap was set and Lev Davidovich started to predict the fall of almost all of the West's progressive forces into the abyss.

Throughout the four weeks he worked on preparing the conference, the pain and fever would not leave him. Many times Natalia tried to tear him away from his work, but he refused, promising that, after the meeting, he would submit to the regimen of her choice. On the brink of collapse, he finished drafting the documents and bid goodbye to van Heijenoort, begging him to forget his wife's orders and keep him up-to-date.

The anxiety soon gave way to disappointment before a predictable fiasco. The parties and groups represented in Paris were a reflection of the dispersal experienced by the European and American left, discouraged by failure and frightened by Moscow's pressures. More than a current, his followers formed small grouplets, the majority being dissidents from communist parties, and they stepped back, scared by that new affiliation that demanded a defined anti-Stalinist position and a philosophical practice that was essentially Marxist, guided by the doctrine of permanent revolution as an ideological principle. Lev Davidovich thought that perhaps

Molinier's unrestrained energy and Liova's inexperience had led to the impossibility of achieving important strategic agreements and because of that, when he found out that only three of the invited parties accepted to join a new coalition, he advised Liova that, to save his honor, he desist from founding the International and announce that the meeting had been just a preliminary conference for the future organization.

Overcome by exhaustion and disappointment, he put his body in Natalia's hands; she began by confining him to a room without a desk, to which all visitors were forbidden, including Liova. Nonetheless, his mind kept going around in circles, and for several days he thought about the reasons for the failure in Paris. That fiasco proved how much his political power had diminished in five years of almost complete marginalization, although he had to recognize that the political situation in which he now had to act was decisive, so different from that of 1917: the revolutionary positions were withdrawing and it was utopian to wait for a situation capable of unleashing a wave of rebellion to advance through Europe and reach Moscow's doors. By any measure, the clamor for permanent revolution and the image of a leader who would subvert the Muscovite order as well as the capitalist one began to seem anachronistic.

A few weeks later, when the French authorities lifted some restrictions on his asylum (now he was prevented only from living in Paris and in the Seine department), Lev Davidovich decided to leave Saint-Palais and cut off his dependent relationship with Raymond Molinier. Due to his limited finances, he chose to establish himself in the outskirts of Barbizon, the small town that Millet, Rousseau, and other landscape artists had made famous. Located on the edges of the Fontainbleau forest and less than two hours from Paris, Barbizon represented the advantage of being closer to his followers, although it forced them to again use a corps of bodyguards.

The house was a two-story building, from the turn of the century, that its owners baptized "Ker Monique," and was only separated from the forest by a dirt path that barely fit a car. Since moving to that place, always perfumed by the scent of the forest, he felt himself regaining his ability to work and was again writing and receiving visits from his followers, to whom he proselytized on an almost individual basis. Thus, he tried to prevent new dissent from forming, as had just occurred in Spain, where the group led by his old friend Andreu Nin had decided to found a party independent of any International, or the one that was led in France by fighters like Simone Weil and Pierre Naville. The most regrettable thing was discovering how much the proposed International had been hurt by Molinier's political ambitions, capable of planting chaos in the French opposition to the point that, he wrote, they would need years of work to bring together the scarcely hundred or so militants who still followed him.

With Natalia, he spent many afternoons that winter walking to the domesticated forest of oaks and chestnuts that made up the hunting grounds of the French monarchy, and even crossed it to visit the Palais-Royal. Some nights, wanting to treat themselves, they went to eat venison at the nearby Auberge du Grand-Veneur, but he almost always dedicated those hours to catching up on new developments in French literature and with pleasure read a couple of novels by Georges Simenon, that young Belgian who had interviewed him in Prinkipo; he discovered the overwhelming Céline of *Journey to the End of the Night*, which had been capable of shaking the vocabulary of French literature; and he enjoyed Malraux's epic *Man's Fate*, the novel that the writer gave him during his visit to Saint-Palais.

However, the book that really moved him at that time had arrived from Moscow and served to reveal to him once again why Mayakovsky had chosen to shoot himself through the heart and, at the same time, to prove the extremes to which the totalitarian system can pervert an artist's talent. This was *Belomorsko-Baltiyski Kanal imeni Stalina* (*The Canal Named in Honor of Stalin*). The book had been edited by and had a prologue by Maxim Gorky and brought together texts by thirty-five writers determined to justify the unjustifiable. Ever since the summer, when the canal uniting the White Sea with the Baltic Sea was inaugurated, the "friends of the USSR" and the European communist press had started to praise the great work of socialist engineering and to deem anyone who merely asked about the enterprise's utility an enemy of the working class. But Gorky's anthology of texts went beyond the limits of abjection. In his previous hyperbolic book, the novelist had already devoted himself to exalting the humanist effort undertaken in the Solovski *lager*, where, according to what was declared in Moscow and happily repeated by Gorky, the Soviet penal system fought at thirty degrees below zero to turn common criminals and enemies of the revolution into socially useful men. And now *Kanal imeni Stalina* proposed to sanctify the horror, documenting the prodigious transformation of the prisoners forced to work on the canal into shining models of the New Soviet Man. The book's immorality was such that it managed to surprise Lev Davidovich when he thought he was immune to that type of shock. If the French gazetteers could save their souls by saying they were unaware of the truth about what happened in the building of that canal and arguing that they were just repeating what was dictated from Moscow, those Soviet writers could not be unaware of the horror lived by two hundred thousand prisoners (unsatisfied peasants, degraded bureaucrats, political and religious opponents, alcoholics, and even some writers) forced for years to build the locks, dams, and dikes of the canal, which included twenty-five miles of path cut through nothing but rock, just so that Stalin could demonstrate the supremacy of socialist engineering that, coincidentally, he also directed. The death toll during the execution of the work could never be calculated, but every Soviet knew that more than twenty-five thousand prisoners had perished in accidents or had been devoured by the cold and exhaustion. Besides, they all knew that the supplier of the physical labor for the canal had been the People's Commissar of Internal Affairs, the maniacal Genrikh Yagoda, and that, for his dedication, Stalin had conferred upon him the Order of Lenin during the inauguration of the canal.

Lev Davidovich was moved to disgust, lamenting the moral degradation of a man like Maxim Gorky, the same Gorky who preferred to go into exile in 1921, still very much convinced that "everything I said about the Bolsheviks' savageness, about their lack of culture, about the cruelty rooted in sadism, about their ignorance of the Russian people's psychology, about the facts that they're carrying out a disgusting experiment with the people and destroying the working class—all of that and much more that I said about Bolshevism is still as potent." What arguments had Stalin used to achieve the return of a man with those ideas from his comfortable Italian exile? Which ones to force him into the humiliation of signing his name to those books and turning into the accomplice of horrifying crimes against humanity, dignity, and intelligence?

The year 1934 brought with it a ray of hope to Barbizon that would keep Lev Davidovich in suspense for weeks. Through the scarce information channels to which he still had access, he received the news from Moscow that Stalin's political rivals had conspired to use the Bolshevik Party's Twenty-Seventh Congress to make the decisive battle for their survival.

Many of the activists who, without mentioning Trotsky's name, continued to support him and considered his return a necessity—in addition to those who had opposed Stalin at some point, and those who for years had been his collaborators and were later expelled by the leader—were thinking of using the congress to remove the Georgian from power through a vote in which they would propose their future politicians. At the head of the heterogeneous group—united only by their hate or fear of Stalin—were old Bolsheviks of various leanings, among them Lenin's oldest comrades—Zinoviev, Kamenev, Piatakov, the unpredictable Bukharin—and Trotskyist oppositionists who had been readmitted to the party after surrendering. The rumors said that they had placed their faith in the election of Sergei Kirov, the party's young secretary in Leningrad, a man whose history wasn't stained with the internal struggles of the 1920s. The reports assured him that Kirov, even though he had refused to reach any agreement with the oppositionists and maintained he was loyal to the general secretary, had criticized Stalin's collectivizing, industrializing, and repressive excesses and, as a Communist, was willing to accept the congress's will.

With the experience of expulsion behind him, Lev Davidovich couldn't stop imagining the tricks Stalin would use to destroy the rebellion in the making, which he followed closely. His ability to divide and use people, blackmail the weakest ones, and terrorize his most committed followers and converts with possible revenge would, without a doubt, shine in those days. Because of that, during the congress's opening session on February 26, when the initial praise for the five-year plan was heard, the ambitious economic plans for the future were proclaimed, and it was decided to call it the "Congress of Victors," he had bet that the general secretary's rivals had lost the battle.

The defeat was confirmed by the summary of the speech by Bukharin, who focused his diatribe on condemning the political position that he himself had led, only to later recognize that "Comrade Stalin was right when, by brilliantly applying the Marxist-Leninist dialectic, he destroyed a series of theoretic proposals from the twisted right, for which I, above all, accept my share of responsibility." Before that tacit acceptance of failure, Lev Davidovich could not help but admire the courage with which a few activists still dared to propose the propriety of Stalin being relieved of his duties and the need to air out the country's political environment. The vote against Stalin, which many delegates joined, ultimately was unable to overcome the majority terrorized by the specter of change, the loss of privileges, and possible reprisals. As Piatakov had done to him, now Lev Davidovich could prophesy to Piatakov himself, to Zinoviev, Kamenev, Bukharin, and even to Kirov, that Stalin would make them pay with blood for their daring and the challenge they had launched.

Barbizon's pleasant season reached its end with spring. The strange arrest of Rudolf Klement (he had broken the speed limit on his small moped) by a policeman who, previously uninformed by the Sûreté, only now "discovered" Trotsky's presence in the area, was able to generate a virulent campaign against the government, led by Communists and fascists, who even managed to make a deportation order against him effective.

Fearful of the reprisals announced by the Stalinists and the fascist Cagoulards, Lev Davidovich and Natalia left Barbizon during the night. In order to disguise himself, Lev Davidovich shaved his mustache and beard and changed his rounded glasses, and they escaped to Paris, where they would consult with Liova about what to do.

They chose to disappear from life in Chamonix, the Alpine village near the Swiss and Italian borders, from where expeditions of climbers to Mont Blanc left. A few weeks later, after they were mysteriously discovered by a journalist, the Trotskys were forced by the region's prefect to go on the move once again. Looking for a lost place on the map, Lev Davidovich made his way to Domène, a small town near Grenoble, where he even decided to go without bodyguards or secretaries. There, he would be a nobody.

Until the end of his life, Lev Davidovich would recall that on the morning of December 2, 1934, he went out to the patio of the house in Domène, where Natalia had hung the recently washed bedclothes. The smell of soap and the morning's aroma painted a peaceful picture that had seemed definitively unreal before the weight of the news he had just heard on the radio: Sergei Kirov had been killed in his office at the Smolny Institute in Leningrad. The Exile's mind envisioned the scenes of commotion that undoubtedly reigned in the Soviet Union and the assumptions about what would happen from that moment on, which, he knew so well, marked a point of no return.

The reports he heard spoke of massive detentions and of preliminary investigations that linked the intellectual authorship of the murder to the Trotskyist opposition (in which they said the assassin, Leonid Nikolayev, had been active) and the plot against the government, which even included the participation of the Latvian city consul, a Trotskyist "agent," according to them. Because of that, when he told Natalia what had happened, the woman asked the question that would pursue the man until the end of his days: "What about Seriozha?"

An entire week of anguish ended when Seriozha's letter arrived, brought from Paris by Liova. In contrast to his previous letters, warm and personal, always directed to his mother, this one was permeated by a cry of alarm. The situation in Moscow had become chaotic, the arrests were endless, everyone was living under the fear of being interrogated, and the apolitical scientist considered his situation "more serious than could be imagined." When she finished reading the letter, Natalia broke out in sobs. What was happening to her son? Why was the situation so serious? Was this simply to be expected because he was a Trotsky? The anxiety to obtain new news of Sergei grew from then on and left his parents' lives in suspense, awaiting any confirmation of his fate.

The path events would take became clearer with the news that on December 2, the GPU had executed about one hundred people—all of them arrested before Kirov's murder—while numerous party members had been imprisoned. Nonetheless, much more light was shed by the series of articles that Bukharin wrote for *Izvestia*, in which he spoke of the illegality of any type of dissidence within the country, while at the same time repeating Stalin's motto that opposition only leads to counterrevolution, and exemplified that degradation with the cases of Zinoviev and Kamenev, labeling them as "degenerate fascists." Because of that, when on the twenty-third of December he heard that Zinoviev and Kamenev had been arrested, accused of being "moral" accomplices to the attack, he had no doubt that a storm had been unleashed of potentially devastating power. Two times Stalin had expelled those old Bolsheviks, Lenin's comrades; two times he had readmitted them to the party, on each occasion devouring pieces of their human and political stature until they became hovering shadows with no weight but the history of their names. Now, however, the moment of truth seemed to have arrived for two ghosts from the past that he would brutally crush because Stalin owed his ascent to power precisely to them. If at Lenin's death they had not allied themselves with the (as they believed) limited and clumsy Stalin, all of them insistent on closing off Lev Davidovich's access to power, Soviet history could have perhaps been different.

Lev Davidovich recalled Zinoviev's murky stare and Kamenev's elusive one (he had never understood how his younger sister Olga had been able to marry him) when they accused him of wanting to take power. Joyous about the success they hoped to achieve, they assumed the visible leadership of the offensive against Lev Davidovich and his ideas, accusing him of being a man anxious to be the protagonist, capable of throwing himself into propagating revolution throughout Europe while putting the sacred fate of the Soviet Union at risk. That tragic duo would never regret enough that Faustian hour in which they accepted the hand of that man from the mountains who, in his other hand, concealed a dagger.

Seriozha's silence hung over the Trotskys in the transition to the year 1935, which arrived with the worst of omens. On the evening of December 31, despite the cold coming down from the mountains, the couple went out for a walk through the nearby fields with the intention of removing themselves from the radio that from Moscow was transmitting patriotic marches, versions of triumphant speeches by the leader, and news such as that the murderer Nikolayev, his wife, his mother-in-law, and thirteen other party members had been executed after they had admitted their links to the Trotskyist opposition and their direct or indirect participation in Kirov's death. At one point in their walk, Natalia asked him to stop and she sat down on the leaves, surprised by her fatigue. He watched her and saw how her suffering was making her age with a betraying swiftness. Nonetheless, she never complained about her fate and, when she heard her husband complaining, pushed him to take up the path again. Lev Davidovich asked her if she felt ill and she responded that it was just a bit of fatigue, then she fell silent again, as if she had imposed a vow of silence on herself that prevented her from speaking of her agonies: her desperation over the lack of news from Seriozha was in a way admitting that that son could also have been devoured by the crushing violence unleashed by a revolution whose first principle was peace.

The anxiety dulled as the days passed, but for weeks Lev Davidovich wandered like a ghost around the house in Domène. He barely came out of his daze when the news arrived from Moscow that Zinoviev, Kamenev, and the others who were "morally responsible" for Kirov's death had received sentences of between ten and five years in prison. Almost immediately, they found out that Volkov and Nevelson, the husbands of the deceased Zina and Nina, deported since 1928, had also received new sentences and that his ex-wife, Alexandra Sokolovskaya, despite her age, would be banished from Leningrad to the colony of Tobolsk, along with Kamenev's wife, Olga Kameneva. All of those sanctions had a positive side that the Trotskyists clung to: if the known oppositionists and other members of the family were just jailed and deported, Sergei should be alive, even if he had been arrested. But why didn't he write? Why didn't anyone mention him?

Adopting her husband's skepticism, Natalia drafted an open letter, directed at international opinion, in which she declared her conviction that Seriozha, a scientist from Moscow's Technological Institute, had no political affiliation, and asked that his activities be investigated and his whereabouts revealed. She asked for the intercession of known figures such as Romain Rolland, André Gide, George Bernard Shaw, and various workers' leaders, since she gauged that the Soviet bureaucracy could not elevate its impunity above public opinion, the leftist intellectuals, and the global working class.

Meanwhile, the voices clamoring against him had become so aggressive that every day Lev Davidovich was expecting to be the victim of a violent act, irrational or premeditated. Because of that, after making his bodyguards come from Paris, he once again mortgaged his hopes of asylum on the stubborn Norway, where the Labor Party had just won the general elections. In his request, he argued that he had health problems but, above all, personal security problems, and as he had done before with France, he reiterated his commitment not to participate in the country's politics.

When he felt the siege of Stalinist and fascist pressures was about to trap him (there was talk of sending him to some colony, perhaps Guyana), the back door opened again with the arrival of the Norwegian visa. In contrast to what had happened two years earlier, when he left Büyükada, no residue of nostalgia accompanied him in the rushed departure from Domène, where he had lived for almost a year without acquiring a single happy memory.

Accompanied by Liova, they traveled to Paris, where they still had to fight to be given a visa that hadn't arrived, while the French authorities demanded that they leave the country within forty-eight hours because he had violated the restriction on traveling to the capital. At the moment of his departure, Lev Davidovich gave Liova a letter to be published in the *Bulletin*. In it he accused the politicians of Democratic France not only of having played dirty with him but also of doing so with the future of the Republic, making shady deals with Moscow while fascism extended throughout the country. "I leave France with a deep love for its people and with unshakable faith in the future of the working class. Sooner or later, they will offer me the hospitality the bourgeoisie has denied me," he said at the end of the letter, showing his usual optimism. But as they crossed Paris, he felt sickened: he wondered whether a possible return to a proletarian France was not an illusion. Undoubtedly, it was: "Socialism has dug its own grave and I sense it will rot there for a long time," he wrote.

The warmth with which the Norwegian journalist Konrad Knudsen welcomed him in his house was like a consolation prize after the months of solitude, tension, and confinement experienced in France. The silence and peace he found in the small town of Vexhall were so compact that he could push them aside with his hands, like a velvet curtain. In summer, the sunsets tended to unfold lazily, as if the day didn't want to leave, while mornings seemed to come forth ready-made from between the tree branches. Ever since arriving at Vexhall, he had acquired the custom of watching those daybreaks as he drank his coffee in the Knudsens' backyard and inhaled the aroma of the forest.

When they were received in Norway, Lev Davidovich had harbored the fantasy that perhaps there he could escape the tensions that had pursued him throughout almost seven years of deportation and exile. Recently arrived in the country, he had found himself subject to the insults that, with nearly the same emphasis and very similar words, the communist and fascist press hurled at him, trying to turn him into a political problem for the Oslo government. But his Labor Party hosts had aborted the campaign with sharp statements, declaring that the right of asylum could not be a dead letter in a democratic nation and that the Norwegian people, and in particular its workers, felt honored by his presence in the country and would never allow any pressure from Moscow against the hospitality extended to a revolutionary whose name was linked to that of Lenin. In addition, to reduce the tension, numerous ministers had offered the assurance that he could consider the six-month visa a formality. The demands were still that he not participate in internal affairs and that he establish residency outside of Oslo. Because of that, faced with the difficulty of finding the right place, they themselves had asked the social democratic politician and journalist Konrad Knudsen to host them at Vexhall, a town close to Hønefoss, thirty miles from the capital.

Lev Davidovich would always remember his first days at Vexhall as strange and confusing. Lodged in a large room, where a splendid mahogany desk had been placed, he and Natalia had to adapt to the rhythms of a house inhabited by a large family who, in the summertime, enjoyed the freedom to forgo schedules and the ability to shrink or grow without warning. The absence of bodyguards, unnecessary in the Labor Party's and Knudsen's opinion, made him look apprehensively at the garden's open gate and think that the Norwegians' trust played with limits that were unknown to Stalin and his secret police henchmen. But the most important adaptation to life in Vexhall was the establishment between Knudsen and his guest of what they called "a nonaggression pact," through which they allowed themselves to discuss politics, but always without questioning their respective positions of Communist and Social Democrat.

If the Exile had any doubts regarding Norwegian hospitality, these disappeared when the minister of justice, Trygve Lie, came to visit him accompanied by Martin Tranmæl, the leader and founder of the Labor Party. Their talk, informal at first, led to an interview that Lie would publish in the *Arbeiderbladet*, the main labor newspaper, and in which the interviewer and interviewee shook hands despite their political differences.

A few weeks later, although Lev Davidovich's mind felt a decrease in tension, his body responded with an ubiquitous discomfort that lasted for months. Nonetheless, he shut himself up in his room each day, resolved to withstand the headaches and joint pains to again take up the biography of Lenin that, with decreasing enthusiasm, his North American editor demanded, the only one who wanted it following his German editor's withdrawal and the lack of interest in his work by the French. But some news that arrived from Moscow, at the beginning of August 1935, led him to wonder whether his efforts should be focused on the leader's biography or if the reigning cynicism in the Soviet Union demanded a reflection about the horror of the present and the need to reverse it. The edition of *Pravda* that had alarmed him featured the chronicle of another one of those parties at the Kremlin in which Stalin, after distributing decorations in abundance, had launched into an inevitable speech. This time his words were reduced to a simple victory cry: "Life is improved, comrades, life is happier here! Let's drink to life and to socialism!" The experience that had allowed him to learn to interpret that man's movements warned him that this could not be a casual phrase but rather the roar of a lion on a devastating hunt.

For months, Lev Davidovich had been considering each act, putting each fact in its place, trying to understand the goals of the policy of détente generated by the Kremlin after the trial at the beginning of 1935 against Zinoviev, Kamenev, and company, with which the investigation into Kirov's murder had been closed. Since then, the arrests had decreased and a wave of official optimism, constantly reinforced by propaganda, had started to run through the country while in Moscow they feted distinguished workers and the representatives of various republics; banquets were offered to scientists, athletes, and distinguished government workers; and party leaders at all levels were recognized. After the hunger and the repression of recent years, Stalin was trying to create a climate of security to spread the idea that the difficult times were a thing of the past because they were already living in the times of socialist prosperity. But once that mirage was created, Lev Davidovich knew that the moment would come when Stalin would strike another blow that would shake the country and consolidate a system in which Stalin could, at last, reign without the interference of any rivals.

Save for the news that Seriozha was alive and sequestered in an apartment in Moscow, nothing good would happen during the final weeks of November and the first of December, when his body declared itself exhausted to the point that he feared the end was approaching in that vulgar manner: "Death by exhaustion, how horrible!" he would write . . . Nonetheless, perhaps the same awareness that he could die leaving so many unfinished projects resulted in working the miracle of getting him out of bed, almost from one day to the next, with his energy practically recovered. Despite his stiff muscles, an overwhelming feeling of rebirth overcame him, and because of that he dared to accept Knudsen's invitation to participate in an outing to the countryside in the north of Hønefoss, ideal for skiing at that time of year. In his memory, the most notable event would be when he sunk in the snow to his thighs and required a rescue operation directed by Knudsen and carried out by Jean van Heijenoort and his new assistant, the recently arrived Erwin Wolf.

Shortly after, in the first weeks of 1936, Lev Davidovich received a letter capable of revealing, better than all the available psychoanalytic literature, the most dramatic and exact notion of what fear could be and the unpredictable human mechanisms that it can mobilize. It was written to him by his former adversary Fyodor Dan, exiled in Paris since shortly after the Bolshevik victory. He had known Dan since 1903, when he had been one of the revolutionary Social Democrats who, at the Congress of Brussels, voted against Lenin and, with the rest of the opponents, established Menshevism within the party. Although Dan had been one of the Mensheviks who worked the most to bring the factions together, his loyalty to his group had placed him in the current that was contrary to the proletarian revolution, since he defended the establishment of a parliamentary system in Russia, to which Lev Davidovich was opposed in the month prior to the October coup. Once the Bolshevik victory was definitively established, Dan tried to engineer a rapprochement and later had the decency to recognize defeat and withdraw in silence.

After greeting him and wishing him good health, Dan explained that he dared to write him, after so many years of physical and political distance, because a mutual friend, Dr. Le Savoureux, had insisted that he tell him something that, on many levels, had to do with Lev Davidovich's past as well as his foreseeable future.

Dan explained to him that Bukharin, despite having been marginalized by Stalin after several castrations, had been sent to Europe with the mission of purchasing some important documents by Marx and Engels that Stalin wanted to deposit in the archives of the former Marx-Engels-Lenin Institute, recently augmented with the inclusion of his own name. Bukharin, with enough money to buy the archives and for his maintenance, had been in Vienna, Copenhagen, Amsterdam, and Berlin before arriving in Paris, where the German Social Democrats possessing the documents had taken the bulk of the archives after Hitler's rise to power. Bukharin was to negotiate in Paris with a former acquaintance of the old Russian fighters, the Menshevik Boris Nikolayevsky, who was also a friend of Dr. Le Savoureux. In conversation, Bukharin had always seemed reserved, nervous, indecisive, like a man under great stress; and although

Nikolayevsky needled him, it was impossible to obtain from him an opinion about what was happening in the USSR, about Kirov's murder or the imprisonment of Zinoviev and Kamenev, whom Bukharin himself had placed on the pillory with his public accusation that they were fascists. "At the beginning he seemed like a man who was gravely mistrustful," assured Dan, who, on two or three occasions, in the company of his wife, had seen him and spoken with him about the only subjects Bukharin allowed: French cheeses and literature, his friendship with Lenin and the documents he had to buy. Dan managed to have him comment on Stalin's politics and, perhaps in a moment of sincerity, Bukharin confessed the great pain he felt about the way the general secretary was demolishing the spirit of the revolution. To anyone knowledgeable about Soviet politics, Dan said, it would have seemed at least curious that Stalin would have picked Bukharin for that operation, more commercial than philosophical or historical, since the direction of the political housecleaning suggested that sooner or later Bukharin, who had dared to defy Stalin at one moment, would be the next victim. But the greatest surprise about Stalin's decision had yet to come: without Bukharin having even dared to suggest it, the dictator had sent Anna Larina, Bukharin's young wife, several months pregnant, to Paris. What kind of strange play was that? Why would Stalin open his captive's door and allow him to desert without leaving his wife behind? Did he prefer to have Bukharin outside of the Soviet Union and not inside the country, where he would always be able to destroy him with the same impunity with which he had expelled Zinoviev and Kamenev, or have him killed like Kirov? Was it a move destined to turn Bukharin into a deserter before he became a martyr? Dan asked himself, forcing Lev Davidovich to ponder this as he read.

A few weeks later, Dan continued, Bukharin received a communiqué from Stalin: he should forget the negotiations, he was no longer interested in Marx's and Engels's papers, and he demanded that he appear in Moscow immediately. Dr. Le Savoureux was present when Bukharin received the order and witnessed the anger that came over the face of the prodigal son of Bolshevism, the most promising revolutionary theorist. Le Savoureux had suggested that Bukharin not return: that unforeseen call could only be geared at retaining him and turning him into the victim of repression. Nikolayevsky was of the same opinion, and he reminded Bukharin that if he remained in Europe, he could become a second Trotsky and, together, lead an opposition with greater opportunities to dethrone Stalin. But Bukharin had begun to prepare for his return: he did it in silence, automatically, like a man who willingly and conscientiously directs himself to the scaffold. Le Savoureux, in a fit of rage, asked him how it was possible for a man, who for years had fought against czarism and accompanied Lenin in the darkest days of the struggle, to return like a lamb, to submit himself to a sure punishment. Then Bukharin gave him the most devastating response: "I'm returning out of fear." Le Savoureux thought he had not understood correctly—perhaps Bukharin's French had been affected by his nervousness—but when he thought twice about it, he was certain he had heard perfectly well: *I'm returning out of fear*. Le Savoureux told him that precisely for that reason he should not return—in exile he was more useful to his country and to the revolution— and then Bukharin at last offered his full reasoning: he wasn't made of the same material as Lev Davidovich and Stalin knew it—and above all, he knew it himself. He would not be able to withstand the pressures Trotsky had experienced for years, and he wasn't willing to live like a pariah, waiting to be stabbed in the back any day. "I know that sooner or later Stalin is going to finish me off; maybe he'll kill me, maybe not. But I'm going to return to cling to the possibility that he not think it necessary to kill me. I would rather live with that hope than with the constant fear of knowing I am a condemned man."

Bukharin returned to Moscow. He took Anna Larina, who was already seven months pregnant. Le Savoureux saw him off at Gare du Nord and later went to meet Nikolayevsky and Dan in the Russian restaurant in the Latin Quarter where they usually ate. The conversation, of course, centered on Bukharin. "Then we realized," Dan continued, "that Stalin had played with him the whole time, like a cat that pretends to be asleep. But Stalin had bet that he wouldn't need to run after his captive. He was sure that the poor mouse, overcome with fear, would return to kiss the claws that would tear him apart and devour him when the cat's appetite required it. It's impossible to conceive of a sicker and more sadistic attitude. It's terrible to know that the man capable of doing this is he who leads our country today, the revolution that you and I dreamed of in different ways but with the same passion, and the one dreamed of by Lenin and so many men who Stalin is annihilating and will continue to annihilate in the future. And I'm sure that amid those sacrificed in the Stalinist slaughterhouse will be Bukharin, who was so afraid that he preferred the certainty of death to the risk of every day having to demonstrate the courage to live."

For weeks, Lev Davidovich fought himself to push the dismal story relayed by Fyodor Dan from his preoccupations. But the image of a pale Bukharin, so different from the exultant and romantic young man who had welcomed him in New York when France banished him in 1916, came back to his mind too frequently; and a few months later, while he was following the trial of a group of old comrades in the newspapers and on the radio, he recalled Bukharin's sentence over and over again: "I'm returning out of fear." Then Lev Davidovich understood the exact proportions of the point to which the country he had helped found had turned into a territory dominated by fear. And when he heard the conclusion of that trial, which seemed more like a farce, he had the painful certainty that, with the decision to shoot many of the men who had worked for Bolshevism's victory, Stalin had poisoned the last ember of the soul of the revolution and one had only to sit and wait for its final agony to arrive, tomorrow, within ten, in twenty years. But the infection was irreversible and fatal.

Ever since he had arrived in Norway the year before, Lev Davidovich frequently commented to Knudsen that, when his health allowed, he would like to go out fishing, and he had told him about his relaxing outings in the Sea of Marmara with his friend Kharalambos. Many things had prevented him from fulfilling that desire until, on August 4, 1936, he got into his host's car and left in the direction of one of the fjords in the south, where there was a small, desolate island that was said to be ideal for fishing. As they left Vexhall, Knudsen had the impression that a car was following them; he then took a side road and managed to leave their pursuers behind, whom he had identified as men from the fascist party of the so-called Commander Quisling.

When they reached the fjord, a speedboat took them to the islet, where there were numerous wooden cabins. The landscape, wild and peaceful, seemed to Lev Davidovich like the very picture of the world in the first days of creation, and he immediately felt in harmony with its desolate grandeur.

The following morning Lev Davidovich got up early; despite the brisk temperature, he left the cabin and, with a pitcher of coffee in his hand, went to the jetty to see the sun rising between a break in the mountains. Immersed in contemplation, he was startled when Knudsen tapped his shoulder to tell him that they had sent him a message from Vexhall: a group of men dressed as policemen, but who were obviously members of Commander Quisling's party, had entered the house to search Lev Davidovich's room. Knudsen's children and sons-in-law, upon realizing they were imposters, sounded the alarm and managed to kick them out, but they couldn't stop them from taking some papers. According to Knudsen, that must have been the reason that they had followed them in the car: they wanted to be sure that they were leaving Vexhall.

When he knew that nothing had happened to Knudsen's family, Lev Davidovich didn't lend much importance to the episode: if they were looking for his papers while he was out, it meant that they weren't too interested in him as a person, at least for the time being.

Three days later, Knudsen, Natalia, and Lev Davidovich saw a small plane land on the island and they understood that something unusual was happening. The head of Hønefoss's judicial police was in it, sent by the minister of justice, Trygve Lie, to interrogate the Exile about the papers that were removed. He wanted to know if in those documents there was any reference made to Norwegian politics, and when Lev Davidovich assured him that in the fourteen months he had spent residing in the country he had not involved himself in its internal affairs, the policeman bid them a good afternoon and returned to the light aircraft. But they couldn't help feeling unsettled by the visit. Despite being convinced that no one could accuse him of having violated his commitment, Lev Davidovich thought that the minister's concern must have had some basis that for the moment eluded him.

The following day, as they had breakfast, Knudsen turned on a small radio to listen to the news from Oslo. As Lev Davidovich had only just started to understand Norwegian, he took no notice of the transmission and went out to the yard. A few minutes later Knudsen approached him with a stony face to tell him that something serious was happening in Moscow: they had just announced that they were taking Zinoviev, Kamenev, and fourteen other men to trial, accused of conspiring against Soviet power, of committing Kirov's murder, and of conspiring with the Gestapo to kill Stalin. The prosecution was asking for the death penalty.

Lev Davidovich looked at his friend and his indignation made him want to slap him. They returned to the cabin and the Exile began to look for some station on the radio that would prove that the information was just a macabre misunderstanding. An hour later, on a German news program, the Soviet agency confirmed what Knudsen had heard and added that the prosecution's case also accused Lev Trotsky of heading and instigating the conspiracy organized by a Trotskyist-Zinovievist cell in favor of a foreign power and claimed they were using Norway as a base for sending terrorists and assassins to the USSR. Lev Davidovich immediately knew that the bloodiest and most devastating wave of terror had been unleashed in Moscow and that its effects would reach even remote Vexhall, where he had spent the most pleasant days of his exile.

During the trials against the sixteen accused, every time he heard the irate voice of prosecutor Viyshinsky, who, in his role as the Soviet people's indignant conscience, asked the court for the execution of the rabid dogs on trial, Lev Davidovich recalled those heroic times in which he and Lenin had handed over the reins of the machinery of revolutionary repression to Felix Dzerzhinsky to apply a Red Terror without law or limits capable of saving, by fire and sword, a stuttering revolution that could barely hold itself up. The terror of Dzerzhinsky's Cheka was the dark arm of the revolution—pitiless as it should have been; as it had to be, one would say—and it annihilated hundreds and thousands of the people's enemies, of the losers in the class struggle who refused to watch the disappearance of their form of life and their culture of injustice. They, the victors, ruthlessly administered their adversaries' defeat, and the party had to function as an instrument of History and of its inevitable massive, albeit impersonal, revenge. It had been a merciless, surely excessive, but necessary violence: that of the victorious class over the loser, the straight choice of "us or them . . ." But the men that Stalin had decided to kill in that dismal month of August 1936 were Communists, comrades of the struggle, and confronted by that affiliation, the machinery of violence led by Lenin and by Lev Davidovich had always stopped, respectful to the utmost limit. The Stalinist terror, perfected in its previous persecutions (peasants, the religious, the country's intelligentsia), now seemed on the verge of crossing a sacred boundary.

Lev Davidovich wanted to trust that the farce would stop at the edge of the precipice: Stalin, with some remains of historic sanity, would prevent the catastrophe and show the world his benevolence. Because now it was no longer about the unknown Blumkin, nor was the punishment hidden behind the dark circumstances in which Kirov had died. Many of

151

the accused had been Lenin's comrades and, for decades, had resisted the czarist repression and deportations; being who they were, they had even submitted to Stalin and played a not-very-credible role in his shocking script: they had incriminated themselves in the most outrageous crimes against the Soviet state and, above all, had admitted that from Turkey, France, and Norway, Trotsky's shadowy hands and his lieutenant Lev Sedov had led the conspiracy devised by a "Trotskyist-Zinovievist center," insistent on assassinating Comrade Stalin and reinstating capitalism on the heroic Soviet soil. An insulting lack of respect for the intelligence emanated from that legal horror show: the shamelessness of the show taking place in Moscow demanded a new kind of ideological faith from the worshippers of the boss of the revolution and a new kind of submission that was capable of overcoming political obedience and turning it into criminal complicity.

Like all dictators, Stalin followed the well-worn tradition of accusing his enemies of collaborating with a foreign power and, in the case of Lev Davidovich, he repeated almost the same arguments that the provisional government of 1917 had hurled against Lenin, with proof fabricated by the secret service, to turn him into an agent of the orders of the German Empire with the mission of handing Russia over to the kaiser. In context, Trotsky's mission was to serve the Soviet Union to the führer. The Exile would later ask himself how he could have been so deluded to have, at times, felt almost calm, to have even convinced himself that the prosecution would find it impossible to present any proof substantiating those accusations. Moreover, the fact that the first claims referred to fifty men arrested and that only sixteen men were brought to trial clearly indicated that they were the ones who had reached an agreement, and in exchange for their self-recriminations Stalin would spare their lives, once the anti-Trotskyist campaign and the annihilation of the opposition had achieved its propaganda purposes.

But raising those implausible accusations without presenting any proof, the court ratified the death penalties for Zinoviev, Kamenev, Smirnov, Evdokimov, Mrachkovsky, Bakayev, and another seven who stood accused, including the soldier Dreitser, who had accompanied Lev Davidovich on his departure from Alma-Ata and who had allowed him (had that been his crime?) to take his papers into exile. In the conclusion to the trial, Lev Davidovich also heard the predictable sentence that he was waiting for: Liova and he were guilty of *personally* preparing and directing—as agents paid by capitalism first, then by fascism—terrorist acts in the Soviet Union and were subject, in the case of being found in Soviet territory, to immediate arrest and trial by the Supreme Court's military college.

When he heard those sentences issued, Lev Davidovich felt a great sadness for the fate of the revolution enveloping him, since he knew that in the Great Hall of Columns of the House of the Trade Unions in Moscow, and under the flag that announced THE PROLETARIAN COURT IS THE PROTECTOR OF THE REVOLUTION, a final frontier had been crossed. Within and outside of the USSR, perhaps many naïve people and fanatics believed something of what had been said during the trial. But people with a bare minimum of intelligence would have to admit that practically every word pronounced there was false and that a lie had been used to kill thirteen revolutionaries. The trial and execution of those Communists would become, through the centuries, a unique example in the history of organized injustice and a first in the history of credibility. It would signify the murder of true faith: the death rattle of utopia. And the Exile knew all too well that it also laid the groundwork for the charge destined to eliminate the People's Greatest Enemy, the traitor and terrorist Lev Davidovich Trotsky.

11

The stubbornly springlike and dizzying weeks of March and April of 1937 would remain in Ramón Mercader's memory like an obscure period in which he felt confused about everything but from which he would suddenly emerge when he came across the most brilliant clarity: that of his solid conviction that ruthlessness was necessary to reach victory.

África's disappearance had been followed by that of Kotov (had it been coincidental?), who, before leaving, had left Ramón orders that left him confined to the Marquis de Villota's palace, where at some point he would meet with a colleague of the adviser's who would introduce himself as Maximus. Due to his strict sense of responsibility he waited, spending his free time in the company of young Luis, with whom he played soccer, and whenever possible providing a little bit of pleasure to the sad-eyed Lena Imbert, with whom he shut himself up in the palace's stalls, where he had installed a stove and a bed. Although he appreciated that parenthesis in the initial days that allowed him to recover from the tensions, hunger, and nights of insomnia of the four months that he'd spent on the front, he soon felt trapped by the inactivity and began to wonder whether Caridad, following young Pablo's death, had used her influence to remove him from the dangers of the war and moved him to that Barcelona where, despite Kotov's prophecies, everything seemed reduced to yelled insults and mandatory slogans, to underground plots, secret meetings, and some execution or other to which the Republican extremists as much as the fascists seemed to be addicted.

In his isolation, Ramón couldn't gain a clear understanding of the events taking place. The newspapers from the different Republican factions that reached his hands were cut in pieces by a crude censorship that contented itself with removing words and leaving blanks in the spaces formerly occupied by the condemned works. Only the communist dailies, free of the censorship that the party exercised over the rest of the newspapers, escaped that orgy of mutilations. Leaving aside their primitive triumphalism, their editorials allowed Ramón to discern the high temperatures reached by the increasingly furious accusations hurled against the POUM's Trotskyist-fascists, the CNT's uncontrollable syndicalists, and the FAI's tempestuous anarchists. But the most significant thing for him was the growing insistence on criticizing the military, the head of government and war minister, Largo Caballero, and his most trusted men. That hard campaign in which truth and lies were mixed up confirmed for him Kotov's prediction that they were headed toward a head-on battle against the hordes of conciliators and extremists.

Caridad, whom he had hardly seen in two weeks, experienced a relapse of angina that kept her in bed for two days with her left arm cramped and suffering. When the woman was able to come out to the mansion's devastated garden, Ramón looked for a way to put the persistent Lena at a distance and be alone with her. He had endured too many days of inactivity, he felt tricked by his mother and by Kotov, and he dared to hurl an ultimatum at her.

"In three days, I'm returning to the front," he said, but Caridad barely moved her head. "This whole business about silence and responsibility is just to keep me here, to control me."

Caridad took a pack of cigarettes out of her coat pocket and the battle she was having with herself must have been agonizing.

"That's going to kill you," he warned her when he saw her remove one of her cigarettes.

"When I feel like this, all I want is to die," she said, and began to unroll the cigarette with her fingers and brought the tobacco to her nose to breathe in its aroma. Finally, she threw her torn-up cigarette to the ground and placed another one between her lips without lighting it.

"Don't look at me like that, don't you dare feel any compassion, because I can't stand it. I hate my body when it doesn't listen to me. And don't come to me with that foolishness about going to the front . . . There are things happening here that you can't even imagine, and sooner than you can believe, your moment will come. But in due time, Ramón, everything in due time."

"I know that story about time by heart already, Caridad."

She smiled, but the pain in her arm cut through her happiness. She waited for a few seconds while the burning cramp receded.

"Story? Let's see . . . Did you believe the story about Buenaventura Durruti getting killed by a stray bullet?"

Ramón looked at his mother and felt that he couldn't say a word.

"Do you think we can win the war with an anarchist commander who's more prestigious than all of the communist leaders?"

"Durruti was fighting for the Republic," Ramón tried to reason.

"Durruti was an anarchist; he would've been one his entire life. And have you heard the story about the translator who disappeared, a certain Robles?"

"He was a spy, wasn't he?"

"A miserable ass kisser. He was the scapegoat in an internal argument between the military advisers and security. But they didn't just pick him at random: that Robles knew too much and could have been dangerous. He was not a traitor; they turned him into a traitor."

"Do you mean to say that they killed him without him being a traitor?"

"Yes, and what of it? Do you know how many they've killed on one side or the other in these months of war?" Caridad waited for Ramón's response.

"A lot, I think."

"Almost one hundred thousand, Ramón. As they advance, the fascists execute everyone they consider a Popular Front sympathizer, and on this side the anarchists kill anyone who, according to them, is a bourgeois enemy. And do you know why?"

"It's the war" was what occurred to him to say. "The fascists made those the rules of the game . . ."

"Necessity. For the fascists, it is a necessity to not have any enemies in the rear guard, and for the anarchists to keep being anarchists. And we cannot allow the war to slip out of our hands. We've also been killing people and we're going to have to kill many more, and you—"

Ramón raised his hand to interrupt her.

"You brought me here to kill people?"

"And what the hell were you doing on the front, Ramón?"

"It's different: it's the war."

"Enough with the fucking war . . . Isn't managing to get the party to impose its policies and for the Soviets to continue to support us the most important thing for us winning this war? Isn't cleaning up the rear guard of enemies and spies part of the war? Isn't eliminating the fifth columnists in Madrid part of the war?"

"In Paracuellos they executed people who had nothing to do with the fifth column, and I know that some from the party were involved in that."

"Who's saying that the dead were saboteurs, you or the Falangists?"

Ramón lowered his head and contained his indignation. In the Sierra de Guadarrama, with a rifle in his hands and a handful of comrades dying of cold and shaking with hunger, and the enemy on the other side of the mountain, everything was simpler.

"This war you're about to get into is more important, because if we don't win it, we won't win the other, and the comrades who were in the trenches are going to fall like flies when the planes, cannons, rifles, and grenades stop coming from Moscow. Ramón, Spain's fate is in the hands of people like you . . . So that you get an idea of what's happening, tonight you'll go with me to La Pedrera. There is an important meeting. It goes without saying that everything that will be discussed there is secret. You cannot speak there or even say your name, is that clear?"

"Is África going as well?"

"Why don't you forget about that woman for a while, Ramón?"

In Caridad's shadow, Ramón crossed the threshold of La Pedrera that night without the guards stopping him. In one of the rooms on the top floor, enveloped in a cloud of smoke, several men were talking and barely noticed the arrival of Caridad and her young companion. Ramón felt disappointed on not seeing África. Of those present, he recognized only one person, Dolores Ibárruri, who was perhaps the only one not smoking at that moment. There was also a man with a Slavic face whom he would later identify as Comrade Pedro, the Hungarian who commanded the Comintern's envoys. His attention nonetheless focused on a loud character, hairy and corpulent, with a large head, bulging eyes, and thick lips that made a smacking noise as he spoke. By his way of addressing himself to the others, you could tell he was an irascible guy, and by what he was saying, it appeared that he was one of those who assume everyone is a traitor and who consider any negligence or ineptitude to be a perverse conspiracy or enemy sabotage. Whispering in his ear, Caridad told him that the man was André Marty, and Ramón understood immediately that he was in the presence of something important: if at that moment of the war Marty was so far away from his post as commander of the International Brigades, it could only be for a more important cause. Thanks to his sister Montse, who for weeks had been working as the secretary for that Comintern leader, Ramón knew that he had the reputation of being a cruel and despotic man, and that night the harangue he issued forth corroborated it, festooned as it was with insults. Marty accused the leaders of the party of being weak and inept, since, according to him, the Central Committee practically didn't exist and the work of the political bureau was terribly primitive and conciliatory: the Spaniards, he said, and pointed to Ibárruri, had to grow up once and for all and stop allowing Codovilla to act like the party was his personal backyard just because he was a Comintern envoy. They should be ashamed that Codovilla was using them like marionettes—and again he looked at La Pasionaria, who lowered her gaze like a beaten dog—and going to the extreme of writing speeches for General Secretary Pepé Díaz and Comrade Dolores Ibárruri just to create the illusion that there was a central committee of Spanish Communists, when in reality it didn't exist or decide anything. The situation didn't allow for any more hesitation: they either went for everything or forgot all about even the most minimal possibility of success.

Indignant, Ramón barely heard the closing of the meeting: according to Pedro, the party had to increase its campaign against the government's management of military operations and internal policies, demand more purges in the military command, and above all be ready to launch an offensive against the saboteurs. The Communists had to assure the success of an operation that would be capable of guaranteeing control over a rear guard free of Trotskyists and anarchists. The Soviet leadership expected that this time the Spaniards would know how to carry out their role.

"It's now or never," Pedro was stating, when Ramón, without waiting for Caridad, escaped from the place in search of the pure air on the streets, deserted at that time of night.

Two days later, Maximus showed up at La Bonanova. Each one of the hours that had passed between that meeting and the arrival of Kotov's envoy, who would at last put Ramón in motion, had served to reaffirm one idea in the young man: the advisers were right in their demands and it was necessary to pull the rug out from under the Republican alliance. Ramón would hand himself over body and soul to that mission and would prove that this Spanish militant was capable not only of obeying but also of thinking and acting, since it wounded his pride as a Communist to have had to listen silently, in his own country, in his own war, how he and his comrades were called feckless revolutionaries by a paranoid who yelled the truth in their faces. It was necessary to act.

Maximus, who, after many weeks of work, Ramón would come to suspect of being Hungarian, turned out to be a specialist in clandestine struggle and destabilization. Under his orders, Ramón joined a six-man action cell (one of the so-called specific groups), all of them Spaniards, of whom only Maximus seemed to know their true identities and whom, because of his presumed admiration for the Roman world, he distinguished with the names of Latin characters—Graco, Caesar, Mario—while he characterized them as praetorians. From that day, Ramón would begin to be called Adriano. It was the first of many names he used, and he felt proud when they renamed him, before he had even the slightest glimpse of the experiences he had to come—not just under other names but in different skins.

Adriano would lament being charged with a mission as innocuous as becoming close with the POUM and establishing the routines of its leaders, especially those of Andreu Nin. Although Maximus had them submitted to a delicate compartmentalization of information and he was unaware of the details of the tasks assigned to the other praetorians, he managed to find out, thanks to his compatriots' loquacity, that some of them were participating in violent and dangerous acts, as corroborated by the mysterious disappearances, some suspiciously definitive, of certain political rivals who were not very noteworthy but without a doubt bothersome, and who were necessary to take out of the game before it entered the critical stages. Because of this, seeing himself limited to walking down Las Ramblas, entering hotels where some of the POUM-ists and their sympathizers were staying and finding out the details of the daily activities of the heads of the Trotskyist party, seemed like something beneath his capabilities. He did not suspect that his work would gain importance in future actions and that his efficiency and chameleon-like abilities, noticed by Maximus, would place him on the path to his extraordinary destiny.

Soon Adriano was convinced that, for the good of the cause, Andreu Nin was a man who had to die. Since before the war started and the political rivalries between the Republicans were so violently stirred, the renegade Nin was a declared enemy of the Communists and had been one of the first (echoing Trotsky's cry of alarm) in declaiming the Moscow trials of 1936 and the others at the beginning of that year as crimes, and in labeling the "friends of the USSR" who defended their legality and propriety as guilty accomplices. He had also been one of those who had most passionately argued for the need for revolution along with the war, for the total struggle against the bourgeois republic, which, in spite of being anti-proletarian, was sustained through the support of those whom Nin called communist collaborators. He disagreed with Soviet aid as if it would have been possible for the government to survive without it. But what had most firmly marked him was his demand, from his post as the *conseller* for the Generalitat government and in the POUM's leadership, that the Republic offer asylum to that traitor Trotsky even after his felony was corroborated in the trials that took place in Moscow. Although Companys, the Catalan president, had been forced to remove Nin from his cabinet, the Trotskyist's arrogance had become so out of control as to make him publicly declare that they would have to kill everyone in the POUM to remove them from the political struggle. Adriano would think that, without a doubt, the best thing would be to make Nin's wishes come true once and for all.

Adriano had picked the Hotel Continental as one of his usual stops. Despite the scarcity devastating the city, you could still have a good coffee there and get a pack of French cigarettes. Many of the members of the POUM were staying there and in the nearby Hotel Falcón, and Adriano proved that, with due caution, his presence in those places could become habitual and not at all suspicious. In the end, the various secret agents who roamed about the building ended up being so visible that he felt he could become transparent or, at most, be taken as just another nosy parker.

Periodically, Adriano reported to Maximus, and they both reached the conclusion that the POUMists were terrified by the rise of the communist press, but its leaders didn't have any possibilities to backtrack nor a full understanding of the abyss they were entering. Between the hotel's guests and visitors, with whom he managed to start occasional conversations, just one English journalist, a POUM militiaman, commented that in the coming days something serious was going to happen in Barcelona: you could read it in the tension floating in the air. The militiaman-cum-journalist, who had been evacuated from the front in Huesca, was a tall guy, very thin, with a horselike face, and bore the unhealthy coloring of an illness that was surely eating away at him. He was always in the company of his tiny wife and he was always looking around him, as if something were continuously lying in wait for him from behind a column. Adriano had introduced himself with his new nom de guerre and the Englishman said he was called George Orwell and confessed to him that he felt more fearful in a Barcelona hotel than in the frozen trenches of Huesca.

"Do you see that fat man who corners all the foreigners and explains to them that everything that's happening here is a Trotskyist-anarchist conspiracy?" Orwell asked him, and Adriano furtively looked at the figure. "He is a Russian agent . . . It's the first time I have seen someone professionally and publicly devoted to telling lies—with the exception of journalists and politicians, of course."

Many years had to pass for Ramón to know who that man was. In 1937 almost no one knew Orwell. But when Ramón read some books about what had happened in Barcelona and found a photo of John Dos Passos, Ramón would have sworn that, just days before everything exploded, he had seen Orwell conversing with Dos Passos in the hotel cafeteria. In those meetings, however, Ramón and Orwell almost never spoke of politics: they tended to talk about dogs. The Englishman and his wife, Eileen, loved dogs and in England they had a borzoi. Through Orwell, Ramón learned of that breed; which, according to the journalist, were the most elegant and beautiful hounds on earth.

What Ramón liked best about his mission was feeling so camouflaged beneath his own skin that, without thinking about it too much, he was capable of reacting like the carefree and simple Adriano. He discovered that using another name, dressing a different way from what he would have considered close to his own tastes, and inventing a previous life dominated by a disillusionment with politics and a rejection of politicians were feelings that he was beginning to secretly enjoy. Thus, with each passing day he felt more like Adriano, was more like Adriano, and could even look at Ramón with a certain distance. He happily discovered that, without África at hand, he could go without his family. Besides, despite his gregarious and partisan spirit, he didn't have a single friend to whom he felt tied. The only compass he clung to was his responsibility, and he tried to carry it out carefully. Because of that, the day on which he handed over to Maximus the summary of the movements, places frequented by and the personal tastes of the heads of the POUM—particularly exhaustive in the case of Andreu Nin—he thought that the congratulations he received were a reward for Adriano and, only remotely, for the Ramón Mercader who had lent him his body.

Kotov looked like an abandoned statue on the bench in the Plaza de Cataluña. The spring was at its height and the warm sun bathed the city. The adviser, with his face slightly raised, was receiving the heat like a lizard slothful from the rays that were injecting him with life. He had even taken off his jacket and the printed kerchief he regularly wore around his neck, and he remained immobile for a few seconds after Ramón sat down at his side.

"What a marvelous country!" he said at last, and smiled. "I could live here for the rest of my life."

"Despite the Spaniards?"

"Precisely because of you. Where I come from, the people are like stones. You are all flowers. My country smells like smoked herring and hops; here, it smells of olive oil and wine."

"Your pals say we're primitive and practically dumb."

"Don't pay too much attention to those lunatics. They confuse ideology with mysticism, and they are no more than walking machines—worse still, they're fanatics. Here they make themselves look tough, but you should see them when Moscow calls for them . . . *Na khuy*. They shit themselves. Don't look to them as an example; you don't want to be like them. You can be so much more."

"What did Maximus say about me?"

"He's satisfied and you know it. But today you will stop being Adriano and go back to being Ramón, and as Ramón, you're going to work with me, for now. Until something else is decided, Adriano doesn't exist anymore; Maximus never existed. Is that clear?"

Ramón nodded and took off his scarf. Heat was rising from his chest.

"Take advantage, kid, breathe in this peace! Get the most out of every peaceful moment. The struggle is hard and doesn't give us many occasions like this one. Do you see the calm? Do you feel it?"

Ramón wondered whether it was a rhetorical question, but Kotov's insistence forced him to look around and answer.

"Yes, of course I feel it."

"And do you see that building over there, in front of us?"

"Telefónica? How could I not . . . ?"

Kotov's laughter interrupted him. The adviser lowered his face and for the first time looked directly at Ramón. His cheeks were glowing, his clear eyes covered to protect them from the intense light.

"It's a hive of fifth columnists who are preparing a coup d'état against the central government," Kotov said, and Ramón had to wake up his neurons to pick up the adviser's thread of reasoning. "Before they do that, we have to fumigate them, like cockroaches, like the enemies they are. We're losing the war, Ramón. What the fascists did in Guernica is not a crime: it's a warning. There will be no mercy, and it seems that not all of you understand it . . . Those anarchists think that Telefónica belongs to them because, when they rebelled against the military, they went in there and said: It's ours. And the government is so soft that it hasn't been able to kick them out. When Guernica was bombed, they went to the extreme of denying the president of the Republic an open line." Kotov smiled again as if he found that story funny. "In a few days, nothing will remain of this peace."

"What are we going to do?"

Kotov stayed silent too long for Ramón's curiosity.

"The fascists keep gaining ground and that midget Franco now has the support of all the parties on the right. Meanwhile, the Republicans are passing the time knocking each other's eyes out and everyone wants to be his own boss . . . No, there can't be any more thinking. If those fifth columnists carry out a coup d'état, you can forget about Spain . . . We have to do something definitive, kid. I'll be waiting for you at eight at the Plaza de la Universidad."

Kotov tied the kerchief at his neck and picked up his jacket. Ramón knew he shouldn't ask anything and saw him walk away with a limp that was more noticeable than on other occasions. From the bench he contemplated, a few feet below him, at the start of Las Ramblas, several sandbags that were once barricades and the carefree or hurried people

163

walking by, dressed as civilians or in the uniforms by which each faction tried to distinguish itself. Ramón felt superior: he was one of those in the know amid a mass of puppets.

Fifteen minutes before eight, Ramón sat on a bench in the Plaza de la Universidad. He saw a parade down Gran Vía, on the way to Sants station, of several trucks filled with recruits from the CNT anarchists' militia, with their banners beaten by the wind. He assumed they would go out to the front that very night and began to understand the strategy of Kotov and the advisers' high command. Half an hour later, when anxiety was beginning to torment him, he felt his stomach growing cold. On the other side of the avenue, he saw her coming: of the millions of people on Earth, her figure was the only one he would never mistake.

África got closer and Ramón felt himself losing what control he had imagined he possessed. He walked to the edge of the street and hugged her almost furiously.

"But where the hell . . . ?"

"Let's go, they're waiting for us."

África's coolness cut through Ramón's anxiety, and he immediately sensed that something had changed. As they walked toward the market, África mentioned she had been in Valencia, where the head of government was now located, and had returned when Pedro and Orlov, the very head of the intelligence advisers, had transferred her command post to Barcelona. She had no recent news of Lenina. She assumed she was with her parents, still in the Alpujarra mountains, she said, and closed the subject to further discussion. Near the market, they entered a building and went up the stairs to the third floor. The door opened without their knocking, and in the room that must have sometimes been a living room, Ramón saw Kotov and another five men of whom he only recognized Graco. Two remained standing, while Kotov and the rest were seated on some boxes. No one said hello.

Kotov was precise: they had been given the mission of capturing a man, not even he himself knew his name; he knew only that they were dealing with an anarchist who needed to be taken out of circulation. The man would come out about ten o'clock from a bar two blocks from there and they would recognize him because he would have a red and black scarf. "You and you"—he pointed out Ramón and a dark-haired man, thirty-something years old, who looked like he came from the south— "dressed as *Mossos d'Esquadra*, you're going to arrest him and take him to a car that she"—he pointed at África—"is going to signal for you." The other three would act as support in case something happened. Kotov insisted that everything should be done as a routine arrest; there couldn't be any shots or drama. The ones in the car would be in charge of driving the man to his fate. Afterward, they would all scatter and wait until he or an envoy of his called them.

The air of mystery and secrecy filled Ramón with joy. He looked at África and smiled at her, since, as he put on the Catalan police uniform, he could feel how his usefulness for the cause was growing. That mission could be the beginning of his definitive entrance into the world of the truly initiated, but working with África was an unexpected reward. He would never remember if he had felt nervous; he would only keep in his memory the feeling of responsibility that overcame him and África's distant attitude.

The facility with which the arrest played out, the transfer of the man to the car (when he heard him protest, Ramón knew he was Italian), and his departure ended up filling him with enthusiasm. Could everything be so easy? After walking a few blocks away, Ramón took off the jacket and threw it in the garbage can. He felt euphoric, desirous to do something else, and he regretted that Kotov's order was immediate dispersal once the operation was carried out. To have África so close just to lose her right away . . . He looked for one of the dark alleyways that led to El Raval, desiring more adventure than the insipid Lena Imbert could provide. When he stopped to light a cigarette, he felt his blood go cold: the cold metal of the barrel of a revolver was pressed into the back of his head. For a few seconds his mind went blank, until his sense of smell came to his aid.

"You're going against orders," he said, without turning around. "You're the only soldier who smells like violets. Shall we take the tram to La Bonanova or do you still have that little room in La Barceloneta?"

África put the gun away and started walking, forcing Ramón to follow her.

"I wanted to see you because I felt I should be honest with you, Ramón," she said, and he sensed a tone in her voice that alarmed him.

"What's going on?"

"There's nothing going on anymore, Ramón. Forget about me."

"What are you talking about?" Ramón felt himself shaking. Had he heard correctly?

"I won't see you again . . ."

"But . . ."

Ramón stopped and grabbed her by the arm almost violently. She let him but gave him a cold, piercing look. Ramón let go of her.

"I never promised you anything. You should have never fallen in love. Love is a weight and a luxury we cannot afford. Good luck, Ramón," she said, and without turning around she walked down the street until she was lost around the corner and in the darkness.

Nearly petrified, Ramón was aware of the commotion affecting his muscles and his brain. What the hell was going on? Why was África doing this? Was she following party orders or was it a personal decision?

He walked to the high part of the city, the unease following him. He felt diminished, humiliated, and in his mind signals began to cross, evidence that until that moment had been brushed away, attitudes that in a new light took on a revelatory dimension. And in that wounded wolf's climb to his lair, Ramón promised himself that África would one day know who he was and what he was capable of.

The explosion that the horse-faced English journalist was waiting for, and that Kotov had prophesied, finally happened. The dry wood of hate and fear, so abundant in Spain, needed only a match, placed precisely, to light the pyre on which, as Caridad would say so many times, the Republic had been purified.

Thanks to the information at his disposal, the playing out of events did not surprise Ramón, although the unpredictable consequences alarmed him. On May 3 the invasion of the Telefónica building by a police contingent, led by the commissar of public order, Rodríguez Salas, bearer of the order dictated by the *conseller* of interior security to empty the place and hand it over to the government, caused the predictable refusal by the anarchists and their entrenchment in the building's higher floors. As was also expected, the confrontation began immediately between the police corps belonging to the Republic and the Catalan government and the CNT anarchists and syndicalists, who were joined by the POUM Trotskyists. The accumulated tension and hardened hate exploded and Barcelona became a battlefield.

A few days before, various contingents of anarchist militia, refusing to obey orders from the joint chiefs of staff, had abandoned the front and, with their weapons, had stationed themselves in the city. The authorities, foreseeing possible confrontations, even decided to cancel the May Day celebrations, but on May 2, some members of the Catalanist party opened fire against a group of anarchists, and the tension increased. The police's plan to empty the Telefónica building was the straw that broke the camel's back and caused such violence that Ramón would ask himself if the government, with the support of the Socialists and the Communists, would be capable of controlling it and emerging victorious.

On the very morning of May 3 and against his expectations, Ramón received the order to remain in La Bonanova, no matter what happened, until one of Kotov's men came to get him. At the first light of day, Caridad went out with Luis in her invincible Ford to place the kid with people who would take him to the other side of the Pyrenees. Ramón said goodbye to Luis with a strange presentiment. Before Luis got into the car, Ramón hugged him and asked him to always remember that he was his brother, and everything that he had done and would do in the future would be so that young people like him could enter the paradise of a world without exploiters or exploited, of justice and prosperity: a world without hate and without fear.

When in midafternoon he learned of the incident that had started at the Telefónica and the violent fratricide that followed, Ramón understood that Caridad was taking those precautions because not even those in the party were sure they could control the situation. The anarchists and POUMists, refusing to hand over their weapons, accused the Communist Rodríguez Salas of having provoked them to bring about a confrontation. The Communists, on the other hand, accused their political rivals of rebelling against the official institutions, of thwarting the central government's work, of generating chaos and disorder, and, directly and indirectly, of planning a coup d'état that would have been the end of the Republic. The bulk of the verbal attack centered on the POUM leaders, who were labeled traitors, instigators, and even the promoters of a planned Trotskyist-fascist coup in collaboration with the Falangists. Ramón understood that he had had the privilege of attending the start of a political game that displayed such a capacity for planning and such mastery for the exploitation of the circumstances that it didn't cease to surprise him. But he also thought that, as never before, the fate of the Republic was dangling from a thread and it was hard to predict the winner of this round.

Many times he was tempted to go down to La Pedrera in search of the evasive Kotov to ask him to revoke his order to remain far away. The hours of the day became interminable for him, and when at night Caridad returned to the palace of La Bonanova with a rifle placed diagonally across her shoulder, she called him down, saying that even if the Telefónica building had not been seized, that it was all merely a question of a few hours, and that the operation had been a success, since the uprising had proven the libertarians' and Trotskyists' crimes. Besides, she trusted that the skirmishes that were still ongoing would soon be under control, since various CNT leaders were mediating them to calm down spirits and an announcement had been made that army contingents were coming from Valencia.

"What I don't understand is why they have me here," Ramón complained as Caridad lit one of her cigarettes and, between drags, swallowed pieces of sausage that she washed down with wine.

"There are already more than enough people to kill fifth columnists and traitors. Kotov must know what he wants you for."

"What's supposed to happen now?"

"Well, I don't know. But when we do away with the anarchists and the Trotskyists, it will be clear who's in charge in Republican Spain. We couldn't keep dealing with the undisciplined and the traitors or waiting for Largo Caballero to leave quietly. We're throwing him out right now."

"And what are the people going to say?"

Caridad put out her cigarette and took another one out of the pack. She took a long drink of wine to get rid of the taste of the sausage in her mouth.

"All of Spain already knows that the POUM Trotskyists, the libertarians, and the Anarchist Federation have gone too far. They've rebelled against the government, and in war, we call that betrayal. There are even documents proving the links the Trotskyists have with Franco, but Caballero doesn't want to accept them. These sons of bitches were slipping maps and even army communication codes to the fascists."

"Hey, hey . . . You know that half of what you're saying is a lie."

"Are you sure? Even so, even if it's a lie, we'll make it the truth. And that's what matters: what people believe."

Ramón nodded. Although it was difficult for him to accept the meanness of that, he recognized how important it was to win the war, and to do so, a purge like that was necessary. Caridad smiled and let her cigarette fall to the ground.

"You have a lot to learn, Ramón. We're going to set up Negrín and Indalecio Prieto's radical Socialists with Largo's conciliators. Rather, we're going to serve them Largo's head on a platter for them to tear apart between them."

"But neither Prieto nor Negrín loves us very much . . ."

"They won't have any choice but to love us. And as soon as they replace Largo and name Negrín or Prieto, we're going to do away once and for all with the POUM. If the Socialists want to rule, they're going to have to help us: either they govern with us or they don't govern at all. We're going to take the anarchists out of their way, and they're going to have to thank us for that."

Ramón nodded and dared at last to ask the question eating away at him:

"And is África involved in all of this?"

Caridad drank two sips of wine.

"She won't leave Pedro's side. So she must be very close to everything . . ."

Ramón nodded. Jealousy or envy? Perhaps both, plus a few drops of despair.

"And what's my role in all of this, Caridad?"

"In time, Kotov will tell you . . . Look, Ramón, you must learn to have patience and to know that you don't beat your enemies while they're standing, but when they are kneeling before you. And you beat them mercilessly, dammit!"

The next morning, after seeing Caridad leave in the Ford, Ramón took the risk of disobeying his orders. He felt smothered in La Bonanova, where the sound of artillery fire barely reached, and went down toward the city, almost without admitting to himself that one of his hopes was to run into África. On the way into town, he avoided the streets where barricades had already been erected and from which sporadic gunfire came. Halted trams and buses cut off traffic, and there were flags unfurled everywhere announcing the political affiliation of the defenders on every corner: Communists, Socialists, anarchists, POUMists, Catalanists, syndicalists, regular troops, militia, and police, in a centrifugal kaleidoscope that convinced the young man of the necessity of the raid: no war could be won with such a chaotic and divided rear guard. The entire city was still on a war footing and the Plaza de Cataluña esplanade looked like the backyard of a barracks. The Telefónica building, where the CNT anarchists were still entrenched, was completely surrounded and in the sights of various pieces of artillery. The besiegers, nonetheless, looked so confident that they were resting, taking advantage of the warm May morning. Avoiding the esplanade, he looked for Las Ramblas and, at the juncture with the Virreina Palace and the Hotel Continental and, further down, by El Falcón, the way was completely empty; only a hurried pedestrian occasionally risked crossing it while waving a white handkerchief. From just around the market, he observed that, on each side of the street, there were men stationed on the roofs, and he assumed that the ones on the Continental were POUM militiamen and leaders. From both sides they shot dispiritedly, and Ramón thought that the fate of the uprising was sealed: the rearguard war looked more like a reenactment than a real confrontation. He felt the temptation to slip back into Adriano's skin and enter the POUM hangouts with it, but he understood that such indiscipline could end up being very dangerous. The ruthlessness he had sworn himself to could turn against him if someone identified him and denounced his presence in the Trotskyist precincts without his having been sent by a superior.

Just a few days later, Ramón would know the extent to which Kotov trusted Caridad, since the woman's predictions began to come true. The sporadic confrontations, violent at times, continued for a couple of days, accumulating a toll of dead and wounded, but they started losing intensity, as if wearing out. Various syndicalist and anarchist leaders asked their comrades to lay down their weapons, and when the bulk of the troops sent by the government finally arrived, the rebels had recognized their defeat, the city was practically pacified, and the majority of the key posts were in the hands of the men chosen by the advisers and the party. The battle was now being waged on verbal grounds, with the continuous exchange of accusations in which the communist means of propaganda, free of censorship, had the upper hand and spread the opinion that the CNT syndicalists, the anarchists, and especially the POUMists had caused an uprising that seemed so much like a coup d'état. Ramón thought that the elusive Cataluña was finally falling under the control of the Soviet advisers and the men from the Comintern, while the government was headed into a crisis and Largo Caballero was as good as dead.

The events unfolded at a dizzying speed once the communist press printed that it had proof of the collaboration between the POUM Trotskyists and the fascists. They wrote and spoke of telegrams and even troop-movement maps passed on to the enemy. Largo Caballero, besieged on all sides—or perhaps accepting at last his inability to resolve the problems of the war and the Republic—tendered his resignation. Then, with the support of the Communists and the advisers, Negrín rose to the leadership of the government and, almost as his first measure, announced the outlawing of the POUM and his intention to try its leaders.

Ramón, who felt bothered by not having been closer to the action, was surprised when Maximus appeared, seeking him out. He was accompanied by two unknown men, obviously Spaniards, but who went without any kind of introduction. In silence they went down to the city, a true field after battle, with troops in the plazas, burned-out buildings, and the remains of barricades on the corners. Soldiers were posted everywhere. Ramón had the conviction that a Republican Spain should take advantage of the shakeup and accept once and for all the only salvation that could come from the most ironclad discipline and from head-on Soviet intervention. He thought perhaps André Marty was right when he had called them primitive and incapable, and when Kotov, in his almost poetic manner, had called them romantic and indolent. The young man felt ensnared by agony over the fate of his country and over the dream for which he had spent four years fighting, but an important step had been taken to save it.

Maximus, in the company of Ramón and the other two comrades, stopped the car on the road to Prat, already in the outskirts of the city, and waited for the arrival of another vehicle, which was also occupied by four men, two of whom looked foreign and another one with a resplendent military uniform, although it was missing his rank. Maximus gave the orders, which seemed directed at Ramón more than at his other two companions: the police were getting ready to take a prisoner out of Barcelona, a spy at the service of the nationalists, and he was entrusting them with the mission of taking that man to Valencia, where he would be interrogated. The information the man possessed was vital for breaking apart the enemy's network and to revealing the extent of the Trotskyist betrayal. But that entire operation had to be carried out with the greatest discretion, and for that reason only men of the utmost confidence were participating.

A few hours later, as night was falling, the police patrol appeared on the road and signaled with its lights. Maximus ordered the men in the second car to place themselves in the rear guard and he, with Ramón and the other two men, placed himself at the front of the convoy and headed toward Valencia. On a few occasions one of the men traveling in the car tried to strike up a conversation, but Maximus demanded silence.

In the predawn hours, they arrived in the outskirts of Valencia, where another patrol was waiting for them. The ones coming from Barcelona stopped and Maximus ordered them not to come out of the car and to remain on guard and, above all, to remain silent. Ramón watched how Maximus went over to the patrol, accompanied by the man dressed in uniform who had traveled in the car that was the last in line. In the darkness he tried to make out what was happening on the highway and he thought he heard Maximus and the men who were waiting speaking in Russian. One of those men looked familiar to him, and although he later thought it could have been Alexander Orlov, head of Soviet intelligence in Spain, the darkness prevented him from being sure. With a flashlight, the uniformed man accompanying Maximus signaled the convoy, and a few minutes later Ramón saw a handcuffed man led by two policemen pass by his car. Despite the sparse light, he was shocked when he was able to identify him: it was Andreu Nin.

At that moment Ramón understood he had been chosen for that mission as a reward for his work involving the POUM. Then the horse-faced English journalist came to mind, as did the words he had said to Adriano in one of their chats at the Hotel Continental a few weeks before:

"Nin is the most Spanish Spaniard I know. If he weren't so Catalan, he would've been a bullfighter or a singer. He exists with just one idea in his mind: revolution. He's the kind who would allow himself to be killed for it. Fanatics scare me away, but I respect that man."

Without looking at his accomplices, Ramón said:

"They're going to have to kill that man."

One of his companions, the older one, dared to comment:

"Remember what the chief said: they're going to make him sing about everything he knows regarding the fifth columnists' plans."

"He won't talk." Ramón felt that conviction so deeply that he was tormented by the desire to get out of the car and tell Maximus and even Orlov himself, if it was Orlov who was now stepping aside to allow Nin into the small covered van. All of that was absurd, and Ramón knew it was going to end in the worst way.

"They can make anyone talk," the man said, lowering his voice, "and all of those Trotskyists are soft."

"Not this one. He won't talk."

"And why are you so sure, comrade?"

"Because he's a fanatic and he knows that if he talks, they're going to kill him anyway, and kill his friends, too. You know something? If I were him, I wouldn't talk, either."

12

Over the years, many of the details of my relationship with the man who loved dogs have faded in my memory, although I don't believe I have forgotten anything essential. What you are reading, in any event, is the reconstruction according to my recollections—subject to the pernicious effects of time—of some conversations and some thoughts that I would only begin to write down, in the form of notes, five years after those encounters on the beach during the year of 1977. In the interim, I had turned into a very different Iván than the one I was when I met Jaime López, and this was, among other reasons and as you will easily come to understand, because of the story that obscure man would tell me. Raquelita was right, as she almost always was: no one could continue being the same person he had been before listening to him.

In the middle of November, precisely on the first day that I returned to the beach after our last encounter, I ran into López again, and I think that for the first time I suspected that perhaps he had been waiting for me. But why? For what? I asked myself, and then I immediately forgot these questions. On that occasion I had gone without Raquel, who tended to work in the afternoons and, at heart, was not too fond of those winter outings to the beach.

After exchanging greetings, we moved on to the subject of the trip to Paris and López's health, but he cut off that line of conversation by telling me that the French doctors couldn't find what was wrong with him, either, and that the climate in Paris had been just as detestable as could be expected from that city. I don't know why that abrupt interruption of a possible chat about something that so interested me—Paris, the dream journey—moved me to ask him the reason he always had his right hand bandaged. Even when I knew that with that question I was brushing the limits of what was permissible in our superficial relationship of insignificant conversations, at that moment I felt a need to know something definitive about him, perhaps moved by the impression that he had made on Raquelita.

"It's a very ugly burn," López responded, without thinking about it too much. "It happened to me a few years ago already, but it's very unpleasant to look at."

I perceived in his voice a regretful tone that I hadn't heard from him before. It must not be, I thought, that it bothers him to talk about the burned hand: perhaps he was upset at having burned it, as if it were still burning? In that instant I regretted my indiscretion, and I have never really known if it was a form of compensation or because I needed to vomit up my pent-up anger that I did something unusual for me and told him about the ups and downs my family had experienced in the previous two months since my younger brother controversially came out as a homosexual. I unleashed all the resentment I felt toward my parents for having punished the kid so cruelly. As I spoke, I noticed that I had been so obtuse that until that exact moment, as I confided the details and feelings I hadn't even revealed to my wife to a person I barely knew, I had concentrated my resentment on my parents' attitude because in reality I had been ignoring the true origins of what had happened: the persistence of an institutionalized homophobia, of an extended ideological fundamentalism that rejected and repressed anything different and preyed on the most vulnerable ones, on those who don't adjust to the canons of orthodoxy. Then I understood that not just my parents but I myself had been the pawn of ancestral prejudices, of the surrounding pressures of the time, and, above all, the victim of fear, as much as or more (without a doubt, more) than William. In me, in addition, I felt a certain rancor toward my brother, precisely because it was *my* brother who had been declared a faggot: I could understand and even accept that two professors may have gone the other way, but this wasn't the same as knowing—and having others know—that the one who went the other way was my own brother. In any event, I silenced the philosophizing that, in the hands of López (who the hell was López? Who did he work for in Cuba? How in the hell could he go see some doctors in Paris?) or anyone who could decide to use them, could be turned against me, as my own past duly reminded me.

López had listened to me in silence, as if ashamed. Ix and Dax, tired from running, had lain down a few feet from their owner, and the tall, thin black man, somewhere between the casuarinas, had also sat down on their roots. In my memory, that instant has remained frozen like a photograph, as if the world had stopped for a few seconds, even minutes, until López said:

"They always fuck somebody . . . I'm sorry for your brother," and he asked me to help him stand up.

This time he was less dizzy, and he confirmed that in recent days he had been feeling much better. When he was already starting to get farther away, López stopped and asked me to come close. With me just barely arrived at his side, the man who loved dogs started to unfurl the bandage on his right hand and showed me the shiny, flat skin that rose from the tip of his thumb to the center of his hand.

"It's pretty ugly, right?"

"Like all burns," I told him, surprised that it was just an old scar.

"It still hurts me some days . . ." and he remained silent until he looked into my eyes and told me: "I wasn't in Paris. I went to Moscow."

That confession surprised me: Why did he lie to me and why was he now confiding the truth to me? Why should I know he had been in Moscow? Didn't dozens, hundreds of Cubans go to Moscow every day, for any number of reasons? I remained silent, unable to answer myself, doing the only thing I could do: waiting. Then López began to bandage his hand and asked me:

"Do you think we could see each other the day after tomorrow?"

I took my eyes off his once-again-covered hand and discovered a brilliant moistness in that man's eyes. Until that day—at least that I knew of—our encounters had been more or less casual run-ins more or less facilitated by the customs or whims of the weather, and had never been arranged beforehand. Why was López asking for another meeting after having shown me that burn hitherto concealed and having confessed to me he had been in Moscow and not in Paris?

"Yes, I think so."

"So we'll see each other in two days . . . It would be better if your wife were not there," he warned me, and slapped his legs so Ix and Dax would walk next to him toward where the tall, thin black man was waiting for them.

The coast was full of gray and brownish algae, the swollen corpses of purplish jellyfish, and worn-out wood and stones thrown out by the sea the previous night. There wasn't a single person visible on the whole swath of sand in the eye's view. The sun warmed the atmosphere, and although on the beach the wind from the north beat coolly, consistently, the light jacket I was wearing that day was enough. Since I had arrived in advance of the time we set for our meeting, I walked along the shore for a bit. I then saw that those darkened pieces of wood, half hidden by shaggy algae, that seemed to make a cross were, in fact, the limbs of a cross. The wood, corroded, announced that perhaps that cross—about sixteen by eight inches—had spent a lot of time at the mercy of the sea and the sand, but at the same time it was clear that it had just recently arrived on the coast, pushed by the waves from the last cold front. Nothing made it special: they were just two pieces of dark wood, very dense, eroded, gouged, crossed, and fixed together by two rusted screws. Nonetheless, that rustic cross, perhaps because of its worn wood, perhaps because it was where it was (where did it come from? To whom did it belong?), drew me so much that, despite my atheism, I decided to take it with me after washing it in the sea. The shipwrecked cross, I called it, even when I had no clue about its origins and before I suspected how long it would stay with me.

As if he were immune to the temperature, López showed up dressed only in a gray short-sleeved shirt adorned with some enormous pockets. The borzois, made for Siberian temperatures, seemed more than happy. The black man, always between the casuarinas, was wearing a military cape and at some point seemed to have fallen asleep.

From the moment in which the man had invited me to meet him, I had barely been able to think of anything else. I had made a mental summary of how little I knew about him and I couldn't find a crack that leaked any speculations about the origin of that need to see me and, as I was expecting, to talk to me about something presumably important (that he preferred, or demanded, that Raquelita not hear). Up until our meeting, I

177

was mulling over many possibilities: that López's son was also gay; that López could use his influence to help William in his case; and, of course, almost instinctively, I thought he was hiding his intention of commenting upon my opinions and was preparing to return with someone who could make trouble for me, just when I had gotten rid of all my dreams and ambitions (I believe that even included my increasingly moribund literary pretensions) and wished for nothing more than a little peace, like the bird trained to happily accept the routine of the cage. Whatever the reasons may be, whatever was going to happen must happen, I concluded, and shortly before four in the afternoon I arrived at Santa María del Mar, without my tennis racket or even a book to read.

López smiled upon seeing me with the wooden cross in my hands. I explained to him how I had found it and he asked to see it.

"It seems very old," he said as he examined it. "They don't make these kinds of screws anymore."

"It came from a shipwreck," I commented, just to say something.

"Of one of those that leave Cuba in washbasins?" His question exuded a mocking irony.

"I don't know. Yes, it could be . . ."

"The cross was there, waiting for you to find it," he said, now completely serious as he returned it to me, and I liked the idea. If I had any doubts about what to do with the cross up until that moment, the possibility that finding it had been more than a coincidence convinced me that I had to keep carrying it, since only at that moment was I sure that it had to have been very important to someone I would never meet. Did things like that occur to me because, despite my problems, I could still react like a writer? When did I lose that capacity and so many others?

Instead of sitting on the sand, we made the most of some concrete blocks very close to the sea. That afternoon, López had brought a bag with a thermos full of coffee and two small plastic cups, in which he served the beverage several times. Each time he drank coffee, he removed from his pocket a box of cigarettes and his heavy gas lighter, which was able to resist the gusts of the breeze.

In addition to the coffee, the man who loved dogs also brought some bad news.

"We have to put Dax down," he told me once we were settled and he looked at the borzois running and splashing in the water.

Surprised by those words, I turned my head to look at the animals.

"What happened?" I asked.

"The veterinarian saw him two days ago . . ."

"How can a veterinarian tell you to euthanize a dog like that? Did he bite someone? Didn't he see how he's running, that he's fine?"

López took his time in responding.

"He has a brain tumor. He'll die in four or five months, and at any moment he'll start to suffer and could become uncontrollable."

Then I was the one who remained silent.

"That was what was making him aggressive, not the heat . . . ," López added.

"Did they run a scan?" I looked at the animals again.

"And other tests. There's no chance that they're mistaken. I'm devastated. No one can fathom how much I love those dogs."

"I can imagine," I murmured, recalling the death of Curry, a tailless terrier who spent all of my childhood and part of my adolescence with me.

"In Moscow and here in Havana, they've been like two friends. I like to talk to them. I tell them everything, my memories, and I always speak to them in Catalan. And I swear they understand me . . . When Dax starts to get worse and I've gotten used to the idea . . . would you be able to help me with this?"

At first I didn't understand the question. Then I understood that López was asking me to help him sacrifice Dax, and I reacted.

"No, I'm not a veterinarian . . . and even if I were, I wouldn't be able to do it."

The man was silent. He poured himself more coffee and took out one of his cigarettes.

"Of course, I don't know why I asked this of you . . . It's just that I have no idea how the hell I am going to . . ."

At that moment I thought I sensed that something more terrible than the fate of his sick dog was pursuing this man, and this was confirmed almost immediately.

"If someone told me I was as sick as Dax, I'd like for someone to help me get out of it quickly. Doctors are sometimes incredibly cruel. When the inevitable happens, they should be more humane and have a better understanding of what it feels like to suffer."

"Doctors do know, but they can't do it. Veterinarians also know and have that license to kill. Look for one who . . ."

I felt that I was entering tricky territory and was losing wiggle room and any possibility for escape. But I was still a long way from imagining the degree to which I would sink into an overflowing pit of hate and blood and frustration.

"I'm also going to die," the man finally said to me.

I tried to find my way out by saying something obvious. "We're all going to die."

"The doctors haven't been able to find anything, but I know that I am dying. Right now I'm dying," he insisted.

"Because of the dizziness?" I clung to my logic and to playing the role of someone stupid. "It's the spine . . . There are even tropical parasites that cause vertigo."

"Don't fuck around, kid. Don't pretend to be dumb. Listen to what I'm telling you: I'm dying, dammit!"

I asked myself what the hell was happening: Why, if we barely knew each other, was that man choosing to confide in me that he was dying and that he wanted someone who was able to cut short that suffering?

"I don't know why you . . ."

López smiled. He dragged his heel across the sand until he made a line. At that moment I was still afraid of what that man's words could say to me.

"The pretext for going to Moscow was that I was invited to the celebrations for the sixtieth anniversary of the October Revolution. But I needed to go to see two people. I was able to see them and I had some conversations with those who are killing me."

"With whom did you speak?"

The man stopped moving his foot and looked at his bandaged hand.

"Iván, I've seen death closer than you would be able to imagine. I think I know everything there is to know about death."

I recall it as if it were yesterday: it was at that exact moment that I really felt fear, real fear, besides the logical surprise at those unfathomable words. Because never in my life had it occurred to me that someone could confess his capacity for understanding everything there is to know about death. What do you do in a situation like that? I looked at the man and said:

"When you were in the war, right?"

He nodded silently, as if my clarification weren't important, and then said:

"But I'm incapable of killing a dog. I swear."

"War is something else . . ."

"War is shit," the man exclaimed almost furiously. "In war, you either kill or you are killed. But I've seen the worst side of human beings, especially outside the war. You can't imagine what a man is capable of, what hate and bitterness can do when they are nurtured . . ."

More or less at that point, I thought: enough with beating around the bush. The best thing I could have done would have been to stand up and end that conversation that could lead to nothing good. But I didn't move from where I was, as if I really wanted to know where the man who loved dogs was going with his argument. Was I interested? Until that moment I was motivated by pure inertia. But then the man ratcheted things up:

"A few years ago, a friend told me a story." López's voice suddenly seemed as if it were someone else's. "It's a story that very few people knew well and almost all of them are dead. Of course, I asked him not to tell me, but there's something that worries me."

I had decided not to speak again, but López was expectant.

"What's that?"

"My friend died . . . and when I die, and when the only other person dies who, as far as I know, is familiar with all the details, that story will be lost. The truth of the story, I mean."

"So why don't you write it down?"

"If I shouldn't even tell it to my children, how am I going to write it down?"

I nodded, and was glad the man was reaching for another cigarette: the action freed me of the need to ask another question.

"I asked you to come today because I want to tell you that story, Iván," the man who loved dogs said to me. "I've thought about it a lot and I've made up my mind. Do you want to hear it?"

"I don't know," I said, almost without thinking about it, and I was completely honest. I would later ask myself if that was the most intelligent answer to one of the most unusual questions I had ever been asked in my life: Is it possible to want or not want to hear a story you don't know, a story about which you don't know a damned thing? But at that moment it was the only response within my reach.

"It's an incredible story; you'll see that I am not exaggerating. But before I tell it to you, I'm going to ask two things of you."

This time I managed to keep my mouth shut.

"First, don't be so formal with me anymore. That way it will be easier to explain everything to you. Also, don't tell anyone, not even your wife; that's why I asked you to come alone. But above all, I don't want you to write it down."

I stared at the man. The fear had left me and my brain was a spiral of ideas, but there was one that made my head spin.

"If you're not supposed to talk about this . . . why do you want to tell me? What are you going to achieve with that?"

The man put out his cigarette by burying it in the sand.

"I need to tell it at least once in my life. I can't die without telling anyone. You'll see why . . . Oh, and don't call me *usted* anymore, *¿vale?*"

I nodded, but my mind could only focus on one thing.

"Yes, that's all fine, but why do you want to tell me? You know that I wrote a book," I added, as if I were raising a paper shield under a steel sword.

"Because I don't have anyone better to tell it to, although sometimes it seems like I met you just to be able to tell it to you. Besides, I think it will teach you something."

"About death?"

"Yes. And about life. About truth and lies. It taught me a lot, although a bit too late . . ."

"You really don't have anyone to tell this story to? A friend, I don't know . . . your son?"

"No, not him . . ." The reaction was too brusque, as if he were defensive, but his tone changed immediately. "He knows some of it, but . . . I told one of my brothers part of it, not all . . . And it has been a long time since I've had friends, what you would call friends . . . But I barely know you, and it's better that way. I know what I'm saying . . . A while back, when I got here, I still wasn't convinced, but later I realized that you were the best person possible . . . So, do you promise you're not going to write it down or tell anyone?"

It goes without saying that, without having a clear idea of why I was doing it or what I was in for, I said yes and became entangled with him. If I had said I didn't want to hear any story or that I couldn't promise that I wouldn't run out and share it that same day, perhaps this whole story, with all of its deep and sordid details, would have been lost with the death of Jaime López and the other individual who, according to him, was the only one who knew it and wasn't going to tell it, either. But as I went over the unpredictable sum of coincidences and games of chance that had led me to be sitting in front of the sea that November afternoon, next to a person who was demanding an answer that was beyond me, I could only arrive at one conclusion: the man who loved dogs, his story and mine, were chasing each other around the Earth, like heavenly bodies whose orbits are destined to cross and cause an explosion.

After hearing my affirmative response, the man took another sip of coffee and lit the cigarette he had in his hand.

"Have you ever heard of Ramón Mercader?"

"No," I admitted, almost without thinking about it.

"That's normal," he murmured, with profound conviction and a small smile, a rather sad one, on his lips. "Almost no one knows him. And others would prefer not to know him. What do you know about Leon Trotsky?"

I recalled my fleeting contact with the name and a few moments in the life of that murky figure, practically disappeared from history, unmentionable in Cuba.

"Very little. That he betrayed the Soviet Union. That he was killed in Mexico." I searched my memory for more. "Of course, that he partici-pated in the October Revolution. In our classes on Marxism, they talked to us about Lenin, a little bit about Stalin, and they told us that Trotsky was a renegade and that Trotskyism was revisionist and counterrevolu-tionary, an attack on the Soviet Union."

"I see that they teach you well here . . . ," López admitted.

"So who is Ramón Mercader? Why should I know him?"

"Well, you should know who Ramón Mercader was," he said, and made a long pause, until he decided to continue. "Ramón was my friend—much more than a friend. We met in Barcelona, and later we fought in the war together . . . A few years ago, we ran into each other again in Moscow. The Soviet tanks had already entered Prague and everyone was speaking in low voices again." The man was looking at the sea, as if the keys to his memory were behind the waves. "The city of whispers. The last action against Khrushchev's détente, against a socialism that dreamed it could still be different. With a human face, they said . . ." He re-membered and rubbed the back of his cloth-bandage-covered hand. "We saw each other again, the day of the first snowfall of 1968 . . . Ramón was fifty-five years old, more or less, but he looked like he was ten, fifteen years older. He was fat; he had aged. We hadn't seen each other since the war . . ." He went silent, as if he were pondering all the time that had passed.

"What war?"

"Ours. The Spanish Civil War."

"And you just ran into each other like that, by coincidence?" The curiosity had already taken hold of me.

"It was as if in some way we had been waiting for each other and suddenly we both went out looking for each other, on that exact day on which snow fell for the first time that year in Moscow." Now he smiled upon evoking it, but I would only understand many years later why he was looking at his bandaged hand again. "We ran into each other on the Frunze, where he lived, in front of Gorky Park. Ramón had gotten fatter, I already told you, but in addition he was very white, and it would have been difficult for someone besides me to recognize in that man the young guy I had said goodbye to in a trench in the Sierra de Guadarrama, with our fists raised, both of us confident we'd be victorious." He paused and lit another cigarette. "Later, when Ramón and I began to talk, I realized that the only thing he had left intact of that beautiful time was that image of happiness. An image that he had to help him survive. And for that reason, when he decided to tell me everything, he confided his life's dream to me: more than anything else in the world, he wanted to return to that Catalan beach at least once before he died. And I think he already knew he was going to die."

Then the man who loved dogs, with his gaze fixed on the sea again, began to tell me the reasons why his friend Ramón Mercader would recall, for the rest of his days, that just a few seconds before pronouncing the words that would change his existence, he had discovered the unhealthy density that accompanied silence in the midst of war. The crash of bombs, gunfire, and engines, the yelled orders and the cries of pain amid which he had lived for weeks, had accumulated in his consciousness like the sounds of life, and the sudden leaden fall of that heavy silence, able to provoke a helplessness too similar to fear, turned into a disquieting presence when he understood that behind that precarious silence could be hiding the explosion of death.

13

The series of events that began on August 26, 1936, clearly revealed to him the often inextricable reasons why Stalin still hadn't broken his neck. Totally absorbed in blind combat from that day on, Lev Davidovich understood that the Great Leader's macabre game still demanded his presence because his back had to serve as a springboard in Stalin's race to the most inaccessible summits of imperial power. At the same time, he had realized that—once his usefulness as the perfect enemy was exhausted, and all the requisite mutilations had been carried out—Stalin would fix the moment of a death that would then arrive with the same certainty with which snow falls in the Siberian winter.

A few months before, foreseeing some incidents that could complicate the delicate conditions of his asylum, Lev Davidovich had begun to eliminate anything that the Norwegian authorities could use against him. More than the aggressiveness of Commander Quisling's pro-Nazi party, he was alarmed by the increasing virulence of the local Stalinists, who had added a disquieting rumor to their attacks: with a pounding insistence they warned that "Trotsky the counterrevolutionary" was using Norway as a "base for terrorist activities directed against the Soviet Union and its leaders." His honed sense of smell warned him that the accusation was not the fruit of some local plots but rather came from farther away and hid the most shadowy ends. Because of that, he asked Liova and his followers to erase his name from the Fourth International executive committee, and at the same time he decided to stop giving interviews and even abstained from participating as a mere spectator in any political act of his host Konrad Knudsen's parliamentary campaign. His relationship with the outside world was reduced to the outings that, once a week, he and Natalia embarked on with the Knudsens to Hønefoss, where they tended to eat in cheap restaurants and later spent the rest of those evenings at the movies, enjoying one of those Marx Brothers comedies that Natalia Sedova liked so much.

That is why he found it so strange when two Norwegian police officers who arrived at Vexhall that afternoon did not display the kind cordiality with which the country's authorities had always treated him. Stiff in their roles, they informed him that they were carrying out Minister Trygve Lie's orders and had only come to hand over a document and return to Oslo with it signed. The younger one, after searching in his folder, extended a sealed envelope. Knudsen and Natalia watched expectantly as he opened it, unfolded the sheet, and, after adjusting his glasses, read it. As he read on, the sheet began to shake slightly. Then Lev Davidovich returned it to the envelope, held it out to the officer who had given it to him, and asked him to tell the minister he could not sign that document and that asking him to do so seemed an undignified gesture on the part of Trygve Lie.

The younger officer looked at his colleague without daring to take the envelope. The policemen were overcome by uncertainty, frozen before an attitude for which they were surely unprepared. At that moment he let the envelope fall, and it came to rest alongside the boot of the older of the two officers, who at last reacted: if Lev Davidovich didn't sign the document, he could be arrested and handed over to the authorities until he was deported, since they had evidence that he had violated the conditions of his residency permit by involving himself in the political matters of other countries.

Then came the explosion. Wagging his finger in a clear sign of warning, Lev Davidovich yelled at the officers to remind the minister that he had promised not to intervene in Norwegian matters but that he wouldn't give up for anything in the world a right that was the reason for him being a political exile: to say whatever he thought convenient about what was happening in his home country. As such, he would not sign that document and, if the minister wanted to silence him, he would have to sew Lev Davidovich's mouth shut or do something to him that would surely bother Stalin greatly: kill him.

A few days later, Lev Davidovich would be forced to recognize that Stalin, political opportunist that he was, had treacherously chosen the most propitious moment to organize the judicial farce in Moscow and try to make him the scapegoat for every conceivable perversity. Hitler's recent entry into the Rhineland had announced to Europe that the expansionist intentions of German fascism were not just a hysterical speech. Meanwhile, the uprising of part of the Spanish army against the Republic, and the start of a war on whose battlefields Italian troops and German planes and ships were advancing, had placed the governments of the democracies (terrified of the possibility of remaining alone in the face of the fascist enemy) in a situation of almost absolute dependency on Moscow's decisions. In that situation, when the fates of so many countries were being decided, no one was going to dare to defend some pitiful souls being tried in Moscow and an exile who had been accused, of all things, of being a fascist agent in the pay of Rudolf Hess. He realized that the pressure on the Norwegian government was surely intense and he warned Natalia that they should prepare for greater aggression.

But Lev Davidovich had decided that, while possible, he would exploit his only advantage: the Oslo government couldn't deport him, since no one would take him, and they didn't even have the option of handing him over to the Soviets, who didn't want him, despite his own request to be tried. Stalin wasn't interested in putting him on trial, even less so when one considered that his repatriation would have to go before a Norwegian court, where he would have the opportunity to refute the accusations made against him and against those who had already been sentenced and executed in Moscow.

Lev Davidovich was certain that a crisis had been unleashed when the court in Oslo summoned him to make a declaration about the raid on Knudsen's house. Everything became clear when the judge who had summoned him revealed the rules of the game, warning him that, since it was a declaration and not an interrogation, neither the presence of Puntervold, his Norwegian lawyer, or of Natalia, or even Knudsen as the owner of the house, was allowed. Alone, in front of the judge and the court's secretaries, he had to respond to questions about the nature of the documents that had been removed, in which, he assured, he had not meddled in

Norway's internal affairs or that of any other country besides his own. Then the judge lifted some papers and he understood the trap that had been set for him: this essay proved the contrary, according to the judge, since, with regard to the Popular Front, Lev Davidovich had made a call for revolution in France.

In the article, written after the victory of the alliance of the French left, Lev Davidovich had commented that Léon Blum, at the head of the new government, was just a minimum guarantee that the Stalinist influence would find pitfalls in establishing itself in the country, and he warned that if France managed to radicalize its politics, it could very well turn into the epicenter of the European revolution that he had been waiting for since 1905, the revolution capable of stopping fascism in its tracks and cutting off Stalinism. Nonetheless, according to the judge, that document was proof of his disloyal conduct toward the government that had so generously taken him in, and constituted a violation of the conditions of his asylum. Lev Davidovich asked if they were investigating his political opinions or the burglary of the house where he was staying, carried out by a group of pro-fascists. As if he hadn't heard him, the judge turned to the court secretary and confirmed that Mr. Trotsky had admitted to being the author of the document that proved his interference in the politics of other countries.

When he was walking toward the door, the police who were guarding him informed him that they had to take him to the nearby Ministry of Justice. Once inside the adjacent building, he was greeted by two functionaries who were so imbued with their character that they seemed to have been plucked from a Chekhov story. After informing him that Minister Lie apologized for not being present, they handed him a declaration that the minister asked him to sign as a requirement for extending his residency permit in the country. As he read the declaration, Lev Davidovich thought his temples would explode if he didn't give free rein to his anger.

"I, Lev Trotsky," he had read, "declare that my wife, my secretaries, and I will not carry out, while we find ourselves in Norway, any political activity directed against any state friendly to Norway. I declare that I will reside in the place the government chooses or approves, and that we will not interfere in any way in political matters, that my activities as a writer will be circumscribed to historical and biographical works and memoirs, and that my writings of a theoretical nature will not be directed against the government of any foreign country. I agree to have all correspondence, telegrams, and telephone calls sent or received by me submitted to censorship . . ."

The Exile stood up as he crumpled the declaration while wondering how soon they would take him to the prison where they would confine him in order to keep him silenced.

Lev Davidovich would prove that the terrified Norwegians didn't need to imprison him to submit him to a silence that, whichever way you looked at it, Stalin demanded, determined to cover up any arguments that could draw attention to the lies and contradictions of the judicial farce that had recently taken place in Moscow. Upon his return to Vexhall, from where his secretaries had been removed under deportation orders, he and Natalia were confined to a room given to them by Knudsen, in front of which a pair of guards were placed to prevent all communication— even with the owner of the house. As if it were a child's game, only more dramatic and macabre, Lev Davidovich slid a formal protest under the door in which he accused the minister of violating the Norwegian constitution with a confinement that was not ordered by any court. The following morning, a policeman handed him a communiqué from Trygve Lie informing him that King Haakon had signed an order that allowed him extraconstitutional extensions in the case of the exiles Lev Davidovich Trotsky and Natalia Ivanovna Sedova. Without a doubt, Lie was determined to allow the silence to cast a shadow of doubt over Lev Davidovich's innocence.

Convinced that even more turbulent times were coming, Lev Davidovich tasked his secretary Erwin Wolf with taking the latest draft of *The Revolution Betrayed* to Liova. Although he had considered the book finished in early summer, the events in Moscow led him to delay sending it to the editors, since he was hoping to add his reflections on the trial against Zinoviev, Kamenev, and their partners in fate. Nonetheless, in view of the uncertainty in his own life, he decided to add just a small preface: the book would be a sort of manifesto in which Lev Davidovich adapted his thinking to the need for a political revolution in the Soviet Union, an energetic social change that would allow the overthrow of the system imposed by Stalinism. He did not fail to notice the strange irony surrounding a political proposal that was never conceived of by the most feverish Marxist minds, for whom it would have been impossible to imagine that, once the socialist dream was achieved, it would be necessary to call upon the proletariat to rebel against their own state. The great lesson to be drawn from the book was that, in the same way that the bourgeoisie had created various forms of government, the workers' state seemed to create its own and Stalinism was proving to be the reactionary and dictatorial form of the socialist model.

With the hope that it would still be possible to save the revolution, Lev Davidovich had tried to separate Marxism from the Stalinist distortion, which he qualified as a government by a bureaucratic minority that, by force, coercion, fear, and the suppression of any hint of democracy, protected its interests against the majority dissatisfaction within the country and against all the revolutionary outbreaks of class struggles in the world. And he ended up asking himself: If the social dream and economic utopia supporting it had become corrupt to the core, what remained of the greatest experiment that man had ever dreamed of? And he answered himself: nothing. Or there would remain, for the future, the imprint of an egotism that had used and deceived the world's working class; the memory would persist of the fiercest and most contemptuous dictatorship that human delirium could conceive. The Soviet Union would bequeath to the future its failure and the fear of many generations in search of the dream of equality that, in real life, had turned into the majority's nightmare.

The premonition that had pushed him to order Wolf to send on *The Revolution Betrayed* took shape on September 2. That day, he and Natalia felt like they were opening the pages of the darkest chapter of the storm that had become their lives and were certain that the Stalinist machine would not stop until it asphyxiated them. The transfer order drily informed them that their destination would be a place selected by the minister of justice and they were allowed to take only their personal effects. The policemen, by contrast, had the deference to allow them to say goodbye to the numerous members of the Knudsen family. The air in the house had acquired the unhealthy heaviness of a funeral, and Konrad's young children cried to see them leave like pariahs after having shared a year with them during which the family had acquired a new member (Erwin Wolf and Hjordis, one of Knudsen's daughters, had married), a preference for coffee, and, as that moment proved, the notion that truth does not always prevail in the world.

The destination chosen for them was a hamlet called Sundby, in an almost uninhabited fjord near Hurum, twenty miles to the south of Oslo.

The ministry had rented a two-story house that the couple would share with a score of policemen devoted to smoking and playing cards, and where the restrictions would end up being worse than those of a prison regime. They were not authorized to leave, and the only person allowed to visit them was Puntervold the lawyer, whose papers were inspected as he entered and again as he left. In addition, they only received newspapers and correspondence after they had been crudely censored with scissors and black ink by a government employee who, like Jonas Lie, the head of the guards watching them, proudly proclaimed his militancy in Quisling's National Socialist Party.

The captives barely had an idea of what was happening outside that remote fjord until Knudsen managed to have their radio, which had been confiscated when they were in Oslo, returned to them. Thus Lev Davidovich was able to get a measure of Stalin's success with his Norwegian collaborators when he heard prosecutor Vishinsky's decrolations that if Trotsky hadn't responded to his ministry's accusations, it was because he had no way to challenge them, and that the silence of the Exile's friends in the socialist governments of Norway, France, Spain, and Belgium only proved the impossibility of refuting the irrefutable. Lev Davidovich understood that he should make himself heard or he would be lost forever: the most blatant of lies, repeated over and over again without anyone refuting it, would end up becoming the truth. He had already thought: They want to silence me, but they will not succeed.

Using the invisible ink that Knudsen had managed to get to him in a cough syrup bottle, he prepared a letter to Liova in which he ordered him to launch a counterattack, and he accompanied it with a declaration, directed at the press, in which he refuted the accusations against him and accused Stalin of having staged the August trial with the goal of suppressing dissatisfaction in the USSR and eliminating all kinds of opposition by means of a criminal offensive that began with Kirov's assassination. In addition, he pointed to the nonexistence of lines of communication with any person in Soviet territory, including his younger son Sergei, whom he had not heard from in over nine months. And finally, he expressed to the Norwegian government his willingness to have all of the accusations against him evaluated and asked for an international commission of workers' organizations to be created to investigate the charges and to try him publicly . . .

On September 15, like a voice from the great beyond, he made himself heard with that cry: it was the warning that Lev Davidovich Trotsky was not giving up.

Even though the Exile had avoided mentioning in his statement the controversy with the Norwegian authorities and the humiliating events of recent days and he had dated it August 27 (the eve of his appearance at the court in Oslo), the ministry of justice forbade him in advance from making any written communications.

For that reason, although Lev Davidovich had been certain for several months that he didn't have enough years left in his life to turn back the political current that had turned him into a pariah and the revolution into a fratricidal bloodbath, he decided to try to make his statement resonate as strongly as possible. To begin with, he ordered Puntervold to sue the editors of the Norwegian newspapers *Vrit Volk* and *Arbeideren*—the former Nazi and the latter Stalinist sympathizers—in hopes of breaking his seclusion and being heard in an open court. The lawyer presented the petition on October 6 and informed him that the process had been initiated to settle it before the month's end. But October would go by without the proceedings beginning. An explanation arrived on the thirtieth: Lie had stopped the trial's process, protected under a new provisional royal decree according to which "a foreigner confined under the terms of the decree of August 31, 1936, cannot appear as a plaintiff before a Norwegian court without the concurrence of the minister of justice."

On November 7, Puntervold traveled to Sundby to give Lev Davidovich, on behalf of Konrad Knudsen, a beautiful cake to celebrate his fifty-seventh birthday and the nineteenth anniversary of the October Revolution. Jonas Lie, the fascist head of the police guards, accompanied the attorney while he handed over the dessert and even said celebratory words to the prisoner, wishing him (he was so conceited that he did so without irony) many years of happiness. They then asked Lie for a little bit of privacy to celebrate the unanticipated gift. As soon as they were alone, Natalia cut the cake and they extracted a small roll of paper. Lev Davidovich shut himself up in the bathroom to read it. Knudsen knew that, in the last two months, this was the story that most intrigued him, but it was only very recently that he had managed to learn the details that he was now revealing to the Exile in tiny script, doing so without adjectives and with many abbreviations.

According to Knudsen, on August 29, three days after Lev Davidovich was confined in Vexhall, the Soviet government asked Trygve Lie, who was substituting for the minister of foreign affairs, to throw out the political exile, since he was using Norway, they insisted, as a base to commit sabotage against the Soviet Union. The extension of his asylum, they threatened, would cause the relations between the two countries to deteriorate. Lie declared that when he shut Trotsky away on August 26, that request had not been made to him yet, and therefore no one could accuse him of having confined Trotsky due to Soviet pressure. Nonetheless, Yakubovich, the Russian ambassador, made sure to comment that several days before, when Lev Davidovich had given an interview for *Arbeiderbladet*, he had verbally conveyed that same message to Trygve Lie. On that occasion, the ambassador had threatened a political crisis and even the rupture of economic relations. The Norwegian fishermen and sailors, conveniently up to speed on the dispute, feared a reprisal that would harm them, and Oslo ceded under the pressure and assigned Lie the role of suppressor. It was then that the minister proposed that Trotsky sign the declaration of submission to him with which Lie hoped to appease the Soviets, but upon not achieving Trotsky's cooperation, he was obliged to order the confinement in Sundby.

Armed with the invisible ink, Lev Davidovich began to prepare a letter to Liova and his French attorney, Gérard Rosenthal. Feeling free of any commitment to the Norwegian politicians, he relayed the details and causes for his isolation and asked his son to step up his responses to Stalin. Now, more than ever, he knew that the only possibility for him was not to surrender—that silence could only result in the victory of the puppet Lie, with Stalin pulling his strings.

By means of the radio and the few censored newspapers that he was allowed to receive, the captive tried to keep himself up-to-date on what was happening beyond the fjord. With a few drops of bitter satisfaction he learned that, just as he had forecast, in Moscow and in the rest of the country the arrests of real or fabricated oppositionists continued. Among those who had been falling was the infamous Karl Radek, just after he had called for the death of the "super-bandit Trotsky" in the press; he also found out about the arrest of that wretched Piatakov, who had thought he had saved himself when he declared that Trotskyists had to be eradicated like carrion. As was predictable, at the end of September, Yagoda had been removed from his post as the leader of the GPU, and this role had been assigned to an obscure character named Nikolai Yezhov, in whose hands Stalin placed the baton so that he could conduct in a new chapter of the terror: Lev Davidovich knew that in Moscow they needed to organize another farce to try to fix the botched August proceedings and to eliminate accomplices who knew too much, such as Yagoda or the infamous Radek.

Another one of his focal points of interest was the development of the war in Spain, which could turn following Stalin's recently announced offer of logistical support to the Republic. But it didn't surprise him to know that along with the weapons—even before them—Soviet agents had traveled to Madrid, establishing guidelines and mining the territory so that Moscow's interests could flourish. Despite the devious nature of that operation, Lev Davidovich thought how much he would have liked to be in that effervescent and chaotic Spain. A few months before, when the nature of the Republic was defined with the electoral victory of the Popular Front, he had written to Companys, the Catalan president, asking him for a visa that, a few days later, the central government roundly denied him. In his way, Lev Davidovich begged for the Republicans to resist the advance of rebel troops that aimed to take over Madrid, although he already sensed that for the Spanish revolutionaries it would be easier to defeat the fascists than the persistent and creepy Stalinists to whom they had opened the back door.

The good news that Knudsen had won the parliamentary elections in his district reached the fjord, reinforced by the release, surprisingly allowed, of *Le livre rouge sur le procès de Moscou*, published by Liova in Paris. Lev Davidovich confirmed that the pamphlet managed to show, in an irrefutable way, the incongruities and falsehoods of the Moscow prosecutors while it warned the world that a trial where no proof is presented, based on self-incriminating confessions of prisoners detained for over a year, could not have any legal value.

The best news for the deportee had been confirming that Liova, when the moment came to make decisions, was also capable of doing so.

In the letters that his son had sent him, before and after the publication of the *Red Book* (letters that Puntervold tried to recite to him from memory), the tension the young man had been experiencing, especially after the August proceedings, filtered through. While the trials in Moscow had had the positive effect of bringing old comrades like Alfred and Marguerite Rosmer closer together and disposed to come out in defense of Lev Davidovich, it had also unleashed in Liova a feeling of being trapped that wouldn't leave him and that led him to worry that he could be kidnapped or assassinated. His situation had become complicated by the exhaustion of funds to pay for the printing of the *Bulletin* and by family tensions, given that ever since the political rupture with Molinier, Jeanne was saying she felt closer to her ex-husband's position than to that of Liova and his father. Nonetheless, his greatest concern, the young man insisted, wasn't for himself or his marriage but rather for something much more valuable: Lev Davidovich's personal and historical archives, kept in Paris. Liova had managed for part of these papers to be donated to the Dutch Institute for Social History, and at the beginning of November he had handed over another part to the institute's French branch. The rest, which contained some of the most confidential files, he had placed under the watch of his friend Mark Zborowski, an efficient and refined Polish-Ukrainian whom everyone called Étienne.

Very soon, the matter of the archives would prove to be more than an obsession of Liova's when, with the new packet barely handed over to the institute, what he had feared so much occurred. On the night of November 6, a group of men entered the building and took some of the files. To the police, it was clear they were dealing with a professional and political operation, since there were no other valuable objects missing from the place. The strange thing was that the burglars had known about the existence of a warehouse that was known only to people in whom Liova had absolute confidence. Furthermore, if the burglars knew about that secret paperwork, why did they enter the institute and not Étienne's apartment, where the most valuable documents were kept? Liova accused the GPU of the theft, but, like the fires in the Prinkipo and Kadıköy houses, his father perceived that a murky story was hidden behind it.

On November 21, Puntervold put an end to the weak hope of the Trotskys: U.S. president Roosevelt had once again rejected the asylum petition submitted by Lev Davidovich. Their last alternatives were now the improbable request by Andreu Nin as a member of the Catalan government that he be received in Spain and the one Liova had initiated through Ana Brenner, a close friend of Diego Rivera's, for the painter to intervene before Mexican president Lázaro Cárdenas so that he would grant Trotsky asylum. For Lev Davidovich, the possibility of going to Mexico—perhaps the most realistic one at that moment—was disquieting: he knew that in that country his life would be in as much danger as if he lay down to sleep naked on the coast of the frozen fjord of Hurum.

At the moment of his strictest confinement, Lev Davidovich received a visit from Trygve Lie, whom he had not seen since the beginning of the crisis. Lie brought some provisions sent by Knudsen, including a bag of coffee that Natalia opened and began to prepare right away. After drinking the beverage, the minister told the captive that he had come to tell him that the trial against Quisling's men would take place on December 11. Lev Davidovich couldn't suppress a smile. Would he be allowed to speak in public? Trygve Lie averted his gaze and told him that the trial would be held behind closed doors. Although Lev Davidovich felt himself bursting with anger, he managed to calm down and asked the minister if in the morning, as he looked into the mirror to shave, he wasn't ashamed to look into his own face. Lie turned bright red, but he waited a few seconds before reproaching his guest's ingratitude: being the politician he was, he should know the demands that politics often imposed. But the other man's clarification was immediate: Lie was a politician; he was a revolutionary . . . Or was Lie willing to endure for his political principles what he had for his? he asked, and Trygve Lie stood up, convinced that he should never allow Lev Davidovich the ability to speak in an open courtroom. Nonetheless, in an effort to revive some goodwill, the minister reached into the pile of books on the table and lifted a volume of one of Ibsen's works: *An Enemy of the People.* Lev Davidovich saw the opportunity to comment on how appropriate that work was in his current situation: Stockmann the politician who betrays his brother was extraordinarily similar to Lie and his friends, and he recited a passage from memory: "It remains to be seen whether evil and cowardice are powerful enough to seal the lips of a free and honorable man." He immediately bid good evening to the minister and held out his hand so he would return the book to him.

Without looking at the confined man, Trygve Lie replied that there were many ways of sealing lips and even sealing off the life of an "honorable" man: in a few days, they would transfer him to a smaller house, far from Oslo, since the ministry couldn't continue to cover the cost of the rent and maintenance of Lev Davidovich and his guards in that place. Then he threw the book on the table and went out into the snow.

Lev Davidovich attended the trial against Quisling's men, even when he knew that the proceeding was just a smokescreen behind which the Norwegian laborites and National Socialists were shaking hands, happy to have cooperated in Lev Davidovich's marginalization. Nonetheless, in his statements, he took advantage of the occasion to denounce the fact that the trial was taking place behind closed doors at Stalin's request to the fascistic minister Trygve Lie.

Because of that, a week later, when he was advised of a new visit from Lie, Lev Davidovich prepared himself for the worst. The minister remained standing, without removing his coat and without looking at Lev Davidovich, and told him that President Cárdenas had granted him asylum in Mexico and the Trotskys would leave immediately.

Although the prospect of moving to Mexico still seemed dangerous to him, the Exile tried to convince himself that it was preferable to die at the hands of a murderer than to continue living in that captivity that threatened to continue until it crushed him. The speed with which the Norwegians rushed to throw him out of the country—they didn't even allow him a brief stay in France to see Liova—revealed the tensions that, because of him, Lie and the other ministers must have been living under for the previous four months. Nonetheless, Lev Davidovich thought that he could not miss his last opportunity and reminded Lie that everything he and his government had committed against him had been an act of capitulation and, like all capitulations, would have its price, since he knew that the day was quickly approaching when the fascists would arrive in Norway and turn them all into exiles. The only thing Lev Davidovich desired was that when that happened, the minister and his friends would find a government that would treat them like they had treated him. Trygve Lie, frozen in the center of the room, listened to that prophecy with a slight smile on his lips, incapable of imagining the overwhelming and dramatic way in which Lev Davidovich's prediction would come true.

Natalia prepared the luggage while Lev Davidovich, still fearful that the hurried departure could be leading them into some kind of trap, devoted himself to setting off warning flares. He quickly drafted an article against the Royal Office's English lawyer, and the French lawyer, a member of the Ligue des droits de l'Homme, who had certified the legality of the Moscow proceedings, and wrote Liova a letter, to which he gave the value of a will. He stated that Liova and Seriozha were his heirs should anything happen to him and their mother during their journey to Mexico or anywhere else. He also entrusted Liova never to forget his brother and asked him, should he meet him again, to tell him that his parents had never forgotten him, either.

On December 19, 1936, enveloped in the opaque light of winter, they got into the car that took them out of the fjord of Hurum. Lev Davidovich contemplated the Norwegian landscape and, as he would write shortly afterward, made a silent tally of his exile, to confirm that the losses and frustrations were many more than the doubtful gains. Nine years of marginalization and attacks had managed to turn him into a pariah, a new wandering Jew sentenced to ridicule and the anticipation of a terrible death that would arrive when the humiliation had exhausted its usefulness and quota for sadism. He was leaving Europe, perhaps forever—and in it the corpses of so many comrades and the tombs of his two daughters. With him, he took the faint hope that Liova and Sergei would be able to resist and, at least, escape that whirlwind with their lives intact; they were leaving the illusions, the past, the glory, and the ghosts, including those of the revolution for which he had fought for so many years. "But with me, I am also taking life," he would write, "and as beaten down as they think I am, while I still breathe, I have not been defeated."

14

Román Pavlovich smiled as if he were coming back to life when Grigoriev deciphered the Cyrillic characters for him and read the name stamped on the passport: R-O-M-A-N P-A-V-L-O-V-I-C-H L-O-P-O-V. The Soviet had moved his index finger over the letters and the recently baptized Román, son of Pablo, after smiling, kept staring at the rigid and unfamiliar symbols as he struggled to etch them in his mind. In the passport photo, taken in the basement of the building occupied by the Soviet Embassy in Valencia, he seemed older, as if he'd been transformed since the last time he'd seen himself in a mirror. But he liked the face of Román Pavlovich: it was more solid, as if molded by the rugged life in the Caucasus where, according to the document, he'd been born. Then Grigoriev held out his hand in a demanding manner, and he returned the passport feeling as if a piece of his soul were breaking away.

Ever since they landed at the military airport, Román Pavlovich had felt himself falling into an impenetrable world. The Russian language surrounded him with the same density as the sour and oily stench given off by the officers who took him to a sealed room where Grigoriev held a brief interview with two of them. Now, settled in the back car seat he was sharing with Grigoriev, he felt his nose clearing with the warm air coming in through the window and, with the caresses of his own language, felt himself recovering a certain equilibrium.

"Are we very far from Moscow?" he asked, looking at the dense pine forest the road crossed through.

"We're closer than we were yesterday," Grigoriev said.

"So when will you take me there?"

"You didn't come to do sightseeing," Grigoriev stated, and Ramón was certain that the man's tone had become harsher for some reason.

Ramón decided to stay silent. He wasn't going to allow anyone to ruin the happiness he'd felt ever since, upon returning to Barcelona, Kotov had told him he'd been selected to travel to socialism's homeland with the mission of preparing himself to fight for the triumph of the world revolution. Without giving him any further details, the adviser warned him that the weeks would be very intense, during which the utmost would be demanded of his body and mind.

The pine forest had become more impenetrable when, at a curve of the road, the coniferous monotony was broken by a concrete wall they rode next to for hundreds of yards until they reached a huge metallic portal that opened with a screech like a prison door. Ramón Mercader's senses were heightened, ready to notice the smallest detail. Behind the door, which closed again as soon as the car cleared the entrance, ran a narrow circular track that they began to follow counterclockwise. To the left, in what appeared to be the center of a gigantic rotunda, were more pines, separated every so often by tracks that, like spokes, were swallowed by the forest's dense center. To the left, set apart by metallic fences flanked by pruned and compact bushes, were some brick cabins on whose doors were numbers that seemed to go in random order: 11, 3, 8, 2, 7 . . . as if the numbers had been dictated by some lottery announcer.

The car stopped in front of cabin 13, and when Grigoriev murmured "We're here," Ramón was convinced that those figures held their own significance: 1913 was the year of his birth. After they got out of the car, it disappeared around the curve of the rotunda and Grigoriev walked to the cabin and opened the door, drawing back the exterior lock. Ramón, who had only a cloth bag into which they had allowed him to throw some underwear, rushed to cross the threshold so that his material and spiritual guide could close the door after him.

The cabin's living room was set up like a classroom for one student, with a desk, a table with a chair, a chalkboard, and a world map unfurled on the wall. To one side, there was a low table and, around it, four leather-covered armchairs. Two uniformed men stood in front of them; one was wearing a standard-issue uniform, with his rank displayed on his shoulders, and the other one had on a pair of black field overalls without any markings. The officer approached Grigoriev and, smiling, hugged him, then kissed him on the cheeks and lips, as they murmured words in Russian. The one in the field uniform gave Grigoriev a martial salute and he, instead of responding, held out his hand and said something to him in that gravelly language. Only then did the officer turn to Ramón and speak in French.

"Welcome to our base, Comrade Román Pavlovich. I'm Marshal Koniev, head of the facility, and this"—he pointed at the man dressed in black—"is Lieutenant Karmin, your official trainer. Please sit down. Some tea?"

Román Pavlovich smiled and took his seat as the other three settled into the remaining ones.

"Is coffee possible, Marshal?" he asked, also in French.

"Of course! Lieutenant, please . . ." As Karmin withdrew to the kitchen, the marshal lit a cigarette and looked at Román Pavlovich. "Tonight, before they bring you dinner, Lieutenant Karmin will explain the internal rules, which must be strictly and absolutely followed. I want you to know beforehand that you will not be able to leave this cabin unless you're accompanied by your training officer, by me, or by your operative officer, Comrade Grigoriev. And I'm also telling you straightaway that for any infraction, there's only one result: expulsion."

The marshal was silent, and as if it had been planned, Karmin returned with a wooden tray on which sat a steaming kettle releasing the aroma of coffee. As soon as he tasted it, Román Pavlovich regretted having asked for that too-sweet and weak concoction and wondered if the rules would allow him to prepare his own infusion.

Without asking permission, Grigoriev and the marshal began to speak in Russian and Román Pavlovich assumed they were going over the details of his stay. Lieutenant Karmin was drinking his tea with his eyes fixed on the mug, as if he expected to find a snake at the bottom. The dialogue went on for several minutes, with Koniev as the main speaker, and ended when Grigoriev gave Román Pavlovich's passport to the marshal, who looked at his new pupil.

"Until we decide your new identity, you'll be Soldier 13," he informed him, and with an almost theatrical gesture, to Ramón's surprise, he ripped up the passport. Ramón suddenly felt himself turning into a nameless ghost, without a compass or any way back, as the marshal's last words confirmed. "Or you won't be anyone."

Grigoriev and Soldier 13 had breakfast in the cabin's kitchen and the latter had the satisfaction of preparing his own coffee. It was a reddish powder without any smell from which it would be difficult to obtain a satisfactory infusion—although, prepared by him, it was at least drinkable. Grigoriev invited him to go for a walk and they left the cabin through the back door. Beyond a few feet of swept dirt, the overwhelming presence of the pine forest came back into view and, through it, about one hundred yards from the house, the metallic fences covered with galvanized planks that separated the terrains of each cabin. As they entered the forest, Soldier 13 noticed that his guide limped slightly.

The night before, Lieutenant Karmin had explained the rules of the base that would have to be followed with absolute obedience. Ramón was told that he wouldn't have any contact with anyone who was not authorized by him and the marshal and it was explained why: in the future, his life could depend on none of the school's students having ever seen his face and him never having seen theirs, either. All who entered that compound were men of exceptional intelligence, and demands would be made of them accordingly. The remaining conditions of his stay, since he was a soldier who was selected for special missions, would be explained to him by Comrade Grigoriev, he said, and he couldn't help but feel a rush of pride that he was part of a select group.

But on that summer day of 1937, Soldier 13 would have a real notion of the point to which his life had changed when he found out what the important mission was that would open the gates of the proletarian heavens. Grigoriev began to sketch out the current situation in the USSR and how it involved them. As Ramón knew, the previous year the party and the government had initiated a battle to the death against the Trotskyists and oppositionists remaining in the country. It had been especially painful to discover, just a few months later, that a group of the Red Army's most prestigious officers, among them Marshal Tukhachevsky, had allied themselves with German intelligence with the intention of carrying out a coup d'état, deposing Stalin, and making a pact with the fascists. The proof found was irrefutable and the soldiers themselves had been tried and shot a few weeks ago, while the removal of dangerous elements from the army continued and the purge of the party was being completed. That operation, he continued, had been led by Comrade Yezhov, the commissar of internal affairs, under Comrade Stalin's direct supervision. So now, Grigoriev said, and despite the fact that they were surrounded only by conifers, he lowered his voice to a whisper: ever since the crisis involving Yagoda, the former commissar of the interior accused of treason and Trotskyism, Yezhov had started a witch hunt within the secret forces themselves, in the NKVD counterintelligence as well as in military intelligence, and out of an excess of zeal or because of his desire to erase former officers from the map in order to replace them with his most trusted men, he was putting at risk the very existence of those organizations.

"Comrade Stalin has let him act because he thinks it's necessary to eliminate any of Yagoda's men who could be linked to acts of treason." Grigoriev stopped walking. "And there is no one better than Yezhov for that job. But at the same time he has moved a lot of responsibilities out of his hands, such as foreign intelligence, and has entrusted them to Comrade Lavrentiy Beria. This base and the plans being made within it, for example. Everything will go well for us as long as that division of labor is maintained, but if Yezhov's purge causes a confrontation with Beria— who at the end of the day is a subordinate—and charges against us, we're going to have a very, very rough time. Although that's not the worst of it: the most serious thing is that the lines of work beginning here could be lost, including ours."

"And why is Comrade Stalin risking something like that happening?"

"He has his reasons; he always has them," Grigoriev said, and spit at a pine. He remained silent for a few seconds. "My situation is especially complicated for two reasons: first, because Yezhov considers me a man from Yagoda's time, although I entered intelligence well before; second, because I'm Jewish and it's obvious that he doesn't like Jews, like many people . . . That's why it's safer for me to go on in Spain and try to make myself indispensable there."

Perhaps overwhelmed by the information he was receiving, because of the words being uttered in Spanish, or because of the uplifting effect of discovering again beneath the dry Grigoriev the Kotov he knew or thought he knew, Ramón felt that he was becoming himself again and that the vertigo of newness and incomprehensible sounds amid which he had lived for the last few days had begun to recede, despite having the impression that they were placing him at the edge of a precipice where they would abandon him without any kind of hold in sight or in reach.

"So what is the mission Comrade Stalin needs us for?"

"The most important one." He paused for some time, as if he were thinking. "That is why I am obliged to tell you now, because whether we move forward or not depends on your willingness."

"Which is?" Ramón didn't want to play guessing games. The best thing, he thought, was to grab the bull by the horns.

"Comrade Stalin thinks the moment has arrived . . . We're going to prepare Trotsky's exit from this world."

Ramón couldn't avoid the shock. He wanted to think he had misheard, but he knew that he had understood perfectly well and that at that same moment, due only to having heard those words of Kotov's, his life had fallen into an extraordinary dimension.

"What do you mean by 'prepare'?" he managed to ask.

"To start working toward it. Putting together the masterstroke. That's why you and other Spanish Communists are here."

"You're going to prepare us to kill him?"

"We're going to prepare you for lots of things."

"So why in the hell do we have to be Spaniards?"

Kotov smiled and moved a giant pinecone with his foot. He said that, in his opinion, Spaniards would never be good secret agents. Although in their favor they had a mixture of recklessness and innate cruelty that made them capable of killing or dying (that is a great virtue) and they were also fanatical (you need a good dose of fanaticism for this job), they also carried the defect of being too spontaneous, at times even friendly and dramatic, and at heart they were all a little bit boastful, and their boastfulness made them talkers, and this was difficult to eradicate . . .

"What you're saying isn't very encouraging. I don't understand—"

"This mission is for men who speak Spanish as their first language. That's the first reason. The second is that they're capable of overcoming any scruples."

Ramón thought to what point those defects and virtues were also his and concluded that Kotov was mostly right, except for the boastfulness.

"But the real reason for all of you being here is because I think you can do it," Kotov concluded.

Ramón looked at the forest. A flame of pride had been lit in his mind, displacing any other fear. What would África have thought if she had overheard this conversation? Would she really have thought he was too weak? What had Kotov seen in him?

"Tell me, Ramón: if necessary, would you be able to kill an enemy of the revolution?"

The young man looked at Kotov and he held his gaze.

"If it were necessary, of course I would do it."

The adviser smiled and his look recovered the twinkle he had lost in the last few days. He pointed at Ramón's chest with one finger.

"Can you imagine the honor of being chosen to take that treacherous scum Trotsky out of this world? Do you know that for years and years that renegade has been working to destroy the revolution and that he is a filthy rat who has sold out to the Germans and the Japanese? That he has even planned massive poisonings of Soviet workers to sow terror within the country? That his adventurist philosophy can put the future of the proletariat in danger, here, over in Spain, in the entire world?"

Ramón looked at the forest again. His mind was blank, as if all the channels of his intelligence had been broken, but he said:

"What I don't understand is why you've waited until now to do away with that traitor."

"You don't have to understand anything. I already told you: Stalin has his reasons and we the duty to obey . . . By the way, how many times have you heard the word 'obedience' in the last two days?"

"I don't know—several."

"And you'll hear it a thousand more times, because it's the most important word. After it come 'loyalty' and 'discretion.' This is the holy trinity and you should tattoo it on your forehead, because after having heard what I've told you, you'll have noticed that there are only two paths for you: one to glory and another to the work camps, where you don't have the least idea of how little the life of a poor guy who doesn't even have a name and is considered a traitor is worth . . . Let's go, they must be waiting for us."

When they entered the cabin, Marshal Koniev and Karmin stood up and gave military salutes. While Soldier 13 settled into his desk, Grigoriev said something to the two soldiers. Then Grigoriev and the marshal sat down on the armchairs in the back. Karmin, with his black suit, went to the blackboard and seemed to melt into it. Ramón noticed that his hands were clammy and he heard Kotov's last words echo in his brain.

"Soldier 13," Karmin said in a clean and southern French that evoked his days in Dax and Toulouse, "your mentor has told us that you're ready to begin training. But before beginning our work, you'll be subjected to a variety of physical and psychological tests so we can get an exact evaluation of you. If the results are satisfactory, as we expect, you'll begin to receive history lessons about the Bolshevik Party, international politics, Marxism-Leninism, and psychology. We'll also teach you survival, interrogation, and hand-to-hand combat techniques and you'll practice parachuting and using a variety of firearms. The most important part of your training, however, will be the work we do on your personality. You'll learn, above all, that you will never again be the person you were before arriving at this base. We're going to completely remake you from the inside out. It's slow and difficult work, but if you're able to overcome it, you'll be ready to receive any of the identities we decide to choose for the mission. This identity still hasn't been determined, but whatever it may be, you will never again be a Spaniard, nor should you speak in Spanish or, less still, in Catalan. For now, you will speak in French and think in French. We'll even try to make you dream in French. Our specialists will help you in this task, but I repeat: your will is essential to obtaining success."

Soldier 13 thought that the expectations were perhaps too high, but he nodded in silence, as he already sensed that all of that knowledge could be useful for the mission Kotov had spoken about to him.

"Good. To begin, we need you to pass a very simple but definitive test, since it will teach you many things. Come with me!"

Karmin walked to the back door and Soldier 13 followed him. Behind them went Grigoriev and Koniev. The morning was now warmer and from the pine forest came a perfumed scent. On a small wooden table, Soldier 13 saw three different kinds of knives and he thought he'd be taught how to use them. From amid the pines at that moment came a soldier, dressed like Karmin, who was dragging a dirty man with greasy hair, dressed in rags, whose stench was stronger than the forest's aroma.

"Take a good look at this man," Karmin said. "He's scum, an enemy of the people."

Soldier 13 barely looked at the destitute man when, without using any other words, Karmin yelled:

"Kill him!"

Soldier 13, surprised by the cry, felt doubly confused: Was the order real? And who was it being given to: Soldier 13, Ramón Mercader, or the ephemeral Román Pavlovich? But he didn't have time to think any further, since Karmin took his standard-issue Nagant out of the case and cocked it.

"*Yob tvoyu mat!* Are you going to liquidate him or do I have to do it?"

Soldier 13 looked at the daggers and took one with a short, wide blade that, without knowing why, seemed the most appropriate. Appropriate? To kill an enemy of the revolution? He felt his legs tremble when he took the first step. He tried to convince himself that this could only be a test: when the moment came, they would order him to stop and would take that beggar out of there. He walked to the stinking man, in whose eyes he noticed a growing fear. The man said something in Russian that he couldn't understand, although he perceived it as a plea in which the word *tovarich* was repeated as he took one, two steps backward, his body trembling. Soldier 13 kept walking forward with the dagger at his hips, waiting to hear the order to stop, the command that wasn't coming, while he got closer and closer to the foul-smelling beggar.

Soldier 13 saw the plea in the man's eyes, just five feet from him, and he could hear the silence. Nothing else. In his mind, a word took shape: "obedience," and a question: "weak?" África's image passed like lightning through his brain. Then he took another step, moved the dagger back to give it momentum, and understood that the other man was incapable of fleeing or even of moving back. Terror had paralyzed him and made him start sweating. Should he kill a man like that, in cold blood, to prove his loyalty to a grandiose cause? Was this the ruthlessness with which you had to treat the enemies of the people in the land of justice? What did that have to do with Trotsky's betrayals, with the excesses of the Spanish fascists? No, he told himself, the order would come, they would stop him, they would all laugh, and he moved the dagger a few more inches until it was in the position to attack. And then he didn't think about it anymore: he launched his weapon hand in search of the beggar's abdomen and found that, at that moment, he was Soldier 13, that Ramón Mercader had disappeared, that he was fulfilling the first sacred principle: obedience. The dagger continued its journey in pursuit of a defenseless man, paralyzed by fear, and when it was about to sink into his abdomen, over which the man's hands were crossed in an attempt to protect himself, those same hands moved at an inconceivable speed, diverted the course of the piece of steel, and Soldier 13 received a very strong kick in the chin, which toppled him backward, unconscious.

In just a few weeks, Soldier 13 became aware of a mutation in the colors of his consciousness. As the theoretical classes were filling his brain with philosophical, historical, and political arguments to make his faith unbreakable, the sessions with the psychologists were draining his mind of the deadweight of experiences, memories, fears, and illusions forged over the course of a life and of a past that he detached himself from as if they were skinning him. He was overwhelmed to see how his personal history was becoming a foggy haze and how even recent events, like Kotov's last recommendations before he returned to Spain, seemed so diffuse that he sometimes asked himself if he hadn't lived them in another remote and murky existence.

During those months was when Ramón really began to stop being Ramón and only became him again when the man they were turning him into was suffocating and, to save him, the former Ramón Mercader had to come to the surface. Or whenever they ordered him to go out and get some sun. But he was never again the same Ramón Mercader del Río.

The man who in his nebulous past had adopted communist ideals through his juvenile romanticism and África's harangues now began to assume a scientifically maintained faith, whose materialization was the new Soviet society where humanity had finally achieved the greatest height of dignity. The revolutionary struggle, intuitive and chaotic, that had been carried out against the oligarchy, the bourgeoisie, fascism, and traitors was made concrete with new coherence and foundations in the historic necessity of the struggle of the proletariat to materialize the utopia of equality and in the mission of the party to lead this great contest. He learned that if that struggle could appear ruthless at times, it was always just. At the root of each of these ideas were Stalinist theories and practices, the wisdom and the strategic vision of Comrade Stalin, the general secretary who stood above history, at the front of the world's proletariat, as the brilliant heir of Marx, Engels, and Lenin. The conviction that the future of humanity belonged to socialism turned into his creed, and he learned that, for the Soviet Union to reach that future, any sacrifice, any act, was historically justified and not even the most minimal dissidence was admissible. On this point they added to his studies lessons about class hatred and, visualizing his class enemies, his convictions became more solid.

October arrived and the temperatures started to drop. Karmin announced that, without stopping the theoretical sessions and the meetings with psychologists, they would begin the physical training. Soldier 13 had the hope that he would at last leave the base and would perhaps see with his own eyes part of the shining reality of the country of the Soviets. However, except for the two weeks during which they moved to the Ural Mountains to submit him to resistance tests in extreme conditions (from which he returned six kilos lighter, but proud of having been congratulated by Karmin), the rest of his education was carried out in the forests of Malakhovka. There he mastered shooting with a rifle, pistol, and machine gun; learned to fight with a knife, a sword, and an axe, acquired personal defense methods that used only his hands and feet, and was taught how to be precise in the lobbing of grenades as well as the art of scaling walls and the processes of demolition. With the first cycle complete, they insisted on his learning how to eliminate one or more enemies with the various weapons he was skilled in using, first identifying the weak points in his opponents' defenses and then the corners of their anatomy where the desired effects might be achieved with the most efficiency. The enemies with whom he trained, specialists in various forms of aggression, were always labeled Trotskyist dogs, Trotskyist renegades, Trotskyist traitors, until the mere mention of that adjective caused a hormonal discharge.

Soldier 13 would recall that the most crucial moment of his conversion and training was when they taught him to resist the psychological methods of torture and interrogation, in which they included, in order to achieve the necessary realism, acts of physical aggression that demonstrated to him the incredible human faculty of invention in inflicting modes of suffering on fellow human beings. The goal of that lesson, nonetheless, was not just the acquisition of the ability to stay silent but rather, and above all, to not allow himself to be manipulated by the interrogators, to cut off any bridge of understanding that could open a channel to his weaknesses, and, further still, to get the interrogators to believe stories that would confuse them and distance them from the truth. They showed him that it was much harder to keep a secret than to get it out of someone, and they educated him in roundabout psychological games, like the evocation of dreams or the reflection of supposed sick obsessions.

When, at the end of November, Grigoriev reappeared on the base, Soldier 13 was already—even the trainers could guarantee it—a man of marble, convinced of the need to carry out whatever mission was asked of him, forged to resist a variety of attacks in silence, gifted with a visceral hatred against the Trotskyist enemies, and ready to be turned into the person they were to assign him. His instructors' satisfaction was obvious, indeed the diamond in the rough found by Grigoriev seemed like a marvelous stone, brilliant in all its facets—political, philosophical, linguistic, physical, psychological—and he had been reinforced with the best armor, because he was a man who was capable of remaining silent, of exploiting his hatred, of not feeling any compassion, and of dying for the cause. He had become an obedient and ruthless machine.

That afternoon Soldier 13 was wearing a black uniform similar to that of his personal trainer, but designed for winter temperatures. Grigoriev, accompanied by Marshal Koniev, entered the cabin, greeted him with a martial salute, and, without removing any of the garments with which he protected himself from the cold, crossed the room in search of the back exit. With an order from Karmin, Soldier 13 followed him and, upon arriving in the snowy yard, was about to smile when he saw, laid out on a small table, three knives similar to the ones he had been offered on the first day of his initiation. Soldier 13 immediately understood what was expected of him, and when he saw the instructor pushing a man from within the forest, dressed in rags, shuddering with fear and cold, he was set to give him the lesson that now, he was sure, he was capable of giving.

"Soldier 13!" Karmin said. "You already know . . . In front of you is a Trotskyist dog, enemy of the people. Kill him!"

Soldier 13 chose the English army field knife. He had barely grasped it when he felt his skin warming up to the point that he didn't feel the cold as his muscles turned into an extension of the steel blade and his feet into snakes slithering toward the victim. The man was begging and Karmin, ten or so feet behind him, was kind enough to translate: "He swears he is innocent, that he hasn't conspired, he says he hates Trotsky, Zinoviev, Kamenev, and all of the traitors of the working class; he insists that Comrade Stalin is his father and asks that proletarian justice be carried out with him, please. Do you believe any of this?" Soldier 13 shook his head and kept walking toward the man, whose tremors seemed as authentic as the plea for mercy in his eyes. At that moment he thought he discovered a different strategy in the begging dog who was protesting with open arms, without retreating, as if he were melted into the snow. When he moved the knife to get momentum, he carried out a quick play of hands and changed his grip. He wouldn't direct his attack at the abdomen but rather the neck, so that the supposed beggar could divert the steel blade's movement but not prevent him from kicking him then with all of his might in his crotch, first, and then, once he was on his knees, digging his heel into his chin, with a half turn of his legs.

Soldier 13 held his breath, ready for attack. He kept his eyes on those of his alleged victim and, with a closed arc, threw his arm from his right side in search of the jugular of the man, whose eyes did not lose their terrorized expression until the knife dug into his neck and, a second later, spurted a stream of blood that came out of his mouth and ended up on the chest of the black, quilted uniform of his executor. Soldier 13 felt the man's deadweight on his shoulder, held up by the knife, until he saw how he crumpled and freed the dented steel, from which a few drops of blood fell onto the already reddened snow. Soldier 13 would never remember whether he felt cold at any point.

As the car moved forward and the forest thinned, Grigoriev recalled his arrival in Moscow, in the chaotic and violent days leading up to the October triumph. Without ceasing to listen, Soldier 13 thought that, just four months before, the young Ramón who had inhabited him would have loved to visit red revolutionary Moscow, the pilgrimage site of all the world's Communists. But he had lost all curiosity and was now making the visit with the same discipline and lack of passion with which he would have followed an order. While he listened to his mentor's words, he impressed on his mind the details of the trip with the meticulousness of a professional.

Grigoriev and Marshal Koniev had commented that they would take a break between his training sessions. Due to his excellent results, he had been given permission so he could enjoy a weekend in the capital. Soon, Soldier 13 would learn that he would be allowed to leave the base with other intentions.

The persistent snow of recent days covered plazas and buildings, cupolas and parks, and the Moscow River was a sinuous mirror. As soon as they began the tour, Ramón felt as if he were entering a city with the air of a feudal town with vast spaces, which caused a feeling of inconsistency between his reality and his ambitions, an impossibility of definition that would only reveal its origins to him years later when he understood that, despite its grandeur and arrogance, the Soviet capital was still a territory in conflict, the meeting point of two worlds with fluid borders there—East and West, Christianity and Orthodoxy, the European and the

Byzantine—that lost their original nature and gave way to something different, definitive and essentially Muscovite. Red Square was, as he expected, the first stop, and, as they crossed it, its dimensions gave the impression of being vaster than the photographs of the parades had forged in his imagination. Although Saint Basil's colorful onion-shaped cupolas surprised him with their colors and shapes, in reality they seemed exotic and indecipherable, as if they were speaking Russian or some other Eastern language; the red walls and towers of the Kremlin, by contrast, seemed closer, more representative of the country's ancestral grandeur. With a special pass, they were able to avoid the line that, in those temperatures of twelve degrees below zero and between the floral offerings petrified by the cold, men, women, and children, from all parts of the USSR and the world, was made in respectful silence to spend a scarce few minutes before the mummified corpse of the founder of the Soviet state. The excitement he expected to feel upon entering that mausoleum, half Pharaonic and half Greek, escaped him, for it took him some effort to absorb, through a glass whose reflections broke the mummy's face into poorly fitted panes, the emanations of grandeur of the man who had achieved the materialization of humanity's most prized and elusive dream: a society of equals.

With another authorization permit, meticulously reviewed by the guards, they walked to the Trinity Tower, through which they entered the Kremlin's walls, against which the snow had been shoveled. While Grigoriev led Soldier 13 through the interior streets that led to the plaza in front of the cathedral, he showed him the places where alterations had been made after demolishing some old chapels from the time of the first czars and nearly stopped the tour to signal, at the closest possible range, the windows of the administrative offices from where the greatest country on earth was led.

"Comrade Stalin works there?"

"Part of the day," Grigoriev responded. "And up until a few years ago, he had his apartment there." He pointed at the old senate building, built under Catherine the Great. "Ever since his wife committed suicide, he left those rooms and always sleeps at his dacha in Kuntsevo. He likes to settle the most important matters there, since he almost always works all night. He sleeps very little and works a lot, but he's strong as an ox."

When they left the walled compound, they went by the huge GUM department store, where people from all over the city came with the hope, often disappointed, of treating their stomachs to a surprise. In front of the Museum of History, they took former Nikolskaya Street, renamed October Twenty-Fifth, to go up the hill leading to the small plaza reigned over by a statue of Felix Dzerzhinsky, behind which rose the nation's most feared building.

Grigoriev pointed. "Voilà, the Lubyanka."

Soldier 13 knew the history of that edifice and devoted himself to contemplating it in silence. The former insurance house, ocher-colored and bleak, had twenty years before received the men—converted into apocalyptic proletarian scourges of the Earth—who had assumed the responsibility of defending the revolution, by any means necessary, when besieged by its internal and external enemies. Just by looking at the building, so dense that it appeared to be set in the ground, and flanked by a sidewalk completely devoid of people, one could feel the force of the most real ruthlessness emanating from it—a ruthlessness that, like the will of an unforgiving god, decides over life and death, without respect for procedure or indeed law. Soldier 13 knew that behind those walls his own fate was being handled, and that, in some way, he had turned into one more brick in that magnificent building that, in darkness, had done so much for the survival of the revolution. The enslaving power of the Lubyanka would soon be his power, he thought.

"As you can see, people avoid passing by here," Grigoriev said, and paused. "This is the plaza of fear. It's a fear that we have cultivated with great care, a necessary fear. A lot of stories about the Lubyanka are told, almost all of them terrible. And you know what? The majority of them are true. The bourgeoisie uses fear very well, and we had to learn it and practice it. Without fear, you can't lead or push a country into the future."

"The proletariat has the right to defend itself in any way," Soldier 13 said, and Grigoriev smiled.

"I see that they've stuffed you full of slogans. You can save them when you're with me."

Limping slightly, Grigoriev led him to the boulevard of theaters and they entered Petrovka Street, where Soldier 13 found a pulsing life that contrasted sharply with the sidereal solitude of the Lubyanka. His mentor had told him they would look for an adequate place to eat and talk, safe from indiscretions. Before a building with a modernist air that reminded Soldier 13 of Barcelona, a man at the top of a flight of stairs that went down to a basement from the sidewalk was marching on the spot to battle the cold. Soldier 13 was certain the man was waiting for them, since he observed them determinedly as he marched: one arm moved to the rhythm, and the hand of his other arm, crossed over his chest in a strange position, moved two restless fingers up by his lapel. As they passed him, Grigoriev mumbled a "*Nyet*," and they went down to the semibasement, whose skylights were on street level, and went into what Soldier 13 would be hard-pressed to qualify as a beer hall. Elbow to elbow at high tables, without any chairs around, were several clusters of men and women shouting as they drank big sips of a hop-colored liquid to which they added generous streams from the small bottles of vodka they carried in whichever of the many pockets of their coats. Without ceasing to talk and drink, they all greedily ate small fillets of smoked herring on pieces of black bread and strips of dark meat from some kind of dried fish that they beat several times against the table in order to facilitate the extraction of the fillets, which they swallowed almost without chewing. The stench of the fish, the stinking draft beer, the smoke of that unbearable Russian tobacco called *mahorka*, and the smell of human sweat under coats that reeked of damp sheepskin resulted in an environment that was too disagreeable, and Soldier 13, prepared to resist a wide variety of discomforts, begged Grigoriev to find somewhere else. Grigoriev smiled understandingly.

"Yes, this requires special training. The truth is that the people chosen by the providence of history need more soap and water, right?"

When they left, the man with two fingers on his lapel was continuing his exercises, but this time he didn't even look at them. As they went back to the boulevard, Grigoriev finally revealed the mystery of the solitary marcher: he was a drinker looking for two companions with whom to share some glasses of *yorsh*, the mixture of vodka and beer that everyone was drinking in the basement.

"Russians are great drinkers, but they're competitive drinkers. There are two things they don't like: beer that isn't loaded with vodka, because it seems like a waste of time and money, and not having a point of reference regarding the quantity of drink they're swallowing. That's why they drink together or compete against each other. And that comrade, as you saw his two fingers, was looking for some partners for the job . . ."

After walking for a few blocks back toward the Kremlin, they went into Manezh Plaza, and Grigoriev, holding on to his arm to stop him, asked him to look at the monumental building rising before them. On the main entrance, Soldier 13 saw a sign in Cyrillic that he was able to read: HOTEL MOSCOW. He contemplated that block of masonry, several stories high (ten, twelve—its structure made it difficult to know), with a colonnade supporting a terraced roof that projected out, and he immediately noticed a strange lack of balance.

"Do you see it?" Grigoriev said, and added, "It's the first great hotel built by Soviet power. A triumph of socialist architecture."

Soldier 13 nodded and remained silent, as he had been taught. The building seemed monstrous, something hideous fallen from the sky and embedded by force into a plaza with whose spirit it painfully contrasted. The most unusual thing was the asymmetry of the two halves of the structure, which opened out behind the façade. One had supporting columns and the other one didn't; the floors above the left tower had arched windows, while the one on the right tower looked strict and square; the two cornices were of different heights—in an incompatible juxtaposition of proportions and styles that produced a disconcerting effect, capable of reaffirming the first sensation of aggressive ugliness.

"It's horrible," he whispered.

"Now I'll explain to you what happened," Soldier 13's guide told him and they crossed over to the hotel's large doors, where, thanks to an ID flashed before the doorman, they were able to enter. After a careful survey by Grigoriev, they settled in at a table in the deserted bar, which smelled like a bar and only vaguely like dried fish, and where Soldier 13 discovered that, after showing another credential (Grigoriev appeared to have all the ones requested in Moscow), it was possible to drink French wine and eat slices of Norwegian salmon and braised veal.

"Why did they make the building like that?" Soldier 13 wanted to know.

"Calm down, kid, I'll tell you about that later," Grigoriev said, and drank his vodka in one gulp and refilled his glass with the small, widemouthed bottle that the comrade waiter had left close at hand. "Three days ago I was at a very, very secret meeting at the Kuntsevo dacha. Since it directly affects you, I'm going to tell you part of what was discussed there. You know that if what I told you in Barcelona was worth your life, and the lives of África, Caridad, and your brothers are worth what you've seen and learned in Malakhovka, then what I'm going to tell you now is priceless. And I'll remind you that if there was no way back before, now your only option is to move forward and keep your mouth shut, with everyone and forever."

Soldier 13 listened to Grigoriev's words and noticed a wave of satisfaction running through him. He wasn't scared, nor did it matter to him that there was no escape except to move forward, since neither fear nor escape in any other way fitted in his mind anymore.

"You can speak," he said, and moved his glass of wine aside after taking a sip.

Grigoriev preferred to take another drink of vodka before getting into things: Comrade Stalin in person had conferred on him the honor of being the one responsible for the operation against the renegade Trotsky, and had given him the order to set it in motion. At the Kuntsevo meeting, the only participants were Comrade Stalin, Vice Commissar Beria, and himself. They had begun by discussing the internal situation at the Commissariat of the Interior and Beria assured him that Yezhov would not intervene in this operation. Furthermore, he added, that that crazy midget's days were numbered and now it was he, Beria, who was at the head of all the special operations that Yezhov, with his persecution mania, would have stopped or dismantled. But the Trotsky operation was born at that moment and Grigoriev, with the necessary discretion, would not only carry it out successfully but also do it with the propaganda effect they wanted.

Upon hearing Beria's last words, Comrade Stalin seemed to wake up from his lethargy and lifted a hand to request silence, Grigoriev recounted. During the conversation, he had been trying some sips from his cup of Georgian wine mixed with Lagidze, a type of lemonade that also came from Georgia; according to what Grigoriev explained to him, he drank that compound under medical authorization, since it had been proven that the mixture of those two ancestral beverages stimulated circulation and relaxed the muscles. As Comrade Beria said so well, the Leader said, the hunt for the degenerate traitor and fascist had begun. He, personally, had decided that Grigoriev would be the director in situ of the operation, but Comrade Beria should receive weekly reports from Grigoriev and, if necessary, daily reports, about which the Leader would be updated when necessary and in any case at least once every fifteen days. Grigoriev, as the official operative in charge of the mission, would have a direct superior within the commissariat, an agent who would answer only to Beria and with whom Grigoriev should discuss all logistical questions, although he wanted him to know that he had all necessary human and economic resources at his disposal, since doing away with that traitor was considered a number one priority by the Soviet state as well as a necessity for the future of international communism. The plan, which should be prepared with the utmost care, would have to meet some important conditions: the first, that it would not be possible to find any trace that would link any Soviet body to the operation; second, that the final action only be carried out when he—Stalin *personally*, he reiterated—gave the order; and then came other conditions—for example, that the best place to carry out the plan was Mexico and that, if possible, the executioners be Mexicans and Spaniards or, as a last resort, men from the Comintern's secret services, although Beria, Grigoriev, and the official operative (we still haven't decided who, Beria had whispered) had to organize various alternatives that Stalin *personally* had also to approve. Grigoriev would work without worrying about collateral effects such as a possible crisis with that imbecile Cárdenas's government, because, once the moment arrived, they would make the Mexican swallow his own arrogance in the way he had acted when he had protested over the asylum granted to the renegade. Stronger democracies, such as France, Norway, and Denmark, had been brought to their knees when they tried to challenge him and he had seen himself forced to turn a few screws.

"Then he explained to me why the moment had come for concocting a plan, but not for carrying it out. The essence of everything is the war, the start of the war and the paths it will follow," Grigoriev said, and served himself vodka again, although he didn't drink it. "The war is going to start at any moment."

"And why should I know all of this?" Soldier 13 asked, stupefied by how everything he'd just heard weighed on his shoulders.

Grigoriev now seemed more relaxed and drank more vodka.

"In a week we have to decide who you will be. We have more than enough Mexicans and Spaniards and we need more Frenchmen, Americans. We're going to create several independent operative groups, and you can be sure that only four people on earth will know of your existence: Stalin, Beria, the official operative, and me."

"Are you thinking it will be me who carries out the mission?"

"You're going to be on the front line, although I still don't know where . . . But since you're going to work with me, I prefer that you know, starting now, what's expected of you should that be the case . . . Experience tells me that the person who knows exactly what he's doing and why he's doing it works better."

Soldier 13 remained silent while Grigoriev tasted the salmon. Outside, the afternoon had given way to night and he could see a stretch of Okhotny Ryad Street, poorly lit and almost deserted.

"Stalin said something else to me . . ." Grigoriev began, and lifted his hand to ask for another *chekushka* of vodka. When the waiter walked away, he looked at his student. "This mission doesn't allow for failure. If I fail, I'll pay for it with my balls."

"He said it to you just like that?"

"Comrade Stalin tends to be a very direct man. And it can bother him very much if his orders aren't followed well . . . So you understand me: what you saw of this hotel is a monument to the obedience he demands and expects . . . Listen closely, it can teach you a lot: when he decided that Moscow needed a new image, he picked this site to have a hotel built to host its most distinguished visitors. Based on his suggestions, he asked that two different projects be presented to him. Since he thinks that Moscow should begin to turn into the capital of proletarian architecture, he has his own ideas about it. He made them known to Shchusev the designer and to the architects Saveliev and Stapran and tasked them with the plans, sure that they would know how to interpret what he had in mind. The architects trembled upon hearing what Stalin was asking of them, and each one, of his own accord, designed what he thought the Leader's ideas could be. But when Shchusev presented the two projects, he couldn't see them right away—he had other problems—and no one knows why, but the following week the plans were given back to Shchusev the designer . . . both of them authorized by Comrade Stalin. How was it possible? they asked themselves. Did he want two hotels or did he want both projects, or had he signed off on both by mistake? The only solution was to ask Comrade Stalin if he had made a mistake, but who dared to bother him during his vacation to Sochi? Besides, the general secretary was never wrong. Then Shchusev was inspired, like the genius he is: they would carry out both projects in a single building, half according to Saveliev and the other half according to Stapran . . . Thus was this freakish building born, and Shchusev, Saveliev, and Stapran managed to come out gracefully. The building is absurd, an aesthetic horror, but it exists and it conforms to Comrade Stalin's ideas and decisions. I learned the lesson, and I hope that you are also capable of understanding it. Cheers, Soldier 13!" he said, and drank to the bottom of his glass of vodka.

Kotov should die, Grigoriev announced. He regretted leaving Soldier 13 at that exact moment, perhaps the most beautiful one of the process of his rebirth, but he had to return to Spain to begin preparing the funeral for his other self. One is born, another dies, that's the dialectic of life, and he explained to Soldier 13 that, before devoting himself body and soul to the new mission, he should transfer his responsibilities in Spain to other comrades. The handoff could only be done on the ground and in a time frame that was perhaps prolonged because of the state of the war: although the nationalists had gained ground, the industrial and most populous part of the country was still in Republican hands, and while they hung on to it, they could hope for victory. Upon hearing this comment, Soldier 13 felt the cunning pull of nostalgia, but he managed to contain Ramón's desires and abstained from asking a single question. But he couldn't deny that the mention of the war and Kotov's imminent departure stirred his still-painful attachment to what had been until very recently *his* war, *his* homeland, and *his* passions. Only the consciousness that none of that belonged to him anymore or would again belong to him, at least in the same way, and the pride of knowing that he was now part of a select group, located at the heart of the struggle for socialism's future, saved him from wavering. He lived for faith, obedience and hate: if it wasn't an order, it didn't exist for him. África included. África most of all.

Karmin and the group of psychologists continued to work with him and Soldier 13 learned to control his anxiety over the delay in announcing his new identity. He knew that he was in the hands of the most capable specialists and, confident in the experience of those masters of survival and transformation, he focused on his training with more determination.

It was already the second week of December when, after a monotonous day in which his only visitor to the cabin was an inexpressive woman tasked with cleaning and bringing him food, there appeared before him two men with appearances and manners very different from those of the ones he had dealt with since his arrival at the base. One said he was called Cicero and the other Josefino. The first impression they gave was of being a comic vaudeville duo: both were dressed in the same awkward way, they had a deep and practiced hardness in their eyes, and they spoke perfect French with a slight accent that Soldier 13 wasn't able to place. Almost in unison, they told him that their mission was to turn him into a Belgian named Jacques Mornard. What did he think of the name? Soldier 13 felt himself swell with pride and satisfaction. Finally, he stopped being a student in order to become an agent. Jacques Mornard, he repeated in his mind, while Cicero removed a folder and several books from the briefcase he had with him, placing them on the table surrounded by armchairs.

"You're going to learn Jacques Mornard's life by heart," he said, and slid the folder toward Soldier 13. "Later, read the books: they have information about Belgium that you also have to include."

The so-called Josefino, who had remained standing, started speaking.

"Write the details you want to include for Mornard, the ones you think should make up part of his personality or his history. What we're giving you is like the skeleton you'll use starting now. We'll add the muscles and blood later."

"Why Belgian and not French?" the man who was still Soldier 13 dared to ask. "I lived in France for several years . . ."

"We know," Josefino said. "But your past doesn't exist anymore and will never exist again. You need to be a totally new man."

"The New Man," Cicero said, and Soldier 13 thought he noticed a touch of sarcasm. "From now on, you need to think of yourself as Jacques Mornard. The success of your conversion and, further still, your life will depend on the solidity of your belief in being Jacques Mornard. But take it easy . . . ," he said, as he stood. The two men left with a smile, without saying any kind of farewell.

Throughout that week of reading and reflection, Jacques Mornard enjoyed the feeling described by Josefino: it was as if his body, empty until now, were taking form and completing its own structure. Once again having parents, a brother, a birthplace, a school where he had studied and played sports, provided the framework over which he inserted his basic interests, his former preferences as a young bourgeois, and even his most remote memories. Like any person, he had attended many soccer games with his father and his brother and had become the fan of one of the clubs, had his favorite café in Brussels, his own ideas about the Walloons and the Flemings, had had girlfriends and a hobby that turned into a profession: photography. He wasn't a member of any party, nor did he have any definitive political opinions, but he rejected fascism because it seemed, at the very least, antiaesthetic. About Lev Trotsky's actions and historic fate, he knew what any educated person did, but all of that debate had to do with communist matters and didn't concern him. He spoke French and English but wasn't fluent in Flemish or Walloon, since he had grown up outside of Belgium, and he didn't speak Russian, either, although he understood Spanish because of all the trips he'd made to Spain before the war. From his family of diplomats, possessors of a certain fortune, he received regular sums that allowed him to live a carefree life with, if anything, a tendency toward waste. He would be a regular old bourgeois guy, a bit boastful, always looking for a good time, with no real worries in life.

Jacques Mornard understood the importance of the work the psychologists had done with him. The old Ramón he knew would not have liked to be like Jacques; he wouldn't have even been interested in being friends with him. Between the intellectual levity he now assumed and the Catalan's political passions and his militant rejection of all ways of bourgeois life, there was an abyss that would have been impossible to bridge without the radical cleaning of his consciousness or the difficult training to which he had been subjected.

When Josefino and Cicero returned, Jacques Mornard felt like he was about half filled to his capacity. The work that those instructors took up from that moment was that of Platonic demiurges: true creators. They spoke about Jacques as if they had known him their entire lives and they implanted memories, ideas, ways of reacting before certain situations, responses to the simplest and the most complex questions. It ended up being a slow process of continual repetitions, interrupted at times to allow the information to take root in Jacques's subconscious; who then welcomed the photography professor brought in to initiate him in the mystery of cameras (Jacques fell in love with the Leica, but in addition, he learned how to use the heavy Speed Graphic, the one preferred by press photographers), of lenses, how to judge the light, and the secrets of laboratory work with the chemicals and printing equipment; and then on to the speech therapist who endowed him with Belgian slang expressions, intonations, and soft *r*'s; to the optometrist who gave him the glasses he would use from then on; to Karmin, who, when Jacques was at the edge of intellectual fatigue, took him out in the snow and, in twelve or fifteen degrees below zero, worked every muscle of his body with an intensity capable of returning him to the cabin physically exhausted but with his mind clear, ready for the next day's session.

When Grigoriev returned to Malakhovka toward the end of January, Jacques Mornard was almost a complete man. The adviser told him that he hadn't managed to conclude his work in Spain and, without Jacques asking him, explained that the state of the war was complicated and desperate, as could be expected, although nothing seemed to indicate that the end was near. The Republican government was confident it could resist until the conflict was swallowed up by the imminent European war and turned into an active part of the antifascist bloc; thus, its situation would be similar to that of the proud democracies who had turned their backs on it under the pretext of nonintervention. But the most important thing, Grigoriev told him, was that he had also had time to take the first steps in the new operation. That is why he would soon leave for New York and Mexico, where he had to hold some important meetings. Before that, however, he wanted to personally work with his new creation.

His mentor's presence encouraged Jacques Mornard. The time for leaving the uterus of the training base was close, and with the adviser's guidance they added the final touches to the Belgian. A hairstylist gave him a new haircut; a tailor prepared a wardrobe of the bare essentials, which would be completed when he traveled to the West; and they added to his profile an enthusiasm for sports cars, whose brands and characteristics, along with the history of European motor racing, he had to study. His prior knowledge of French cuisine and of table manners acquired at the École Hôtelière de Toulouse saved him those lessons, although they instilled a taste for certain Belgian dishes. In response to Jacques's own proposal, they added a weakness for dogs to his nature. That remote passion of Ramón Mercader's, located in a deep recess of his consciousness, was compatible with Jacques's nature and upbringing, and his teachers allowed it. The Labradors of his childhood changed their names of Santiago and Cuba to Adam and Eve, and being able to feel love for dogs made Mornard feel happier with himself.

Before leaving for America, Grigoriev decided to take him to Moscow again, where he publicly acted like a curious Belgian journalist visiting the mecca of communism. The adviser charged himself with testing for his own satisfaction the solidity of the new personality, and throughout the days on which they shared Grigoriev's free time, Jacques was on trial the whole time, responding to a variety of questions, and displaying the reactions most suitable to his new personality.

Enjoying his freedom (he knew he was being watched at a distance), Jacques went beyond the Boulevard Ring that enclosed the prerevolutionary city and went into the proletarian neighborhoods, where his presence nearly caused stampedes by alarmed neighbors and where he found a steely, homogenous grayness capable of stirring his insides. He

222

knew that those men, almost all of them émigrés from the countryside during the difficult times of land collectivization, lived in minimal, poorly heated spaces (the so-called *kommunalka*s), sometimes without running water. Wrapped in coats of the same cut and color, worn out already by the winters, they barely ate from the monotonous and scarce offerings at the empty markets and combated boredom and exhaustion with devastating doses of vodka. But those men were also, like him, soldiers in the battle for the future, whose constant sacrifice constituted the only guarantee that the humanity of the future would enjoy true freedom. The lives of those Moscow inhabitants (looked down upon by true Muscovites) and his (yes, he who was wearing warmly threaded clothing from the West and eating delicacies that had disappeared even from the dreams of those proletarians) were on the same path, on the same battlefront. Only, while their responsibility was daily and modest, his had to be dark and, when the moment came, cruel, but was equally necessary. That was the price that the present charged the men of today for the light of tomorrow.

On one of those afternoons, seated on a bench in the recently inaugurated Gorky Park, in front of the frozen Moscow River, Grigoriev and Mornard were watching the kids who, with improvised sleighs, were gliding over the layer of ice, happy and oblivious to life's great sorrows.

"We're fighting for them, Jacques," Grigoriev said, and the Belgian sensed deep sincerity in his mentor's voice. "And it's a hard fight."

"I know, that's why I'm here. But I'd like it if they knew that I'm like them, and not some shitty capitalist."

Grigoriev nodded and, after a period of silence, spoke with his eyes fixed on the river.

"Imagine a horse race," he said, scratching his chin. "That's how we're going to work . . . Everyone leaves the gate at once, but some will get closer to the finish line before the others. The conditions on the ground, the opportunities, and each one's capacities are going to have an influence, but the orders the jockey receives will decide who goes toward the goal first. If he reaches it, the work is over. If he fails, the next one in line has to go."

"What number am I?"

"You'll be the ace up my sleeve, kid. You'll always work with me, directly with me. For now, you're at the end of the line, but that doesn't mean you're the last one. It means that you'll be the surest card, and that I won't risk you until I have no choice."

"And why don't I go out first and that's that?"

"For a lot of reasons that I can't explain to you now, or perhaps ever. Just understand that's how it is."

Jacques Mornard nodded and lit another one of the French cigarettes he now smoked and that a few days earlier had prompted him to cough and choke.

"You will be my masterpiece," Grigoriev continued. "I'm going to put together a real chess game for you. We're going to start to play thinking about move twenty, thirty, checkmate, from the beginning. It's going to be an intellectual challenge, something truly beautiful." The man appeared to be dreaming when he moved and placed himself in front of Jacques. "There's only one thing that worries me . . ."

"My obedience? My silence?"

Grigoriev smiled, shaking his head.

"I'm worried about whether, when the moment for checkmate arrives, Jacques Mornard isn't going to lose heart. I know that Ramón and Soldier 13 wouldn't lose heart. But Jacques . . . It's a mission that could end up being very difficult: perhaps you have to think not only about killing but about dying as well . . ."

Jacques threw his cigarette to the side and thought for a few moments.

"It's strange," he began. "Jacques Mornard fills me almost entirely, but there are spaces he can't reach. My hate and my fury are intact; my faith is the same. And those things aren't going to melt away. I know what I am doing and I feel proud. I also know that I will never be able to express that pride, but that, in and of itself, makes me stronger. If the moment comes, I'll be the truth of the proletariat, the hate of the oppressed. And I'll do it for them . . ." He pointed at the children playing. "You can rest assured. Jacques is a wretch. But Ramón will always be ready for anything. Dying included . . ."

Jacques Mornard possessed a peculiar ability to face time. He had internalized that each action should be carried out at a precise moment and that the anxiety to rush events was something foreign to his nature and his mission: his time had historic dimensions, it ran over human time-scales, and its proportions sprouted from philosophical necessity. Several years later he would ask himself whether that ability that had spared him from the daily ruts, hardships, and tedium hadn't been instilled in him intentionally, in anticipation of just how necessary it would be for him to resist sanely and in silence the long years of his imprisonment.

Ever since Grigoriev left and he returned to the Malakhovka base without an exact idea of the weeks and months he'd have to wait to go into action, he dove into the task of polishing the visible and even invisible edges of his new identity. In the company of Josefino and Cicero, he took long walks through the forest, repeating his family and his own life's history while he used his Leica to find suggestive compositions, expressive light, daring approaches. He devoted many hours to reading newspapers and studying Belgian city maps and tourist guides until he felt like he was capable of walking through Brussels or Liège without getting lost. He brought himself up-to-date on the tumultuous political situation in France and studied Mexico's recent history. That time, which he would have found exasperating at another point, now seemed pleasant, free of any trauma.

In the French newspapers they had started to give him, he read about how the Soviet prosecutor was preparing a case against twelve former party members and former state civil servants accused of serious crimes that went from treason against the homeland to anti-Bolshevik behavior and murder. The most mentioned names were those of Nikolai Bukharin and Alexei Rykov, former leaders of the so-called rightist opposition within the party; that of Genrikh Yagoda, the dismissed commissar of the interior who was responsible for the investigation of the trials in 1936 and 1937; and that of the Christian Rakovsky, the most stubborn of the Trotskyist oppositionists. On the bench would also be ambassadors and even doctors, such as Dr. Levin, Lenin and Stalin's personal doctor since the revolution, accused of having poisoned, among others, Gorky and his son Max under Yagoda's orders. The entire country knew that the accused had been detained for several long months and that their trial was imminent. Nonetheless, Jacques Mornard could not cease to be alarmed by the extent to which the crimes of those men, like those of the traitors judged in 1936 and 1937, had placed the very existence of the country, in which they held the highest positions and against which they had worked, in danger, according to what he read, from the very start of the revolutionary process. All of them, allied with the Trotskyist opportunists, were the very essence of the most concealed betrayal, of the worst felony.

One article he read in those papers surprised him even more than the news of the trial. It spoke of the death in Paris of Lev Sedov, Trotsky's son and closest collaborator, and it discussed the strange circumstances of that event, which was being investigated by local police. Jacques Mornard was convinced that his death, just when they were setting into motion the machinery to do away with the old traitor, couldn't be an act of coincidence or nature, and when Grigoriev finally returned to Malakhovka, he dared to confirm his suspicions.

"Do you think it could have been us?" Grigoriev sighed in exhaustion as he settled into one of the cabin's armchairs.

"I would think it very strange if it weren't."

"Yes, it would be strange. But coincidences exist, my dear Jacques; postoperative complications are frequent . . . Why would we risk killing that wretch who was already half-dead and living like a pauper in Paris, trying to find followers that don't exist? To alarm the old man and make things more difficult for ourselves?"

Jacques thought for a few moments and dared to ask something that the demiurges didn't manage to erase from his mind.

"So why did you kill Andreu Nin?"

"Because he was a traitor, and you know that," Grigoriev said in a rush.

"You didn't kill him because he wouldn't talk?"

The other man smiled weakly. He looked exhausted.

"Forget about that. Come on, grab your things. We're moving to Moscow."

The apartment where they stayed was close to the Three Stations Square, on Groholsky Lane, close to the Botanical Gardens. It was an old house with three floors that had belonged to a tea exporter whose family, decimated by exile and the rigors of the new reality, had been crowded onto the ground floor. Grigoriev and Jacques installed themselves in an apartment with its own bathroom on the second floor, and only then did the mentor tell him that they would leave for Paris in two days.

On March 2, Jacques followed the information on the radio about the opening of the first session of the Military Council of the Supreme Court of the Soviet Union. According to reports, there were about five hundred people in the room, and their focal point was the aged and stammering Bukharin. Prosecutor Vyshinsky presented the charges, already known by all: The accused, in alliance with the absent Lev Davidovich Trotsky and his deceased son and deputy, Lev Sedov, were not only murderers, terrorists, and spies, but they had also been counterrevolutionary agents since the start of the revolution and even before. In 1918, Trotsky and his accomplices had already conspired to assassinate Lenin as well as Stalin and the first Soviet president, Sverdlov. In the prosecutor's possession were legal statements declaring how Trotsky had become a German agent in 1921 and a British intelligence operative in 1926, along with some of his comrades in conspiracy there present. In his treacherous degradation, his last criminal efforts had been selling information to the Polish secret services and conspiring, with some of the accused, to cause mass poisonings of Soviet citizens, fortunately impeded by the tireless actions of the NKVD.

Since Grigoriev came and went from the apartment without offering Jacques any explanations, the latter decided to take advantage of his time by taking long walks around Moscow, and wherever he went, the Belgian found a city that was shocked and outraged. Throughout those days of terrible revelations, the people even seemed less concerned by the awful quality of the bread or the lack of shoes and happy to know that their leaders had managed to dismantle another conspiracy. The people's indignation grew as the accused admitted to ever more shocking crimes. But the surprise reached its climax when Bukharin admitted the monstrosity of his crimes and recognized that he was responsible, politically and legally, for promoting defeatism and planning acts of sabotage (even when he personally, he clarified, did not take part in the preparation of any concrete act and denied his participation in the most sinister acts of terrorism and sabotage). What was clear was that Bukharin had finalized his declaration in such a way that only made him a traitor. "Kneeling before the party and the country," he said, "I await your verdict." Jacques noticed that Bukharin's declaration included a great number of present and past evils, almost inconceivable in a man who, until two years earlier, was moving at the highest levels of the party. But that night in the beer halls, streets, metro cars, in the lines and amid the drunks who milled around the sordid triangle of the three stations (Leningradsky, Kazansky, and Yaroslavl), Jacques heard the same words again and again: "Bukharin has confessed," and the same conclusion: "Now they're really going to shoot him."

When Grigoriev announced the following morning that he had a gift for him, Jacques thought that the time of their departure had come.

"Today we're going to the trial," Grigoriev said, to Jacques's great surprise, and added, "Yagoda is taking the stand."

It was just a little after eight when they exited Okhotny Ryad Station and walked toward the House of the Trade Unions. On the boulevard of theaters, at the plaza where the Bolshoi Theater rose up in front of the Hotel Metropol, a protest was taking place and people were shouting and waving signs demanding the death of the Trotskyist, anti-Bolshevik traitors. Their indignation was vehement but not chaotic, and Jacques confirmed that the groups were organized by unions, factories, and schools, and that their slogans came directly from *Pravda* editorials.

Through the line of soldiers stationed at the top of Pushkinskaya Street, they managed to make their way toward the building where, prior to the October victory, the indolent Russian aristocracy had taken its pleasures. They went up the staircase, a tremendous display of marble, bronze, and glass, in search of the historic Hall of the Columns, where the geniuses of Russian music had played their scores and the great figures of the previous century had danced. Thanks to the revolution, the compound's fate had changed, like that of the entire country: in it, the Bolsheviks had made many of their revolutionary speeches, and even between the twenty-eight magnificent marble-covered wooden columns to which the hall owed its name, Lenin's corpse had had its wake before being moved to the mausoleum where he now rested; the trials of August 1936 and February 1937 had also been carried out there, marking the beginning and continuing the painful but necessary purge of a party, a state, and a government resolved not to stop even before history in order to give birth to a new History.

Moved to silence, Jacques took the seat Grigoriev pointed out to him. Party civil servants, leaders of the Komsomol, directors of the Comintern, foreign diplomats, and accredited journalists were filling the hall when, at nine on the dot, the judges, the prosecutors, and finally the accused and their lawyers made their entrance. The tension in the air was dark and unhealthy, when Jacques Mornard leaned toward his mentor to whisper in his ear:

"Is Comrade Stalin coming today?"

"He has too many important things to do to waste his time listening to these treacherous dogs confess."

When Vyshinsky called Genrikh Yagoda to make his statement, a murmur went through the hall. Jacques Mornard saw a man stand who was rather small, nearly bald, with a Hitleresque mustache that made him look like a ferret. It was difficult to recognize in that individual, incapable of keeping control over his hands, the man who for many years possessed the power to decide the life and death of so many citizens and who, for many years, had hidden a traitor.

"Are you willing to confess the crimes of which you are accused, Genrikh Yagoda?" Vyshinsky inquired.

"Yes," the prisoner said immediately, and paused before continuing. "I confess because I have understood the perversity of what I and the rest of the accused have done and because I believe that we shouldn't leave this world with such terrible crimes on our conscience. With my confession, I hope to serve the Soviet brotherhood and inform the world that the party has always been right and that we, criminals outside the law, have been wrong."

Vyshinsky, satisfied, began the interrogation with questions laced with sarcasm, and each one of Yagoda's responses caused a stir or a cry of indignation in the room. Jacques Mornard, still capable of being surprised before certain Russian attitudes, noticed the theatricality emanating from those figures, from their words, their outfits, their gestures, and even from the scenery: their actions reminded him of certain puppet and marionette tableaus that he had enjoyed in the South of France, those mise-en-scènes in which, with necessary haughtiness, the inexhaustible tales of Robert the Devil, Roland, and the Knights of the Round Table were told.

Yagoda admitted to having conspired to carry out a coup d'état, in collusion with the German, English, and Japanese secret services; he admitted his participation in the Trotskyist plot to make an attempt on Stalin's life, in some poisonings, and in the murder of Maxim Gorky; he accepted having planned a restoration of the bourgeoisie in Russia and, carrying out one of Trotsky's plans, of having committed an excess of repressive operations aimed at destabilizing the country. But when Vyshinsky, more than happy over what he had reaped, asked him about his role in the murder of Max, son of Gorky, Yagoda didn't answer. Vyshinsky demanded a response, but the prisoner maintained his silence. The tension became thick and the prosecutor's voice resonated between the columns when he yelled at the prisoner to confess his role in Max's murder. From his chair, tensely, Jacques noticed that Yagoda's hands were trembling in an uncontrollable way when, looking at the court, in a barely audible voice, he denied having participated in the murder of Gorky's son and added, in a pleading tone:

"I want to confess that I lied during the proceedings. I haven't committed any of the crimes I am accused of and that I admitted to. I ask you, Comrade Prosecutor, not to interrogate me about the motives for my lie. I was always loyal to the Soviet Union, to the party, and to Comrade Stalin, and as a Communist, I can't incriminate myself in crimes I didn't commit."

Jacques Mornard understood that something strange was happening. Vyshinsky's face, those of the judges, the expressions around the courtroom and even of the accused, revealed a bewilderment that, from the public area, had turned into a wasp's nest of voices revealing disbelief, surprise, and indignation, when the principal judge's voice rose above the cacophony and declared a recess until the afternoon.

"How interesting!" Grigoriev said to him, excited. "Let's go and eat. I promise that this afternoon you're going to see something you will never forget."

When they returned, Jacques Mornard saw entering the Hall of Columns a Yagoda who appeared to have aged ten years in just five hours. When the judge demanded it of him, the accused rose with difficulty. He looked like a corpse.

"Does the accused maintain this morning's declaration?" the judge wanted to know, and Yagoda shook his head in the negative.

"I recognize my guilt for everything of which I am accused," he said, and made a long pause until the applause, whistles, and cries of "Death to the treacherous dog" from many of the spectators were silenced by the judge's gavel. "I don't think it's necessary to repeat the list of my crimes and I don't expect to tone down the seriousness of my crimes. But since I know that Soviet laws know no revenge, I ask for forgiveness. I address you, my judges; you, from the Cheka; you, Comrade Stalin, to say: Forgive me!"

"No, there will be no forgiveness for you!" Vyshinsky yelled at that moment, unable to hide his satisfaction and his hate. "You will die like a dog! You all deserve to die like dogs!"

Grigoriev nudged a pale-faced Jacques with his elbow and motioned with his head, standing up.

"There's nothing else to see anymore," he said to him, leaving the hall.

Jacques Mornard couldn't help feeling confused. It took great effort to find any reasoning behind Yagoda's disparate actions. Out on the street, Grigoriev asked the chauffeur driving them around the city to take them directly to the safe house. When they got out, he bid goodbye to the chauffeur with the order to come pick them up in a couple of hours. Instead of going up the stairs, Grigoriev motioned to Jacques and they went out to the building's courtyard, through which they accessed a street by which, always in silence, they walked toward the crowded Three Stations Square. Without stopping, Grigoriev made his way to Leningradsky Station. Nearly elbowing their way through, they entered the only place serving alcoholic beverages and the adviser asked for two pints of beer.

"What did you make of what you saw?"

Jacques Mornard immediately knew that the question had too many layers and that his response could be of value to his future.

"Do you want the truth?"

"I expect the truth," the other man said, and served himself a second glass, which he filled with a stream of the vodka he carried in his pocket.

"Yagoda didn't confess of his own volition. Everything sounded like a play."

Grigoriev looked at him, pensive, drank a big sip of the *yorsh*, and, his eyes fixed on Jacques Mornard's, poured more than half of the *chekushka* of vodka into his pitcher and drank it.

"Yagoda knows all the methods in existence to make someone confess. He invented many of them and I can assure you that he was very creative. Of course, some were already applied to him before the trial. Didn't you notice how his teeth moved? Who knows who that set of teeth belonged to . . . But that wretch, in his delirium, believed he could resist . . . Three days ago, Krestinsky thought the same thing and ended up confessing everything . . . Yezhov didn't even need three hours to convince Yagoda that it's not possible to resist if one is guilty. Only absolute innocence can save you, and even then, many innocents are capable of confessing that they crucified Christ as long as you leave them alone and kill them as soon as possible."

"Are you telling me that Yagoda is guilty of everything the prosecutor says?"

"I don't know about everything, or almost everything, or just a part, but he's guilty. And that made him weak. Despite that weakness, he fought; you can't deny his determination. Today has been a good day for you, Jacques. I wanted to show you how a man grovels, but you've had the privilege of seeing how he collapses and sinks. I hope you've learned the lesson: no one resists. Not even Yagoda. Neither will Yezhov when his turn comes."

Jacques Mornard drank almost his entire pint of beer in one gulp. He felt his lungs congest, threatening to suffocate him, until his nasal passages snorted like a locomotive starting up; he still had to wait a few seconds to recover his breath. That lesson might have been extremely arduous, but he at least learned that ethyl alcohol vapor had the advantage of removing the stench of the atmosphere from his nose.

"Are you going to tell me now what happened with Andreu Nin?" he asked when he was at last able to speak.

Grigoriev smiled while he shook his head.

"You're so stubborn . . . What do you want me to say? That Catalan was so crazy that he didn't confess. He pissed off everyone and—"

"I knew all along he was not going to confess," he said, and moved the pitcher of beer to Grigoriev. His mentor dropped a stream of vodka into it. "Not even if you'd drowned him in vodka . . ."

15

Throughout the last week of November and the month of December 1977, I had six meetings, all arranged beforehand, with the man who loved dogs. The winter, an indecisive one, would dissolve toward the end of the year in two or three cold fronts that exhausted themselves in their transit through the Gulf of Mexico, bringing only a few drizzles to the island that were incapable of altering the thermometers and some murky waves that broke the peacefulness of the sea in front of which we held our conversations. Captivated by the man's words, I would run from my job to the beach barely thinking about anything but our next agreed encounter. Listening to and trying to digest that story, in which nearly all the incidents constituted revelations of a buried reality, of a truth that wasn't even imagined by me or by the people I knew, had turned into an obsession. What I was discovering as I listened, added to that which I had started to read, deeply disturbed me, while the flame of a visceral fear devoured me, without being able, despite everything, to burn away desire to know.

Ever since the man began to paint the journey of his friend Ramón Mercader, starting with his childhood and youth in Barcelona, the doors began to open for me to a universe of whose existence until then I'd had only vague and orthodox notions, with categorical distinctions between the good and the bad but whose inner workings I didn't know: professions of a sincere and all-consuming faith mixed with intrigue, dirty games, lies always believed as truth, and never-suspected truths that highlighted my innocence and ignorance with dazzling flashes. As López moved through his story, on several occasions I was on the verge of refuting him, of yelling at him that that couldn't be, but I always held back and limited myself to asking some question when I felt things went beyond my credulity or understanding, and I kept listening to an account that melted away many of my beliefs and reorganized some of the other notions that they had instilled in me.

After the second conversation, I drew the insidious conclusion that something very important didn't click in the story of the man who loved dogs. Although I still hadn't completely developed the cosmic mistrust that I would acquire precisely as a consequence of those meetings (that vocation for suspicion that would bother Raquelita and my friends so much, since it led me to react in an almost mechanical way and to qualify any story capable of minimally challenging plausibility as impossible, as sheer lies), as I listened there was a disquieting but ubiquitous lack of logic that, to begin with, would make me wonder whether some of the episodes of Ramón's history weren't being manipulated by his friend and storyteller Jaime López. But only at the end of the third conversation, already in the middle of December, did I discern with certain clarity the crack through which the logic was escaping: How was it possible for López to have such precise information about his friend's life and feelings? No matter how explicit or detailed Ramón was during the conversations held in Moscow over ten years before, when they met after such a long time without seeing each other and the deceived Ramón Mercader opened all the channels to the most incredible corners of his life to his old comrade Jaime López, the knowledge displayed by the narrator seemed undoubtedly exaggerated and could only be due to two reasons. The first possibility had been cooking in my mind since our initial exchange: López was an out-and-out fabulist who could be coloring the story with brushstrokes from his own palate; the second struck me like a bolt of lightning as I was traveling on the bus to Havana after our third meeting, and it almost drove me to madness: Was Jaime López Ramón Mercader himself? Could that phantasmagoric being relegated to a stormy and lost corner of history, that faceless protagonist of a past plagued by horrors, still exist? Although the only possible responses to those questions was a resounding no for each, the seed of doubt had fallen on fertile ground and would remain there because a persistent suspicion prevented me from cultivating it: If the man who loved dogs was Ramón Mercader, what the hell was he doing in Cuba? Why in the devil was he telling *me* his story? What was all that bullshit about Jaime López and his mystery?

One of the considerations that had encouraged my doubts about Jaime López's role in that story arose from the fact that at the time I was listening to him I had some clues that I did not have when I first met him. It was after the second conversation, knowing already where the story was leading, that I decided to go and see my friend Dany in the offices of the publishing house where he had started to work as a "specialist in promotion and distribution." Although it wasn't the job Dany had dreamed of, he had accepted it with the hope that, once his two years of social service were over, a coveted editor's position would become available, and he would have better chances of filling it if he positioned himself in the publishing house's administrative department.

Since Daniel Fonseca has already appeared and will continue to appear at various points of this story, I should say something about this friend who had been, in a way, my only literary pupil, if I can call him that. Dany had enrolled in the literature program at the university just when I was doing my last year in journalism. Recommended by a cousin of mine who was his neighbor, one day he showed up at my house in Víbora Park with the always dangerous intention of borrowing some of the books he needed for his classes. Against all logic, I lent them to him, and in order to underline that in the future everything would be as it should be, he pushed the limits of logic even further by returning them to me when his exams were over. Thus his visits started, generally on Saturday afternoons, and we went from textbooks to novels that I suggested to him and with which he began to fill his encyclopedia of ignorance. Around that time Dany listened to me and looked at me like I was a goddamned guru, only because he was an absolute ignoramus, although intelligent, and I was a guy who was five years older, several miles of reading ahead of him, and above all, with a book of stories already published. Neither Dany nor I could have dreamed then that one day that voracious animal, who, before enrolling for a degree in the arts, had spent every hour of his life playing baseball, would end up being a writer—what's more, a wise and noteworthy writer, which is equal to being something more than acceptable and several levels below brilliant—who at times seemed gifted with a greater literary ability than shown in his published books.

Despite the fact that, by the time of my conversations with López, Dany and I barely saw each other, he didn't find it strange to see me show up at the large house in Vedado where the publishing house was located. But he was shocked by the reason that brought me there: I needed to find a biography of Trotsky, and among the people I knew, he was the one who seemed most likely to have one. Before Dany could get over his surprise at my unusual request, I explained to him that at the National Library and the Central at the university, there were only some books about Trotsky published by the Progress publishing house, in Moscow, in which the authors devoted themselves to devaluing each act, each thought, even each gesture, the man had made in his life and even in death—the false prophet, the renegade, the enemy of the people, they called him, and it was always several authors, as if one alone couldn't handle the task of so many accusations—and I was interested in finding something that wasn't such flagrant propaganda, so blatant that it forced me to question its accuracy. And if anyone would have the material I needed to read, it was the uncle of Dany's wife Elisa, an old journalist and militant Communist, very active in the country since the 1940s, who in the convulsive times of the sixties had even spent several weeks in prison, with a group of Trotsky sympathizers with whom he maintained personal and, they said, even philosophical relationships.

Now it's important to remind you that this was in 1977, at the apogee of Soviet imperial grandeur and at the height of its philosophical and propagandistic inflexibility, and that we lived in a country that had accepted its economic model and its very orthodox political orthodoxy. With those important clarifications, you'll have the more exact context of the dreadful drought of reading materials, information, and even ways of thinking when it came to subjects such as this one, that were particularly sensitive for our beloved Soviet brothers. So you will imagine the terror caused by the mere mention of anything critical—and Trotsky was political criticism personified, ideological evil multiplied to the nth degree. Due to all of this, you'll understand Daniel's response:

"What the fuck are you talking about?" He leaped up at learning my intentions and immediately added, in a lower voice and with a look of clinical concern, "Have you gone crazy, my friend? Are you drinking again? What the hell is wrong with you?"

In those years, almost no one on the island, at least that I knew of, had the least acknowledged interest in Trotsky or Trotskyism, among other reasons because that interest—if it came out or surfaced in someone who was crazy enough to reveal it—could not lead to anything more than complications of all kinds. Lots of complications. If listening to certain kinds of Western music, believing in any kind of god, practicing yoga, reading certain novels considered to be ideologically damaging, or writing a shitty story about some poor guy who felt afraid could represent a stigma and even involve punishment, getting into Trotskyism would have been like tying a rope around your own neck, especially for people who moved in the world of culture, teaching, and the social sciences. (I would later learn that some Uruguayan and Chilean refugees who lived on the island around that time dared to talk about the subject with a certain knowledge, although even they, subject to the surrounding pressure, did so in whispers.) Hence my friend's nearly violent reaction.

"Don't be ridiculous, Dany," I answered when he started to calm down. "I'm not going to become a Trotskyist or any shit like that. What I need is to know . . . k-n-o-w, you get it? Or is it also forbidden *to know*?"

"But you already *know* that Trotsky is fire!"

"That's my problem. Get me some book that Elisa's relative must have and don't fuck around. I'm not going to tell anyone where I got it from . . ."

Despite his protests, I had touched a fiber of Dany's intellectual curiosity: faster than I expected (given the not-very-close relationship he maintained with the old former Trotskyist), he introduced me to an author and a biography that I had never heard of: Isaac Deutscher, and his trilogy about "the prophet" unarmed, armed, and outcast, in editions published in Mexico in the late 1960s. The morning on which he handed over the three volumes, after forcing me to make every conceivable promise that I would return the books as soon as possible, I went by my workplace and asked for the rest of the month as vacation. Besides the trips to the beach, what I remember best about those days was the consuming intensity with which I read that voluminous biography of the revolutionary named Leon Bronstein and the subsequent proof of my monumental ignorance of the historical truths (truths?) of the times and events amid which that man had lived, events and times so Russian and so far-off, starting with the October Revolution (I've never understood very well what happened in Petrograd that seventh of November, which was really October 25, and how the Winter Palace that no one wanted to defend in the end was taken and that automatically marked the triumph of the revolution and handed power over to the Bolsheviks) and followed, among other things, by some also very strange dynastic battles between revolutionaries in which only Stalin seemed willing to take power and by some nearly silenced proceedings in Moscow (that seemed never, ever to have existed to us) in which the prisoners were their worst prosecutors. At the end of that parade of manifestations of the "Russian soul" (if we don't understand something about the Russians, it always seems to be because of their souls) was the corroboration of the old leader's assassination, something that had disappeared in the Soviet books devoted to him, since Trotsky (perhaps because he was Ukrainian and not Russian) seemed rather to have died of a cold or, better yet, been consumed one day by a trembling fit, as if he were a character in an Emilio Salgari novel.

Thanks to that biography, the person who traveled to the beach from the third meeting onward was just beginning to be someone capable of processing elements of that story through a different lens. Now my ears insisted on interpreting information that, with summary knowledge of the events and their actors, I intended to place on a board whose coordinates were becoming familiar.

A few days after being bit by the bizarre but logical suspicion that López may not be López and that Mercader may not be dead, I arrived at the beach ready to try to force the man to confess the truth about his identity—if that truth existed, something of which I was not sure. I cautiously waited for the right moment to voice my doubts and I found the occasion when López was talking about the commotion the controversial Molotov-Ribbentrop pact caused in Ramón and his mother, Caridad del Río.

"You know what?" I asked without looking at him. "Of everything you've told me, there's something I can't believe."

López lit one of his cigarettes with a gas lighter. Before his silence I continued:

"No one could know this much about another person's life. No matter how much the person told you. It's impossible."

López was smoking unhurriedly, and I got the impression that he hadn't heard my words. Later I would understand that a guy like me would barely have been able to move that rock: the man was a specialist in answering only what he wanted to, and his strategy was to take the frying pan out of my hands, grip the handle, and beat me over the head with it.

"What are you thinking? That what I've been telling you is a lie?" He took his glasses off for a few moments, held them up to the light, then wet them with his tongue to clean off the salt spray that had clung to them.

"I don't know," I said, and hesitated. His voice had taken on a tone capable of freezing my impulses, and that's why I chose my words very carefully: "How is it possible that you know so much about Ramón? Isn't it too much of a coincidence that Caridad and your mother, both of them, were born in Cuba? I'm thinking that—"

"That I'm Ramón's brother? Or that I was his boss?"

I quickly weighed those possibilities without realizing that, with them, the man did nothing more than make me weaken in my convictions. But he didn't leave me too much time to think, since he immediately cut to the chase.

"Or perhaps you think I am Ramón?" he asked.

I looked at him in silence. In the previous weeks the man who loved dogs had been noticeably losing weight, his skin had become much more opaque, greenish, and he frequently suffered from a sore throat and was overcome by coughing fits that he managed to control with sips of water sweetened by honey from a bottle that now always accompanied him. But at that moment there was a burning intensity in his eyes, and I have to admit, it scared me.

"Ramón is dead and buried, kid. And the worst thing is that he has turned into a ghost. If you look in all the cemeteries in the Soviet Union, you won't ever find his grave. I myself don't even know the name under which he was buried . . . I already told you: among the things Ramón gave to the cause were his name and his freedom to make decisions . . . Besides, if I'm telling you all of this, why would I deceive you about the rest of it? What does it matter who I am? Further still: What would change if I were Ramón?"

The answers came to my mind: it matters because what you're telling me is the History of Deception and everything would change if you were Ramón, since nobody (at least I thought) would have wanted to be Ramón Mercader. Because Ramón caused disgust and engendered fear . . . But it goes without saying that I didn't dare to say these things.

"I know what you're thinking, and it doesn't surprise me," the man said, and I felt a new current of fear. "This is a repulsive story that in and of itself devalues millions of speeches made over the course of sixty years . . . And it's also true that many people ended up finding Ramón repugnant."

239

He paused, although he remained immobile. "But try to understand it, dammit, even if you can't justify it. Ramón is a man from another era, from a really fucked-up time, when even doubting wasn't allowed. When he told me his story, I placed it in his world and in his time, and then I understood it. Although, to be clear, don't ever feel pity for him, because Ramón hated that sentiment."

"If you never saw his grave or went to his burial, how are you so sure that Ramón is dead?" I asked, throwing out my last chance for perseverance, despite the fact that I already knew I'd been defeated by López's argument.

"I know that he is dead because I saw him several weeks before he died, when he had already been declared terminally ill . . . ," he said and smiled, with visible sadness. "Look, for your peace of mind, I'm going to give you a reason you won't be able to deny: Do you think Ramón, after promising that he would remain silent for the rest of his life, and after having maintained that commitment against every tide, would tell his story to the first . . . to the first person he met? If I were Ramón, do you think I would have risked doing it? And besides, for what?"

In a second, I counted ten things López could have called me (from the Cuban *comemierda*—shit eater—and *sapingo*—bullshitter—to the Spanish *gilipollas*—asshole, which he himself had used on occasion), and I thought of so many other reasons to refute López's last questions (a man who, according to himself, was dying: What could he be afraid of? The only affirmative response would imply that fear is also transmitted, like an inheritance, and includes the fate of those same children who, perhaps to protect them, López, or Mercader—if in fact that man was Ramón Mercader—had decided not to tell the story). But I realized that if I wanted to continue listening, my only option was to believe him; in fact, at that instant, I did believe him. I forced myself to forget or at least put off my doubts until I somehow had the complete certainty that López was López and that Mercader was a ghost without a grave. Or the opposite. But how in the hell was I going to arrive at any of those certainties if I didn't even know whether a man named Ramón Mercader del Río had existed?

The story's interruption cut the man who loved dogs' narrative momentum, and that afternoon he bid me farewell long before the sun set. Although we agreed to meet on Monday, I remained awhile on the sand, fearing that the relationship may have fallen apart due to my suspicions. And if that was the case, I would be left without knowing how the events took place that were to seal the absolute devotion of Ramón Mercader.

In any event, I spent that weekend devoted to the marathon of reading the last volume of Deutscher's biography, *The Prophet Outcast*, to try to immerse myself in the time in which López's story was taking place. I remember that when the theatrical figure of Jacques Mornard appeared in the book's final pages I felt my heart leap in my chest, as if the murderer had entered my room. My brain then began to play tricks on me: the image of Mornard that came to mind was that of López, with his heavy tortoiseshell glasses. I knew that didn't make sense, since between the young and handsome Mornard and the sallow and, according to him, moribund López, the distance was great. But my imagination insisted on juxtaposing the real and live visage of the owner of the borzois with the elusive body of the Belgian who showed up at the fortress in Coyoacán with the mission of killing the man who, alongside Lenin, had achieved the unthinkable: that the Bolsheviks seized power in 1917, and, further still, held on to it afterward by overpowering imperial armies and internal enemies.

Between the pages of the biography's final volume, I found three newspaper clippings that betrayed the owner of the book's interest in the relationship between Trotsky and his assassin. One was from the Cuban daily *Información* where, under a large headline, the very owner of the book gave news of the attack suffered by Trotsky on August 20, 1940, and the seriousness of the state he was in at the time the paper was going to print (to a Communist in 1940, that would have seemed like a pro-Trotskyist comment, only because the author didn't voice his opinion on the event); the second one must have come from a magazine and contained a commentary about the parodies of Trotsky's murder that Guillermo Cabrera Infante had included in his book *Three Trapped Tigers* (never published in Cuba and, as such, almost unfindable for us); and the last one, a longish undated column with no reference, I found the most revealing, since it spoke of the presence of Ramón Mercader in Moscow after leaving the Mexican jail where he'd served his sentence. The author of the column relayed that a person very close to Mercader—had López been guilty of another breach of trust?—had told him that, since the day of the attack, the assassin carried in his ears the sound of his victim's cry of pain.

It was the following Monday, December 22, when I had, without yet knowing it, what would be my last conversation with the man who loved dogs. I remember that afternoon perfectly, as never since López started to tell me the story of Ramón had I felt subject to a pressure that until then I had managed to skirt: For my own good, I asked myself a thousand times, shouldn't I tell someone official what was happening to me with that Jaime López who insisted on telling *me* a story so terrifying and politically compromising? The fear that was already engulfing me, reinforced by what I read about Trotsky's end, was a more sordid, much crueler feeling than I even confessed to myself at that moment, as in reality it had not so much to do with the story of horror and betrayal that I was listening to than with the more than probable fact that it would be known that I had spoken to that strange man for several days without deciding to "ask for advice," as they used to say, which was regarded as my duty. But the very idea of looking for the "*compañero* who minded" at the information center that edited the veterinary magazine (everyone called him that—"the *compañero* who minded"—and everyone knew who he was, since it seems important that we should *all* know of his diffuse but omnipresent existence) and telling him about a conversation that, no matter who López was, I had promised not to talk about, seemed so degrading to myself that I rebelled at the thought of it. I decided at that moment to accept the consequences (was there a less important and ambitious job than mine? Yes, of course, they could, for example, send me back to Baracoa), and for years I covered up that story with a wall of silence, and not even Raquelita knew—she still doesn't know today, and besides, she would not give a shit to know—what Jaime López told me.

On that afternoon of my runaway fears, having barely arrived at the beach, López confessed that he felt terribly sad: Dax had started to have problems in moving ("He gets dizzy, like me," he said) and the day that he would have to put him down was growing imminent.

"I know you're not a veterinarian and I shouldn't ask this of you," he said to me without looking at me, "but if you help me, I think it will be easier . . ."

"I would like to help you, but I really don't know how to do it, nor can I," I said to him, watching the two dogs run on the sand. Dax, it was clear, had lost the elegance of his trot and was stumbling.

"I don't know how I'm going to deal with this . . ." The man was talking to himself more than with me, his voice on the verge of breaking. "I want to be sure he doesn't suffer . . ."

The evidence of an approaching death and the revelation of those feelings placated my doubts about López's identity and, particularly, made me decide to face, in silence, any consequences that could come from my decision, an undoubtedly ideologically questionable one. Death has that capacity. It is so definitive and irreversible that it barely leaves any room for other fears. Even a man like the one I had in front of me that afternoon—a connoisseur of everything about death, according to what he had told me—was frozen before it; he was shaken up in its presence, even when it involved only the death of a dog.

After drinking coffee, smoking a cigarette, and suffering a coughing fit, López at last started on the story of Ramón Mercader, and he relayed to me the way in which his friend had definitively become a part of history. I listened to him, with my judgment lost, beyond any surprise, and even with a certain delight when the story agreed with the information obtained from my recent reading. At one moment I also discovered that a bothersome and enigmatic mixture of disdain and compassion was taking possession of me—yes, *compassion*, and I've never had any doubts regarding the word or what it denotes—disdain and compassion for that Mornard-Jacson-Mercader willing to carry out what he had assumed as a duty and, above all, as a historic necessity demanded by the future of humanity.

López seemed to be on the edge of exhaustion when he reached the story's climax. It had been dark for a while and I could barely see his face, but I clung to his words, excited by what I was hearing.

"What remains of the story is your New Year's gift," he said at that moment, and he seemed emotional and as though he was feeling a great sense of relief. I still close my eyes today and I can see him in those final minutes of his narration: López had spoken with a whistle in his voice and his left hand over the bandage that always covered his right hand. "My wife is the strangest Communist I know. Even in Moscow she insisted on celebrating Christmas Eve and Christmas Day. To her they're sacred, and never better said . . . And she won't want to let me go this week, so it will be difficult for me to come until after the New Year. I have to please her."

"What should we do, then?" I was feeling anxious and frustrated. An accumulation of terrible evidence and burning questions was suffocating me, but I knew it was best not to touch on them in order to avoid their muddying my relationship with the man, since I still had to go over a decisive phase in the life of Ramón Mercader and, due to everything I had heard, I was anxious to know about it. "Do you want me to call you on the phone?"

He responded immediately:

"No. We'll see each other January eighth. Can you?"

"I think so."

243

"I'll come on the eighth. If I don't see you, I'll come back on the ninth."

"Uh-huh," I said, accepting in the absence of any alternative. "What about Dax?"

"I can't do it now," López said to me, and held out his hand so I could help him stand up. "Careful, my arms hurt a lot . . . Dax is strong, he'll hang on. I'm going to wait as long as I can, until the beginning of the year. If I had a friend who would help me . . ."

"Poor Dax," I said when I saw where the conversation was headed and upon confirming that the borzois were getting closer, wanting to leave already, for their dinnertime had come and gone.

López held out his bandaged hand to me. Without a thought, I smiled at him and shook it. Later, as I kneeled down to pick up the bag with the thermos and give it to him, I dared to voice one of the questions that had been tormenting me:

"I read in a newspaper that Ramón heard Trotsky's cries for the rest of his life. Did he talk about that cry?"

López coughed and ran his bandaged hand over his face. I would have liked for there to have been more light so I could see his eyes.

"He still heard it when he told me the story, about ten years ago," he said to me, and began to walk away. "I think he heard it until the end . . . Have a merry Christmas."

"*Lo propio*," I managed to say, flooded by emotion, and I immediately realized that it had been a long time since I had pronounced or heard those words that, in Cuba, were only used as a formula to return Christmas greetings, that holiday banished years ago by the scientifically atheistic island that was too needy of each workday to allow itself the luxury of wasting days off.

López made his way across the sand, compacted by the previous day's rain. Alongside him walked Ix and Dax at a slow pace. The darkness didn't allow me to see the tall, thin black man, but I knew he was still there, between the casuarinas, waiting patiently. López approached the trees and his figure went blending into the night until he disappeared. As if he had never existed, I thought.

PART TWO

PART TWO

16

What feelings went through him when he saw the silhouette of the most absolute question rising above the line of the horizon? He observed that sea whose scintillating transparency could damage one's pupils and surely thought that, in contrast to Hernán Cortés, thrown upon that unknown land in search of power and glory, he, if anything, could aspire to find there a point of support for the final days of his existence and the grotesque possibility of vindicating a past in which he had already reached and exhausted his quota of power and glory, of hope and fury.

That nightmarish crossing had lasted twenty days. Ever since they had boarded the *Ruth* and its horns announced the call for departure along the rugged Norwegian coast, that tanker that regurgitated the unhealthy vapors of petroleum from its cisterns had turned into a physical extension of the imprisonment they suffered in the desolate fjord. Despite the fact that Lev Davidovich, Natalia, and the police escorts were the only passengers on the vessel, the inevitable Jonas Lie and his men made sure to keep the deportees isolated, preventing any radio communication and keeping watch on them even when they were seated at the table of Captain Hagbert Wagge, who was so proud to have a piece of history on board. Confined in the commander's cabin, Lev Davidovich and Natalia spent the days reading the few books about Mexico they had obtained, thanks to Konrad Knudsen, trying to make out what was waiting for them in that violent and exalted New World, where the price of life could be a simple look interpreted the wrong way and where, as far as they knew, no one was waiting for them.

When the coast took on all its clarity, his fears rose to the surface and Lev Davidovich made a final demand of Lie: he would only leave the oil tanker if someone he could trust came to meet him. Who? he was thinking, when Jonas Lie gave him the surprising reply that they were going to honor this request, and then he also concentrated on observing the coast.

As the boat approached the port of Tampico, the restless crowds dotted with the blue uniforms of the Mexican police became visible. Although it had been a long time since Lev Davidovich had overcome his fear of death, exultant throngs always forced him to remember those that had surrounded Lenin in August 1918 and from which the pistol of Fanny Kaplan had emerged. But a wave of relief washed over his apprehensions when he discovered, at one end of the jetty, Max Shachtman's features, George Novack's good-looking face, and the radiant levity of a woman who could be none other than the painter Frida Kahlo, Diego Rivera's lover.

As soon as they docked, the Trotskys fell into a whirlwind of rejoicing. Several friends of Frida and Diego's, in addition to the North American followers who had come with Shachtman and Novack, enveloped them in a wave of hugs and congratulations that achieved the miracle of making tears run down Natalia Sedova's face. Taken to a hotel in the city where a welcome dinner had been organized in their honor, the couple listened to the jumble of information that had been kept from them by Jonas Lie, undoubtedly because of the nature of the news: General Lázaro Cárdenas had not only granted Lev Davidovich indefinite asylum but also considered him his personal guest and, with this welcome message, was sending the presidential train to take them to the capital. At the same time Rivera, who excused himself for not having been able to go to Tampico, offered them, also indefinitely, a room in the Casa Azul, the building he inhabited with Frida in the capital neighborhood of Coyoacán.

The French wines and the strong Mexican tequila aided Lev Davidovich and Natalia in the gastronomical jump from the *mole poblano* to the *puntas de filete a la tampiqueña*, from the fish *a la veracruzana* to the bumpy consistency of the tortillas, colored and enriched with chicken, guacamole, peppers, jitomates, refried beans, onions, and cola-roasted pork, all of it sprinkled with the fiery chili that demanded another glass of wine or a shot of tequila capable of putting out the fire and clearing the way for a taste of those fruits (mango, pineapple, sapodilla, soursop, and guava), pulpy and sweet, indispensable to topping off the party for European palates overpowered by the textures, smells, consistencies, and flavors that were alien to them. Overwhelmed by that banquet of the senses, Lev Davidovich discovered how his preoccupations dissolved and the tension gave way to an invasive tropical voluptuousness that wrapped him in a beneficial tenderness which, so he wrote, his exhausted body and mind greedily received.

Following their siesta, they resolved to go for a drive with Frida, Shachtman, Novack, and Octavio Fernández, the comrade who had worked the hardest to get them asylum. Nonetheless, the guests soon returned to reality when they saw that the car was placed in a convoy headed by a convertible jeep in which members of the presidential guard, rifles in hand, were traveling. Lev Davidovich thought that not even in paradise would they be completely free.

On the train, Frida brought him up-to-date on the reactions caused by his arrival. As could be expected, General Cárdenas's decision had been an act of defiant independence, since it had been taken at a moment of great political tensions, right in the middle of an agrarian reform process and with oil nationalization on his agenda. The decision to accept him—the only and understandable condition of which was that the Exile abstain from participating in local political matters—had been an act of sovereignty through which the president expressed his loyalty to his own political ideas more than his sympathy for those of the political refugee. But that decision had turned Cárdenas into the object of a variety of accusations that went from cries of traitor to the Mexican Revolution to fascist ally (uttered by the Communists and the leaders of the Confederation of Workers, the president's traditional supporters), even of "red anarchist under Trotsky's orders" (put forward by a bourgeoisie for whom Trotsky and Stalin meant the same thing and for whom the arrival of the former confirmed the ascendance of "the Russians" over the president).

An exultant Diego Rivera was waiting for them in a small station close to Mexico City, and from there—accompanied by other policemen and many friends armed with bottles of cognac and whiskey—they took the path toward that strange residence painted telluric blue.

Lev Davidovich's first encounter with Rivera's work had been in Paris, during the years of the Great War, when the echoes of the Mexican Revolution reached Europe and, with them, the works of its revolutionary painters. Later, he had closely followed the cultural phenomenon of muralism, of which he even received news during the days of his exile in Alma-Ata, when Andreu Nin sent him a beautiful book about Rivera's painting that perished in the fire at Prinkipo. In contrast, he had just a superficial notion of Frida's tormented and symbolic work, but from the moment he found himself surrounded by her paintings, he discovered that his sensibility communicated much better with the woman's anguished art than with Rivera's explosive monumentality.

Their hosts had prepared for them the former room of Cristina Kahlo, Frida's sister. When Rivera had decided to receive them, he bought the young woman a dwelling close to the Casa Azul, by which he announced to the Trotskys that they could use the bedroom to their liking. The painters' friendliness and the critical state of their finances forced Lev Davidovich to accept what would be, he thought, just a temporary accommodation.

La Casa Azul quickly took on the aspect of a besieged fortress. Several windows had to be covered and some of the walls reinforced, and as soon as the exiled couple arrived, guards started turns of duty. The inside of the home was entrusted to young Trotskyist Americans, while the outside was handled by the local police. Nonetheless, just barely settled in, Lev Davidovich began to feel himself surrounded by an optimism he thought he had already lost, although he forced himself, more for the exhausted Natalia than for himself, to take a break before launching himself back into the struggle that called out to him.

As it had done so many times in his life, politics shook him and reminded him that not even the possibility of the briefest repose had been given to Prometheus and those who dared to be near his rock. And that was the fate that would pursue him to the last day of his life.

The radios and newspapers began to announce that the criminal court put together in Moscow's House of the Trade Unions was again opening its doors to dramatize a new episode of the Stalinist farce. At first, the number and names of those on trial was unknown, until it was specified that there were thirteen, headed by Radek, who, with his resounding capitulation, had thought himself safe from Stalin's rage. Also summoned were the redheaded Piatakov, Muralov, Sokolnikov, and Serebriakov, although it was again Lev Sedov and Lev Davidovich who were the main defendants, in absentia.

Ever since the new proceedings were initiated on January 23, 1937, Lev Davidovich had closed himself up with the radio to try to unearth the logic of that absurdity in which the accused seemed to compete with confessions that were more and more humiliating and unhinged, which were then added to the conspiracies to overthrow the system or assassinate Stalin, the existence of industrial sabotage plans, of massive poisoning of workers and peasants, and even the signing of a secret pact between Hitler, Hirohito, and Trotsky to tear apart the USSR. The saboteurs took on their shoulders all economic failures, hunger, and even railway and industrial accidents with which they had attacked the country and its heroic workers and betrayed the Leader's trust. One of the accusations in the proceedings placed one of the prisoners in Paris, receiving orders from Trotsky at the moment he was in Barbizon without permission to visit the capital. But the cornerstone of the aborted conspiracy rested on the confession of Piatakov, who declared he had traveled from Berlin to Oslo in 1935 to attend a counterrevolutionary summit with the renegade Trotsky.

Forced to explain their responsibility in that matter, the pusillanimous Norwegian government issued a denial with proof that Piatakov's presumed plane, coming from Germany, had never landed in Norway in the places or on the dates declared by the prosecutor and accepted by the accused. But it was already known that the angry curses by the former Menshevik Andrei Vyshinsky against the degenerate, rabid, stinking dogs for whom he was asking the death penalty were going to overcome any obstacle or evidence from obstinate reality ... Lev Davidovich knew, nonetheless, that those unsustainable proceedings hid some objective that went beyond the need to repair the contradictions of the previous proceedings and eliminate another group of old Bolsheviks: something of that goal was becoming clear to him as the names of Bukharin and his companions in the faded opposition of the right were repeated. It was darker and more difficult for him to understand, in contrast, the mention of certain Red Army officers, supposedly linked as well to the Trotskyist conspiracy, treason, and sabotage.

With that political earthquake, the calm of the Casa Azul disappeared. The Exile organized a press conference and, anticipating the foreseeable sentences, declared his purpose of refuting the accusations with undeniable proof. That declaration, of course, did not stop the court, and before Lev Davidovich could put together his testimony or obtain a single document of proof, the judges in Moscow issued sentences that carried the death penalty for almost all of the prisoners and the surprising sentence of ten years for the indefatigable Radek, who again saved his own skin, at a price known only to him and to Stalin—and only Stalin knew until when.

Overwhelmed by the news that so many old comrades in arms were going to be executed, Lev Davidovich brandished the only weapon he had at his disposal and again asked Stalin to extradite him and put him on trial. But as he expected, Moscow remained silent and executed the sentenced men with its habitual speed and efficiency. Then he threw the next stone and asked that an international investigative committee be created and repeated his willingness to appear before a Terrorism Commission of the League of Nations and to hand himself over to the Soviet authorities if any of those bodies proved a single one of the accusations. But again the world, fearful and blackmailed, was silent. Convinced that he was playing his last card, the Exile decided to organize a counterproceeding himself where he would denounce the falsity of the charges against him and, at the same time, would turn himself into the accuser of Stalin's henchmen.

Deep down inside, Lev Davidovich knew that the counterproceeding, if anything, would just scratch the surface, but he threw himself into it with the faith and desperation of a shipwrecked man. For several nights he worked on the idea and had long talks with Rivera, Shachtman, Novack, Natalia, and the recently arrived Jean van Heijenoort, while Frida Kahlo came and went like a restless shadow. Covered with ponchos, watching how Rivera's pantagruelian voraciousness made bottles of whiskey evaporate and how he devoured dishes of meats burning with chili, they tended to settle in around the orange tree that dominated the backyard of the Casa Azul and debated all the possibilities, although the main challenge lay in finding people with enough moral authority and political independence to legitimize if not legally, at least ethically, a counterproceeding that could perhaps still stir some consciences in the world.

It was the Americans who proposed inviting the nearly octogenarian professor John Dewey to preside over the court. Despite his prestige as a philosopher and pedagogue, to Lev Davidovich he seemed, nonetheless, a man too removed from the intricacies of Soviet politics. Meanwhile, Liova had begun to work in Paris, trying to obtain proof to refute the accusations. The materials Liova sent, in addition to the documents that Natalia, van Heijenoort, and Lev Davidovich had taken from the archives that they had brought to Mexico with them, implied an overwhelming amount of analysis.

Lev Davidovich was working feverishly and desperately and demanded from his collaborators, especially Liova, a superhuman effort. Overcome with anxiety, any carelessness enraged him and he began to label certain failures and delays from his son as negligence, without paying attention to calls to reason from Natalia, that were aimed at reminding him of the precarious conditions in which Liova lived in Paris, where he had even been forced to publish a statement in which he warned of the surveillance he was subject to by the Soviet secret police. In reality, what most bothered Lev Davidovich was receiving a letter in which his son commented that the enormous effort seemed pointless. Even if they managed to get the world's most prestigious people to testify to his father's innocence, the results wouldn't mean anything to those who thought him guilty, and it would bring very little to those who already knew he was innocent. On the other hand, Liova thought that the circulation of the pamphlet *Stalin's Crimes* that his father had started to write could be more effective than a trial requested by the accused himself. In a fit of anger, the former commissar of war called the young man a defeatist and even threatened to take away his position at the front of the Russian section of the opposition. Liova responded by asking for forgiveness for not always being able to rise to the heights demanded of him.

At that moment Lev Davidovich received news that gave him some hope that he and Natalia clung to tooth and nail. Thanks to a deserter from the former GPU who had seen himself threatened by the purges also initiated within the repressive apparatus, Liova had managed to learn that his brother, Sergei, had been arrested in Moscow during the witch hunt that preceded the last trial. The informant assured him that he had been sent to a forced labor camp in Siberia, accused of planning the poisoning of workers. In the midst of the prolonged lack of news in which the couple had assumed the worst, the news that the young man (doubtless, after being tortured) had been thrown into the hell on earth of a work camp fell on the Casa Azul like a blessing. Seriozha was alive! In the privacy of their room, they went through the painful motions of encouraging each other, and spoke for many nights about the survival strategies that the young man's logical mind would rely on and of the integrity he must have shown in order to not accept the confessions that in all certainty they had tried to make him sign in order to take him to trial. They avoided, however, the stabbing images of Sergei tormented by the cruelest systems and didn't dare to pose the most piercing questions: How had he withstood it without caving in? (What is caving in: confessing to something you haven't done, going mad, allowing yourself to die?) Where must the limits of Sergei's resistance have taken him? (Does the brain give in first or does the body?) Which of those imagined tortures had they applied to him or which of the unimaginable ones? (Was Seriozha one of the few who withstood and preferred to die rather than grovel?)

Lev Davidovich did not dare to reveal to Natalia, and less still to Liova, that pessimism was beginning to defeat him when he understood the limited reach of the counterproceeding for which they had worked so hard. Neither the trade union organizations nor the progressive intellectuals, controlled by Moscow's propaganda and money, had agreed to participate, and only national committees made up of professed anti-Communists and anti-Stalinists dared to offer their support, while men such as Romain Rolland proclaimed Stalin's integrity, certified the GPU's humanitarian methods to get confessions, and even denied that there was any intellectual repression in the USSR.

But Lev Davidovich knew that, even in those conditions, he should wage the battle. During the recent meeting of the Central Committee, with the bodies of the most recently executed still warm, the dark Nikolai Yezhov, turned into the dazzling star of the repression, had accused Bukharin and Rykov of training terrorist groups destined to assassinate the Great Leader, for whom they felt "a perverse hate." Anastas Mikoyan, another one of the red czar's hunting dogs, made a speech full of cruel comments about the two old Bolsheviks in which he claimed that the much trumpeted closeness between Bukharin and Lenin had never existed. At the end of the session—which, it was reported, Stalin had followed in silence and with his face in consternation over those "revelations"— Bukharin and Rykov were arrested and led to the Lubyanka's chambers of horror, and it was decided to create a commission of thirty-six militants, including all of the members of the Politburo, with the mission of dictating a partisan verdict against the accused. Among the members of the commission, Lev Davidovich painfully discovered the names of Nadezhda Krupskaya and Maria Ulyanova, Lenin's widow and sister. The two women, whom Stalin had begun to attack and marginalize even during the leader's life, had seen Vladimir Ilyich talk and speak with Bukharin countless times and now accepted Mikoyan's lies, developed by Stalin, in silence. That sordid move allowed Lev Davidovich to see something that had escaped him in previous trials: Stalin had also resolved to turn the few figures of the past that were still with him not just into submissive extras to his lies but into direct accomplices of his criminal fury; whoever was not a victim would be an accomplice and, moreover, would be a henchman. Terror and repression had been established as the policy of a government that adopted persecution and lies as resources of the state and as a lifestyle for all of society. Is that how a "better" society was made? he would ask himself, although he already knew the answer.

When John Dewey arrived in Mexico, under infinite political pressure, he asked for information on the case, which he had yet to read, and refused to meet with Trotsky. He reminded the press that, ideologically, he did not share the accused's theories and, as president of the commission, would only limit himself to offering some conclusions on the basis of the proof and testimonies presented, and that the only value of those results would be of a moral nature.

On March 10, the Casa Azul looked like a military camp. Inside the building, the harmony of objects and colors had disappeared when the potted plants, wood-grained furniture, and works of art were removed to make space for the members of the jury, journalists, and bodyguards. Outside the mansion, barricades had been erected and dozens of policemen spread out. The morning of the opening, already awaiting the arrival of Dewey and the members of the jury, Diego Rivera observed the yard and, smiling, spoke to his guest about the sacrifices that had to be made for permanent revolution.

Dewey demonstrated an energy that belied his seventy-eight years. As soon as he entered the house, after greeting Diego and Lev Davidovich, he asked to begin. His role and that of the members of the jury, he said, would consist of listening to any testimony that Mr. Trotsky had to offer them, interrogating him, and later offering some conclusions. The pertinence of those sessions, in his opinion, was based on the fact that

Mr. Trotsky had been sentenced without the opportunity of making himself heard, which constituted a reason for serious concern to the commission and to the entire world.

That moment initiated perhaps the most intense and absurd week in the life of Lev Davidovich. He could not remember ever having been subjected to the physical and intellectual effort required to contend for hours and hours with the sick logic of the accusations fashioned in Moscow. As the entire counterproceeding was held in English, he constantly feared not being as precise or explicit as he needed and desired to be. At night he barely slept two or three hours, and only when his body overpowered his mind; his stomach, affected by the tension and liters of coffee he drank, had turned into a fiery stone embedded in his abdomen; while his blood pressure, already disturbed by the altitude, had produced a buzzing in his ears and a bothersome pain at the base of his skull. At the end of the sixth day, he was under the impression of being in a strange place, among unknown people talking about incomprehensible matters, and he thought he would pass out, but he knew that speaking before those people was his only alternative, perhaps the last occasion to fight in public for his name and his history, for his ideas and for the mortal remains of a revolution betrayed.

When the time came for his statement, on April 17, the members of the commission saw before them an exhausted man who had to ask Dewey's permission to remain seated. Nonetheless, when he began his speech, the vehemence of old times returned and those gathered at the Casa Azul saw some of the sparks of the Trotsky who had moved the masses in 1905 and 1917, of the passion that had earned him the devotion of so many men and the eternal hatred of others, from Plekhanov to Stalin. His first conclusion was that, according to the present Soviet government, all of the members of the Politburo that brought triumph to the revolution and accompanied Lenin in the most difficult days of war and hunger and had founded the state—men who had suffered jail, exile, endless repression—in reality had always been traitors to their ideals and, further still, agents at the service of foreign powers who wanted to destroy what they themselves had built. Wasn't it a paradox that the October leaders, all of them, had ended up being traitors? Or was there perhaps only one traitor and his name was Stalin? He wouldn't waste time to demonstrate the falseness, let alone the absurdity, of the acts attributed to him, he said, but he pointed out that the governments of Turkey, France, and Norway had corroborated that he had not engaged in any anti-Soviet activities in their territories, since he had remained removed and even confined under police watch. Forgetting his physical weaknesses, he stood up. The ideas bursting within him acted as an impulse that moved him and gave him the strength to go on to the end. His life experience, he reminded them, in which neither triumphs nor failures were scarce, had not destroyed his faith in the future of humanity; on the contrary, they had given him indestructible conviction. He still possessed the faith in reason, in truth, and in human solidarity that at the age of eighteen he brought with him to the neighborhoods of the provincial city of Nikolayev; it had become more mature but no less ardent, and no one nor anything could ever kill it.

His breathing agitated and his head hurting, he took his seat again. His eyes met those of the old American professor and, for a few thick seconds, held his gaze. The silence was dramatic. Before Lev Davidovich's plea, Dewey had promised to offer some provisional conclusions, but now he froze as if petrified. A sob from Natalia Sedova broke the spell. Finally, Dewey lowered his gaze and looked at his notes and whispered that the session was closed until they reached their conclusions. And he added: anything he might have said would have been an unforgivable anticlimax.

The session barely closed, Lev Davidovich, on Natalia's orders, decamped to a country house in the beautiful city of Taxco. Although he had asked the secretaries to take the hunting rifles, his fatigue was such that he could only go for a few walks around the city and, almost at the end of his stay, go on an excursion to the Pyramids of the Sun and the Moon in Teotihuacán. Fortunately, the headaches, the high blood pressure, and the insomnia began to recede, but Natalia's strict vigilance kept him in a reclusion that included the blocking of his correspondence.

When they returned to Coyoacán, Lev Davidovich was surprised by a feeling he hadn't experienced since his days in Prinkipo: he was returning to a place he desired to be. For a man who had lived his entire existence in constant motion, the traditional notion of home had been substituted by the necessity for a place that was propitious for working, and the Casa Azul, with its charms and exotic atmosphere, exercised a beneficent magnetism, to which was added (though Lev Davidovich would never admit to it in his writings) the attractive flitting of the Kahlo sisters, whose attentions had awoken instincts that the years of struggle and isolation had put to sleep. The enjoyment of Cristina's beauty and Frida's mysterious charm, the aroma of youth that emanated from both of them and the conversations in which he tended to let compliments slip out that were sometimes awkward and banal, gradually turned into a kind of adolescent game that made his confinement unpredictable and turned the kitchen, the hallways and the yard of the house into places for smiling encounters, while he felt the gaiety also turning back his encroaching old age.

While waiting for Dewey's conclusions, Lev Davidovich continued to submit evidence that refuted the charge that he had participated in an anti-Soviet conspiracy. He regretted that many of those documents had not reached him weeks earlier, and the idea that Liova had been indolent about sending them set him at the edge of fury. Resolved to punish that unforgivable inefficiency, he delegated his correspondence with Liova to his secretaries, knowing that the young man would immediately get the signal he was transmitting with his silence.

One night at the end of March after dinner, Natalia, Jean van Heijenoort, and Lev Davidovich, along with the residents of the Casa Azul, prolonged one of the pleasant evenings in which the Exile was frequently asked to narrate the most remarkable memories of his life. Since he felt encouraged, he launched into a story about his relationship with Marshal Tukhachevsky, the young and elegant officer who in the days of the civil war, thanks to his capacity as a strategist, was nicknamed "the Russian Bonaparte." Natalia, who knew those episodes and understood very little English, was the first to retire, and Rivera, who was already storing an impressive quantity of whiskey in his blood, immediately followed her. Frida, overcome by tiredness, was next, and then van Heijenoort discreetly disappeared.

Cristina's smile, the wine in his system, and the tensions accumulated over several weeks of proximity caused the foreseeable explosion. More than once, at dinners and in outings, Lev Davidovich had slid a hand across Cristina's legs or arms, only as an affectionate gesture, and she, while flirtatious, had delicately, always with a smile, prevented any advance, yet without completely dissuading him, suggesting perhaps that these flirts and smiles were part of a ritual of approach, so that at last the man made a pass that night. Then, to his surprise, she stopped him and asked that he not confuse admiration and affection with other feelings. Without understanding the reaction of a woman who had seemed to accept his overtures until that moment, Lev Davidovich was struck dumb, his desires frozen.

Annoyed by the failure, ashamed at having given in to an impulse that put his relationship with the owners of the house and, worse still, the stability of his marriage in danger, the man implored his reason to conquer the hormonal rush that had overtaken him. He forced himself to consider whether his intentions with the young woman had not been more than a fleeting intoxication caused by the magnetism of her smooth skin. It was all just an absurd manifestation of a midlife crisis, he told himself.

When Frida found out about what had happened, she assumed the role of confidante and offered the paltry consolation of setting him straight about her sister's sexual fecklessness; Cristina was so fond of arousing males, and even of the most sordid deception: she had exceeded all limits when she went to bed with Diego himself, something that Frida had accepted, although she would never forgive either her husband or her sister. The painter's tenderness and understanding, peppered with coquettishness, led Lev Davidovich to ask himself whether he hadn't miscalculated his possibilities, and he began to redirect his intentions, which soon acquired an overwhelming vehemence, capable of altering his waking and sleeping hours with the image of the woman who had confided such intimate revelations to him.

Wrapped in the dense spiderweb of desire, Lev Davidovich had to rely on all of his discipline to concentrate on his work. Frida's presence and the very atmosphere of the Casa Azul led him to inertia and digressions when so many political commitments and economic problems called on him. Perhaps the fact of having postponed the drafting of Lenin's biography in order to devote himself to Stalin's, for which he had already received an advance, also affected the rhythm of his work. Researching in the archives and searching his memory for everything related to that dark being was a thankless task, and although he intended to turn the book into a grenade against the Grave Digger, at root he felt that he was degrading himself by dedicating his intelligence and his time to it.

A strange and confusing event that occurred in Barcelona on May 3 managed to focus his attention on what was happening in Spain. For several months the civil war had turned into a field for political confrontation between the groups fighting for the Republic, and Lev Davidovich noticed Moscow's hand behind the accusations and debates between the factions. It could not be a coincidence, he would write, that shortly after the initiation of the Moscow purges and the announcement of military support for the Republic, in the form of Soviet weapons and advisers, a campaign was unleashed against the real and supposed Spanish Trotskyists, who were besieged with the same viciousness and in almost the same words with which the Bolsheviks in the USSR had been accused. His old friend Andreu Nin, from whom he had distanced himself over tactical differences, was one of the first to be thrown out of the governmental apparatus, while his party, the POUM, was turned into the target of propaganda attacks more scathing than those made against the fascist soldiers.

In the tumult of censored and contradictory information coming from Barcelona, the old revolutionary sensed that what had happened regarding the military control of the Republic's communications building had been just the first step toward achieving the objective of the *corrida*: to kill the bull of the opposition and bend the government to Soviet will, which would allow Stalin to take the leading role in the European political game. Because of that, he was not surprised when he learned that the first to be placed on the pillory had been the POUM militants. It was clear to him that the aggressiveness with which the Spanish Communists threw themselves at wiping out the POUM was due, more than to old rivalries or the need to achieve a unified government, to the obsession of the master of the Kremlin (who desired the defeat of the POUM even more than the military defeat of Franco and his second-class fascists).

In the final days of that turbulent May, several editions of the recently published *The Revolution Betrayed* arrived in Coyoacán. The Riveras, to celebrate it, invited the Trotskys and other friends to dine at a restaurant in the city center. Since his spirits had been restored, Lev Davidovich had begun to use the freedom of movement that the Mexican authorities granted him. With some frequency, he traveled to the colorful city in the company of two or three bodyguards, camouflaged in the backseat of a car and covered by a hat and handkerchief that hid even his goatee. Even so, he enjoyed those excursions, and some nights he even devoted himself to wandering the streets to examine and appreciate the cathedral's heavy Baroque style, the atmosphere of the cantinas and their mariachi music, and the elegance of the old viceregal palaces, always pursued by the smell of tortillas placed over the fire on every corner of the city. The liveliness of Mexico seemed like that of a thriving world sustained by deep cultural mix that, nonetheless, would not be capable, for centuries, of eliminating the barriers separating the races that cohabitated there.

On the night of the celebration, following dinner, the invitees walked the center's alleyways and read the political proclamations covering the walls, which either accused Cárdenas of being a traitor and a Communist or gave him their support and encouraged him to continue to the end. Trotsky's name, as could be expected, appeared on several of the painted walls, and went from *viva* to calls for his death, from "Welcome" to "Leave Mexico." But that night Lev Davidovich was interested in neither the signs nor the discoveries of the city: he was really searching for intimacy with Frida. The vertigo of the senses into which he had fallen demanded a release that he began to pursue vehemently. Although the painter's body imposed the barrier of a deformity that had to rely on orthopedic corsets and a cane to help the more affected of her legs, perhaps precisely because of those limitations the woman took on sex and sensuality in an aggressive, effusive way. When Lev Davidovich learned that her open morality had even allowed homosexual relationships, the perverse imp of his virility had unleashed itself in licentious imaginings, creating more urgent needs than those he had experienced in his youth, and than those he had felt in his days as a powerful commissar, when so many female comrades in arms had offered him a release of the accumulated tensions and fervors in solidarity.

Through poems and love letters hidden between the pages of the books he recommended to Frida, Lev Davidovich already demanded an ascent to the physical. The fire that moved him burned with such intensity that he had even managed to overcome the fear that Natalia would suspect an affair. So on that night of revelry, as Diego, Natalia, the friends who joined on the walk, and the secretaries entered the building where one of Rivera's murals was on display, he purposely stayed behind and, without exchanging any words, pushed Frida against the wall and kissed her on the lips as, between breaths, he repeated how much he desired her. With complete awareness, at that moment, Lev Davidovich was throwing himself into a well of madness and putting in danger every significant thing in his life. But it made him happy, proud, and without the least feeling of guilt, he would tell himself later, convinced that, at the end of the day, it had been worth it to waste in that orgy of the senses the last reserves of his virility.

17

Ramón Mercader was convinced that Paris was the most fatuous city in the world and that the French and their socialist government were betraying Spain, denying it the saving support that the Republic was screaming for. But he felt satisfied when Tom opened the door of the apartment on the top floor of rue Léopold Robert and he discovered how from the windows facing north he could see the boulevard du Montparnasse while from the balcony, looking south, he could make out the boulevard Raspail, where the Café des Arts was.

"It's good, isn't it?" Tom commented as he handed him the keys. "Central and discreet, very bourgeois but a little bohemian, as befits you."

"Jacques likes it," he admitted, and looked at the wooden tables and bookcases, soulless without any decorations, the empty walls where he should hang some photos. "He has to start to make it his."

"You have time to get settled. Two or three months, I believe."

Jacques lit a cigarette and went through the bedroom, the water closet, the bathroom, and the small kitchen, where a glass door permitted a view of the service balcony that led to the building's interior courtyard. He returned to the living room with a small plate that would serve as an ashtray until he acquired the necessary accessories, in line with his personality. At that moment he was overcome by an unfamiliar feeling, for ever since Caridad had begun running away more than ten years earlier, he had never had anything resembling what the bourgeois call a home.

"I'm going to my hotel," Tom said, yawning. "Are you going to rest?"

"I need to buy some food. Milk, coffee . . ."

"Very well. We'll see each other tonight. At eight, in front of the Fontaine Saint-Michel. I have a surprise for you." With more difficulty than at other times, he stood up.

"When are you going to tell me what happened to that leg of yours?"

Tom smiled and left the apartment.

Jacques opened his only suitcase. He took out his shirts and the English cashmere suit and draped them over the armchair so they would air out and recover their shapes. He went down to the street and crossed the boulevard Montparnasse to enter La Closerie des Lilas, nearly empty at midmorning. He asked for a glass of hot milk, a croissant, and a cup of coffee. He used his best Belgian accent and remembered that there was no need to exaggerate. In any event, he would have time to polish those minor defects, he told himself, as he slipped the ashtray from the neighboring table, engraved with the café's name, into his jacket pocket.

Before leaving, Grigoriev had explained that during his trip to New York he had put into motion the plan that would move Jacques Mornard toward the renegade Lev Trotsky. It seemed so far-fetched and improbable to Ramón that he started to wonder whether it was all made-up. Grigoriev had told him how, under the identity of Mr. Andrew Roberts, he had gotten in touch with Louis Budenz, the director of the *Daily Worker*. On other occasions, Budenz had collaborated with the Soviet secret services, and now Roberts needed something as simple and as difficult from him as sending to Paris a young woman named Sylvia Ageloff, an active member of the U.S. Trotskyist circles and sister of two other fanatics who had even worked very closely with the Exile. Of course, he didn't say why he needed Sylvia in France, and although Budenz would only know of the need to move this Trotskyist, Roberts emphasized that everything had to be done with the utmost discretion and he thought it sufficient warning to remind him that, regarding that request, no one besides the two of them could know a single word. Louis Budenz promised to give him an answer as soon as possible.

That night, when he left the bus and passed by Odéon on the way to the Fontaine Saint-Michel, Jacques Mornard felt himself entering the heart of a city in its effervescence. For the Parisians, the war happening on the other side of the Pyrenees and the one to come on the European horizon were as far away as the planet Mars. *La nuit parisienne* was just as animated as always, and while he waited alongside the fountain, Jacques felt surrounded by life.

Perhaps it was his instinct or a telluric call of his blood that made him turn around. Immediately he saw her among the people as she approached him on Tom's arm. He noticed how his new identity was thrown into confusion by the mere presence of that battle cry who responded to the name of Caridad del Río. When the woman was in front of him, smiling and proud, dressed with an elegance that seemed out of place (those crocodile-skin high heels, for God's sake), and whispered in Catalan, "*Mare meva, quin home mes ben plantat!*" he guessed what was coming: she took him by the neck and kissed his cheek with malevolent precision, placing the heat of her saliva at the edge of his lips. Although Jacques Mornard tried to keep himself afloat, Caridad had cast off the ropes of a Ramón who continued emerging from the depths, dragged up by the invincible taste of aniseed.

At Tom's suggestion, they looked for Brasserie Belzar, on the rue des Écoles, where someone was waiting for them. Caridad walked between the two men, satisfied, and Ramón decided not to weaken, at least not in an obvious way and certainly not in front of Tom. He wanted to ask about young Luis, who he supposed was still in Paris, and about Montse, who had mentioned to him at some point her intentions of traveling to France. Would Caridad know anything about África, about little Lenina?

Upon entering the brasserie, a man with his head shaved stood up and their party, led by Tom, walked to his table. After shaking the man's hand, Tom introduced them, speaking in French.

"Our comrade Caridad. This is George Mink." He turned to his pupil: "Jacques, George will be your contact in Paris."

"Welcome, Monsieur Mornard. I wish you a pleasant stay in the city."

As they drank their aperitifs, Caridad talked about how things were going in Spain. According to her, the Popular Army was still showing weaknesses, which she attributed to enemy sabotage. Mink, as if he didn't understand, commented that with the Trotskyists and the anarchists crushed, he couldn't fathom what enemies she was referring to, and she leaped up: the incompetents still in the government.

"The army is now armed by the Soviets and eighty percent led by communist officers," Caridad pointed out, looking directly at Tom, "but even so, we're still losing battles and the fascists have reached the Mediterranean; they've split the peninsula in two. The only explanation is that the heart of the Republic is lacking the necessary ideological purity to win the war. In Spain we need more purges."

"Poor Spain," Tom said, and at first Jacques didn't know what he meant. "There are even Soviet advisers in the public bathrooms already, and the Spanish Communists are the ones flushing the toilets. If we practically control the army, the intelligence, the police, the propaganda, who are they going to purge now?"

"The traitors. We already got rid of Indalecio Prieto. All that time he was waging war on us. He was spending all his time saying that Communists are like automatons who obey the orders of the party's committee. He was worse than any fifth columnist."

"Sometimes Prieto seemed enlightened to me," Tom said, sighing. "I had never seen a minister of war more convinced that he wasn't going to win the war . . . But the real problem is that you, the Spanish Communists, don't know how to win. Have you listened to yourself speak, Caridad? You sound like a fucking newspaper editorial. All of you talk like that . . . And who's going to pay for the disaster in Spain? Us: Pedro, Orlov, me, and the rest of the advisers. But the truth is that we're getting tired of hearing you talk and talk and having to push you every day."

Jacques Mornard had felt the lashing on Ramón's back. Reasonably or not, the blows were always going to fall on Spanish heads, but he remained silent.

"I don't know what kind of Communists you are," Tom continued, as if spitting out old resentment. "You let other people tell you what you should do and they treat you like children. The Comintern wolves are still cutting the cake. Why are they doing that? Because you can't decide to tell them to go to hell and do things as they should be done."

"So if we tell them to go to hell," Ramón began, unable to contain himself at that moment, "them and you, how do we stand up to the Italian units and German aviation? You know we depend on you, that we have no alternative . . ."

Tom looked directly into his pupil's eyes. It was a penetrating and easy-to-decipher look.

"What's wrong, Jacques? You seem upset . . . a man like you . . ."

Jacques Mornard noticed the piercing tone of voice and felt overcome by his impotence, but he made one last effort to save his dignity.

"It's just that we're always to blame . . ."

"No one said that," Tom replied, his tone changed. "Almost out of nowhere, you've made it to where you are: today you are the most influential party in the Republican alliance, and you will always have our support. But you have to grow up once and for all."

"When do you return to Spain?" Mink asked, taking advantage of the more relaxed moment, and Tom sighed.

"In two days. I'm setting things up here and then I leave again. Yezhov insists that I keep working with Orlov. But it's taxing to have my mind on two different matters . . . I only have one head and I'm trying to put it in two places."

Caridad looked at him and, with a caution that was uncharacteristic of her, said:

"There's a rumor among the people that the advisers are going to leave us to our fate. They even talk about the ill will of some . . ."

"The ones saying that are ungrateful . . . I want to leave because I have another mission. I've sweat blood in Spain and put my own skin in front of Italian tanks in Madrid when no one could give a damn about the city . . ." Tom drank from a glass of wine that had been served and looked at the tablecloth, startlingly white, as if he were looking for a nonexistent stain. "No one can say that I want to abandon you."

Silence settled over the table and Mink seized upon it as he refilled his empty glass.

"I know that the situation in Spain hurts, but we have some other minor problems, like what we're going to order, right? I recommend the Alsatian *choucroute*; the sausages are first-rate. Although I'm opting for the *cassoulet*, I love duck . . ."

Before Tom stepped back into Kotov's skin and returned to Spain, Jacques received advice that was really an order: he was to erase Spain and the war from his head. To Jacques Mornard, what was happening to the south of the Pyrenees was just news read in the papers. Ramón could not allow that passion to crack his identity, not even in the most intimate circles, and as a preventative measure Tom forbade him from seeing or talking to

Caridad until he authorized it. The subtle machinery that he had put into motion made Ramón's sentimental, patriotic gaffe unacceptable. Ramón Mercader had proven to be capable of placing himself above those weaknesses and his passions should not see the light of day until they were called upon for a greater cause, perhaps the same greater cause.

George Mink, the son of Ukrainians who emigrated to France in the days of the Russian Civil War, became responsible from then on for placing Jacques in the Parisian world that befitted him. They spent weeks going to the bohemian haunts of the Rive Gauche, and the Hippodrome, where Jacques practiced his theoretical knowledge of betting; they wandered the historic and now dilapidated streets of Le Marais, got close to the chorus girls of the Moulin Rouge, inviting them to champagne; and they surveyed at the steering wheel the streets of Paris learned from the maps Jacques studied in Malakhovka. As if he were visiting a sanctuary, George took him to Le Gemy Club, where Louis Leplée was presenting his great discovery, *La Môme* Piaf, a volatile and rather scruffy little woman who, with an enormous voice, sang songs full of vulgar phrases and daring metaphors that, nonetheless, left the Belgian bored and speechless. With Jacques at the wheel, they visited Brussels and Liège, the fabulous castles of the Loire basin, and trained the young man's palate with Belgian chocolates, French wine and cheeses, hearty Norman plates, and the subtle aromas of *provençal* cuisine. The apartment on rue Léopold Robert took on a bourgeois and informal air, and Jacques dressed himself in the wares of some German Jewish tailors recently installed in Le Marais, ending up with twelve hats in his closet. The whole time they remained removed from French political circles, the world of Russian émigrés, and the haunts of Spanish Republicans, where the spies of the whole planet's secret services milled about as if they had been gathered for a general convention of the shadow world.

When Tom returned at the beginning of June, he observed with satisfaction how his creature had progressed and felt pleased at having known how to find in a primitive Catalan Communist that diamond he was now polishing to perfection. Once his time in Spain was up, Tom had returned to New York, to learn that the Sylvia Ageloff line had been activated and that it would begin to run in the month of July when the girl, a high school teacher, took her summer vacation and, thanks to the enthusiasm and economic generosity of her old friend Ruby Weil, embarked on the trip of her dreams to Paris. Without telling him who the person in the photograph was, Tom gave Jacques a picture of Ruby Weil and saw that the young man's eyes lit up.

"She's not bad," he admitted.

Tom smiled and, without saying anything, gave him a second photo of a woman close to thirty, with rounded, Coke-bottle glasses, a thin face covered in freckles and straight hair falling gracelessly, through which the points of her ears stuck out.

"Every wine is not a Bordeaux, Jacques," Tom said, continuing to smile. "This is Sylvia Ageloff, your hare. If you cook her well enough, she'll even taste good."

To soften the shock, Tom told him that he had also been in Mexico, where other parts of the operation had been set in motion. While the men from the Comintern had assigned the Communist Party the mission of raising popular spirits against the presence of the renegade in Mexico, four agents, all of them Spaniards, had been planted in the capital to carry out the operation if the order was given and if the possibilities for success were considered real.

"You are perhaps living the best vacation of your life, in Paris, far from the war, with money to burn. If you have to gnaw that bone"—he tapped the photographed face of Sylvia Ageloff with his nail and smiled— "and in the end you're not the one to carry out the job, we'll give you a good discount on your debts."

Jacques thought there were worse sacrifices, and with that consolation he resolved to await the arrival of the woman who, if he was lucky, would be his channel to the remote Coyoacán and, perhaps, to history.

At the beginning of July, Tom and Mink disappeared and those days of pleasant summer waiting for moment zero were for Jacques Mornard slow days, darkened by the galloping crisis affecting the government coalition of the Popular Front in France. Above all, he was bothered by the worsening news that came from Spain, where the evacuation of International Brigade volunteers had begun without the Popular Army, despite the intrepid campaign of the Ebro, managing to push back the pro-Franco troops or kick them out of the strip they'd opened up to the Mediterranean. The vestiges of Ramón still beating within Jacques couldn't help but be irritated by those failures, but his discipline allowed him to keep himself far from the places where the evacuated volunteers gathered before returning to their respective countries. Ramón would have liked to have heard their stories.

On July 15, without Jacques expecting him, a pale and agitated Tom went to see him at the apartment on rue Léopold Robert. Without even saying hello, Tom told him that a serious complication had arisen: everything seemed to indicate that Orlov, head of the Soviet intelligence advisers in Spain, had deserted. At that moment, for the first time, Jacques would see a streak of weakness in that man whom he admired so much for his aplomb in any circumstance. But very soon he understood the dimensions of the disaster tormenting him.

"We're after him, but the son of a bitch knows all our methods and how we do things. We know he's in France, perhaps even right here in Paris, and the truth is that I think he'll escape us."

"Are you sure he deserted?"

"He had no other choice."

"Wasn't he your right-hand man?"

"So much so that he knows the entire network of Soviet espionage in Europe."

Jacques felt a tremor go through him.

"Does he also know about me?"

"No," Tom reassured him. "You're beyond his reach. But not the comrades who are in Mexico. You can't imagine what Orlov knows. As they say in Spain, that swine left us with our asses hanging in the air . . . It's a disaster."

"I swear I don't understand. Orlov was a traitor?"

Tom lit a cigarette, as if he needed that break.

"No, I don't think so, and that's the worst part. They forced him to desert. What happened was that crazy Yezhov sent Orlov a telegram telling him he should come to Paris, take a car from the embassy, and show up in Antwerp to board a ship where there would be a very important meeting with an envoy of his. Orlov didn't even need to be too intelligent to realize that if he showed up, he would end up dead, like Antonov-Ovseyenko and other advisers that Yezhov had called for. On the eleventh, he left Spain and disappeared."

Jacques Mornard felt his head spinning. Something too sick and out of control was happening and, based on what Tom was saying, the consequences could be unpredictable.

"If Beria and Comrade Stalin don't stop Yezhov, everything is going to get fucked up."

"So why don't they just stop him, goddammit?" Jacques cried out.

"Bloody hell, because Stalin doesn't want to!" Tom yelled, throwing his cigarette to the floor. "Because he doesn't want to!"

Tom stood up. The fury possessing him was unfamiliar to Jacques, who remained silent until the other man, back in control of himself, again spoke.

"Your plan is still on. Orlov doesn't even know you exist and that's our guarantee. Now it's more important than ever that you do everything right. As long as we don't know where Orlov is and what information he's going to release, we're up in the air. For now, we've put three of the comrades in Mexico in quarantine and have taken the other one out for good . . . Orlov knew that agent personally. He himself recommended him for a job with the utmost responsibility."

Jacques remained silent. He knew that Tom needed to get out all of those tensions and that he was doing it in front of him because he trusted his discretion and required his intelligence, perhaps more than ever before.

"I'm going to tell you something you were going to find out at some point, and it doesn't make sense anymore for you not to know. The agent we removed from Mexico is a woman and she was working under the name Patria. When the time came, if it had been necessary, you and she would have worked together . . ."

Ramón gave a start. Was it possible that Yezhov's foolish act had deprived him of something so beautiful that he couldn't have even dreamed of it?

"Are you talking about . . . ?"

"África de las Heras. When you arrived at Malakhovka, she was in cabin 9. She left there two months before you. Orlov doesn't know where she is, but he knows her and we can't risk her. She's too valuable."

Ramón Mercader stood up and went to the window from which he could see the boulevard du Montparnasse. Evening was falling and the cafés, with their tables in the sun, had filled with locals, carefree and pleasant, who would talk about the great and small things in their lives, perhaps anodyne, but theirs. To know that for weeks he had had África thirty yards away from him without being allowed to see her was not a comforting piece of news. It was a mutilation, one more, of the many he'd had to endure to reach the dark point of his life in which he found himself: without a past, without a present, with a future in which he would depend on others, on the impalpable paths of history. Ramón turned around and looked at Tom, who, with his head down, was smoking again.

"Don't worry. I'll take care of my responsibilities. I'm not going to fail you . . . So, is she well?"

Behind the bar's counter was the longest, cleanest, and most precise mirror Ramón Mercader would see in his whole life. It was the mirror against which he would compare every other mirror in the world, the mirror in which he wanted to see himself, especially the frozen Moscow morning of 1968 that, feeling the abrasive pain in his right hand and observing his reflection in the new glass walls of the mausoleum of the god of the world's proletarians, he saw the emptiness pursuing his shadowy life. He thought that if he'd been in front of that magic mirror at the Ritz, he would have surely seen himself, as he did on those afternoons in 1938, when he was Jacques Mornard and he walked around with his faith and his health intact, wearing a suit of muslin or twill that was crisp because of the starch, swollen with pride at knowing he was at the center of the battle for the future of mankind.

Before he left, Tom had explained to him, with his usual meticulousness, how that first meeting with Sylvia Ageloff and Ruby Weil would go. On the afternoon of July 19, Jacques would run into the women at the bar of the Hôtel Ritz, where Ruby and Sylvia would go in the company of the bookseller Gertrude Allison, so that he, taking advantage of his client relationship with Allison, would be introduced to the tourists and invite them for a drink. At that moment, Sylvia would fall in the Belgian's sights; from that moment on, the way in which she was gunned down would depend only upon the abilities and the steady hand of Jacques Mornard.

But that afternoon, seated in front of the gin and tonic barely sprinkled with gin, he was again thinking that perhaps África's brusque change in attitude, when they separated in Barcelona, had nothing to do with other men and was only due to orders to cut off her old relationships before getting involved with her new mission. Relieved by that thought, he watched, through the mirror, the noisy and smiling entrance of four women. He recognized Allison, the blond Ruby Weil, and told himself that the tall, young one must be Marie Crapeau, a French friend of the bookseller's.

271

He then focused on the freckly one with glasses, with milky skin, who hid her extreme thinness below a wide, pleated skirt and a flounced blouse, and he felt how the glass perfectly reflected back the overwhelming ugliness of Sylvia Ageloff. He saw her sit at a table and decided to turn around in order to observe, like the other patrons, the women who came in with such a ruckus. He understood at that moment that Jacques Mornard was about to grow up.

Gertrude Allison gave a cry of authentic surprise:

"But look who's here! Hi, Jacques!"

Smiling, with his glass in hand, he approached the women, allowing his personal charm, his elegance, and his cologne to spread and start his work. Gertrude made the introductions and when he shook Sylvia's hand, he had the feeling of touching a small and feeble bird. Gertrude Allison explained to him who her friends were, two Americans on holiday in Paris, and invited him to sit down. He didn't want to interrupt their party, but if she insisted . . . on the condition that they allow him to buy them all drinks.

"Jacques is a photographer," Gertrude explained. "Are you still working for *Ce Soir*?"

"Whenever they ask me to," he said nonchalantly.

Gertrude turned to the women and explained:

"He's one of those lucky ones who doesn't have to work to live."

"It's not like that," he clarified modestly.

"But let me tell you that these friends here"—she pointed at Sylvia and Ruby—"prefer workers, all sweaty and hairy . . . They're Marxists, Leninists, and several more '-ists' . . ."

"Trotskyists." Sylvia barely smiled, but she couldn't help herself. "I'm a Trotskyist," she repeated, and the woman's warm but sharp voice entered Jacques's ears.

"She sings 'The Internationale' in the shower," Gertrude Allison concluded, and they all, even Sylvia, smiled, relaxed.

"I congratulate you," he said, making his lack of interest obvious. "I love people who believe in something. But for me, politics . . ." and he backed up the phrase with a shrug of his shoulders. "I'm more interested in shower songs . . ."

The table was set and Jacques took charge of ordering the dishes and distributing the silverware. Half an hour later, when Gertrude and Marie left, he decided to stay in the company of the tourists for a while longer, and when they said goodbye, they agreed to meet to go to the Hippodrome, where he had to take some photos of the races the next day. And if they didn't have any other engagements, he offered to show them the Parisian night life once his work was done.

Jacques Mornard's charm, his splendid way of spending money, his car, his knowledge of Parisian night life, and his apartment with a bohemian air just off the boulevard du Montparnasse, where they ended the night drinking a glass of port, turned out to be irresistible, especially for someone like Sylvia Ageloff, who didn't understand why that young man (who obviously was not even twenty-eight years old, as he said he was) seemed to prefer her over Ruby Weil when it came to directing his flirtatious comments.

The following morning, a phone call from Tom got Jacques out of bed and they agreed to meet for a meal at La Coupole. As they drank an aperitif, Jacques told him all was going according to plan and the only thing left for him to do was ask Sylvia Ageloff to take off her pants. So that everything would work as efficiently as possible, the best thing to do would be to take Ruby far away from Paris, and Tom told him George would take care of it.

"Now let's eat something, I don't know when I'll be able to sit down at a table again." Tom placed the cigarettes alongside the ash tray. "Orlov showed up."

Jacques waited. He knew Tom would only tell him what he could.

"He's in Montreal, requesting a visa to enter the United States. When he came through Paris, he realized we have people watching the U.S. embassy, so he went to the Canadian one. He had more passports on him than a consular office and they were all very good . . . I had gotten them for him myself."

"And how did you learn he was in Canada?"

The waiter arrived and they ordered their food.

"Orlov is the most son-of-a-bitch son of a bitch there ever was in the world." Tom's voice was a mixture of anger and admiration. "Just barely arrived, he sent a communiqué to Comrade Stalin with a copy to Yezhov. He proposes a deal: if they don't take any reprisals against his mother and his mother-in-law, who live in the USSR, he'll give the U.S. secret services just a little bit of bait and keep the big stuff to himself. And what he knows is very, very big. He could destroy years of our work. But if something happens to one of those women, his wife, his children, or him, a lawyer will be in charge of making a public statement of everything he knows that is already being kept in the vault of a bank in New York."

"So what do they say in Moscow? Do they think he'll keep his end of the deal?"

"I don't know what they're saying there, but I think so. He knows we can make his mother and his mother-in-law's lives very difficult and that we can find him wherever he goes. You know what? Because of Yezhov, we've lost the most intelligent and cynical devil we had. I think Beria is about to reach an agreement with him."

"What about the operations in Mexico?"

"That whole operation is being quarantined, until we see how things fall. Comrade Stalin asked me, in the meantime, to go to Spain and try to fix the disaster Orlov left behind."

"What do I do, then?"

"You're still the great white hope. The chess game has already begun and the opening moves are usually decisive . . . and unrepeatable. You have all my trust, Jacques. Take care of Sylvia. We'll take care of the rest."

Sylvia Ageloff looked at Jacques Mornard's nakedness and thought she was living a fairy tale. She knew that to think like that was tremendously corny, but it was impossible to come to terms with it in any other way. If that young man, the son of diplomats, refined, educated, beautiful, and worldly, was not Prince Charming himself, what else could he be? The passion with which Jacques awoke the rusted springs of her libido had pushed her beyond all imaginable ecstasy, to the degree of accepting his condition that they abstain from discussing politics, the one constant in her loveless militant's life.

The days spent wandering around Paris, Chartres, and the Loire Valley; the weekend in Brussels, where Jacques showed her the sites of his childhood, although he refused (to Sylvia's passing annoyance) to take her to his parents' house; her lover's limitless understanding (he agreed to take her to Barbizon so she could see, at the edge of the Fontainebleau Forest, the house called Ker Monique that had housed her idealized Lev Davidovich three years before)—all of this, complemented by nights in the most luxurious restaurants and the most popular cafés where bohemian Parisian intellectuals gathered (at the Café de Flore, Jacques showed a gowned Sylvia the table around which Jean-Paul Sartre, Albert Camus,

Simone de Beauvoir, and other young people who called themselves existentialists drank and argued; at Le Gemy Club, he made her listen to Édith Piaf two tables away from Maurice Chevalier) and, above all, with those predawn hours in which Jacques Mornard's virility hammered into the center of her life—in just a few weeks, turned her into a marionette whose movements originated from and ended with the fingers of one man.

Just one concern had remained with Sylvia during those days of glory. When she had just arrived in Paris, in mid-July, there had been a commotion in Trotskyist circles over the disappearance of Rudolf Klement, one of Trotsky's closest assistants and the executive secretary of the planned Fourth Communist International. From Mexico, the Exile had sent his protest to the French police, since the letter in which Klement said he was resigning from the International and Trotskyism was, according to him, a crude hoax by the Soviet intelligence services. For that reason, when Klement's dismembered corpse was found on August 26 on the banks of the Seine, Sylvia Ageloff fell into a state of depression from which she would only emerge to attend, as an interpreter, the founding meeting of the Trotskyist International in Périgny, in the outskirts of Paris.

In one of his fleeting appearances, Tom advised Jacques to support Sylvia emotionally and politically, to finish forging his dominion over her.

"There's a problem," Jacques said, looking at the waters of the Seine that had washed over Klement's corpse. "Sylvia has to go back to her high school in October. What's better, let her go or keep her here?"

"Orlov is already in the United States and it looks like he's going to fulfill his end of the deal. But Beria has stopped special operations until they get Yezhov out of the way. I think the best thing is for you to keep her here and consolidate your position. Is it difficult?" Jacques smiled and shook his head as he threw his cigarette butt in the river. "So Sylvia is at peace, let's get her some job. It's better if she keeps herself busy and earns a few francs."

"Don't worry, Sylvia won't make any trouble for us."

Tom observed Jacques Mornard and smiled.

"You're my hero . . . and you deserve a story I've owed you for a long time. Shall we have some vodka?"

They crossed the place du Châtelet toward rue de Rivoli, where some Polish Jews had set up a restaurant specializing in kosher dishes, Ukrainian and Belorussian, served in an abundance that would scare off their

French competitors. Once the vodka was served, Tom suggested to Jacques that he allow him to order, and the young man agreed. After having two stiff drinks, Tom lit one of his cigarettes.

"Are you going to tell me how you ended up lame?"

"And two or three other things . . . Let's see, the limp I owe to a Cossack from Denikin's white army. He slashed me in the calf with a saber and severed my tendons. This was in 1920, when I was head of the Cheka in Bashkina. The doctors thought I wouldn't walk again, but six months later, all I had left was this intermittent limp that you see . . . It had been a year since I'd left the Socialist Revolutionary Party and I'd become a member of the Bolshevik Party, although since the civil war started I was enlisted in the Red Army, always with the idea that I'd be moved on to the Cheka. Do you know why? Because a friend who had entered the Cheka overwhelmed me with what he told me. They were the whip of God, they had no law, and they got two pairs of boots per year, cigarettes, a bag of sausages. They even had cars for work. When I was able to enter, I saw that it was true, the Chekists gave us carte blanche and good shoes! But don't go thinking it was easy to make my way up, and don't think that I'm going to tell you the things I did to get my first stripes and make it to chief in a city within one month . . . When the war ended, they took me to Moscow, so I could go to the military school, and when I got out, they called me from the Department of Foreigners. As it happened, in 1926, I was working in China, with Chiang Kai-shek. When the coup against the Communists happened in Shanghai, we Soviet advisers fell into disgrace and they started killing us like rabid dogs. They put my boss, Mikhail Borodin, as well as other colleagues, in jail, accusing them of being 'enemies of the Chinese people,' and they were torturing them before killing them. I managed to rescue them and get them out of the country, but I had to return to Shanghai to avoid those sons of bitches razing the Soviet consulate to the ground . . . That really cost me. Chiang Kai-shek's men beat me so badly, they left me for dead. *Bliat!* I was lucky. A Chinese friend picked me up: I traveled for twenty-two days in an oxcart, covered with straw, until they left me for dead at the border . . . For rescuing Borodin and the others, they gave me the Order of the Red Flag, which, incidentally, I should now return because they just executed Borodin after accusing him of being 'an enemy of the Soviet people.' " Tom smiled sadly and threw back his vodka. "I had barely recovered when they sent me here, so I could start to penetrate what would be my destiny, the West. Then something happened that you may already suspect . . ."

"You met Caridad," Ramón said, who at some point in the conversation had ceased to be Jacques Mornard.

"She was a different woman. She was seven years older than me, but even when she denied it, had a fit, rolled around on the ground, you could see she had class. I liked her and we began to have a relationship."

"That still continues."

"Uh-huh. At that time, she was a little lost, although she sympathized with Maurice Thorez's Communists. And I was working with them . . ."

"Did she join the party because of you?"

"She would have joined anyway. Caridad needed to change her life; she was screaming out for an ideology to center her."

"Is Caridad a collaborator or does she work with you?"

"She started collaborating with us in 1930, but she became part of the staff in 1934 and did her first work in Asturias, during the miners' uprising . . . That will clarify many things about her that perhaps you didn't understand before."

The young man nodded, trying to place certain memories of Caridad's actions.

"That's why she returned to Spain when the Popular Front won. And that's why she's here, in Paris. Or is it because she's your lover?"

"In Spain she worked for us, and now she's here because she will be very useful in this operation and because things there are going from bad to worse . . . The Republic is falling to pieces. In a few days, Negrín is going to propose the exit of the International Brigades. He still believes that Great Britain and France can support them, and that with that support they can even win the war. But Great Britain and France are shaking with fear and are courting Hitler and aren't going to bet a dime on you. Forgive me for bringing the subject up, but I should tell you so you don't have any illusions. The war is lost. They're never going to manage to resist until a European war starts, as Negrín wants."

"And you're not going to give them any more help?"

"It's no longer a question of weapons, although we don't have enough to just go around wasting them. All of Europe is going to deny them everything, even water. And within the Republic, morale is fucked. When Franco decides to take on Barcelona, it's all over . . ."

Ramón perceived the sincerity of Tom's words. But he refused to give him the pleasure of getting scolded for talking about the fate of his country. He felt how his usual fury gripped him and he preferred to move on to something else.

"You have a wife in Moscow, right?"

Tom smiled.

"Not one, two . . ."

"So you picked me because I'm one of Caridad's sons?"

The adviser was quiet for a few seconds.

"Would you believe me if I said no? . . . Ever since I saw you the first time, I knew you were someone special. I've been watching you for years . . . And I always had a hunch about you. That's why, when Orlov received the order that we should look for Spaniards suitable for working in secret missions, I immediately thought that you were the best candidate. But something warned me that I shouldn't discuss you with Orlov or the others. Now I know why. You're too valuable to be put in just anyone's hands . . ."

Ramón didn't know whether he should feel flattered or offended at having been chosen like a stud. Besides, despite what the man said, Caridad's shadow kept lurking in the background of that story. But the possibility of being at the epicenter of a great event based on his own merits gave him a burning satisfaction.

"If you can, tell me something else, just to know . . ."

"The less you know, the better."

"So, well . . . are you ever going to tell me your real name?"

Tom smiled and finished swallowing one of the meat pies served as appetizers and drank more vodka, staring at the young man.

"What's a name, Jacques? Or are you Ramón now? Those dogs you like so much have names. So what? They're still dogs. Yesterday I was Grigoriev, before I was Kotov, now I'm Tom here and Roberts in New York. Do you know what they call me in the Lubyanka? . . . Leonid Alexandrovich. I gave myself that name so they wouldn't know mine, because they were going to notice that I'm Jewish, and many people in Russia don't like us Jews . . . I am the same and I am different each moment. I am all of them and I am none of them, because I'm just one more person, so very small, in the fight for a dream. A person and a name are nothing . . . Look, there's something very important they taught me when I had just entered the Cheka: a man can be relegated, substituted. The individual is not an unrepeatable unit but rather a concept that is added to and makes up a mass that is real. But man as an individual isn't sacred and, as such, is expendable. That's why we've charged against all religions, especially Christianity, that state that foolishness about man being made in the likeness of God. That allows us to be ruthless, to let go of the compassion that gives way to pity: the worst sin doesn't exist. Do you know what that means? . . . It's better that neither you nor I have a real name and that we forget we ever had one. Ivan, Fyodor, Leonid? It's all the same shit; it's nothing. *Nomina odiosa sunt.* The dream is what matters, not the man, and even less the name. No one is important; we're all expendable . . . And if you end up touching revolutionary glory, you'll do so without having a real name. Perhaps you will never have one. But you will be a formidable part of the greatest dream humanity has ever had." And, raising his cup of vodka, he toasted, "Here's to the nameless ones!"

As soon as he opened the door, he had the feeling that something terrible had happened. He thought of young Luis; that an order was canceling the operation or Jacques Mornard's existence. It had been six months since he had seen her and he had enjoyed that distance. All he felt was relief when Caridad smiled at him as if they had sat down for dinner together the night before. She placed a cigarette at the edge of her mouth as she observed his naked and recently showered torso.

"*Malaguanyada bellesa!*" she said in Catalan as she caressed her son's nipple and walked into the apartment.

Ramón couldn't help getting goose bumps and, with all the delicacy allowed by his anger and his weakness, he moved Caridad's warm hand away.

"What are you doing here? Didn't we decide that no—" Without thinking about it, he had also spoken in Catalan.

"He sent me. I know better than you what can and can't be done."

Caridad had changed in the months that had passed since their only meeting in Paris. It was as if she had gone back in time and buried the holster-wearing Republican combatant who had walked around Barcelona and who she still dragged along despite the tight clothing and the crocodile-skin shoes. She now dressed with the elegant informality of a bohemian woman; her hair was lighter and the waves were distinct; she wore makeup on her face, her nails were long, and she smelled like expensive perfume. She exerted control over high-heeled shoes and even smoked with different movements. It was possible for Jacques to see in Caridad the last remains of the Caridad Ramón had known many years before, before the fall that led to her depression and suicide attempt.

"How's it going with your Trotskyist lizard?" she continued in Catalan as she took off the silk *foulard* covering her neck and shoulders. With measured movements she settled into one of the leather armchairs, in front of the window through which one could see the already ocher-colored tops of boulevard Raspail's trees.

"As it should," he said, and went to his room in search of a satin robe.

"Make some coffee, please."

Without answering, he went to the kitchen to prepare it.

"What does Tom want?" he asked from the kitchen.

"Tom has to stay in Spain, so he sent me . . ."

"And what's the matter with George?"

"He's in Moscow."

"Did Yezhov send for him?" Ramón looked into the living room and saw Caridad with a cigarette in one hand and a lighter in the other, her gaze fixed on the window as if she were addressing the panes.

"Yezhov isn't going to send for anyone anymore. They've taken him out of the game. Now Beria is in charge."

"When did that happen?" Ramón took one step into the living room, his attention divided between the brewing coffee and what Caridad was telling him.

"A week ago. Tom asked me to come and tell you, because things could go into motion at any moment. As soon as Beria cleans up Yezhov's shit and Comrade Stalin gives the order, we'll go into action. When Mink comes back, we'll know more . . ."

Ramón felt his muscles tense. It was the best news he could have received.

"Have they told you anything about Orlov?"

"He's in Washington, singing like a canary. He still presents a threat to many projects, but not for ours. In the end, it wasn't because of him that we took the other comrades out of Mexico who were already there."

"The Spaniards?"

Caridad lit her cigarette before responding.

"Yes. With Yezhov, almost the entire New York and Mexican networks went down. A disaster . . ."

Ramón Mercader tried to place himself in the new puzzle of betrayals, desertions, purges, and real or fictitious dangers and, as tended to happen to him, he felt lost. The ultimate reasons for Moscow's decisions were too intricate, and perhaps not even Tom himself could know all of the complexities of those witch hunts. He just reaffirmed the necessity to himself, often repeated by Tom, of discretion as the best immunization to guard himself against betrayals. But in the welter of tensions at play, he noticed more clearly what his mentor had considered to be the value of his actions. It was a contradictory feeling, of fear at the responsibility and joy over knowing he was closer to the great mission. He took the coffee off the flame and started to serve it.

"What about Tom? Will he stay in Spain?" he asked in French.

"Yes, for now." She continued to speak in Catalan. "There's not much to do there, but he has to stay until the end. Negrín is fighting with him, but he can't live without him . . . the Republican army keeps sliding back. Spain is lost, Ramón."

"Don't say that to me, goddammit!" he yelled, again in French, and the coffee spilled on one of the small plates. "And don't speak to me in Catalan!"

Caridad didn't flinch and he waited to calm down. He didn't know if it was the news of Spain or the uncertainty this added to Luis's fate—weeks before he had crossed the border to join the Republican army—or simply his mother's malevolent insistence on stirring up the past and poking at the cracks in Jacques Mornard's identity. He finished serving the coffee and entered the living room carrying the cups on a tray. He sat down in front of her, taking care that his robe not open.

"What does Tom think will happen?"

"Franco's troops are going for Catalonia," she answered, now in Spanish. "And he thinks they're not going to be able to stop them. Ever since these French faggots and those shitty Brits signed that pact with Hitler and Mussolini, not only did Czechoslovakia get fucked but we also got fucked: no one can help us anymore . . . *Estem ben fotuts, noi. T'asseguro que estem ben fotuts . . .*"

"So what are the Soviets going to do?"

"They can't do anything. If they meddle in Spain, a war will start that would be the end of the Soviet Union . . ."

Ramón listened to Caridad's argument. In some way he agreed with her, but it was painful for him to confirm that the Soviets were withdrawing as Hitler swallowed up Czechoslovakia and gave Franco more and more support. Perhaps the Soviet tactic of allowing the sacrifice of the Republic was the only possible one, but it was still cruel. The party, at least, had accepted it, and La Pasionaria herself said that if the Republic had to be lost, it would be lost: they could not compromise the fate of the USSR, the great homeland of communism . . . But what was going to happen to those men, Communists or mere Republicans, who had fought, obeyed, and believed for two and a half years for nothing? Would they be left at the mercy of the pro-Franco forces? Where could young Luis be fighting right now? Ramón preferred not to ask his questions out loud. He observed how Caridad finished her coffee and returned it to the tray. Then he leaned over and tasted his. It had gone cold.

"Tom doesn't want me to talk about Spain. Jacques isn't interested in Spain." He tried to pull himself together.

"Jacques reads the papers, doesn't he? What's he going to say when his Trotskyist girlfriend tells him that Stalin is going to make a pact with Hitler, as well as with the French and the English? Because that's what that renegade louse is writing in that fucking bulletin of his."

"Jacques would tell her the same thing: Change the subject; that's not his problem."

Caridad looked at him with that green and piercing intensity that he had always feared so much.

"Be careful. That woman is a fanatic, and Trotsky is her god."

Jacques smiled. He had a card up his sleeve to defeat Caridad.

"You're mistaken. I'm her god, and Trotsky, if anything, is her prophet."

"You've become sarcastic and subtle, kid," she said, smiling.

Caridad stood up and started to place the *foulard* over her shoulders. Ramón was pulled between wanting her to stay and wanting her to go. Speaking in Catalan again had been like visiting a closed-off region of himself that he hadn't wanted to enter but, once inside, provoked a sense of comfortable belonging. Besides, he knew she was in touch with Montse and, above all, with young Luis, and perhaps even knew something about África. But now was the least appropriate time to roll over before her and show his weaknesses. It was the first time that he had felt truly superior to her and he didn't want to squander the feeling.

Caridad's visit left him full of expectations regarding the orders that could come from Moscow, but also the bitter taste of the fate of the Republic that, as much as he tried, Jacques Mornard could not remove from the mind of Ramón Mercader. Because of that, on that early December afternoon, he had to call on all his discipline to bury Ramón's passions deep inside himself when Sylvia asked him to accompany her to see some U.S. comrades who had fought in Spain, members of the international troops evacuated by the government of the Republic, who were now in Paris.

"What do I have to do with those people?" he asked, making clear his annoyance at the proposal.

Sylvia, surprised and perhaps even offended, tried to convince him.

"Those people were fighting against fascism, Jacques. Although there are many beliefs I don't share with them, I respect them and I admire them. The majority of them didn't even know how to march when they went to Spain, but they've been able to fight for all of us."

"I didn't ask them to fight for me," he managed to say.

"They didn't ask you, either. But they know that many things are decided in Spain, that the rise of fascism is a problem for everyone, you included."

Winter had come quickly and the air was sharp. Jacques took her by the arm and made her enter a café. They sat down at a table to the side, and before the waiter could approach them, Jacques shouted:

"Two coffees!" He focused on Sylvia. "What did we agree?"

The girl took off her glasses, steamed up by the change in temperature, and rubbed the lenses with the edge of her skirt. At that moment Jacques realized he was afraid of himself. How could she be so ugly, so stupid, so much of an imbecile as to tell him who was fighting for what? How long could he stand to be next to a being who disgusted him?

"I'm sorry, my love. I didn't mean to—"

"It doesn't seem like it."

"It's just that it really is important. In Spain, a lot is decided and Stalin is again letting Hitler and the fascists get their way. Stalin never wanted or allowed the Spaniards to make the revolution that would have saved them and . . ."

"What are you talking about?" Jacques asked, and he immediately understood that he had made a mistake.

Jacques simply couldn't care what Sylvia was talking about and he made himself regain his control. Neither those loathsome accusations nor Sylvia Ageloff's ugliness would get the best of him. They were served their coffee and the break helped him regain his composure.

"Sylvia, if you want, go see those saviors of humanity and talk to them about Stalin and your beloved Trotsky. You have every right to. But don't involve me in it. I'm just not interested. Can you understand that for once, dammit?"

The woman shrunk into herself and sank into a long silence; finally she took a sip of coffee. Two months before, Sylvia's insistence on talking about politics had caused the couple's first serious argument. That afternoon, Jacques had accompanied her to the villa of the Trotskyist Alfred Rosmer, in Périgny, so the girl could serve as the secretary at the meeting that, according to Sylvia herself, had signified the abortion rather than the birth of the Trotskyist International. As they were returning to Paris, after castigating her and making her promise she wouldn't speak of those matters again, Jacques took advantage of the situation to try to make her give up her return trip to New York at the beginning of the new school year and to drop the hint—as if he were placing a noose around Sylvia's neck—that they should be formally engaged. But political passion was once again betraying Sylvia, who, fearful of her lover's reaction, murmured:

"Yes, my love. I appreciate you letting me go. But if you don't want me to, I won't go."

Jacques smiled. Things were returning to normal. His preeminence had been reestablished and he understood that he could be very cruel with that defenseless being. Further still, he found it satisfying to do so. Something malignant within him revealed itself in that relationship and he was discovering how much he enjoyed the possibility of bending wills, of generating fear, of exercising power over other people until they crawled in front of him. Would he ever have the chance to exercise that control over Caridad? Though he didn't have a name or a homeland, he was a man gifted with hate, faith, and, in addition, a power he was going to use as long as possible.

"Of course I want you to go, if that makes you happy," he said, satisfied, magnanimous. "I have to go shopping to send my parents some presents for Christmas. What do you want me to give you?"

Sylvia relaxed. She looked at him and in her myopic eyes were gratitude and love.

"Don't worry about me, dear."

"I'll see what I find to surprise you," he said, and took her hand atop the table and forced her to lean toward him to give her a kiss on the lips.

Jacques felt the woman was overcome with emotion and told himself that he should administer his power carefully or he could kill her with an overdose.

Less than two years later, Ramón Mercader would come to understand that the tests of psychological strength he was subjected to during the last bitter weeks of 1938 and the first of 1939 were to be a grotesque rehearsal for the worst experiences that he went through at the most critical moment of his life, and it required all his powers of resistance in order to prevent a total breakdown.

Although the news arriving from Spain throughout December sketched out the magnitude of the disaster, Jacques Mornard managed to maintain a façade of distant political skepticism. With greater vehemence, he avoided the discussions of politics before him and on one occasion left a meeting when those present insisted on steeping themselves in the unpleasant and silly matters of the war, fascism, and French politics.

In the solitude of his apartment, however, he read all of the press articles that could reveal something to him about the situation in Spain and listened to the radio news programs as if looking for a ray of hope amid the shadows. But each piece of news was a knife through the heart of his illusions. There he gave free rein to his contained anger, his impotence, and screamed curses, kicked the furniture, and swore to take revenge. Those outbursts, nearly hysterical, left him exhausted and showed him the weakness of Jacques Mornard against the passions of Ramón Mercader, but they reaffirmed his disdain for everything that hinted of fascism, the bourgeoisie, and the betrayal of the proletariat's ideals. His hidden desires to change places with his brother Luis, who was still fighting with the remains of the Popular Army amid the chaos and the capriciousness of Spanish politicians, turned into an obsession for him, and he swore to himself that when the time came to act against the enemies, he would be implacable and ruthless, like the enemies of his dream were being with that attempt to build a more just world.

The lack of news from Tom added to his uncertainty. He feared for the fate of his mentor, so prone to involving himself and transgressing limits. If they killed him or made him a prisoner in Spain, all of their efforts and the structure they had helped put together could come crashing down, as had already occurred with other operative lines. Among his worries was also the fact that the time for Sylvia's return was upon them. The girl said she had to return to her job the second week of February and had set the first day of the month as her departure date. Although Jacques knew that a little bit of pressure could dissuade her, he felt that living with Sylvia any longer would require an effort he wasn't prepared for and feared that the woman's sickliness could make him explode at any moment.

The reappearance of George Mink in the second week of January brought some relief to Jacques Mornard's anxiety. They met at the Montparnasse cemetery and, on learning the details of the meeting, Jacques thought that he would never completely understand the Soviets: the night before it had snowed relentlessly, and this was supposed to be the coldest day of the year.

As they had agreed, Mink was waiting for him next to the tomb of Prince D'Achery, Duke of San Donnino, and Madame Viez, in the seventh division of the avenue d'Ouest. The snow had made a compact layer of ice over which he had to walk carefully. The cemetery, as could be expected, was deserted, and upon seeing Mink's dark figure amid that white landscape, flanked by two lions who made up the prince's singular mausoleum, Jacques told himself that nothing could seem more suspicious than a meeting at that place in that weather.

"Good day, Jacques, my friend."

"'Good day'? Wouldn't you like to have a coffee somewhere warm?"

"It's just that I love cemeteries, did you know? For years I've been living in a world where no one knows who's who, what's real and what's a lie, and, less still, how long you'll be alive . . . Here, at least, you feel surrounded by a great certainty, the greatest certainty . . . Besides, what we have today isn't cold, not real cold . . ."

"Please, George. Does it have to be here?"

"Did you know that when Trotsky and Natalia Sedova met, they used to come here to read Baudelaire in front of his tomb?"

"Even in this shitty cold?"

"Baudelaire's tomb is over there. Do you want to see it?"

They left the frozen cemetery and walked to place Denfert-Rochereau, where Jacques had had coffee before. Even inside the café they picked, Jacques kept his coat on, since he now felt as if the cold were coming from inside of him.

Mink had returned four days before with orders he had received from Beria personally. Besides, as he expected, in the embassy in Paris they also had guidelines sent by Tom from Spain.

"What have you heard about Tom? The French are threatening to close the border."

"That's no problem for Tom. He always gets out."

"What are the orders? What do I have to do? Should Sylvia leave?"

"Let her go. But with something to bring her back to you. Promise her marriage."

Jacques breathed a sigh of relief at that authorization.

"So what do I tell her? That I'll go see her, that she should come in the summer . . . ?"

"Don't assure her of anything. Tell her you'll tell her your decision in a letter. The order from Moscow could come tomorrow or in six months, and you have to be ready for that moment. When Tom returns, he'll organize things. Beria wants him to focus only on this work from now on. Stalin's orders. Incidentally, Stalin himself named the operation: Utka."

"Utka?"

"*Utka*, duck . . . And any method would be good to hunt him: poisoning his food or his water, an explosion in his house or car, strangulation, a knife in the back, a blow to the head, a gunshot to the base of his skull." Mink took a breath and concluded: "Even an attack by an armed group or a bomb dropped from the air haven't been ruled out."

Jacques asked himself into which square of that chess game he would fit. It was obvious that something was finally starting to take shape, although the reasons for the slowness with which the operation was moving escaped him.

"What did they say in Moscow when they brought down Yezhov?"

Mink smiled and drank his tea.

"Nothing. In Moscow, those things aren't discussed. People were so afraid of Yezhov that they won't be cured for a long time."

Jacques looked toward the *place*. He couldn't be bothered to face the cold again to return to his apartment, where Sylvia was waiting for him. He understood that he needed action. At that exact moment, where was África? What was his brother Luis doing? What adventures had Tom embarked on? He didn't have any alternative but to wait, inactive, acting like a lovestruck man who doesn't want his lover to leave.

"When will we see each other again?"

"If there's nothing new, when Tom returns. If you have anything urgent to ask, go look for me at the cemetery. I always pass by there."

In the days prior to Sylvia's departure, Jacques behaved in a way that Josefino and Cicero, his Malakhovka professors, would have admired. Overcoming his low spirits and his desire to be far from that farce, he exploited the relief getting rid of that woman represented to him to the utmost and showered her with attention and gifts for her and her sisters, and he had the fortitude to make love to her every day until an ecstatic and satisfied Sylvia returned to New York. Jacques had done his job and was happy with the space and freedom he'd recovered.

From Spain, by contrast, only news of the painful death rattles of the war came. Barcelona's fall seemed to be the final act, and the reports that Franco had entered a city that cheered him filled Ramón Mercader with bitterness. Starting at the end of January, the French papers were picking up, with various degrees of alarm, the news of the scattering of combatants, officers, politicians, and desperate people fearful of reprisals who had leaped to cross the border. There was already talk of hundreds of thousands of people, hungry and without any resources, who would burst the logistical capacities of the forces of order and the possibility of being taken in by the French. Some politicians, at the height of cynicism, recognized that perhaps it would have been better to help them win the war than to be forced now to receive them, feed them, and dress them for who knew how long. The right-wing newspapers, meanwhile, called out their solution: Send them to the colonies. People like that were what was needed in Guyana, in the Congo, and in Senegal.

Changed by Ramón's passions, Jacques Mornard noticed that he needed to break out of his inertia, even at the price of sacrificing his discipline. He knew what was at risk if he disobeyed strict orders to stay far away from anything having to do with Spain, but the anger and the desperation won him over. Besides, Tom still hadn't shown up, and if he did, he would have no reason to tell him. So, on February 6, he took his car, his cameras, and his journalistic credentials and headed toward Le Perthus, the border town that had the largest concentration of refugees.

At noon on the eighth, when the Belgian journalist Jacques Mornard managed to reach the closest point to the border that the army officers and the French police allowed, the malignant stench of defeat welcomed him. He confirmed that, from the promontory where the press reporters were, he wouldn't be recognized by any of the people who, already on French territory, were led like sheep by the Senegalese soldiers who were in charge of watching and controlling them. The scene ended up being more pathetic than he was capable of imagining. A human wave, covered with rags, traveling with a few cars or hanging on to the rickety carts pulled by starving horses, or simply on foot, dragging suitcases and bundles in which they had stuffed all of their lives' belongings, accepted in silence orders that were incomprehensible to them, shouted in French and punctuated by warning gestures and threatening truncheons. Those were people launched into an exodus of biblical proportions, pushed only by the will to survive; beings weighed down with an enormous list of frustrations and tangible losses with gazes from which even dignity had disappeared. Jacques knew that many of those men and women were the same ones who had sung and danced for every Republican victory, the same ones who for a variety of reasons had placed themselves behind the barricades that periodically went up in Barcelona, the same ones who had dreamed of victory, revolution, democracy, and justice, and had, on many occasions, ruthlessly practiced revolutionary violence. Now defeat had reduced them to the condition of pariahs without a dream to hold on to. Many were wearing the uniforms of the Popular Army and, their weapons handed over, were silently following the Senegalese orders ("*Reculez! Reculez!*" the Africans insisted, enjoying their bit of power) without caring about maintaining a minimum of composure. Jacques learned from a British correspondent, recently arrived from Figueres, that the majority of children escaping from Spain were arriving sick with pneumonia and many of them would die if they didn't receive immediate medical attention. But the only order the French had was to take all weapons away and lead the refugees, big and small, to some camps enclosed by barbed wire, where they would remain until each one's fate was decided. A feeling of suffocation had started to take over him and he wasn't surprised when tears blurred his vision. He gave a half turn and walked away, trying to calm himself down. He forced himself to think that it had been a predictable but not a definitive defeat. That revolutions must also accept their setbacks and prepare themselves for the next attack. That the sacrifice of those defenseless beings, and of those who—like his brother Pablo—had died during those almost three years of war, barely represented a minimal offering before the altar of a history that, in the end, would vindicate them with the glorious victory of the world's proletariat. The future and the struggle constituted the only hope at that moment of frustration. But he discovered that the slogans weren't helping him and that at some moment he couldn't pinpoint in that piercing afternoon, he had lost Jacques Mornard in some corner of his consciousness and had again become, fully and deeply, Ramón Mercader del Río, the Spanish Communist. It was satisfying to him to know that at least Ramón had a higher mission to fulfill in that ruthless world tightly divided between revolutionaries and fascists, between the exploited and exploiters, and that scenes like this one, far from damaging him, strengthened him: his hate was becoming more compact, armored and complete. I am Ramón Mercader and I am full of hate! he yelled in his head. When he turned around to look for the last time at the wretched scene of the debacle that underpinned his convictions, he felt how his cameras moved and remembered that that idiot Jacques Mornard had forgotten to take a single image of the failure. It was at that moment that a French journalist, almost with disgust, pronounced those words that were to change the shape of his smile:

"What a disgrace! They weren't able to win and now they come to hide here!"

The blow Ramón served him was brutal. Of the four teeth he knocked out, two fell on the damp earth and two were lost in the stomach of the unfortunate journalist, who would surely ask himself, for the rest of his life, what terrible thing he had said to provoke the ire of that unleashed madman who, to top it all, had disappeared like a breath of air.

18

Of all the battles he'd waged, which did he remember as the most arduous? Those with Lenin in the days of the split between Bolsheviks and Mensheviks? The tense and dramatic ones of 1917, when the revolution's birth or abortion was decided? The furious battles of the civil war, always doomed to fratricidal violence? The cruel ones for succession and for control of the party? The ones for physical and political survival in those days of exile and marginalization? And who had been his most fearful adversary: Lenin, Plekhanov, Stalin? When Lev Davidovich looked at the blank page over which he didn't dare to move his pen, he thought, no, the battle had never been as arduous nor the opponent as tricky, for he had never seen himself forced to fight for something so essential.

Ever since Natalia Sedova left the Casa Azul and he took refuge with the bodyguards in the cabin in the hills of San Miguel Regla, under the pretext of the need for physical exercise, but so pressed to gain distance from the Casa Azul in order to stew in the solitude of his desperation and shame, he had been looking for the most elegant way to initiate a reconciliation with his wife with the knowledge that his dignity should be the first piece he would have to sacrifice in the service of his supreme objective.

The feeling of guilt that had been absent until then had unleashed itself, and not only because of the damage he had done to Natalia. During that infamous month of June 1937, the lives of two of his dearest and most constant friends had been devoured by Stalin's fury, while he, submerged in the renewed waves of his libido, dedicated the best part of his intelligence to engineering ways to mock Diego and Natalia's presence, to run behind Frida to Cristina Kahlo's nearby house, on Calle Linares, the site of their sexual encounters. Van Heijenoort and the young bodyguards had been made to serve as facilitators of the meetings, lending themselves to the fictions that Lev Davidovich's feverish brain devised: from hunting and fishing to trips to the mountains, even as far as the search for documents that he had to track down personally, he had used every excuse. For his protectors, the situation had proven to be agonizing, since they knew the physical risks of each escapade and, above all, in a scandalous venting of an affair that could destroy the Exile's marriage and affect his prestige as a revolutionary generously welcomed in the Casa Azul, or even could provoke a violent reaction from Rivera. But he had decided not to think about anything else, and was concerned only with giving in to his cravings and receiving Frida's uninhibited sexuality, capable of revealing to him, at his fifty-seven years, means and practices the existence of which he had barely suspected. Never as in those days of lust had madness spun around Lev Davidovich's mind so forcefully and when he looked at himself in the mirror, he saw the image of a man whom he barely recognized and who, nonetheless, continued to be none other than himself.

On the afternoon of June 11, after a morning round with Frida, he had dedicated himself to documenting one of the darkest passages of his relationship with Stalin: the day in 1907, exactly thirty years before, when they had met in London and, perhaps, when the war between them had commenced. Natalia, who already perceived the density of deceit in the air, entered the room and, without saying a word, placed the newspaper over the page he was writing. Without looking up, Lev Davidovich read the headline and felt the anguish growing in his chest as he devoured the report taken from *Pravda*. In Moscow, the case had been initiated against eight high-ranking Red Army officers, led by Marshal Tukhachevsky, the second in command in the military hierarchy, and the trial had been set for sentencing. The court judging them, the dispatch relayed, was a special section of the Supreme Court and was made up by "the cream of the crop of the glorious Red Army."

The former commissar of war noticed that, in contrast to the trials carried out in the previous year, Tukhachevsky and the other generals were not accused of Trotskyism but rather of being members of an organization in the service of the Third Reich. Even when it was already known that the old officers of the Red Army were in Stalin's sight, Lev Davidovich had not been able to imagine that, unless they had more solid proof of the existence of the conspiracy, the Grave Digger would dare to decapitate the country's military cupola at a moment in which war seemed inevitable. He knew that ever since Tukhachevsky's substitution as deputy commissar of defense two months before, many detentions must have been ordered among the high officers; furthermore, he was sure that the fate of those soldiers had been decided when it was made public that the administrative and political person responsible for the army, the old Bolshevik Gamarnik, had committed suicide, while four of his advisers mysteriously disappeared.

The next morning, Moscow reported the summary execution of the accused, who, they assured, had confessed their treason. Stupefaction and pain had paralyzed Lev Davidovich: he knew that perhaps Stalin was right in fearing that the leaders of the army could plot a conspiracy to remove him from power, but it was inadmissible to accuse those men—military mainstays of the revolution from its darkest days—of being the agents of a fascist power, especially when the list of prisoners was headed by, precisely, Communists and Jews such as generals Yakir, Eidemann, and Feldmann. But if in reality the soldiers had conspired, why hadn't they acted? Why had they delayed the coup when they were warned that they were sought after?

Never before had Lev Davidovich felt fear like that for the future of the revolution and the country, at the same time that he was convinced that if Stalin dared to take that mortal leap, it was because he had Hitler's promise in hand to respect the borders of the USSR in case of war. If that was not the case, the fascist leaders had to think that Stalin was definitively crazy to accept the story of a conspiracy that no rational being would believe, since the mere fact of placing three high-ranking officers of Jewish origins as the heads of a pro-German plot would have been incredible even for the Nazis themselves, the supposed friends of the traitors. The inevitable conclusion had been that, with that process, Stalin was taking another step in his rapprochement with Hitler, whom he had denounced so many times since the electoral rise of Fascism.

For several days Lev Davidovich had ceased to look for Frida in order to take refuge in the sure comfort of his Natasha, for whom the death of Tukhachevsky, like so many others who stirred in her memory, were losses of people for whom she felt affection. How many more was Stalin going to kill? Natalia asked him one night as they drank coffee in their room, and he offered his response to her: as long as there remained one Bolshevik with the memory of the past, the henchmen would have work. The war to the death was no longer against the opposition but against history. To do it right, Stalin had to kill all those who knew Lenin, and those who knew Lev Davidovich, and, of course, those who knew Stalin ... He had to silence all those who had been witnesses to his failures, to the genocide of the collectivization, of the murdering madness of his work camps ... and then he would still have to remove from the world those who had helped annihilate the opposition, the past, history, and also annoying witnesses ... "And Sergei? Liova? Why hasn't he already come for us?" the woman then asked herself. He saw that Natalia Sedova's eyes had the vague glimmer of pain and felt in his chest the pressure of the shame over his weaknesses and refused to tell her that his sons were as condemned to die as the two of them. Perhaps tormented by the pain, at that moment he committed one of the most unforgivable slips of his life and asked Natalia if she was afraid of dying. From dull blue, her eyes went to the color of steel, like that of a wet dagger, and he felt a fear that he had never had of anything in his life: no, she didn't fear death, the woman said. She worried only that respect and trust might die.

Feeling himself drowning in shame, Lev Davidovich thought the time had come to put an end to his relationship with Frida.

Days later, Lev Davidovich would tell himself that another piece of news, this time arriving from Spain, had been the one to blame for delaying the decision to cut off his clandestine affair. The confirmation that his old colleague Andreu Nin had disappeared after being detained, accused of charges similar to those used in Moscow, threatened to drown him in depression and prevented him from overcoming his compulsive need for the voracious sex of Diego Rivera's wife.

The story of Nin's detention and disappearance was full of contradictions and, as usual, challenged credulity. Through various sources, the Exile managed to establish that on June 16 the police had taken the Catalan Communist out of Barcelona to Valencia. The last confirmed news placed him, on the night of June 22, at a special prison in Alcalá de Henares, from where, according to the official press, he had been bizarrely rescued by a German commando, charged with taking him to fascist territory and, later, of sending him to Berlin.

The accusation that Nin was one of Franco's spies was crude and unsustainable: Stalin's men in Spain hadn't even concerned themselves too much with the believability of their accusations. The disappearance and almost certain death of that friend who more than ten years earlier Lev Davidovich had met in Moscow and who had joined the opposition without ever renouncing his own political criteria as a convinced and anarchic Communist could only be due to the shocking capacity Nin had to resist the tortures of the GPU without signing the statements that, with all certainty, were placed before him. A fighter like Nin would've known, from the beginning of his Calvary, that his fate was decreed, but that the prestige of his party and the lives of his comrades, accused of promoting a coup d'état, depended on his lips. So conquering Stalin must have become his last obsession as he was tortured and he refused to sign the condemnation of the Spanish left and of his own memory.

The image of a young, always war-like Tukhachevsky who had become one of the mainstays in the middle of the civil war of the recently created Red Army, and Andreu Nin's awkward and passionate image, that of a man dazzled by the Soviet reality but always questioning it, would accompany Lev Davidovich to the burial of his last grasp of youth. Yet after the first erotic encounters, Frida had started to send him signals that could be read as holding back that the man, drunk with sex, had refused or been incapable of understanding, even when it hadn't gone unnoticed that, after the first meetings, she had tried to evade him (her political and sexual curiosity perhaps satisfied, her possible revenge against Rivera's infidelities fulfilled), causing him to pursue her with even more fury. When at last they lay down in intimacy, she tried to finish quickly as he confessed over and over again how much he loved her, desired her, dreamed about her.

The tension went up like a barricade inside the Casa Azul, and it was Natalia Sedova who, at the beginning of July, lit the fuse when, without consulting with anyone, she moved to an apartment in the city center, giving Rivera the excuse that she preferred to be alone as she underwent medical treatment for "feminine problems." Faced with that situation, Frida must have understood that their foolishness was beginning to reach the limits of what could be controlled, and that same afternoon had entered the guest room and attacked her lover along the flank he least expected: they had to clarify things once and for all, and he should make a definitive decision: was he leaving his wife or staying with her? The challenge had stirred the man, but he responded without thinking and he told her he had never thought of making such a choice. With difficult steps, Frida approached him and caressed her lover's face and, calling him Piochitas—from the name Mexicans give to a goatee—told him the game had ended. It was no longer fun and they could hurt other people who didn't deserve it, and she didn't say it because of Diego, an alcoholic pig, nor because of herself, whom Diego had turned into an untamed pig; she said it because of Natalia, who was a queen.

At that moment Lev Davidovich had understood that perhaps he would never manage to know through exact science what chemical reaction had burned inside Frida to make her throw herself into their affair. He would ask himself whether he had been used just as an instrument of revenge against Rivera (was it possible that the painter hadn't noticed anything?); whether his historic halo might have motivated the young woman's dazzling curiosity; even whether pity at seeing him suffer before her sister's rejection had convinced Frida, who was so liberal, that indulging the sexual appetite of a man who was twice her age was just an act of enjoyable pity that didn't impact her relaxed morality at all. But when Frida's perfume had gone from the air in the room, Lev Davidovich managed to smile. Had the game really ended? Only for Frida. It was now up to him to clean up the filth dammed up in his spirit and try to salvage, with the least amount of damage possible, Natalia Sedova's trust and love. But thirty years of companionship warned him that he would have to deal with an indomitable animal who devoted the same vehemence to her solidarity as to her hate, to her love as to rejection. I'm scared, he thought.

A few days later, observing the arid mountains of San Miguel from his window, a Lev Davidovich already resolved to sacrifice his dignity and overcome his fears took a piece of paper and began the most intense and strange correspondence, of up to two letters per day, in which he recognized his emotional and biological dependence on his wife. When she left the Casa Azul, Natalia had left him a note capable of wounding him like a dagger. She had looked at herself in the mirror, she said, and seen the death of her charms at the hands of old age. She didn't reproach him for anything, but she stated that what he had done was an irreversible act. Lev Davidovich had understood the meaning of the message: that her old age was coming at the end of thirty years of a life in common, throughout which Natasha had lived by and for him. At that moment he began to write pleas, often signed as "Your faithful old dog," a sort of increasingly plaintive knocking on the doors of a heart he was trying to reconquer with memories of yesterday and sentimental and physical needs of the present, expressed at times in language so direct that he surprised himself . . . When at last he received a letter from her, concerned by the pessimism that prevented her husband from focusing on his work, he knew the battle was won and that the victor had been his dear Natasha's sense of kindness: "You will continue to carry me on your shoulders, Nata, as you have carried me throughout your life," he wrote to her, and on the following day, with the inevitable entourage, he took the road to the capital in search of the woman of his life.

An event in Paris, of which Liova informed him, attracted his attention when they returned to the Casa Azul. Ignace Reiss, the nom de guerre of one of the heads of the Soviet secret service in Europe, had approached Lev Sedov to communicate his intention to desert. The young man, with understandable caution, held two meetings with the agent, who told him, among other horrors, that Yezhov and several soldiers designated by Stalin had been the ones who, in agreement with the Germans, fabricated the false accusations used to try the heads of the Red Army. According to Reiss, the purge of soldiers, which was still in progress, was not only necessary for Stalin's political security but also part of the collaboration sustaining Stalinism and Nazism, under the cover of their respective hates, and had the objective of facilitating the alliance with which they would arrive at the war. The secret services were playing the most active role, for the time being, in that cooperative effort, and what most horrified Reiss was the betrayal that such a machination represented for all the revolutionaries in the world who were enlisting in the antifascist struggle along with the USSR—for the Communists who, despite what happened in Moscow, still obeyed.

As Trotsky read the reports about Reiss, the Exile felt growing disgust at the betrayal of the most sacred principles. And despite the disgraces that Reiss had surely committed due to his profession, he couldn't help but feel admiration for a man who, he knew well, had placed his neck under the executioner's axe. His greatest fear, however, was that Reiss's break had implicated Liova and the Fourth International, and that when in anger Stalin let loose his henchmen, the Trotskyists were going to once again be his scapegoat.

Lev Davidovich didn't have to wait much longer to find out the denouement of that story that would end up touching the very center of his life: on September 6, Liova gave him the news that, a few days earlier, Reiss had been killed on a highway close to Lausanne. The police suspected that the committee for the repatriation of Russian citizens, one of the NKVD fronts created in Paris, was responsible. That same day, by a parallel route, he received another letter, sent by his collaborator Rudolf Klement, in which he commented that Reiss had assured him that one of the plans of the Stalinist police was the elimination of the Trotskyists outside the USSR and that Lev Sedov topped the list. Thus, Klement advised the evacuation of the young man, who was already on the edge of a physical and nervous breakdown due to the political and economic tensions under which he was carrying out his work, exacerbated by personal complications ever since his wife, Jeanne, had declared herself a supporter of her ex-husband Raymond Molinier's political faction. Because of that, following a conversation with Natalia in which they weighed the options for the young man's future, Lev Davidovich wrote to Liova, asking his opinion regarding Klement's fears, before proposing any alternative measures to protect his life.

As they waited for Liova's response, the long-awaited verdict of the Dewey commission finally arrived. As Lev Davidovich had foreseen, Dewey and the rest of the members of the jury had reached the conclusion that the Moscow trials of August 1936 and January 1937 had been fraudulent and, as a result, declared him and his son innocent. Excited, he sent a telegram to Liova, demanding that he get as much publicity for the results of the counterproceeding as he could, and that he gather journalists and reporters to initiate a propaganda offensive. At the same time Lev Davidovich would devote himself to preparing the articles to accompany the text of the sentence in a special edition of the *Bulletin*.

Just a few months later, Lev Davidovich would try to clarify the ways in which his personal life and history became intertwined in those moments until they drove him to his greatest tragedy, because in the middle of the storm of optimism unleashed by the verdict they received Liova's response. The young man (like his father) considered that for the time being he was irreplaceable in Paris and could not delegate his duties to Klement, who was already tasked with coordinating the Fourth International, or to Étienne, his most responsible collaborator. It was true, he confessed, that he had financial problems, that he was living in a cold attic, that his relationship with Jeanne had become complicated, and that what had happened in Moscow had affected him more than he originally thought it would, since practically all of the men he had grown up surrounded by and who had been his role models had gone down one by one after admitting to horrible betrayals. Natalia and Lev Davidovich again discussed Liova's fate, and at that moment it seemed to them unfair to ask him to come to Mexico, almost certainly without his wife, to shut himself away, since, if he didn't hide, he would just be substituting one danger for another. Lev Davidovich then told his wife that he trusted in Liova's ability to take care of himself, and that perhaps Stalin would think that killing him would be excessive. "Nothing is excessive for him," Natalia commented. Despite agreeing with her husband, she would have preferred to have the boy closer to them.

It was around that time that a certain Josep Nadal showed up in Coyoacán. The man said he was Catalan, a POUM militant, and a very close friend of Andreu Nin. In light of the repression unleashed in Spain against his party, Nadal had preferred to get as far away as possible. Since he was asking for an interview with Comrade Trotsky, van Heijenoort held a meeting with him and, upon returning, confessed to Lev Davidovich that he had felt a stinging in his back as he talked to the man. The deaths of Nin and Reiss warned Lev Davidovich and his inner circle of the new Stalinist offensive outside the USSR, and they all knew that any humble Spanish worker, any German refugee, any French intellectual, could be the black angel sent by Moscow. But, motivated by what the Catalan seemed to know about Nin's disappearance, Lev Davidovich decided to see him on the condition that Jean van Heijenoort be present during the interview.

The Catalan ended up being a loquacious man with sharp reasoning who, despite his excessive love of cigarettes, captivated Lev Davidovich. According to him, there was no doubt: Nin was dead and his murderers had been directed by the men in Moscow who were imposing their rule on the Republican alliance. The comments he had heard pointed at a Soviet adviser named Kotov and the French Communist André Marty, famous for his brutality, as the organizers of the operation charged with kidnapping Nin and eliminating him when he refused to sign confessions of his collaboration with Franco's supporters.

Nadal, who, due to his proximity to Nin, was familiar with many political secrets, would confirm to Lev Davidovich several of his suspicions about Moscow's strategy in Spain. For him, it was clear that Stalin was playing for the domination and eventual sacrifice of the Republic with several cards, and one of them was financial. After getting Negrín, in his days as the minister of finance, to authorize the Spanish treasury to be moved to Soviet territory, an enormous amount of money seemed to have evaporated and now new payments in cash were demanded of the Republican government for military assistance. The weapons received, Nin had told him, were sufficient for the Republic to resist in the short term but insufficient to stand up to the fascists supported by Hitler and Mussolini, and the real reason that they didn't sell more war matériel to the government was that Stalin wasn't interested in a Republican army that was well enough equipped to aspire to victory; once they reached that point, they could end up being uncontrollable . . . But since the financial yoke didn't guarantee control, Stalin had also ordered the political manipulation of the Republic.

The offensive against the POUM's "Trotskyists," the anarchists, syndicalist groups, and even the Socialists who did not agree with Moscow's policies had begun in 1936, but the great repression had started after the events in Barcelona in May. According to Nadal, the results of that operation could already be felt; the Communists now dominated the three sectors that most interested Stalin: domestic security, the army, and propaganda. Meanwhile, the Comintern advisers and the men from the GPU were working out in the open, deciding political positions and directing the repression. The two most visible representatives of the Communist International had been, until a few weeks before, the Frenchman Marty and the Argentinean Vittorio Codovilla, the former in charge of the International Brigades and the latter in control of the Communist Party. The hatefulness of these men was so palpable that Marty was called "the Butcher from Albacete" because of his cruelty with the international volunteers, and Codovilla was such a dictator that the International itself had to replace him with the more discreet Palmiro Togliatti.

Lev Davidovich listened to the POUMist's statement without asking any questions. Nadal was smoking with old-fashioned relish; the abstinence he had been subject to in Spain still made him anxious. Calling him Comrade Trotsky, he then asked what would remain of the dream of the Soviet society, the dream of justice, democracy, and equality, when it became known that it was the men from Moscow who had ordered the murders of Nin and of other revolutionaries? What would happen when they found out that the men from the USSR had manipulated the Communists and ordered the political and even physical destruction of those who were opposed while at the same time demanding more money in return for weapons and advisers? What would survive when it was known that they were stopping the proletarian revolution? . . . Lev Davidovich bid farewell to Nadal almost convinced that at least that man would not be the murderer Stalin would send for him. And no, he had told him as he shook his hand: he didn't know what was going to be left standing of the poor communist dream.

That November, the revolution celebrated its twentieth anniversary and Lev Davidovich turned fifty-eight. Since his birthday nearly coincided with the Day of the Dead, which Mexicans celebrated with a party that aimed to bring the deceased back to life and give the living a peek over the threshold of the great beyond, Diego and Frida filled the Casa Azul with skulls dressed in the strangest ways and built an altar, with candles and food, to remember their deceased. That Mexican proximity to death seemed healthy to Lev Davidovich, because it familiarized them with the only goal all lives shared, the only one from which it was not possible to escape, even for Stalin.

But Lev Davidovich was not in the mood for a celebration. A few days earlier, information had reached him that, following Marshal Tukhachevsky's fall, Yezhov had been merciless with his family. While two of his brothers, his mother, and the marshal's wife were executed, one of his daughters, who was thirteen (and whom Lev Davidovich had carried as a newborn), had committed suicide out of pure terror. The family purge didn't surprise him too much, as it seemed to be a habitual practice. His own sister Olga had been arrested and her oldest son executed for being guilty only of being the wife and son of Kamenev, who led the Soviet council in October 1917; three brothers, a sister, and Stephan, the oldest son of Zinoviev himself, who protected Lenin in the most difficult days of 1917, had also been executed, while another three brothers, four nephews, and who knew how many relatives of that old Bolshevik remained in the so-called gulags that were really death camps. And poor Seriozha: What had happened to his son?

Ever since Yezhov had taken over for Yagoda, the wave of terror unleashed ten years before with forced land collectivization and the struggle against the peasant landowners had reached levels of insanity that seemed poised to devour a country made prostrate by fear and the practice of denunciation. It was said that in state offices, schools, and factories, one out of every five people was a habitual GPU informant. It was also known that Yezhov boasted openly of his anti-Semitism, of the pleasure he received from participating in interrogations, and that his greatest joy was hearing a detainee, beaten by torture and blackmail, incriminate himself. He and his interrogators warned the victims that, if they didn't confess, their relatives would be executed or deported to camps where they would not survive. "You will not be able to save yourself and you will condemn them" was the most efficient formula to obtain the confession of crimes that had never been committed. Would his son Sergei have been able to withstand those threats, the physical and mental pain? he used to ask the people with whom he spoke. "Should I still nurse the hope that he has survived in a prison camp in the Arctic, almost without food, with work-days that even the toughest can only withstand for three months before kneeling down like living corpses?"

Lev Davidovich's most recent sorrow had arrived from an unexpected source. For several weeks, a group of writers and political activists who claimed to be close to the positions of the old revolutionary had devoted themselves, in the fervor of the twenty-year October anniversary, to finding the defects of the Bolshevik system that led to the birth of Stalinism. To that end, they had wanted to examine the bloody repression of the Kronshtadt sailors' uprising and decided to publicize Trotsky's responsibility for the event. The most repeated argument had been that this repression could be considered the first act of "Stalinist terror" and compared the military response and the execution of the hostages with Stalin's purges. Because of his responsibility, they considered the then commissar of war the father of those methods of repression and terror.

It had been so painful for Lev Davidovich to learn that men like Max Eastman, Victor Serge, and Boris Souvarine held those opinions about an act that had been hounding him for years, but above all it bothered him that they took a military mutiny, which occurred during times of civil war, out of context and placed it alongside rigged trials and summary executions of civilians occurring in times of peace. But it hurt him even more that they did not realize that the discussion only served to benefit Stalin just when Lev Davidovich was most insistent on denouncing the terror in which those who opposed the man from the mountains—and many men and women who hadn't even dreamed of opposing him—lived and died.

For weeks Lev Davidovich would get caught up in that historical dispute. To begin to refute them, he had to accept the responsibility that, as a member of the Politburo, he had approved the suppression of that uprising. He refused to admit that he personally had brought about the crackdown and encouraged the cruelty that accompanied it. "I'm willing to consider that civil war is not exactly a school for humanitarian conduct and that, on one side and the other, unforgivable excesses were committed," he wrote. "It is true that in Kronshtadt there were innocent victims, and the worst excess was the execution of a group of hostages. But even though innocent men died, which is inadmissible at all times and in all places, and even when I, as the head of the army, was ultimately responsible for what happened there, I cannot admit a comparison between the suffocation of an armed rebellion against a weak government at war with twenty-one enemy armies and the cold and premeditated murder of comrades whose only charge was to think and, perhaps, say that Stalin was not the only or the best option for the proletarian revolution."

But Lev Davidovich knew that Kronshtadt was going to forever remain a black chapter of the revolution and that he himself, full of shame and pain, would always carry that guilt. He also knew that if in Kronshtadt the Bolsheviks—and he included himself as well as Lenin—had not repressed that rebellion mercilessly, it would have perhaps opened the doors to the restoration of the czar. Revolution and its options could be so simple, so terrible, and so cruel. He thought it then and would think it to the end of his life, and nothing would make him change his mind.

When at the end of November, a letter from Liova arrived with the news that the *Bulletin*'s publication would be delayed in order to include the findings of the Dewey Commission, Lev Davidovich preferred not to respond. In the last letters they exchanged, they had been on the verge of a break. He simply could not believe that Liova had needed four months to prepare the most important edition of the *Bulletin*. All of his excuses were inadmissible and he came to think that there had been negligence and even incompetence on his son's part. In one of those letters, he had even commented whether it would be better to transfer the publication to New York and place it in the hands of other comrades. Natalia, who had received other missives from her son, told him that Liova felt offended, since he didn't understand how his father could be so insensitive, knowing the problems hounding him. Insensitive! A man with Liova's experience didn't understand what was at stake? "Liova is an excellent soldier and we're at war," he added, without suspecting how much he would very soon regret his outbursts and his lack of sensitivity.

It was at the beginning of the year when they decided that Lev Davidovich would spend some time far from the Casa Azul. Rivera maintained he had seen some suspicious men prowling around and, to be safe, they chose to move him to the house of Antonio Hidalgo, a good friend of the Riveras who lived above the forest of Chapultepec. Lev Davidovich welcomed the idea, since he wished to make the most of his isolation to move forward in the biography of Stalin: he needed to take that dark mist out of his head. Natalia, meanwhile, would stay in Coyoacán, and they agreed that she would visit only if his stay was extended. How long will we live fleeing, hidden, even provoking the paranoia of men like Diego Rivera? he thought as he entered the forest of cypress trees.

The days lived at Antonio Hidalgo's house soon blended into each other, and of that time he would only clearly remember the afternoon of February 16, 1938. From the window of the studio assigned to him, he saw Rivera cross the garden with his hat in his hand. Lev Davidovich was writing an article at that moment in which he used the Kronshtadt controversy to make a defense of the communist ethic. When Diego reached the studio, he could tell from his face that something serious had happened.

Liova had died in Paris, Rivera said. When Lev Davidovich heard those words, he felt the earth open, leaving him hanging in the air like a marionette. He would never remember if he attacked Diego physically, only that he yelled "Liar! Swine! . . ." until he collapsed in a chair. When he began to recover, Rivera told him that, after reading the news in the afternoon papers, he had telegraphed Paris in search of confirmation. Hidalgo then suggested that Trotsky call Paris to get more information, but he refused. Nothing was going to change the fate of his dead son and the only thing he wanted at that moment was to be with Natalia.

Before starting back, Lev Davidovich demanded that Diego share all the information that he had. What had happened was and would continue to be confusing. On February 8, one of Liova's illnesses flared up and the doctors diagnosed him with appendicitis and decided on an emergency operation. To avoid any GPU agents, Liova entered a private clinic in the outskirts of Paris run by Russian émigrés. His location was known only by Jeanne and his collaborator, Étienne. Taking extreme cautions, Liova registered himself at the clinic as Monsieur Martin. The operation was a success, but four days later, for reasons that were still unknown, the young man suffered a strange setback. According to the witnesses, he was wandering the clinic, delirious and screaming in pain. The doctors operated on him again, but his body, overcome by exhaustion, did not withstand the second surgery.

As they drove to Coyoacán, Lev Davidovich felt his temples pounding and his body shaking. He couldn't stop thinking that his son had died alone, far from his mother, without having seen his daughters again, lost as they were in the Soviet Union. And that Liova had been barely thirty-two years old. When he entered his room, he saw Natalia Sedova seated on the bed, looking at old family photos. As never before in his life, he wished to die that very second, disappear forever before being forced to give his wife the news. When she saw him (never had she seen him so defenseless and aged, she would tell him weeks later), she rose, lifted up by the only two questions she could formulate: Liova? Seriozha? The human mind is a great mystery, but without a doubt it is at the same time wise and sibylline, since at that moment, the Exile felt he would have preferred to say "Seriozha" instead of "Liova." Sergei's life, if he still had it, belonged to Stalin; Liova's seemed more his, more real. The pain he was going to cause Natalia was so great that he didn't dare say "has died" and stammered that little Liova was very sick. Natalia Sedova didn't need more in order to know the truth.

They spent eight days shut up, without receiving visitors or condolences, barely eating, just he and Natalia. She read and reread the letters from her dead son and cried; he, lying down next to her, cried with her, lamenting the young man's luck, speculating about how he should have protected him, how he should have treated him, blaming himself for not having acknowledged his work every day, for not having forced him to leave France. But he decided that he didn't want to forget the pain, either. It was the third child he had lost and he didn't know if he should cry over Seriozha, who was perhaps already dead, also destroyed by the hatred of a criminal.

Slowly, they began to unravel the sordid knot that had wound around Liova's mysterious last days and understood that there was something dark in his death, and that those shadows could only have come from one place: the Kremlin. The doctors at the clinic continued to be unable to explain the reasons for his setback, but one of them had confessed to

Jeanne that he suspected Liova had been poisoned with some unknown substance. To Jeanne and Étienne, it seemed strange that Liova had decided to camouflage his origins at a Russian clinic, of all places, and said they didn't know who could have suggested that place. Furthermore, they didn't know who, besides themselves and Klement, knew of his location.

Lev Davidovich was convinced that the guilt he felt would never leave him. The boy's death, whatever the reason for it was, seemed more linked to his father's fate than his own; it was a direct consequence of his father's life and acts. Liova's absence had left him and Natalia in unfathomable pain, since they felt that none of their children had been closer to them. "He was our young part. And I can't forgive myself that we weren't able to save him," he wrote as a farewell homage. "The old generation with which we once embarked on the road to revolution has been swept from the stage. What the deportations and the czarist jails, the deprivations of exile, war, and illnesses didn't do has been achieved by Stalin, the worst scourge of the revolution," he wrote in the final lines of Liova's obituary, convinced that, sooner or later, the world would know with certainty that Stalin had killed the boy who, during their cold and impoverished Paris mornings, on the way to school, turned in at the printer the calls for peace and the proletarian revolution for which he lived and now has died . . . "Let the pain turn into anger, to give me the power to go on!" he wrote and wept again.

19

January 8, 1978, might have been the coldest day that winter, and I blamed the temperature and the intermittent rain sweeping the sea for the absence of the man who loved dogs. Had he perhaps gotten sick, and for that reason missed our prearranged meeting? The following afternoon I had barely handed in the corrected proofs at the printer's when I ran to the line for the Estrella bus and returned to the beach. Although it was still cold, the sky had cleared and the sea was unusually calm for that time of year. Walking on the shoreline or leaning against some casuarina, I waited, again in vain, until night fell. The following ten days, resisting Raquelita's protests, crossing the city like a man condemned, I repeated that routine and returned to that stretch of beach six times and prayed for the appearance of that man, his dogs, and the conclusion of that absorbing story.

As I played tricks with my mind in order to summon his return—I threw coins in the air, closed my eyes for ten minutes, counted the seconds, things like that—I weighed each of the possibilities that could justify López's absence, although Dax's announced sacrifice and the man's health problems seemed to me the most probable. On the sixth or seventh fruitless day I began to consider whether the best thing wouldn't be to find out how to get to López—the trail of the singular borzois, actors in a film, seemed the most plausible—but a few days later I decided I had no right to do so and that the best thing for me was not to try: it was already dangerous enough to play with fire, but it was quite another thing to jump into it. Finally, on the verge of a crisis with Raquelita and already well into February, I started to space out my trips to the beach, and as if I were curing myself of another addiction, I looked for every way possible to overcome the anxiety that the expectant void had left me.

Many years later I would confess to my friend Dany that the day I went to return his books about Trotsky I was on the verge of overcoming my fears and telling him the story of my meetings with the man who loved dogs. The fact of being the only repository of a story capable, in and of itself, of bringing down the foundations of so many dreams urged me to drain myself of the horror with which I'd been infected and produced in me a kind of mental vertigo, worse than the vertigo López himself suffered. That murky handling of ideals, the manipulation and hiding of the truth, crime as state policy, the cynical construction of a big lie, caused me indignation and more and new fears.

At that moment, what really still intrigued me was not knowing the final fate of Mercader, of whom I only knew—due to the folded article in the Trotsky biography—that he had gone to jail in Mexico and then been received in Moscow in such a way that was hostile to him and his acts; a city where, according to López, his friend had died, confined to an anonymity that included his grave.

As I could not get the man who loved dogs out of my mind, I started to think that I ought to do something to find out what Ramón Mercader must have thought, felt, and believed during all those years of punishment and imprisonment, and then later when he returned to a world that no longer seemed (though it continued to be the same) like the world he had left more than twenty years before, full of faith, convictions, and with a death mission in his hands.

What still hadn't occurred to me, nor would occur to me until a few years later, was the possibility of putting López's confession in black and white and less still of writing a book about Mercader's crime and the history and the interests of his demiurges. Perhaps it was because the story had been left incomplete and many of the details from the part I knew escaped my comprehension and my ability to relate them and situate them in a historical context; or perhaps it was because I didn't know if López would reappear at some point and, no matter who he might be, I had promised not to tell or write his tale. Perhaps I didn't think about it because, in reality, I had so forgotten that I had wanted to be a writer at one time that I almost didn't think like a writer. But the fact was that the idea of writing that inconclusive story did not come to mind, and if it did, it did so in a manner that was too timid—and you'll see immediately that I'm not picking just any adjective. Only several years later, when I started to squeeze my memory to try to reproduce the details that López had told me, did I learn that the true cause for the long postponement, the only and real cause, had been fear. A fear greater than I could imagine.

In the months that followed the disappearance of the man who loved dogs, in the most devious ways, almost always in whispers, I pursued the few existing books on the island capable of helping me understand the dramatic relationship between Stalin and Trotsky and what that sick confrontation and Stalin's success represented for the fate of the Utopia. Searching in the mountain of Stalinist literature that continued to come to the country from Moscow, dusting off chewed-up pamphlets from the 1950s that went from the most basic Trotskyism to the fervent anticom-munism of the Cold War—gasping as I read Solzhenitsyn's *One Day in the Life of Ivan Denisovich*, published in Cuba years before—I started putting together a fragmentary and diffuse knowledge that, despite everything that had been hidden (there were still almost ten years left until glasnost and the first round of revelations of some of that inner world of terror), brought with it an inevitable feeling of surprise and incredulity (disgust would come to the surface soon after), above all because of the crude ma-nipulation of the truth to which so many men had been subjected.

Meanwhile, whenever I could, I went out to the beach, convinced that I should tempt fate; and many times, when I heard the phone ring, I won-dered if it wasn't López calling me.

It was a tremendously painful although not so unexpected event that brought me out, abruptly, from the paralysis of waiting, speculation, and reading to which the man who loved dogs had abandoned me. My brother William had fought for two years to overturn the decision to remove him definitively from the medical school. In that battle of letters—almost al-ways unanswered—and interviews with lower-rung civil servants, William had taken a dangerous and challenging path. He demanded that he be ac-cepted at the university and that he not have to hide his irreversible and totally gay sexual orientation. Fearful of what could happen to him ("What else could happen to me, Iván?" he asked me; I answered, "There can always be something else"), I tried to convince him that the ancestral national homophobia, with all of its social, political, cultural, and religious cruelties, wasn't prepared to take that challenge, but it was prepared to crush whoever launched it. Perhaps my brother and his former anatomy professor, also enrolled in the crusade, had been confused about not only their capacity for withstanding looks of disdain and a variety of humiliations but, above all, their chances of success. The degradation, marginalization, and offenses they saw themselves subject to in the places they went in search of a justice in which they believed ended up devastating them, and at the end of two years of bloody combat they gave up in the worst way: trying to escape by the route that would carry them to possible salvation or an inevitable precipice.

William's disappearance took on all of its tragic dimensions when two police agents went to the house in Víbora Park and informed my parents that, according to investigations, their son William Cárdenas Maturell and citizen Felipe Arteaga Martínez, former anatomy professor of the School of Medicine, who, according to a custodian at the marina of the Almendares River, had stolen a motorboat with the purpose of traveling across the Straits of Florida to the United States. The boat, overturned and without the engine, had been found by some fishermen two days ago, about twenty-five miles north of Matanzas, and, according to the U.S. Coast Guard, no one meeting the description of William Cárdenas or Felipe Arteaga had been rescued in the previous ninety-six hours. Had they heard from their son? Did they know anything about his plans?

My parents, Sara and Antonio, clung to the hope that William was in one of Cuba's northern keys, on a lost beach in the Bahamas or aboard some ship that, for whatever reason, had not given news of the rescue. But as the days passed and hope began to founder under its own weight, a feeling of blame over not having supported their son and, they more than anyone, having made him feel the weight of rejection, started overtaking their spirits until they were thrown into a depression. For my part, I regretted not having shown William enough solidarity and of having left him alone in that disproportionate battle in which he aspired only for the recognition of his freedom of sexual choice and his right, as a homosexual, to study what he wanted.

The environment that had been, until then, tense in the house at Víbora Park, became funereal. In just a few months, my parents turned into old people who lived practically enclosed in their bedroom. My house smelled of the grave and guilt, and to escape that atmosphere, I turned into a kind of fugitive who spent as much time as possible at my job and, when I got out, went to sit at the National Library to read about the life and work of writers who had committed suicide (I got into that and I still don't know where that almost necrophiliac need came from). The sick atmosphere in my house and the physical and mental distance with which I tried to evade it damaged my relationship with Raquelita in a first period of crisis—it appears I attract crises—that hit rock bottom when we decided that the best thing to do would be to separate for a while. As never before in the previous five years, I feared that my loneliness, desperation, the urgency to escape reality, would lead me to the bottle and I would again fall into the well of that addiction.

The disasters came a year and some odd months following William's disappearance, and more than two years after my last meeting with the man who loved dogs—I always remembered that a phrase as tender as "*Lo propio*" was the last thing I said to him, wishing him a Merry Christmas—when in March 1981 my father died and, four months later, it was my mother's turn. I didn't call the friends I had left, or the majority of my relatives, or my work colleagues, and because of that, their wakes were attended only by a few neighbors and the relatives who somehow found out what happened.

I now saw the true dimensions of my solitude and how the decisions of history can come in through the windows of some lives and destroy them from the inside. The family house in Víbora Park, built by my father when I was a boy and William was not born yet, turned into a kind of mausoleum about which ghosts and memories wandered, with echoes of laughter, tears, greetings, and conversations that had taken place there throughout twenty-five years, when we were a family. If we had not been a happy family, we had at least been a normal one, a clan that, by the logic of life, could even grow with Raquelita joining it and the predictable arrival—at the beginning, demanded by my father—of some grandchildren who would rejuvenate those walls made with his efforts, his love, and his own hands.

Dany was one of the friends who came to my mother's wake. Raquelita had called him and he came to keep me company. I remember that at that time Dany was exultant and removed, since his first book of short stories had just been published after having won the same contest in which I had received a mention . . . ten years or ten centuries before. Two days after the burial, Dany came back to my house and asked forgiveness for the disloyalties that, according to him, he'd racked up against me: not having been by my side when William disappeared, when my father died, when Raquelita and I separated, and, above all, for my not having been the first person to receive a copy of his published book, since, as he said, everything he could do and achieve as a writer he owed to me, to my advice, to the books I had made him read.

As we talked and drank coffee, seated on the terrace that looked over the backyard of my house, I told him that there was nothing to forgive: life is a vertigo and everyone has to manage his own. Since I needed to do so with someone, I confessed to him that a great feeling of guilt was following me and he tried to convince me that I wasn't responsible for any of what had happened and told me something I hadn't thought of until then.

"Iván, the problem is that you've spent your life blaming the easiest targets. And you almost always pick yourself, because it's simpler and that way you can rebel, although what you're doing is self-flagellation. Do the math and you'll see that you stopped writing, you became an alcoholic, you buried yourself in that shitty magazine and didn't even try to get a job you're worthy of. When I met you, you were an ambitious guy, people said you showed great promise, they put your stories in all the anthologies of young writers being published . . ."

"I was a fake, Dany: I wasn't a writer or anything promising. They used me when it was useful because they had already done away with all the real writers. And they punished me when they had to."

"But you should have kept writing, dammit!"

"Brother, I lost all desire."

I am sure that at that moment Dany was comparing himself to me. The pupil's star was beginning its ascent, while that of his teacher, so bright at one time, had gone out and it was already impossible to point out the place in the sky where it had once blinked. I am sure that he felt pity for me. And I didn't care if that was what he was feeling.

I think that Dany's presence saved me from depression and, perhaps, from something worse. Resolved to get me out of that stupor, my friend invited me to readings of his stories and there I saw many of my old writer colleagues, some of them still insistent on being so. Above all, I discovered the existence of a new legion of "young narrators," as they were called then, who were shyly beginning to write in a different way, tell different stories, with fewer heroes and more fucked-up, sad people, like in real life.

312

Dany started to lend me books that had never been published on the island that he got from his friends who traveled abroad, and even when I knew he didn't like it very much, he went with me several times to play squash on the courts at the beach, without imagining my second (or was it really my first?) intention of peering out onto the sand with the hope of seeing two Russian wolfhounds followed by a man with tortoiseshell glasses and a bandage on his hand. A few months later, I even allowed myself to be dragged to some literary parties soaked in the abundant alcohols of the illusory bonanza of the eighties (since I didn't drink, they nicknamed me "Waterboy"), intellectual meetings where you felt that people were beginning to free themselves of certain chains of orthodoxy but, above all (because this was the most interesting to me), where you could always find ethereal poetesses wearing sheer cotton dresses (they said they were Hindu) who refused to wear bras and who were in a state of constant desperation to forget transcendental poetics and receive what we then called, à la Lezama Lima, a "male offering," or, simply put in good Havanese, "*pinga* [cock] any which way."

I followed Dany through all of those places without much enthusiasm, but at the same time I was feeling, by pure infectiousness rather than out of any real desire, an increasingly perceptible lashing, that started to awaken the monster locked up within me: the desire to write again. It was then, already convinced that López would never return, that I started to write, on some pads of yellow paper I had taken from the magazine, the story that the man who loved dogs had told me. I did so without having the slightest idea what ending I would give to those notes of a story whose avenues were constantly blocked by a lack of knowledge and the impossibility of overcoming it; and, above all, I did it pursued by a growing feeling that I was playing with fire.

Fortunately for me and the peace of my spirit, the literary heat that Dany's proximity was causing abandoned me when Raquelita returned to live with me at the beginning of 1982. That same year, we had Paolo, and in 1983 Francesca was born, and I dedicated myself to the illusion that we could still make an ordinary life, with a family and the vivid sound of laughter and the inconsequential tears of children.

That was an interval of calm. In the country, life was getting better, and I was able to devote myself to raising my children and forging the illusion of a future that would perhaps smile upon them. In Moscow, meanwhile, they even began to talk about changes, of improvement, of transparency, and many of us thought that, yes, it was possible to do it better, live better, indeed, even the Chinese, after having been through a cultural revolution of which we knew nothing or very little, recognized that you didn't have to live poorly in order to be Socialists. Who would have thought?

The first hole through which water began to sink the ship of my tranquillity was made when Raquelita asked me for a divorce, in 1988. Although she had tried for years to hold together a marriage that, however you looked at it, didn't work: what Raquelita called the (shitty) apathy with which I dealt with everything, and what she considered to be my loss of will to fight to defend the most basic things in my (also shitty) life, had ended up disappointing and defeating her. Raquelita had always aspired to things in life, to promotions and rewards, to cars and comforts that seemed ever more possible for everyone in a socialism that was maturing and being perfected. But, according to her—and it was true—I was merely content with holding on to hopes for the future (of everyone else) from a corner of the present where I had huddled up with the single hope that they would leave me alone to live in peace.

"You're miserable, a loser, a good-for-nothing," she said to me (many times) in those days. "You're not a writer or anything. You tricked me and I can't take it anymore."

And she tended to add when she really wanted to bring me down even further:

"If you don't want to live your life, hang yourself from a tree, because I'm going to do everything possible to live mine and even the impossible to guarantee that my children live theirs."

Even though she was partially right in her fits of anger—I was and am a wretch: a misery—Raquelita suffered a semantic betrayal: more than a loser, I was defeated, and between one state and another, there was (there is, there will always be) an abyss of connotations and implications. And, despite that, with her flight, she was also paying the price of her poor aim: I had never been the man she was looking for, and I still don't understand how someone so perceptive when it came to calculations made that enormous error of appreciation.

The real blow was being separated from my children, and I suffered their absence bitterly when they became prolonged absences. This time even Dany had to admit how right I was when I picked myself to blame for what had happened, despite the fact that, as always, I wasn't the only one at fault. This new fall—what number was this already? Could it be twelve?—into the solitude and the void was completed when, without any will to put up a fight, I accepted, with the divorce petition, the *permuta*, or trade, of the house in Víbora Park for two lesser spaces: a little house with a backyard and two bedrooms in the neighborhood of El Sevillano for Raquelita and the kids, and a small apartment, damp, with cracked walls and little natural light, in Lawton for me. I recognize, nonetheless, that I felt a certain freedom when I said goodbye to the family home, full of memories, and started my hermit's life, from which I was brought out two years later, by that girl who looked like a tiny fragile bird and who, with tears in her eyes, begged me to save her poodle, affected by an intestinal obstruction.

When I no longer expected it, I had a new, alarming and clarifying contact with the man who loved dogs. It was in 1983, a few months before Francesca was born, and I can place it exactly because I clearly remember when Raquelita came to tell me that someone was looking for me and I can see her with that sprawling belly, so different from the one that had accommodated Paolo. If, a few years before, I'd tortured myself by asking myself what astral conjunction had led me to López and turned me, according to him, into an exceptional repository for the story of his deceased friend Ramón Mercader, at that moment I was tormented by the certainty that the man who loved dogs had not arrived in my life only by chance, but rather that he had pursued me intentionally and continued to pursue me even after, by basic logic, I believed him dead and buried—even after, for my own good and through my idleness, I had managed to forget about him and the adverse reactions caused by the story he'd told me: rancor, fear, curiosity, disgust, and the increasingly dormant but still latent and dangerous desire to write.

The letter—if that's what you could call a parcel of more than fifty sheets in a cramped, almost infantile handwriting but a better than well-composed style—reached me through the hands of a thin, very black woman. According to what she told me, she had been one of the nurses who had taken care of López when his illness worsened. The woman, who barely sat down in the living room of my house and didn't even dare to make up a name for me to call her, started by demanding the greatest

315

discretion. She told me that she'd been keeping those papers since the middle of 1978, when *compañero* López, as she called him, gave them to her before leaving Cuba. By that time, the man's condition had reached a state of utmost severity and he had to leave to receive shock treatment. The woman didn't know—she said—what the illness was or where López had gone, nor whether he was still alive or if he had died, although she was very sure that the latter had to have happened to him, since he had been doing so badly. She explained that, before leaving, the sick man had asked her, very discreetly, to do him the favor of handing that manila envelope to a young man with whom he'd become friends, and given her my name and the address where I lived. The nurse promised to carry out what he had entrusted to her, but she had taken almost five years to do so because she was afraid it could put her or me at risk. Put me at risk? Why? Wasn't López merely a Spanish Republican who worked and lived in Cuba with all the imaginable authorizations? Or had the nurse read those papers and discovered other truths? The woman, slippery and precise at the same time, only responded to my third question and added a revelatory afterthought: no, she hadn't read the letter, nor had she spoken to anyone of its existence, and she was expecting similar discretion from me, above all regarding her role in that story. And before leaving, she made a request that sounded like a warning: if anyone ever asked me where those papers came from, she had never seen anything like them and had never been in the house of the recipient. And she disappeared.

As soon as I started reading the manuscript, I understood two things. First, that the strange nurse had undoubtedly read it and, as a consequence of this act, it had taken her five years to resolve to bring it to me. Second, when I finished reading, I understood even less what had conquered her fears and made her resolve to come see me, but I appreciated that she hadn't destroyed the letter, as I might have done in that situation.

In a note introducing the document, Jaime López apologized to me for not having returned to the beach, but first his spirits and then his health had prevented him from doing so. The deterioration of Dax's health and that animal's impending death had affected him much more than he had expected, and the vertigo he suffered had become so violent that he practically couldn't walk. It even prevented him from concentrating, and he'd had new encephalograms done and switched his treatment to pills that kept him in a drowsy limbo all day. But he had always kept in mind that he owed "the kid" that part of the story and, excusing his handwriting—I should have seen the round and beautiful calligraphy he used to have, he said—and any digressions he would surely make, he went into the story about the final years of his old friend Ramón Mercader's life, thanks to the unexpected meeting with that ghost of the past, right on the day that the first snowfall of the winter of 1968 was falling in Moscow.

As I read, I felt the horror spilling out of me. According to the man who loved dogs, during that coincidental meeting Ramón had told him the details I already knew about his entrance into the shadow world, his spiritual and even physical transformation, and his actions as Jacques Mornard and under the name of Frank Jacson. But he had also confided everything that, with the passing of years, he had managed to learn about himself, and of the machinations and the most sinister purposes of the men who took him to Coyoacán and put an ice axe in his hands. If before I had thought that López frequently exceeded the limits of credibility, what he relayed in that long missive surpassed the conceivable, despite everything that, since our last meeting, I had been able to read about the dark but well-covered-up world of Stalinism.

As is easy to infer, that story (received a few years before the glasnost revelations) was like an explosion of light illuminating not only Mercader's dismal fate, but also that of millions of men. It was the very chronicle of the debasement of a dream and the testimony of one of the most abject crimes ever committed, because it not only concerned the fate of Trotsky, at the end of the day a contender in that game of power and the protagonist in various historical horrors, but also that of many millions of people dragged—without their asking, many times without anyone ever asking them what they wanted—by the undertow of history and by the fury of their patrons, disguised as benefactors, messiahs, chosen ones, as sons of historical necessity and of the unavoidable dialectics of class struggle . . .

But when I read Jaime López's letter, I couldn't suspect that another ten years would have to pass—almost sixteen since my last meeting with him—for me to hit upon the clues that would finally allow me to put together all the pieces of that puzzle made with cards of misery and tons of manipulation and concealment: the components that shaped the times and molded the work of Ramón Mercader. Those ten years ended up being the ones that saw the birth and death of the hopes of *perestroika*. Those years caused for many the surprises that the opening of Soviet glasnost generated; exposure of the true faces of characters like Ceaușescu and the change in China's economic path, with the subsequent revelation

317

of the horrors of its genocidal Cultural Revolution, carried out in the name of Marxist purity. Those were the years of a historic rupture that would change not only the world's political balance but even the colors on maps, philosophical truths, and, above all, it would change men. In those years, we crossed the bridge that went from enthusiasm for what could be improved to disappointment at confirming that the great dream was terminally ill and that, in its name, genocides had been committed like that in Pol Pot's Cambodia. For that reason, in the end, what once seemed indestructible finished up undone, and what seemed to us incredible or false resulted in being just the tip of the iceberg that hid in its depths the most macabre truths about what had happened in the world for which Ramón Mercader had fought. Those were the revelations that helped us bring the blurry shapes into focus that, for years, we had barely been able to make out in the shadows or give a definitive outline to, as shocking as it is now easy to see. Those were the times when the great disenchantment set in.

20

Jacques felt that he was going backward in time. As soon as he saw him, he remembered the meeting with Kotov, two years before, in the still-pleasant Plaza de Cataluña. Now Tom, with the top of his jacket open and holding in one hand that patterned handkerchief with which he usually covered his throat, was taking in the miserly March sun with the eagerness of a bear recently awoken from his winter slumber. But in those two years, everything had changed for Ramón. That meeting, on a bench at the Luxembourg Gardens, was proof of many transformations, including the disappearance of the Spanish dream and the kilos lost by the adviser since the last time they had met.

"What a blessing! Isn't it?" Tom said, without moving from his position.

"At least you prefer parks and not cemeteries," he commented, and settled down next to his boss. Before him was an extensive view of the pond, the palace, and the gardens, where some yellow flowers with purple stems, born in the last islets of snow, fought to announce the end of winter. With the gift of the first rays of spring sun, the elderly and their nursemaids had taken over the benches, and Tom seemed proud and happy.

"Moscow was an ice floe."

"Did you come from there?"

The Soviet barely nodded. Jacques lit a cigarette and waited. He already knew these rituals.

"I wanted to go to Madrid with what was left of the Republic but they ordered me out. Well, there's not much left to do. The end is a question of days . . . *Bliat!*"

Jacques felt Ramón's indignation besieging him again, but he knew to hold back the fit of anger that could end up being inappropriate. For several days, he had been carrying the rage it caused him to know that Great Britain and France had reached the extremes of cynicism by recognizing the fascist caudillo as the legitimate leader of Spain. And now the French, always proud of their republican democracy, were not only interning the refugees in concentration camps, but they had gone and named Pétain their ambassador to Franco's government, even when the Republic still existed. What hurt him most, nonetheless, was having read in the Parisian newspapers that the Soviets had also disengaged from Spain when they saw the final disaster arrive.

"What are they saying in Moscow?" he dared to ask.

"You and I know that without unity you can't beat the enemy. And it's true. Right now the Republicans are killing each other in Madrid, while Franco is getting his boots shined to go parade down La Gran Via. Poor Spain, what's in store for it isn't easy . . ."

Jacques regretted asking. For defeat, there was invariably one reason and one predictable culprit, always the same one.

Tom stayed silent, still immobile, as if the only important thing was to receive those weak rays of sun.

"I met in Moscow with Beria and Sudoplatov, the operative officer who will serve as our link. Stalin asked us to get the machinery going."

"Are we leaving for Mexico?" Jacques Mornard immediately regretted that his anxiety betrayed him.

"You're not going anywhere, not yet. I'm leaving in a few days. The Duck bought himself a house and is going to move. I have to do reconnaissance of the terrain, make some adjustments, organize a few things . . . The chess game."

"So what do I do?"

"Wait, my dear Jacques, wait. And meanwhile, don't think of doing anything crazy. That whole thing about showing your face in Le Perthus and going about punching men . . ." Tom had slowly lowered his head and, after wiping his handkerchief across his face, rested a cold and distant stare on Jacques Mornard, who felt himself go cold inside. "I always know everything, *mudak* . . . Don't play around with me. Never. One day I can rip your balls off and . . ."

The young man kept silent. Any reasoning could worsen his situation.

"I know it's hard for a man like you," Tom continued as he knotted his handkerchief around his neck, "but discipline and obedience come first. I thought you had learned that . . ." He looked at his pupil again. "What's more important, a personal impulse or a mission?"

Jacques knew it was a rhetorical question, but Tom's pause forced him to respond.

"The mission. But I'm not made of stone . . ."

"What's more important," the other man continued, raising his voice, "holding on to the terrain you've gained or losing someone from whom we expect so much? Don't answer me, don't answer me, just think . . ." Tom gave him time to think, as if it were really necessary, and added, "We're going to create other options for Mexico. We practically have to start from the beginning, planting the possible operatives and deciding in a few months which one of them we'll use. But you'll go on your own path; you're still my secret weapon. And I don't have the luxury of losing you. I know you're not made of stone . . . I spoke of you to Comrade Stalin and he agrees that we should hold on to you as our ace in the hole."

Ramón couldn't believe it. Comrade Stalin knew about him? He knew of his existence? Amid his infinite number of concerns, he counted among them? He was hard-pressed to control his pride to rise to the circumstances, confessing what he considered to be his greatest weakness.

"Excuse me, Tom, but there are days on which I can't stop being Ramón Mercader."

"I already know that, and it's logical it should be that way. But Jacques Mornard needs to know how to control Ramón Mercader. That's the point. Can you release or retain Ramón Mercader at your will?"

"I don't know . . ."

Tom moved his lower body for the first time. He tried to find the best position to look at the young man and smiled at him.

"A very important moment is coming for you now: you're going to be Ramón Mercader and Jacques Mornard at the same time. You have to learn to take one or the other out at each specific moment, because when the time comes, you're going to have to get out of Jacques to become

Ramón almost without thinking about it. For the people who know you in Paris, you will continue to be Jacques Mornard. In the meantime, Ramón is going to again be in touch with Caridad, his siblings, and to that intimate circle he will be a Spanish Communist full of hate for the fascists and fifth-columnist Trotskyists and bourgeois traitors who finished off the Republic and who would give anything to make the Soviet Union disappear."

"Don't worry. I have that hate nailed right here," and he pointed at his own chest, where he felt hate beating, very close to where his pride was throbbing.

"Starting now, Caridad is part of the operation. She, you, and I are a team. What we do, only we will know about. George Mink will be outside this circle . . . Listen to me, kid: we're at the center of something very big, something historic, and perhaps life will give you the opportunity to render a priceless service to the struggle for the revolution and for communism. Are you ready to do something that could be the greatest glory for a Communist and the envy of millions of revolutionaries around the world?"

Ramón Mercader watched Tom's eyes for a few moments: they were so transparent that he could almost see through them. He then remembered Lenin's corpse and the glasses in which he had seen himself, superimposed on the face of the Great Leader. And he knew he was privileged.

"Don't doubt it for a second," he said. "I'm ready."

Ramón felt more comfortable ever since he could live with Jacques Mornard as if he were a suit that he only wore on special occasions.

During the weeks of waiting, which turned into months, he forced the Belgian to write frequently to Sylvia, always promising a quick reunion. He walked around Paris and visited the woman's friends, especially Gertrude Allison the bookseller and the young Marie Crapeau, with whom he went to the cinema several times to see Marx Brothers comedies, where he laughed so much that he cried. Jacques went to the Hippodrome, which had turned into a meeting point for the hundreds of spies of all possible nationalities who milled around the city, and to Les Deux Magots and other sites favored by the Parisian bohemia, wonderfully removed from the dangers on the horizon.

In the meantime, Ramón, in Caridad's company, traveled with young

322

Luis, recently returned from Spain, and with the reappeared Lena Imbert to Antwerp, where the young people left for the Soviet Union so that Luis could continue his studies and grow as a revolutionary in the homeland of the proletariat and amid the Spanish Communists trapped in exile. On several occasions they visited his sister Montse, living in Paris with her husband, Jacques Dudouyt, whose only notable quality, according to Caridad, was his ability to cook.

Looking for signs of the new times, Ramón and Caridad followed with interest the information coming from Moscow, where Comrade Stalin was leading a new party congress before which, with his usual bravery, he dared to criticize the excesses of certain civil servants during the purges and proceedings of previous years. As they already expected, the greatest reprimands came down on Yezhov's head and they foretold a fate similar to that of his predecessor, Yagoda. But the most important thing for the Soviet Union, at that time before the threat of imperialist wars, was obtaining the perfect unity of the people behind a monolithic party, like the one that emerged from a congress in which the general secretary dismissed more than three-quarters of the members of the Central Committee elected four years before and substituted them with men of unbreakable revolutionary faith. The demands of the present had imposed themselves and Comrade Stalin was preparing the country for the most ironclad ideological resistance.

Ramón discovered in that time that his relationship with Caridad was taking on a different nature. The fact that he was now the one at the center of a mission whose proportions she couldn't even fathom on the morning that she presented it to him in the Sierra Guadarrama, placed him at a height that his mother could not reach. In the face of powers that were beyond her, she had to check her habit of trying to control his destiny. Perhaps Tom's influence had contributed to that change, demanding that she remain in a triangular relationship that depended so much on the balance of all of its parts. To see how Caridad ceased to be an oppressive presence relieved him and helped to make his period of forced inactivity less complicated by unnecessary quarrels.

As frenetically mobile as ever, Tom had left for New York and Mexico at the beginning of April, shortly after the definitive entrance of Franco's troops in Madrid. When he returned, at the end of July, the agent came back with a mix of satisfaction and concern over the progress of an operation that was still unfolding at a cautious rhythm.

During a week that, at Tom's suggestion, they all spent in Aix-en-Provence, as well as going over Cézanne's route and enjoying the subtleties of Provençal food, which the adviser adored, Ramón and Caridad learned the details of the machinery that had been put into motion. In parallel to what they were doing, Tom explained, Comrade Grigulievich (from the beginning, Ramón would ask himself if that was George Mink's new name) had established himself in Mexico and begun to work with the local group that would eventually carry out an action against the Duck. Relying on a Comintern envoy, they had begun by trying to obtain the Mexican party's support, only to discover (to no great surprise) that two of its leaders, Hernán Laborde and Valentín Campa, didn't dare to join a possible action, holding up the excuse that they considered Trotsky to be a political corpse and that any violent act against him could complicate the party's relations with President Cárdenas. That hesitancy by the leadership had not prevented them from achieving two other objectives: finding a group of militants willing to carry out an armed attack against the renegade, and the preparation of a massive campaign rejecting Trotsky's presence in Mexico, with which they sought to create a state of hostile, even aggressive opinion against the Exile.

Meanwhile, in the United States, Tom's colleagues had managed to infiltrate several young Communists into the ranks of the Trotskyists with the intention of getting one of them sent as a bodyguard to the Duck's lair. That man, if he managed to be placed inside the renegade's home, would have the mission of informing on his movements and, according to one of the prepared plans, would even facilitate the entrance of a commando or solitary agent charged with perpetrating the attack. As Tom himself had been able to confirm, Trotsky's new house was practically impregnable. Apart from the features of the house itself (high walls, bulletproof doors, a river running alongside it that made it nearly impossible to access it by one side), there was also a watch system composed of seven armed men, in addition to which there were Mexican policemen protecting the residence, and an electric mechanism that activated lights and sounded alarms.

"Until we have a man inside there, the cook who works in the Duck's house will keep us informed. She's a party agent."

"And where does Jacques fit into those plans?" Ramón wanted to know; he didn't see himself anywhere on that mortal chessboard, sketched out in all its details, in which the renegade seemed perfectly surrounded, without the possibility for escape.

"Everyone has his place. Jacques is going to keep moving forward, don't worry," the adviser said, and drank from his glass of wine.

Tom, Caridad, and Ramón sat at one of the tables that the restaurant owners, taking advantage of the summer season, had placed on the sidewalk on the town's main street. They had already selected their dishes— Ramón, out of pure coincidence, had opted for a duck-based dish—and ordered a light, fresh wine that awakened their palates. They conveyed the image of three pleasant middle-class people on holiday and Caridad and Ramón's table manners, Tom's Panama hat, and the worldly gastronomical tastes each one had would have placed them in the category of the illustrious bourgeois, people familiar with the pleasures of life that are bought with money.

"When they give me the orders, the three of us are going to Mexico," Tom said, and looked at Ramón. "Jacques Mornard's role in this hunt will depend on many things that are still far-off. But it could be crucial for Sylvia to be able to get him into the house. We still don't know if we will get the American spy in there, so the possibility of Jacques being close could be important. And, if necessary, if everything we're planning fails or is not safe for one reason or another, then Jacques would go into action."

"Why not use the cook?" Caridad asked. "She could poison him . . ."

"That's a last resort. Stalin has asked for something resounding, an exemplary punishment."

"But couldn't the American do it?" the woman insisted.

Tom looked at her and served himself more wine.

"In principle, yes. He could be a disillusioned Trotskyist who fought with his leader . . . but what if it fails and he's detained? Who can guarantee that man's silence?" Tom allowed for an expectant pause before answering himself. "It's a risk we can't take . . . Never, in any case, can the Soviet Union and Comrade Stalin be visibly involved in the action. Do you hear me, Ramón?" The man's voice had broken its monotonous rhythm to turn emphatic. "That's why we're working with Mexicans, so it looks like something to do with politics and local quarreling. The Mexicans would have no information about Grigulievich's connection to me and even less of my own connection to Moscow. We're thinking that some man of ours, a supposed Spanish Republican who met them in the war, will help Grigulievich and control things from the inside. If they do things well, then congratulations, the work is done and we'll have had a vacation in the tropics."

"Mexico City isn't quite tropical, shall we say," Caridad dared to correct him, and Tom laughed heartily.

"My dear, the tropics are anywhere you don't have to spend half of the year cursing and damning the cold to hell and walking in the fucking snow."

Paris seemed to be at the point of melting under the sun and fear. The temperatures of war, incredibly high during that hot August, had at last put an end to the politicians' indifference and had given way to a nervous preoccupation with the growing aggressiveness of Nazi speeches, which had already caused the mobilization of the army and the reserves. Alarming news of great concentrations of troops in Germany circulated and people were discussing what the next objective could be of an aggressive empire that had already swallowed up Austria and part of Czechoslovakia and now had an exhausted but loyal ally to the south of the Pyrenees. After many delays and self-deception, the imminence of war settled into the fears of the Parisians.

Tom had disappeared again without announcing where he was going. Ramón, using Jacques Mornard more often, insistently wandered the world he had shared with Sylvia, as he found in Trotskyist circles a level of alarm that bordered on hysteria. From Mexico, the Exile had launched a warning campaign about the looming military conflagration, and on each occasion he expressed his fears over Soviet defensive weakness caused as a result of the purges to which the Red Army had been subjected in the past two years. Jacques Mornard, always removed from political passions, listened to those arguments and couldn't help but notice in them an underground incitation to the enemies of the Soviet Union to take advantage of the situation about which the renegade was so insistent.

On the morning of August 23, a nervous and shaken Caridad, appearing as if she had returned to the murky days of the past, turned up at Jacques's apartment. The young man, who was drinking a pot of coffee to try to dispel the effects of the champagne he had consumed the night before, guessed the gravity of the events that the woman would immediately reveal and snapped out of his fog through pure alarm.

"The Soviet Union and the Nazis signed a pact," Caridad whispered in Spanish, and although the young man didn't understand what those words meant, what madness they referred to, he felt that it was Ramón who, already completely lucid, was listening to his mother. "They're saying it on all the stations. The newspapers are going to run a midday edition. Molotov and Ribbentrop have signed it. A pact of friendship and nonaggression. What the hell is happening?"

Ramón tried to process the information, but he felt that something eluded him. Comrade Stalin had made a pact with Hitler? What the Duck predicted had happened?

"*What else are they saying, Caridad? What else are they saying?*" he yelled, standing before the woman.

"That's what they're saying, *collons*! A pact with the fascists!"

Ramón waited a few seconds, as if he needed the shock to dissolve amid the reasons he desperately started to search for, like those pigs who sniffed for truffles in the Dax of his adolescence, and he clung to the most solid argument he had at hand:

"Stalin knows what he's doing; he always knows. Don't rush into things. If he signed an agreement with Hitler, it's because he has reason to do so. He must have done it because of something . . ."

"At Concorde and on Rivoli, they've burned Soviet flags. Many people are saying they're going to resign from the party, that they feel betrayed . . ." Caridad licked her wound.

"The fucking French can't speak of betrayal, dammit! Ribbentrop was chatting with them here in Paris while Franco was massacring the Republicans."

Caridad let herself fall on the sofa; she lacked the energy to refute or support Ramón's words, who, despite the conviction he had just expressed, could not overcome the dizziness that had taken hold of him. Where the hell was Tom? Why wasn't he here with his reasoning? How could he have left now, of all times, when he most needed him?

"*So when in the fuck is Tom coming?*" he yelled at last, without being fully conscious of the extent to which he depended on his mentor's words and ideas.

For years Ramón would remember that bitter day. With all of the preconceptions underpinning his beliefs broken, he faced the inconceivable. The rapprochement between Stalin and Hitler was what Trotsky had prophesied for years. As he would come to know a few months later, the deception ended up being so painful that various Spanish Communists, imprisoned in Franco's jails, committed suicide out of shame and disillusionment upon learning of the accord. It was the last defeat their convictions could take.

The following day, when Ramón, full of doubts, with his radio on and surrounded by newspapers, opened the door certain that he would find Caridad there again, the smiling face he ran into had the effect of immediately returning the calm he had lost for a day and a half.

"A master move," Tom said, and patted Ramón's shoulder as he walked by his side. "An incredible move . . ."

"Were you in Moscow?" The anxiety still ruled him.

"Would you make some coffee?" The recently arrived swept the newspapers on the sofa aside with one hand without putting any special emphasis on this action: he was just cleaning a place where trash had accumulated in order to make himself more comfortable, with a sigh, as if he were very weary. "I've barely slept in two days," he remarked, and Ramón understood the order. He went to the kitchen to make some coffee and listened to Tom from there. "Tell me the truth. What did you think? It will stay between you and me."

Ramón noticed that, despite the heat, his hands were cold.

"That Stalin knows what he's doing," Ramón said.

"Really? Then I congratulate you, because Comrade Stalin has never been more sure of anything. He's even sure of the European Communists' doubts."

"I'm a Spanish Communist," Ramón replied, and heard Tom roar with laughter.

"Yes, of course, and you'll recall that a year ago, the European democracies silently accepted it when Hitler bit off a piece of Czechoslovakia. And now they don't want Stalin to protect the Soviet Union?"

Ramón came out with the coffee, served in two great mugs, and almost in a hurry Tom began to drink his.

"Listen to me, kid, because you should understand what happened and why it happened. Comrade Stalin needs time to rebuild the Red Army. Between spies, traitors, and renegades, they had to purge thirty-six thousand officers from the army and four thousand from the navy. There was no other choice but to execute thirteen of the fifteen troop commanders, taking out more than sixty percent of those in command. And do you know why he did it? Because Stalin is great. He learned the lesson and now he can't allow the same thing to happen to us that happened to you in Spain . . . Now, tell me, do you think you can fight against the German army like that?"

Ramón tasted his coffee. A hint of logic was beginning to slice through the thickness of his doubts. Tom leaned toward him and continued.

"Stalin cannot allow Germany to invade Poland and reach the Soviet border. First would be the morale factor: that would be like handing over a piece of us. And, from Poland, the fascists would be just one step from Kiev, Minsk, and Leningrad."

"So what guarantees the pact?"

"For starters, that eastern Poland will be ours. It's the best way to keep them far from Kiev and Leningrad. With the Germans that far away and with a bit of time for Stalin to better prepare the Red Army, perhaps they'll decide not to attack the Soviet Union. That is what Stalin is seeking with the pact. Are you beginning to understand?" Ramón nodded and Tom, leaning back, continued: "The numbers are clear. The German army has eighty divisions. They have enough to launch an attack against the West or the Soviet Union, but not both fronts at the same time. Hitler knows it and that's why he agreed to sign it. But that piece of paper doesn't mean anything; it doesn't mean we'll renounce anything. Look at it like a tactical solution, because it has just one goal and that is to gain time and space."

"I understand," Ramón said as he felt his tensions diminishing. "In any event—" he began, but Tom interrupted him.

"I'm glad you understand, because you're going to have to accept many things that could seem strange to other people. The war is just around the corner, and when it begins, we're going to have to make very serious decisions. But remember that the Soviet Union has the right and the duty to defend itself, even at the expense of Poland or whoever . . . Fortunately, we have Comrade Stalin, and he sees farther than all the bourgeois politicians . . . so far that he gave the order for you to go into action."

Ramón felt a shudder go through him. The unforeseen twist in the conversation, which suddenly included him in a gigantic political maneuver, erased the last trace of doubt and filled him with pride.

"He already gave the order?"

"We're getting close . . . It all depends on what happens in the coming months. If the Germans sweep Europe, we'll go into action. We can't run the risk of the Duck staying alive. The Germans can use him as the head of a counterrevolution. And he is so desperate for power, so full of hate for the Soviet Union, that he wouldn't hesitate for a second to lend himself as Hitler's puppet in an offensive against us."

"So what do we do?"

Tom fished in the pocket of his shirt and removed a passport.

"We can't risk you getting stuck if they seal the borders . . . You're going to New York . . . Jacques Mornard is leaving because the war is about to start and he's not willing to fight for others. You bought this Canadian passport for three thousand dollars and you're going to see Sylvia before you go to Mexico, where you have a job as the agent for a businessman, a certain Peter Lubeck, importer of raw materials . . ."

"Will I then be Jacques Mornard again?"

"Full-time, although with two names. According to this passport, you're Frank Jacson . . . And don't worry, Caridad and I are going to be nearby the whole time."

Ramón looked at the passport. Beneath his photographed face, he read his new name, and he felt happy knowing that he was getting close to the battlefront where the future of the socialist revolution could be decided. When he lifted his gaze, he saw that Tom had fallen asleep, with his head hanging over his shoulder. From his mouth, a deep snore began to reverberate. Ramón left him to recover his energy. For them, the war was about to begin.

In the days pierced by the doubts that would arise, and in the very difficult years that would follow, Ramón Mercader spent many hours recalling the life of Jacques Mornard and came to discover that he felt admiration and pity for him in similar measure. What Jacques did on that occasion, for example, was something mechanical, a decision that, at that moment, seemed to be the only possible one: as soon as he disembarked in New York, he went to see Sylvia. He didn't even consider the possibility of taking a couple of days to enjoy the city without having to drag around the deadweight of that taxing woman. Definitively, Jacques was a little foolish and obeyed Ramón's puritanism and Tom's orders too closely, he would think when he was in a position to examine Jacques from a critical distance and see how he could have acted differently.

When she opened the door and saw him, Sylvia was on the verge of passing out. Despite the letters in which he confirmed his love, his promise of matrimony, and the proximity of their next encounter, that woman—dazzled as she was and would be until she was brutally removed from her dream—had trembled every day their separation lasted, fearing that that gift from the sky would disappear and return her to the solitude of an ugly thirty-something with no expectations. During those months of distance, she had suffered every moment thinking that Jacques could fall in love with another woman or that he wouldn't fit into her regular life, so full of meetings and political work, or that Jacques was too much of a man for so little a woman . . . Now the happiness of having him before her made tears spring to her eyes, and she kissed him as if she wanted to make him definitively real with the warmth of her lips.

"My love, my love, my love," she kept repeating, like a woman possessed, as she began to drag Jacques toward the bedroom of her small Brooklyn apartment.

That night, her appetites fulfilled, Sylvia was at last able to find out that her lover had turned into a deserter. He explained that his sustained decision not to enlist in the army had led him to buy a passport on the black market, thanks to which he was able to leave France. His mother's generosity had provided him the money for the purchase of the passport ("They've gotten so expensive because of the war," he said) and for the trip, along with a few thousand dollars more to bring with him so that they could live on in New York until something economically satisfactory came up. Faced with the decision of her man who had come searching for her after burning all his bridges, Sylvia felt giddy with happiness.

Jacques insisted they go out to dinner. She suggested a nearby restaurant, as she planned the outings they would make to familiarize her lover with New York. At the newsstand, the vendor was ready to close the blinds and Jacques hurried to buy an evening paper. As he arrived at the stand, the headline repeated on all the evening papers burned itself into his retinas, Germany had invaded Poland.

With various newspapers in their hands, they entered the humble restaurant, furnished with Formica tables, settled in, and commented that that was, without a doubt, the start of the war. The British and French reactions to the German invasion were of a tone that could only lead to a formal declaration of war, and there was speculation about whether the United States would join. As he read, Jacques understood that, once again, Tom had analyzed the Soviet strategy keenly and knew that he now found himself a few steps closer to carrying out his mission.

Sylvia ended up being an excellent guide to the city. Because of her political work and her community-based activities, she knew every inch of the metropolis. Jacques could see with his own eyes the cohabitation, in a limited space, the dazzling splendor and miserable poverty on which that mirror of capitalism sustained itself. With Tom still in Europe, he dedicated all of his time to Sylvia and felt proud that he was able to satisfy the needs of a constantly hungry woman.

As he and Tom had decided, starting on September 25, Jacques went on alternate days to a bar on Broadway where, at some point, Tom would find him to pass on his new instructions. The pretext he gave Sylvia for his absences was that he needed to find an old classmate who had been living in the city for years and who was connected enough to find him a good job.

The afternoon of October 1, when he saw Andrew Roberts enter, dressed in overwhelming elegance and displaying very sophisticated manners, Ramón felt a wave of envy. How many faces could that man use? Which of the stories he had told him could be true? As well as his loyalty to the cause, what visible part of him was real? Now he seemed like an actor from those Chicago mobster movies that Americans liked so much. Even his laughter fit his appearance, cinematographic and gangsterlike.

"Lots of work?" he asked in English when he sat down next to Jacques.

"I would say too much, Mr. Roberts. That woman always wants more."

"Use your Spanish fury. If you were Swedish, you'd be fucked." And he laughed sonorously as he addressed the bartender: "The usual, Jimmy. For my friend, too."

"What about Caridad?" Jacques asked, hiding his surprise over the familiarity with which Roberts treated the bartender.

"For now, forget about her. I want you to spend all your time living and thinking like Jacques Mornard."

"Why did it take you so long?"

"With the war, everything got complicated. I had to look for a new passport. I couldn't leave as a Pole."

"Any news from Mexico?"

"Everything is on. I need you there in two weeks."

332

"To do something?"

"You have to become familiar with the terrain. Ever since the Red Army entered Poland, things have been going as Comrade Stalin foresaw. I have a feeling the order is about to be given."

Mr. Roberts accepted his frozen vodka and, before the bartender could place the small glass before Jacques, he was already returning his, empty.

"You're thirsty today, Mr. Roberts," said Jimmy, who refilled his glass and withdrew.

"In a few days, Europe is going to turn into an inferno," Roberts sighed.

"Do I take Sylvia with me?"

"For now, it's preferable to leave her here. You have a job in Mexico at an importing company. Your Belgian friend put you in touch with Mr. Lubeck, who needs someone who speaks several languages and is able to inspire more confidence than a Mexican. It's an easy and well-paid job . . . We'll need Sylvia in Mexico later on, when you control the terrain."

"What about the American spy?"

The bartender returned with another vodka and Roberts gave him his successful, tough-guy smile.

"Nothing yet. But it's better that way. If he arrived now, it would be too soon. Grigulievich is having a hell of a time with the Mexicans. Each one wants to do things his own way and do them straightaway."

Jacques tasted his vodka and Roberts downed his.

"From now on, you're Jacson for all legal matters; to Sylvia and the people you meet through her, you're Jacques. Be careful with the way you speak. The idea is that little by little you start improving your Spanish."

The bartender removed his empty glass and returned it full. Roberts smiled at him. Slowly, Jacques finished his vodka.

"You seem worried, kid," Roberts said.

"Sometimes I am afraid that all of this"—Jacques Mornard opened his arms, indicating the bar, the city—"is all just for fun. I've spent two years preparing myself for something I might never do. I left my comrades in Spain, I don't have a single friend, I've turned into someone else, and it could all be in vain."

Mr. Roberts let him finish and stayed silent for a few moments.

"This work is like that, kid. Lots of lines are cast, even though there's just one fish. Each one of us is a line. One of us will have the possibility of getting the fish and the others will return empty, but they'll have carried out their role in the water. It will be crucial for you to manage to get close to the Duck. Everything we learn about how that house works will help us a lot. But meanwhile, you'll still be a fishing line with a hook at the end. And I assure you that you're the one who will be closest to the fish, with the best bait. At the definitive moment, perhaps you won't take all the glory, but you'll have done your job in a disciplined way, silently, and although no one will ever know that you were so close to the great responsibility, the men of the future will have a better and surer world thanks to people like you."

"I appreciate the consolation. Lately, you talk like Caridad."

"It's not a consolation or a speech, it's the truth. So go to Mexico and get ready . . . Remember that from the first time I saw you in Barcelona I had a very strong feeling about you, and I'm not the kind who makes mistakes. That's why we are here. Of the ones in Mexico, do you know how many know I exist? None. And they will never know. If they're not the ones in charge of getting the Duck out of the way, no one will ever know there was a certain Roberts—no, a certain Tom . . . bah, no, it was Grigoriev; or was it Kotov? Anyway, there should have been a man who placed them before history. Who was it? . . . I am a soldier who fights in the shadows and only aspires to fulfill my duty." Mr. Roberts took out some bills and placed a glass on top of them. "Let's go around the corner: they're showing the latest Marx Brothers film."

Jacques smiled and looked at his mentor.

"I'm sorry, Mr. Roberts, I have a dinner date with my fiancée. I hope we see each other soon. Thanks for the drink."

"You're welcome, Mr. Jacson. Good luck with your girlfriend and your job."

The men shook hands and Roberts saw Jacques walk away toward the door. Then he went back to his chair and leaned with his elbows on the bar.

"Jimmy, I think my glass is empty."

He signed the name "Jacques Mornard" and carefully folded the sheet. When he tried to slip it into the envelope engraved with the Hotel Montejo's letterhead, Ramón was again certain that the makers of loose sheets of paper and the makers of correspondence envelopes should come to an agreement: either one side cuts a few millimeters off the sheets or the other adds a few to the envelopes. Nothing bothered him more than when something he wished to remain pure was unnecessarily damaged, and because of that, he used the utmost care when placing the sheet in the envelope. With his tongue, he wet the glue and closed the packet, wedging it under the lamp to get it perfect.

He finished getting dressed and, before putting on his hat, wrote his name below the letterhead and, in the middle of the envelope, Sylvia Ageloff's address. He went downstairs, gave the letter to the reception desk, and went out onto Paseo de la Reforma. Amid the usual noise, he walked on the sidewalk in search of the garage where he liked to park his sparkling Buick and looked distantly at the Indian woman who was selling hot tortillas on a stone dish. The sweetish smell of the corn flour stayed with him until he entered his car, shiny and black. Without looking at the city map, he headed to Coyoacán.

It had been a week since Jacques Mornard, with a passport issued in the name of the Canadian citizen Frank Jacson (why not Jackson? Who the hell had lost that *k* that forced him to explain so much?), had arrived in Mexico City. Besides the various letters he wrote to Sylvia, he began to prepare the indispensable logistics of his mission and had been fine-tuning his identity. After buying the car secondhand but in perfect condition, he opened a mailbox in an office building on Calle Bucareli, giving the concierge the excuse that, while he looked for a place, he needed to receive correspondence somewhere that wasn't a hotel. In addition, he had wandered around offices, restaurants, and businesses in the city center, practicing his Spanish with a French accent, and spent hours reading the newspapers with the greatest circulation, seeking to bring himself up-to-speed on the nuances of local politics until he had an approximate idea of the way that, when the time came and before different interlocutors, he should be able to talk about every issue. He had noticed, as usually occurs, that while the parties on the right were very clear about their purposes, the ones on the left were absorbed in the most uncontrollable controversies. Finally, he had again studied the recently purchased maps of Mexico (the ones he had handled in Paris he had ripped apart before leaving, to keep Sylvia from seeing them in his suitcases) and regained an image of the city, now putting a face to some of its streets, plazas, and parks.

Despite the chronic lack of signs, he drove without making a single wrong turn until he reached the intersection of Londres and Allende, in Coyoacán. He stopped the car and locked it. Protecting himself from the sun with the dark gold-rimmed glasses he bought in New York, he observed the Casa Azul, Diego Rivera and Frida Kahlo's property, where the Exile had lived for over two years. It was a building surrounded by high walls painted in exultant colors, and he noticed that on one of the side walls he could tell the different texture of the squares that must have been windows but were covered, out of fear, perhaps, long after the walls were built. Smoking a cigarette, he walked away in search of Calle Morelos to access Avenida Viena, which was really a stony alleyway that ran parallel to the moribund Churubusco River. Two blocks before reaching the fortress, he approached a small business and asked for a soda from a sleepy, toothless salesclerk. The house, ocher and walled, took over the block it rose from. The watch towers, soaring over the high fences, gave a privileged view of the men who, at that moment, were speaking animatedly and, at intervals, looking inside the dwelling as if they were expecting something. On the corner, they had built a wooden shack in front of which was a policeman, and he discovered two other uniformed men milling in front of the steel-sheeted gates for cars to enter. A smaller door to the right served to allow access to visitors and inhabitants. The air around it breathed secular poverty, and the image of a medieval castle surrounded by serfs' huts came to Jacques Mornard's mind.

Having drunk just about half the soda, he walked toward the fortified house. He tried to fix in his mind every detail, every tree and sunken stone in the earth, of that so-called avenue. Without stopping, with his hat and his glasses on, he passed in front of the Duck's lair. If at the Casa Azul he had noticed the signs of fear, now he had beside him a monument to anxiety. The man who had cloistered himself behind those walls was convinced that his life had been marked and should know that, when the time came, neither steel nor stones nor the guards would be able to save him, because he was condemned by history.

As he turned the corner and discovered two more policemen at that part of the wall, he heard a metallic screeching and slowed down to look over his shoulder. The gate opened and a car—a Dodge, he noted immediately—peeked out onto the stony street. A stocky blond man was at the wheel and another man, with a hard look and a rifle raised between his legs, was in the passenger seat. From one of the towers came a voice that, in English, announced everything was clear, and the Dodge was barely on the street when the gate began to close. Jacques walked two steps toward the closest building and, violating a basic rule, turned around to watch the car pass by, through the back windows of which he saw a woman with light hair who fit the well-studied image of Natalia Ivanovna Sedova, and behind the driver, just a few feet from his hands, he sighted the graying hair, the sharp face made longer by the goatee, of the Great Traitor. The car sped up, lifting dust in the street, and made its way toward the road leading out of the city. Jacques started walking again, regaining the rhythm of a carefree man, without much interest in what surrounded him.

Back in his Buick, on the highway heading back toward the city, Jacques Mornard tried to imagine how he would feel if he ever met that malevolent man who, so long ago, had managed to place himself so close to revolutionary glory and now survived justly detested, sentenced by the infinite betrayals he had committed due to his lust for power and his basic deceitfulness. If Jacques made it in front of him, would he be able to control himself and not throw himself at the neck of that louse who had encouraged the POUM fifth columnists and who was now shouting about supposed Soviet military weakness? Like an eruption, Ramón Mercader came out of Jacques Mornard's pores. With all his energy, he wished at that moment for life to offer him the great chance to be the ruthless arm of the most sacred and just hate. He was willing to pay whatever price was necessary, silently, without aspiring to anything. And he felt convinced that he was ready to fulfill history's mandate.

Tom and Caridad were a couple from Marseille, comfortable but not rich, who had decided to get some distance from the events in Europe and await the evolution of a war that the fascists would eventually take to France. Life in Mexico was sufficiently cheap for their finances to withstand (doing some business or other with a brother of Tom's based in New York), and while they looked for an appropriate house, they lived in the Shirley Court apartments, on Calle Sullivan, which was, coincidentally, very close to the Hotel Montejo. They spoke Spanish perfectly but were very reserved, very little given to socializing, although they loved small trips, in which they could invest several days.

It was the beginning of November when Frank Jacson answered a call from his old friend Tom, inviting him to visit him at Shirley Court. When he arrived at the appointed time, Caridad was waiting for him in the apartment's small entryway. Inside, seated at the dining room table,

Tom was reviewing some papers when Jacson entered. The adviser was dressed very informally, with a denim jacket, a handkerchief around his neck, and hiking boots. Even the smile with which he welcomed the young man was different from the one that, a month before, had lit up the face of the man who had then called himself Mr. Roberts.

"My friend Jacson!" He stood up and pointed at the armchairs in the living room. "How's the city treating you?"

Jacques settled in and observed that Caridad disappeared behind a partition where he assumed the kitchen was.

"The coffee is disgusting."

"We're already fixing that, right, *ma chérie?*"

Caridad said "Of course" without leaving the kitchen, and Tom added:

"Cuban coffee, you'll see."

"Anything new?" Jacques wanted to know as he took out his cigarettes.

"Everything's moving forward; the siege is starting to take shape."

"What should I do in the meantime?"

"Same as you've been doing. Get to know the city and, if possible, come to understand a little bit about how Mexicans think. Keep Sylvia in New York for a few more weeks. Tell her you have a lot of work piling up at the office, since your boss is traveling outside Mexico for a few weeks."

Caridad came in with the tray and small cups. It smelled like real coffee. The men took their cups and Caridad sat down to drink from hers as well. The cigarette smoke created a cloud in the room. Caridad's silence warned Jacques that something was going on, and he didn't have to wait too long to find out.

"Ramón," Tom said, and paused. "Why do you insist on disobeying me?"

Surprised by the question and by hearing his name, Ramón searched for the possible infraction in his mind and immediately found it.

"I wanted to get a first impression of the terrain."

"*What the fuck kind of impression?*" Tom yelled, and even Caridad was startled in her seat. "*Yob tvoyu mat!* You do what I tell you to do and nothing else besides what I say! *Suka!* It's the second time you go beyond your limits and it will be the last time. If you try to do what you feel like again, your story is over, and in truth, kid, then you won't want to be in any of your guises."

Ramón was ashamed and confused. Who could have noticed his

presence in Coyoacán? The toothless salesclerk who sold him the soda? The man with the crutches sleeping on the street? Whoever it was, Tom seemed to have eyes everywhere.

"It was a mistake," he admitted.

"Kid, I expect mistakes from everyone else. I'm going to have to live with all the blunders from that bunch of Mexicans we're putting together, with those made by those imbeciles from the Comintern who think they own the revolution and are nothing more than *vedettes* whom we can leave with their asses hanging in the air with just one breath. But not you . . . Get it into your head for once and for fucking all that you don't think, you just obey; you don't act, you just execute; you don't decide, you just fulfill. You're going to be my hand on that son of a bitch's neck and my voice is going to be that of Comrade Stalin, and Stalin thinks for all of us . . . *Bliat!*"

"It won't happen again, I promise."

The adviser looked at him long and intensely, and his face began to relax.

"What did you think of the coffee?" he then asked, in a friendlier voice and even with a smile.

Since that afternoon, Jacques Mornard felt as never before the viscous density of the days of passivity. It was as if he had a lottery ticket in his hands whose drawing was delayed and, with it, his future. He lacked the concentration to read anything besides newspapers, his character kept him far from cantinas and brothels, and he opted for sleeping the greatest quantity of hours possible. He even found himself hoping that they would order him to bring Sylvia; that way, at least he would have something to focus on, someone with whom he could use his Jacques Mornard brain and even experience a mediocre but sure release of his diminished sexual appetites. In Tom and Caridad's company, he took trips to the pyramids of Teotihuacán, to Lake Xochimilco, and to the city of Puebla, which reminded him so much of some Castilian towns, with more churches than schools. A couple of times, he went out with Tom to the San Ángel area, to practice shooting a handgun and hone his skills with sharp-edged weapons. One night a week, accompanied by Caridad as well, they went out to eat together at some restaurant in the city center, where Tom eagerly devoured dishes loaded with that hot sauce capable of making Ramón and Caridad cry. They talked about the war (the Soviet army had finally launched itself into what should be a crushing expedition against Finland), about Grigulievich's group's advances, about the escalation of the campaign orchestrated by Vittorio Vidali, the Comintern man, against the renegade's presence in Mexico, and about the Mexican Communist Party purges that would soon be carried out. Loyal to his role, Ramón Mercader only spoke and acted like Jacques Mornard, but the events seemed to be moving in slow motion and anxiety was taking over the repressed but burning Ramón. When he was alone, without the obligation to look like a wasteful and fun playboy, the young man spent many of his nights going to the movies where they played new Westerns and films with his beloved Marx Brothers. Groucho's *boutades*, which he liked to repeat in front of the mirror, still seemed like the height of the verbal genius he'd never had and that he admired so much in those who did.

When, in the middle of December, Tom told him it was time to make Sylvia come, Ramón Mercader knew that something had at last started to move. The strike could happen at any moment and the smell of risk cleared his mind of the mist of forced inactivity. The Duck hunt had begun.

21

The House of the Trade Unions in Moscow is a great work of nineteenth-century Russian architecture. The architect Kazakov had turned the eighteenth-century building into a club for the Muscovite aristocracy, and in its luxurious Hall of Columns, Pushkin, Lermontov, and Tolstoy had danced, and Tchaikovsky, Rimsky-Korsakov, Liszt, and Rachmaninov had played their music. After the revolution, the hall, with its excellent acoustics, was used for party meetings and press conferences. There Lenin's voice was heard dozens of times; there the funeral chapel was erected from which the remains of the leader would exit toward the mausoleum on Red Square. But Lev Davidovich was convinced that the compound was going to pass into posterity for having housed the most grotesque judicial farce of the century, and on March 2 of the already disastrous year of 1938, when the Hall of Columns' doors were opened again, he also knew that death was returning to that historic building ready to gather another harvest.

Ever since they began to cry over the fate of their son Liova, Natalia and Lev Davidovich had learned in too painful a way what it meant to harbor one last hope, since they now had only one—Seriozha's life—to cling to. Although it had been months since they'd received news of the young man, the fact that they didn't know if he was dead allowed them to embrace the improbable but still conceivable hope that he was still alive. Their only other hope was Seva. Besides them, the boy was the only member of the family living outside the Soviet Union, and they begged Jeanne to bring him to Mexico, at least for a few months, and, with his presence, help them lessen the pain of the loss they had suffered.

But Jeanne wanted to request a more exhaustive investigation into Liova's cause of death and was willing to hire an attorney, a friend of the Moliniers, despite Rosenthal, the Trotskys' legal representative in France, being of the opinion that they shouldn't mix the Molinier group up in the case. In the most diplomatic way, Lev Davidovich asked the woman to leave the investigation request in his hands, but she insisted on moving forward and had decided that Seva would remain with her in Paris, since, she said, he had turned into her best support. Natalia Sedova was the first one to foresee that devastating conflicts were coming from that flank.

Meanwhile, the efficient Étienne had committed himself to continuing the work of the *Bulletin* in Paris. In his last months, Liova had assured his father that the publication was in circulation often thanks to Étienne's dedication. Liova's trust in the young man was such that, in case of emergency, he had given him a key to the mailbox where he received personal correspondence. Now Étienne offered to continue the task begun by Liova, along with Klement, on the planned constitution of the Fourth International. "Hopefully, Étienne will be half as efficient as our poor Liova," Lev Davidovich commented, knowing how much he was fooling himself.

The news that the Military Council of the Supreme Court would go into session again in the Hall of Columns didn't surprise him. Lev Davidovich expected that at any moment the machinery of terror would again be set in motion, since Stalin needed to complete his work of erasing the collective memory that he had initiated with Kirov's murder and carefully and efficiently continued over the last three years. In a way that made him feel miserable, Lev Davidovich tried to concentrate on the details of the new judicial farce, trying to remove from his mind the obsessive feeling of guilt and pain that had plagued him since his son's death.

When the list of the twenty-one accused was unveiled, Lev Davidovich found many predictable names: Rykov, Bukharin, Rakovsky, Yagoda, and Trotsky himself, in absentia. They would also try the memory of Lev Sedov, his eternal deputy, and lesser-known characters, including doctors, ambassadors, and civil servants. Of the accused, thirteen were of Jewish origin, and such an insistence on subjecting Jews to those proceedings could be read as another sign of compliance toward Hitler and as a testimony of Stalin's visceral anti-Semitism. The charges were none too original, since they repeated the accusations of the previous trials, although there were more, since there always had to be more: terrorism against the people and the party leaders, poisonings . . . The greatest novelty was that several of the accused had fallen so low in the markets of espionage and crime that they were blamed for serving not just German and Japanese intelligence but also Polish intelligence, and not only for wanting to assassinate Comrade Stalin but also for having poisoned Gorky and his son Max. Since they didn't seem to be criminal enough, the crimes now expanded to the time of the revolution and even previous dates, when the state that would try them didn't yet exist. The prosecutor's master move was to accuse Yagoda of having acted as an instrument of Trotskyist aggression by which, throughout the ten years that he had pursued, imprisoned, and tortured Lev Davidovich's comrades and confined thousands of people to death camps, his criminal excesses were due to counterrevolutionary orders that came from Trotsky himself and not at the disposition of Stalin.

Feeling how that aggression for the truth was giving him back his energy, the Exile wrote that the Grave Digger of the Revolution was going beyond all his previous experience and the limits of the most militant credulity. The irrationality of the accusations was such that it was nearly impossible to conceive of a counterattack, although at the beginning he decided to respond with sarcasm: he wrote that he had such power that under his orders, given from France, Norway, or Mexico, dozens of civil servants and ambassadors with whom he had never spoken turned into agents of foreign powers and sent him money, lots of money, to maintain his terrorist organization; leaders of industry became saboteurs; respectable doctors devoted themselves to poisoning their patients. The only problem, he would comment, was that those men had been chosen by Stalin himself, since it had been many years since he'd appointed anyone in the USSR.

The incredible confessions heard during the ten days that the proceedings lasted, and the way in which they humiliated men loaded with history, such as Bukharin and Rykov, didn't surprise Lev Davidovich. He was greatly saddened to read the self-incriminations of a fighter like the radical Rakovsky (so close to death that he was allowed to sit while making his statement), who acknowledged having allowed himself to be led by Trotskyist theories, despite the fact that Trotsky had confessed to him in 1926 that he was a British agent. What extremes had they gone to in order to break the dignity of a man who had withstood years of deportations and imprisonments without giving up his convictions and who knew he was at the end of his life? Did any of them really think that, with his confession, he was rendering a service to the USSR, as they were forced to claim? Lev Davidovich was incapable of understanding those displays of submission and cowardice.

One prime setback in the proceedings showed the seams in their fabrication, and Krestinsky was at the center of it. For an entire afternoon he dared to maintain that his confessions, made before the secret police, were false and declared himself innocent of all charges. But the following morning, when he took the stand, Krestinsky admitted that the previous accusations and some more, surely developed in a hurry, were true. What means had they used to break a man who was already convinced he would be executed? The new GPU was developing methods that would horrify the world the day it found out about them, methods thanks to which the most spectacular revelation of the proceedings was produced when Yagoda, after declaring himself innocent and receiving the same treatment as Krestinsky, confessed to having prepared Kirov's murder under Rykov's orders, since the latter was envious of the young man's meteoric rise.

But the star of the trial, as to be expected, was Nikolai Bukharin, who, at the end of a one-year stay in the pits of the Lubyanka, seemed ready to undertake the last act of his political and human self-demolition. Although he denied being responsible for the most dreadful acts of terrorism and espionage, Lev Davidovich thought he noticed that his tactic was to accept the unacceptable with a conviction and emphasis with which he hoped to show the most perceptive observers the falsity of the indictment. The old revolutionary nonetheless noticed the error of perspective Bukharin was committing by trying to give a cry of alarm to the alarmed, for whom (despite the silence they maintained) all of those accusations would be as hard to believe as those of previous trials. But the great masses, the ones who followed the course of the proceedings in Moscow and in the world, came to just one conclusion from his words, which validated the charges and destroyed the prisoner's strategy: Bukharin confessed, they said, and that was what was important. To end up kneeling and sobbing, admitting to fictitious crimes, Bukharin had preferred to return to Moscow? Lev Davidovich asked himself, recalling the dramatic letter that Fyodor Dan sent him three years before.

To Lev Davidovich, it seemed clear that in the proceedings Stalin demanded more than a truth: he demanded the human and political destruction of the accused. When he executed the accused in the previous trials, he had forced them to die conscious that they had not only debased themselves but had condemned many innocents as well. For that reason it surprised him that Bukharin, who without a doubt had learned the lesson of the Bolsheviks who had preceded him in that moment of peril, should retain the deluded hope of saving his own life. In one of the many letters that he wrote to Stalin from the depths of the Lubyanka and that the Grave Digger was sure to have circulated in certain circles, Bukharin finally told him that all he felt for him, for the party, and for the cause was a grandiose and infinite love, and he bid farewell embracing him in his thoughts . . . Lev Davidovich could imagine Stalin's satisfaction upon receiving messages like that one, which turned him into one of the few executioners in history to receive the worship of one of his victims as he pushed him toward death . . .

On March 11 the trial closed for sentencing. Four days later, *Pravda* confirmed those sentenced to death had been executed . . .

Ever since that spectacle started to unfold, Lev Davidovich had been shutting himself up in his room, as it was painful to try to answer the questions posed to him by journalists, followers, secretaries, and bodyguards, all in search of some logic beyond the hate, the conspiratorial obsession, and the criminal insanity of the man who governed over one-sixth of the earth and influenced the minds of millions of men and women around the world. Lev Davidovich knew that Stalin's only possible objective in these proceedings was to discredit and eliminate real and potential adversaries and blame them for every one of his failures. What escaped them was that the discrediting was directed *inward* at Soviet society, which undoubtedly believed everything that was propagated, no matter how difficult it was to take in. The other great purpose was to make fear extensive and omnipresent, especially in those who had something to lose. Because of that, the first targets of those purges had been, in reality, the bureaucrats. Following that strategy, Stalin beat dozens of his acolytes, including various members of the Politburo and party secretaries in the republics, Stalinists who, from one day to the next, were labeled traitors, spies, or inept. If the oppositionists of other times had been publicly dishonored, the Stalinists, by contrast, tended to be destroyed in silence, without open proceedings, in the same way that the Communists of various countries taking

345

refuge in the USSR were decimated along with those whom Stalin, after using them, seemed to have turned upon.

The most terrible thing was knowing that those sweeps had affected all of Soviet society. As could be expected in a vertical and horizontal state of terror, the participation of the masses in the purges contributed to its geometric diffusion because it was impossible to undertake a witch hunt like the one experienced in the USSR without exacerbating people's basest instincts and, above all, without each person being terrified of being caught in the net for any reason, even no reason. Terror had the effect of stimulating envy and the desire for revenge; it created an atmosphere of collective hysteria and, worse still, of indifference before the fate of others. Once the purge was unleashed, it fed on itself and released infernal forces that made it keep growing and moving forward . . .

Weeks before, Lev Davidovich had received dramatic proof of the horror endured by his compatriots when an old friend, miraculously escaped to Finland, wrote him: "It's terrible to confirm that a system born to rescue human dignity has resorted to rewards, glorification, the encouragement of denunciations, and feeds on everything that is humanly vile. I feel the nausea rise in my throat when I hear people say: they've shot M., they've shot P., shot, shot, shot. The words, after hearing them so much, lose their meaning. The people say them with greater calm, as if they were saying: we're going to the theater. I, who lived these years in fear and felt the compulsion to denounce (I confess so with terror, but without any feeling of guilt), have lost in my mind the brutal semantics of the verb 'to shoot' . . . I feel that we've reached the end of justice on earth, the limits of human dignity. That too many people have perished in the name of what, they promised us, would be a better society . . ."

André Breton's arrival brought Lev Davidovich out of the well of his personal and historic sorrows. Diego and Frida received him with enthusiasm. Breton was the guru of surrealism, the eternal nonconformist capable of challenging the most sacred dogmas, such as when he noted that he and his friends were affiliating themselves with the French Communist Party and accepting party discipline as citizens . . . but not as surrealists.

At the conclusion of their first meeting, weighed down with condolences, Lev Davidovich asked the poet for a few days to organize his thoughts before beginning to work on the project that had brought him to Mexico:

346

the creation of an International Federation of Revolutionary Artists. Lev Davidovich knew he would work passionately, but that it would require great effort, since not even for someone like Lev Davidovich was it easy to handle the weight of so much death and pain. In addition, the heated situation in Mexico continued to worry him. When President Cárdenas announced the nationalization of oil interests and the U.S. secretary of the treasury responded with the threat of not buying any more Mexican silver, one million people gathered in the Zócalo to express their support for Cárdenas, but at the same time there was talk of possible uprisings against the government. Lev Davidovich knew that these circumstances put him and Natalia in a critical situation, as the NKVD murderers could take the opportunity, in the midst of so much chaos, to pounce on them, indeed he was convinced that, after the last trial, the purge of his former Bolshevik leadership completed, his existence had ceased to be useful to Stalin.

Before Breton and his wife, Jacqueline, left, the Communists in France and Mexico had begun a campaign against him. The French, from which Breton had separated himself in 1935, were accusing him of being a Judas and, of course, something worse, a Trotsky sympathizer; in Mexico, meanwhile, the local Stalinists, with Lombardo Toledano and Hernán Laborde at their head, launched even more aggressive propaganda against the poet and against Lev Davidovich—so aggressive, in fact, that van Heijenoort decided to take some of the bodyguards for Breton's protection during the conferences he would be giving in the country.

To discuss literature and art, surrealism and vanguardism, political commitment and creative freedom, was a balm for the Exile. Breton's presence and his literary encouragement reminded Lev Davidovich that ever since his childhood, and later on, when he was a young student, his life's dream had been to become a writer, although soon after he would subordinate that passion and all others to the revolutionary work that marked his existence.

Guided by Diego, the Bretons and the Trotskys walked around the pre-Columbian ruins and visited museums and local artists who accepted the Exile's presence. The high priest of surrealism confessed to his astonishment before the multicolored markets, the cemeteries, and the manifestations of popular religiosity, in which he tended to find a "surrealism in a pure state," more revealing than the shock of the umbrella and the sewing machine on the dissection table, and for that reason he considered Mexico "the chosen land of surrealism."

When they began to work on the manifesto of writers and revolutionary artists with which they would bring the international federation into creation, Lev Davidovich and Breton must have felt the explosive tension that two stubborn souls could generate, but at the same time the possibility of an understanding born of shared need. From the beginning, Diego made it clear that the theoretical statements would be left to them, although they could count on his signature, since the three were operating with the urgency of offering a political and intellectual alternative to the left that would allow them to reconcile themselves with Marxist thinking at a moment in which many believers, disillusioned by the repression unleashed in Moscow, were beginning to turn their backs on the socialist ideal.

In those conversations, Breton maintained the need to make a major distinction: the intellectuals on the left that had linked their thinking to the Soviet experiment were making a serious conceptual error, since it wasn't the same to march alongside a revolutionary class as in the steps of the victorious revolution, more so when that revolution was represented by a new leadership insistent on suffocating artistic creation with a totalitarian grip . . . But despite the accusations by the Stalinists, his own distance from the party had not been a break with the revolution and, less still, with the workers and their struggles, he said. His great disagreement with Lev Davidovich revolved around a concept both considered fundamental to establish clearly, and about which the Exile's position was definitive and nonnegotiable: "Everything is permitted in art." Upon hearing this, Breton smiled and showed his agreement, but only if an essential clarification was added: everything except attacking the proletarian revolution. Breton recalled that Lev Davidovich himself had said that, and the Exile explained that when he wrote *The Revolution Betrayed*, the aesthetics deformations in the Soviet Union had certainly reached alarming levels, but the events of the last three years had broken the dike. While a proletarian revolution might inevitably pass through a period that was not Thermidorian but rather a terror that negated its own essence, it still had no right to impose conditions restricting artistic freedom: everything has to be permitted in art, he insisted, to which the French man again added: everything except attacking the proletarian revolution. This was the only sacred principle.

Breton was the kind of sharp adversary who brought Lev Davidovich so much pleasure. The challenge of persuading the surrealist reminded him of Alexander Parvus of his youth, when discussing Marxism became his obsession. To reinforce his arguments, Lev Davidovich evoked for Breton the fates of Mayakovsky and Gorky, the forced silences of Akhmatova, Osip Mandelstam, and Babel, the degradations of Romain Rolland and of various former surrealists loyal to Stalinism, and insisted that they shouldn't admit any kind of restrictions, nothing that could lead to the acceptance of things that a dictatorship could impose on the creator with the excuse of political or historic need: art had to follow its own demands, and only those. By accepting political conditions that Lev Davidovich himself had defended (at this point he truly regretted having done so), presently it was impossible to read Soviet poems and novels or see paintings created by the obedient, without feeling horror and disgust. Art in the USSR had turned into a pantomime in which civil servants armed with pens and brushes—watched by civil servants armed with guns—could glorify their great genius leaders. That's where the slogan of ideological unanimity had led them: the pretext that they were under siege by class enemies, and the eternal justification that it was not the right time to talk about problems and the truth, to give poetry freedom. Artistic creation in Stalin's time, he thought, would remain the expression of the deepest decadence of the proletarian revolution, and no one had the right to condemn the art of the new society at the risk of repeating that frustrating experience. "For art, freedom is sacred, its only salvation. For art everything has to be *everything*," he concluded.

In those conversations in which they attempted to fix the world, Lev Davidovich discovered with some surprise that, more than any theory, Breton was fascinated by the drama of life itself, and that he frequently brought up the subject of fate and its role in the events that marked one's destiny. It was during one of these conversations, seemingly insignificant and without anyone recalling how they got to talking about it, that Lev Davidovich confessed to the poet how much he loved dogs. He expressed his regret to Breton that his wandering life had prevented him from having one ever since he said goodbye to his Russian wolfhound at the cemetery wall in Prinkipo, and he spoke to him of Maya's goodness and the devotion that, in general, dogs of that breed felt for their owners. Then Lev Davidovich realized that the most surreal of the surrealists was a strictly logical man when Breton refuted that idea and claimed that Lev Davidovich was allowing himself to be led by his emotions. Breton explained that, upon speaking of the love that dogs feel, Lev Davidovich was trying to attribute feelings to these beasts that belong only to humans.

349

With arguments that were perhaps more passionate than rational, Lev Davidovich tried to convince the Frenchman that a dog feels love for its owner. Hadn't many stories about that love and friendship been told? If Breton had met Maya and seen her relationship with him, perhaps he would have a different opinion. The poet said that he understood it and clarified that he also loved dogs, but the feeling came from him, the human. A dog, at best, could show that it made a distinction based on how humans treated it: by being afraid of the human being who could cause him pain, for example. But if they accepted that the dog was devoted to someone, they had to also admit that the mosquito was consciously cruel when it bit someone, or that the crabwalk was deliberately retrograde . . . Although he didn't convince him, Lev Davidovich liked the surrealist image of the purposefully retrograde crab.

A few days later, they had a less pleasant discussion and with very strange consequences. It happened when Lev Davidovich was waiting for Breton to show him the draft of the manifesto, and the poet said the ideas weren't coming and that he hadn't been able to finish it. Perhaps due to all his stress, Lev Davidovich at that moment went into a fit of rage. He reproached Breton for his negligence (he would later regret it, recalling the times he accused Liova of the same) and his inability to understand the importance of getting that document circulating in a Europe that was closer to war every day. Breton defended himself and reminded him that not everyone could live with just one thought in mind. Lev Davidovich's passion was "unreachable" for him. That he should be called "unreachable" annoyed Lev Davidovich even more, and they were on the verge of a breakup, which Natalia prevented by placing herself on the poet's side.

The following day, Lev Davidovich received the news that Breton had suffered an unusual physiological phenomenon: he had fallen into a kind of general paralysis. He could barely move, he couldn't write, and he was aphasic. The doctors diagnosed him with emotional fatigue and recommended absolute rest. But according to van Heijenoort, Lev Davidovich was the one to blame for Breton's physical and intellectual freeze: the secretary called it "Trotsky's breath on your neck," which, he said, was capable of paralyzing anyone who had a relationship with him since, according to van Heijenoort, exposure to his way of living and thinking unleashed a moral tension that was almost unbearable. Lev Davidovich didn't realize this, because he had been demanding that of himself for many years, but not everyone could live day and night facing all the powers in the world:

fascism, capitalism, Stalinism, reformism, imperialism, all religions, and even rationalism and pragmatism. If a man like Breton confessed to him that he was out of reach and ended up paralyzed, Lev Davidovich had to understand that Breton was not to blame; rather, Comrade Trotsky, who had withstood everything he had to withstand all those years, was an animal of another species. ("I should hope I'm not a cruel mosquito or a reactionary crab," Lev Davidovich commented to the secretary.)

Despite the discussions—or perhaps thanks to them—Breton's presence had a positive effect on Lev Davidovich, whose concern increased, as Natalia had predicted, by Jeanne's refusal to separate herself from Seva. Any way he looked at it, the woman appeared affected by neurosis, and perhaps had been influenced by someone who had turned her against Liova's parents: her attitude was so aggressive that she had not allowed Marguerite Rosmer to have a conversation with the boy. Faced with that situation, they had no alternative but to file a lawsuit for Seva's custody.

On July 10, the Trotskys, the Bretons—the poet had already recovered—and Diego Rivera left for Pátzcuaro. The manifesto was almost ready and Breton wanted to add the final touches. Some fisherman friends of Diego's had promised them the best of their catch since Lev Davidovich had a weakness for the fish from Lake Pátzcuaro. Jacqueline and Breton also had a taste for them, which the poet baptized "André Masson's fish." The fishermen in mid-task reminded the Exile, with more nostalgia than he could have predicted, of the years in Prinkipo, when he still had faith in the future of the opposition within the Soviet Union and the energy and motivation to go out fishing with kind Kharalambos. What was his friend doing now? he asked himself. Did he still return each evening navigating over the reddish wake drawn by the setting sun on the Sea of Marmara?

With the manifesto still unfinished, the politician and the poet argued a lot about the effects of Stalinism on artistic creation inside and outside the USSR. Lev Davidovich reminded him how much disgust he felt for Stalin's sycophants, especially authors such as Rolland, and Malreaux, whom Trotsky had praised so much on reading their first novels and who were now typical of those writers in Paris, London, and New York who were signing statements supporting Stalin without having (or wanting to have) any idea of what was really happening in the USSR. Lev Davidovich would submit each one of them, so convinced of the regime's goodness, to a test: he would make them live with their families in a sixty-square-foot apartment, without a car, with bad heating, and force them to work ten hours a day in order to succeed in an emulation that produced nothing, earning just a few devalued rubles, eating and wearing what was assigned by their ration books and without the least possibility of traveling abroad or the freedom to express opinions on anything. If at the end of a year they still defended the Stalinist regime and espoused its great philosophical principles, then he would shut them up for another year in one of the penal colonies that Gorky had considered to be the factories of the new man—that would be the true test (excessive, really, he told himself)—and then they would see how many Rollands or Aragons still raised Stalin's flag in a Paris bistro.

They had just returned from Pátzcuaro when Lev Davidovich received the news that on July 14 his collaborator Rudolf Klement had disappeared in Paris without a trace. His previous experiences made him fear deeply for the fate of the young man, for whom he felt great affection. Although the reports he received were untimely and sparse, from the start he felt that there was some connection between Klement's disappearance and Liova's death, and he let the French police know in a letter protesting the negligence with which they had handled the investigation.

Finally, on July 25, the *Manifesto for Independent Revolutionary Art* was ready. Since Lev Davidovich felt that his name could taint the document politically, he refrained from signing it. For that reason, he asked Rivera to undersign it along with Breton, and the painter agreed. Lev Davidovich believed this to be a first step toward a Federation of Revolutionary and Independent Artists, so necessary for a world trapped between the two most devastating totalitarian systems that had ever existed.

To send off Breton, Diego and Frida planned a surrealist party. Although the Trotskys were feeling far from festive, they tried not to dampen everyone else's high spirits. Frida designed for Breton as "high priest of surrealism" a robe adorned with Dalí clocks, Masson fish, and Miró's colors, and covered it with a Magritte hat. Several of the guests read surrealist poems and Diego toasted with mescal, which was, according to him, the most surrealist liquor.

Lev Davidovich was trying to fill the void left by the extraordinary Breton by concentrating on writing the resolutions and planning the program of the Fourth International, when an alarming letter arrived from the South of France. It was signed by none other than Klement himself, informing him of his political break with him in aggressive terms, full of invective. The Exile had the terrible feeling that the letter had not been written by his collaborator, unless Klement had written it under duress. One week later his worst fears came true when, on the banks of the Seine, Klement's dismembered corpse was found.

Under the dark cloud of Klement's murder, the constituent assembly of the Fourth International was held at the Rosmers' villa in Périgny. Although the meeting did not come close to being what Lev Davidovich had wished for, what mattered was that the International existed at all. Following the deaths of Liova and Klement, the assembly was presided over by his old collaborator Max Shachtman, but barely forty delegates attended. The Russian contingent, as had previously been decided, was represented by the practically unknown Étienne.

Although Lev Davidovich didn't dare confess it even to Natalia, he knew that act had been, if anything, a cry in the dark. The times they lived in were not particularly propitious for workers' and Marxist associations without ties to Stalinism, and to prove it, one needed only to take one look at the world: within the USSR, Trotsky had barely any followers left, all of them imprisoned; Europe was rife with defections and Molinier-style divisions, and Socialists and Communists were squashed en masse in Germany and Italy; in Asia, the workers went from failure to failure. Only in the United States had the Trotskyist movement grown with the Socialist Workers Party, thanks to leaders such as Shachtman, James Cannon, and James Burnham. Meanwhile, the communist parties, routinely bowing before Moscow's demands, had been silenced, and in the United States they had even bent to Roosevelt's New Deal policy. "But if there's a war, there will be a revolutionary shakeup," he wrote. And there would be the Fourth International to prove that it was something more than the dreams of an obstinate man who refused to give up.

His predictions about the imminence of war seemed more accurate when Hitler, after meeting with Chamberlain, called a conference in Munich on September 22 and told the European powers that either they gave him a piece of Czechoslovakia or there would be war. As could be expected, the "powers" sacrificed Czechoslovakia, and Lev Davidovich could see on the horizon, more clearly than ever, the completion of an agreement between Hitler and Stalin that the two dictators had worked on in secret (and not so much) in recent years. For now, he wrote, they should agree to the division of Europe. Hitler was devoted to Aryan supremacy and turning the eastern part of the continent into his field slaves; Stalin dreamed of having a greater empire than any of the czars ever had. When these ambitions collided, there would be war.

It was around then that the Exile received a letter, this time posted in New York, that would cause him persistent anxiety. Its author introduced himself as an old American Jew of Polish origin who, without practicing his political faith, had followed his history as a revolutionary. He explained to him that he had learned the news relayed to him through a Ukrainian relative, a former member of the GPU, who a few weeks before had deserted and asked for asylum in Japan and had asked him insistently to get in touch with Trotsky. For his security, that would be the only letter he would send and he hoped it would be useful, he said.

Although that scenario seemed fantastic, the letter had a distinct air of truth. The letter centered on the existence of a Soviet agent, planted in Paris, whose code name was Cupid. That man had come to assume an important role within the French Trotskyist circles, thanks to the infinite naïveté of his followers, who had even permitted him access to secret documents. Meanwhile, Cupid maintained contact with an operative at the Soviet embassy the entire time and collaborated with the Society for the Repatriation of Émigrés, a front for the NKVD that was linked to the deaths of Reiss and Klement. The former agent taking refuge in Japan could not prove it, but due to Cupid's proximity to the Trotskyist leadership, he thought he must have a more or less direct connection to the death of Lev Sedov. What he did know with certainty was that his mission, besides espionage, would consist of approaching Trotsky and murdering him, if conditions allowed it. He was sure that the Kremlin had already given that order following the March proceedings against Bukharin, Yagoda, and Rakovsky.

The old Jewish man ended his letter with a revealing story. His relative said he had been present at the interrogation to which they subjected Yakov Blumkin following his trip to Prinkipo. The truth about Blumkin's arrest was that his wife, also a GPU agent, had been the one to inform on him and accuse him, not only of having contacted the Exile, but even of having given Trotsky a certain amount of money realized from the sale of old manuscripts Blumkin had taken to Turkey. The rumor that Karl Radek had been his informant was a maneuver by the Lubyanka to destroy Radek's prestige, making him seem like a rat. In that whole proceeding, the former agent stated, Blumkin had acted with integrity and dignity that, in similar circumstances, he had seen in very few men. Despite the brutal torture sessions, Blumkin had refused to sign any type of confession, and the day on which he was executed, he had refused to kneel.

Lev Davidovich read and reread the letter and consulted with his secretaries and with Natalia. They agreed that there were only two ways to interpret the document: either it was a GPU provocation, behind which they could not see a clear objective, or it had been sent by somebody who knew the purposes of the secret police very well and who, by revealing the presence of an agent in Paris, was pointing precisely at Étienne. Although it was difficult for them to admit that Liova could have let in an enemy (Sobolevicius had introduced them, Lev Davidovich recalled), the very idea that Étienne was in reality one of Stalin's men made him nauseous. Because of that, in his innermost being, Lev Davidovich wanted the letter to be a trick by the NKVD. Nonetheless, behind the smokescreen, he smelled a whiff of genuineness, and what made him believe in the authenticity of the information was the story of Blumkin's detention, since until the arrival of the letter not even Natalia had known of the money the young man had given him. But what most led him to believe what the letter said was a certainty that, after the last trial, Stalin needed him much less to bolster his accusations and, as a consequence, his time on earth had begun its final countdown.

That is why Lev Davidovich did not find it strange that, following the creation of the Fourth International, the campaign against him organized by the Mexican Communist Party increased in pressure. The worst thing, however, was the fact that the political heat generated by the founding of the new meeting of parties also entered the Casa Azul, something that bothered Rivera very much. The painter was mad because Lev Davidovich had not supported his candidacy to become the secretary of the Mexican section of the Fourth International. But the reason the Exile had withheld his support was that he didn't think it would be beneficial for Rivera to sacrifice his creativity for a bureaucratic job that, even if it gave him political direction, would have taken up all his time in meetings and in drafting documents. The second reason—which he was less likely to confess—was that he did not think Diego had sufficient political savvy. Nonetheless, Rivera aspired to political preeminence and felt betrayed by his guest.

A few days before his birthday, Lev Davidovich received a report from his former correspondent V.V., who told him that now his boss at the NKVD, that midget Yezhov, had been removed and, shortly after, jailed under charges of abuse of power and treason. Like Yagoda, Yezhov was going to die, and the real reason was that, as always, Stalin needed a scapegoat in order to make his own innocence shine.

V.V. told him in detail how, under Yezhov's command, the labor camps had ceased to be Yagoda's prisons, managed cruelly and with disdain, where people died from hunger and the elements. Under Yezhov, the propaganda about the excellence of the Soviet reeducation of criminals had been forgotten, and the so-called gulags had been turned into camps of systematic extermination, where the prisoners were forced to work until their deaths, or were murdered, in unprecedented numbers. But Yezhov's terror had not been as irrational and sick as it seemed. For example, in February 1937, Stalin told his peon Georgi Dimitrov, the Comintern general secretary, that the foreign Communists received in Moscow were "playing with the enemy" and immediately tasked Yezhov with solving the problem. One year later, of the 394 members of the executive committee of the International who lived in the USSR, only 170 were still alive, the rest having been executed or sent to death camps. There were Germans, Austrians, Yugoslavs, Italians, Bulgarians, Finns, Balts, British, Frenchmen, and Poles among them, while the proportion of sentenced Jews was once again noteworthy. In that witch hunt, Stalin eliminated more leaders of the German Communist Party from before 1933 than Hitler himself had. Of the sixty-eight leaders who, after obeying his policies and allowing fascism to rise, fled to seek refuge in the homeland of communism, more than forty had been executed or died in the camps; so many Poles were eliminated that their faction in the party had to be dissolved.

As he read and wrote notes on V.V.'s letter, Lev Davidovich felt himself sinking under the weight of the revelations. Could he hold out hope that someday humanity would come to know how many hundreds of thousands of people had been executed by Stalin's henchmen? How many true Communists had he taken out? He was convinced that both totals were dizzying, to which one had to add the millions of peasants who had died of hunger in the Ukraine and other regions due to the catastrophe of collectivization, and the millions who had perished in the resettlement of entire towns ordered by the former commissar for nationalities. In all certainty, he thought, we're dealing with the greatest massacre in peacetime history, and the worst thing is that we will never know the true and terrible proportions of the genocide, since for many of those sentenced there was no criminal proceeding, trial, or sentence. The majority had died in jails, suffocated in trains, frozen in the Siberian camps, or been executed on the banks of rivers and precipices so that the corpses would be dragged under by the waters or covered by avalanches of earth and snow . . .

The feeling of finding himself at the mercy of that terror was accentuated when Victor Serge and other friends from Paris confirmed that Étienne was the agent Cupid, linked to the deaths of Liova, Reiss, and Klement. In addition, they accused the young man of having manipulated Jeanne to cause the break that ended in the trial over Seva's custody (favoring the Trotskys, fortunately) and of intervening in the investigation of Liova's death, slowing down the police's work rather than helping it. But, at the same time, the Rosmers and other comrades had tried in vain to find a gap in Étienne's behavior, and Lev Davidovich still refused to accept the conclusion of his other friends. During all of those months, Étienne's efficiency had been prodigious: never before had the *Bulletin* come out so regularly, and in all of his work prior to and following the establishment of the International, his dedication had been exemplary. He knew, nonetheless, that all of that diligence could have been a mask behind which an enemy agent was hiding. He decided that the only solution was to confront Étienne with the accusations against him and demand that he prove his innocence.

Jeanne, in turn, refusing to acknowledge the court's verdict, had fled from Paris, taking Seva and the part of the archives Liova had kept, reasoning that they belonged to her, since she had been his wife. Marguerite Rosmer, willingly and kindly, had taken it as a question of honor to find the boy and guaranteed Natalia that she would bring him to Mexico. Poor Seva! The woman then exclaimed that with his biological father in a concentration camp; his mother dead by suicide, practically in front of him; his adoptive father dead under strange circumstances that pointed to Stalin; his tutor seemingly gone mad, turning all of his frustrations against him; his grandparents in exile; another grandmother confined to a prison camp; dead aunts and disappeared uncles, siblings, and cousins who were never heard from again . . . was there ever a victim more innocent and at the same time more exemplary of Stalin's hate than that small Vsevolod Volkov?

Despite so many losses and the charged atmosphere in the Casa Azul—especially since Frida's departure for New York, where an exhibit of hers had been organized—Natalia Sedova decided to celebrate her husband's fifty-ninth birthday. A few trusted friends came to see him (Otto Rühle, who had stayed to live in Mexico; Max Shachtman; Octavio Fernández; Pep Nadal; and others), joined by secretaries and bodyguards. Natalia had prepared various dishes, mostly Mexican but also Russian, French, and Turkish. Rivera's bad taste was on display when he gave him a Day of the Dead candied skull with the label "Stalin" on its forehead. Meanwhile, Shachtman gave a sort of speech, half in jest, half-serious, and made a portrait of the feted man: "His hair is messy, his face tan, his blue eyes are as penetrating as always. L.D. is still a good-looking man. A dandy, as Victor Serge says, who gave me this tidbit, with which Lenin tried to explain who our beloved Trotsky was, and is. 'Do you know what Lev Davidovich's response will be when the dour-faced officer in charge of his execution squad asks him his last wish?' Lenin asked. 'Well, our comrade will look at him, approach him respectfully and ask him: is there any chance, sir, that you have a comb so I could smooth my hair?'"

But the real portrait was sketched by the person who knew him best, Natalia Sedova, who wrote: "L.D. is alone. We walk through the small garden in Coyoacán, and are surrounded by ghosts with their foreheads riddled with holes . . . Sometimes I hear him, when he's working, and he sighs and talks to himself out loud: 'how exhausting . . . I can't go on!' Many times friends surprise him talking alone with famous shadows, their skulls broken by the henchmen's bullets, friends of yesteryear become penitents, overshadowed by infamy and lies, accusing L.D., Lenin's companion . . . He sees Rakovsky, his beloved brother who, like a prince, offered his enormous fortune to the revolutionary movement. He sees Smirnov, brilliant and happy; Muralov, the general with the enormous mustache, a Red Army hero . . . He sees his children Nina, Zina, Liova, his beloved Blumkin, Yoffe, Tukhachevsky, Andreu Nin, Klement, Wolf. All of them dead. All of them. L.D. is alone."

22

Jacques Mornard truly felt happy when he saw Sylvia Ageloff's thin figure in the airport hall. She was wearing one of those black dresses that, on Gertrude Allison's advice, she had begun to wear ever since her stay in Paris, since, according to the bookseller, that color highlighted the whiteness of her skin. Since then, so conscious of her ugliness, the woman had followed the advice with the hope of offering something more enticing to her adored Jacques, against whose chest she threw herself, shuddering with emotion.

The week before, with the year 1940 barely begun, Tom had told Jacques that the Spanish agent Felipe, one of those who was frozen after Orlov's desertion, had arrived in Mexico. Felipe was coming back from Moscow to take charge, as the operative officer at the head of the action, of the group of Mexicans—former combatants in Spain—who were training to strike against the renegade. The Spaniard, who had been turned into an ambiguous French—or was it Polish—Jew, would be to his local subordinates a man without a name, he would just be the Jewish Comrade. Grigulievich, who had remained in the shadows the whole time, would pass the reins on to Felipe, while Tom would begin to devise and prepare other actions. The second piece of encouraging news was that, if everything went as planned, the American spy would arrive in two to three months to take the place of one of the bodyguards whose period of service in the Exile's house was about to end. Tom assured him that the operation was entering the adjustment period, but was careful to mention to him that at that moment Jacques Mornard had moved back to the second or third line of attack. In other words, his stock had fallen.

For several days, Jacques and Sylvia lived a kind of honeymoon in their room at the Montejo. At Jacques's insistence, the woman delayed her Coyoacán visit more than she wanted in order to say hello to her admired Lev Davidovich, for whom she brought correspondence and to whom she wanted to reiterate her willingness to help in anything he needed while she was in Mexico. When Sylvia made the appointments to be received at the house on Avenida Viena, Jacques offered to take her in his car, but only on the condition that under no circumstances would he mix himself up with her friends. It was that he simply wasn't interested, and just as he respected Sylvia's political passions, he wanted her to accept his lack of interest in that whole pathetic story about Communists fighting with other Communists.

"You don't understand anything," Sylvia said, smiling, enjoying the superiority she felt, at least in that terrain.

"More than you know," Jacques refuted her. "Have you already read in the papers what the Mexican Communists are doing to each other?"

"It's a Stalinist purge. They removed the general secretary, Laborde, and Valentín Campa not because they were bad Communists but because they didn't want to obey some order from Moscow. It's the usual . . ."

Jacques laughed, so much that tears came to his eyes.

"My God, they're all the same. That side says that everything bad that happens is due to agents and Trotskyist provocations, and all of you see Stalin's ghost and his policemen even in your soup."

"The difference is that we are right."

"Please, Sylvia . . . The world can't live between Stalinist and Trotskyist conspiracies."

"Do me the favor of not comparing the two. Stalin is a murderer who has killed with hunger and executed millions of Soviets and thousands of Communists throughout the world. He invaded Poland and now Finland in agreement with Hitler and he's obsessed with murdering Lev Davidovich and . . ."

Jacques gave a half turn and entered the bathroom.

"Let me finish! Listen to me for once!"

Jacques returned to the room and stared at her. He got close to her and, with the tips of his fingers, forcefully, he tapped her two or three times on the temple. He felt an almost uncontrollable desire to hurt her and Sylvia didn't know how to react to his new attitude.

"Get it well into your head that I could care less about all of these stories. Are you going to Coyoacán or not?"

Already in the car, Jacques assured her that he had an approximate idea of how to get to the suburb where the Exile lived, although he had to ask a few times to be sure that he was going the right way. When at last they turned onto Avenida Viena, a quagmire because of the recent rains, he couldn't avoid exclaiming, "My God, where has this man put himself?"

"The only place he was given asylum. And if he lives like this, it is because, as you say, he's obsessed with Stalinist conspiracies."

Jacques had stopped the car in front of the building and a Mexican policeman approached him. When the woman got out of the car, they yelled from the watchtower it was okay. Then Jacques moved the car to the opposite side of the road and parked it farther away from the armored gate. Sylvia, in front of the visitors' door, waited for them to open it, and just as she entered, the heavy barrier closed behind her.

Despite the fact that the temperature was fairly low, Jacques got out of the Buick and, with a cigarette at his lips, leaned against the hood, willing to wait.

When Sylvia emerged, three quarters of an hour later, she came in the company of a man as tall as Jacques but perhaps stockier. Sylvia introduced him as Otto Schüssler, one of Comrade Trotsky's secretaries. Jacques held out his hand, introducing himself as Frank Jacson, and exchanged the usual polite phrases with Otto. He had the impression he was being examined and opted for an attitude halfway between shyness and arrogance, a bit stupid and boisterous, the one that best seemed as if it could express his ignorance of politics and his indifference to everything that place signified.

"Sylvia tells us that you're going to be here for a while," Otto noted casually.

"Well, I don't know for sure; it depends on business. For now, everything's going well. And if there's easy money to be made, then I'm here."

"Jacques—" Sylvia said, and stopped herself, conscious of her mistake and a little embarrassed by her lover's words. "I mean Frank . . . came to open an office in Mexico."

Otto Schüssler arched his eyebrows. Jacques didn't give him time to think about it any further.

"My name is Jacques Mornard, but I travel as Frank Jacson. I am a Belgian army deserter and I don't know when I'll be able to return to my country. I'm not willing to fight for something the politicians didn't know how to take care of when they had the chance."

"It's a point of view . . ." Otto paused. "Mornard . . . Jacson?"

"If you're not the immigration police, however you like."

"Jacson, then." Otto smiled and held out his hand. "Take good care of little Sylvia. All of us here love her and her sisters a lot."

"Don't worry," he said, and, after opening Sylvia's door, walked around the car, avoiding the mud, and took his place behind the wheel.

"Nice car," Otto commented through Sylvia's window.

"And very safe. Since I have to travel throughout the whole country . . ."

Schüssler patted the roof softly and Jacques began to drive away.

"Will they approve of me to be your boyfriend?"

Sylvia looked ahead, her cheeks flushed.

"I couldn't avoid it, dear. It's not the bodyguards' paranoia. They are expecting something. Things have gotten really heated. Please understand."

"I understand. A Stalinist conspiracy," he said and smiled. "So how's your boss?"

"He's not my boss . . . And he's fine, working a lot. He wants to finish the biography of Stalin as soon as possible."

"Trotsky is writing a biography of Stalin?" Jacques's surprise made him slow down.

"He's the only one who can tell the truth about that monster. The rest are dead or are his accomplices."

Jacques moved his head, as if he were denying something remote, and sped up.

"I am dying of hunger. What do you want to eat?"

"Whitefish from Pátzcuaro," she said, as if she had already thought about it.

"Where have you tasted it?"

"I just learned that it's one of Lev Davidovich's favorite dishes."

"I know somewhere where they make it . . . Let's go see if your boss has good taste."

"You're an angel," Sylvia said, and moved her left hand between Jacques Mornard's legs. It appeared that being so close to her admired Lev Davidovich awoke all of her appetites.

Tom and Caridad had disappeared again. A few days before, at the Shirley Court apartment, Tom had warned Jacques that at any moment he would leave Mexico to receive orders, perhaps definitive ones. During the length of his absence, the young man would have just one mission: to get closer, with the most carefree attitude, to the Duck's house and become familiar with his guards. Under no circumstances should he ask Sylvia to introduce him into the fortress, but if they invited him, he should not refuse. If he had the opportunity to meet the Exile, he should demonstrate respect and admiration, but in rather low doses, and he should even act a little shy. In his mind, he should photograph the territory and start to plan an exit strategy in case he or anyone else was tasked with carrying out the mission. The escape was just as important as the action, Tom insisted. His eventual entrance should be gained on the belief that a guy like him could never be a threat against anyone.

Jacques had a glimpse of how his fate was linked to that of the renegade when Sylvia was required by her idol to assist him in his work for two or three weeks: Mademoiselle Yanovitch, tasked with transcribing the recordings of articles the Exile dictated in Russian, had taken ill, and Sylvia's presence in Mexico was a blessing. Jacques, who had a few days free, since Mr. Lubeck was in the United States on important business, offered to take her every morning to the house on Avenida Viena and return in the afternoon to pick her up. While she helped her "boss," he would be updating papers and correspondence in the rented office of the Ermita building. The only problem was that if Sylvia finished early, she had to wait for him, because, with typical Mexican inefficiency, the phone Jacques had requested two months earlier had yet to be installed.

Throughout the month of February, the couple showed up in front of Trotsky's house three or four days a week, and Jacques, without getting out of the car, blew his horn a few times to announce Sylvia's arrival; the door was immediately opened for her. In the afternoons, when he returned, Sylvia was rarely waiting outside, and because of that he had to park the car and smoke a cigarette as she finished her work. In those first days, Jacques Mornard smoked without paying too much attention to the house. He became a regular presence for the guards, who, always seeing him dressed so elegantly, took to calling him "Sylvia's husband" or "Jacson." Thus the distance between them faded. Otto Schüssler, a car enthusiast, was the one who returned to break the ice and, whenever he could, went out to the street to speak with him, since the Belgian man was practically an expert on race cars. More than once Sylvia, sitting in the Buick already, had to wait for Jacques, Otto, and even some of the other guards covering the tower to finish their conversation about engines, clutches, and brake systems.

One of the first afternoons on which they became involved in one of these talks, Jacques had turned around when he heard some joyful barking. He discovered an adolescent boy (the renegade's grandson, Seva Volkov, whom he recognized immediately) going out to the street in the company of a dog of an unknown breed. The image of the dog and the young boy disturbed him for a moment and, forgetting the conversation with Schüssler, he took a few steps toward the house and whistled to the animal, who observed him with his ears raised. Jacques snapped his fingers at the dog, who, indecisive, looked at the adolescent boy. Seva then patted him on the neck and took two steps toward Sylvia's husband, who kneeled down to pet the animal.

Jacques Mornard patted the straight reddish fur with the pads of his fingers with real satisfaction. He allowed his hands to be licked and, in a voice inaudible to the rest, said some words of affection in French. For a few moments he was disconnected from the world, in a corner of time and space in which only he, the dog, and some memories he had thought buried existed. When he regained his bearings, still kneeling, he lifted his gaze toward Seva and asked him the pet's name.

"Azteca," the kid said.

"He's beautiful," Mornard admitted. "So he's yours, right?"

"Yes, I brought him when he was a puppy."

"When I was a boy, I had two. Adam and Eve. Labradors."

"Azteca is a mutt. But my grandfather always had Russian wolfhounds."

"Did he have borzois?" The question was filled with admiration.

"They're the most beautiful hounds in the world. I would've given anything to have one."

"The last one was called Maya. I knew her."

"So you're going for a walk with Azteca?" he asked as he petted the ecstatic animal's ears.

"We're going to the river . . ."

Jacques stood up and smiled.

"I'm sorry, I haven't introduced myself. I'm Jacson, Sylvia's boyfriend."

"I'm Seva," the young boy said.

"Have fun, Seva . . . Goodbye, Azteca," he said, and the dog wagged his tail.

"He likes you," Seva said, smiling, and walked toward the nearby intersection. At that moment Jacques Mornard could feel in the air how the fortress's bulletproof door was beginning to melt before him. He was making more and more friends behind those walls.

One afternoon at the end of February, when he turned down Morelos toward Viena, he noticed that Sylvia was waiting for him by the door to the house, in the company of a couple he immediately recognized thanks to the photographs he had studied so many times. As he always did, he stopped the car on the other side of the street, got out, and kissed Sylvia. She introduced him to Alfred and Marguerite Rosmer, reminding him that a year and a half before, when he had taken her to Périgny for the founding meeting of the Fourth International, he had been in front of the couple's house.

"Yes, of course . . . Beautiful house," Jacques said with his usual lightness. "Are you vacationing in Mexico?"

Alfred Rosmer explained to him that he had traveled to accompany Seva Volkov, who until recently had lived in France ("I already know him, him and Azteca," the Belgian pointed out, smiling). They spoke about the situation in Paris, of the military mobilization of young Frenchmen, and when they said goodbye fifteen minutes later, the Rosmers and the Mornards promised to dine together at one of the city's restaurants the young man knew. With a touch of bourgeois boastfulness, Jacques made it clear that he was treating.

When Mademoiselle Yanovitch was able to return to her job, Sylvia ceased to be indispensable, but Jacques and his Buick returned frequently to the fortress on Avenida Viena, where no one thought his presence unusual anymore. Once a week they stopped by to pick up the Rosmers to go and dine in the city center or, if they were willing, to the nearby city of Cuernavaca, and on the occasional Sunday to the farther-off Puebla. During those outings, they talked about the human and the divine and Jacques had to listen, with admiring attention, to stories about the great friendship between the Rosmers and the Trotskys, begun before the Great War—"Huh, when I was learning to read," Jacques commented one day, though in reality he had already studied the details of that relationship—and, with obvious boredom, the conversations between the Rosmers and Sylvia about the disastrous Soviet invasion of Finland and the imminent Nazi offensive in Western Europe, the growing aggressiveness of Mexican communist propaganda against Lev Davidovich, and even matters of internal politics of the not-very-healthy Fourth International. He showed greater interest when he learned that Trotsky owned a hardy collection of cacti and devoted a couple of hours a day to raising rabbits. But Mornard's favorite topic was bohemian life in Paris, to which he had introduced Sylvia during the months they lived in France, and about which he ended up being much more in the know than the Rosmers.

One night after Jacques had gone down to get cigarettes and returned to the hotel room, Sylvia told him that a Mr. Roberts had called him: he needed to see him urgently over a business matter. The following morning, when Jacques arrived at the apartment in Shirley Court, Tom himself opened the door to him. His mentor informed him that Caridad was in Havana and would return in a few days. He had had some very important meetings, he added, his eyes fixed on Jacques.

"The time to hunt the Duck has come," he said.

Ramón felt the impact of those words in his stomach. Tom gave him time to process the news and then told him about his most recent meeting with Comrade Stalin, this time at a dacha he owned about sixty miles from Moscow, where he held the most secret meetings. In addition to Tom, Beria and Sudoplatov had been there, and regarding what was discussed there, Ramón only had to know—he noted that he had called him "Ramón" but always spoke French—what concerned him directly, since they were vital matters for the Soviet state. The young man nodded and lit a cigarette, consumed by anxiety.

"The renegade is preparing the great betrayal," Tom began, looking at his hands. "An agent of ours passed on the fact that the Germans and the traitor are reaching an agreement to use him as the head of a takeover government when the Nazis decide to invade the Soviet Union. They need a puppet, and there is none better than Trotsky. Through another channel, we learned that he's willing to collaborate with the Americans if they're the ones who, if the war goes in that direction, end up invading the Soviet Union. He's even willing to make a pact with the devil."

"Goddamn him!" Ramón said, unable to control himself.

"There is more . . . ," Tom continued. "In the Soviet Union, we've arrested two Trotskyist agents under orders to assassinate Comrade Stalin. They have both confessed, but this time it has been decided not to publicize it, because with the war you have to move with the greatest caution."

"So what's the order?" Ramón asked, wishing to hear only one response.

"The order is to take him out of the game before the end of the summer. Hitler is now going to attack the West and he's not going to try anything against the USSR, but if he advances through Europe as quickly as we think he will, in a few months he can turn against us."

"Despite the pact?"

"Do you believe in the word of that crazy protector of Aryan purity?"

Ramón shook his head for a long time. Hitler was not his concern and his mentor's subsequent words confirmed it.

"In a few weeks, our American spy arrives in Mexico. From that moment everything is going to move quickly. First we'll play the Mexican group card. Last night I was already with Felipe and he thinks that if the American does his job, they will be able to do theirs."

"So what do I do?" Ramón's disappointment was obvious.

"Keep moving forward as if nothing has happened. I know you have become close with the Rosmers, and they and your beloved Sylvia are going to open the doors of the house for you."

"Sylvia has to go back to New York in a few days . . ."

"Let her go. You will go on like you have until now, and when the Mexicans' attack takes place, whatever happens, you will continue that routine. If things turn out as we expect, then we all leave in a few days. If it fails, you bring Sylvia and we start with another plan."

Ramón looked at the adviser and said, with all his conviction, "I can do it better than the Mexicans." Tom's blue eyes were like two precious stones: happiness made them shine and gave them that sharp, translucent clarity.

"We're soldiers and we follow orders. But don't feel sorry for yourself: this is a long struggle and you are worth a lot . . . Comrade Stalin knows you are the best we have. That's why we want you on the bench: so that if we need to, you can go in and score the goal. And in the future, remember, every damned second of your life, that the most important thing is the revolution and that it deserves any sacrifice. You are Soldier 13 and you have no mercy, you are not afraid, you do not have a soul. You are a Communist from head to toe, Ramón Mercader."

Jacques Mornard spent several days examining himself: he wanted to know where he had gone wrong for Stalin to order, and Tom to allow, that others be in charge of the operation. He was so close! Sylvia's return to New York was a relief and allowed him to wallow in his depression. He lamented how Orlov's desertion had prevented África from being with him in Mexico at that moment. With her at his side, he would at least have had a real consolation and more concrete possibilities of having been selected. He and África, together, would have been capable of bringing down the walls of the traitor's house and freeing the world of that louse who had sold himself to the fascists.

Before traveling, Sylvia had made him promise that he would not go to the Exile's house until she returned. The unbridled aggression of the Mexican Stalinists forced the fortress guards and the police to be on maximum alert, and Jacques's presence, with a false passport and without any concrete motive to go to the house, could cause problems with the Mexican authorities that she preferred to avoid. He promised her that he would not go to Coyoacán, since he had plans to take advantage of his beloved's absence to travel to the south, where Mr. Lubeck wanted to set up some new business.

As soon as Sylvia left, Tom ordered Ramón to leave the Hotel Montejo and move to a tourist complex located near the Buenavista train station. At some point in the next few weeks, Tom would bring him some of the weapons that he could use in an attack on the Duck's house, and the complex, with its wide tree-lined gardens, interior paths, and separate bungalows where different people came and went every day, was ideal for first hiding and then removing a travel trunk. Tom confirmed that none of those participating in the operation knew of his existence and that he personally would take care of bringing in and taking out the weapons.

Ramón stayed in his cabin for several days, smoking, sleeping, and barely eating. An inertia caused by disappointment and forced inactivity lowered his spirits. He felt duped. It seemed unfair that almost two years of work, of planned movements, should only serve to make him the custodian of the weapons that others would use. Convinced that with a little more time he would be in a position to execute the order and even of leaving the act unscathed, he considered himself the best choice. That story about sending the Mexicans so it would look like a matter of local disputes was difficult to swallow. Was Caridad behind that decision? Did she doubt his ability or had she tried to keep him far from danger, with her unbearable propensity to control and decide the lives of her children? After several days of being holed up, the morning that he read in the papers that the German armies had begun their advance to the west, invading Norway and Denmark, he felt his anguish rising and decided that he, too, should go into action and besiege the enemy.

The afternoon he showed up in Coyoacán, it was Harold Robbins, the head of the renegade's praetorian guard, who greeted him from the watchtower. A smiling Jacques explained that he had returned to the city the day before and needed to see the Rosmers. Robbins sent notice to Alfred and Marguerite and asked if he wanted to enter the house to talk more comfortably. Jacques felt so happy his chest burst, but he immediately told him not to worry, he would just be a few minutes.

Alfred and Marguerite received him at the door. He told them about his work trip and the letters in which Sylvia sent her regards, and gave Marguerite a sculpture of an indigenous goddess with a feline face and the body of a woman, purchased that morning in one of the city's markets, telling her that he had seen it in Oaxaca and had immediately thought she would like it. Meanwhile, there was a change of guard in the watchtower and Robbins, before coming down to say goodbye to Jacson, ceded his place to a young man with light-colored hair and very pale skin whom the Belgian was seeing for the first time.

"Is he new?" he asked the Rosmers as he waved at the unknown man.

"He arrived a few days ago. His name is Bob Sheldon and he comes from New York," Alfred Rosmer explained, and Jacques wondered whether that wasn't the man Tom had been waiting for to release the pack of Mexicans.

Since he now had free time again, Jacques proposed seeing the Rosmers in two days for dinner. They had mentioned a French restaurant recently opened in the city center and he was eager to try it, but he didn't feel like going alone. The Rosmers accepted and said he should come pick them up on Friday at seven in the evening.

That Friday, April 18, two seemingly unrelated events confirmed for Ramón Mercader that his fate was to enter history as a servant of the cause of the world's proletariat. In the morning, as he was walking through the gardens of the tourist complex, he found a mountaineer's ice axe driven into a mahogany tree. The complex owner's son, a kid with a slight stutter with whom he had spoken a couple of times, had told him he practiced mountain climbing and even insisted on showing him his equipment. The ice axe driven into the tree was with all certainty the mountain climber's and, given the various wounds on the mahogany's bark, the young man had undoubtedly used its straight, compact trunk for his training. Ramón had to pull hard to dislodge the ice axe from the tree trunk. When he had it in his hands and hefted it, he felt a current of emotion run through him. The spike was a lethal weapon. Ramón chose a place in the mahogany where the bark was a few inches thick. He stepped back and brought the ice axe down, sinking it just above the place he had aimed at. Again he worked hard to free the steel point from the tree, and when he had the ice axe in his hand again, he thought that it was the perfect instrument of death. When he returned to his cabin, he wrapped it up in a towel and put it in the suitcase he usually kept locked.

The second proof of his fate revealed itself when, upon arriving at the fortress on Avenida Viena to pick up the Rosmers, Otto Schüssler told him that Alfred was laid up with a severe attack of dysentery. Lev Davidovich insisted he should go to the hospital, since it could be an appendicitis attack under the diarrhea. Jacques didn't think twice about it, telling Otto that he himself would take Alfred to the doctor; that way none of them would have to leave the house.

Jacques spent almost the entire night with the Rosmers. The doctors at the French clinic, following a series of tests, declared that Alfred was suffering from an especially aggressive parasite, aggravated by a lack of antibodies for tropical predators in Europeans. Montezuma's revenge, they called it. After paying the bill and buying the medicines, Jacques returned to Coyoacán with Marguerite and Alfred, who was much improved thanks to the IV he had been given. As he usually did when he came for Sylvia, Jacques beeped the horn of his Buick twice, and from the watchtower they called out that Jacson was coming back with the Rosmers. Robbins and Schüssler opened the bulletproof door and went out

370

into the street to find that everything seemed to have been resolved. Between the two bodyguards, they helped Alfred enter the house, while Marguerite, her attention divided between her husband and the kind Jacques, hesitated before the open door, through which the young man could see Natalia Sedova and, behind her, the unmistakable head of the renegade, who was dressed in a bathrobe. At that moment Natalia Sedova came to the door to congratulate Marguerite on the incident's happy resolution and to thank Mr. Jacson for being at their disposal. It was then that Natalia asked him if he wanted to come in to have coffee or eat something.

"No, thank you, madame. It's very late and Alfred has to rest."

"Please, Jacques," Marguerite Rosmer insisted. "You've been so kind."

"No, don't worry, it was my duty," he said, and immediately threw his hook into the water: "Another day, when Sylvia's back." Then he began to walk away, smiling, as Marguerite reiterated her gratitude and Alfred's.

The following morning Jacques wrote to Sylvia, telling her he had found himself forced to break his promise not to visit the Trotskys' house, sharing the details of what had happened, and declaring how anxious he was to have her back in Mexico. His brain, meanwhile, was buzzing with satisfaction, because the bulletproof doors of the fortress on Avenida Viena were now merely curtains that he could part softly with the back of his hand.

Tom and Caridad showed up one night at the end of April and unleashed the earthquake that would change Ramón Mercader's life forever. They had called midafternoon announcing they would visit at 9:30 that night and asking him to be ready when they arrived in a dark green Chrysler. Sensing that their reappearance would have profound implications for his life, he had eaten very little and was seated on the wall of the flower bed, smoking a cigarette, thinking that he would like to have a dog—no, two would be better—with whom he could run, rolling around in the sand of some beach, caressing their fur. He became angry as he remembered that the last one he had had a relationship with had been Churro, who came from no one knew where and was part of the Republican army, when the lights of the car turning toward his cabin shined on him and moved forward until the vehicle stopped in front of him.

Tom got out, jingling the car keys in his hand, and motioned to

Ramón to follow him. Caridad got out on the other side and, after unsuccessfully trying to kiss her son, walked to the cabin. Tom opened the back and Ramón saw the trunk inside. Tom warned him it was heavy, and between the two of them they lifted the long chest and walked toward the cabin, where Caridad was holding the door open for them. As if he had already thought everything out, Tom steered them to the bedroom and they placed the trunk to the side of the closet.

Caridad was waiting for them in the living room, sitting in an armchair. It seemed to Ramón that she had gained weight in recent weeks and looked strong and energetic, as she had in the ever more distant days in which she wandered the streets of Barcelona in a confiscated Ford and demonstrated her toughness by shooting a dog. Ramón cursed the ambiguous feelings his mother generated in him. Meanwhile, Tom, sitting in front of Ramón, explained that the trunk would be there for no more than two weeks.

"The wheels are turning," he concluded.

"Is the spy Bob Sheldon?" Ramón asked.

"Yes, and as I imagined, we can't expect much from him. The Jewish Comrade is working on him and is confident that at least he'll be good enough to open the door."

The young man kept his silence. His situation bothered him.

"What's wrong, Ramón?" Caridad asked him, leaning toward him. "When you get strange like this . . ."

"You and he already know. But don't worry. After all . . ."

"Are you going to have a tantrum?" Tom's tone was sarcastic. "I'm not going to repeat what you already know. You and I follow orders. It's that simple. Everyone serves the revolution where and when the revolution decides."

"What do I do in the meantime?"

"Wait," Tom said. "When the attack is about to happen, I'll tell you what to do. Go by Coyoacán every once in a while and say hi to your friends. If you find out anything that could be useful, find me. If not, we'll keep our distance."

"It's better like this, Ramón," Caridad said. "Tom knows you can do it, but this is a very complicated political problem. Killing that son of a bitch will have consequences and the Soviet Union cannot afford to be implicated . . . That's all."

"I understand, Caridad, I understand," he said, and stood up. "Coffee?"

From that night on, Ramón lived feeling like his insides had been emptied. He felt that, after having to put so much of himself beneath the false skin of Jacques Mornard, it had rebelled and trapped his real and neglected self. Now it was Jacques wandering the city streets, traveling in his black Buick at suicidal speeds, passing by the fortress on Avenida Viena to ask about Alfred Rosmer's health and have trivial conversations with Robbins, Otto Schüssler, Joseph Hansen, Jake Cooper, and even with the recently arrived Bob Sheldon, whom he had invited to have a beer more than once in the noisy cantina where the toothless salesclerk had disappeared and was replaced by a young woman; it was Jacques who smiled, wrote love letters to Sylvia Ageloff and looked with interest at the shop windows of shoe stores and tailors of a city as splendid as it was besieged by misery that was, to a guy like him, invisible. Meanwhile, Ramón, a ghost, conjugated the verb "to wait" in all of its tenses and possible uses, which in Spanish can also mean to expect and to hope, and felt how life was passing by him without even deigning to look at him.

On the morning of May 1, he had gone all the way to Paseo de la Reforma, where workers and union members were marching, to see the signs and sheets asking not for the renegade's expulsion but rather for the death of the fascist traitor, and he felt that claim didn't include him. Disoriented, without expectations, he spent hours in bed smoking, looking at the ceiling, repeating the same piercing questions, asking himself, After everything happens, then what? This sacrifice and self-denial, for what? The glory he thought he had at arm's reach—where had it gone to? Ramón had handed over his soul to that mission because he wanted to be the main player, and it didn't matter to him that he had to kill, or even be killed, if he achieved his goal. He felt prepared to remain in darkness his entire life, nameless and without his own existence, but with the communist pride of knowing he had done something great for others. He wanted to be chosen by Marxist providence and at that moment he thought that he would never be anyone or anything. So, two weeks later, when Tom returned to reclaim the trunk, Ramón felt he would never play an important role in that plot.

"When will it be?"

They had placed the weapons in the Chrysler's trunk and were sitting in the cabin's armchairs, looking each other in the eye.

"Soon." Tom seemed annoyed.

"Is something wrong?"

Tom smiled sadly and looked at the floor, where he was lightly tapping the tiles with the tip of his shoe.

"I'm afraid, Ramón."

His mentor's response surprised him. It didn't escape his notice that Tom was calling him Ramón again as he confessed something he never expected to hear from that man's lips. Should he believe him?

"Grigulievich and Felipe have prepared everything as best as they can, but they have no confidence in their men. Sheldon can do his job, but the others . . ."

"Who will be at the front?"

"The Jewish Comrade."

"And he doesn't have any confidence in himself?"

"It's going to be an attack with many people, many shots. A Mexican-style show . . . They are men with experience in war, but an attack like this is something else."

"So why don't you cancel it?"

"You remember the Hotel Moscow, right? Who is going to tell Stalin that the attack will be canceled?"

Ramón leaned forward. He could hear Tom's breathing.

"And what will you say to him if they fail? . . . Let me go with them, goddammit . . ."

Tom looked him in the eye. Ramón felt anxiety in his chest.

"It would be a solution, but it's not possible. When they identify you, they're going to realize that it's not an action planned by the Mexicans but rather a conspiracy coming from elsewhere."

"So what if someone identifies Felipe?"

"He would be a Spaniard who was with the Mexicans in the civil war. That front has already been established."

"I'm also a Spaniard . . . And Belgian, and—"

"It can't be, Ramón! The attack is perfect, but something unexpected could always happen: they could injure the Duck and he could survive, I don't know. I myself told Comrade Stalin that he should consider the possibility of failure. And I also told him that if that happened, you would enter the game. But it can't be canceled, nor can I send you . . ." Tom stood up, lit a cigarette, and looked toward the garden. "You should be happy to not have to participate in this. You know that the lives of all who enter that house can be very difficult from that moment on. All they have to do is capture one and the rest will fall like dominoes. And they're going to catch them, that's certain . . . Besides, from the beginning I told you that you are my best option, but not the first. If they do things well, it's better for everyone; that's how we planned it. Did you see what happened on May Day, how the Trotskyists and the Communists fought in the street? Who is going to suspect us when a group of Mexican Communists execute a traitor who is even collaborating with the Americans to carry out a coup d'état in Mexico? And in any event, even if they tell the police whatever they want to, there will be no evidence that those men were mixed up with us . . ."

"I understand what you're saying. But you can't ask me to be happy to have worked for three years for nothing."

Tom at last smiled. He crushed the cigarette butt in the ashtray and walked to the door.

"I hope you never lose that faith you have, Ramón Mercader. You can't imagine how much you'll need it if your turn comes to enter the scene. I assure you, it is not easy to kill a man like that son of a bitch Trotsky."

Jacques Mornard put the water for the coffee on the stove and adjusted the belt on the boxing robe he used around the house. When he went out to the small entryway he confirmed that the morning papers had not arrived. The previous week, he had doubled the tip for the kid who brought the papers on the condition that they be left at his door before seven in the morning. He returned to the kitchen, percolated coffee, and drank a small cup. He lit a cigarette and walked to the caretaker's office. The month of May was almost over, but the morning was cool thanks to the previous night's rain. He walked down the gravel path and cursed as he felt his slippers becoming damp. At the door to the cabin that served as the concierge's office, the morning caretaker was placing gardening tools in a wheelbarrow.

"Good morning, Mr. Jacson, how can I help you?" The man was smiling and making small bows.

"The paperboy, what happened to him today?"

The caretaker's smile widened. His teeth were incredibly white and, miraculously, he wasn't missing any.

"It's that the papers haven't come out yet. They're waiting."

"What kind of thing is it that the papers haven't come out yet?"

"Oh, *señor*, it's because of what happened last night." The caretaker smiled again. "They tried to kill that bearded Trotsky. They're saying it on the radio."

Ramón gave a half turn and, without saying goodbye to the caretaker, returned to his cabin. If he understood correctly, the man had been talking about an attack, not an execution. He turned on the radio and searched until he found a station reporting the news. An armed commando unit had entered Leon Trotsky's house just before dawn that morning and, despite the numerous shots fired, had not achieved their purpose of killing the exiled revolutionary. The attackers—they said that Diego Rivera, gun in hand, was among them—had managed to flee, and President Cárdenas himself had ordered an exhaustive investigation until the perpetrators of the aborted crime were found. As he digested those words—Diego Rivera was part of the attack?—and tried to predict the consequences, Ramón felt a strange mixture of anxiety and happiness coming over him. As he dressed hurriedly, he continued to listen and learned that there was talk of one wounded, of attackers dressed as soldiers and policemen, of the kidnapping of one of the renegade's bodyguards.

He dialed the number of Tom's apartment in Shirley Court and didn't get an answer. What should he do now? Jacques Mornard took some time to reflect. Tom had put together a plan that escaped his comprehension. Had he managed to use the political differences between the renegade and fat Rivera so that the latter would take the helm of a killer commando unit, or had he simply threatened him with airing his problems with his wife? They spoke of twenty armed men, of hundreds of shots fired but no one killed. How was that possible? With a professional like Felipe inside the house, how was it possible for the Duck to still be alive? There was something murky in the attack that defied the most basic logic. In any event, he thought, the attack's failure placed him at the front line, where he had fought so hard to get. Tom's fears regarding the success of the operation were now powerfully highlighted, and he came to wonder whether in reality that failure did not have a purpose. But what? To enter the Duck's house, have him at the mercy of ten rifles and not kill him— for what? Had he, Ramón, always been the one tasked with the real mission? He felt as if his head were about to explode. The evidence that he had turned into the true alternative continued to bring him remote revolutionary joy, but with it the ghost of an unexpected fear surreptitiously came to the surface at the responsibility that came with it. He drank more coffee, smoked two more cigarettes, and, when he felt ready to move, put on his hat and climbed into the Buick.

As he drove to Shirley Court, Ramón noticed that his chest was about to burst with anguish. He had never felt that oppression so clearly, and he wondered if it wasn't angina like the kind Caridad experienced. When he asked the caretaker at the apartments if Mr. and Mrs. Roberts were in, the man explained that they had left the night before.

Ramón Mercader left the Buick in the apartment parking lot and went out toward Reforma, which was congested with pedestrians, vendors, cars, beggars, and even prostitutes with flexible schedules: a multicolored humanity surrounded by engine exhausts and the cries of newspaper boys announcing the miraculous salvation of the "bearded" Trotsky. The city seemed crazed, on the verge of exploding, and the young man felt dizzy amid the crowd and their rejoicing. Leaning against the wall, he lifted his gaze to the clear sky, wiped clean by the previous night's rain, and was certain that his fate would be decided beneath that bright, clear sky.

23

On May 2, 1939, the Trotskys moved the beds and the worktable and put coal in the ovens. The house at number 19 Avenida Viena was now their house. Although it meant little more than changing prisons, Lev Davidovich felt that with that move he was gaining enormous freedom. Can I feel happy? Do I have the right to that human emotion? he asked himself upon sitting in *his* office and looking around. The yard he could see from the window was ruined and the main work hadn't been finished yet, since, despite Natalia Sedova's strict management and the secretaries' Stakhanovite efforts, the funds had been exhausted. But he couldn't live under the same roof as Rivera for one more day. Over the last two months, they hadn't even spoken, and he regretted the way in which that friendship had ended, since he would never be able to forget that, for whatever reason, Rivera had helped him travel to Mexico, had offered his hospitality, and had contributed to his recovery after the terrible experiences at the end of his Norwegian exile.

Ever since he was very young, he had thought that the worst aggression against the human condition was humiliation, because it disarmed the individual, attacking the essence of his dignity. He, who throughout his life had suffered all the insults and slanders possible, had never felt so close to the verge of humiliation as when Natalia and Jean van Heijenoort prevented him, after his last birthday, from leaving the Casa Azul and going to yell at Rivera about the disgust he felt at his exhibitionism, his macho Mexican positions, his inconsistencies as a political clown. For a long time Lev Davidovich had known that if Rivera had welcomed him into his house, and perhaps even accepted that Rivera's wife went to his bed, it had only been to use it as a platform for his phony radicalism, a trampoline to the newspaper pages. But when tensions had reached the boiling point, his kindness had come undone and he had shown his true face.

The tension had been aggravated by the inevitable collision between Rivera's ambitions and Lev Davidovich's sense of responsibility when the latter opposed the painter assuming the role of Mexican secretary of the Fourth International. But things went beyond the permissible limit when Rivera announced his break with General Cárdenas and his decision to support the right-wing presidential candidate Juan Almazán. Although the Exile knew that it was all due to his own insolence, he tried to warn the painter of how damaging his defection would be for Cárdenas's progressive project, and the response he received had been so offensive that, that very day, he decided to end his stay at the Casa Azul. Trotsky could not give anyone political lessons, his host had told him; only a lunatic could think of organizing an International that was nothing but a vainglorious effort to become the leader of something.

If in another time he had left the Kremlin itself, why not leave the Casa Azul now? If they went somewhere less protected, his life would be in danger, but that did not matter too much to him; however, van Heijenoort reminded him that he was also putting Natalia's life at risk. Lev Davidovich had to lower his head, although he announced his break with Rivera and his disagreement with the painter's political about-face, not wanting to be associated with an action that directly affronted General Cárdenas, to whom he felt so committed.

At the beginning of the year, Lev Davidovich had written to Frida, who was still in New York, with the hopes that she would be able to allay the crisis, but she never responded. Meanwhile, Rivera, who now declared himself a supporter of Almazán, was announcing his break with Trotskyism because he considered it a harebrained ideology that played into the fascists' strategy against the USSR.

Jean and the other secretaries intensified their search for a safe place for them to live and finally opted to rent a brick house with an ample shaded yard on the nearby Avenida Viena, a dusty street where there were only a few shacks. The house had the advantage of high walls and of being inaccessible from the back, where the Churubusco River ran. But the building had been empty for ten years, and it required a lot of work to make it inhabitable. Once they decided to move, Lev Davidovich tried to offer Diego rent for the months that the renovation of the house would take, but the painter wouldn't even receive him, making his intention of humiliating the Exile obvious. The tension then reached such a level that van Heijenoort confessed to Lev Davidovich that he even feared Rivera could commit violence.

That domestic crisis barely allowed Lev Davidovich to follow events happening outside the Casa Azul with the care he desired. With much difficulty he had managed to concentrate on the reorganization of the American section and discuss with Josep Nadal the seriousness of Spanish events following Franco's offensive toward Catalonia, the last of the Republican strongholds apart from Madrid. In Mexico, meanwhile, the attacks against his presence were entering a dangerous spiral, and at the same time that Hernán Laborde, the secretary of the Communist Party, demanded that the government expel him threatening a political rupture if it did not, the right tinged its protests with a dark fascist-inspired anti-Semitism. Lev Davidovich lived surrounded by the feeling that the siege was closing in, that the knives and guns were getting closer and closer to his graying head.

The renovation was turning out to be more complex than they had originally thought, as Natalia had ordered one of the walls be made higher, watchtowers to be built, the covering of all entrances with steel sheets, and the installation of an alarm system. At one point Lev Davidovich had asked if they were preparing a house or a sarcophagus.

Since he spent almost the whole day holed up in his room at the Casa Azul, he made the most of his time by writing an analysis of the foreseeable end of the Spanish Civil War. Spain's revolutionary movement, if successful, could perhaps have delayed and even prevented the European war. Nadal had told him that, in the final months of the previous year, the Spanish government had asked for more weapons from its allies in a desperate attempt to save the Republic. The Soviets made a shipment through France, but Paris refused to allow the weapons through its borders, and that failure had been definitive. The Soviets, tired of a war without the prospect of a victory, decided to cut off all their commitments, and from that moment Spain was lost. While the fascists were rolling their military power over Spanish soil, Stalin was turning a blind eye and beginning to concern himself with what had always been his true interest, his neighbors in Eastern Europe.

There had been no information about Seriozha for many months when an American journalist who had recently arrived in New York after a stay in Moscow wrote the Trotskys, telling them that a colleague of his had managed to interview a prisoner just released by the new head of the NKVD, Lavrentiy Beria. The former prisoner had relayed that, a few months before, he had seen Sergei Sedov alive, and another detainee had told him that Seriozha had been in the Vorkuta camp in 1936, during the Trotskyists' strike, where he had been on the verge of dying of hunger; but in 1937 he had been transferred to the shadowy prison of Butyrka, in Moscow, where he had been subjected to torture to force him to sign a confession against his father: he was one of the few prisoners who withstood it without surrendering. The anonymous prisoner said he had met him in a camp in the subarctic, where other inmates talked about Sergei Sedov as if he were an unbreakable man.

Natalia and Lev Davidovich had believed the news heart and soul, even when their minds thought it would be difficult for their son to have been able to escape Vorkuta or Butyrka with his life, places that were worse than the sixth circle of hell. But Lev Davidovich couldn't avoid feeling proud when they kept hearing the same description of Seriozha's attitude; the only thing about which there was no doubt was that he had resisted the interrogations without signing confessions against his father. So they consoled themselves by thinking that if Stalin had preyed upon his innocent life, Seriozha had conquered him with his silence.

A new congress of the Communist Party of the Soviet Union, held at the beginning of the year, had left Lev Davidovich several certainties. On the international level, it had made Stalin's willingness to seek an alliance with Hitler more obvious; on the national level, it underscored the cynical pretension of carrying out yet another revision of history by blaming the expelled heads of the GPU for the excesses of the purge. To the indignation of very few and to popular acceptance of his good intentions, the "great captain" criticized those who carried out the purge, since it had been accompanied by "more mistakes than expected" (his own words). So everything would have turned out okay if only the expected mistakes had been committed? How many was it acceptable to execute by mistake? The most alarming thing was that none of those in the world who recognized Stalin's honesty seemed to recall that, a few months earlier, the man from the mountains had sent pompous congratulations to Yezhov and the heads of NKVD. It only seemed to matter to them that the genius had warned them about the existence of "deficiencies" in the operation, such as the "simplified investigation procedures" and the lack of witnesses and proof. So where was Stalin while that was happening? the Exile had asked a world that would not respond to him.

In reality, the most dramatic of the revelations of the congress was the proof that the general secretary had finally ascended to the heights of power. The terror of those last years had allowed him to remove from the scene, in one way or another, eighteen of the twenty-seven members of the Politburo elected in the last congress presided over by Lenin, and to leave the heads on just twenty percent of the members of the Central Committee elected in 1934, the last time the situation was on the verge of slipping out of his hands. Stalin had proven to be a real genius of political chicanery, and his successful elimination of any opposition within the party (relying on the agreement promoted by Lenin over the illegality of factions) turned into his most efficient political weapon to make democracy disappear and, later, to establish terror and carry out the purges that gave him absolute power. Perhaps the first mistake of Bolshevism, Lev Davidovich thought, was the radical elimination of the political tendencies opposed to it, and once that policy went from outside society to inside the party, the end of the utopia had begun. If freedom of expression had been allowed in society and within the party, terror would not have been able to take root. That was why Stalin had embarked on the political and intellectual purge in such a way that everything would fall under the control of a state devoured by the party—and a party devoured by the general secretary. This was exactly what Lev Davidovich, before the aborted revolution of 1905, predicted to Lenin would happen.

To top off that series of defeats, one afternoon in March, Josep Nadal arrived at the Casa Azul with several newspapers in his hands and a look of disappointment on his face. The Republican army had surrendered and Franco's troops were marching through Madrid. Lev Davidovich knew that in the coming months the reprisals would be terrible and he felt pity for the Republicans who had not been able to or had not wanted to flee Spain. The saddest thing was seeing how a courageous country that had had the revolution at the tips of its fingers had been sacrificed by the owners of the revolution and socialism, just as years before they had done to the Chinese Communists and the German workers. Was it so difficult to see that series of betrayals? he asked, looking into Nadal's face.

Their new lives at the house on Avenida Viena forced the family to depend only on their own economic resources. Lev Davidovich's author royalties were smaller every day: only the advance paid for the English edition of *Stalin* and his contributions to newspapers allowed them to stay afloat. He was bitter that part of that money had disappeared in the effort to turn the estate into a trench, because no matter how high the walls were, no matter how impregnable the doors seemed, when the GPU order was given, they would find a crack in the defenses and reach him. And he sensed—in fact knew—that the order had been given: the more imminent the war, the closer his death.

Natalia and the bodyguards tried to extend their vigilance to every single person who visited them, but Lev Davidovich refused to be so suspicious as to succumb to paranoia. The great advantage of living in his own house was being able to deal freely with the people who interested him, and from the moment they moved in, he had begun to receive visits from politicians, philosophers, university professors, Mexican sympathizers and those from other countries, including recently arrived Spanish Republicans, many of whom had felt uncomfortable around Rivera or, simply, had preferred not to visit Trotsky at the Casa Azul. Those meetings and the friends he kept were his contact with the world, and their opinions served to inform him, to reaffirm or temper his ideas.

Regularly, the Trotskys went out of town in the car they had purchased. They made the decision to leave randomly, almost by surprise, and the employees of the house never knew when it would happen, and on occasion not even the bodyguards—whom van Heijenoort alerted about the outings with very little notice—knew their schedule. Since the situation in Mexico was getting more and more explosive (from the start of the electoral campaign, the Exile's presence had become a hotly debated issue), they barely visited the city, and when they did, Lev Davidovich hid himself in the backseat. But decidedly the outings to the countryside were the ones Lev Davidovich most enjoyed. He took long walks that stimulated his body, dulled by so many hours of sedentary work, and he devoted himself to what would become one of his favorite hobbies, collecting rare cacti, which he replanted in the yard of his home. The marvelous variety of those plants turned the search for specimens into an adventure that sometimes took the Trotskys over difficult terrain and gave them many hours of exercise as they dug up the cacti with picks and shovels and transported them to the car. Natalia called those outings "days of forced labor," but returning to the house with specimens that they planted with the utmost care was the prize for that work. One afternoon, as they planted one of the most singular cacti in his collection, Lev Davidovich remembered the order not to sow a single rosebush in the house at Büyükada. Were those cacti the image of his defeat?

When the house was minimally set up for work, Lev Davidovich decided to make a final push to complete his Stalin biography. Natalia, so radical in her attitudes, insisted that he was debasing his talents by dedicating himself to deconstructing the Georgian, and she thought that many would have doubts about his objectivity due to the confrontation between the two of them over so many years. His editors had also encouraged him to write a biography of Lenin and spoke of sizable advances. But Lev Davidovich wanted to show the world the red czar's true face. Even when he knew he was blinded by his passion, he didn't reach the point of distorting the truth. Moreover, the monstrosities and crimes of Stalin's era disgusted him, and he wanted that feeling to pervade the work. If from his pages a sinister figure rose almost reptilelike, it was because Stalin was in fact that way. Stalin's years of infighting had given him that capacity to work for his promotion behind the scenes and one day take all power— aided by Lenin's indolence, by Zinoviev's, Kamenev's and Bukharin's congenital fear, and by Lev Davidovich's own damned pride, he said. Or was the dictatorship an unavoidable historical necessity, the system's only possibility? But what most encouraged Lev Davidovich to dedicate himself to writing that devastating book was the belief that, as had happened to the also deified Nero after his death, Stalin statues would be brought down and his name erased from everything—because history's revenge tends to be more thorough than that of the most powerful emperor who ever existed. Lev Davidovich was sure that, when Louis XIV declared "*L'état, c'est moi*," he was pronouncing an almost liberal formula in comparison with the reality of Stalin's regime. The totalitarian state he had created went well beyond Caesar's—and for that reason the general secretary could say, with all honesty, "*La societé, c'est moi.*" But the world should remember that both Stalin and the society custom built for him were deeply sick beings. The terror of those years had not been just a political instrument but also personal pleasure, an orgy of the senses for the Grave Digger and the dregs of Russian society. No one should find it strange that the terror should have come to include his own family and those closest to him (Why did Nadezhda Alliluyeva commit suicide? Give me a convincing answer that doesn't have Stalin pointing the gun, he thought). The most terrible thing was the certainty that the terror had reached Lenin himself, whom, Lev Davidovich was convinced, Stalin had poisoned, since he knew that Vladimir Ilyich, if his devastated body and mind allowed it, would have named Lev Davidovich his successor as general secretary.

As the summer of 1939 went on, Lev Davidovich was certain that the start of the war in Europe was a question of days. The atmosphere in his own surroundings was also heating up, and he agreed with his secretaries and friends that he needed to be more careful about his movements. The animosity of local Stalinists was growing, and that was bound to result in more attempts on his life. Over the last year, the demands that he leave Mexico had turned into a campaign for his head. He knew that if the war started, Stalin would do almost anything to destroy him, since, even in his isolation, he was the only one capable of challenging him and Stalin could not run the risk that Lev Davidovich would return to Soviet territory and organize opposition to the system.

Natalia continued the work of fortifying the house and decided to reduce the visits of journalists, professors, and sympathizers who requested meetings. The number of men who protected him increased, although they faced the problem that those young men came to Mexico for a few months and, just when they had become familiar with their duties, had to return to their countries. The result of that collective paranoia was that he returned to living practically sequestered and his marginalization became especially painful in those summer days, the most pleasant for walking and fishing. Resolved to find a distraction from his many hours of work, he then had the idea of raising rabbits and hens, and began to ask for books on those subjects, for if he was going to try it, he would do so scientifically.

What most worried Natalia Sedova was that her husband's health, so weakened in recent years, was suffering at an altitude that could cause a permanent state of high blood pressure. His digestion was difficult, and only light food, at set hours, saved him from greater ills. Definitively, the life of a pariah lived for so many years was taking its toll, and when he was on the verge of turning sixty, Lev Davidovich himself had to admit that he had turned into an old man, to the point that many people called him simply "the Old Man."

When Lev Davidovich wrote about the impending war, he couldn't help but warn that the USSR would perhaps end up being an easy victim of German tanks and aviation. Stalin, who accused Trotsky of being an opportunist and a traitor when he published this analysis, had weakened the military power of the country to the point that, everyone knew, only a miracle could save them. And that miracle—nobody could say it better than Lev Davidovich—was the Soviet soldier, whose capacity for sacrifice was unrivaled in the world. But the price to be paid would be many lives that could have been saved. What did Stalin need to withstand a German attack? Above all, time, he wrote. Time to reinforce the borders and rebuild the leaderless army. And he also needed for Western Europe to resist the fascist onslaught, at least for a while. Because of that, when on August 23, 1939, the news broke, Lev Davidovich was not really surprised, although he felt deep disgust. The radio stations, the world's newspapers on the left and the right, communist or fascist, big or small, all had the same headline that day: the Soviet Union and Nazi Germany had signed a pact of nonaggression, a pact of understanding . . .

The news that von Ribbentrop and Molotov, as foreign ministers, had reached an agreement, of which, obviously, only a part had been made public, surprised more people in the world than Lev Davidovich would have imagined. A treaty that left Hitler's hands free to attack the West was incomprehensible for those who willingly and even unwillingly had, despite the terror and the criminal proceedings, continued to defend Stalin as the great leader of the working class. For that reason, the Exile dared to predict that for centuries that date was going to be remembered as one of the most extraordinary betrayals of man's fate and gullibility.

Lev Davidovich knew that Stalin would soon argue that the defense of the USSR was the priority, and that if the West had given free rein to German expansionism with the Munich Pact, the USSR, too, had the right to avoid a war with Germany. And he would be partially right. But the muddy trail of humiliation could never be erased, he wrote; seeing that the USSR's radical antifascism was not what it seemed would cause massive disappointment, and the faith of millions of believers, who had resisted all tests, might be lost forever. But the demoralized workers and militants would perhaps soon have the opportunity to turn shame into an impulse to achieve the postponed revolution. Days of pain were coming, he concluded, but perhaps also times of glory for a new generation of Bolsheviks armed with the bitter experience of life, both inside and outside the Soviet Union.

Less than ten days later, when the Wehrmacht invaded Poland, Lev Davidovich noted that the Germans seemed to penetrate Polish territory with too much caution, as if their tanks were advancing with the brakes on. But when, two weeks later, Soviet troops entered Poland, the Exile understood the conditions of the pact. The two dictators, as he had assumed, were spreading their hands over the once again sacrificed Poland. The curious thing was that the Western powers that had declared war on the Nazis accepted, without great protest, that Stalin would do the same as Hitler. The hypocrisy of the policy, he thought, would have disastrous consequences.

At that moment, Lev Davidovich was a man with his soul divided in anguish. Someday, he told himself, they would recognize that it was the mistakes of revolutionaries, more than the pressures of imperialism, that had delayed the great changes of human society; but even with that conviction and after so much infamy, political lows, and crimes of all kinds, he continued to believe that defense of the USSR against fascism and imperialism constituted the great duty of the workers of the world. Because Stalin was not the USSR, nor the representative of the true Soviet dream.

It shamed him, because of what it meant for the socialist ideal, to know that after invading Poland, Stalin was imposing the Soviet order there with the same fury with which Hitler exported fascist ideology. That crude imposition of the Soviet model on Poland and the Western Ukraine would bring about the demoralization of European workers once they saw the political opportunism of Stalinism. The inhabitants of those conquered regions, historic victims of the Russian and German empires, surely already asked themselves what differences existed between one invader and another, and Lev Davidovich would not be surprised if, very soon, many of those people came to consider the Nazis their liberators from Stalinist tyranny.

Even so, Lev Davidovich felt the contradiction like an overwhelming weight, not knowing if it was possible to oppose Stalinism while still defending the USSR. It anguished him not to be able to discern whether all of that bureaucracy was already a new class, incubated by the revolution, or just the excrescence that he had always thought it was. He needed to convince himself that it was still possible to show the difference between fascism and Stalinism and try to show all honest men, dumbfounded by the low blows of that Thermidorean bureaucracy, that the USSR still contained the essence of the revolution and *that* essence was what had to be defended and preserved. But if, as some said, won over by the evidence, the working class had shown with the Russian experience its inability to govern itself, then one would have to admit that the Marxist concept of society and socialism was mistaken. Was Marxism just one more ideology, a form of false consciousness that led its supporters and the oppressed classes to believe they were fighting for their own ends when in reality they were benefiting the interests of a new governing class? . . . Just thinking of it caused him intense pain. The victory of Stalin and his regime would be raised like the triumph of reality over philosophical illusion and as an inevitable act of historical stagnation. Many, himself included, would see themselves forced to recognize that Stalinism did not have its roots in Russia's backwardness nor in the hostile imperialist atmosphere, as had been said, but rather in the proletariat's inability to become the governing class. He would also have to admit that the USSR had been no more than the precursor of a new system of exploitation and that its political structure had to breed, inevitably, a new dictatorship, albeit adorned with a different thetoric . . .

The Exile knew that he could not change his way of seeing the world. He would not tire of exhorting men of good faith to remain alongside the exploited, even when history and scientific needs seemed to be against them. "Down with science, down with history! If necessary, we must redefine them!" he wrote. "In any event, I will remain on Spartacus's side, never with the Caesars, and even against science I am going to maintain my trust in the ability of the working masses to free themselves from the yoke of capitalism, since whoever has seen the masses in action knows that it is possible." Lenin's mistakes, his own equivocations, those of the Bolshevik Party that permitted the deformation of the utopia, can never be blamed on the workers. Never, he would keep thinking.

No matter how great his unease, Lev Davidovich felt that life, so arduous, was still capable of compensating him with happiness when Seva at last arrived in Mexico. If his grandparents had not seen photos of the boy, they never would have recognized him. Between the little boy they had said goodbye to in France and the confused and shy thirteen-year-old who arrived in Coyoacán, there was a terrible and devastating story that made them fear for his mental health. But he and Natalia were convinced that love could cure even the deepest wounds, and love was what they had more than enough of, they who did not tire of hugging and kissing him, of admiring his youth in full bloom, despite the fact that both knew the boy's life would not be easy in a country where he didn't speak the language, where he had no friends, and where, to top it off, he lived in a fortress.

Alfred and Marguerite Rosmer, after rescuing Seva from the religious boarding school in the South of France where Jeanne had sent him, had traveled with him from France to Mexico fearful of possible attacks. Those friends, the only ones they had left from the days of uncertainty before the revolution, had been one of the great blessings in Lev Davidovich's existence and made him ask himself how he could have ever been so obtuse as to mistake Molinier's opportunism for sincere friendship.

Natalia and the Rosmers took charge of showing Seva around the city, and his grandfather insisted on being his guide on an outing to Teotihuacán. Lev Davidovich demanded that only the bodyguards go with them, since he wanted Seva all to himself. Although they couldn't climb to the summit of the Pyramid of the Sun, they made a deep journey to the past. They talked about his father, Plato Volkov, of whom Seva did not have specific memories, since he had been deported when the boy was three years old; about his mother, Zina, a victim of horrible revenge; about his uncle Liova, about whom the boy dreamed on many nights; they talked about what were for him the misty days of Prinkipo and Istanbul, of which his mind kept memorable flashes of the fires, the fishing, but above all the company of Maya. He kept a photo of himself at age five with his grandfather, his hair and beard still dark, and the beautiful borzoi, who gave the impression of looking right into the camera in order to eternalize the kindness of her eyes. During the years he lived in Berlin and Paris, Seva had wanted to have another dog, but his nomadic life would not allow him that pleasure. So Lev Davidovich promised him that he could have a dog now, and that it would help him like nothing else to feel that something belonged to him and that he belonged to a place. Poor boy! How much hate had consumed the best part of his life! he would say that night to Natalia Sedova.

Meanwhile, the Red Army had invaded Finland and the international community was finally comparing Stalin to Hitler. In the article that he wrote on that episode, Lev Davidovich weighed his opinions with extreme care, certain that he would sow confusion and dissent among his followers, who would even label him a Stalinist for expressing an idea that did not seem negotiable even to him, even after that invasion: even with Stalin at the helm, he wrote, the defense of the integrity of the USSR continued to be the priority of the world proletariat.

A couple of weeks after his arrival, Seva asked Harold Robbins, the new head of the bodyguards, to accompany him on a walk through the neighborhood. Although Natalia and Marguerite were not in favor of it, Alfred and Lev Davidovich thought they should give the child a little freedom, since Seva had shown himself to be a strong boy, and life's blows did not appear to have affected him. An hour after they left, Seva and Robbins returned . . . with a dog. On one of their drives, the boy had seen his dog's mother, with a litter, in front of a shack, and of course the dog's owners were happy for someone to take one of the pups. Upon arriving at the house, he had already been baptized "Azteca," and he was one of those mutts in possession of an intelligence gained over generations by the struggle for survival.

The happiness that Lev Davidovich felt over Seva's presence was clouded over by his break with his old friend Max Shachtman, the collaborator who, ever since his first visit to Prinkipo in 1929, had offered him so much affection and devotion. The defection was a consequence of the separatist fever that was undermining the American Trotskyists, the same as that which had affected the French ten years earlier that preventing the gestation of a unified opposition right at the moment of the fascist ascent. Now the heat of the war and the adoption of the most radical positions regarding the USSR had exacerbated the divisions and new parties were emerging, a little bit closer to or further from the left than others in regard to "matters of principle." Max Shachtman and James Burnham had turned into leaders of their own party, an offshoot of the Socialist Workers that was reduced to a mere handful of followers with that split.

Although he asked Shachtman to come to Mexico to discuss his disaffection, Max did not show up, and Lev Davidovich knew the reason: Shachtman knew that he would not be able to stand "Trotsky's breath on his neck." At the end of the day, the Exile realized that he had always been bothered by a certain superficiality in Shachtman, but he also had to admit that he had come to love him and that he should at least appreciate the straightforwardness with which Max had announced his break, so different from the enigmatic way in which Molinier and the Pazes before him had done.

The year 1939 was ending and the war was continuing. Lev Davidovich had turned sixty, and despite everything that had happened, it was the most peaceful New Year he had celebrated ever since he went into exile. He had Seva and Azteca with him, and the dog followed him faithfully when he went outside to care for the rabbits and hens. His beloved Alfred and Marguerite were with them and, together with other friends, bodyguards, and secretaries, they helped him better spend the nighttime hours in intelligent, relaxing conversations, so necessary for his soul. Although the house looked more and more like a fortress and his escapes had become more sporadic, he had the freedom to write and opine, and he did so incessantly, despite the censorship of some editors, like the ones from *Life* magazine who had feared repercussions from publishing an excerpt from the forthcoming *Stalin* in which Lenin's possible poisoning was mentioned. Mexico's festive atmosphere, despite the war, reached all the way to the walls of Coyoacán, and although it didn't manage to put out all the embers of the sadness the Trotskys carried with them, it reminded them that, even in the most difficult circumstances, life always tended to put itself back together and make itself tolerable . . .

Among the visitors he received that season was Sylvia Ageloff, the sister of the efficient Ruth and Hilda, who occasionally assisted him as translators or secretaries in his relations with American Trotskyists. Just like her sisters, Sylvia proved to be a dedicated militant but, above all, a very useful person because of the help she rendered when Fanny Yanovitch fell ill. In addition to English, the girl spoke French, Spanish, and Russian perfectly and was a quick typist . . . But poor Sylvia was also one of the least graceful women that Lev Davidovich had ever met. She was just a little over five feet high, she was thin to the point of emaciation (her arms looked like strings and he imagined that her thighs were the width of his fist), and her face was full of reddish freckles. To top it off, she wore thick glasses, and although her voice had a warmth that was almost seductive, without a doubt she had less taste in fashion than any woman he had ever met. Sylvia's physical shortcomings were so noteworthy that Natalia and the Exile discussed them more than once (they had also been the subject of conversation among the bodyguards), and it caused quite a stir when it was learned that Sylvia had a boyfriend . . . and not just *anyone*, they said, but one who seemed to be well-off, the son of diplomats, and, as Natalia herself would add, very good-looking and five years younger than she was. It went to show that, in questions of love, nothing is written in stone, and beneath any skirt a beast could be hiding. There was so much gossip over the discovery that Lev Davidovich was curious to see the trophy the young woman had snared.

On March 12, the Soviet Union had to sign an onerous peace treaty with Finland, through which they obtained just a few strips of the original territory they were after. The Red Army's fiasco had turned into the proof of its weakness. Lev Davidovich saw that episode as a warning: while Stalin was failing in Finland, Hitler and his divisions had invaded and occupied Denmark in just twenty-four hours.

Later, when Norway was invaded by the Nazis and fell in just a few days, Lev Davidovich knew that the prophecy he had hurled at Trygve Lie three years earlier was on the verge of fulfilling itself: his repressors of yesteryear were turning into political exiles themselves and suffering the humiliation of being refugees with conditions imposed on them. He was sure that their hosts would not be as cruel with them as they had been with him, but the king and the Norwegian ministers would perhaps remember him and the way in which they had treated him.

In those first months of 1940, the temperature of the war of the Mexican Stalinists against the Exile rose. Laborde and Campa had been thrown out, and now other leaders were being decapitated for the same sin: that of not being sufficiently "anti-Trotsky." His instinct told him that something was being planned, and it wasn't good. Amid those purges, they celebrated May Day with a parade strikingly similar to the ones the Nazis and the fascists were organizing in Berlin and Rome: twenty thousand irate Communists gathered by the Mexican Communist Party and the Workers' Central, but instead of yelling slogans against the war, they had written on their flags OUT WITH TROTSKY! TROTSKY FASCIST! TROTSKY TRAITOR! Perhaps out of a remote sense of modesty they had not written what they yelled most arduously: "Death to Trotsky!" . . . That negativity had put the inhabitants and guards of the fortress-house on alert, since people wrote and yelled like that when they were willing to brandish a gun. The bodyguards adopted new precautions (they placed machine guns in the small windows), they brought more volunteers from the United States, and outside the house they put together a ten-man police guard. Would all of these measures be worth anything? Could they stop the insidious hand that would find its way in through a crack that would be impossible to see with the naked eye? Lev Davidovich asked himself when he watched that armed multitude that surrounded him. And it bothered him, knowing the response beforehand: he was a condemned man and, when they wanted to, they would kill him.

One day, when Alfred Rosmer got sick, Lev Davidovich finally saw Sylvia's boyfriend, since it was the young man who took Alfred to the clinic and insisted on paying for his medicine. According to Marguerite, Sylvia had not wanted to introduce her boyfriend because he had problems with his papers and was in Mexico illegally; according to Natalia, always sharp, the girl's fear was due to the boyfriend being involved in certain murky businesses from which he earned the money that he spent so freely. Hopefully, poor Sylvia won't lose him, the Exile would remark to his wife.

May 23 had been a routine day in the house. Lev Davidovich had worked a lot and he felt exhausted when he ran out in the afternoon to feed his rabbits, helped by Seva and accompanied by Azteca. At some point he spoke with Harold Robbins and asked that they not maintain their habitual educational talks with the new guys in the guard that evening, since he was exhausted and had slept poorly for several nights. After dinner, he talked for a while with his wife and the Rosmers, then returned to his study to organize the documents that he intended to work with the following morning. A little earlier than usual, he took a sleeping pill to find the rest he needed so much and went to bed.

Despite the fact that he had spent twelve years waiting for it, on occasion he was capable of forgetting that, that very day, perhaps during the most peaceful moment of the evening, death could knock on his door. In the best Soviet way, he had learned to live with that expectation, to carry its imminence as if it were a tight-fitting shirt. And he'd already decided that he should keep moving forward in the meantime. Although he didn't fear death, and at times even desired it, an almost sick sense of duty compelled him to take a variety of measures to evade it. Perhaps because of that same mechanism of self-defense, when the explosions woke him, he thought that they were fireworks and rockets being set off in some *feria* being celebrated in Coyoacán around that time. He understood that they were gunshots and that they were coming from very close by only when Natalia pushed him from the bed and threw him to the floor. Had the hour of his departure arrived, just like that, when he was dressed in a nightgown and curled up against a wall? Lev Davidovich even had time to consider it a very undecorous way to die. Would he end up laid out with his nightshirt raised and his privates exposed? The condemned man closed his legs and readied himself to die.

24

One tiring and typically sweaty afternoon in 1993, the screw that kept me connected to Ramón Mercader's story turned again. I had barely left the bag loaded with bananas, malangas, and mangoes on the floor, and put away the bike on which I had gone to and from Melena del Sur in search of those provisions, when Ana gave me the strange news that I had received a package in the mail. I don't even know how many years it had been since I received so much as a letter, less still a package. The friends who left the island wrote once, at most twice, and never did so again, urged to separate themselves from a past that pierced them and that we reminded them of. As I gulped down a liter of sugar-spiked water, I examined the manila envelope with the CERTIFIED notice stamped across it and read the name of the sender written in the corner, Germán Sánchez, and the address of the post office in Marianao, at the other end of the city.

With a cigarette in my mouth, I opened the envelope and immediately noticed that the name of the sender was false. The item sent was a book, published in Spain, and it was written precisely by someone named Germán Sánchez and by Luis Mercader—a book in which, according to the title, Luis relayed, with the help of the journalist Germán Sánchez, the life of his brother Ramón. The first thing I did, of course, was flip through the book and, upon discovering that it had photos, look at them until I ran into an image that stirred my insides. That big-headed, almost square man with aged features behind his tortoiseshell glasses, that man whose eyes looked at me from the work by Germán Sánchez and Luis Mercader was—there was no longer any doubt—an assassin and also, of course, the man who loved dogs.

I think I'd had the greatest suspicion that Jaime López was not Jaime López at the moment in which he confirmed that Ramón had continued to hear Trotsky's scream forever. The tone of his voice and the dampness of his look warned me that he was talking about something intimate and painful. A few years later, the letter brought by the nurse moved me a little closer to the belief that the man who loved dogs could be none other than Ramón Mercader himself, no matter how extraordinary the palpable existence, on a Cuban beach, of that character whose presence seemed inconceivable, since reason told me that he had been devoured by history many years before. Weren't Trotsky, his life and his death, bookish and remote references? How could someone escape from history to wander around with two dogs and a cigarette in his mouth on a beach in *my* reality? With those questions and suspicions, I had tried to leave some room for doubt, I think, above all, with the intent of protecting myself. It wasn't pleasant for anyone to be convinced that he had a relationship of trust and closeness with a murderer, that he has shaken the hand with which a man was killed, that he has shared coffee, cigarettes, and even very private personal discomforts with that person . . . And it is less pleasant for it to turn out to be that that murderer was precisely the author of one of the most ruthless, calculated, and useless crimes in history. The margin of doubt that I had preserved had given me, nonetheless, a certain peace that ended up being especially necessary when I decided to delve into that story through which, among others, I searched for the reasons that had moved Ramón Mercader—the last truths that perhaps his omniscient friend Jaime López would have never confessed to me. But with the fall of the last parapet, when I found that image, I would always have the certainty that I had never spoken with Jaime López but rather with that man who had once been Ramón Mercader del Río, and also the certainty that Ramón had told me, precisely me (why the hell was it me?), the truth of his life, at least in the way that he understood it—*his* truth and *his* life.

That same night, after dinner, I began to read the book. As I went on, I concluded that only one person could send me that work and put the last details of that story in my hands—justifications, hypocrisies, silences, and revenge through Luis's mouth—including the painful exit from this world of Ramón Mercader, which I was still unaware of until that moment. And that person could not have been anyone other than the very black supposed nurse, unnamed and squalid, who, obviously, had to have known much more about her "patient" than, ten years before, she had told me in her sole and very brief visit. If the woman now (perhaps still connected to the family, perhaps with the sons of the man who, now without a doubt—for her as well—was a murderer) took on that work, it couldn't be solely due to her desire to eliminate the last corners of the ignorance of that "kid" who had shared some afternoons chatting with Jaime López, in another life called Ramón Mercader, in another Jacques Mornard, in another Román Pavlovich . . .

When I read the biography, I found that some of what I knew was confirmed by information that Luis Mercader must have known firsthand, since he had been a witness to the episodes of which he spoke. Meanwhile, other stories contradicted what I knew, and for some reason that I was unaware of at that moment, it turned out that I knew about attitudes and episodes Ramón lived through that his brother omitted or was unaware of. But the most important thing was that, once Jaime López's identity was confirmed, Ramón Mercader's final fate known, and the downfall of the world that had cultivated him like a poisonous flower was a reality, I felt completely free of my commitment to maintain my silence. Above all because, with that book sent by a ghost, the certainty had also reached me that the siege to which the man who loved dogs had subjected me while alive—and even after his death—could only have a reason calculated by the mind of a chess player and that was to push me silently but inexorably to write the story he had told me, though he made me promise the opposite.

Luis Mercader's book not only freed me of my promise to remain silent but also allowed me to add the last letters to the scattered crossword puzzle of a murderer's life and work. My first reaction to the news was to feel sorry for myself and for all of those who, tricked and used, had ever believed in the validity of the utopia founded in, then ruined by, the country of the Soviets; more than a sense of rejection, it caused me a feeling of compassion for Mercader himself, and I think that for the first time I understood

397

the proportions of his faith, of his fears, and the obsession with the silence he would maintain until his last breath.

The second reaction was to tell Ana the entire story, since I felt I would burst if I didn't pop the pus-filled pimple of fear once and for all. So I told her that, if Luis Mercader had relayed a part of his brother's life, I at last felt willing and in the intellectual and physical condition to write the story, whatever may happen.

"I don't understand, Iván, I don't understand, for God's sake I really don't," Ana would say to me emphatically and (I knew) full of bitterness over the part of the deception that she had to live through herself. "How is it possible for a writer to stop feeling like a writer? Worse still, how can he stop thinking like a writer? How is it that in all this time you didn't dare to write anything? Didn't it occur to you to think that at twenty-eight, God had put this story in your hands that could be turned into your novel, the big one . . ."

I stopped talking, nodding my head for each of her statements and questions, and then I responded:

"It didn't occur to me because it couldn't occur to me, because I didn't want it to occur to me, and I searched for every excuse to forget it every time it tried to occur to me. Or do you not know what country we live in right now? Do you have any idea how many writers stopped writing and turned into nothing or, worse still, into anti-writers and were never again able to take flight? Who could bet on things ever changing? Do you know what it is to feel marginalized, forbidden, buried alive at the age of thirty, thirty-five, when you can really begin to be a serious writer, and thinking that the marginalization is forever, to the end of time, or at least until the end of your fucking life?"

"But what could they do to you?" she insisted. "Did they kill you?"

"No, they didn't kill me."

"So . . . so . . . what terrible thing could they do to you? Censor your book? What else?"

"Nothing."

"What do you mean, nothing?" She jumped, offended, I think.

"They make you *nothing*. Do you know what it is to turn into *nothing*? Because I do know, because I myself turned into *nothing* . . . And I also know what it is to feel fear."

So I told her about all of those forgotten writers who not even they themselves remembered, those who wrote the empty and obliging literature of the seventies and eighties, practically the only kind of literature that one could imagine and compose under the ubiquitous layer of suspicion, intolerance, and national uniformity. And I told her about those who, like myself, innocent and credulous, earned ourselves a "corrective" for having barely dipped our toes, and about those who, after a stay in the inferno of nothing, tried to return and did so with lamentable books, also empty and obliging, with which they achieved an always-conditional pardon and the mutilated feeling that they were writers again because they once more saw their names in print.

Like Rimbaud in his days in Harar, I had preferred to forget that literature existed. Further still, like Isaak Babel—and it's not that I'm comparing myself with him or with others, for God's sake—I had opted *to write silence*. At least with my mouth closed, I could feel at peace with myself and keep my fears in check.

When the crisis of the 1990s became more intense, Ana, Tato the poodle, and I were on the verge of dying of starvation, like so many people in a dark country, paralyzed and in the midst of falling apart. Despite everything, I think that for six or seven years, the most difficult and fucked-up of a total and interminable crisis, Ana and I were happy in our stoic and hungry way. That human harmony that saved me from sinking was a true life lesson. In the last years of my marriage with Raquelita, when that bonanza of the 1980s was becoming normal and everything seemed to indicate that the bright future was beginning to turn on its lights— there was food, there was clothing (socialist and ugly, but still clothing and food), there were buses, sometimes even taxis, and houses on the beach that we could rent with our salaries—my inability to be happy prevented me from enjoying, along with my wife and my children, what life was offering me. In contrast, when that false equilibrium disappeared with the end of the Soviet Union and the crisis began, Ana's presence and love gave me a will to live, to write, to fight for something that was inside and outside me, like in the distant years in which, with all my enthusiasm, I had cut sugarcane, planted coffee, and written a few stories pushed by the faith and the most solid confidence in the future—not just mine but the future of everyone . . .

Because urban transport had practically disappeared, from the beginning of the nineties, five days a week I pedaled on my Chinese bicycle the six miles to get there, and six to return, that separated my house from the veterinary school. In a few months I ended up so thin that more than once, looking at my profile in a mirror, I couldn't do anything but ask myself if a devouring cancer hadn't invaded my body. As far as she was concerned, Ana would suffer—as a result of the daily exercise on her bicycle, the lack of necessary calories, and bad genetic luck—the worst consequences of those terrible years, since, like many other people, she was diagnosed with a vitamin-deficient polyneuritis (the same one that spread across the German concentration camps) that, in her case, would later turn into an irreversible osteoporosis, a prelude to the cancer that would eventually kill her.

Devoted to taking care of Ana at the start of her illnesses (she was almost blind for a few months), in 1993 I chose to leave the job at the veterinary school when I received the opportunity to establish a first aid clinic in an unoccupied room close to our house. From that moment on, with the consent (but not a shred of support) of the local powers, I turned into the neighborhood amateur veterinarian, tasked with the immunization campaigns against rabies. Although in reality it wasn't a lot of money, I earned three times as much as my old salary, and I earmarked every peso obtained to finding food for my wife. Once a week, to stretch out my scarce funds, I climbed upon my bike and went to Melena del Sur, twenty miles from the city, to purchase fruits and vegetables directly from the countryside and to trade my abilities as a castrator and worm remover of pigs for a bit of meat and some eggs. If a few months earlier I had seemed like a cancer patient, the new efforts had turned me into a ghost, and to this day even I can't explain to myself how I came out alive and lucid from that war for survival, which even included everything from operating on the vocal cords of hundreds of urban pigs to silence their shrill cries to getting into a fistfight (in which knives even came out) with the veterinarian who tried to steal my clients in Melena del Sur. At the bottom of the abyss, accosted on all sides, instincts can be stronger than beliefs, I learned.

Besides the slow and stumbling work of writing to which I returned after receiving Luis Mercader's book—I had never had any idea of how difficult it could be to really write, with responsibility and a view of the consequences and, to top it off, trying to get into the head of someone who existed, and resolving to think and feel like him—that dark and hostile period had the reward of allowing me to completely bring forth from within myself what should really have been my life's vocation: from the rustic and basic clinic I had established in the neighborhood, not only did I vaccinate dogs and castrate or silence pigs, but I was also able to devote myself to helping all of those who, like myself, loved animals, especially dogs. Sometimes I didn't even know where to get the medicines and instruments to keep the clinic doors open, and there were days on which even aspirin disappeared from the island and the School of Veterinary Medicine recommended curing skin diseases with chamomile fermentations or feverfew and intestinal problems with massages and prayers to St. Luis Beltrán. The nominal fees I charged the animals' owners barely covered my expenses and would not have been enough for Ana and me to survive. My reputation as a good person, more than as an efficient veterinarian, spread in the area and people came to see me with animals as thin as they were (can you imagine a thin snake?) and, almost against all reason in those dark days, gave me medicines, stitches, bandages they had left over for some reason, as a display of solidarity between the fucked, which is the only true kind. And being a part of that solidarity in which Ana involved herself whenever she could—many times she was my assistant in the vaccinations, the sterilizations, and the massive worm removals that I organized—removed from me any pretension of recognition or personal transcendence and was elemental in making me the person who seemed like the one I had always wanted to be, the one who, even now, I have most liked being.

Although I still hadn't begun to go to church with Ana, Dany, Frank, and the few other friends I saw told me I seemed to be working toward my candidacy for beatification and for my ascent to heaven. What was true was that reading and writing about how the greatest utopia men had ever had within their reach had been perverted, diving into the catacombs of a story that seemed more like divine punishment than the work of men drunk with power, eager for control, and with pretensions of historical transcendence, I had learned that true human grandeur lay in the practice of kindness without conditions, in the capacity of giving to those who had nothing, but not what we have left over but rather a part of what little we have—giving until it hurts without practicing the deceitful philosophy of forcing others to accept our concepts of good and truth because (we believe) they're the only possible ones and because, besides, they should be grateful for what we give them, even when they didn't ask for it. And although I knew that my cosmogony was entirely impractical (so what the hell do we do with the economy, money, property, so that all of this works? And what about the predestined ones and those born sons of bitches?), it satisfied me to think that perhaps one day humans would be able to cultivate that philosophy, which seemed so basic, without suffering labor pains or the trauma of being forced, out of pure and free will, out of the ethical need to show solidarity and be democratic. My mental masturbations . . .

Because of that, in silence and also in pain, I was letting myself be dragged toward writing, although without knowing if I would ever dare to show anyone what I had written, or to seek out a greater destiny, since those options didn't interest me too much. I was only convinced that the exercise of recovering a vanished memory had a lot to do with my responsibility to face life—rather, to face my life. If fate had made me the repository of a cruel and exemplary story, my duty as a human was to preserve it, to extract it from the tsunami of oblivion.

The accumulated need to share the weight of that story that pursued me—along with the repulsion of memories and blame that the visit we made to Cojímar would cause—were the reasons for which I decided to also tell my friend Daniel the details of my relationship with that slippery individual whom I had named "the man who loved dogs."

Everything came to a head on a summer afternoon in 1994, just when we had hit bottom and it seemed that all the crisis needed was to chew us a few more times in order to swallow us. It wasn't easy, but that day I pulled Dany out of his apathy and we went to Cojímar on our bicycles, set to witness the spectacle of the moment: the massive exodus, in the least imaginable boats and in daylight, of hundreds, thousands of men, women, and children who were making the most of the border opening decreed by the government to throw themselves to the sea on any floating object, loaded with their desperation, their exhaustion, and their hunger, in search of other horizons.

The establishment, for three or four years, of blackouts lasting eight and even twelve hours daily had served to enable Dany and me to become close again. Since his blackout area (Luyano I) was on the border with mine (Lawton II), we discovered that, in general, when there was no electricity at his house, there was at mine and vice versa. Always on our bicycles, and most times with our respective wives on the back, we tended to transfer ourselves from darkness to light to watch a movie or a boring baseball game on television (the announcers and the baseball players were thinner, the stadiums almost empty) or simply to talk and be able to see each other's faces.

Dany, who around that time was still working at the publishing house as the head of the marketing department, was now the one who'd stopped writing. The two short story collections and the two novels he had published in the 1980s had turned him into one of the hopes of Cuban literature, always so full of hope and . . . The fact is that, reading those books, you noticed that in his storytelling there was a dramatic force capable of penetration, with narrative possibilities, but someone with my training could also see that he lacked the necessary daring to jump into the void and risk everything in his writing. There was in his literature something elusive, an intention to search that was suddenly interrupted when the precipice came into view, a lack of final decisiveness to cross the curtain of fire and touch the painful parts of reality. Since I knew him well, I knew that his writings were a mirror of his attitude in the face of life. But now, overwhelmed by the crisis and the almost certain impossibility of publishing in Cuba, he'd fallen into a literary depression from which I tried to bring him out during our nighttime talks. My main argument was that Dany should make the most of his empty days to ponder and write, even if it was by candlelight. That's how the great Cuban writers of the nineteenth century had done it; besides, his case wasn't like mine, since he was a writer and couldn't cease to be so (Ana looked at me silently when I touched on this subject), and writers write. The saddest thing was that my words didn't seem to produce (actually, didn't produce) any effect at all, and the passion that pushed him forward in his literary calling must have left him, so that he, always so disciplined, just let the days float by, busy perfecting his strategies of survival and the search for his next meal, like almost all of the island's inhabitants. On one of those nights, while we were talking about the matter, I proposed that we make an excursion to Cojímar the following day to see with our own eyes what was happening there.

The spectacle we found turned out to be devastating. While groups of men and women, with tables, metal tanks, tires, nails, and ropes devoted themselves along the coast to giving shape to those artifacts on which they would throw themselves into the sea, other groups arrived in trucks loaded with their already-built boats. Each time one of them arrived, the masses ran to the truck and, after applauding for the recently arrived as if they were the heroes of some athletic feat, some threw themselves at helping them unload their precious boats, while others, with wads of dollars in their hands, tried to buy a space for the crossing.

In the middle of the chaos, wallets and oars were stolen. Businesses had been set up and were selling barrels of drinking water, compasses, food, hats, sunglasses, cigarettes, matches, lights, and plaster images of the protecting Virgins of La Caridad del Cobre, the patroness of Cuba, and of Regla, Queen of the Sea, and there were even rooms to be rented for amorous goodbyes and bathrooms for greater needs, since the lesser ones were taken care of on the rocks, shamelessly. The police who had to guarantee order watched with their eyes fogged over by confusion, and only intervened reluctantly to calm people down when violence broke out. Meanwhile, a group of people were singing alongside some boys who had arrived with a pair of guitars, as if they were at a camping ground; others argued over the number of passengers that could be taken on a balsa raft so many feet long and talked about the first thing they would eat upon arriving in Miami or about the million-dollar businesses they would start there; and the rest, close to the reefs, were helping the ones launching their craft into the sea and bidding them goodbye with applause, cheers, promises to see each other soon, over there, even farther: way over there. I think I will never forget the big, voluminous black man with his baritone voice who, from his floating balsa raft, yelled at the coast: "*Caballero*, last one out has to turn off the light in the Morro," and immediately began to sing, in Paul Robeson's voice: "*Siento un bombo, mamita, m'están llamando . . .*"

"I never imagined I would see something like this," I said to Daniel, overcome by a deep sadness. "It's come to this?"

"Hunger rules," he commented.

"It's more complicated than hunger, Dany. They lost their faith and they're escaping. It's biblical, a biblical exodus . . ."

"This one is too Cuban. Forget about the exodus, this is called escaping, going on the lam, getting the hell out 'cause no one can stand it anymore . . ."

Almost fearfully I dared to ask him:

"So why don't you go?"

He looked at me, and in his eyes there wasn't a drop of the sarcasm or cynicism with which he tried to defend himself from the world, but that was no use when he tried to protect himself from himself and his truths.

"Because I'm scared. Because I don't know if I can start over. Because I'm forty years old. I don't know, really. And you?"

"Because I don't want to leave."

"Don't fuck around; that's no answer."

"But it's true: I don't want to leave and that's it," I insisted, refusing to give any other reason.

"Iván, were you always this weird?"

Then I kept looking at the sea in silence. With that atmosphere and the unhealthy conversation we had had, an old feeling of blame rose to the surface that was giving me a lump in my throat and bringing tears to my eyes. Why did fear always show up? How long would it pursue me?

"The worst thing that happened to me when William disappeared," I said, when I at last managed to speak, "was that I blocked myself in and couldn't vent. I had to pretend with my parents, tell them there was hope, that maybe he was alive somewhere. When we all convinced ourselves that he was at the bottom of the sea, I could no longer cry for my brother . . . But the most fucked-up thing has been thinking about what a son of a bitch luck is. If William had decided to do that two or three months later, he would've left through the Mariel. With the expulsion papers from the university, where it said he was an antisocial faggot, they would have put him in a speedboat and he would have left without any trouble."

"No one could even dream that what happened was going to happen. Even this right now, did you ever imagine that we were going to see something like this? People leaving and the police watching them as if it were nothing?"

"It's as if William was marked by tragedy. Just for being a homosexual or for being my brother . . . I don't know, but it's not fair."

At sunset we decided to go back. I felt too overcome by that human stampede capable of creating in my mind the closest image to my brother's last decision and of stirring the dirty waters of a never-resolved memory—never buried, like William's body.

Night had already fallen when we arrived at Dany's house, where, fortunately, there was electricity that day. We drank water, mixed grain coffee, and ate some sandwiches with fish *picadillo* rounded out by boiled banana peels. Daniel knew that for two or three years I had been allowing myself to drink alcohol again, although only on certain occasions and in reduced quantities. So, since he knew me, he knew that at that moment I needed a drink. He opened the closet where he kept his strategic

405

reserve and took out one of the bottles of *añejo* rum that Elisa, whenever she had a chance, stole from work. Seated on the chairs in the living room, with two fans on high speed, we drank almost without looking at each other, and I felt that what had happened that day had somehow prepared me for what I had thought of doing and finally did.

"I'm trying to write a book" was the way in which it occurred to me to bring up the subject, and immediately it seemed cruel to say that you're writing to a writer who has dried up; it is like insulting his mother. I know it all too well. But I didn't stop myself and I explained that for a while I had been trying to give shape to a story I had run into sixteen years before.

"So why didn't you write it before?"

"I didn't want to, I couldn't, I didn't even know . . . Now I think that I want to, I can, and, more or less, I know."

So I told him the basics of my meetings in 1977 with the man who loved dogs and the details of the story that, through the strangest ways and in pieces, he had given me since then. I don't quite know why, but before doing so I imposed a condition and asked him to please respect it: he should never speak to me about that matter if I didn't bring it up. Now I know I did it to protect myself, as was my custom.

When I finished telling him the story, including the search for the Trotsky biography in which I had involved him, I felt, for the first time, that I was really writing a book. It was a feeling between joy and torment that I had lost many years before, but that had not left me, like a chronic illness. The terrible thing, nonetheless, was that at that moment I was also fully conscious that Ramón Mercader was causing me, more than anyone else, that inappropriate feeling that he himself rejected and that frightened me by the mere fact of feeling it: compassion.

The conversation with Daniel and the immediate effects it generated served to dust off and revise what I had already written. I perceived, as a visceral necessity of that story, the existence of another voice, another perspective, capable of complementing and contrasting what the man who loved dogs had told me. And very soon I discovered that my intention of understanding the life of Ramón Mercader implied trying to understand that of his victim as well, since that murderer would only be complete, as an executioner and a human being, if the object of his act accompanied him, the repository of his hate and the hate of the men who induced and armed him.

For years I had dedicated myself to gathering the little information existing in the country about the twisted conspiracy to kill Trotsky and about the awful, chaotic, and frustrating epoch in which the crime was committed. I recalled the joyful tension with which many of us searched for the few glasnost magazines that during those years of revelations and hopes entered the island, until they were removed from the news-stands—so we wouldn't be ideologically contaminated by certain truths that had been buried for so many years, said the good censors. But my need to know more, at least a little more, threw me into an obstinate and subterranean search for information that would take me from one book to another (obtained with more difficulty than the previous one) and to confirm for myself that we had lived in programmed ignorance for de-cades, our knowledge and credulity systematically manipulated. To be-gin with—and a couple of conversations with Daniel and Ana reaffirmed this—very few people in the country had any idea who Trotsky had been, what the reasons for his political downfall were, the persecution he had suffered, and the death they gave him; fewer still were those who knew how the revolutionary's execution had been organized and who had car-ried out the final mandate; practically no one knew, either, the extremes reached by Bolshevik cruelty in the hands of that same Trotsky in his days of maximum power; and almost no one had an exact idea of the sub-sequent felonies and massacres of the Stalinist era—all that barbarity jus-tified by the struggle for a better world. And the ones who did know something kept quiet.

Thanks to books that revealed the diverse horrors archived for decades in Moscow, and the capacity for judgment that those revelations extended to the experts, I came to the conclusion that now we were getting to know or at least could learn about Mercader's world and the ins and outs of his crime more than Mercader himself had managed to discover. Only with glasnost first, and then with the inevitable disappearance of the USSR later, and the ventilation of many details of its perverted, buried, covered up, rewritten and rewritten-again history, was a coherent and more or less real image obtained of what the dark existence of a country had been that had lasted exactly seventy-four years, as long as the life of a normal man. But all of those years, according to the evidence that I was reading—going from surprise to surprise—(and to think that Breton said to Trotsky him-self that the world had lost its capacity for surprises forever), all of those years, I was saying, had been lived in vain from the moment in which the

Utopia was betrayed and, worse still, turned into the deceit of man's best desires. The strictly theoretical and so attractive dream of possible equality had been traded for the worst authoritarian nightmare in history when it was applied to reality, understood, with good reason (more, in this case), as the only criterion of truth. *Marx dixit.*

So when I thought I was starting to have a more or less complete understanding of that entire cosmic disaster and what Mercader's crime had signified in the midst of so much criminality, one dark and stormy night—as you could expect in this dark and stormy story—at the door of my house came knocking the tall, thin black man who, in 1977, had accompanied Ramón Mercader and his Russian wolfhounds when they entered my life.

25

Jacques Mornard felt a hair-raising chill go down his spine: Harold Robbins, smiling, let him in after shaking his hand. With a paper bag in one hand and dressed as if he were going out for a stroll, he crossed the fortress's threshold without the bodyguard bothering to look at what he had in the bag. When the lead door closed, Ramón Mercader heard how History was falling prostrate at his feet.

After the attack by the Mexicans, he had returned on two occasions to the house in Coyoacán to ask about the state of its inhabitants. It was during the second visit that they confirmed that the Rosmers would leave for France from the port of Veracruz on the afternoon of May 28, and since, coincidentally, he had to travel to that city for some business by the end of the month, he proposed to Alfred Rosmer, with Robbins and Schüssler's authorization, to be the one to take them. That way none of the bodyguards (two of them were still being held by the police) would have to leave the house, something that was especially dangerous after what had happened in the early hours of the twenty-fourth.

The police investigations had already dismissed the presumed participation of Diego Rivera in the attack, and despite the fact that they persisted in their hypothesis of a self-attack, the renegade's insistence on pointing to the Soviet secret police as the author of the assault kept the Mexican authorities in check. With anxiety, Jacques waited for Tom's return with his explanations and, above all, with the orders and final adjustments for his call to action.

Despite the fact that several people had spoken to him of what existed inside the walls, that afternoon Jacques Mornard was surprised to see the layout of the fortress's central yard. His first impression was that he had entered the cloister of a monastery. To his left, close to the stone wall, were the rows of rabbit cages. The part not covered with asphalt had been taken over by plants, mainly cacti, between which one could still see the effects of the massive invasion a few days earlier. The main house, to the right, was smaller and more modest than he had imagined. Its windows were closed and the walls were pockmarked by the bullets shot a few days before. Alongside a small building that he identified as the guards' sleeping quarters rose the tree from which, he presumed, the attacker with a machine gun fired into the yard. How was it possible for that assault to have failed?

Robbins pointed at a wooden bench while he alerted the Rosmers of his arrival. In the main watchtower, from which there was a privileged view of the street as well as the yard, Otto Schüssler and Jake Cooper were talking without worrying too much about him, and Jacques asked himself why the tower's machine gun hadn't neutralized the attackers. He lit a cigarette and, without making his interest too obvious, studied the structure of the house, the distance separating the renegade's study from the exit door, the garden paths through which a man could move less exposed to gunfire from the towers. Like someone who is waiting, he walked looking for a better place to observe the whole scene and turned around when he heard a voice behind him.

"What can I do for you?"

Despite having seen him in hundreds of photos and fleetingly in a passing car, the tangible presence of the Exile, just six yards away from him, stirred Jacques Mornard's senses. There he was, armed with a bunch of grass, the most dangerous adversary of the world revolution, the enemy for whose death he had been preparing himself for almost three years. What had begun as a confusing conversation on the side of the Sierra de Guadarrama had finally led him to the presence of a person condemned to die long ago—and he, Ramón Mercader, would be the one in charge of executing him.

"Good day, sir," he managed to say as he tried to force his lips into a smile. "I'm Frank Jacson, Sylvia's friend, and—"

"Yes, of course," the old man said, nodding. "Did they alert the Rosmers?"

"Yes, Robbins . . ."

The Exile, as if he were annoyed, stopped listening to him and gave a half turn to open one of the compartments and place the fresh grass in the basket from which the rabbits would take it.

As he felt his emotions calm down, Jacques observed the nape of his enemy's neck, unprotected and easy to break, like any neck. The man, seen up close, seemed less aged than in the photos and bore no relation to the caricatures that represented him as an old and feeble Jew. Despite his sixty years, the tensions and physical ailments, the renegade emitted firmness and, despite his multiple betrayals of the working class, dignity. His graying, pointed goatee, the wavy hair, the sharp Jewish nose, and, above all, the penetrating eyes behind the glasses emitted an electric force. It was true what many said, he looked more like an eagle than a man, Jacques thought as he remained immobile, the paper bag in his hand. What if he had brought a revolver with him?

"The grass must be fresh," the renegade said at that moment, without turning around. "Rabbits are strong animals, but delicate at the same time. If the grass is dry, their stomachs become ill, and if it's wet, it causes mange."

Jacques nodded and only then did he realize that it was difficult for him to speak. The old man had started to take off the gloves with which he protected his hands and placed them on the roof of the rabbit cages.

"But they're going to be late," he said, and walked toward the house. When he passed, barely three feet away from him, Jacques noted the soapy smell coming from his hair, perhaps in need of a cut. If he had stretched out his arm, he could have taken him by the neck. But he felt paralyzed and breathed in relief when the man walked away from him and said, "Good, there they are."

Marguerite Rosmer and Natalia Sedova were going out to the yard by the door that, according to what Sylvia had told him, led to the dining room and toward which the Exile walked. The women exchanged greetings with Jacques, and Natalia asked if he wanted a cup of tea, which he accepted. When Natalia turned around, Jacques stopped her while digging into the paper bag.

411

"Madame Trotsky . . . this is for you," he said, and held out a box tied with a mauve ribbon that made the shape of something resembling a flower.

Natalia looked at him and smiled. She took the package and began to open it.

"Chocolates . . . But . . ."

"It's my pleasure, Madame Trotsky."

"Please, Jacson, you can call me Natalia."

Jacques also smiled, nodding.

"Does Madame Natalia sound all right?"

"If you insist . . ." she accepted.

"Seva's not here . . . ? I've also brought something for him," he explained, raising the bag.

"I'll send him right away," she said, and walked to the dining room.

The boy took a few minutes to come out, and he was wiping his mouth as he walked. Without giving him time to greet him, Jacques held out the bag. Seva ripped the paper covering the cardboard box, from which, at last, he extracted a miniature airplane.

"Since you told me you liked airplanes . . ."

Seva's face shone with joy and Marguerite, next to him, smiled at the boy's happiness.

"Thank you, Mr. Jacson. You didn't have to go to the trouble."

"It was no trouble, Seva . . . Hey, listen, where's Azteca?"

"In the dining room. My grandfather has gotten him used to eating bread soaked in milk and now he's giving him dinner."

Marguerite excused herself, as there were some things left to pack and it was getting late. With Seva and the recently arrived Azteca, the visitor walked around the area with the rabbit cages until he saw Alfred Rosmer exit the house and, behind him, the renegade. His nerves started to settle and the certainty that he could enter that sanctuary, carry out his mission, and exit while saying goodbye to the watchtower guards calmed him. Jacques shook Rosmer's hand and reassured him that they had enough time to reach Veracruz by the appointed hour. Natalia then came out with a cup of tea and Jacques thanked her. The renegade watched them all but only spoke again when he sat down on the wooden bench.

"Sylvia told me you're Belgian," he said, focusing on Jacques.

"Yes, although I lived in France for a long time."

"And you prefer tea to coffee?"

Jacques smiled, moving his head.

"In reality, I prefer coffee, but since I was offered tea . . ."

The renegade smiled.

"And what's this story about you being called Jacson now? Sylvia said something, but with so many things in my head . . ."

Jacques observed that Azteca was coming back from the rabbit cages and he snapped his fingers to call him over, but the animal kept going and settled in between the legs of the old man, who mechanically started to scratch his head and behind his ears.

"I have a falsified passport in the name of Frank Jacson, a Canadian engineer. It was the only way to leave Europe after the general mobilization. I have no intention of allowing myself to be killed in a war that isn't mine."

The Exile nodded and he continued:

"Sylvia didn't want me to come here because of that passport. In reality, I am illegal in Mexico and she thought that could hurt you."

"I don't think anything hurts me anymore," the Exile assured him. "After what happened a few days ago, every morning when I wake up I think I'm living an extra day. Next time, Stalin isn't going to fail."

"Don't talk that way, Lev Davidovich," Rosmer interjected.

"All of those walls and guards are just scenery, Alfred, my friend. If they didn't kill us the other night, it was a miracle or for reasons that only Stalin knows. But it was the penultimate chapter of this hunt, of that I am sure."

Jacques abstained from participating. With the tip of his shoe, he moved some small rocks among the gravel. He knew that the renegade was right, but the calm with which he expressed that conviction disturbed him.

The two men talked about the situation in France, whose defeat at the hands of the German army seemed imminent, and the renegade tried to convince the other not to leave. Rosmer insisted that now, more than ever, he had to return.

"I'm turning into an old egotist," the Exile said, as if he were concentrating only on the caresses he was lavishing on the dog. "It's just that I don't want you to leave. I am more and more alone, without friends, without comrades, without family . . . Stalin has taken them all."

Ramón refused to listen and tried instead to concentrate on his hate and on the nape of the man's neck, but he was surprised to discover that he was surrounded by an ambiguous feeling of understanding. He suspected that he had spent too many months in the skin of Jacques Mornard and that using that disguise for much longer could be dangerous.

Tom's silence turned into a dense cloak that began to crush Ramón's will. It had been more than two weeks since he had heard any news, and he still hadn't received his orders. As the days of inactivity went by, he began to fear more insistently that, after the failure of the Mexican assailants, the operation had been postponed, even called off. Enclosed in the cabin at the tourist complex, he immersed himself in the most diverse reflections, convincing himself that he was ready to carry out his mission and that nothing would be able to impede it after having accomplished the most complicated part of his work, penetrating the Trotsky sanctuary. He knew he could and should overcome his nerves, and he had managed to keep them under control in front of the renegade, although they had played a bad trick on him when he left the fortress in Coyoacán and when he missed the road to Veracruz a couple of times, which caused Natalia Sedova to ask whether he traveled frequently to that city or not.

"It's that my mind is somewhere else," he said, almost with all sincerity. "I'm not too interested in politics, but there's something about Mr. Trotsky . . . Sylvia had already told me."

"You were touched by Trotsky's breath on your neck," Alfred Rosmer told him, and, smiling, explained the manifestations of that paralyzing spell and the way it had affected, for example, a man as hardened and sure of himself as André Breton.

On June 10, when he picked up the phone and heard his mentor's voice, Ramón felt his hands nearly trembling as he received the order to leave for New York in a couple of days. What was happening?

"Should I travel with all of my things?" he asked.

"Only what's necessary. Keep the cabin. Madame Roberts will get you at the airport," Tom said, and hung up without saying goodbye.

If they were ordering him to leave his belongings, it meant that the operation was still in motion. His spirits lifted immediately, and as he separated out the clothing he would send to the dry cleaners, he removed the mountaineer's ice axe from the locked suitcase. He took it in his hands, weighed it again, struck the air three or four times, and convinced himself that it could be the ideal weapon. The only problem was that its downward motion was complicated by the length of the grip, which prevented the wrist's free motion at the time of the blow, but cutting the wood would resolve that difficulty. The problem was what to do with it during his stay in New York. Leaving it in the cabin, at the mercy of the cleaning ladies, was dangerous, and he decided to search for a hiding place. Although he could have bought a similar one at any sports store, Ramón felt that that ice axe was his.

The morning of the twelfth, by previous agreement with Harold Robbins, he took the Buick and drove to Coyoacán. Since one of the cars of the house had been damaged when the Mexican attackers fled in it, Jacques had decided to leave them his for the time he would be in New York, so they could use it if there was an emergency. With his suitcase in the trunk, he stopped by the complex's offices, turned in his keys, and paid in advance for the rest of June. A few miles from the camp, he turned down a dirt road he had covered on other occasions, and between some porous rocks placed on one side of the path he hid the ice axe.

As they had agreed, Jake Cooper was waiting for him to take him to the airport and go back to Coyoacán in the Buick. All the guards, with the exception of Hansen, who was assigned to the main tower at that moment, came out to the street to say goodbye. Jacson said that he hoped to return as soon as possible, since everything seemed to indicate that, thanks to the war, Mr. Lubeck had some promising business lined up in the country. That night, when it was beginning to get dark, the airplane in which the Canadian Frank Jacson was traveling took off for New York.

Ramón couldn't remember the last time that a meeting with Caridad brought him happiness. His mother, dressed with the elegance befitting Mrs. Roberts, received him with her usual disquieting kiss, and Ramón could taste that she had been drinking some cognac. Roberts was waiting for them at nine at a restaurant very close to Central Park, Caridad said, and immediately announced that everything was on the verge of going into motion.

"I'm afraid, Ramón," the woman said, taking refuge in the Catalan language, which would be difficult for the Irish-looking taxi driver to understand.

"Afraid of what, Caridad?"

"Afraid for you."

"What chance does Tom think I have of getting out?"

"He'll tell you eighty percent, but he knows that you barely have thirty percent. He's going to convince you of the opposite, but he can't fool me. They're going to kill you . . ."

"You're just realizing that now?"

Ramón thought about his mother's words. He knew that she was as capable of telling the truth as she was of lying to make him desist and, in her strange way, protect and control him. But if she herself had pushed him in that direction, why was she trying to dissuade him now, when she knew it was impossible to turn back? Ramón was convinced that he would never fully understand his mother's paradoxes.

"I know I'll manage to get out," Ramón said. "I've been there and I can get out if I have support. You worry about getting me that; leave the rest to me."

"I couldn't stand it if they killed you," Caridad said, and looked away at the illuminated windows of Fifth Avenue, in which, with tiresome frequency, American flags were displayed. Those flags and the uniformed servicemen who could be seen every once in a while were the only obvious signs of the war, so far off for most New Yorkers.

"Do any of us really matter that much to you?" Perhaps due to the certainty that he would very soon die, Ramón felt petty and powerful. "I would've never imagined. Don't you still think that the cause is above everything, including family? Are you losing heart?"

They left the suitcase at the hotel on Lexington Avenue and walked the seven or eight blocks to the restaurant. The June night was pleasantly cool and he placed his raincoat on his arm. Caridad was walking so close to him that their shoulders touched frequently and it was difficult to look at each other as they spoke.

"Sometimes I think I should've never gotten you involved in all of this," she said.

"Are you going to tell me once and for all what in the hell is wrong with you now?"

"I already told you, dammit, I'm afraid."

"Who would've imagined!" Ramón said sarcastically, and remained silent for a few moments.

"Don't be an imbecile, Ramón. Think a little bit. Doesn't it seem strange that the Mexicans who organized all of that shooting weren't able to kill anyone?"

Ramón agreed and had been thinking the same thing since the day of the attack, but he preferred not to involve Caridad in his doubts regarding what had happened that predawn morning.

The brasserie had an authentic air and reminded Ramón of the place where, two years before, they had met with George Mink in Paris. Roberts welcomed him with a hug like an old, dear friend. Loyal to his habits, he prompted Caridad and Ramón to try the dishes he considered to be the most attractive and picked the wine, a full-bodied 1936 Château Lafite Rothschild with a delicate bouquet that left a faint taste of violets on the palate that brought back memories of Ramón's buried life. Roberts announced that they would not talk about work, but it was difficult to avoid the subject that had brought them together. According to the latest news, the Germans were at Paris's door. The Soviets, Roberts stated, were not going to stand by with their arms crossed and were preparing to complete the reinforcement of their borders with the occupation of the Baltic republics. That was war, he said.

The following morning Roberts picked up Frank Jacson at his hotel and they traveled to Coney Island. Roberts preferred that Caridad not be present, and Ramón appreciated it. In view of the sea, over which some gulls were flying, Roberts opened the collar of his shirt and slid down the wood of the bench. It appeared that the only motive for that excursion was his eternal eagerness to drink in the sun.

"Why didn't you call me or say anything to me before leaving?"

"Kid, you have no idea what's happened."

The failure of the Mexicans' attack had forced them to evacuate several people who had participated in the preparations, among them Grigulievich and Felipe. Later he had to prepare a detailed report, send it to Moscow, and await new instructions.

"Can you imagine a very, very put-out Stalin? Asking for blood, hearts, heads, and testicles, including yours—I mean mine?" he said, and lowered his hand to between his thighs, as if to confirm that his testicles were still there. "I had to convince him that the failure had not been our fault and that, in any event, the commotion doesn't hurt us."

"So why did those imbeciles fail?"

Roberts turned his gaze from the sun and focused on Ramón.

"Because they're idiots and cowards. They did everything with fear. They got drunk before entering the house. They thought that it was some kind of Wild West movie and that everything could be solved with a lot of gunshots. Felipe tried to impose order, but he couldn't do it alone with all of those scared, drunk animals. It was a disaster. They couldn't even burn the old man's papers. The one who was supposed to lead the action said at the last minute that he would wait outside, and the one who had the order to enter the house and kill the Duck was one of the first to go running out when he heard the engine of the car start. When Felipe wanted to take on the task, he was almost killed by them. Their shots crossed and no one could get close to the house."

"What about Sheldon?"

"He did his part; he's not to blame for everyone else's failure . . . We're going to get him out of Mexico as soon as possible. He's the only one who knows anything and we can't risk the police getting their hands on him." Roberts fell into a long silence. He lit a cigarette. "Now it's your turn, Ramón. If you don't complete the mission, neither you nor I are going to find any fucking place in the world to hide. Can I trust in you?"

Ramón recalled his conversation with Caridad the previous night and the superiority that he felt the whole time.

"What do you think my chances are of getting out?"

Roberts thought. He was looking at the sea and smoking.

"Thirty percent," he said. "If you do everything right, I think fifty. I'm going to be honest with you, because you deserve it and I need you to know what you're going to do and what you're risking. If you do things as you should, you have a fifty percent chance of leaving that house on your own feet. If not, two things can happen to you: either they kill you right there or they hand you over to the police. If they hand you over, you go to jail, but you can count on all of our support to the end. You'll have the best lawyers and we're going to work to get you out somehow. I give you my word. I'll ask you again: Can I trust in you?"

The sea off Coney Island is different than that of El Empordà. One is the open Atlantic, cut through by great waves, and the other one is the warm and peaceful Mediterranean, Ramón thought, and concluded that he preferred the beaches of El Empordà. Observing the coast and the restless gulls, he said:

"This sand looks dirty," and added: "Yes. Of course we're going to do it."

With a bouquet of roses in his hands, Jacques Mornard realized that, in all his life, Ramón had never bought flowers for any woman. He felt a little sorry for him, for the commitments and struggles that his times had pushed him toward, robbing him of the carefreeness of youth and many of the stressful maneuvers of love. It was all the more sad that Jacques was traveling in a taxi with that splendid bouquet of flowers in order to give them to a woman he was using like a marionette and with whom he had to make love with his eyes closed, his secret mission hiding behind every caress. He recalled the women with whom Ramón had been involved in his youth, furious militants who tended to be as removed from romantic gestures as he was. His great love, África, would not have allowed him that romantic expression, which she would have labeled decadent while labeling him weak. Perhaps Lena, the one with the sad eyes . . . Jacques Mornard, knowing the crossroads of fate that Ramón was approaching, regretted that he had never confronted those insults of África's, just for the sake of having the ridiculous but kind memory of having bought her at least a rose, a dahlia, a carnation from the ones that perfumed some of the flower stands along Las Ramblas, which was getting more distant every day. Would he ever again walk along those places of his memory?

They had spent two days discussing the different plans that he and Tom were developing. Ramón was certain that the different variants were complicated by Tom's insistence on increasing his pupil's possibilities for escape. From the start, they agreed that taking out a gun and shooting the renegade in the head was a quick but impractical solution. The same went for cutting his throat in front of the rabbit cages where the Duck often lost himself. As they went on discarding options or considering others to revise them more slowly, Ramón asked himself what moved Tom, whose ultimate intentions he could never be sure of, to complicate the operation so that he would be able to leave the attack alive. Did they want him alive to silence him once the mission was completed? Was it possible to imagine that there was a bond of affection between them? Or perhaps they feared that he would weaken and confess the true source of the execution order and that was why they were searching for ways to escape. The images of the cards put on the table, and the ones that with all certainty were still hidden, bumped around in his head as Tom debated with him how they would carry out the job. It had also become clear that poison, which could guarantee his flight, was also practically impossible to use, at least in the span of a brief time period and taking into account the scarce level of intimacy that Jacques could reach with the condemned man. Left on the table were the most violent but silent methods, strangulation and an attack with a knife. Of these two, due to its quickness, Tom preferred the second one. For execution with a knife, they would need what presented itself, whichever way you looked at it, as the greatest difficulty: a private meeting between the renegade and Jacques Mornard. They calculated that the efficacy with which he could stab him determined whether the thirty percent chance of escape would rise to more than fifty or even sixty. What about the ice axe? Ramón proposed. Tom moved his head, without deciding to accept or reject the option. He liked the ice axe, he had to admit, because of the symbolism of its use. It was cruel, violent, revengeful, and a lethal fusion of the hammer and sickle, he said. Could he even enter the house armed with an ice axe? In any event, if Ramón managed to step on the street once the act was consummated, his chance of escape reached eighty percent; and if he got in the car and put it in motion, Tom guaranteed him escape either by air, by sea, or by land to Guatemala, the United States, or Cuba, where they already had safe places for him. Tom would handle the details, and in a week Jacques would return to Mexico with Sylvia on his arm and would stay again at the Hotel Montejo.

On June 27, when they landed in Mexico, Jacques and Sylvia were met with the news that, two days before, the corpse of Bob Sheldon had been found in an abandoned ranch in the desert of Los Leones. The reporters, citing the head of the secret police Sánchez Salazar, said that the American had died with two bullets to the head and his corpse had been buried in quicklime under the floor of the same cabin where, presumably, the attackers of the exiled revolutionary's house had been hiding. Having just finished reading the news, Jacques felt a shock. Could the order to kill him have come from Tom or one of his men, or could it have been the initiative of the Mexicans? Was Sheldon's silence more important than his life? Had Tom tried to deceive him by telling him that they were going to get Sheldon out, but thinking that the body would never be found?

That night, while Sylvia slept, Jacques went down to the street and walked along the Paseo de la Reforma. The city was moving at a calm rhythm in those hours, but inside, the man was buzzing with doubts. Sheldon's death demonstrated to Jacques that knowing too much could be dangerous. And he, precisely he, was the one who knew the most. He thought that if that same night he went to Coyoacán and rescued his

Buick and the next morning withdrew the money in his name at the bank, he could perhaps disappear forever in a peasant town in El Salvador, or a small Honduran fishing town, with nearly legal papers bought at a very low price. Perhaps he would save his life, but was that a life worth aspiring to when the door of history was just within reach? Tom had not lied to him; Tom would explain what happened; Tom had molded him for years for this mission, and it made no sense that Jacques would risk glory and even his life with a decision like that. But none of those conclusions, so dazzling, managed to displace the ghost of doubt that, prophetically, had installed itself in Ramón Mercader's mind.

Jacques Mornard struggled to regain his routine. Every morning he said goodbye to Sylvia with the excuse that he was going to the office he told her he had opened in a suite of the Ermita building when, in reality, he only had a mailbox where, by arrangement, Tom would send the new instructions. Two and even three times a day he checked the mailbox and on each occasion left frustrated upon not finding new messages. He spent the rest of the day wandering around the city, but his spirits asked for some solitude that he could find only between the trees of the Chapultepec Forest.

On various occasions, he accompanied Sylvia to the renegade's fortress without expressing the desire to cross the threshold a single time. On the street, leaning against his Buick, he had long talks with the bodyguards. The one who most frequently came out to see him was the young Jake Cooper, always interested in the secrets of the stock market, to which the worldly Jacques Mornard was dedicated. In an almost imperceptible way, subjects like the European war, the Soviet annexation of the Baltic republics, the need for the United States to finally enter the war on the side of its British allies, filtered into their talks. To Jacques, the faith of those young men in their cloistered idol's sermons was almost touching, and he even liked to hear them talk about the need to strengthen the Fourth International to promote a working class consciousness regarding the options for world revolution. To demonstrate an incipient sympathy for his friends' political cause, Jacques proposed that they mention to their boss his willingness to carry out some operations in the stock market that, with his information and experience, could generate important gains that would economically help the Trotskyist International.

When, on July 18, it was announced that thirty members of the Communist Party had been arrested as suspects for participating in the attack against the Exile, Jacques knew with certainty that his lucky date would be decided in the coming days. For that reason he wasn't surprised when, the following morning, he found a note, unsigned, in his mailbox: "Since you like forests so much, shall we go for a walk today at four in the afternoon?"

At three o'clock, Jacques had settled in beneath the cypresses in Chapultepec, ordered to be planted eighty years before by the ephemeral empress Carlota. From there, one could see the path that led to the overbearing summer palace of the emperor Maximilian and the road going down to the Paseo de la Reforma. His doubts had turned into anxiety and he had to rely on what Soldier 13 had learned in Malakhovka, to regain control of himself and feel ready for the conversation.

At exactly four o'clock, he spied Tom. He was wearing a white shirt with a narrow collar from which a ridiculous polka-dotted handkerchief peeked out. From the path he made a signal and Jacques started moving.

"They had to kill him," he said without exchanging any greetings, his sight set on the curve in the road. Ramón remained silent, but all the alarms in his head rang. "His nerves failed him, he became aggressive, he wanted them to get him out of Mexico, he threatened to go to the police and say he had been kidnapped . . . The Mexicans were desperate and didn't think about it too much. If you need it, I can give you my word that we had nothing to do with it. From the beginning, I told you that the American could be efficient, although he wasn't trustworthy, but killing him . . ."

Ramón thought for a few moments.

"You don't have to give me your word; I believe you," he said, and realized how much he wanted to utter that phrase, and that doing so brought him patent relief.

"We can't wait anymore. While the Mexicans accuse each other and the police look for the French Jew, we're going to finish this shit."

"When?"

"Moscow wants it to happen as soon as possible. Hitler's campaign in Europe has been a walk in the park and he is becoming more daring; he thinks he's invincible."

Ramón looked at the cypress trees. Tom's demands resounded in his stomach. The time for waiting and strategizing was behind him, the time for reality was beginning, and he immediately felt that he must carry a difficult and heavy load. Would he be able to move it after clamoring so much for that honor?

"What's the plan?" he managed to ask.

"You have to see the Duck one or two more times. You will know how to do it. At those meetings you're going to start to court him. The idea is for him to think he can convert you to Trotskyism. Without exaggerating, make him feel like you admire him. We're going to exploit his vanity and his need to amass followers. When the opportunity presents itself, you tell him you'd like to write something about the situation in the world, something that occurred to you while talking to him. You're going to prepare an article that will force him to work with you. The idea is for you to be alone with him in his study. If you manage that, the rest should be easy."

"Do you think he'll want to receive me alone?"

"You have to manage it. Your possibilities of escaping will be much greater. That day you're going prepared to eliminate him and to use a weapon to escape if necessary."

"How many things should I enter with?"

"A gun in case you need it. A knife for him."

Ramón thought for a few moments.

"A knife would force me to cover his mouth, to grab him by the hair . . . I prefer the ice axe. Just one blow and I leave . . ."

"You don't want to touch him?" Tom smiled.

"I prefer the ice axe," Ramón replied, evasive.

"Okay, okay . . . ," the other one conceded. "That day Caridad and I will be with you. As soon as you step out onto the street and leave in your car, I'll take care of the rest. Do you trust me?"

He didn't respond and Tom untied the handkerchief from his neck and dried his cheeks.

"We're going to put together a letter for you to drop when you leave. You're going to be a disillusioned Trotskyist who has understood that his idol is no more than a puppet who, to return to power, has even been willing to place himself under Hitler's command . . ."

Ramón felt confused and Tom noticed that something wasn't working right. Taking him by the chin, he forced him to turn around and look him in the eye and Ramón saw a glimmer of excitement.

"Kid, we're getting closer . . . It's going to be us, you and me, the masters of glory. We have to prevent that son of a bitch from plotting with the

Nazis. Always think that you're working for history, that you're going to execute the worst of all traitors, and remember that many men in the world need your sacrifice. The bravery, hate, and faith of Ramón Mercader have to sustain you. And if you can't escape, I trust in your obedience and in your silence. It's no longer your life or mine at play, but rather the future of the revolution and of the Soviet Union."

From his eyes, more than from his mentor's words, Ramón received the message he needed. The doubts and fears of recent days began to disappear, as if that look had evaporated them, while he felt how his life got closer to its resounding culmination.

The door of fate opened with one of Natalia Sedova's ideas. In order to thank Jacson for his care with the Rosmers and his frequent gifts to Seva, the Trotskys invited him and Sylvia over for tea. They proposed the date of July 29, at four in the afternoon. In their room at the Montejo, Jacques reviewed the small notebook where he wrote down his business meetings and told Sylvia to call Natalia and tell her that they would be delighted to attend. The young woman's face shone with excitement and she immediately ran to the phone to confirm the appointment.

On the twenty-ninth, at exactly four in the afternoon, the Buick stopped in front of the fortress in Coyoacán. Jacques had put on a light cream summer suit, and Sylvia, despite the sun and the heat, had insisted on wearing black. She was nervous and happy, and had spent an hour in front of the mirror in a futile struggle to make her face pretty.

Jake Cooper greeted them from the watchtower and Jacson joked that he would give him a tip if he took care of the car. The Mexican policeman smiled at him and Corporal Zacarias Osorio, the most senior among the guards, practically bowed down to the guests. Harold Robbins opened the door to them and, as they talked, guided them to the forged-iron furniture that Natalia had placed in the yard, under the shade of the trees.

When the hostess came out, they greeted her affectionately and the young man gave her the box of chocolates he had bought her. He learned that Seva, upon returning from school, had gone fishing in the river and that Azteca, as always, had gone with him.

"Lev Davidovich asks your forgiveness," Natalia Sedova said. "An emergency came up and he's dictating some work he has to send tomorrow. He'll come to say hello to you in a little bit."

Jacques smiled and discovered that he felt relieved. It didn't bother him that the rhythm of penetration had to be slow, even when he knew that Tom needed him to act as soon as possible.

After the Mexican servant placed the tea and cookies on the table (could she be the party comrade infiltrated into the house?), Natalia told them that they were worried by the lack of news from the Rosmers. With the Nazis in Paris, their friends' situation was much compromised, and many times they feared the worst. Jacques nodded with his usual shyness and, following a silence that threatened to make itself infinite, made a comment about the weather.

"It looks like this summer is going to be very hot, doesn't it? I imagine you and Mr. Trotsky prefer the cold," he said to Natalia.

"When one starts getting old, the heat is a blessing. And we've experienced so much cold in our lives that this climate is a gift."

"So you wouldn't like to return to Russia?"

"What we like or don't like hasn't decided anything for a long time. We've spent eleven years wandering the world, without knowing how much time we can spend in one place or even if we will wake up the next day." She pointed at the walls where the gunshot marks remained. "It's very sad that a man like Lev Davidovich, who has done nothing in his life but fight for those who don't have anything, has to live fleeing and hiding like a criminal . . ."

Jacques nodded in agreement and, when he lifted his gaze, felt a jolt, for the Duck was approaching them. First his shadow and then his shape became visible.

"Thank you very much for coming, Jacson. Hello, little Sylvia."

Jacques stood up with his hat in his hands, wondering whether he should or shouldn't step forward and hold out his right hand. The Exile, who seemed distracted, walked to where Natalia was and the dilemma seemed resolved.

"I am so very sorry, I regret not being able to accompany you. It's that I have to finish an article today . . . Will you serve me tea, Natushka?"

While Natalia served it, the man looked at his garden and smiled.

"I've managed to save almost all the cacti. I have some very rare species. Those savages almost did away with them."

"Are you going to do new renovations after all?" Sylvia asked while their host drank his first sips of tea.

"Natasha insists, but I can't decide. If they wanted to come in again, they're capable of blowing up a wall . . ."

"I wouldn't think that they would attack like that again," Jacques said, and they all looked at him.

The old man broke the silence. "What would you think, Jacson?"

"I don't know . . . a lone man. You yourself have written it: the NKVD has professional murderers . . ."

The renegade looked at him with intensity, his cup frozen at chin height, and Ramón asked himself why he had said that. Was he scared? Did he want someone to stop him? He thought and always gave himself the same response: no. He had done it because he liked to use that power of playing with fates that were already decided.

The renegade, after drinking a sip of tea, finally left his cup on the table and nodded.

"You're right, Jacson. A man like that could be unstoppable."

"Please, Liovnochek," Natalia interrupted, trying to change the course of the unpleasant conversation.

"Dear, we can't be like ostriches," he said, smiling, and observed his visitor. "Don't smoke so much, Jacson. Take care of that marvelous youth you have." And with a wave of his hand to indicate he was leaving them, he took the path leading to the dining room and from there added: "Don't let him smoke, Sylvia. You can't find a good man like that every day. Will you forgive me? Goodbye! . . ."

Sylvia's face reddened and Jacques smiled, also embarrassed. He crushed his cigarette and looked at Natalia, who seemed amused.

Less tense already, Jacques Mornard told several stories about his Belgian family, brought to mind by the recollection of his father, a smoker of Cuban cigars. Natalia spoke of Lev Davidovich's first exile in Paris and how they had met, and the three smiled hearing about the Exile's observation that Paris was fine but Odessa was much more beautiful.

"Mr. Trotsky should rest more," Jacques remarked when the conversation was flagging. "He works too much."

"He's not a normal person . . ." Natalia looked at the house before continuing. "Besides, we live off of what the newspapers pay. That's what we've come to," she finished, her voice thick with nostalgia and sadness.

When the sun set, Jacson and Sylvia bid goodbye. Natalia again apologized for her husband and promised to find an opportune moment for another meeting. They had so few friends left, so few they received, and she would love to have them at the house again, of course with Lev Davidovich tied to a chair, she said, and shook Jacson's hand and kissed Sylvia's cheeks twice.

When they returned to the hotel, Jacques found that Mr. Roberts had called him and was begging him to get in touch, urgently. From his room he asked for a number in New York and Roberts himself answered.

"It's Jacques, Mr. Roberts."

"Are you alone?"

"No. Talk to me."

"Come tomorrow. I'll wait for you at eight o'clock at the Hotel Pennsylvania bar."

"Yes, tell Mr. Lubeck I'll fly tomorrow . . . Thank you very much, Mr. Roberts."

Smiling, he turned to Sylvia and said to her:

"We're going to New York for a few days. Lubeck is paying."

The stay in New York ended up being brief and had precise goals: the time for preparations had ended and Moscow was demanding that the operation be carried out at the earliest opportunity, keeping in mind the progress of the war, which had already allowed Hitler to dominate Europe almost without shooting. The greatest novelty was that Mr. Roberts gave him a new raincoat that had three interior pockets of a very curious design.

On August 7, Jacques and Sylvia settled in at the Hotel Montejo once more, and the following morning the young man ran out with the excuse that he had to see the contractors tasked with remodeling the offices. At the wheel of his Buick, he went in the direction of the tourist complex and looked for the unpaved road that he had traveled a few weeks before. The mound of porous rocks where he had left the ice axe was to the right of the path, and as he entered through the road he asked himself whether he hadn't confused the place, since according to his calculations, the rocks were two or three minutes from the highway, and he had already gone for more than five and he still had not located them. He thought of going back and confirming that it was the right road, although he was sure it was. Anxiety began to overcome him, and to calm down he told himself that in any store in the city he could buy a similar ice axe. But not finding that exact ice axe seemed like a disastrous omen. Where could the fucking rocks be? He continued on and, when he was ready to turn around, discovered the pile and breathed in relief. He climbed the rocks and saw the metallic shine. When he managed to take the ice axe out and have it in his hands, he felt something visceral unite him to that steel weapon, and the act of holding it gave him confidence and certainty.

Back in the city, he parked his car in front of a carpenter's shop in the Colonia Roma and asked the salesclerk to saw off about six inches from the ice axe's wooden grip. The man looked at him strangely and he explained that he felt safer climbing with a shorter grip. Twine in hand, the man measured the six inches Ramón had indicated, made a mark in pencil, and returned it to him to confirm whether that length was more comfortable for him. Ramón took the ice axe and made a gesture as if he were driving it into a rock over his head.

"No, it's still too long. Cut it around here," he said, and pointed to the place.

The carpenter shop salesclerk shrugged his shoulders, walked over to a saw, and sawed the wood. With a piece of sandpaper he smoothed the edges and handed the ice axe to Ramón.

"How much is it?"

"It's nothing, *señor*."

Ramón put his hand in his pocket and withdrew two pesos.

"That's too much, *señor*."

"My boss is paying. And thank you." He said goodbye.

"Climbing with a grip that short is dangerous, *señor*. If you slip . . ."

"Don't worry, comrade," he said and lifted the ice axe to eye level. "Now it looks like a cross, right?" And without waiting for a response, he walked to the corner where he had left the Buick, out of the carpenter's sight.

He went in the direction of Chapultepec and entered the forest. From the car's trunk, he withdrew the bag where he kept the khaki-colored raincoat that Tom had given him in New York and dropped the ice axe into it. He walked between the trees until he found a place where he assumed no one would see him and put on the raincoat. On the left side, below the waist, they had sewn a long narrow lining, almost in the shape of a knife. At stomach height, on the same side, was a smaller pocket designed to hold a medium-caliber revolver. On the right side, running from the armpit, was the third lining, triangle-shaped, with the narrowest angle below. Ramón placed the ice axe in the pocket and confirmed that, with the trimmed grip, it sank farther than he considered comfortable for rapid extraction. He verified, nonetheless, that if he kept his hands crossed over his abdomen, his own right arm hid the weapon's lump, and that was the most important thing. He placed the raincoat over his forearm and noticed that the depth of the pocket prevented any movement. He carried out several tests and concluded that if the renegade had his back to him, he could extract the ice axe in just a few seconds without taking his eyes off his objective.

Ramón folded the raincoat over his arm when he got close to his car. During that whole morning, he had barely thought of Jacques Mornard, and that memory lapse worried him. To cross all of the barriers to enter the fortress in Coyoacán and to be ready at the instant in which he would extract the ice axe, he needed the Belgian man's entire presence, his clumsy comments, his shyness, his insipid smile. Because Jacques was the only one capable of leading Ramón to the most grandiose moment of his life.

When they met in Moscow, almost thirty years later, and talked about what had occurred in those days as well as what happened later, Ramón asked his mentor if he had conceived of that perfect concatenation of events or if coincidence had worked in his favor. The man assured him, with the greatest seriousness, that he had planned it all, but that the devil had been collaborating with them. Each detail sketched out two, three years before had been shaped and would fit in such a perfect way that no man, only an infernal plan, could have made it thus, because in the end the events happened as if that ice axe, Ramón's arm, and Trotsky's life had been pulling at each other like magnets . . .

On Tuesday, August 13, Sylvia at last decided to face the difficult moment of going to Coyoacán and communicating to Lev Davidovich some important messages that she had received during her stay in New York. Two hours later the woman left the house with a smile on her lips. Jacques, who was waiting for her in the street, had spoken to almost all of the bodyguards in turn, showing a loquacity that only a few days later would seem significant to those men for whom Frank Jacson was an innocuous presence. He had even made plans with Jake Cooper to have dinner the following Tuesday when Cooper's wife, Jenny, would be arriving from the United States. Jacson was treating, of course, and he would take care of picking a restaurant that would be to Jenny's liking.

Sylvia had reason to feel happy, although her relations with the renegade were going through a period of crisis caused by her attraction to the new political group that Burnham and Shachtman, Lev Davidovich's former comrades, had formed in the United States. Nonetheless, the old man, so sensitive to splits—more so at a time when he needed all of his sympathizers—did not seem put out with her and, after hearing that Sylvia had spoken with Shachtman in New York, had asked her to come back in two days, with her boyfriend, for tea, since he wanted to apologize for not having attended to them during the previous visit.

"I think you made a good impression," she said as they left rocky Avenida Viena and turned onto Morelos.

"Do you want me to tell you something?" Jacques smiled. "I thought that the old man was a proud and arrogant guy. But ever since I met him, I think he is a great person. And the truth is, I don't know how it occurred to you to ally yourself with Burnham and Shachtman."

"You don't understand these things, dear. Politics is complicated . . ."

"But loyalties are very easy, Sylvia," he said, and pressed on the accelerator. "And, please don't tell me what I understand and what I don't understand."

The following morning Jacques went over to Shirley Court, where Tom and Caridad were staying. His mother received him with a kiss and offered him recently made coffee, which he refused. He felt jittery and only wanted to consult his mentor about the strategy they would follow the next day. When Tom came out of the bathroom wrapped in a robe, the three sat down in the armchairs of the small living room. Seeing how Tom and Caridad were drinking their coffee, Ramón perceived that some distance was opening between them, invisible but to him very tangible: it was the distance between the first and the second lines of command.

"You're going to cause an argument about that matter of Burnham and Shachtman," Tom said when he finished listening to his pupil. "You'll take the Duck's side against Sylvia. What he most wants to hear is that those dissidents are traitors, and you're going to give him the pleasure. At some moment, tell him that you want to write about that split and about what is happening in France with the Nazi occupation."

"He knows that Jacson isn't interested in politics."

"But he is so interested in it that he will open the doors of his house to

430

you again. Besides, he is so alone that if you write something in his favor, he'll receive you again. And that will be our moment. You have to be careful, but at the same time you'll seem resolved."

"Sylvia could view it all as strange . . ."

"That imbecile doesn't see anything," Tom assured him. "If everything goes well, in two or three days you'll go back to Coyoacán with your article . . ."

Caridad was following the dialogue in silence, but her attention was focused on Ramón. It was obvious that Tom's enthusiasm and certainty clashed with her son's patent lukewarmth.

"I'm going to get dressed," Tom said. "I want you to practice with the Star revolver that you're going to take the day of the party."

Caridad served herself more coffee and Ramón decided to have a cup. Then the woman leaned forward and, as she poured his coffee, whispered, "I want to talk to you. Tonight. At the Hotel Gillow at eight."

He looked at her, but Caridad's eyes were fixed on serving coffee and handing him his cup.

Tom was able to prove that the abilities of Soldier 13 remained intact. In the small forest in the San Angel area where they had their practice, the young man fired at difficult targets and made three out of every four shots, despite the tension he was feeling. Tom talked nonstop about what would happen once the attack was carried out. The easiest escape would be through Cuba, where Ramón could lose himself among the thousands of Spaniards milling about Havana and Santiago. On the island, a pair of agents would be waiting for him with money and connections to guarantee his needs and protection. Perhaps he and above all Caridad, who adored the country where she had been born, would also drop in there and the three would cross the Atlantic together. Tom's certainty, and the fact that his prognostics and plans tended to come true with surprising regularity, pushed aside Ramón's doubts and fears until he was nearly convinced that escape was certainly possible.

The Hotel Gillow, in the area near the Zócalo, was a colonial building that had originally been built to house the nuns destined to serve the neighboring church of La Profesa. At midday, many of the workers from government offices tended to have lunch in the restaurant. In the evenings, in contrast, it was a place where successful hustlers and high-class prostitutes filled their stomachs before going out to face the night. It had a large hall, discreet lighting, and many tables covered with checked tablecloths.

As soon as he entered the place, Ramón recalled that afternoon of rejoicing and victory when, with África at his side, he had entered an old café in Madrid to meet with Caridad. Now he could make out his mother, who was huddled at a table, smoking with her head down. Ramón moved his chair and it was as if Caridad were waking from a nap.

"Thank goodness you came. I told Kotov I was going to the movies, so we don't have too much time and there's a lot to discuss . . . Call the waiter over."

When the waiter approached, Caridad ordered a bottle of cognac, two glasses, and two bottles of Tehuacán sparkling water, and requested that they be left alone.

"And to eat?" The waiter was puzzled.

"We should be left alone . . . ," the woman repeated, and looked at him intensely.

Ramón waited in silence for the waiter to bring their order and leave.

"To what do we owe so much mystery?"

"You're on the verge of doing something very big and very dangerous. Although you don't care what I think, I feel responsible for what you're going to do and what happens to you, and I want to tell you some things."

Caridad poured two glasses of sparkling water and another two with cognac. She raised her glass a bit, smelled the liquor for a few seconds, then drank it in one long swallow.

"At least drink." She pushed the cognac to Ramón. "It will do you good."

Ramón looked at the glass but didn't touch it.

"I'm going to start at the end," she said as she lit a cigarette. "If they put you in jail, I will move heaven and earth to get you out. Even if I have to blow up the fucking jail. You can count on that. The only thing I ask you in return is for you not to fail when you have the old man in front of you and that, if they catch you, never say why you did it or who ordered it. If you fall apart, then I will not be able to help you, and neither will Kotov, because his life and I think mine depend on your silence."

"That's what matters to you? That I could complicate things for you?" Ramón enjoyed the possibility of hurting her.

"I'm not going to deny that matters to me, but believe me, it's not the most important thing. What you have the possibility to do can change the world, and that's what matters." Caridad took another sip. "And this shitty world needs a lot of changes. You know that." She observed Ramón's untouched glass for a few seconds. "Your life depends on your silence. Look what happened to that Sheldon . . ."

"The Mexicans killed him," Ramón said.

"That's what Kotov says . . . And we have no choice but to believe him."

"I believe him, Caridad."

"I'm happy for you," she said, and poured more cognac into her glass but didn't drink it. "Listen closely to what I'm going to tell you. Perhaps later you will understand why we're in this restaurant, counting the hours left until we kill a man."

At some point in the conversation, Ramón drank his glass of cognac in one shot and, without having any idea when he refilled it, again drank, in short sips, as he felt his insides turning. What he least expected was to hear that story of the humiliations and degradations that Caridad had been subjected to by her privileged and bourgeois husband, Pau Mercader. Although Ramón already knew pieces of the story, this time his mother went into the most shocking details, and spoke to him of the visits to brothels where her husband forced her to watch; the way he had induced her to try drugs in order to later throw her into bed, where a young man was paid to penetrate her while her husband penetrated the young man; the beatings he gave her when she refused to have anal sex; the threats, finally carried out, to separate her from her children and civilized life, confining her to an asylum where they nearly drove her mad and where, in order to not die of thirst, several times she had to drink her own urine. Those were the experiences that she had to go through in her sanctified bourgeois marriage, and hate was the seed that was planted in the center of her soul, that was barely relieved when she could direct that hate against those who maintained a miserable morality that allowed an abject and sick being like Pau Mercader to be considered a respectable man. Since then, Caridad had taken revenge with the weapons she had at hand and, more than once, upon returning to Barcelona after the electoral triumph of the Republican left, spent nights awake in front of the dark apartment on the Calle Ample where her husband then lived. The idea of going up the stairs and blowing his brains out with six shots from the Browning she always had at her waist turned into an obsession, and if she didn't do it, it was not out of fear or compassion, it was because she understood that knowing he was poor and the employee of other men who could humiliate and exploit him was the greatest punishment that Pau Mercader could receive, and it would be better the longer it lasted.

As he listened to her, Ramón felt how the human and political superiority he had felt over his mother for some time began to disappear. He remembered the poisoning episode in the restaurant in Toulouse and the suicide attempt from which he and his brother Jorge saved her. His mother was a destroyed being full of hate who was beginning to put herself together like a puzzle with pieces to spare.

"If I am a Communist with defects, Ramón, it's because of all of that," Caridad continued after serving her son a third drink and pouring a fourth one for herself. "My hate will never allow me to work to build the new society. But it's the best weapon to destroy that other society, and that is why I've turned all of you, my children, into what you are: the children of hate. Tomorrow, the day after tomorrow, in two days, when you are in front of the man you have to kill, remember that he is my enemy as well as yours. That everything he says about equality and the proletariat is all lies and that the only thing he wants is power. Power to degrade people, to control them, to make them grovel and feel fear, to fuck them up the ass, which is what those who enjoy power most take pleasure in. When you kill that son of a bitch, think that your arm is also mine, that I will be there, supporting you, and that we are strong because hate is invincible. Have that drink, dammit! Take the world by the balls and bring it to its knees. And get this into your head: Don't have compassion, because no one will have it for you. And when you're fucked, don't allow compassion; let no one pity you! You are stronger, you are invincible, you are my son, *collons!*"

26

In the early hours of May 29, while the gunshots whistled over his head, Lev Davidovich had a revelation: Death could not touch him because Natalia would protect him.

Just at that moment of enlightenment, he had heard Seva's voice and, with an unknown fear that didn't include the possibility of losing his own life, he had yelled: "Under the bed, Seva!" while Natalia pinned him down, pressing him against the corner of the room. The gunshots that had been meant to kill him and had filled the night with sparkling lights came from Seva's room, from the door to the study and through the bathroom window. From his corner, he could see the flight of an incendiary bomb going toward his grandson's room, but he had not tried to move, since above them, bursts of machine-gun fire made the stuffing of the mattress fly out. On the wall, almost at his back, the condemned man had felt the impact of the lead in search of his body. Finally, they heard voices, car engines, silence between gunshots. At that moment he had almost forgotten his previous conviction, since he was thinking: They're going to come in; now they're going to kill us both. Since he knew he would have no alternative, he closed his eyes, squeezed his legs shut, and waited. How long? Two, three minutes? he would ask himself later, since they were the longest ones of his life. His greatest concern had been Seva's fate and, above all, Natalia's, who was going to die because of him.

Lev Davidovich only recovered his senses when Seva's voice broke the silence. As soon as he confirmed that Natalia was not wounded, he ran to his grandson's room, where he didn't find him, but he saw bloodstains on the floor and his heart stopped. Robbins, who had entered the house to remove the incendiary bomb and prevent the fire from spreading to the work study, asked the Exile if he was wounded and calmed him down with the news that Seva was outside with the Rosmers. In the yard, as the bodyguards who had gone out after the assailants came back, the house's inhabitants had started to get an idea of what had happened. There had been between ten and fifteen men dressed as soldiers and policemen, and they had begun this attack by neutralizing the agents watching the outside, then they cut the cables of the alarms connected to the powerful lights inside and outside the house, ripped out the telephone lines, and cut the electric circuits that communicated with the police in Coyoacán. When the group had invaded the garden, one of them, armed with a machine gun, had climbed up a tree, where he took position and shot a burst at the area where the secretary slept. The rest of the assailants had gone toward the house, firing against the windows and closed doors. The bulletproof shutters diverted some of the bullets, whose marks were visible. The policeman and the bodyguards who had been closest to the assailants confirmed that several of them seemed to be rather drunk, but without a doubt they knew what they were doing and how to do it: so many bullets in one bed could not be a coincidence.

To Lev Davidovich it would always seem significant that the assailants had not attacked any of the bodyguards, whom they only pointed guns at. They had only directed fire against his room while they threw incendiary bombs (and even an explosive one that fortunately did not burst), which demonstrated that he and his papers had been their only objective. But why hadn't those ten or twelve assailants, who knew how to use weapons and had as their goal the death of one man, who controlled the situation inside and outside the house, gone in to see if they'd fulfilled their mission before giving the order to withdraw? It seemed incongruous to him that there should have been more than two hundred shots, sixty-three of them at his bed, with only Seva's superficial wound, and that had been caused by a bullet that ricocheted. Perhaps everything had failed because it had been botched, because of drunkenness or fear? Or was there behind that spectacle something darker that could still not be explained? He asked himself and would continue to ask himself, since a malignant essence, whose perfume he knew, was floating in that strange attack.

To escape, the assailants had opened the gates and gotten in the house's two cars, which always had the keys inside, in case of an emergency. In the middle of the confusion, Otto Schüssler, one of the secretaries, returned from the street commenting that the assailants had taken with them young Bob Sheldon, one of the new bodyguards. They had all formulated the same question: Had they kidnapped Sheldon or had he left with them? One of the Mexican policemen would later assure them that the young man was driving one of the cars (they abandoned the Ford a few blocks later, when it got stuck in the river's mud, and the Dodge showed up in Colonia Roma), but Lev Davidovich thought that, in the darkness, frightened as he was, it would be difficult for the policeman to recognize someone in a car going at top speed.

The great mystery was how the assailants had managed to enter the compound. The missing Bob Sheldon had been in charge of guarding the main door, and there were two reasons he would have allowed the assailants to enter without consulting with the head of the guard: either Sheldon, previously infiltrated, had always been part of the commando unit, or he had opened to someone who was so familiar that he thought it was unnecessary to consult with anyone.

When the police arrived, Lev Davidovich was still dressed in his nightshirt. Before talking to his old acquaintance Leandro Sánchez Salazar, the head of the secret police in the capital, he asked that they let him change, although he warned Salazar that he knew who was responsible for the events in the house, which still smelled like gunpowder . . .

General José Manuel Núñez, director of the national police, assured Lev Davidovich that General Cárdenas had instructed him to personally follow the investigations, and the officer had guaranteed the president that he would find and arrest those responsible. As he did with Salazar, the Exile responded that the task should be easy, since the intellectual author of the attack was Joseph Stalin, and the material authors were agents of the Soviet secret police and members of the Mexican Communist Party. If they arrested those responsible for the party, they would have in their hands the executors of the attack.

General Núñez did not like those words very much (the same ones the Exile would repeat to the press), nor did Colonel Sánchez Salazar, with whom Lev Davidovich had already had to speak several times since his arrival in Mexico and who had always seemed to him like a typical smart aleck who had opinions about everything. Sánchez Salazar's opinion, on this occasion, was insulting, since the policeman thought the attack could have been nothing other than an assault prepared by the Trotskys themselves to call attention to themselves and put the blame on Stalin . . . If his experience had not taught him to seek ulterior motives behind everything, the Exile would have been able to understand that Salazar would think that way: what had happened was suspicious and Sheldon's disappearance didn't help. The colonel also commented that he didn't understand how it was possible that, following such a violent attack, the old man could be so calm and in control of his actions and thoughts. It was obvious that the colonel didn't know him.

Looking to corroborate his thesis, Salazar detained the secretaries Otto Schüssler and Charles Cornell with the excuse that he needed to interrogate them to collect as much information as possible. He also left with all of the servants: the cook Carmen Palma, who cried when they took her away; Belén Estrada, the cleaning lady; and Melquíades Benítez, the handyman.

Lev Davidovich would read with shock that the press was initially reporting that Diego Rivera was the possible leader of the attack. That rumor came about because while he was neutralizing the policeman watching the house, the one who seemed to be the head of the assailants had launched cries against Cárdenas and yelled "Viva Almazán!" But Sánchez Salazar's declarations, that the attack had been staged by the Trotskys, got more attention than the Rivera possibility, and the communist press used the theory of a fake attack to accuse the Exile of wanting to destabilize the government and create a crisis in the Soviet Union—arguments that served them marvelously as they asked for his expulsion from Mexico with renewed fury. What most outraged Lev Davidovich was the realization that, with his version, Salazar was insulating himself from failure. After all, the attack had been prepared and executed without the secret police having the least idea of what was happening.

Nonetheless, despite the sixty-three shots in the bed, Lev Davidovich would continue to harbor doubts about the intentions of that attack. He came to wonder whether it had not been just a bluff, like the fires in Turkey, and that this time the purpose was to prepare the setting for a definitive action. When he confessed his worries to Natalia, she immediately began to take new security measures, and he reproached her for spending so much money, since it was obvious that when the assassins wanted to come in, they would enter. Besides, he was convinced that the next attack was not going to be the same. As he warned in his letter to the *American Jew*, the next time it would be a lone man, a professional, who would come from underground, like a mole, without them being able to do anything to avoid it.

Just one week after the attack, Lev Davidovich said goodbye to the Rosmers. If at another time he would have lamented very much a departure that deprived him of the proximity of good and old friends, at that moment he was almost happy, since he felt responsible for their lives while they were with him. Friendship, like almost all the simple and necessary human satisfactions, had ended up turning into a burden for him. He lived with the memory of those who were his friends, more than those who were capable of resisting the pressures, the attacks, and his own political stubborness. The wake of affections he had left behind was painful: many had died, violently; others had rejected him, and in the cruelest ways; others still had moved away from him, out of sincere or feigned distance from his ideas, his past, his present. Because of that he had come to wonder whether the fate of all those who handed themselves over to political causes was to die in solitude. That tended to be the price of altruism, of power, and, above all, of defeat. But not because of that did he cease to lament the losses of friends for which he had been to blame owing to his political fundamentalism; when blinded by the glitter of politics, he was incapable of understanding the difference between the circumstantial and the permanent. The most insidious trap, he told himself, had been turning politics into a peremptory passion, as he had done, and of having allowed its demands to blind him to the point of placing it above the most human values and conditions. At that point in his life, when very little was left of the utopia for which he had fought, he recognized himself as the loser of the present who still dreams and consoles himself with the reparation that could come in the future.

The evening before the Rosmers' trip, Lev Davidovich learned that, from the day in which Alfred got sick, the couple had become friends with Sylvia's boyfriend and the youngster had offered to take them to Veracruz, where they would take the ship to New York on their way to France.

Jacson, as that Belgian man said he was called, appeared to be a handsome man, although a little slow catching on. The morning of the departure, Lev Davidovich was feeding the rabbits for the first time when the young man approached him, interested in the animals' breed. Lev Davidovich had then felt rage against the presence of a stranger in the house, but he recalled that the Rosmers had invited him and, by his looks, deduced who he was. Still annoyed, he responded anyway, making his disgust obvious, and Jacson had discreetly withdrawn. Later on, he would see him talking to Seva, for whom he had brought a gift, and he was ashamed of his attitude. It was then that he told Natalia to invite him to breakfast, but the young man accepted only a cup of tea.

The decision to return to France with the Nazis knocking on Paris's doors had seemed to him an attitude worthy of Alfred Rosmer's greatness. As he tended to do, that morning he shook his friend's hand, gave a kiss to Marguerite, asked them to take care of themselves, then went to his study, since he didn't want to see them leave. At his age and with the GPU breathing down his neck, he assumed all farewells were definitive . . . At the house, with more men on watch and more tension, the couple's absence was immediately noticeable.

Finding that his cacti were the main victims of the attack caused Lev Davidovich real disgust. Several had been stepped on, others had lost their arms, and he worked for days to save them, although he knew well that with all his effort he was only looking to bring back a certain normalcy to the life of a house that had never had it and, until the end, would live in a permanent state of war.

During all those events something had made a favorable impression on the Exile: Seva's character. The boy was just fourteen years old and behaved with integrity. He didn't seem nervous and said he was worried about his grandparents, not himself. Just thinking that something serious could have happened to him made Lev Davidovich feel sick. To have made him come from France just so they could kill him here would be something he couldn't withstand. Because of that, when he saw him playing in the yard with Azteca, he felt great pain over the fate that without meaning to he had saddled him with. It was ironic that he had fought to build a better world and that around him he had only managed to generate pain, death, and humiliation. The best testimony to his failure was the heartbreaking presence of a boy confined within four bulletproof walls when he should be playing soccer in a field in Moscow or Odessa.

Thanks to Lev Davidovich's persistence, President Cárdenas ordered the release of his assistants and Lev Davidovich wrote a statement trying to put things in perspective. In addition to accusing Stalin and the GPU—as he insisted on calling the Kremlin's secret police—of attacking his house and of the deaths of Liova and Klement in Paris, of Erwin Wolf in Barcelona, of Ignace Reiss in Lausanne, he asked for the interrogation of the Mexican communist leaders, especially Lombardo Toledano and the painter Alfaro Siqueiros, who had been missing since the day of the attack. Would the Mexican judges be brave enough to do what the French and the Norwegians had never done? Would the investigators take the truth by the horns?

As could be expected, his new article was met with fury by the Stalinists. *El Popular*, the newspaper of the Workers' Confederation, published an essay by a certain Enrique Ramírez in which he asserted that Trotsky had organized the whole attack in order to blame the Communists. Meanwhile, from his hiding place, Siqueiros made a sarcastic statement in which he also accused Trotsky of having attacked himself. The way in which those men, who called themselves Communists, rolled around in lies and used them even to defend crimes deeply disgusted him.

But Lev Davidovich's statement achieved the desired effect when Sánchez Salazar saw himself forced to admit that "new" evidence had led him to discard the hypothesis that Lev Davidovich himself had orchestrated the attack. That evidence, nonetheless, also managed to fill the Exile with doubt, as the policeman insisted that only with collaboration on the inside would it have been possible for the assailants to enter. They believed the inside man was Bob Sheldon.

That young man had arrived at the house seven weeks before the attack. Like other bodyguards whom Lev Davidovich had employed in Mexico, he came "certified" by his comrades in New York, but Salazar insisted that it was impossible for Trotsky to guarantee that Sheldon had not been trained by the NKVD. Although the policeman's logic was irrefutable, Lev Davidovich responded that it was absurd to consider Sheldon an infiltrated man. What he didn't tell him, nor would he ever tell him, was that he couldn't accept that theory because it would prove that not even his closest collaborators were trustworthy. It would also show the plausibility of the Soviet secret police's favorite trick: making it seem that his death was the work of a Trotskyist militant who had attacked him over some political disagreement.

In the middle of that wave of accusations, allegations, and insults, some American followers proposed to Lev Davidovich that he travel clandestinely to the United States, where they would hide him. Without even thinking about it, he refused. His time for clandestine struggle had passed and he had no right to disappear to save his own life, especially at a moment in which the future of human civilization was being decided. "My naked head has to withstand until the end of the infernal black night: it is my fate and I must accept it," he wrote to them as he forced himself to return to normalcy, even when attempting it seemed absurd. He lived in a house that reminded him of the first jail he had been held in, forty years before, since the bulletproof doors made the same noise. But at the same time he felt strong and animated, and because of that, when he felt that he was suffocating in his imprisonment, he defied all of his protectors' safeguards and took up his excursions to the countryside again.

With that impulse, which he knew was epilogical, he sat down to give shape to his final will and testament. "For forty-three years of my conscious life, I have been a revolutionary," he wrote, "and for forty-two, I have fought under the banner of Marxism. If I had to begin all over again, I would try to avoid this or that mistake, but the general course of my life would remain unchanged. I shall die a proletarian revolutionary, a Marxist, a dialectical materialist and an irreconcilable atheist. My faith in the communist future of mankind is not less ardent, but rather more firm today, than it was in the days of my youth."

At that point he must have lifted his gaze from the page. It had to appear to him so revealing that the entire life of a man who had been at the summit of his epoch could be summarized in those few words: surely he was at the point of laughing—for the first time in many days. All of the struggles, the suffering, the successes, and the vanities could be expressed with such simplicity? What resistance could the monuments, the titles, the fury and glory of power, offer before that incorruptible reality, more powerful than any human will? He was thinking this at the precise moment when he saw his wife approaching across the patio, making a small gesture of greeting. She opened a window wide to permit a breeze to enter his study. From his seat he could see the grass border at the foot of the wall, a flowering bougainvillea, the profile of some cacti, the Mexican sky of that clear blue, and the light of the sun everywhere. "Life is beautiful, the senses celebrate its festival . . . May the future generations cleanse it of

442

all evil, oppression and violence, and enjoy it to the utmost," he added to what was written, calling up the vital burst of that moment.

Lev Davidovich had never imagined that preparing himself for his end through the writing of his last will could provide him with such compact calm. With very few words he managed to resolve the practical things in his life: he left his wife, Natalia Ivanovna Sedova, his literary rights, since the money that his books would yield was the only material thing he could bequeath her, and she was the only beneficiary possible after the profound sifting to which his family had been subjected. The house, which they had at last managed to buy, had been put in Natalia's name, and his archives had already been sold to protect them from the GPU. There was nothing else. When he thought about what he had and what he had lost, the losses were so numerous that he felt he had died several years before and was now enjoying an extension, something like a coda to the history of his life in which his will no longer intervened. He felt as if he was enjoying an extemporaneous lucidity that had been awarded to him so he could take a look at events that didn't come to a close with the exit of the main character.

"I am sixty years old and my body wants to collect payment for the excesses to which I submitted it. I hope it gives me a quick end, that it doesn't force me to suffer a long agony, like Lenin. But if this were the case and I find it impossible to lead a life that was moderately normal, I want to reserve a decision to put an end to my existence: I have always thought that a clean suicide is preferable to a dirty death." But Lev Davidovich didn't write that the origins of that feeling of a bad end came from very far away, both in time and in space. His death, planned many years before in an office of the Kremlin, was now among Stalin's priorities, but not, as some said, out of fear of the words Lev Davidovich poured into the biography he was writing: Stalin felt himself above words. Why, then? For years the man from the mountains had devoted himself to exterminating his party followers to make sure, like the gangster he had always been, that an avenging hand would not be able to come for him out of the darkness; besides, he had isolated Lev Davidovich and knew very well that, for the Exile, it was more and more difficult to place himself at the front of the new communist movement, as demonstrated by the farce that the Fourth International had become. The danger to the life of the political exile had begun precisely when Stalin felt that he had squeezed all the juice out of him that he needed to feed his repressions inside and outside the Soviet Union. And, like an obsolete machine, he had decided to send him to the junk yard and avoid any risk of a reactivation.

"My squalid material legacy completed," he started to write again, "I want to take advantage of this testament to remember that, besides the happiness of having been a fighter for the socialist cause, I've had the fortune of being able to share my life with a woman like Natalia Sedova, capable of giving me sons like Liova and Seriozha. Throughout almost forty years of shared life, she has been an inexhaustible source of tenderness and magnanimity. She has experienced great suffering. But I find some consolation in the certainty that she has also known days of happiness. I lament not having been able to give her more of these days: it only brings me relief to know that, in the essential things, I never deceived her. Ever since I met her, she knew that she was committed to a man led by the idea of the revolution, and she never felt like this was an adversary, but rather a companion in the journey of life, that has been that of the struggle for a better world." He signed each one of the pages, sealed them, and tried to forget them.

In reality, it was his wife's support that most encouraged Lev Davidovich to keep going. He knew that she suffered, but she did so in silence, because her character prevented her from weakening. She continued directing the fortification of the house (the walls were made higher, all of the doors were made bulletproof, and the windows were covered with steel curtains), organizing life in the house, and helping Seva regain the Russian language while she kept waiting for, against all evidence, some news that would confirm that Seriozha was still alive. When he saw his Natasha, hardworking and tenacious, and remembered his past indiscretions, a cold shame ran through his body and he concluded that only while affected by transitory madness could he have committed acts that made her suffer.

Outside of his personal sphere, the world was also falling apart. That fourteenth of July, "The Marseillaise" had not been sung at the place de la Bastille, since the Nazis were already in Paris. The campaign had been so devastating that they barely needed thirty-nine days to bring proud France to its knees. Lev Davidovich couldn't stop thinking about Alfred and Marguerite, since he didn't have any idea of what could be happening to them and to the rest of his French followers. But it was more painful for him to listen to the declaration of support for the Third Reich formulated by the Soviet chancellor, the infamous Molotov, and to see the proof of the agreement to repartition Europe concluded by Hitler and Stalin the previous year, as shown by the "annexation" of the Baltic republics to the Soviet empire.

The result of those imperial conquests was that the old Europe was being crushed by the weight of Hitler's swastika and the Soviet hammer and sickle. Which of the two, when the moment came, would take the first swipe at the other? Lev Davidovich asked himself. He sensed that times of great suffering for his people were approaching. Relying on the scarce optimism he had left, he came to consider that perhaps the country needed a new quota of pain in order to wake up and put the revolutionary dream back in its place.

Lev Davidovich was surprised to receive a visit from General Núñez and Colonel Sánchez Salazar, who came to inform him that thirty people, almost all of them members of the Mexican Communist Party, had been arrested in connection with the May 24 attack. Salazar asked his forgiveness for not forwarding the evidence that allowed them to continue the investigation, and Lev Davidovich responded that if the results warranted it, he not only forgave him but he also congratulated him . . . on his luck.

According to Salazar, shortly after the Exile's public statement, the police had the incredible good fortune of hearing the comments of a drunk that had put them on the trail of the men in charge of obtaining police uniforms used in the attack. Following this thread, they started to find accomplices until they came to one of the attackers, David Serrano, who led them to discover, on one side, two women tasked with watching the house and distracting the police guards and, on the other, a certain Néstor Sánchez, who, upon being arrested, gave the crucial information that the attack had been led by the painter Siqueiros and a French Jew whose identity none of the detained seemed to know. They already knew that in the attack the brothers-in-law of Siqueiros had been involved, along with his assistant, Antonio Pujol, and the Spanish Communist Rosendo Gómez, all veterans of the Spanish Civil War. Although the statements were confusing, Salazar thought that the French Jew and Pujol had been the ones directly responsible for the attack, since Siqueiros had remained outside the house, next to the police cabin. The order to arrest the painter had been issued, but they didn't have the least idea where he could be and they feared he was already far from the country. Regarding the French Jew, perhaps the real architect of the plot, only Siqueiros and Pujol seemed to have been in contact with him. The arrested men even contradicted each other, with some claiming he was Polish.

As he listened to Salazar, Lev Davidovich thought about the degree of perversion that Stalin's influence had injected into the souls of men like those who, after embracing the Marxist ideal and living through betrayals like those committed in Spain, continued to follow Moscow's orders and were even capable of attacking other human beings. What made him laugh, in contrast, was the nerve of "El Coronelazo" Siqueiros, who, after organizing the attack, didn't dare enter the house and direct it. It was regrettable that an artist of his scale had turned into a third-rate gunman, terrorist, and liar.

A few days later, the worst hypothesis was confirmed when the police found the corpse of Bob Sheldon buried in the kitchen of a hut up in Santa Rosa, in the desert of Los Leones. At four in the morning, some of Salazar's emissaries went to get Lev Davidovich to identify him, but Robbins refused to wake him up and sent Otto Schüssler instead. Nonetheless, in the morning, when Natalia told him what had happened, he asked to go to Santa Rosa, where he met Salazar and General Núñez.

Bob Sheldon's corpse was on a coarse table in the yard of the house. Although they had washed him, he had remnants of the dirt and lime that had covered him. His body was perfectly preserved, and on the right side of his head were two bullet holes. When Lev Davidovich saw him, he felt deeply moved, since he was certain that, in collusion with the GPU or not, Bob Sheldon had been another victim of Stalin's fury against him, and that that corpse could just as well have been that of Liova, to whom he couldn't say a final goodbye, or little Yakov Blumkin, or the efficient Klement, or Sermux or Posnansky, his old and close secretaries from the days of the civil war, or perhaps the obstinate Andreu Nin or the kind Erwin Wolf—all of them devoured by terror, all of them murdered by Stalin's criminal fury. The police respected his silence and remained silent themselves for a few minutes. Salazar concluded that Sheldon's death confirmed his participation in the attack, but Lev Davidovich again refused to accept that theory and asked to return home. He wanted to be alone, with his guilt and his thoughts.

There was no longer any doubt that fate or Stalin's inscrutable designs had given him an extension, even though he was convinced it would be a short one. He fluctuated between a rush to tie up outstanding issues and depression over the certainty that everything would very soon be over and his work and dreams would remain in the hands of the unforeseeable fate that posterity would award them. For too many years he had been a pariah, a captive who should behave so as not to bother his hosts. He had been converted into a puppet at whom the rifles of lies were aimed, into a man who was completely alone, who walked through the walled yard of a far-off country, in the company of just a woman, a boy, and a dog, surrounded by dozens of corpses of family members, friends, and comrades. He didn't have any power, he didn't have millions of followers, nor did he have a party; barely anyone read his books anymore, but Stalin wanted him dead and in a short while he would swell the lists of Stalinism's martyrs. And he would do so leaving behind an enormous failure: not that of his existence, which he considered a barely significant circumstance for history, but that of a dream of equality and freedom for the majority, to which he had given his passion . . . Lev Davidovich trusted, nonetheless, that future generations, free of the yoke of totalitarianism, would do justice to that dream and, perhaps, to the stubbornness with which he had maintained it. Because the greater struggle, that of history, would not end with his death and with Stalin's personal victory—it would start again in a few years, when the statues of the Great Leader were knocked down off their pedestals, he wrote.

Although Lev Davidovich knew that he should forget this turbid attack, each revelation pulled him back to it like a magnet. The story of the supposed Polish or French Jew seemed to lead the Mexican and U.S. police to the trail of an NKVD officer with years of experience in missions carried out in France, Spain, and Japan. Salazar had found out that, under the Jew's orders, they had rented two houses in Coyoacán to use as support for the attack. Despite those advances, Lev Davidovich was convinced that the identity of the mysterious Jew would remain unknown, as would be the reasons for which a professional like him had not gone into the room and executed the condemned man himself.

The tension experienced in the fortress at Coyoacán turned into a quicksand that sucked in the days. Lev Davidovich couldn't go back to his previous routine, abnormal in and of itself, but to which he had become accustomed. Nonetheless, whenever he could, he escaped that prison in search of a horizon. The worry over his safety had reached the point that some of his American friends sent him a bulletproof jacket, but he refused to wear it, just as he also forbade that every person who visited him be frisked or that one of his secretaries be present with him for interviews, be they with journalists or with friends like Nadal, Rühle, or others who came by occasionally.

Around that time Sylvia Ageloff returned from New York, and at Lev Davidovich's insistence she was invited to come over one afternoon, with Jacson, to have tea. He wanted to thank Jacson for his care with the Rosmers and apologize for not having received him as he should have that afternoon on which, pressed by work, he couldn't sit down to talk. On that more relaxed occasion, they had a pleasant meeting. Sylvia, who had always revered Lev Davidovich, seemed to be on cloud nine over his deference to her and her companion, while Jacson, loyal to his bourgeois education, had brought Natalia a box of fine chocolates and a gift for Seva.

After that meeting, Lev Davidovich commented to Natalia that Jacson had come across as a peculiar guy. First of all, it was unusual that, without the least shame, he claimed that he didn't care at all about politics, but when he and Sylvia had argued about her sympathies for Shachtman's faction, he had taken Lev Davidovich's side and, with a certain vehemence, had reproached her for her Yankee attitude of thinking Americans are always right. Shortly before leaving, when they were talking about dogs and he had touched on the topic of raising funds for the International's work, Jacson offered him his experience in the stock market and even the credit and contacts of his affluent boss. At that moment Lev Davidovich recalled that one of his secretaries had commented on that offer of Jacson's, which he had rejected, convinced that he couldn't get mixed up in monetary speculations even to support the most idealistic of political projects. In the face of the Exile's reaction, Jacson excused himself, saying he understood. Lev Davidovich felt at that moment that there was something in that man that didn't quite come together: the story of the passport bought in France so he wouldn't have to fight in the war, his willingness to use his boss's capital to earn money for him, his apathy toward politics despite having worked as a journalist and being the son of diplomats, his open talk about his financial possibilities . . . No, something wasn't coming together. Although the Exile thought the origins of that inconsistency perhaps came from his bourgeois talkativeness, he told Natalia that perhaps it was worth learning more about Jacson. For now, his care of the Rosmers repaid, the best thing would be not to receive him again, he added.

Sánchez Salazar went to see him to inform him that they had arrested

Siqueiros in a town in the interior. According to the police, since the initial interrogations, always very petulant (and, Lev Davidovich thought, convinced that someone would rescue him from justice's hands), Siqueiros had denied that the NKVD had been involved in the attack and refused to admit that any French or Pole had participated. He assured them that the idea for the attack had been conceived of by him and his friends in Spain when they learned of the Mexican government's betrayal of the world proletariat by giving asylum to Trotsky, an apostate capable of ordering his followers to rise up against the Republic in the midst of a civil war. They had resolved to carry out the attack when the war in Europe started, since they believed that they could prevent the traitor from returning to a USSR eventually occupied by his allies, the Nazis. On that point, Lev Davidovich even smiled and asked the policeman if Siqueiros knew that he was a Jew and a Communist. Sánchez Salazar himself admitted that the contradictions were blatant, since the painter had added that the objective of the attack was not to kill him (we would have done so if we had wanted to, he repeated) but to pressure Cárdenas to throw him out of the country. He assured the police that they had prepared the assault without the party's support, which seemed even more incredible, since all of the commando members were militant Communists. The only thing that made Lev Davidovich happy about that arrest was thinking that probably there would be a trial, and it would provide him the occasion denied to him by the Norwegians to denounce Stalin's criminal methods and the lies of his regime in a public forum.

It was the afternoon of August 17, while Lev Davidovich was set to distract himself with the rabbits and Azteca, when Sylvia's boyfriend showed up. The reason for his visit was that, after the conversation he had heard between the girl and the Exile, he had written an article about the defection of the American Trotskyist leaders Shachtman and Burnham. And he recalled that he had mentioned his interest in writing something about those subjects to him and desired to get the old revolutionary's verdict. Lev Davidovich himself, before they said goodbye, had told him he would review the draft, although he no longer remembered that commitment.

For the next four days, several times Lev Davidovich would ask himself why he had agreed to receive Jacson when he had already decided not to see him again. He would comment to Natalia that he felt sorry for the young man's political naïveté and for the resounding way in which he had refused to accept his financial assistance. Whatever the reason, he had allowed the Belgian into his study and started to read the article in order to convince himself definitively that the guy was a fool. Jacson's piece repeated the four ideas Lev Davidovich had said in the conversation with Sylvia and suddenly jumped to the situation in occupied France without in any way linking one story with the other. What kind of journalist was this character?

In his anxiety to hear Lev Davidovich's opinion, Jacson had stood behind him the entire time, leaning on the edge of the worktable, reading over the Exile's shoulder what he was marking in the text. That warm pressure over the back of his neck soon provoked the Exile's fear. As he folded the pages, he called Natalia so she would accompany Jacson to the door and he explained to the young man that he had to rewrite the article if he intended to publish it. The man took the pages with the face of a beaten dog, and, upon seeing him, Lev Davidovich again felt sorry for him. Perhaps because of that, when the Belgian asked if he could bring him the rewritten text, he said yes, thinking that the appropriate and necessary response was no. Nonetheless, during dinner he told Natalia that he didn't want to receive him again; he didn't like that man, who, for starters, could not be Belgian, since no Belgian with the least education (and this one was the son of diplomats) would even think to breathe down the neck of a person he barely knew.

On what would be the second-to-last sunrise of his life and the last of which he would be conscious, Lev Davidovich awoke with the feeling of having slept like a child. The sleeping pills he had been prescribed had a relaxing effect that allowed him to sleep and awaken with energy, in contrast to the ones he had taken a few months before, which caused a sticky inertia. In the morning, he spent more time than usual with the rabbits, since just to see them confirmed how much he had abandoned them since the doctor had recommended rest in light of his elevated blood pressure. He had tried to explain that being with the rabbits and with Azteca, far from exhausting him, comforted him. But the doctor insisted that he not make physical efforts, and even prohibited him from writing. The bastard must be from the GPU, he thought.

The work morning lasted longer than usual. He had insisted on drafting an article for his American comrades about the theories of revolutionary defeatism and the way to adopt it in a situation different to that of 1917, keeping in mind that the current imperialist war, as he had declared on more than one occasion, was a development of the previous one, a consequence of the deepening of the capitalist conflicts, for which it was necessary to look at reality with a new lens.

The good news of the day had been the cable brought by Rigualt, his Mexican lawyer, confirming that his papers were finally in safe hands at the Houghton Library at Harvard University. Rigualt had also brought him a gift, two tins of red caviar. At lunchtime he asked Natalia to open one and he himself served it. As soon as the caviar touched his taste buds, he felt a wave that took him back to the first days of the Bolshevik government, when they had just installed themselves at the Kremlin. In those days he and his family lived in the Knights' House, where before the revolution the czar's civil servants had lived. The house had been divided into rooms, and in one of those lived the Trotskys, separated by a hallway from the rooms occupied by Lenin, his wife, and his sister. The dining room they used was common to both rooms, and the food they were served was terrible. They didn't eat anything but salted beef, and the flour and the pearl barley they used to prepare the soup were full of sand. The only thing that was appetizing and abundant (because they couldn't export it) was red caviar. The memory of that caviar had forever become associated with those first years of the revolution, when the political tasks they faced were so big and unknown that they lived in perpetual vertigo and, even so, Vladimir Ilyich, whenever he could, dedicated some minutes to playing with Lev Davidovich's children. That final midday, as he devoured the caviar, he again asked himself if all great dreams were condemned to perversion and failure.

After a brief siesta, he returned to his study, determined to finish various projects in order to dedicate himself fully to revising the biography of Stalin. Now he wanted to include in the book what was apparently the last letter that Bukharin had written to the Grave Digger while he waited for the verdict to his appeal. They were a few lines, very dramatic, even worse, sullen, that some friendly hands had sent on to him and that, ever since then, he had not been able to stop thinking about. In the letter, Bukharin, sentenced to death, didn't even ask for clemency anymore but rather for a reason: "Koba, why do you need me to die?" Bukharin didn't know? Because he knew why Stalin wanted them dead—all of them.

He took up his work again, dictating some ideas for an article with which he intended to respond to the new verbal attacks of the Mexican Stalinists, but at some point he lost his concentration and remembered that Jacson, Sylvia's boyfriend, had announced he would return that afternoon with his rewritten article. Just thinking about seeing that man and reading his string of banal remarks disgusted him. I'll get rid of him in a couple of minutes and then I'll give the definitive order that I will not receive him anymore, under any pretext, he thought.

While he was waiting for Jacson, he observed that, outside his study, it was a beautiful afternoon. The Mexican summer could be hard but not cruel. Even in August, at least in Coyoacán, there was always a breeze. Lev Davidovich lamented that the windows facing the streets were covered and cut off the flow of fresh air and the possibility of seeing people pass by, the fruit and flower vendors with their perfumes and colors. He knew that, despite the misery, the war, and death, beyond the walls he lived between there crawled a normal and small life that tried to make do day by day, a life he had dreamed of many times as if it were a great privilege that had been taken away from him.

Since Seva still hadn't returned from school, Azteca was sleeping at the door of his study. The mutt had grown into a beautiful dog, though a beauty different from Maya's aristocratic one, but definitively attractive. Who does Azteca love more, Seva or me? he asked himself, and smiled. Observing the dog, he remembered that he had to feed the rabbits. He went out to the yard and put on his thick gloves, and for several minutes his mind was occupied only with the activity he was carrying out. His rabbits were also beautiful, he thought, and for a few moments he felt far away from the world's sorrows. It was then that he heard the jail-like screeching of the door. Jacson, he confirmed, as he cursed the moment when he had agreed to see him again. I'll finish with him as quickly as I can, he thought, and for the last time in his life Lev Davidovich Trotsky caressed the rabbits' soft fur and directed some words of love to the dog by his side.

27

The moment he crossed the armored threshold of the fortress in Coyo-acán and saw, in the middle of the yard, the table covered by a tablecloth of bright Mexican colors, he felt how he was regaining control of himself. The fury that had accompanied him all day disappeared, like dust swept away by the wind.

Ever since Ramón returned to the hotel the night before, the dry aftertaste of the cognac and the bitterness of an explosive rage had settled in his stomach, inducing him to vomit. The belief that his will, his capac-ity to decide for himself, had evaporated began to besiege him and lead him to feel like an instrument of powerful designs in whose mechanisms he had been enshared, refused any possibility to turn back. The certainty that in three, four, five days he would enter the murky current of history as a murderer caused him an unhealthy mix of militant pride over the action he would carry out and repulsion toward himself over the way in which he had to do it. Several times he asked himself if it wouldn't have been preferable, for him and for the cause, for his life to have ended be-neath the tracks of an Italian tank at Madrid's doors, like his brother Pablo, before thinking that his mission would only be that of draining the hate that others had accumulated and had guilefully injected into his own spirit.

That morning, when he woke up, Sylvia had already ordered breakfast, but he barely tasted the coffee and, without saying a word, got in the shower. Ever since the last trip to New York, the woman had noticed that her lover's affable nature had begun to turn, and the fear that the fantastic relationship could falter made her tremble with anxiety. He had explained to her that business wasn't going well, that the renovation of the offices was delayed and cost too much, but her feminine instinct yelled that other problems were weighing down the soul of her beloved Jacques.

Without speaking he got dressed. She, with her black slip, observed him in silence, until she dared to ask: "When are you going to tell me what's wrong, dear?" He looked at her, almost surprised, as if only at that moment had he noticed her existence.

"I've already told you: business."

"Just business?"

He stopped adjusting his tie.

"Can you leave me alone? Can you shut up for a while?"

Sylvia thought that never in almost two years of their relationship had Jacques spoken with that hostile tone, loaded with hate, but she chose to stay silent. When he opened the door, she decided to speak again.

"Remember that they're expecting us today in Coyoacán."

"Of course I remember," he said, violently tapping his temple, and went out.

Ramón wandered the streets of the city center. On two occasions he drank coffee, and almost at noon his body demanded a hit and he entered the Kit Kat Club. Against his habit, he drank a glass of Hennessy advertised by the mirror behind the counter. At two in the afternoon, he opened his second packet of cigarettes that day. He wasn't hungry, he didn't want to talk to anyone, he only wanted time to go by and the nightmare in which he was involved to reach its end.

A little after three he picked up Sylvia at the hotel and at four on the dot he was looking at the multicolored tablecloth spread over the forged-iron table on which they would soon take tea. At that moment he noticed how he was regaining his ability to confine Ramón under the skin of Jacques Mornard.

Jake Cooper had accompanied them to the table, told a couple of jokes, and confirmed their dinner on Tuesday the twentieth, his day off.

They agreed to see each other at Café Central at seven, since Cooper wanted to make the most of his day walking around with Jenny through the Zócalo area and the markets. The silence Jacques had maintained until that moment seemed to disappear and Sylvia would tell him that night that, evidently, visiting the fortified house in Coyoacán had been a balm for his worries.

Just five minutes later the renegade and his wife came out of the house. Jacques Mornard observed that the old man looked exhausted and stood up to shake his hand. At that moment he understood that for the first time he was touching the incredibly soft skin of the man he would kill.

"So at last . . . Jacson or Mornard?" the Exile asked with a sarcastic smile on his thick lips and a disquieting shine in his eagle eyes.

"Don't be impertinent, Liovnochek," Natalia reprimanded him.

"Whatever is easier, sir. 'Jacson' is an accident that will follow me for I don't know how long."

"For quite some time," the old man said. "This war could go on for another few years. And you know what? The longer it lasts, the more devastating it is, the more possibilities that workers will at last understand that only revolutionary action can save them as a class," he said, as if a soapbox had been placed under his feet.

"So what role could the Soviet Union have in that action?" Jacques dared to ask.

"The Soviet Union needs a new revolution to bring about a great social and political but not economic change," the renegade began. "Although the bureaucracy took all the power, the economic base of society is still socialist. And that's a gain that can't be lost."

Sylvia coughed, as if asking to change the conversation. "Lev Davidovich . . . I, like many, think that ever since Stalin signed the friendship pact with Hitler, the Soviet Union cannot consider itself a socialist country but rather an ally of imperialism," she said. "That's why it's invading all of Eastern Europe."

The arrival of the maid with the tray, cups, pot of tea, and plate of pastries made the Exile pause for a moment. But as soon as the woman placed the tray on the table, the man jumped like a spring.

"Dear Sylvia, that's what the long-standing anticommunists say and now also Burnham and Shachtman to justify their break with the Fourth International. I continue to maintain that the duty of all the world's Communists is to defend the Soviet Union if it's attacked by the German fascists or any imperialists, because the country's social bases are still, in and of themselves, an immense progress in the history of humanity. Despite the crimes and the prison camps, the Soviet Union has the right to defend itself and the Communists have the moral responsibility to stand together with Soviet workers to preserve the essence of the revolution . . . But if the social explosion that I expect occurs and the socialist revolution triumphs in several countries, those same workers will have the mission of helping their Soviet comrades free themselves of the gangsters of Stalinist bureaucracy. That's why it's so important to strengthen our International and why your friends' attitude is so regrettable . . ."

Jacques Mornard observed how Natalia Sedova served the tea. For a moment the smell of the recently baked pastries had alleviated his stomachache, but the Exile's words had taken away his appetite. That man had just one passion and was always talking as if he were leading the masses, pushed by a disproportionate vehemence regarding his diminished audience, but with a very convincing and seductive logic. Ramón concluded that listening to him for too long could be dangerous and he took refuge in the evidence that the last door on the way to the fulfillment of his mission was coming into view, and he decided to focus on opening it. Within an effusiveness Sylvia was unfamiliar with, he then launched into supporting the Exile's theory and criticizing the inconsistent attitudes of Burnham and Shachtman, who were removing themselves at the moment when unity was needed. Echoing his host, he criticized Stalin but defended the idea that the USSR maintained its socialist nature, and agreed with the Exile about the necessity of universal revolution, until, through some twists in the conversation, they ended up on the difficulties of the French resistance against a German army that practically controlled the whole country.

Natalia Sedova asked the maid for a second pot of tea at the moment the front door opened and young Seva entered the yard, preceded by the joyous Azteca, who, without paying any attention to the visitors, went to the Exile. The old man smiled, petting the animal and speaking to it in Russian.

"Do you always speak to him in Russian?" Jacques, smiling, asked after greeting Seva, over whose shoulders he even threw his arm.

"Seva speaks to him in French, in the kitchen they speak to him in Spanish, and I speak to him in Russian," the old man replied. "And he understands us all. The intelligence of dogs is a mystery to human beings. In many ways I think that they're intellectually far superior to us, since they have the capacity to understand us, even in several languages, and we are the ones who do not have the intelligence to understand their language."

"I think you're right . . . Seva says you've always had dogs."

"Stalin took many things away from me, even the possibility of having dogs. When they kicked me out of Moscow, I had to leave behind two, and when I went into exile, they wanted me to leave without my favorite dog, the only one I was able to take to Alma-Ata. But Maya lived with us in Turkey, and we buried her there. With her, Seva learned to love dogs. It's true that I have always loved dogs. They have a kindness and a capacity for loyalty that go beyond that of many human beings."

"I also love dogs," Jacques said, as if he were ashamed. "But it's been years since I've had one. When all of this is over, I'd like to have two or three."

"Find yourself a borzoi, a Russian wolfhound. Maya was a borzoi. They're the most loyal, beautiful, and intelligent dogs in the world . . . with the exception of Azteca, of course," he said, winking and caressing the dog's ears more, then hugging him against his chest.

"You know? You're the second person to tell me about those dogs. An English journalist I once met told me he had one."

"Listen closely, Jacson: if you ever have a borzoi, you'll never forget me," the old man proclaimed, and looked at his watch. He immediately patted Azteca's side and stood up. "I should take care of the rabbits and I am also behind on some work. It has really been a pleasure talking with you and with the stubborn Sylvia."

"Would you like me to help you with the rabbits?" Jacques offered.

Sylvia and Natalia smiled, perhaps since they knew the answer.

"Don't worry, thank you. The rabbits are not as intelligent and they get nervous with strangers."

Jacques stood up. He looked at the ground, as if he'd lost something, and suddenly reacted.

"Mr. Trotsky . . . I was thinking . . . I would like to write something about the problems of the political parties in the French resistance. I know France very well, but your ideas have made me understand things differently and . . . would you do me the favor of reviewing it?"

The old man turned toward the rabbit cages. The sun was beginning to set. With gestures that seemed mechanical, he popped the buttons on his cuffs to roll up the sleeves of his Russian shirt.

"I promise not to steal too much of your time," Jacques continued. "Two or three pages. If you read them, I would be more sure of not making a mistake in my analysis."

"When will you bring it to me?"

"The day after tomorrow: Saturday?"

"All I want is that you not steal a lot of my time."

"I promise, Mr. Trotsky."

With the edge of his shirt, the Exile cleaned the lenses of his glasses. He stepped toward Jacques and, with the glasses back on, looked him in the eye.

"Jacson . . . You don't look Belgian. Saturday at five. Make me read something interesting. Good day."

The renegade turned toward the rabbit cages. Jacques Mornard, with a smile frozen on his lips, was incapable of responding to his farewell. Only that night, when he placed a sheet in the typewriter, did he understand that, with his last words, the man he had to kill had breathed on his neck.

He awoke with a headache and in a bad mood. He had barely slept despite the exhaustion he was pushed into by those three hours of effort, at the end of which he had only managed to write a couple of messy paragraphs with poorly put-together ideas. How was he going to write something that would end up being interesting to the old man? He was certain that he had again dreamed of a beach and some dogs running on the sand, and he remembered that he had awoken in anguish during the night. The conviction that everything would be over the following day, when he sank the ice axe in the skull of that renegade traitor, instead of calming him, filled him with disquiet. He took a pair of painkillers with his coffee and, when Sylvia asked him where he was going, whispered something about the office and the construction workers, and with his smudged pieces of paper he went out onto the street.

His mentor was waiting for him in the apartment at Shirley Court, and after Ramón had relayed the details of the previous afternoon's visit, his anxiety exploded.

"I know how I have to kill him, but I can't write a fucking article! He asked that it be something interesting! What interesting things am I going to write for him?"

Tom took the pages that, almost imploringly, Ramón handed him, and told him not to worry about the article.

"I have to do it tomorrow, Tom. Prepare things to help me escape. I can't wait any longer. I'll kill him tomorrow," he repeated.

Caridad was listening to them, seated in one of the armchairs, and Ramón, in his daze, thought he noticed her hands shaking slightly. Tom, the sheets in hand, was looking at the typed lines, full of cross-outs and additions. Then he crumpled the pages, threw them in a corner, and commented, as if it weren't important, "You're not going to kill him tomorrow."

Ramón thought he misheard. Caridad leaned forward.

"If we've worked for three years," he continued, "and we've gotten to where we are, it's for everything to turn out right. You're not the only one who is risking his life in this. Stalin forgave me the disaster with the Mexicans because we never trusted them too much to begin with, but he is not going to forgive me a second failure. You cannot fail, Ramón, that's why you're not going to do it tomorrow."

"But why not?"

"Because I know what I'm doing; I always know . . . When you are alone with the Duck, you'll have all the strings in your hands, but you have to be hanging on to them tightly."

Ramón shifted his head. As always, he felt Tom's aplomb touch him, and the anguish began to melt away.

Tom lit a cigarette and stood before his small group of troops. He asked Caridad to make coffee and ordered Ramón to go to the pawnshop to buy a typewriter, the portable kind.

When he returned with the typewriter, Caridad offered him coffee and told him Tom was waiting in the bedroom. Ramón found him leaning over the chest of drawers he used as a desk and saw that on the floor there were crumpled pages written in Cyrillic. The adviser demanded silence with a gesture, without ceasing to repeat *"Bliat! Bliat!"* Standing, Ramón waited until the man turned around.

"Come on, I'm going to dictate the article to Caridad and the letter that should accompany it."

"What letter?"

"The story of a disillusioned Trotskyist."

"What do I have to do tomorrow?"

"Let's say it's a dress rehearsal. You're going to the traitor's house with all of your weapons on you, to see if you can get in and out without anyone suspecting anything. You're going to give him the article and you're going to be alone with him. The article will be so bad that you'll have to make a lot of corrections and he himself will give you the option of returning with another draft. That will be the moment, because you'll have calculated the way in which you're going to hit him, the way to get out . . . You have to be sure you will do each thing very calmly and very carefully. You already know that if you can get out to the street, I'll guarantee your escape; but while you're inside the house, your fate and your life depend on you."

"I won't fail. But let me do it tomorrow. What if I can't see him again?"

"You won't fail and you won't do it tomorrow—and you will see him again, that is sure," Tom said, taking him by the chin and forcing him to look him in the eyes. "The fate of many people depends on you. And it depends on our shutting the mouths of the ones who didn't trust in us, the Spanish Communists, do you remember? You're going to show what a Spaniard who has two balls and an ideology in his head is capable of," and with his right hand he tapped Ramón's left temple. "You're going to avenge your dead brother in Madrid, the humiliations your mother had to endure; you're going to earn the right to be a hero and you're going to show África that Ramón Mercader is not soft."

"Thank you," Ramón said, without knowing why he said it, as he felt the pressure of his tutor's hands turning into a sweaty heat over his face. At that moment he convinced himself that Caridad's story of her humiliations, mentioned in passing by Tom, in reality was part of a strategy concocted by his mother and the agent to sharpen his hate; that was the only explanation for Tom knowing of the conversation in the Gillow. How was it possible that Tom also knew that África had accused him of being too soft?

"Come on, to work." Tom patted him on the shoulder and brought him out of his thoughts. "You have to memorize the letter we're going to write. When you're done, you drop it on the floor and leave. But if they catch you, that letter is your shield. You have to say that your name is Jacques Mornard and repeat what that letter says. But they are not going to get you—no. You're my boy and you'll get out. I'm telling you . . ."

They went back to the living room. Caridad, standing, was smoking. The tension had made the worldly woman she had been in recent months

460

disappear; her features were sharp again, hard, androgynous, as if she were also preparing herself for war.

"Sit down and type," Tom ordered, and she threw her cigarette butt in a corner and settled down in front of the typewriter placed on the table. She ran a sheet through the roller and looked at the man.

"What are you going to write?"

"The letter." Tom dropped into the armchair, with a pained look on his face. He stretched his body on the seat, read something from the pages he had filled with Cyrillic characters, and closed his eyes. "We'll put a date on it later. Begin! 'Dear Sirs: Upon writing this letter, I have no other objective, in the event that something should happen to me, than to clarify . . .' No, wait . . ." And he held out his hand like a blind man feeling his way around. "Better: 'than to explain to public opinion the motives that brought me to execute the act of justice I have set out to do.'"

Tom interrupted himself, his eyes still closed and some sheets in his hands, deciding his next words. Ramón was standing and smoking, and he observed his mentor and his mother and saw two different beings concentrating, doing a job responsibly. The phrases that the man was inventing and the woman was imprinting on the pages were a human being's sentence and a murderer's confession, but Tom and Caridad's demeanor displayed such comfort with the idea of death that they seemed like two actors in a play.

Through Tom's mouth, Jacques Mornard was beginning to speak about his origins, his profession, the political inclinations that led him to participate in Trotskyist organizations.

"'I was a devoted student of Lev Trotsky and would've given my last drop of blood for the cause. I started studying as much as had been written about the different revolutionary movements in order to instruct myself and that way become more useful to the cause,' period."

"Same paragraph?" Caridad asked. Tom shook his head. "Just a moment," she said, and placed a new sheet in the roller.

"Read me what's already written," Tom asked, and Caridad complied. At the end the adviser opened his eyes and looked at Ramón. "What do you think?"

"Sylvia will challenge it."

"When Sylvia speaks, you're going to be very far away. Caridad, read it again."

Tom closed his eyes again, and as soon as Caridad finished her reading,

461

he began to put together the story of a member of the Fourth International committee who, after various conversations in Paris, had proposed to Jacques a trip to Mexico with the objective of meeting Trotsky. Mornard, excited, accepted, and the member of the International ("You never knew his name," he clarified to Ramón; "That's not believable," he replied; "I could give a shit about believability," the other one sighed) gave him money and even a passport to leave Europe.

Suddenly Tom stood up, ripped up the pages he still had in his hands, and uttered a Russian curse. Ramón noticed that his limping, absent in recent months, had returned. At that moment he had the feeling that it was Kotov who was going to the kitchen and returning with a bottle of vodka. He placed a glass on the table where Caridad was working and served himself an overlarge amount. He made it disappear in one swallow.

"We have to give the idea that Trotsky was already waiting for Jacques because he wanted something from him. And Jacques has to seem very sentimental, a little dumb . . ."

"Ramón is right. No one is going to believe that story," Caridad said.

"When have we ever worried about people's intelligence? We have to tell them what interests us. What they believe is their concern. What has to remain clear is that Trotsky is a traitor, a terrorist of the worst kind, that he's being financed by imperialism . . ."

Tom returned to his armchair and continued dictating. Ramón felt himself getting lost in the labyrinth of lies that his mentor was weaving so easily, as if he were telling some truth in which he had lived. He rejoined the story's narrative thread when Tom was going into the section about the young Trotskyist's disillusionment: the famous revolutionary revealed himself to be a cruel and ambitious being when he proposed to him, whom he barely knew, that he travel to the USSR to commit acts of sabotage and, above all, to assassinate Stalin. Tom added that his anti-Soviet action would rely on the support of a great foreign nation, which obviously was financing the traitor. Ramón felt that those words seemed familiar, as if he had read them or heard them before.

"That's the tactic, not only eliminate the enemy, but cover him in shit, lots and lots of shit; let the shit overflow." Tom got excited and elaborated on the Exile's intrigues against the Mexican government and its leaders, seeking the destabilization of the country that had given him refuge. But Trotsky had to be even more corrupt, and so he had expressed to Jacques his disgust for all the members of his own group who didn't think exactly as he did and even confided in him the idea of eliminating those dissidents. Although Mornard had no proof, he was sure that the money to buy and fortify the house where Trotsky lived did not come from those blind followers but rather came from another source and the person who knew it was the consul of that great imperialist nation who visited him frequently.

"Has anyone seen that consul?" Caridad asked.

"This is a country of blind people," Tom responded, "and we're going to give them some of what they like."

Tom shifted to melodrama when he had Jacques travel to Mexico with the young woman he loved and whom he wished to marry. If he went to Russia to commit the crimes planned by Trotsky, he would have to break his engagement, which the Exile encouraged him to do, since he considered the young woman a traitor to the true Trotskyist cause. And he finished off the letter with an unexpected twist:

"'It's probable that this young woman, following my act, will not want to have anything else to do with me. Nonetheless, it was also for her that I decided to sacrifice myself by taking the head of a man who didn't do anything but harm the workers' movement, and I am sure that not only the party but also history will agree with me when they see the most incarnate enemy of the world proletariat disappear . . . In case something should happen to me, I ask for the publication of this letter,' period."

With the last keystroke, the apartment became silent. Ramón, still standing, felt a shudder come from the depths of his soul. He no longer had the impression that he had heard those words before, since the lies accumulated by his mentor had the same tone as the accusations that, for years, in successive proceedings, articles, and speeches, had been launched against Trotsky and other men who were tried and sentenced. Didn't truths, real events, exist on which to base a young revolutionary's decision to sacrifice himself and commit a crime to free the proletariat of the influence of a traitor? Something murky emanated from each one of the words of that letter, and Ramón Mercader understood that his shaking was not only due to the fear caused by the act of falsification that he had just witnessed. He had discovered that he feared the ones who were sending him to execute a man as much as the consequences that his act could bring. If he still needed it, that letter was the last proof that, for him, there was no other way out of the world than to become a murderer.

He stopped the car near Coyoacán. He opened the trunk, removed the raincoat, and placed it over his shoulders. At that moment, as if the weight of the raincoat were trying to drown him, Jacques Mornard felt revulsion and barely had time to lean over to avoid being stained by vomit. The liquid, a mixture of coffee and bile, smelled of rancid tobacco, and its stench caused a new bout of dry heaving while his skin broke out in a cold sweat. When his stomach had calmed down, he cleaned himself with his handkerchief and opened the bag in which he kept the English dagger and the ice axe and moved them to the interior pockets of his raincoat. The Star revolver with nine bullets he placed in the small of his back, tucked in the waistband of his pants. He confirmed that the sheets of the article were in the left outside pocket of the raincoat and returned to the car.

He remembered that there was a pharmacy on the way and, upon seeing it, stopped the car. He bought a bottle of mouthwash, another one of cologne, and a box of painkillers. On the street, he rinsed his mouth several times, to get rid of the taste of vomit, and chewed a pair of pills. He never experienced headaches and suspected that perhaps his blood pressure was responsible for that pressure in his skull that hadn't left him for the past two days. He rubbed the cologne on his neck, his forehead, and his cheeks, and got back behind the wheel.

When he took the dusty Avenida Viena, Ramón understood that he still hadn't gained back control over Jacques Mornard. The conviction that it was just about a rehearsal, that he would enter and leave the house as quickly as possible, did not provide him with the expected relief. He still doubted whether it wouldn't have been better if Tom had allowed him to carry out his job that very day. What was going to happen would happen, and the sooner the better, he told himself. His hate for the renegade, which should have been his best weapon, was dissolving amid fear and doubts, and he didn't know anymore whether he was moved by irreversible orders (the imprisonment of the painter Siqueiros and the possibility of a public trial had alarmed Moscow, according to Tom) or by a deep conviction that was getting more and more difficult to recover in his mind. Because of that, upon seeing the ocher-colored fortress, Ramón decided that that would be his last visit to Coyoacán.

He stopped the car after turning around and placing it in the direction of the highway to Mexico. He doused the handkerchief with cologne and cleaned his face again. He took several deep breaths and left the car. From the front tower, Jake Cooper waved hello and asked about Sylvia. Jacson responded that he was only coming for a few minutes and, considering how talkative Sylvia could be, had preferred to leave her at the hotel. Cooper, smiling, confirmed that his wife was arriving Monday evening.

"So we'll see each other on Tuesday," Jacques yelled as the bulletproof door opened before him.

Joe Hansen, the renegade's secretary, shook his hand and let him in.

"My mother always used that German cologne," he remarked. "Was the Old Man expecting you earlier?"

"I'm ten minutes late. I got delayed because of Sylvia."

"He's working now. Let me ask him if he can still see you."

Hansen left him in the yard. He took off his raincoat and folded it carefully over his arm. In a corner of the garden, close to the fence that overlooked the river, he saw Melquíades, the handyman, at work on the house. The rooms occupied by the secretaries and bodyguards had their windows open, but no movement could be seen. He then had a very strong feeling that, yes, definitely, this was his day. In order not to think about it, he concentrated on contemplating the bullet holes in the house's walls, until he noticed a presence very close to him. He turned around and found Azteca, who was sniffing at his shoes, and saw that they were splattered with vomit. Being careful with the position of the raincoat, he bent down next to the animal and with his free hand caressed his head and ears. For a few minutes, Jacques lost all sense of time, place, and what he had set to do as the animal's fur ran between his fingers, causing a feeling of well-being, confidence, and calm. His mind was blank when he heard the man's voice and he reacted with surprise.

"I'm very busy," the renegade said as he wiped his glasses with a red handkerchief that was embroidered in one corner with a hammer and sickle.

"I'm sorry, I got delayed," he said, standing, as he looked for the typed pages in the outside pocket of his raincoat, careful that the garment, pulled down by the weight of the weapons, would not fall from his arm. "I won't take much of your time."

Jacques handed him the pages, still devastated by the poor quality of the text. Without taking them, the Exile gave a half turn.

"Come on, let's see the article."

Jacques Mornard entered through the doors of the house for the first time. From the kitchen came the sounds of activity and the smell of cooking, but he didn't see anyone. Following the renegade, he crossed the dining room, where there was a large table, and entered the workroom. He observed that on the desk were several papers, books, fountain pens, a lamp, and a bulky dictaphone, which the man moved aside to make space.

"And your wife?" he dared to ask.

"She must be in the kitchen" was the dry response of the renegade, who was already sitting in front of the desk. "Let me see this article."

Jacques handed the sheets over and the man, with a thick grease pencil, began to correct, quickly, the first lines. Ramón managed to place himself behind his prisoner and observed the room. Behind him, against the wall, there was a long, low set of drawers on which were piled typed papers and where a globe rested. On the wall, a map of Mexico and Central America. On the desk was a folder with a label in Cyrillic that he managed to read: PRIVATE. From his position, he spied in the half-open drawer the dark shine of a revolver, perhaps a .38, and thought about how little the caliber of a weapon mattered to him that was not going to defend its owner. He stopped inspecting the site and forced himself to think about the fact that he was three steps behind the man, and his condemned head was a few inches below Jacques's own shoulder. He always thought he'd have a more elevated position, but even so, if he managed to raise his arm, he could bring down a brutal blow in the middle of that skull on whose crown the hair was just beginning to thin. He stuck his hand in his raincoat and touched the metallic part of the ice axe. He could take it out quickly, in just a few seconds, and hit forcefully in the exact place where the scarcity of hair allowed him to see the white skin, almost shining, provocative. He closed his hand around the shortened grip and resolved to extract the weapon just at the moment in which he realized he had not removed his hat and the sweat had accumulated on his forehead, threatening to run into his eyes. He thought of looking for his handkerchief but desisted, to avoid a sudden movement. The window overlooking the garden was open, to make the most of the afternoon breeze, and from that angle he could only see the cactus pots and some flowering bougainvillea. He calculated that, if he hit him with precision, he would need just one minute, with rapid steps, to reach the exit door and ask that they open it for him, talk to the guard on duty for a few seconds, and leave the house. Until he got in the car, it would be two, maybe three minutes in which his salvation would depend on his cool head and no one discovering the Duck's body. But if the man didn't die from the first blow or if his nerves faltered and he rushed too much, the fortified house would turn into a tomb from which he would never escape. He clutched the ice axe forcefully and concentrated on the skull in front of him. The old man was working, using his pencil frequently, crossing out or adding words, as his throat admitted sounds of disapproval. His head, nonetheless, was still there, in reach of Ramón's arm.

"The poor French," the Exile murmured.

At that instant, through the window, Ramón could hazily see Harold Robbins. The head of the bodyguard corps was looking at the study and then up at the watchtower. Slowly he took his hand out of his raincoat and decided to look for the handkerchief in the back pocket of his pants. His glasses had become damp with sweat. Without letting go of the coat, he dried his face and, with difficulty, took his glasses off and cleaned them.

The renegade's head became clear again. It was still challenging him. In that head was everything that man possessed, and now Ramón had it at his mercy. Why hadn't Kotov given him the letter he should drop as he went out? To Ramón, with his gaze fixed on the place where he was going to drive in the steel point, it now seemed obvious that the best thing would be to forget about the damned letter. He couldn't keep on thinking; he was wasting the golden opportunity that had taken years to create—an occasion that was perhaps unrepeatable. But at the same time he understood that at that moment he wasn't capable of executing the order, although his confusion prevented him from knowing why. Was it fear? Obedience to Tom's orders? The letter he didn't have? The need to prolong that sick game of power? Doubts about the probabilities of reaching the street? He discarded this last one, since, despite the solitude the renegade enjoyed, it was obvious that the chance of escape mentioned so many times by Tom had never gotten to thirty percent. Only if a miraculous combination of coincidences occurred would he manage to leave the house after dealing the blow, and he was certain that, if he dared to administer it, something would happen and he would be cut off from his escape options. The next time he entered the fortress, he would perhaps conquer his nerves and kill the most pursued man in the world, whose breathing he could hear two steps away from him, whose skull kept enticing him. Nonetheless, he was now completely sure that he would not

467

manage to escape. In reality, was the escape ever really foreseen? He convinced himself that his bosses without a doubt preferred that he leave the house, but whether he managed to or not was not important, and Ramón understood that they had destined him to commit a crime that, at the same time, would mean his death. Furthermore, his mentor had designed everything with such mastery that, in the end, the condemned man himself would be in charge of fixing the date of his own death and, to reach the maximum perfection, also that of his executioner. He understood that his inability to move was a result of that macabre situation that controlled his body and his will.

"This needs a lot of work," the Exile said without lifting his gaze.

"Does it seem very bad to you?" Jacques Mornard asked after a few seconds, fearing his voice would fail him.

"You have to rewrite it completely and—"

"All right," Jacques interrupted him, and approached the table. "I'll rewrite it this weekend. Now I have to go. Sylvia is waiting for me to go eat and . . ."

Jacques needed to leave that oppressive space. The Exile still held sheets in his hand and had turned toward the visitor, to whom he gave an incisive look.

"Why didn't you take off your hat?"

Jacques brought his hand to his forehead and tried to smile.

"Since I'm in a rush . . ."

The old man looked at him even more intensely, as if he wanted to penetrate him.

"Jacson, you're the strangest Belgian I know," he said, and handed him the sheets at last, then called in a loud voice, "Natasha!"

Jacques took the pages and folded them any which way as he noticed how the cold damp of his hands stuck to the paper. Preparing a smile for the woman's arrival, he managed to return the sheets to the pocket of his raincoat, which was on the verge of getting away from him due to the weight of the instruments of death it was carrying. He mechanically moved his hand until he touched the knife's handle. The sound of steps getting closer stopped that impulse. Natalia Sedova, with an apron covering her chest and lap, peeked into the studio and, upon seeing Jacques, smiled.

"I didn't know that—"

"Good afternoon, Madame Natalia," he said, and clutched the knife.

"Jacson is leaving, dear. Please, see him out."

Ramón felt that, instead of a goodbye, the Exile's words sounded like an expulsion order. He had the knife in his right hand, thinking that it was impossible for that man, accosted by death for so many years, to remain impassive at the bottom of the net in which he had been caught, as if calling for his own end. It wasn't logical; it was almost incredible that, with his intelligence and his knowledge of the methods of his pursuers, he had believed that whole story about a Belgian deserter dedicated to doing no one knew exactly what business, who worked in a nonexistent office and met with a phantom boss, who said inappropriate things and committed errors en masse, or claimed to be a journalist and wrote an article full of banal remarks—a Belgian who, to top it off, while visiting indoors, forgot to remove his hat. Without looking into his eyes, he asked the Exile, "When can we see each other again?" The silence lasted for an agonizing amount of time. If the renegade said "Never," his own life would be prolonged while Ramón Mercader would have an unpredictable future, without glory, without history, perhaps without too much time; if he gave the date, he would name the day and time of his death, and of Ramón's almost certain death. But if he said "Never," he also thought, the revolver could be the most expedient alternative: two shots for the old man, one for the woman, another for himself. The work would be done and there would be five bullets left over.

"I'm very busy. I don't have time," the condemned man said, and tipped the balance in his favor.

"Just a few minutes; you already know the article," mumbled Ramón, and with that plea, both of their lives fell into a precarious balance.

The Exile took a few seconds to decide his fate, as if he had intuited the tremendous implication his words would have. His future murderer moved his right hand to his waist, resolved to take out the revolver.

"Tuesday. At five. Don't do what you did today . . . ," he said.

"No, sir," Ramón murmured, and, without breathing, dragged Jacques Mornard to the garden, in search of the street and the fresh air his lungs, congested by desperation, clamored for. Death was in no hurry; it was taking three days to return by Ramón Mercader's hand to the fortified house in Coyoacán.

Ramón would have to wait twenty-eight years to get the answers to the most worrying questions that, from that moment, had begun to take root in his mind. Throughout those years, lived in skins that became all the more outrageous, as befitting a creature born of deceit and the manipulation of feelings, he would always remember those seventy hours—the time period decreed by the condemned man—like a murky journey toward his fate, which had been placed in someone else's hands ever since that predawn morning in the Sierra de Guadarrama, when Caridad made her request and he said yes.

That night, when exhaustion overcame him, he managed to sleep for a few hours without being attacked by nightmares. When he awoke, he saw Sylvia, seated at the vanity table, the black slip and her myopic glasses on, and prayed that the woman would not speak. He worried that his fear and rage would explode on that pathetic being whose life he had used. Since the previous afternoon, he had discovered that his hate, far from disappearing, in reality had multiplied and it could now expand in unforeseeable directions: he hated the world; he hated every single person he saw, with their lives (at least on the surface) ruled by their wills and decisions; and above all, he hated himself. When he returned from Coyoacán, he had gotten into an argument with a driver who tried to pass him. At the next intersection, when they were stopped at a red light, he got out of his car and, with the Star in his hand, completely worked up, had run up to the other car and pointed the barrel of the gun at the head of the trembling driver as he yelled insults, as if he needed to get out the explosive violence that was burning inside him. Now, upon remembering the scene, he felt a deep shame at the lack of control that could have ruined the work of three years.

"Order coffee; I'm going to work," he said, and went to the bathroom. When he returned, breakfast was on the vanity table and he drank his coffee and lit the first of many cigarettes he would smoke that day. Sylvia looked at him, disconcerted, her eyes wet, and he warned her, "Don't talk to me, I'm worried."

"But, Jacques . . ."

His eyes must have had such violence in them that the woman stepped away from him, crying, and shut herself up in the bathroom.

Ramón had decided not to see Tom or Caridad, at least on that day. With the article corrected by the renegade, he sat down in front of the portable typewriter that Tom had demanded he use and felt how much he hated Trotsky's arrogance at marking the text with comments such as *foolish! banal! unsustainable!* as if he were rubbing his superior intelligence in his face.

Slowly, he tried to make a clean draft, changing just a few words. He knew that what he said was no longer important, or even how he said it, just that it have the appearance of being the result of revision, to obtain from the renegade the few minutes of attention that he needed. Nonetheless, his fingers trained to squeeze throats, hold weapons, wound and kill, got tangled in the keys, and forced him to rip up the pages and start again.

Sylvia came out of the bathroom completely dressed and, without talking, left the room. When Ramón managed to finish the first page, he felt exhausted, as if he had cut down an entire forest with an axe. He ate some crackers, drank the rest of the cold coffee, and threw himself on the bed, a fresh cigarette between his lips.

At some point, he fell asleep and awoke with a start when the door to the room opened. Sylvia Ageloff, thinner and more vulnerable than ever, was looking at him from the foot of the bed.

"My love, what's wrong? Is it because of me? What did I do?"

"Don't say such stupid things. I'm worried. Can't I be worried? And can't you shut up? Are you such an idiot you don't understand what it means to *shut . . . up*?"

Sylvia burst into tears and Jacques felt the desire to hit her. As he got dressed, he remembered África. How would it have been if she had been there with him in that difficult time? Would she have reinforced the conviction that was cracking? Would she have had the necessary power to remove him from that well of doubts, fears, misdirected hate? It only managed to shore him up to think that África, wherever she was, would surely tremble with pride when she knew that he was the one who would carry out the mission for which so many of the world's Communists, including her, had been willing to give their lives. With that image in mind, he ran out onto the street and wandered until he exhausted himself. For the first time in three days he was hungry and entered a restaurant, where he ordered the Pátzcuaro fish and a glass of French white wine. Later he walked to the cathedral and looked at the beggars clustering in its porticos, like beings thrown away by the earth and the heavens. The night's fresh air and the clear firmament managed to calm him down, and Ramón remembered the beach he had dreamed of a few nights before and wished he were on the sand, in front of the crystal sea of that cove.

When he returned to the hotel, Sylvia was sleeping. He turned on a light, sat down in front of the typewriter again, and at the end of two hours had the article ready that would return him to the fortress in Coyoacán.

Perhaps due to the long nap he had taken in the middle of the day, sleep didn't come to him until past four in the morning. The hours of wakefulness turned into a maddening parade of visions about the execution that his brain was creating, uncontrollably. About what would happen afterward, by contrast, he had just one image: a dark void that he could only associate with his own death.

He woke up when the sun was rising and noticed his broken body was almost inert. He cursed time, which wasn't moving, which seemed to have stopped at that torturous impasse, as if insistent on making him lose his mind. He dressed and went down to the hotel restaurant, where he drank coffee and smoked until eight o'clock and got into the Buick heading in the direction of Shirley Court.

Tom had just woken up, his eyes still puffy with sleep. He offered him coffee and Ramón refused: if he drank another cup, his heart would explode. Caridad came out of the bedroom wrapped in a robe and with her hair wet. While Tom was taking a shower, Caridad and Ramón sat in the living room, looking into each other's eyes.

"I know they're going to kill me," he said. "I have no way to escape."

"Don't think like that. We'll be waiting for you. You just have to get one foot out onto the street and we'll take care of the rest. Under gunfire if necessary . . ."

"Don't say that to me again! You know it's a lie, that everything is a lie."

"We'll be there, Ramón! How could you think that I'm going to abandon you?"

"It wouldn't be the first time."

"This is different."

"Of course it is. I'm not going to get out of there alive."

The door to the bedroom opened and Tom popped his head in, although Ramón could see his whole body, naked, and his pubis, covered in saffron-colored curls.

"Enough with the stupidities, dammit!"

Ramón and Caridad remained in silence until Tom returned dressed and took Ramón by the arm.

"Walk," he demanded, and almost ripped him from the armchair.

472

They got into the dark green Chrysler and Tom headed for Reforma, toward Chapultepec. The morning was warm, but as they entered the forest, a cool, perfumed breeze came in through the car window. They left the car and walked until they found a fallen trunk on which they sat.

"Why didn't you come to see me yesterday?"

"I didn't want to see anyone."

"You're not going to have an attack of hysteria, are you?"

Ramón stayed silent.

"Tell me what happened."

"We agreed I would come back tomorrow, Tuesday, at five."

"I already know that. Give me the fucking details," the adviser demanded, and with his eyes fixed on the grass he listened to Ramón's story, which stuck to the facts and left out his thoughts.

Tom stood up and limped a couple steps.

"*Suka!* This fucking leg . . . It cramps up every once in a while." From his pocket he brought out the letter written three days before. "Sign it as 'Jac,' so it will be more confusing: Jacques, Jacson . . . And date it tomorrow. When you have to talk about the letter, you say that you wrote it before entering the house and that you threw out the typewriter on the way. You have to get rid of it . . ."

Ramón put the letter away and remained silent.

"Don't you trust me anymore?" Tom asked him.

"I don't know," Ramón answered, in all honesty.

"Let's see. As you can imagine, I've never told you the whole truth, because you can't nor should you know it. For your own good and for that of other people. But everything I have told you is true. Everything we planned has come about in the way I've told you it would. Until today. And tomorrow, what we want to happen will happen. I never guaranteed you that you would escape from that house or that you would get out unscathed after killing the Duck. I talked to you about a historic mission and my responsibility to get you out of this country if you managed to get out of the house. You have my word that I will get you out, but if you don't believe it, forget it and think of what's necessary. The important thing is to kill that man and, if possible, to not fall into the hands of the police. My trust in you is infinite, but you've seen with your own eyes how the toughest men in the world, who seem to withstand everything, will confess to what they haven't done. So the best thing would be for you to get out, because I can't be completely sure of your silence. What I am

473

sure of is that if you talk, your life will be worth less than a gob of spit," he said, and spit on the grass. "And your mother's life even less; and, it goes without saying, mine, who will be the first to have his head cut off. If you don't talk, we will always be with you and guarantee you our support at all times, wherever you are . . . It couldn't be clearer."

The young man looked at the forest, trying to process those words.

"I would like to be the Ramón I was three years ago, before the lies started," he said, without realizing that he had begun to speak in Spanish. "I would like to enter that house tomorrow and smash the life of a renegade traitor and be sure that I'm doing it for the cause. Now I don't know the difference between the cause and lies."

Tom lit a cigarette and focused on the blades of grass he was moving with a stick. When he spoke, he continued to do so in French.

"Truth and lies are too relative, and in this work that you and I do, there's no border between the two. This is a dark war and the only truth that matters is that you follow orders. It's all the same if, to get to that moment, we climb a mountain of lies or truths."

"That's cynical."

"Perhaps . . . Do you want a truth? I'll remind you of one: the truth is that the Duck is a threat to the Soviet Union right now. We are at a point in which everything that is not with Stalin is in favor of Hitler, without any in between. What do a few lies matter if they save our great truth?"

Ramón stood up. Tom discovered that the fear and doubts had made an obvious mark on his pupil's soul. But he was certain that Ramón had understood the essence of his situation: there was no turning back for him.

"What you told me about África, that thing about me being soft . . . Did she tell you that?"

Tom dropped the stick he was moving around in the dirt.

"África is a fanatic, a machine, not a woman. Don't you realize that a person like that cannot love anyone? For her, everything is a fucking competition to see who says more slogans. And if that crazy woman ever thought you were soft, now she's going to know how wrong she was . . ."

Ramón felt the effect of those words. His muscles relaxed.

"Kid, go to your hotel, eat something, try to sleep. Think only that you're going to leave that house alive and that once you get to Moscow you'll be a hero . . . I'll take care of the rest. We're going to take you to Santiago de Cuba. I wanted to get you out to Guatemala, but Caridad wants to go with you to Santiago, because she hasn't been back since they took her to Spain. She tells a whole story about how her father was the first one to free the black slaves."

"Another tall tale," Ramón said, and nearly smiled. Tom shook his head, smiling. "My grandparents were shameless exploiters and that's how they got so rich . . . When will we see each other again?"

"I have to arrange a lot of things. I hope we'll see each other tomorrow when you finish your work at the Duck's house. Incidentally, do you know what you're going to be called when you leave there? Juan Pérez González. Original, right?"

Ramón didn't answer. Tom stood up and, in silence, they went down to where the Chrysler was parked. The adviser drove to the city center, his eyes fixed on the road. When they entered the parking lot of Shirley Court, he looked for the Buick and stopped next to it.

"I worked with you the best I could. I have taken you to the door of the most protected man on earth and I've shown you that it's possible to do it. Now everything is left to you, and the rest depends on luck. That's why I wish you all the luck in the world. We'll see you tomorrow when you leave the house . . . Incidentally, Caridad says that the best rum in the world is in Santiago de Cuba and that her grandfather, the one who freed the slaves, was a business associate of the first Bacardis. I hope the three of us together can confirm it. The thing about the rum, of course."

Ramón recalled the conversation he had had with his mother a few days before. He then asked himself if Tom had ordered Caridad to tell that sordid story from which, if it was true, the hate marking their lives was born.

"We'll see each other tomorrow," he said, and when he went to get out of the car, he felt Tom's hand clutching his arm. The adviser leaned toward him and Ramón let himself be kissed on both cheeks, and finally he felt the man's lips on his own. Tom released him and patted his shoulder.

Ramón Mercader had to wait twenty-eight years to get another kiss from the man who had led him to the shore of history.

Sylvia insisted that they go to the hospital. Jacques took two more painkillers and, with a damp handkerchief over his eyes, leaned his head on the pillow and begged her to leave him alone. The tiredness, the pain,

475

and, at last, the relief brought by the pills plunged him into sleep, and when he awoke the following morning, he didn't know where or who he was. The hotel room, Sylvia, the typewriter on which he had placed the pages of the article, brought him back to reality and into the soul of Jacques Mornard.

He took a long shower and, despite his lack of appetite, managed to ingest the café au lait, fresh bread smeared with butter and strawberry jam, and a strip of fried bacon. He drank coffee and got dressed. Sylvia watched him the whole time, like a little scared animal, without daring to speak. The woman stopped hesitating when she saw him take his hat.

"Dear, I—"

"I'm going to the office to see what those damned construction workers are doing."

"What time are we meeting Jake Cooper and his wife?"

"At seven."

"Where are you thinking of taking them? Wouldn't you like to go to Xochimilco?"

"It's not a bad idea," he said. "Oh, I had forgotten . . . Tomorrow we have to travel to New York."

"But—"

"Pack our bags. In New York, I'll go back to my usual self. I think the altitude and the food in this inferno of a country are making me sick . . ." And he got closer to Sylvia. He kissed her on the lips, just brushing them, but the woman couldn't contain herself and embraced him.

"Dear, dear . . . I don't like to see you like this."

"Neither do I. That's why we're leaving tomorrow. Will you let go of me, please?"

She loosened her arms and Jacques Mornard stepped back. He took the typed pages and the portable typewriter. He observed Sylvia Ageloff, her scared-bird face, and remembered the carefree days in Paris, when everything seemed like a game of hunters and gazelles, of cold calculations that set off multicolored lights when they fitted in the predetermined places, while they went on giving shape to a story that, step-by-step, led him to a heroic climax. Without knowing why, he then said:

"At twelve I'll pick you up and we'll go eat something."

There were eight hours left until his meeting with the condemned man. What would he do until five in the afternoon, the moment set to kill a man called Lev Davidovich Trotsky? He drove the Buick to the outskirts of the city and thought of África again and, for the first time in many months, of his daughter, Lenina, of whose life and fate he had never received any news. She must be six years old already and perhaps was still in Spain, without the least idea who her father was. What would it have been like to live with his daughter? The damned fascists and the blasted war had cut off that possibility.

He drove in the direction of the tourist complex where he had lived for several months. He looked for the path on which he had hidden the ice axe and stopped his car next to the porous rocks. He opened his trunk, took out the typewriter and the envelope in which he kept the letter written by Tom. He sat down in the shade of the tree and began to read it. He couldn't concentrate: each word led him to lost memories, the singing of the birds bothered him, even the murmur of the nearby stream—and because of that he had to go back over the text several times until he felt that, like other lies, he could also absorb these, inject them into his blood and take them out of his brain at will. Next to him, the cigarette butts piled up and his stomach had turned into a boiling cauldron. Fortunately, the headache that had irritated him so much was gone.

He recited the letter from memory and replayed in his mind, with utmost care, the chain of actions he would have to execute that afternoon. His victim's skull and thinning hair were the point he always reached; then he got lost in confusion. In reality, he didn't even know if he would try to escape. He feared that his legs wouldn't respond and that, if he managed to get to the yard, he would give himself away with his confusion. What most bothered him was not being able to clearly discern his feelings, since he was convinced that it would not be a normal fear that could paralyze him or induce him to betray himself by running. It was a new and sharper fear that grew within him, a terror over the certainty of having lost it all, not just his name and control over his own decisions but the solidity of his faith, his only support. And cursed time wasn't moving . . .

Ramón would always remember the end of that morning and the beginning of the afternoon of August 20, 1940, those agonizing and turbid hours. The entire arsenal of psychological resources they had armed him with in Malakhovka had become jammed in his mind and the only thing that remained of his training was the hate—but no longer the central and basic hate they had instilled in him; rather, it was one that was getting all the more dispersed and difficult to control, a complete hate bigger than himself, visceral and all-consuming. Close to one o'clock he remembered that he had made plans with Sylvia. He knew that a strange anticipation had led him to arrange that meeting. If he didn't want to go crazy, he needed to fill his time, and Sylvia could once again be useful. He stood up and beat the typing machine against the rocks, threw its fragments toward the stream and returned to the car.

Sylvia was waiting for him at the door of the hotel, in the company of Jake Cooper and the woman who had to be his wife, a young woman so blond she seemed yellow. Ramón would always think that he had never managed to exercise greater self-control than during the conversation he maintained for a few minutes with Jake, Jenny, and Sylvia. After introducing his wife, Cooper explained that he had coincidentally walked by and seen Sylvia. Ramón would remember vaguely that he had smiled, perhaps even made a joke, and confirmed the date they had that night at seven. He bid them goodbye and went with Sylvia to the Don Quijote restaurant at the Regis Hotel, where they served Spanish food. As soon as he ordered, he lit a cigarette, told the woman his head hurt, and fell silent.

Sylvia told him something relating to Cooper and his wife, talked about some people she had to visit in New York, and told him that, before leaving, she would like to say goodbye to Lev Davidovich. Jacques, who could barely taste the food (he would never be able to remember what they had served him, only that he could barely swallow), told her he would pick her up at five so that they could stop by the house in Coyoacán for a few minutes. Then he felt an urgent need to be alone. He calculated that in less than three hours he would kill a man. He took out some bills and handed them to the woman.

"You pay. I have to go get the plane tickets," he said, and drained his glass of water. He stood up and looked at Sylvia Ageloff. At that moment Ramón noticed a warm feeling of relief running through him. He leaned over and pressed the woman's lips with his own. She tried to take his hand, but he avoided it with a rapid gesture. Sylvia had carried out her last function and wasn't worth anything anymore. Sylvia Ageloff belonged to the past.

At four in the afternoon, tormented by a persistent beating in his temples and sweating that came and went, he decided it was time to put an end to his agony. He left the movie theater, where he had spent almost two hours thinking and smoking, and returned to the car. He took the raincoat from the trunk, adjusted the Star at his waist, and confirmed that the other weapons were in their place. He placed the pages of the article in the outside pocket and put away the letter in the summer sportcoat he had chosen that morning. With the raincoat on the passenger seat, he drove, paying as much attention as he was able to, convinced that he had more than enough time to get to Coyoacán. When he passed in front of the small stone chapel, he was tempted to stop and enter it. It was a fleeting idea, arising from the most remote area of his unconscious, and he discarded it immediately. God had nothing to do with his story; besides, he wasn't fortunate enough to believe in a God. He no longer believed in many things.

It was eight minutes to five when he turned down Morelos and made a half turn onto Avenida Viena before stopping the car in front of the house, pointing it again toward the Mexico highway. He put his hand in the pocket of his jacket and took out the letter, wrote the date on the first page—August 20, 1940—and his signature—*Jac*—on the last one. He folded the papers and pressed his temples, ready to burst, and repeated twice that he was Jacques Mornard. He took a deep breath, put the letter in his pocket, dried the sweat off his forehead, and got out of the car. Charles Cornell, the guard on duty in a tower, greeted him, and he tried to smile at him while making a gesture with his hand. The Mexican policeman posted next to the bulletproof door gave him a nod, but he didn't deign to respond. The door's mechanism activated and Harold Robbins, with a rifle slung over his shoulder, shook his hand. When Robbins let him pass, Ramón remembered something. He took one step back and looked out to the right side of the street. About 150 yards away, he saw a dark green Chrysler, although he couldn't make out its occupants.

"Mr. Trotsky is expecting me," he said to Robbins.

Jacques arranged the raincoat over his left arm again, searching for a balance between the length of the fabric and the weight of the weapons.

"I already know . . . He's at the rabbit cages," Robbins said, and pointed to where the Exile, his head covered with a straw hat, was tending to the animals.

"Sylvia and I are leaving for New York tomorrow."

"Business?" Robbins asked.

"That's right," Jacques said, and Robbins returned to the door.

479

Ramón looked at the yard. He could see only the figures of the Duck and Azteca the dog. He walked toward them slowly.

"Good afternoon."

The old man didn't turn around. He had just placed the fresh grass in the metal basket of one of the compartments.

"I've brought the article," he said, taking the typed pages from his raincoat pocket and holding them out as if they were a safe-conduct pass.

"Yes, of course . . . Let me finish," the condemned man asked.

Jacques Mornard took a few steps toward the center of the yard. He was overcome by dizziness and thought of sitting on the iron bench. At that moment Natalia Sedova came out of the kitchen and walked over to him. At the door's threshold, Jacques saw Joe Hansen, who waved at him and went back into the house.

"Good afternoon, Madame Natalia."

"To what do we owe you coming around here again?"

"The article, don't you remember?" he said, and immediately added: "Tomorrow, we're going to New York."

Azteca had gotten close to him and he looked at the dog as if he couldn't see him. His stomach was in flames; he was sweating again; he feared losing his concentration.

"If you had told me before, I would've given you correspondence for some friends," the woman said sadly.

"I can come back tomorrow morning."

Natalia thought about it for a moment.

"No, don't worry . . . So you brought the article?"

"Yes," he said, and handed it to the woman.

"At least it's typed. Lev Davidovich doesn't like to read things that are handwritten," she said, and pointed at the raincoat. "Why are you carrying that around?"

"I thought it was going to rain. Here the weather changes in just a few minutes . . ."

"In Coyoacán, it has been sunny and hot all day. You're sweating."

"I don't feel very well. My lunch didn't agree with me."

"Do you want a cup of tea?"

"No, I still have food at the top of my stomach. It's suffocating me. But I would love a little water."

The condemned man had come closer and heard the end of the conversation.

"I'll go get the water," Natalia said, and returned to the house.

Jacques turned to the old man.

"It's the altitude and the spices. They're going to kill me."

"You have to take care of your health, Jacson," the Exile said, taking off his gloves. "You don't look very well . . ."

"That's why we're going to New York: to see a good doctor."

"A sick stomach can be a curse; I'm telling you because I did mine in by mistreating it for so many years."

The renegade slapped his legs so that Azteca would come over to him. The dog stood up and put his front feet on the old man's thighs. He patted the animal with both hands below his ears.

"Sylvia is about to arrive. She's coming to say goodbye."

"Little Sylvia is very confused," the Exile said as he cleaned his glasses with the edge of the light blue shirt he was wearing.

Natalia Sedova returned with a glass of water, placed on a small plate, and Jacques thanked her and drank two sips.

"Let's see this famous article," the renegade said, and without further ado he walked to the dining room entrance but stopped, and Jacques almost bumped into him. He addressed his wife in Russian: "Natasha, why don't you invite them for dinner? They're leaving tomorrow."

"I don't think he'll want to eat," she answered, also in Russian. "Look at his face: he's practically green."

"He should have had some tea," the man said, now in French, and resumed walking.

Jacques followed him to his workroom. When they passed the dining room, he saw the table set for dinner, and it seemed an incongruous image. When he entered the office, he saw that the dictaphone had been moved to the side of the desk; in its place before the renegade's chair were a dozen books, all of them thick and dull looking. The window to the garden was open, as on the previous occasion, and he could see the plants, beaten by the sun, still strong at that hour of the afternoon. The condemned man again cleaned the lenses of his spectacles and, as if he were annoyed, held them up to the light. Finally he moved his chair and Jacques handed him the pages. The man pulled toward him the folder on the desk labeled with Cyrillic characters, perhaps to use it to lean on.

"Do those letters mean 'Private'?" Jacques asked, without knowing why.

"Do you know Russian?" the Exile asked.

"No . . . but . . ."

"They are some notes. A kind of diary that I write when I can . . ."

"And does it say anything about me?"

The condemned man sat down and said:

"It's possible."

Ramón asked himself what that man could say about a man like Jacques Mornard, and he realized that he was worrying too much about something insignificant. Even though the conversation had served to definitively displace Jacques and his mind was now occupied only by Ramón, for a few seconds he had almost forgotten his mission. Nonetheless, a piercing desire to read those papers made him think of the possibility of taking them with him when he escaped: it would be like reaching the ultimate degree of perfection to appropriate the body and also the soul of his victim.

Ramón Mercader regained control when, from his position, he again saw the head, the white skin under the sparse hair that, he thought fleetingly, always seemed to need a trim at the bottom. Almost without realizing it, his mind began to work automatically, with simple reasoning, leading to just one purpose; no matter how hard he tried, for many years he could not remember having thought of anything but the mechanics designed to place him behind the seated man. He would not even remember if the beating in his temples or the shortness of breath were bothering him at that moment. Days later, he would start to recover the details and even believed he had embraced, at some moment, the dream of escaping and saving himself. Perhaps he also thought of África and her inability to love. Perhaps about the tumultuous way, in a matter of seconds, he was going to enter history. If it was not a trick of his memory, the image of a beach where two dogs and a boy were running passed through his head. In contrast, he would always remember with shocking clarity the feeling of freedom that began to run through him when he saw the renegade prepare himself to read those typed pages. He noticed how a kind of weightlessness invaded his body and his mind. No, his temples weren't beating anymore; he wasn't sweating anymore. Then he tried to recover the hate that that head had to provoke in him and enumerated the reasons he was there, a few inches away from it: the head of the revolution's greatest enemy, of the most cynical danger threatening the working class; the head of a traitor, a renegade, a terrorist, a reactionary, a fascist. That head held the mind of the man who had violated all the principles of revolutionary ethics and deserved to die, with a nail in the head, like an animal at the slaughterhouse. The condemned man was reading and, once again, he was crossing out, crossing out, crossing out, with brusque and annoyed gestures. How dare he? Ramón Mercader took out the ice axe. He sensed it hot and exact in his hand. Without taking his eyes off the victim's head, he placed the raincoat on the low shelves behind him, next to the globe, which tottered and was about to fall. Ramón noticed that his hands were again bathed in sweat, his forehead was burning, but he convinced himself that to end that torture he just needed to lift the metallic spike. He observed the exact spot where he would hit him. One blow and everything would be over. He would be free again: essentially free. Even if the bodyguards killed him, he thought, his freedom would be absolute. Why hadn't he hit him already? Was he afraid? he asked himself. Was he expecting something to happen that would prevent him from doing it? That a guard would enter, that Natalia Sedova would come in, that the old man would turn around? But no one came, the globe didn't fall, the ice axe didn't slip out of his sweaty hand, and the old man didn't turn around at that moment—but, in French, he said something definitive:

"This is garbage, Jacson," and he crossed the page with his pencil, from right to left, from left to right.

At that moment Ramón Mercader felt that his victim had given him the order. He lifted his right arm, brought it well behind his head, squeezed the trimmed grip forcefully, and closed his eyes. He couldn't see, at the last instant, that the condemned man, with the typed pages in his hand, turned his head and had just enough time to discover Jacques Mornard while he was bringing down the ice axe with all of his might in search of the center of his skull.

The cry of horror and pain shook the foundations of that useless fortress on Avenida Viena.

28

I don't know at exactly what moment I started to think about that; I don't know if I already had it in my head at the time that I met the man who loved dogs, although I suppose that it must have been afterward. What I am very sure of is that, for years, I was obsessed (it sounds a little exaggerated, but that is the word and, moreover, it is the truth) with being able to determine the exact moment at which the twentieth century would conclude and, with it, the second millennium of the Christian era. Of course, that would in turn determine the moment that would start off the twenty-first century and, also, the third millennium. In my calculations (I always counted by the age) I would be—fifty or fifty-one?—upon the awakening of the new century, according to the date on which the end of the previous one was established—in the year 1999 or in 2000? Although for many the crossroads of the centuries would only be a change of dates and diaries among other, more arduous concerns, I insisted on seeing it another way, because at some moment in the terrible preceding years, I began to expect that that leap in time, as arbitrary as any human convention, would also propitiate a radical turn in my life. Then, against the logic of the Gregorian calendar, which closes its cycles in years with zeros, I accepted, as part of a convention and like many people in the world, that December 31, 1999—soon after my fiftieth birthday—would be the last day of the century and the millennium. As the date approached, I was excited to know that computer programmers around the globe had worked for years to avoid the computer chaos that the radical alteration of numbers could produce that day, and that the French had placed an enormous clock on the Eiffel Tower counting down the days, the hours, and the minutes to the Great Leap.

That's why I took it as a personal affront that, when the date arrived, in Cuba a more logical calculation was made and it was decided, more or less officially and without appeal, that the end of the century would be December 31 of the year 2000 and not the last day of 1999, as the majority thought and wanted. Because of that almost state decree, while the world celebrated the (supposed) arrival of the third millennium and the twenty-first century with great fanfare, on the island we bid the year farewell and greeted the newly arrived one like any other, with the usual anthems and political speeches. After having dreamed for so long of the emergence of that date, I felt that they had swindled me of my excitement and anxiety, and I even refused to watch the brief news flashes on television of the celebrations that, in Tokyo, Madrid, or next to the Eiffel Tower, were greeting the perfect four-figured sign on the historic clocks. My malaise lasted for several months, and when, on December 31, 2000, some Cuban newspaper announced without much interest that the world was truly and Gregorianly arriving at the new millennium, it barely surprised me that no one could be bothered to celebrate what almost all of humanity had already feted. At that moment, I knew all too well that, besides some shitty numbers, nothing would change. And if it did change, it would be for the worst.

I bring up this episode that for many would be insignificant and seemingly removed from what I am telling, because it seems to me that it captures the perfect metaphor: at this moment, I don't think there are many people who will deny that history and life have treacherously shown no mercy to us, to my generation, and, above all, to our dreams and individual wills, subjected to the straitjacket of decisions that were impossible to appeal. The promises that had fed us in our youth and filled us with faith, participative romanticism, and a spirit of sacrifice turned to salt and water as we were besieged by poverty, exhaustion, confusion, disillusionment, failures, escapes, and upheaval. I'm not exaggerating if I say that we have traversed almost all the possible phases of poverty. But we have also witnessed the dispersal of our most resolved or most desperate friends, who took the route of exile in search of a less uncertain personal fate, which wasn't always so. Many of them knew what it meant to be uprooted and the risks of chronic nostalgia that they were throwing themselves into, how many sacrifices and daily concerns they would be subject to, but decided to take on the challenge and set forth for Miami, Mexico, Paris, or Madrid, where they arduously began to rebuild their lives at an age at which, in general, they are already built. The ones who, out of conviction, a spirit of resistance, the need to belong, or simple stubbornness, apathy, or fear of the unknown, chose to stay, more than reconstruct anything, dedicated ourselves to awaiting the arrival of better times while we tried to erect stanchions to avoid collapse (in my case, living between stanchions has not been a metaphor but rather the daily reality of my little room in Lawton). At that point at which life's compasses go mad and all expectations are lost, so too are all our sacrifices, obediences, deceits, blind beliefs, forgotten slogans, atheisms and cynicisms more or less conscious, more or less induced, and, above all, our battered expectations of the future.

Despite that tribal destiny in which I include my own, many times I've asked myself whether I have not been specially chosen by that son of a bitch providence: if in the end I haven't ended up being something like a branded goat designated to receive as many kicks as possible. Because I received the ones that were due to me generationally and historically and also the ones that they gave me cruelly and treacherously in order to sink me and, in passing, to show me that I would never have peace or calm. Because of this, in what was perhaps the best period of my adult life, when I began my relationship with Ana, I fell in love completely for the first time and, thanks to her, I regained the desire and the courage to sit down and write until my wife's illness began to worsen, crushing any hope I had left. And on December 31, 1999, when they told us that the day of the great change I had been dreaming of for so long would not change anything, not even the disgusting century in which we had been born, I saw the bluebird of my last hope fly out the window of the little apartment in Lawton—an insignificant bird, but one I had raised with care and that the winds of high decisions were taking from my hands. Because the authorities had not even allowed me that innocuous dream.

At the end of the 1990s, life in the country had begun to regain a certain normality, lost during the hardest years of the crisis. But while that new normality returned, it became clear that something very important had come undone along the way and that we were in a strange spiral in which the rules of the game had changed. From that moment on, it would no longer be possible to live on the few pesos of the official salaries, the times of equitable and generalized poverty as a social achievement had ended, and what was starting was what my son Paolo, with a sense of reality that superseded mine, would define as every man for himself (and which he, like many of the children of my generation, applied to his life in the only way within his reach: by leaving the country). There were people like Dany who, relying on cynicism and a better spirit of survival, had more or less managed to adapt themselves to the new reality. He had left his job at the publishing house and bagged all of his literary dreams and now earned much more money as a hired driver of the 1954 Pontiac that he had inherited from his father. Besides, his wife had an attractive job at a Spanish company (where they paid some dollars under the table and gave out a couple of bags of food twice a month) and they lived with some comfort. But the ones who didn't have anything to hold on to or anywhere to steal from (Ana and I, among many others) began to see things for ourselves as even darker than in the years of the endless blackouts and the breakfasts composed of orange-leaf teas. With Ana retiring early and with my demonstrated incapacity for practical life, the rope we had around our necks did nothing but get tighter, until it had us continuously on the verge of suffocating, from which we were saved only by the gifts that the owners of dogs and cats presented to me for my services and the additional pesos that the pig breeders gave me as payment for the castrations, worm removal, and other jobs for which I charged the ridiculous price of "give me what you want." But it was clear that we had fallen to the bottom of an atrophied social scale where intelligence, decency, knowledge, and capacity for work gave way before craftiness, proximity to the dollar, political placement, being the son, nephew, or cousin of Someone, the art of making do, inventing, increasing, escaping, pretending, stealing everything that could be stolen. And cynicism, bastard cynicism.

I knew then that for many in my generation it wasn't going to be possible to come out of that mortal leap unscathed without a safety net: we were the gullible generation; the one made up of those who romantically accept and justify everything with our sights on the future; the ones who cut sugarcane convinced that we should cut it (and, of course, without charging for that infamous work); the ones who went to war because the proletariat and internationalism required it, and we went without expecting any recompense except for the gratitude of Humanity and History; we were the generation that suffered and resisted the ravages of sexual, religious, ideological, cultural, and even alcoholic intransigence with just a nod of the head and many times without filling up with the resentment or the desperation that leads to flight—that desperation that now opened the eyes of the younger ones and led them to opt for escape before they even got their first kick in the ass. We had grown up seeing (that's how myopic we were) in each Soviet, Bulgarian, or Czechoslovakian a sincere friend—as Martí said—a proletarian brother, and we had lived under the motto, repeated so many times on school mornings, that the future of humanity belonged completely to socialism (to that socialism that, if anything, had only seemed to us a little ugly aesthetically—only aesthetically grotesque—and incapable of creating, shall we say, a song half as good as "Rocket Man," or three times less lovely than "Dedicated to the One I Love"; my friend and buddy Mario Conde would put Creedence Clearwater Revival's "Proud Mary" on the list). We went through life removed, in the most hermetic way, from the knowledge of the betrayals that, like that of Republican Spain or invaded Poland, had been committed in the name of that same socialism. We didn't know anything about the repressions and genocides of peoples, ethnicities, entire political parties, of the mortal persecutions of nonconformists and religious people, of the homicidal fury of the work camps, and the credulity before, during, and after the Moscow trials. Nor did we have the faintest idea of who Trotsky was or why they had killed him, or of the infamous subterranean and even the evident agreements of the USSR with Nazism and imperialism, of the conquering violence of the new Muscovite czars, of the invasions and geographic, human, and cultural mutilations of the acquired territories and of the prostitution of ideas and truths, turned into nauseating slogans by that model socialism, patented and led by the genius of the Great Guide of the World Proletariat, Comrade Stalin, and later patched up by his heirs, defenders of a rigid orthodoxy with which they condemned the smallest deviation from the canon that sustained their excesses and megalomania. Now, with great difficulty, we managed to understand how and why all of that perfection had collapsed like a giant meringue when only two of the bricks of the fortress were moved, a minimal access to information and a slight but decisive loss of fear (always that infamous fear, always, always, always) with which that structure had been

488

glued together. Two bricks and it came down. The giant had feet made of clay and had only sustained itself thanks to terror and lies. . . . Trotsky's prophecies ended up coming true and Orwell's futurist and imaginative fable *1984* ended up turning into a starkly realistic novel. And there we were, not knowing anything . . . or is it that we didn't want to know?

Was it pure coincidence or did he consciously pick that horrid night of 1996, after almost twenty years? In the afternoon, a storm of rain and thunder had been unleashed that seemed to announce Armageddon, and when night and the blackout came, there was still a cold and persistent drizzle falling. Because of that, when he knocked at the door, I supposed it was someone pressed to have their animal looked at and, lamenting my luck, went to open the door with one of those little kerosene lanterns in my hand.

And there he was. Despite the time, the darkness, the fact that he had gone completely bald and that he was the person I least expected to find at the door of my house, I recognized the tall, thin black man at first sight and immediately had a very strong certainty that, throughout all those years, he had been watching me in the shadows.

Faced with my silence, the black man said good evening and asked me if we could talk. Of course, I invited him to come inside. Ana was with Tato in the room, trying to listen to a soap opera through the modulated frequency band of our battery-operated radio, and I shouted to her not to worry, I would take care of our guest. With my usual clumsiness, augmented by my surprise, I told the man to be careful with the bowls placed around the room to collect the rain that leaked from the ceiling and I asked him to sit down on one of the iron chairs. After settling in the other chair, I stood up again and asked him if he wanted to drink some coffee.

"Thank you, no. But if you would give me a little bit of water . . ."

I served him a glass. The black man thanked me again, but he drank only a couple of sips and left the glass on the table. Despite the half-light, barely broken by the lantern's flame, I noticed that in those minutes he had studied the apartment's atmosphere, as if he needed to formulate an overall opinion about who I was or look for a way to escape in the face of any dangerous situation. Since the black man was thinner, older, without a hair on his head, in the scarce light of the lantern, his face looked like a dark skull—a voice from beyond the grave, I thought.

"*Compañero* López asked me to come see you sometime," he began, as if it was taking a lot of effort to get started. "So here I am."

You took some time to come, I thought, but I kept my mouth shut. Coming out of the shadows and the past, he would only tell me what he decided to tell me, so it wasn't worth the trouble of trying to force any specific conversation.

"Did you receive Luis Mercader's book? At the post office, they guaranteed that if you didn't receive it, they would return it to me."

"So how did you know my address?"

"You know that here everything is known," he said, elusive. And without further ado, as if he were repeating a libretto he had studied for a long time, he explained that in 1976 he was working as a driver for an army leader. One day they called him and told him that, since his superior was being sent to the war in Angola and he was a man of complete confidence, a party militant, a veteran of the clandestine struggle, they were going to entrust him with a special mission, that of driving and to a certain extent taking care of Jaime López, an officer of the Spanish Republican army living in Cuba whom doctors had prohibited from driving his car. They also warned him that in that job he should keep his mouth shut—with everyone. And they asked him if he saw anything strange around the man, he should inform them immediately, and they specified that, when it came to that Spaniard, anything could be strange . . .

When he began to work with López, there were already other *compañeros* tasked with taking care of him, of taking him to a special clinic and even of driving him when he went to certain meetings or very specific visits. They never told the black man who López was and, of course, he hadn't dared to ask, although from the beginning he assumed that with so many people around him dedicated to his care (and to keep watch on him? he wondered), he thought he couldn't be just any López . . . Almost two years later, when the man was already doing very poorly and some nephews and, later, his brother showed up in Cuba, he learned at last that Jaime López was Jaime Ramón Mercader del Río. Since he had never in his life heard anyone talk about Ramón Mercader and almost nothing about Trotsky, and since he couldn't ask anyone anything that had to do with that man, he realized that he was involved in something too big for a simple driver, no matter how much of a party militant or army veteran he was. And if they had told him he had to keep quiet, he knew that the best thing was to keep quiet.

490

The tall, thin black man confirmed for me that Jaime Ramón López had traveled to Cuba in 1974. Although he didn't know it at the time, he would later come to be certain that they had opened the Soviet cage and allowed Mercader to come to the socialist island, the birthplace of his ancestors, because death had already marked him. Just when the arrangements for his trip were being finalized, suddenly the first flare-up of the strange illness had come up. The doctors at Moscow's most select clinic, where they treated the Kremlin's highest in command, diagnosed a hemorrhage caused by a pulmonary infection. Ramón, who until that moment had possessed a constitution capable of resisting twenty years of prison and its attendant horrors, spent three months at the hospital. Later, even when the diagnosis was favorable, he felt that something inside him had come undone. From that moment on, despite the temporary improvements, his body would never again respond to him the same way and he would live until his death with those dizzy spells, intermittent fevers, headaches and sore throats, and a permanent difficulty in breathing. But he still did not know that in reality he had a cancer that would end up corroding his bones and his brain.

"They had run thousands of tests on him," the black man said to me, and in his voice I seemed to notice a touch of sadness. "I don't even know how many analyses, encephalograms, X-rays, without finding anything. But when the Cuban oncologists finally saw him, they immediately diagnosed cancer . . . Doesn't it seem strange?"

"Luis Mercader says that Eitingon was sure that in Moscow they had poisoned his blood with radioactivity. With the gold watch that his comrades from the KGB gave him . . . Activated thallium."

"Yes, that's precisely why I'm telling you it's strange."

"But I don't believe it," I said. "If they had wanted to kill him, they would've killed him and that's that. They had lots of time and opportunity."

"Yes, that's also true." He nodded and almost seemed relieved to accept the possibility. "Well, the doctors found the cancer at the beginning of 1978, after he had spent a few months in bed because the dizzy spells barely let him walk. When that crisis began, he said that it was all because of the pain it caused him to sacrifice his dog, Dax, the male, remember? Because of those dizzy spells, he couldn't go see you as he had arranged. And a few weeks later, when he didn't know if he would ever be able to go back outside, he began to write those papers I sent to you years ago, until he couldn't write anymore, almost couldn't even move . . . The poor man was screaming like a madman at the end because of the headaches, and every time he moved, he could break a bone. Morphine kept him alive until October."

"Just hearing about it gives me pain," I commented.

"You don't know anything about pain . . . The worst thing about it was that he never lost his lucidity. In August he was so bad that his brother Luis came to be with him when he died. But Luis had to leave at the end of September because the Soviet permit that, after much struggle, authorized him to return to Spain with his wife, was expiring. Two weeks after his brother left, Ramón received a letter from him: he was in Barcelona already . . . I heard him say that he was going to die with the satisfaction of knowing that at least one person from the family had managed to return . . ."

"So he had asked to come to Cuba?"

"It appears so. It's not like he had too much to pick from . . . On the one hand, the Soviets didn't want to release him, and on the other, it wasn't easy for someone to decide to take him. Of course, no one wanted him . . . I think that coming here was the only alternative. I don't know how all of this was negotiated, but the condition for him to live here was that he live incognito. Despite that, some people recognized him, but the majority of people who were close to him—almost all of us who tended to him when he was sick and even visited his house, his children's friends, the doctors—we didn't know who *compañero* López was in reality. I found out because of the level of trust we came to have. Because I was with him until the end . . ."

At that moment, I felt that an old and dormant fear was waking in some part of my memory, and I dared to ask him: "And you didn't tell your bosses that López was seeing me? Wasn't I one of those 'strange' things?"

That was the only time the whole night that the black man smiled.

"No, I didn't have time to inform. The first time you saw each other, I think you met by coincidence, and I didn't think much of it. The second time, after you talked, he asked me not to say anything so that you wouldn't be scared away and he could talk to you. Seems as though he liked you, no?"

"I think something else, but it doesn't matter . . . So the nurse . . . ?"

"She's my sister. She did me the favor . . . The poor woman, now she's very ill, she's going to die at any moment . . . The problem is that López had tasked me with giving you those papers, but I didn't dare come . . . Although I didn't make any report, they learned that you were seeing each other and I imagine they were watching you a little bit and . . ."

In another time, that news would have paralyzed me, but in 1996 it seemed folkloric, even comical because it had been a while since I'd crossed over the borders of nothing and almost reached invisibility. That was why I was more interested in knowing what that man thought and felt than trying to understand what was meant by "watching you a little bit."

"And now . . . why did you decide to come now, after so many years?"

The tall, thin black man looked at me and I knew I had stepped on a landmine. By what I could see of his face, I realized that he was deciding whether he should stand up and leave my house. Later I thought of the motives for which, at the end of so much time, that man dared to disobey a mandate that perhaps no one remembered and fulfill the promise of coming to see me. Maybe he was dying, like his sister, and he decided that it no longer mattered what could happen to him. Or because things had changed so much, and he was less fearful. Perhaps he dared because, after reading Luis's book, he understood that it didn't matter too much if he told me something, since I could get my hands on the information in other ways . . . Or he simply decided because he thought it was his duty to tell me after having promised a dying man: it seemed that someone, for once, had done something normal in this whole story . . .

"Do you think I was a coward?"

I tried to smile before responding.

"No, of course not. I was the one who was shitting myself with fear. And that's even when I wasn't sure that they were watching me 'a little bit' . . ."

But my response didn't satisfy him, because he continued with his interrogation.

"Why do you think Luis waited almost fifteen years to write the book? He was already living in Spain. Who could he have been afraid of?" he asked me, maintaining the same timbre, the same intonation, as if he were playing a fixed dramatic role in that frame of mind. "Why did Luis wait until the Soviet Union and the KGB and everything hanging on it disappeared?"

"Out of fear," I answered, and then I did what I could to look into his eyes when I asked: "So why did you put the book in the mail to me? Nobody asked you to . . ."

"When I read it, it seemed that if there was someone who had to read it, it was you. Especially because Mercader was dead and you didn't know it. But also to give you an idea of what fear is, how great and long it can be . . ."

"You're telling me all this because you read López's letter, right? So tell me, why does it end like that?"

The black man thought again. And he decided to answer me.

"Because López—I mean, Mercader—couldn't write anymore. In April, when they discovered the cancer in his glands, they sent him for radiation, but it had already spread. In June or July, he was so fucked up that he broke an arm when he went to lift a glass of water. His bones started to shatter. He couldn't write anymore . . . That's why it ends like that: suddenly."

"And do you know if he saw Caridad again?"

"One of the people who worked with López from the beginning told me that his mother had come to see him here at the end of 1974 and that she had ruined his holidays and, in passing, those of his wife and his children. She was a crazy and unbearable woman, he told me. She had friends in Cuba, old Communists she had met here in the 1940s and later in France, and she even passed herself off as a Cuban . . . That must have been the last time they saw each other, because the following year she died in Paris, I imagine desiring to return to Barcelona, like all of the Mercaders, because Franco beat her in the battle against death by a month and kept the doors of Spain shut to her. Through López's wife I learned that she had died alone and that her neighbors discovered the corpse because of the smell . . ."

While I listened to the stories of abandonment and death that that man was telling me—that man who, despite his decision to come to see me, was still surrounded by fear—I discovered that again a bothersome unease was threatening me, a surreptitious feeling that was too close to compassion.

"Bad luck pursued them. It was like a punishment," I said.

The black man barely nodded but remained silent, observing the buckets and the cans collecting the water dripping from the roof.

"This house is going to fall down on you," he said at last.

"You really don't want coffee?" I asked him again, since I had gotten lost in the conversation, although I knew that I had several holes yet to fill in and I was certain that was the last time I would speak with him.

494

"No, thank you, really, no. I have to leave already . . . Let me see if I can grab a bus."

"So why do you know so much about Mercader? Why did he trust you and give you those papers?"

"When we went to walk the dogs, he talked to me a lot. Sometimes I think he told me all of that so that I would then tell someone. Although he never confessed to me who he was or what he had done . . . That, I had to discover on my own. He told you more things than me . . ."

"So what about the borzoi bitch, Ix? What happened to her?"

"You see? Because of that I think that he trusted me a lot. López gave her to me, because his wife didn't want to keep the dog. It was like the inheritance he left me, right? . . . Ix lived with me for four more years . . ."

"And what about Dax? How did they sacrifice him?"

Again the black man looked at the ceiling of the apartment, dark and agonizing, as if he feared that its collapse could be imminent.

"In reality, they all ended up fucked-up, even Stalin," he said, as if that same night, in my ruined and shadowy house, he had had that revelation. He took his eyes off the ceiling and looked at me. "López felt very bad, but one day he asked me to take him with Dax to a little beach that is near Bahía Honda. There's never anyone there, but since it had recently rained it was a little cold and there wasn't a single soul around. López let him off the leash, let him run a little while, but Dax got tired right away and started to cough. He spent a lot of time caressing him, talking to him, until his cough went away and he lay down. Dax loved to have his belly dried. After a while, he put the towel over his head and took out a gun . . . López was sure that his dog had died in the best way, without knowing it, almost without having time to feel any pain . . . That was at the end of January. We never went back to the beach . . ." The black man stood up, and at that moment he didn't seem that tall. "How long has it been since the lights went out?"

"About five hours . . . I try not to keep track. After all . . ."

As we spoke, the man was digging in one of his pockets.

"*Coño*, I almost forgot."

He took out a piece of cloth, smaller than a handkerchief, and opened it. He took something out and put it on the table: even in the weak light, I was able to recognize the valiant gas lighter that had belonged to Jaime López.

"It's yours," he said, and cleared his throat. "That's your part of the inheritance."

The end of the century and the millennium were approaching when, of nothing more than old age, Tato, Ana's poodle, died, and my wife's osteoporosis entered its most aggressive period with the sustained crisis that left her practically an invalid, with very strong pain, for three months. We had still not imagined the true seriousness of her illness, and all my friends, inside and outside Cuba, began to look for what seemed to be the only remedy for her: vitamins—calcium with vitamin D and B complex, above all—and bone enhancers, including the supposedly miraculous shark cartilage and those Fosamax tablets with such strong effects that, after ingesting them, the patient had to remain upright for an hour. So Ana improved, at the same time that Truco, the mangy stray mutt that I had picked up shortly after Tato's death, was getting fatter, turning into the family's happiest and liveliest member.

The expected change of century and millennium passed and the world, having turned into a place that was getting more and more hostile, with more wars and bombs and fundamentalisms of all kinds (as could be expected, after going through the twentieth century), ended up turning into a remote place for me, repellant, with which I was cutting ties, as I let myself drift along on skepticism, sadness, and the certainty that solitude and the most resounding neglect awaited me just around the corner.

What most pained me was seeing how Ana, despite passing improvements, was gradually dying within the four damp and flaking walls of the propped-up little apartment in Lawton. Perhaps because of it, first as a companion to my wife's desperation, and then as a practicing member, I approached a Methodist church and tried to pin my hopes on the great beyond, where perhaps I would find everything that had been denied to me in the great over here. But my capacity to believe had been ruined forever, and although I read the Bible and attended worship, I constantly broke the rules of a rigid orthodoxy demanded by that faith which had too many unappealable obligations for one lifetime, too many desires to control the faithful and their ideas for a freely chosen religion. Control, damned control. What ended up complicating my credulity was the demand for a necessary Christian humility proclaimed from the pulpits by a theatrical hierarchy, whose sincerity I began to doubt when I learned of the existence of cars, trips abroad, and privileges acquired in exchange for forgetting the past, for complicity and silence. If it had not been for

Ana, more than once I would have told all those pastors where to go and shove it. But she always told me that God was above men, who were sinners by definition, and so I shut my mouth, as was habitual in my life. Then I grabbed onto the essentials that offered me escape and forced myself to believe in what mattered. I didn't succeed. I didn't care about the great beyond or the salvation of my immortal soul. Or about the great over here with its manipulated promises of a better future at the cost of a worse present. I would have preferred other compensations.

Looking for medicine for my wife, smoking cigarettes with a suicidal intensity, taking care of Truco after each accident or street fight for which he had such a propensity, practicing a tyrannical religion without faith, looking stoically at the chinks in the walls and ceilings that would eventually lead to the collapse of our small apartment, and curing dogs as poor and scruffy as their owners—these turned into the limits of my shitty life. Each night, after putting Ana to bed (she could no longer do it herself)—and without any desire to read, much less to write—I acquired a taste for climbing my neighbor's wall and sitting, whether it was hot or cold, on the fork made by the branches of his mango tree. There, under the gaze of Truco, who followed each one of my movements from the hallway, I smoked a couple of cigarettes and felt the plentitude of my defeat, of my anticipated old age, of my cosmic disillusion, and examined the almost dead conscience of the regrettable being that turned into the same man who had once been a boy who was pregnant with illusions, and seemed gifted to tame fate and make it bend down at his feet. What a disaster.

In that incorruptible spirit I asked myself, as I observed the infinity of the universe, who the hell cared what I could say in *one* book? How was it possible that I had let myself be convinced by Ana, but above all by myself, and had tried to write *that* book? Where had I gotten the idea that I, Iván Cárdenas Maturell, wanted to write it and perhaps even publish it? Where, at some point in a far-off life, had I pretended and thought I was a writer? And the only answer within my reach was that the story had pursued me because *it* needed someone to write it. And the bitch had picked me.

PART THREE

Apocalypse

29

Moscow, 1968

A second time they summoned the man who had been
  blind.
"Give glory to God by telling the truth," they said. "We know
  this man is a sinner."
He replied, "Whether he is a sinner or not, I don't know.
  One thing I do know. I was blind but now I see!"
John 9:24–25

Moscow could also be infernally torrid, and the afternoon of August 23, 1968, had to have been the hottest of the season. But, thanks to their medals, they didn't have to show any kind of credentials for the doors of the decrepit Hotel Moscow to open to them and for the fresh air of the screeching air conditioners to welcome them.

In recent years, Ramón Pavlovich had resorted to the tactic of hanging the powerful medals of Hero of the Soviet Union and the Order of Lenin on his lapel, which managed to force open, without violence, almost all of the doors in the greatest and most closed country in the world. In reality, it had been Roquelia who made that fabulous discovery, one winter morning in 1961, as she shivered in an endless line that snaked all the way toward October Twenty-Fifth Street, in front of the windows of a shop in the GUM gallery. Cursing her luck, the cold, the lines, and the shoving that she had to stoically withstand, Roquelia had seen a man with crutches and a missing leg pass in front of the crowd of aspiring purchasers and, without asking permission, enter the store and leave with six packages of the coveted Hungarian salami and twelve cans of the elusive crabmeat from Kamchatka. The impunity with which the wounded man passed before the combative Russian matrons at the head of the line—who limited themselves to pressing their faces against the establishment's window to count, in agony but in whispers, the number of salamis the man was dropping into his bag (terrified at the possibility of hearing the cry most feared by the Soviets: "It's all gone, comrades!")— had moved her in a proletarian way, since even in Mexico, or in any other capitalist country, there had never been deference like that toward an invalid. Because of that, when the man dropped the last item in his bag (into which two bottles of vodka had also fallen), Roquelia made use of gestures and her rudimentary Russian and discussed the matter with the woman who was behind her in line; she was surprised to find out, or in reality thought she found out, that the man's mutilation had nothing to do with his privilege, which actually came from the medal hanging on the pocket of his frayed cloak. The wounded man was a hero of the USSR and, as such, he was authorized to go in front of everyone else in every line, even when they had slept on the sidewalk overnight to have the certainty of obtaining the desired product. What Roquelia was sure of was that the man's decoration (she approached him almost to the point of impertinence and nausea, because of the stench he gave off) was similar to one her husband had in a drawer at home. Because of that, the following night, when she attended a party with Ramón organized by the Casa de España, Roquelia asked the old exiled Republican women and was certain that her life in Moscow had changed. From that day on, whenever she went out in search of some product in deficit (the list could be interminable), she made her husband go with her. From his jacket she hung the prestigious medals to obtain Bulgarian sausages and Hungarian salami and toilet paper, oranges and tickets to the Bolshoi alike.

The previous afternoon, the phone had rung while Ramón Pavlovich was reading an issue of *L'Humanité* that, every morning, he bought at the newsstand located on the north exit of Gorky Park, next to the Frunze Quay. Roquelia, always resistant to lifting the apparatus and speaking in Russian, shouted to him from the kitchen to answer the phone. Ramón hated any interruption in the rhythm of his reading or when he was listening to Bach, Beethoven, and Falla, and it was especially annoying that afternoon, since he was caught up in an article that showed how the Czech revisionists had worked cunningly for an onerous capitalist restoration, turning their backs on the will of the country's workers and peasants. The Red Army, with its opportune entrance into Prague, invited by the leadership of the Czechoslovak Communist Party, only meant to guarantee the continuity of the socialist option chosen by the great masses of that country, the piece argued.

Ramón Pavlovich took off his thick tortoiseshell glasses and still had time to tell himself that that article showed that nothing had changed, not even the rhetoric. With difficulty, he stood up. No matter how much Roquelia insisted that he eat vegetables, he didn't lose weight, and with the passing of years he had become a slow and wheezing man. He lifted his feet to step over Ix and Dax, his two Russian wolfhound puppies, who, despite their youth, had turned lazy with the summer heat. Ramón was almost sure that the phone call was for his son Arturo, who, in his adolescence, had taken over the phone. On the tenth ring, he managed to raise the heavy receiver.

"*Da?*" he said in Russian, almost annoyed.

"*Merde!* You already know how to speak in Russian?" The voice, sarcastic, French, was an arrow that went through the heart of Ramón Pavlovich's memories.

"Is it you?" he asked, also in French, feeling his chest and his temples beating.

"Twenty-eight years without seeing each other, eh, kid? Well, you're no longer a kid."

"Are you in Moscow?

"Yes, and I'd like to see you. I've spent three years wondering if I should call you or not, and today I made up my mind. Can we see each other?"

"Of course," Ramón Pavlovich said, after thinking for a few moments. Of course he wanted to see him, although for a thousand reasons he doubted it was appropriate. For starters, he presumed that their conversation was being listened to, and that the meeting would be monitored by security agents, although he decided it was worth the risk.

"Tomorrow at four, in front of the beer hall in Leningradsky Station. Do you remember? Bring money: now we pay out of our own pockets. And mine aren't exactly healthy."

"How have things gone for you?" Ramón Pavlovich dared to ask.

"So fucking well," the man said in Spanish, and repeated before hanging up: "So fucking well. See you tomorrow."

Having barely hung up, Ramón Pavlovich heard the scream again. In all those years, that cry of pain, surprise, and anger had pursued him; and although in recent times its insistent presence had dissipated, it was always there, in his mind, like something latent that resolved to activate itself, sometimes by some reminiscence of the past, and many other times without any discernible motive, like a spring he had no ability or possibility of controlling.

Ever since he'd arrived in Moscow eight years before, he had been wishing to meet with that man (what the hell was his name now? What could his name have originally been before he turned into a perpetually masked man?), and only feared that the death, of one or the other, could prevent the necessary conversation that would get him closer to the truths he had never known and that influenced the path of his life so much. And now, when he already thought that nothing would happen, at last the meeting seemed about to become real, and as usual the initiative had come from his always evasive mentor.

"Who was it?" Roquelia asked when she came out of the kitchen, drying her hands on her apron. "What's wrong, Ramón? You're pale . . ."

He put his glasses back on, took a cigarette from the pack lying on the table next to his reading chair, and lit it.

"It was him," he said at last.

With a cigarette in his hands, Ramón went out to the tiny balcony from which he enjoyed a privileged view of the river and, on the other side, of the tree-lined park. From the heights of his apartment, if he looked to the south, he could see the buildings of the university and the Church of St. Nicholas; if he turned to the north, he could make out the Krymsky Bridge, where he usually crossed over to Gorky Park, and beyond that he could make out the highest towers and palaces of the Kremlin. Ix and Dax followed him and, seated on their hind legs, dedicated themselves to panting and contemplating the tiny pedestrians going back and forth across the quay. Ramón felt a lost feeling of fear return and squeeze his chest. Almost mechanically, he observed his right hand, where, an inch or so from the wound he received in the first days of the war, he had the indelible half-moon-shaped scar. He didn't like to look at those four marks hanging on his skin, since he preferred not to remember; but memory was like everything in his life ever since that remote early morning on which he said yes—it also acted with insolence independent of the reduced will of its owner.

First he had heard the shrill cry and, when he opened his eyes, saw that the wounded man, with his glasses twisted on his nose, had managed to throw himself at his weapon-holding hand and clung to it to sink his teeth in and force him to release the ice axe stained with blood and brain. What happened in the following minutes had turned into an amalgam of images where some vivid memories were confused with the stories he would hear and read through the years. The stories agreed that, perhaps paralyzed by the scream and the wounded man's unexpected reaction, he had not even tried to leave the office, and they said that while the bodyguards beat him with their hands and the butts of their revolvers, he had yelled in English: "They have my mother! They're going to kill my mother!" From what recess of his mind had those unforeseen words come? He remembered, in contrast, having managed to cover his head to protect himself from the blows, and that he started to cry upon thinking he had failed. He could not believe that the old man had resisted the blow and leaped upon him with that desperate force. Then he yelled, begging for them to kill him. He wanted and deserved it. He had failed, he thought.

Ramón could still feel in his chest a renewal of the oppression that had crushed his breath when, along with the confirmation of the condemned man's death, he heard the policeman in charge of his interrogation assure him that his victim, already fatally wounded, had saved his life by demanding that his bodyguards stop beating him, since it was necessary to make him speak. That information gave meaning to what happened that afternoon and, in a strange way, fed the cry of pain and horror clinging to his eardrums. From that moment on, he was able to evoke with greater clarity the surprising relief he felt when he stopped being hit on the head with the rifle butts, and he also managed to remember the look of disgust that at that moment Natalia Sedova directed at him and the moment in which Azteca the dog came into the room and approached the wounded man, lying on the floor with a pillow under his head. Ramón was sure he'd seen him caress the dog and heard him say not to let Seva enter.

In reality, Ramón had only completely regained consciousness when, as it was getting dark already, they had taken him out of the house, handcuffed. Before getting into the ambulance that would take him to the

Hospital Cruz Verde, he had looked to his left and, between the blood and the swelling that shot through his right eye, he was able to confirm, beyond the police cars lining Avenida Viena, that the dark green Chrysler had disappeared. In the ambulance, he told the head of his escort to take the letter he had in the pocket of his summer jacket. The pain he felt in his hand, where he had been bitten, and in his bruised head and face did not prevent, while the policeman opened the letter, a wave of relaxation from enveloping him, nor one sole idea, clear and precise, from taking control of his mind: my name is Jacques Mornard, I am Jacques Mornard.

Tom had warned him that the letter would be his only shield and, whatever happened, he should take cover from lightning and thunderbolts behind it. And so he did throughout the twenty years he spent in the hell on earth of the three Mexican prisons of his sentence. The saddest times were without a doubt the intense months in which they held him in the bulletproof cells of the Sixth Delegation, submitting him to interminable interrogations, periodic beatings, constant slaps, and daily kicks; confrontations with Sylvia, which always included the woman spitting on his face; confrontations with the renegade's bodyguards and even with several of the participants of the massive attack directed by Siqueiros ("directed by" was figuratively speaking), who, as was foreseen, could not identify him and even less still connect him to the disappeared French Jew. Later came the interviews with Belgian civil servants who demonstrated the falseness of Jacques Mornard's supposed family and national origins, and the incisive psychological tests, bordering on torture, that demanded all of his physical resistance, his intelligence, and the use of the full arsenal received in Malakhovka to keep his shield raised. The process of re-creating the attack had been especially arduous, when they forced him to represent, with a newspaper rolled up in his hand, the way in which he had hit the condemned man. Behind the mahogany desk, with his newspaper raised, he had the certainty at last that the ice axe had missed its target by a few inches because the renegade, with the pages of the article in his hands, had turned toward him. This also meant that he had had time to see the lethal point coming down and breaking his skull. That vision—which clarified why the forensics determined that the victim had received the blow from the front and explained why the old man had been able to stand up, fight with him, and even live another twenty-four hours—was so brutal that he passed out.

He also remembered the difficult moment in which the instructing judge spoke to him of the evidence that his real name was Ramón Mercader del Río, Catalan in origin, since some Spanish refugees had recognized his photo in the newspapers, and even put a snapshot in front of him, taken in Barcelona, in which he appeared dressed as a soldier. The existence of that proof came with more interrogations and torturers with the purpose of wresting from him the confession that everyone wanted to hear. The head of the secret police, Sánchez Salazar, seemed to have taken a personal interest in the need to hear that confession from his lips, and hundreds, thousands of times he repeated the same questions: "Who provided you with the weapon? Who were your accomplices? Who sent you here? Who helped you? Who provided the funds for the attack? What is your real name?" His answers, in every case, every year, and in every situation, had always been consistent with the letter: no one had armed him; he had no accomplices; he had traveled with the money supplied to him by a member of the Fourth International whose name he had forgotten; his only contact in Mexico had been a certain Bartolo, he didn't remember if it was Pérez or Paris; he was called Jacques Mornard Vandendreschs and had been born in Tehran, where his parents, Belgian diplomats, were posted, and with whom he later lived in Brussels; and he didn't know anything about any Mercader del Río, and although they looked a lot alike, he could not be the man from the photo.

His ability to resist in silence and almost arrogantly maintain what everyone knew was a lie gave him back the power and convictions lost in the days before his act. From inside, a feeling of superiority was growing in the certainty that they would not break him. More than once he thought of Andreu Nin and of the hard work he made for his captors when he wouldn't admit to the faults they tried to lay on his head. Ramón knew that if the promised protection arrived, and if none of those venal policemen or the prisoners with whom he would soon live received the order to eliminate him, he could resist for as long as necessary, in the conditions and with the specifications they imposed on him, since he knew that his life depended solely on that resistance. And, at least at the beginning, Kotov seemed to have come through, although he could only see that at the end of seven months of isolation and harassment, when they allowed him at last to receive a visit from his lawyer, Octavio Medellín Ostos, hired the day after the fatal assault by a woman named Eustasia Pérez. That woman, whom the lawyer had not seen again, had handed

507

him a large sum of money for him to use for Ramón's case until she or a designee of hers got in touch with him. Ramón then understood that he was not alone, and when Medellín Ostos asked him to tell him the truth in order to help him, he repeated again, word for word, the content of that letter he had handed to the police.

"Do you expect me to believe you, Señor Mornard?" the lawyer said to him, looking into his eyes.

"I only expect you to defend me, Counselor. In the best possible way."

"It has already been proven that everything you're saying to me is nothing but lies. You're not Belgian, nor does Jacques Mornard exist; you were never a Trotskyist, nor did you plan the murder a week before. It's very difficult this way . . ."

"So what can I do if, despite what everyone wants to believe and say, that is the only truth?"

"We got off on the wrong foot," the man lamented. "Let's break it down: the Mexican government is going to push until you confess, because your crime has caused an international scandal. For weeks here, people even forgot about the war. Did they tell you that Trotsky's funeral had the largest crowds seen in this country for the death of a foreigner? They know that your identity is false and that you understand Spanish as if it were your native language. All of this they have demonstrated by conceding you the honor of giving you the first polygraph test done in Mexico. They've proven that the story of your meetings with Trotsky to prepare attacks in the Soviet Union is a lie, since the house's visitors book confirms that you didn't spend more than two hours total with him, the majority of that time in front of other people. Everyone knows that your friend Bartolo Paris is a ghost and that the letter you handed over and have repeated to me is a mockery. Whoever wrote that letter is a cynic with the greatest disdain for intelligence, since he knew that those lies would be discovered in ten minutes. With all of this against you and with the government insistent on getting the truth, how can you expect me to defend you if I know that you're a liar?"

"You're the lawyer, not me. I killed him for the reasons I say in the letter. That is all I can say. And I need you to do me a favor. Buy me some prescription glasses, since I can't see anything lately," he said, willing to face all the consequences.

Ramón experienced a shock when Roquelia came out to the balcony with a glass of water and a cup of coffee on the colorful Uzbek tray.

"What does that man want from you now?" she asked while Ramón Pavlovich drank the water.

"To talk, Roque, only to talk," he said, and gave her back the glass, ready to drink the coffee.

"Do you need to roll around in the past? Isn't it better to live in the present?"

"You don't understand me, Roque. It's been twenty-eight years of silence . . . I have to know . . ."

"Ramón, you have to recognize that things are not good. Look at Czechoslovakia . . . Do you think they'll ever let you leave here?"

"Forget about that already, please. You know they'll never let me leave. Besides, I don't have anywhere to fucking go . . ."

He took the first sip of coffee and looked at his wife. Not even Roquelia, after fifteen years together, could understand what that meeting with his old mentor meant to him. From the beginning, even when he was convinced that Roquelia had been sent to him by his distant bosses, he had decided to keep the woman at the margin of the deepest details of his relationship with the world of shadows, since not knowing was the best way to be protected. He had taken the same attitude with his brother Luis, since they had met again in Moscow and the latter had confided in him, very secretly, his aspiration of one day returning to Spain.

"Don't worry, they can't do anything to me anymore. They already did it all," he said, and finished his coffee.

"They can always do more. And now we have children . . ."

"Nothing's going to happen. If I don't talk . . . I'm going out to walk the dogs."

With a cigarette in one hand and the leashes in the other, he got into the elevator with his wolfhounds and pushed the button for the ground floor. That building on the Frunze Quay, where he had moved just two years before, was inhabited by local party leaders, heads of business, and a couple of high-level foreign refugees, and had the privileges of an elevator, an intercom on the ground floor (diligently operated by the soldier employed as a doorman), granite floors, a bathroom in every apartment, a washing machine, and, above all, a magnificent location on the banks of the Moscow River, in front of Gorky Park and fifteen minutes by foot from the city center. Arturo and Laura, his children, were the ones who most enjoyed the park, where they ice-skated in winter and played sports in the summer. Ix and Dax also benefited from the park in the mornings, but in the afternoons their walk was limited to the tree-lined path that ran next to the avenue on the quay, where their owner had taught them to run and jump without getting close to the street.

Ramón let the dogs go and made the most of an unoccupied bench under the shade of some lilac trees, their branches still loaded with bells of flowers. He liked to watch his wolfhounds run, observing how their brownish hair moved while their long legs seemed to barely touch the grass, how they trotted with perfect elegance. Ever since the absurd and cruel death of Churro, the shaggy little dog who got into his trench in the Sierra de Guadarrama, he had not had another opportunity to care for a dog. In the first years in Moscow, before the adoption of Arturo and Laura, he wanted to have a puppy, but the arrival of the children, so wished for by the sterile Roquelia, had forced him to postpone that desire, since space did not exactly abound in the Khrushchevesque building in the Sokol neighborhood where they were then living. Nonetheless, when his brother Luis, perhaps fulfilling some mysterious and unappealable mandates, appeared at his Frunze apartment with the two small borzois, Ramón knew that those dogs were a reward and at the same time a punishment he had to take on, like another burden of that enduring past—from the man who, with patience and treachery, had molded his fate.

Ramón remembered that, when they issued the sentence of twenty years' incarceration, the maximum penalty allowed by the Mexican penal code, and transferred him to the dismal prison of Lecumberri (they were justified in calling it "the Black Palace"), the certainty that had sustained him until that moment suffered an upheaval; and in the creaking of that circular building, overpopulated by murderers of all kinds, his life was entering a suffocating tunnel. Only if Kotov's promise still stood, and the silence maintained during those almost two years mattered, would his life find any support. Otherwise, he would be like a shipwrecked man in the place where a man's life was valued at only a few pesos. The fear of dying, which had barely figured among his weaknesses, from that moment on came to accompany and torment him. Ramón knew that if he were dead he would be much less compromising for the men who, as the policeman Sánchez Salazar said, had provided his hands with the weapons. Nonetheless, the worst thing was thinking that protecting him or preparing his escape was no longer among the priorities of those same men, and less still of Kotov, who was surely enmeshed in other missions more important than protecting a soldier captured by the enemy and considered a casualty of battle. With that painful certainty he faced each new day, and more than once he would open his eyes, with his pupils fixed on the oppressive ceiling of his cell, appropriating the words he had heard his victim say: "I've been given another day of grace. Will it be the last?" Ever since then, the impression that his fate and that of the man he was ordered to kill had become confused thanks to a macabre confluence had pursued him without rest, just like the incorruptible scream that resounded in his ears or the half-moon-shaped scar that, for exactly twenty-eight years and two days, he wore on his right hand.

The beer hall at Leningradsky Station had not changed much in the last thirty years. Perhaps the steam produced by sweat in the August heat had increased that afternoon to a new level, but it continued to be accompanied by the stink of fish, yeast, and the rancid urine of drunks fighting over a pitcher of beer to fill it with a stream of vodka. The floor was still sticky, and the faces of the locals, with their noses crossed by dark veins and their eyes degraded behind a hepatic veil, were like a photograph immune to the passing of time; that in reality did not move, as if it feared the future promised so many times, in the same manner as those men (once upon a time hopeful of being *new*) fled from sobriety and the evidence that it usually reveals. Only the figures of a limping being, some time ago called Leonid Alexandrovich, or Kotov, or Tom, or Andrew Roberts, or Grigoriev, and one who was over a hundred kilos and had never again been called Ramón Mercader testified that things were no longer the same.

"You've turned into a fatso, kid!" the first man said, and leaped into a hug that Ramón knew would end with a nauseating kiss from which he managed to escape.

"And you're an old baldy!" he countered, and gave him the opening to trap him in a second immobilizing hug that prevented him from resisting the Russian's kiss.

"Time and sorrows," the Soviet man said, now in Spanish.

"Let's leave; this is a goddamned latrine."

"I see you've become picky. What do you think of our proletariat? They still need soap, right? But look at how you're dressed! That clothing is foreign, right? It smells of the West and decadence . . ."

"My wife brings it from Mexico."

"Does she have some to sell me?" he said, and laughed, guttural and sonorous.

"*They* also know that Roquelia brings clothing to sell?"

"*They* always know everything, kid. Always and everything."

They went out onto the street and Ramón placed the medals on the lapel of his jacket and they were able to take the first taxi in the noisy line at the station. They ordered the taxi driver to leave them at Okhotny Ryad, in front of the Hotel Moscow.

"Why do you want to go in there? That hotel is full of microphones," the Soviet man said in French when they saw the building's façade, which the passing of years had turned even more incongruous and opaque.

"Make sure you avoid them." Ramón smiled. "Wait a minute, what is your name now?"

The former Kotov again launched into his guttural laugh of old times.

"*Nomina odiosa sunt.* Remember? How do you feel about me being called Lionia, Leonid Eitingon?"

"They didn't put you on trial with that name . . . Wasn't it Nahum Isaakovich? Are you going to fucking tell me once and for all what the real one is?"

"All of them are as real as Ramón Pavlovich López. You even owe your name to me, Ramón . . ."

The Hotel Moscow was a symbol of the past that was still alive, like the two men who, thanks to their high-ranking insignias, entered the refrigerated bar that freed them from the Muscovite dogs. Leonid stopped Ramón and sniffed the air. He pointed at a table and, his limp more accentuated, led the way.

"We even have spaceships already, but the KGB microphones and the razors they sell us are from the Paleolithic age . . . Look, here's something that I'm sure no one has told you." Lionia smiled. "Many of the walls of this hotel are double, do you understand? They're made up of two walls, between which a man fits. They built the hotel like that to hear what certain guests were saying. What do you think of that?"

Ramón asked for a pitcher of orange juice, a bottle of chilled vodka, a plate of strawberries, and slices of a Polish sausage that was only sold in stores for diplomats and foreign technicians.

"And bring us caviar and white bread too," Eitingon demanded of the surprised waiter.

"Why did you call me? I thought you didn't want to talk to me anymore."

"You know I got out of jail three years ago, right?" Eitingon asked, and Ramón nodded. "When they let me out, they told me not to look for you, and I don't need to tell you what the word 'obedience' means. But a while ago I asked a friend who still works for the apparatus if anyone cared much if we saw each other and talked about old times . . . So a week ago, when they let Sudoplatov out, the friend called me and told me that, no, it didn't matter too much if I saw you . . . as long as I told them a few things later."

"So are you going to tell them something?"

"After what they did to us, do you think I'm going to help them? Did you know that they had Sudoplatov put away for fifteen years?" he said, and added in Spanish: "They can go fuck themselves and their super-whore mothers . . . I'll see what I make up for them. Is it wrong to say 'superwhores' to indicate there's a lot of them and they really are whores?"

When Ramón arrived in Moscow, in May 1960, the KGB officer assigned to him during the first months had the deference to inform him that his former mentor sent his greetings of welcome from the prison where he was confined, carrying out a sentence of twelve years for the crime of participating in a conspiracy against the government. But before that, through various letters that Caridad sent him through the lawyer Eduardo Ceniceros (who took care of Ramón after Medellín Ostos's death), the prisoner in Lecumberri had learned a little about his mentor's strange run of luck. Although the letters were intentionally confusing, incomprehensible for someone without any background, Ramón managed to gather that when his mentor returned to the USSR, after fulfilling the most important mission of his life, he had been promoted to general and given the first of his orders of Hero of the Soviet Union, awarded to him personally by Comrade Stalin. Mr. K., or the Gimp (as Caridad would call him in those letters), continued working with Sudoplatov in the so-called foreigners' department of the secret service, training the agents charged with infiltrating and sabotaging the German rear guard. For that work (what things must he have done? Ramón asked himself, although he could guess the response) he would again be decorated as Hero of the Soviet Union and promoted to brigadier general. But in 1946, Beria was transferred from the intelligence agencies to the department of investigations, and the development of nuclear weaponry turned into the greatest obsession of Stalin, who was preparing himself for atomic war. This left Mr. K. up in the air, and he was immediately withdrawn from service by the new director of the Cold War espionage and sabotage agencies. According to other letters from Caridad, who was already established in Paris by that time, everything was apparently normal in the life of that agent until, in 1951, he was imprisoned under Stalin's orders, along with his sister Sophia, a doctor, both of them caught in the net of the most recent raid of doctors, scientists, and high officers (led by the very same minister of state security, Abakumov), all of them of Jewish origins. This time they were accusing them of nothing more and nothing less than trying to poison Stalin, Khrushchev, and Malenkov in order to take power for themselves. The case had come out in the newspapers and in Lecumberri Jacques Mornard could read French, English, and Mexican dailies that gave the details of the so-called conspiracy of the Jewish doctors discovered by Muscovite intelligence, which had prevented the assassination of Comrade Stalin and the deaths of a great number of Soviets. The tone of those accusations, laden with the same rhetoric as the trials of the 1930s, awoke the fear that Ramón had managed to exorcise after more than ten years of a relatively peaceful stay in prison. For him, the story of that dismal conspiracy could only have one lesson: behind the charges of a plot lay plans to eliminate men who knew uncomfortable secrets about Stalin's past. And it was precisely his mentor, who moreover was Jewish, who knew one of the most compromising secrets. If they killed Kotov, how much time would Ramón have left? Would the kindness of the prison officials continue to be purchased by Moscow? The prisoner spent two years living with that anxiety, waiting each day to receive the news of the execution of general Nahum Isaakovich Eitingon, as the official journalistic dispatches called him. Until, in March 1953, the news of Stalin's death arrived at his prison.

Around that time, Roquelia started to take him the messages sent by Caridad from Paris. In one of the first, his mother told him that Mr. K. and all of the supposed authors of the plot, imprisoned since 1951, had been released by Beria. Ramón breathed in relief. But not for long. When the new Soviet leadership team headed by Khrushchev brought down and executed Beria, Eitingon was swept up in the raid, now accused of conspiring with his old boss to perpetrate a coup d'état, and he was sentenced to twelve years in prison. Caridad assured him in a letter that that was how Soviet gratitude was expressed and warned him to never let his guard down, since that gratitude could cross the Atlantic.

"What have you been doing with your life since they released you?" Ramón served himself the juice while Leonid drank his first swig of vodka.

"They insinuated that Khrushchev's treatment of me and other old soldiers of Beria's had been excessive. They gave me back my pension, but not my medals; they got me a job as a translator; and they gave me an apartment in Golianovo—a shell without its own bathroom. Those buildings aren't made with cement but with hate . . . Haven't you ever heard the song of the taxi drivers?" he asked, smiling, and immediately sang in Russian: "'I'll take you to the tundra, / I'll take you to Siberia, / I'll take you any place you want to go, / but don't ask me to take you / to Golianovo . . .'"

Leonid tried to smile but couldn't manage it.

"Was it very hard?" Ramón, his own prison experience behind him, felt he had the right to ask that question.

"Surely harder than your jail, and I know that a Mexican jail can seem like the closest thing to hell. But you knew you were protected and I didn't even have a nail to hang on to; you knew that you were going to be there for twenty years, but I had no expiration date. And while the Mexicans could kill you and go out to party, they're not capable of conceiving of the things that occur to our comrades when they want you to confess something, whether you've done it or not. And the worst is when you know that you are paying for faults that aren't yours. And worse still when it's your own people turning the screws . . . Add to that the fucking cold . . . How I hate the cold . . ."

Leonid wolfed down two slices of the Polish kielbasa and drank his second vodka, perhaps to warm up the cold of his memory. He moved his head, denying something remote. In reality, he said, since 1948 he had felt his luck could change. That year, Stalin started the purge of the old European antifascist fighters who were not adapting to the new Stalinist bureaucratic model demanded by socialism in expansion and by the rules of the recently debuted Cold War. The Prague purge was the sign that the clowns of the past had to be sacrificed, but Eitingon made the mistake of thinking that those new trials had nothing to do with men like him, true professionals, so useful in times of hunting.

The failure experienced by the Great Helmsman in his attempt to gain influence over the nascent state of Israel (which, after receiving support and Soviet money, opted to go under Washington's sphere) took the lid off of his passionate, long-standing hatred of the Jews. The general secretary pulled the conspiracy of the poisoning doctors out of the air and, with his sense of economy, made the most of the trial to take out of circulation other Jews and non-Jews who were potentially dangerous because of their ideas or their knowledge of troublesome secrets.

"Stalin knew he was in decline and began to identify the survival of the revolution with his own. He really thought that he was the Soviet Union. Well, he almost was. He was close to seventy years old, and after fighting so long to gather all the power in his hands, after having turned into the most powerful man on earth, he felt exhausted and began to sense what was going to happen: that when he died, his own dogs were going to villify him. No one can generate so much hate without running the risk that at some point it will overflow onto the recipient, which is what happened when he died. That's why he entered a sick world of obsessions. After the war, with the euphoria of having won and with so many things to rebuild, people were calmer and better controlled. That son of a bitch Stalin knew very clearly that, to reign until the end, he would have to make sure that no one could feel safe—ever. I really think that period after the war was much harder than the years 1937 and 1938. You don't think so? Look, kid, although he had men who had enjoyed his trust, such as Beria, Zhdanov, Kaganovich, and that son of *superwhores* Vyshinsky— and other useless ones like Molotov and Voroshilov—he suspected all of them, because he was a man sick with mistrust and fear, lots of fear. Can you imagine that, when they interrogated us, they always asked if any of those men, the ones in the highest positions, the ones he trusted, were implicated in our anti-Soviet plot? Do you know that each one of them was submitted to a terrible test? He put Polina, Molotov's wife, in a gulag for being Jewish. Kalinin's wife was imprisoned while he was president of the country, and when she got sick he had to ask Stalin, as a personal favor, for a better bed than the straw mattress on which he found her nearly dead . . . The president of the Union of Soviet Socialist Republics, kid! At that time I understood that Stalin's cruelty not only obeyed political necessity and the desire for power, it was also due to his hatred of men— worse still, to his hatred of the memory of the men who had helped him create his lies, to fuck and rewrite history. But the truth is, I don't know who was sicker, Stalin or the society that allowed him to grow . . . *Suka!*"

"This was the same Stalin whom you adored and taught me to adore?"

Every time he entered those waters, Ramón felt dislocated, as if he were hearing a story removed from his own, of a reality different from the one Ramón himself had created in his head.

"He was always the same, a son conceived by Soviet politics, not the abortion of human evil . . . ," Leonid replied, and paused. "When they took me to Lefortovo Prison, I knew everything was over. They told me that they would subject us to a public trial and asked me to sign statements in which I admitted, among a thousand other things, being up-to-date on the murderous plans of the doctors and of having given them political and logistical support. But I told them I wasn't going to sign."

"So how did you get out of signing?"

"Oh, Ramón," Leonid laughed. "Why was I going to sign? Let's see, so that you understand. How many sons did Trotsky have?"

"Four."

"I have three and several stepchildren . . . What happened to Trotsky's children?"

"They were killed, they committed suicide . . ."

"Do you remember if Trotsky had a sister?"

"Olga Bronstein, the one who had been Kamenev's wife."

"And?"

"They say she disappeared in a work camp."

"Well, I also have a sister who was one of the accused doctors . . . They sentenced her to ten years . . . Do you remember the day we went to the trial to hear Yagoda's statement?"

"Of course."

"Do you think it was worth it for me to cover myself in shit, thinking that I was going to save my wife, my children, and my sister that way? That incriminating myself in any infamy was going to help the Republic of the Soviets and, maybe, save me? What happened to Zinoviev and Kamenev? Did they save their families when they confessed that they were Trotskyist conspirators? Stalin changed the penal code to kill their children who were minors . . . If I confessed something, not only was I killing myself, but I was also going to kill other people. So I told myself I was going to take it all, and I took it, without talking. Do you know how? Well, by letting myself die bit by bit, turning myself into a skeleton that could come apart in their hands. It was the only way to avoid them torturing me . . ."

Ramón stayed silent. He remembered the upheaval he felt when he read Khrushchev's speeches, which Roquelia brought him, in which

Stalin's excesses were recognized. As soon as they put names and faces to them, the "excesses" began to be called crimes. He would never forget when, already established in Moscow, his brother Luis again stirred that pot: very secretly they had given him Bukharin's letter "To a Future Generation of Party Leaders" to read, which the Bolshevik's wife had kept in her memory for twenty years. It was the political testament of a man who, after labeling Stalinist terror an infernal machine, warned the henchmen—he must have been looking at Ramón, Kotov, and others like them—that "when dealing with indecent matters, history can't stand witnesses," and that the time of their sentencing was getting closer and closer.

"Just like them, I wasn't completely innocent, either. In the new logic, no one in this country is completely innocent . . ." Lionia had lost part of the vibrating depth of his voice. "Beria had his plans for the future and had told me about them. But not having signed that confession and Stalin's death saved me from the firing squad. Because they were going to execute me. I was the only one who knew everything about you, and also some other things that were more or less shocking, like the attack in Ankara against German vice chancellor von Papen and certain medical experiments with prisoners during the war."

"What are you talking about?" Ramón looked at his old mentor and thought that not everyone could cross the broad steppe of jail and torture with a lucid mind.

Eitingon cleaned his fingers several times with a greasy paper napkin as if he were trying to get rid of some especially adhesive substance.

"Poisons with no trace. Tests of resistance to radiation, activated thallium, uranium. They were traitors or war criminals; they were going to die anyway . . . Stalin was obsessed with the idea of making the atomic bomb. There were many tests . . . It was disgusting and cruel . . ."

Ramón looked him in the eye and saw that the old Kotov had kept that sharpened transparency of his pupils that prevented knowing when he was lying and when he was telling the truth. On that occasion, something warned Ramón that Leonid was being more honest than ever.

Eitingon took a cigarette and began to stroke it.

"When Stalin died, Beria got me out of jail. They gave me back my party card and my rank. And despite everything they had done to me—I had dropped forty kilos, I knew terrible things—I thought justice existed and that the party would save us. That's why, when I got to my house and my children told me that in those two years a couple of my friends had

had the courage to go see them and offer them some help, I told them that those comrades and they had committed a grave mistake: if I was in prison, accused of being a traitor, nobody should worry about me or sympathize with me, not even them ... What do you think? ... That was my second-to-last act of faith. I was convinced that, without Stalin and his hate, the party would be just and the struggle would regain its meaning ... But forget it, I was wrong again. Everything was rotten. How long had it been rotten?"

"What do I know? Why are you telling me all of this?"

Lionia lit the cigarette at last and moved the glass across the table as if he wanted to distance it from himself.

"Because I think I owe you my whole story. I made you what you are and I feel indebted. I was a believer, and I forced you to believe in many things, knowing they were lies."

"That Stalin wanted to kill Trotsky not because he was a traitor but because he hated the Exile?"

"Among other things, Ramón Pavlovich."

A few months after Stalin's death, when Beria fell into disgrace, Eitingon was arrested again. In reality, his old boss was aspiring to power, but he had committed, according to Leonid, the same mistake as Trotsky, that of underestimating his adversary, thinking he was better equipped, the master of information that guaranteed his ascent and impunity. Beria had seen Khrushchev dance like a clown to amuse Stalin, although they all knew that he hated the Georgian for not giving clemency to Khrushchev's son who had fallen into German hands during the war and for whom the Great Helmsman refused to trade other prisoners. Beria had seen Khrushchev cry after being scolded by the great man and had in his hands hundreds of orders of execution from the years of the purges in which Khrushchev's signature appeared as the secretary of the party in the Ukraine. Beria considered Khrushchev miserable, of limited ambitions, and that was his mistake. Khrushchev proved to be more astute, and before Beria realized it, Khrushchev had already devoured him.

The card up Khrushchev's sleeve had been the army, Eitingon said, bringing a piece of bread to his mouth. The soldiers had not forgiven Beria for having been involved in the purge of the marshals in 1937, and they saw in Khrushchev the possible successor to a Stalin who had stolen all the credit for the military victory over fascism—obtained despite Stalin, sometimes even against Stalin. Khrushchev knew how to use to his advantage the ongoing investigation into the great spoils of war that many of the generals had taken from the occupied zones of Eastern Europe. Beria had in his hands the document from the council of ministers that itemized hundreds of leather coats, dozens of paintings from the Potsdam palace, the furniture, tapestries, rugs, and other valuable objects (thousands of yards of different kinds of fabric—he loved fabric!) that the hero Zhukov had brought back with him at the end of the war. That document had cost the marshal a demotion and his removal from Moscow, and he could still be tried by a civil court. But Lieutenant General Kriukov and General Ivan Serov had also taken their share of the spoils and knew that the great marshal's fate awaited them. It was Serov, in agreement with Khrushchev, who incited his companions to carry out a coup de main against Beria, and because of that he was promoted to head of state security and head of military intelligence. The new school of generals created by Stalin did not much resemble the humble and poorly dressed officers of Lenin and Trotsky's time.

"With Beria, we all went down. Sudoplatov, me . . . my trial lasted one day, and the next I was in the first of the prisons I went through in those twelve years. I still ask myself why they didn't kill me. Perhaps it was because they knew that I knew and that perhaps at some point they would need what I knew . . ."

"So what does a man like you do when he no longer believes in anything?"

Lionia poured himself more vodka and lit another of his foul-smelling cigarettes.

"What *can* I do, kid? Flee, like Orlov? If I could do it—which is very improbable, since if I get within sixty miles of any border I get shot or they send me back to a work camp—could I leave with my children? Would I have the possibility of making a deal and offering my silence in exchange for my family's life? Would someone dare to take me in? Let's see, how many countries denied you a simple transit visa when you left jail?"

"All of them. Except for Cuba, which gave me seventy-two hours."

"Do you understand that we're like the plague? Do you realize that we're Stalin's worst creation and that, because of that, no one wants us, not here or in the West? That when we accepted the most honorable mission, we were condemning ourselves forever, because we were going to execute the revenge that Stalin's sick mind thought was necessary to hold on to power?"

"Stalin wasn't sick. No sick man leads half the world for thirty years. You yourself said that: 'Stalin knows what he's doing . . .'"

"It's true. But part of him was sick. They say he killed about twenty million people. A million could be a necessity, the other nineteen million are an illness, I say . . . But I already told you that Stalin wasn't the only sick one."

In his long years in prison, Ramón had had a lot of time to think about his life's actions and dream about that parallel existence, created by his mind in the vain attempt to overcome depression and agony. In the beginning, he managed to control his fear when he discovered that they would not withdraw the promised protection and that they were forging some plan to get him out of prison; then he forced himself to discard all of the doubts he had had when he made his way to Coyoacán that twentieth of August 1940. If he fulfilled his promise of keeping his mouth shut, he thought, his bosses, and with them history, would reward him for what he was: a man capable of sacrificing his life for the great cause. But the years passed and the escape never went further than being an idea in Caridad's mind, although the protection remained and Ceniceros the lawyer always had money to ease his life in jail as much as possible. From that point on, resignation was his only mainstay, and he tried to fight to keep his mental balance.

"I'm going to tell you something that no one knows," Ramón said, and this time poured himself a glass of vodka. He drank it Russian-style, in one shot, and felt it cut his breath short. He waited to get his breath back as he watched how Leonid devoured the slices of sausage, placing them on rounds of white bread as the starved do. "In 1948, my lawyer managed to get a letter through to me inside a book. It came from a Jew living in New York, but as soon as I read it I knew who—"

"Orlov," Eitingon jumped in, and Ramón nodded. "That faggot loves writing letters."

"It was signed by a certain Josue I-don't-know-what and it said that he was going to tell me something that an old Soviet counterintelligence agent, a close friend of his, had confided in him, things he thought I should know . . . In truth, he didn't say anything I hadn't thought, but, said by him, everything took on a different dimension and made me think . . . He told me about deception—deceptions, actually. He said that Stalin had never wanted for the Republicans to win the war and that his

521

friend had been sent to Spain precisely to avoid, first of all, a revolution and, of course, a Republican victory. The war only lasted long enough for Stalin to use Spain as a chip in his discussions with Hitler, and when the time came, he abandoned us to our fate, but with the honor of having helped the Republicans and, as an additional reward, having the Spanish gold in his hands. He also told me about Andreu Nin's murder. His friend participated in that whole show, and he told me that the supposed proofs against Nin, like the ones against Tukhachevsky and the marshal, had been put together in Moscow and Berlin as part of the collaboration with the fascists."

"That's exactly how it was," Leonid said, and drank another shot of vodka. "Stalin and his people, that son of a bitch Orlov among them, put everything together. And the best part is that they even managed to keep many people believing in them . . . Those old and unconditional 'friends of the USSR,' do you remember? How we pulled the wool over their eyes! How they liked for us to pull the wool over their eyes!"

"And he talked to me about Trotsky . . ." Ramón went silent, lit a cigarette, rubbed his nose. "He told me something that you knew very well. The old man had never made any agreements with the Germans. The proof had been the Nuremberg trials, in which not a single trace of Trotsky's supposed collaboration with the fascists appeared . . . He told me that I had been an instrument of hate and that, if I didn't believe him, he hoped I would live long enough to see how that drama would come to light . . . When I read Khrushchev's speech, in 1956, I thought of that letter a lot. The most difficult thing about all of those years was knowing those truths and being certain that, despite the deception, I couldn't say anything."

"Do you know why? Because at heart, we are cynics, like Orlov. But above all, we are cowards. We've always been afraid and what has motivated us is not faith, as we told ourselves every day, but rather fear. Out of fear, many kept their mouths shut: what else could they do? But we, Ramón, went beyond that, crushing people, even killing . . . Because we believed, but also out of fear," he said, and to Ramón's surprise he smiled. "We both know that there's no forgiveness for us . . . But luckily, since we don't believe in anything anymore, we can drink vodka and even eat caviar in this dialectical, materialist hell that is our lot because of our actions and our thoughts . . ."

———

They had agreed to meet at five, at Gorky Park, since at seven they would cross the river and go up to Ramón's apartment, where Roquelia (begrudgingly, as she always did when her husband invited someone over) would "lavish" Lionia with a Mexican meal.

That afternoon, his old mentor arrived with the news, obtained from a very reliable source, that two days before, while they were talking at the Hotel Moscow, six Soviets, holding up small signs, had gone down to Red Square to protest what they called the Soviet invasion of Czechoslovakia. Of course, neither the newspapers nor the television commented on the event, which was quickly brought under control and squashed, and had not reached the ears of the foreign accredited correspondents in Moscow. Save for the very few people in the know, that protest had never existed nor would it ever exist.

"What nerve! You have to be crazy to do that," Ramón commented.

"Or have some balls and be very, very tired of everything," Eitingon answered. "Those six guys knew they wouldn't get anywhere, they knew what was in store for them, they were sure they would never again be people in this country, but they dared to say what they were thinking. Something you and I and I don't know how many millions of other Soviets would never do, right? . . . Maybe we passed them when we were going into the hotel . . ."

"So what's going on in Prague?"

"It's the beginning of the end . . . Brezhnev went at it with all his might, twenty-nine infantry divisions, seven thousand five hundred tanks, a thousand airplanes . . . A show of force. The myth of the unity of the socialist world died in Prague, and also the possibility of renewing communism. Stalin had already fucked it up when he butted heads with Tito, and later Khrushchev crushed the Poles and the Hungarians, and even attacked the Chinese and the Albanians for being too Stalinist . . . But this is the requiem. The next time something similar arises—and it will arrive, sooner or later—it will not be to revise anything but rather to destroy it all. Don't look at me like that. This is a sick body, because Stalin invented everything that exists here and Stalin's only objective was that no one could take power away from him. That is why we are going to keep swimming, even though we will arrive dead on the shore at the end . . . And to think that Khrushchev planned the jump from socialism to communism for 1980. *Na khuy!* The things he thought of . . ."

As they killed time until dinner, they wandered the park's paths, watching the wolfhounds trot. Ramón—his former mentor's predictions gnawing away at him—had begun to think back on the time of his arrival in Moscow and his difficulties in finding his bearings in the world to which he had given the best part of his life and the loss of his soul.

When the Mexican minister of the interior agreed to the petition of inmate Jacques Mornard, to bring forward his release from prison by a couple of months, and thus avoid the scandal that journalists willing to travel to Mexico on August 20, 1960, would cause, Ramón had the conviction that he would just be going from one prison to another. His exit from the Santa Marta Acatitla jail, where he had spent the last two years of his long sentence, had been fixed for Friday, May 6, at the end of strange negotiations. Because inmate Jacques Mornard did not legally exist and, as such, did not have Belgian nationality but continued to deny his Spanish origins—proven ten years before with fingerprints from his police record prior to the Spanish Civil War—the Czechoslovak consulate agreed to issue a passport for him with the name under which he had entered prison and served his sentence. Ramón had an exact idea of his situation when Great Britain, the United States, and France refused to even give him a transit visa for the necessary layover on his way to Prague . . . Just as had happened to the renegade thirty years before, now for him the world had turned into a planet for which he had no visa. Again the macabre conjunction of fate between victim and murderer, which had exploded with the point of an ice axe, was stalking Ramón once more, only he wasn't accompanied by the remains of glory or the disproportionate hate or fear that the Exile would provoke for years. He was pursued and marginalized by disdain, disgust, the useless blood, and his role in a story that everyone wished to forget. His only refuge was a Soviet Union where, he knew well, his presence wouldn't be gladly accepted, either, since at the end of the day he was merely one of the more annoying proofs of Stalinism that the country was fighting to shake off. Throughout the last weeks of his imprisonment, avidly reading Khrushchev's new speeches in which other "excesses" of the Stalinist period were revealed, he came to fear that not even the possibility of traveling to the USSR would materialize. Would they now publicly and ostentatiously admit that Jacques Mornard or Ramón Mercader had always been an obedient Spanish Communist recruited as a soldier of the Soviet ideal to commit the most hateful and repulsive crime? Did anyone ever think he would survive that attack and all the dangers of prison, and that one day he would return from the great beyond? . . .

But Moscow was waiting for him, domineering, willing to challenge the world. The transit through a revolutionary and presocialist Cuba was so brief that he barely had a fleeting vision of Havana when the immigration police took him out of the Cubana de Aviación machine, coming from Mexico, and took him to the Soviet ship in which he would travel on to Riga. From the porthole of the cabin to which they took him, he observed the rocky image of the city's buildings, castles, and churches, its resplendently green trees and overwhelmingly clear sea, and he could feel the effects of the nostalgia for that mystical country, acquired through the memories of his maternal family, rooted for years in that land where even Caridad had been born.

The first impression he had when he arrived in Moscow was of having entered a place that smelled of cockroaches and where he would never again find the man he had once been, since the city in 1960 was no longer the capital of the same country he had visited twenty-three years before. Renamed Ramón Pavlovich López, he was confined to a KGB building in the outskirts of the city, until one morning they sent him a new suit and ordered that he be ready to be picked up at six in the evening. That night, Ramón Pavlovich entered the Kremlin again and received from the hands of head of state Leonid Brezhnev the orders of Lenin and of Hero of the Soviet Union, the plaque that proved he was among the most honorable in the KGB, a huge bouquet of flowers, and the inevitable kisses. Meanwhile, from a small record player, the melody of "The Internationale" blasted again and again. And Ramón felt calm, proud, and rewarded. The KGB officer taking care of him, and with whom he dined following the ceremony in a small hall of the Great Palace of the Kremlin, promised him that they would soon give him the keys to an apartment where he could receive his companion, Roquelia Mendoza, but at the same time he warned him that his movements in the USSR should be approved by a special office of the KGB. He could maintain contact only with the Spanish émigrés and with his relatives residing in the USSR. He was still required to remain silent, said that dinosaur, without a doubt a survivor of Beria and Stalin's times, kindly but clearly.

That conditional freedom was joined by, from the beginning, the distance with which Soviets of all ages and conditions treated him, which made him feel doubly a foreigner.

"But you *are* a foreigner!" Eitingon lit one of his cigarettes. "Or did you think that because of who you are and because you spent years in prison studying Russian that you were going to be less of a foreigner? . . . The majority of the Soviets will never leave the country, and for them what is foreign is forbidden, damned. Although they feel curiosity and even envy (all you have to do is look at how you dress, Ramón: Did your wife also bring you that shirt? No one in Moscow has one like it), above all, you inspire fear. This is a country isolated from the world, and our leaders have made sure to demonize what lies beyond the reach of their power—in other words, everything having to do with damned foreigners. Remember that by your having unauthorized contact with foreigners, Stalin could order your execution or send you to a gulag for five, ten years. The genius of the Russian people lies in their capacity for survival. That's why we won the war . . ."

"It doesn't happen to me so much anymore," Ramón recalled, "but at the beginning, when I went out on the street, I looked at people and asked myself what they would think if they knew who I was . . ."

"*Think?*" Leonid said and pointed at the sky, more or less from where the supposed order to think something should come. "Here, people almost never think, Ramón! Thinking is a luxury that is forbidden to the survivors . . . To escape the fear, it has always been best not to think. You don't exist, Ramón; neither do I . . . Even less still, those six guys who protested over the invasion of Czechoslovakia . . ."

The park, nonetheless, existed and exuded life. The Muscovites were making the most of the last month before the cold spending their hours in the open air: people were reading lying on the grass and there were even families that deluded themselves into thinking they were having a picnic in the forest. Because of that, the discovery of an open bench, protected by the shade of a linden tree, aroused suspicion in the two secret service veterans. While Ramón played with his dogs, Eitingon inspected the place and concluded that there were no microphones installed; despite what Stalin had always maintained, he said smiling, it was proven that coincidences could exist.

Settled in on the bench, Ramón chose to change the subject and told him how he had met Roquelia Mendoza and how he immediately suspected she was part of the promised help. Roquelia, a girl from the middle class who had been a folkloric dancer, was the cousin of another Lecumberri prisoner named Isidro Cortés, who had been sentenced for killing his wife. Roquelia's insistence on striking up a friendship with him revealed her true motivations.

"It was the last thing I could do for you." Eitingon smiled. "Beria authorized me to look for a sympathizer willing to help you. We sent Carmen Brufau, Caridad's friend, to Mexico, and she found Roquelia, who accepted right away because she admired you and loved Stalin. They set aside a certain quantity of money to her for your needs, besides what your lawyer was receiving."

"In 1953, they stopped sending her money for almost a year, but she kept helping me. She's ugly and rather unbearable, but I owe her a lot."

"Yes, I can imagine."

"Roquelia helped me withstand all of that . . . In prison, many people visited me, under many pretexts, but the truth is that they came to see me because they thought I was a strange bird . . . Once, a Spanish Communist came with the most beautiful woman I've ever seen in my life. Now she's very famous because of her movies. Her name is Sara Montiel."

"I've heard of her," Lionia said, distracted. "They say she's beautiful."

"You can't imagine what it's like to see an animal like that three feet away from you . . . She's one of those women who makes you want to eat dirt, to do anything . . ."

Eitingon tried to sound casual.

"How long has it been since you last saw Caridad?"

"She came to see me when I arrived and she has come back through three times. The last time, last year."

"Does she look well?"

"She's strong, with the same personality, but she appears to be two hundred years old. Well, I've turned fifty-five and I seem to be about a hundred and ten. Even though you're bald, you look better than we do."

"I must be embalmed in cynicism," Eitingon said, and laughed thunderously. "What's she doing in Paris?"

"Nothing . . . Well, now she has gotten into painting"—Ramón smiled— "and into being a grandmother to my sister Montse's children, despite Montse. The truth is that no one wants her around . . . She spent five or six years working at the Cuban embassy, I imagine as a KGB informant. She said that the Cubans are a bunch of thrill seekers who don't understand what the hell socialism is and are unappreciative misers. According to what she says, she bought the ambassador's newspapers with her own money so he would find out what was happening in the world, and now they don't even invite her to receptions. But she blames Brezhnev; she said that he gave the order to have her removed from everything. Although she still receives the pension they send her from here . . ."

"Times change. Caridad, you, and I are hot potatoes that no one wants to have in their hands. If they haven't killed us, it's because they trust that nature will soon do its job . . . ," Eitingon stated, and lifted the bottom of his shirt to show a reddish scar. "In prison, they operated on me for a tumor. It's a miracle I am alive, but I don't know until when . . ."

"Anyone who sees Caridad in Paris, posing as a grandmother and painting ugly, colorful landscapes, would they be able to imagine what kind of demon she is?"

The borzois were running through the park and Ramón was watching them, proud of his dogs' tangible beauty, when Leonid spoke again.

"I owe you many stories, Ramón. I'm going to tell you some that perhaps you don't want to hear but that I feel belong to you."

Ramón discovered at that moment that the person at his side was Kotov. His old mentor took the same position that years before he adopted in the Plaza de Cataluña, that of an alligator at rest, with a handkerchief in his hands that he used to dry his sweat.

"You once asked me if we had something to do with the death of Sedov, Trotsky's son, and I told you no. Well, it was a lie. We sent him off ourselves, thanks to Cupid, an agent we had placed very close to him. We also executed his other son, Sergei, after having him for a time in the Vorkuta camp and here at the Lubyanka, trying to get him to sign documents in which he admitted that his father had given him instructions to poison Moscow's aqueducts . . . Like us, the ones who killed those kids were following direct orders from Stalin."

"Why did you lie to me? I could have understood it was necessary."

"Because you had to be as pure as possible when you went to the sacrificial altar. The letter I gave you to carry with you that day was a string of lies, and it didn't matter whether anyone believed it or not. The plan was that you kill Trotsky and that the bodyguards kill you, as should have happened. Everything was going to be easier that way. That was how Stalin requested it. He didn't want any loose ends and he could give a shit about your life. But Trotsky saved you . . ."

Ramón felt bowled over by emotion. To hear, directly from the man who had plotted that operation with Stalin, the admission that not only had he been used to carry out revenge but that he was considered a more than dispensable piece brought down the last mainstay with which he had withstood the passing of those years full of disappointments and painful discoveries.

"But you were waiting for me . . ."

"The possibility always existed that you would manage to get out. Besides, I couldn't tell Caridad that I had sent you to the slaughterhouse, and less still that if you managed to escape, the order was to leave you in the hands of other comrades."

"Just like Sheldon, right? So, did you kill him?"

"Not directly. But nobody was killed without our authorizing it."

"If you were going to kill me, why did you protect me in jail, why did you pay for lawyers, why did you send Roquelia?"

"Because if we killed you in jail after what we had done, everyone would know where the order came from. What saved you was that you kept your silence. With the Old Man dead, Stalin didn't care very much about the rest, and least of all at that moment, with the Germans just around the corner . . ."

"So why did the Mexicans' attack fail?"

"That was botched, but that was what Stalin wanted, something spectacular, with lots of noise, so no one would forget. I saw those people two or three times and realized that Trotsky was too big for them, they were wimps and they lacked balls. That's why I didn't mix you up with them or let them know about me or you . . . What I never understood was that our man in the group—Felipe, remember?—didn't go in to confirm whether they had killed the Duck or not . . . That is a mystery I still haven't solved . . ."

Ramón lifted his gaze toward the edge of the park, where the river flowed. He felt the disappointment eating away at his insides and he felt empty. The remains of pride to which, despite the doubts and marginalization, he had clung tooth and nail started evaporating in the heat of the all-too-cynical truth. The years of confinement in prison, fearing every day for his life, had not been the worst part. The suspicions first and the evidence later that he had been the puppet of a dark and miserable plan had robbed him of sleep more nights than the fear of being knifed by another prisoner. He painfully recalled the impression of having been deceived when he read the not-so-secret report of Khrushchev to the Twentieth

Party Congress and the feeling of unease that seized him from that moment on: What would become of his life when he got out of prison?

"So why didn't they shoot me when I got to Moscow? . . . Until they gave me the medals, I was waiting for them to take me out . . ."

"You yourself said it: you had arrived in a different world. If Stalin and Beria had still been alive, you wouldn't have crossed the Atlantic. But Khrushchev would even have thanked you for telling the truth, although he could not encourage you because Stalin's spirit was alive—no, is alive—and Khrushchev didn't want to nor could he wage that war, so he preferred to look the other way and leave you alone. Now that Khrushchev has been defeated by Stalin's spirit, you don't matter to anyone anymore . . . As long as you remain silent and don't try to leave the Soviet Union."

"So what did Caridad know?"

"More or less the same as you. Remember, we never trusted too much in the nature of you Spaniards. When she returned, she tried to convince Beria to help you escape. After giving her the runaround many times, Beria finally said yes, that they would help you, but that she herself had to take care of arranging things in Mexico. Caridad was given a passport and a lot of money, and Beria sent a thug from the Comintern to give her a good scare as soon as she arrived in Mexico. Caridad just barely saved herself. She learned her lesson, went to Paris, and has laid low, without protesting again. So now she's taken to painting pictures?"

"Must I believe all of these atrocities? Were you always this cynical? Did you know they were going to kill me? Did you apply yourself to that?"

"You have to believe what I tell you: we were more cynical than you can imagine. You weren't the only one who was going to die for an ideal that didn't exist. Stalin perverted everything and forced people to fight and die for him, for his needs, his hate, his megalomania. Forget that we were fighting for socialism. What socialism, what equality? They tell me that Brezhnev has a collection of antique cars . . ."

"And you, why did you fight?"

"At the beginning, because I had faith, I wanted to change the world, and because I needed the pair of boots they gave to the Cheka agents. Afterward . . . We already talked about fear, right? Once you enter the system, you can never leave. And I kept fighting because I turned into a cynic—me, too. But after spending fifteen years in prison for having been an efficient cynic, with a few deaths under my belt, you begin to see things in a different light."

"So how can you live with that?"

"Just like you, Ramón Mercader! The day you killed Trotsky, you knew why you were doing it, you knew you were part of a lie, that you were fighting for a system that depended on fear and on death. You can't fool me! . . . That is why you entered that house with your legs shaking but resolved to do it, because you knew well that there was no way back. When you talk to Caridad again, ask her what I told her when you arrived in Coyoacán. I told her: 'Ramón is shitting himself with fear, but he's already like us, he is one of the cynics.'"

"Shut up for a while, please," Ramón said, though he didn't know if it was a demand or a plea.

With the edge of his shirt, he cleaned the lenses of his glasses, which had fogged up. In the hands that had held the ice axe, that tortoiseshell frame, purchased by Roquelia on one of her trips to Mexico, seemed like a strange and remote object. At the end of the day, Eitingon was right, he had wrapped his faith tightly around himself, in the conviction that he was fighting for a better world, to then use that faith to avoid the truths about which he did not want to think: the murders, among others, of Nin and Robles; the party's manipulations before and during the civil war; the murky stories surrounding Lev Sedov, Bob Sheldon, and Rudolf Klement; Yagoda's strange confession that he himself had witnessed; the manipulation of the events of May 1937 in Barcelona; the vagabond he'd had to kill like a pig in Malakhovka; the lies about Trotsky and his collaboration with the fascists; the malevolent use of Sylvia Ageloff . . . just one of those truths would have been enough for him to recognize that not only was he a ruthless being but he had turned into a cynic.

"In jail, I read Trotsky," he said, when he adjusted his glasses and observed, with regained clarity, the half-moon scar on the back of his right hand. "All of the prisoners knew I had murdered him, although the majority had no idea who Trotsky was or understood why I had murdered him. They killed for real reasons: the woman who cheated on them, the friend who stole from them, the whore who found herself another pimp . . . One day, when I returned to my cell, I had on my bed a book by Trotsky. *The Revolution Betrayed*. Who had left it there? The fact is that I started to read it and I felt very confused. About a month later another book appeared, *Stalin's Crimes*, and I read that as well, and I was even more confused. I thought about what I had read and for months I waited for another book, but it never came. I never found out who put them in my cell. What I did know is that if, before going to Mexico, I had read those books, I believe I would not have killed him . . . But you are right, I was a cynic on the day I killed him. That's what all of you turned me into. I was a puppet, a wretch who had faith and believed what people like you and Caridad told him."

"Kid, they fooled all of us."

"Some more than others, Lionia, some more than others . . ."

"But we gave you all the clues so you could discover the truth, and you didn't want to discover it. Do you know why? Because you liked being the way you were. Don't come to me with any stories, Ramón Mercader . . . Besides, things were clear from the beginning: ever since you knew what your mission was, there was no going backward. It didn't matter what you would read later . . ."

For Ramón, walking around Moscow during the month of September was like entering a concert when the last movement of the symphony is being executed. The volume of the music rises, all of the instruments participate, the climax is reached, but the notes reveal a sad tiredness, like the warning of an inexorable farewell. As the foliage on the trees changed colors, filling the air with ocher tones, and the sleepy afternoons began to get shorter, the threat of October and the arrival of the cold, the darkness, and the forced enclosure became palpable to Ramón. When the winter came, the old feeling, discovered thirty years before, that the Soviet capital was an enormous village stuck between two worlds would become more agressive, oppressive. The forests that grew within the city, the steppe that seemed to infiltrate itself through its disproportionate avenues and squares, would become painted with snow and ice, turning Moscow into an inscrutable territory, even more remote, populated by wrinkled brows and gross insults. Then his dream of returning to Spain would attack him with renewed insistence. With increasing frequency, as he read or listened to music, he discovered how his mind would escape from the letters or the notes and go to a Catalan beach, with rocky sand, enclosed between the sea and the mountains, where he would find himself again, free from the cold, the loneliness, the rootlessness, and the fear. He was even again called Ramón Mercader and his history disappeared like a bad memory that is finally exorcised. But Spain's doors were shut to him with a double lock, one on each side. That he had to spend the rest of his days in that world, always feeling like a prisoner between the impassable four walls of the earth's largest and most generous country, had turned into an underhanded sort of punishment from which, he well understood, there was no redemption. In search of a relief that he knew to be false, many summer afternoons Ramón escaped from his apartment, with or without Roquelia, and dragged his frustration and disappointment toward the monument to the defeat and the nostalgia of the Spaniards left stranded in Moscow.

"So, at the beginning, how did it go with your compatriots?" Eitingon wanted to know when, on the following Sunday, they met in front of the old *kofeinia* on the Arbat, which was shut down in Stalin's time because the general secretary came and went down that avenue every day on his way to his dacha in Kuntsevo. By decree, on that whole route there could not be any meeting places, or even trees: in the country of fear, even Stalin lived in fear. In Khrushchev's time, the place had been turned into a record shop where Ramón had become an assiduous seeker of symphonic treasures at laughable prices.

As they walked without a specific destination, smoking some Cuban cigars that Caridad had sent from Paris (Ramón had to wrap them in damp cloth to bring back something of their Caribbean softness), Ramón told his former mentor that a few months after his arrival in Moscow, taken by his brother Luis, he had begun to visit the Casa de España. He remembered perfectly his disappointing first incursion in that unreal territory, built with calculated doses of memory and unmemory, where the shipwrecked of the lost war swam, encouraged by the vain illusion of reproducing, in the middle of that strange country of the future, a piece of their homeland of the past. Although a good number of the refugees who remained in the USSR were members of the Spanish Communist Party, selected, welcomed, and maintained by their Soviet brothers, Ramón had also found a notable number of the so-called children of the war (renamed Soviet Hispanics) who left the peninsula when they were less than ten years old and came to the Casa de España in search of the best espresso to be had in Moscow and of a fractured cultural identity, to which they obstinately clung.

Luis had warned him that for many years the boss of that displaced tribe was Dolores Ibárruri, already known around the world as La Pasionaria. The woman was so addicted to power and command in the Stalinist sense that the simple possibility of differing with her opinions was ruled out, at least between the walls of the building and her party, of which she had been president since handing over the—shortened—reins of the general secretaryship in 1960 to Santiago Carrillo. As he listened to his brother, Ramón could not help but remember the night he went with Caridad to La Pedrera and heard the insults André Marty heaped upon La Pasionaria, her head lowered and obedient. But Ramón feared in particular the way in which his former comrades would receive him, and the fact that he could hang on his jacket the two most coveted orders of the USSR would surely not be enough to overcome the suspicions that his personal history would cause in many of them.

"The majority of them are hypocrites," Ramón said, now using Spanish. "They congratulated me on returning, on my medals, and gave me my membership card as a militant in the Spanish Communist Party, but deep in their eyes I discovered two feelings that the bastards couldn't hide: fear and disdain. For them I was the living symbol of their great mistake, when they swung like weather vanes at the orders from Moscow and Stalin's policies and many of them became—we became—hangmen; but I was also the most pathetic proof of that useless obedience . . . Some have never said a word to me. Others have become my friends . . . I think. What really bothers me the most is that they consider themselves the 'pure ones' and I am the 'dirty one,' the man of the sewer, when the truth is that more than one of them has shit all the way up to his eyeballs."

"And even further up," the former Soviet adviser confirmed.

They turned left in front of the statue of Gogol, as if they had agreed without any need for words.

"Did La Pasionaria recognize you?" Eitingon wanted to know.

"Yes, she recognized me, but she made it look like she didn't. She has always acted like I am not worthy of her. Caridad says she'll throw herself at her neck one of these days . . ."

"I should go with you one day . . . if they would let me. A few of those telling tales there would shit themselves if they saw me. They know that Kotov knows many, many stories. And if you killed Trotsky it is because we sent you to kill him. Some of them snuffed out other people because we sent them—and sometimes without our sending them—because they thought they were more worthy of being our friends if they were ruthless . . ."

The almost physiological urgency to move through known territory, no matter how thorny, had turned Ramón into a regular at the Casa de

España. Moscow continued to be for him a city of codes and difficult languages to process, and at least there, amid Stalinist Communists, some Khrushchevists, and simple Republicans weighed down by nostalgia and frustration, they had a perverse language that united them: defeat. Thanks to his brother Luis and to his own capacity for hiding his feelings, Ramón established closer relationships with old comrades from the romantic days of the struggle in Barcelona and with a few new acquaintances who, despite everything, respected him, or at least tolerated him, not as much for what he had done but for the way in which he had withstood twenty years of imprisonment and had proven he was a Spaniard, a Catalan of the kind who cannot be broken, who, moreover, preferred a fragrant stew to a solianka stinking of cabbage.

"Solianka doesn't stink of cabbage," Lionia protested. "One day I'll treat you to one, prepared by me, of course."

"Something very fucked-up happened to me when I asked to be part of the group in charge of drafting the history of the civil war, the one they started to publish in 1966 to commemorate thirty years from the start of combat."

"I already read it and what I found didn't surprise me. Franco's crimes and those of his people are the most terrible episode of what happened in Spain, what gave the war its tone—everyone knows that. But they're not the only bad stories."

"And you know that all too well, correct?" Ramón attacked, and Eitingon shrugged his shoulders. "Of course, the whole rigmarole of writing the book would be directed by La Pasionaria, and she didn't seem very happy with my being part of the team. But others insisted; I don't know if it's because they felt bad for me. In the end—so I would leave them alone, I think—they assigned me the task of interviewing veterans of the war and gathering their remembrances and interpretations of the events they lived through or knew of firsthand. As I already expected, every one I interviewed insisted on telling it the way it best suited them, sometimes without any shame, and only remembered what meshed with their political ideas, with their version of the war. Do you know how many spoke to me of the 'removals' of prisoners in Madrid and Valencia, of the executions in Paracuellos?"

"None."

Ramón looked at his former mentor and had to smile.

"It was as if they hadn't existed . . . Fear still hounded them and they didn't dare utter any truth. The worst was seeing how they twisted stories that I myself lived, that you lived when you were Kotov. The executions in Paracuellos were an anarchist thing, according to them. And the taking of the Telefónica is still a necessary action to get rid of the Trotskyists and the fifth columnists that had been found. They justify or don't speak of Nin's disappearance; some insist on minimizing the importance of the International Brigades in the defense of Madrid; they don't remember anything about the plans you prepared for them to get the other groups out of the way . . ."

As a member of the research committee, Ramón made a decision that he only shared with his brother Luis. He went to the Academy of History of the USSR, which was financing (and controlling) the project and its future publication, and began to study the documents placed at the disposal of historians. Since at that time, Roquelia, horrified by the Muscovite winter, had made her first trip to Mexico with Arturo and Laura, Ramón had more than enough time to devote to the research, and he discovered, at first puzzled and then shocked, that the documentation available to him was not only partial—overwhelmingly favorable to the Soviet and Comintern's collaboration with the Republic—but also on occasion manipulated and differing from the experience he had lived through.

"What were you expecting, kid? The true history of the conquest of New Spain?" Leonid sucked on his cigar and found it had gone out. "Haven't Franco's men done the same thing, but less gracefully and more shamelessly? . . . Here all Khrushchev's thaw did was move around a little bit of leftover snow. Neither the Spanish Communists nor the Soviet government were in a position to get to the bottom of things, nor did they want to, because, even when it's frozen, that dark thing hiding underneath is all shit. It's like the petrified mammoth shit they found a little while ago in Siberia, thousand-year-old shit, but shit nonetheless."

Long before Eitingon put it into paleontological terms, Ramón had understood that the order had been given that the shit, no matter how old, could not and should not come to the surface. He knew it the morning he arrived at the Academy of History and the kind archivist who had helped him was not at her post. She was out sick, the substitute commented to him, and then took his slip and returned five minutes later with the information that the files requested by Comrade Pavlovich López had been transferred to a closed section and could only be accessed by those with an authorization from the Kremlin office in charge of the History and Social Research Institutes. Ramón was not even surprised that when the first volumes of *War and Revolution in Spain, 1936–1939* were published, bearing the logo of the Progreso publishing house, his new name did not appear among the members of the research committee, presided over by Dolores Ibárruri and made up of her most loyal squires.

"How did you feel?" Eitingon wanted to know.

"Frustrated, but what the hell, I'm already used to it."

"Yes . . . Now, just remember that rewriting history and putting it wherever is most convenient to those in power was not something Stalin invented, although he used it, in his rough and contemptuous way, to the utmost. And talking about 'revolution' in Spain, when that was the first thing that was impeded, and without going into the Republican alliance's cruelties . . . well, that's really making a bitch of history. That's why it's better to have a muzzle on historical controversy . . ."

Eitingon made an effort and managed to light his cigar again. Ramón looked at his: it was still burning evenly and happily.

"Things have been going on at the Casa de España lately."

Although many refugees had managed to return to Spain starting in 1956, the ones who still remained fought to gain power. La Pasionaria, who had the loyal Juan Modesto as her deputy, felt that in recent years her absolute preeminence had come under question: Enrique Líster, who carried the record of his legendary participation in the civil war, the Great Patriotic War and in the Yugoslav guerrillas behind him, and Santiago Carrillo were becoming more notably opposed to the famous Stalinist militant's power. "It's the same song over and over," Luis had said to him when the break was becoming visible. "The day we stop fighting amongst ourselves, we'll have ceased to be Spaniards."

"It's not that you are or are not Spaniards, kid, it's that you're politicians," Lionia said, this time in Spanish. "Franco's end is on the horizon, and the time for the harvest is near. You have to be ready in case there's a new division of power. You have to improve your image, keep up with the times!"

They both knew that the waters of the Casa de España, before whose walls they stood at that moment, had become very murky in recent months. Due to the Soviet intervention in Prague, some of the leaders of the Spanish Communist Party had dared to express doubts regarding the pertinence of the invasion, which caused a schism in the party's leadership. To Eitingon, that attitude responded to the need to distance itself from the darker side of Soviet influence and put on a more seemingly democratic face; to Ramón, it was just a propitious although dangerous opportunity to gain some power within the colony, but above all, in a future Spain. The most daring refugees, incited by Santiago Carrillo and Ignacio Gallegos, had even decided to dig around in the Casa's archives and in the personal records of each one of the Spaniards settled in the USSR. That proposal had been like bringing a flame to dynamite. If certain documents zealously guarded on the second level of the Zhdanov Street building were circulated, many of the plots and cruel maneuvers would come to light in which many of the refugees, turned into informants and betrayers of many others, were involved. And so comrades of so many years moved this time by the fear of being discovered, again divided into bands to launch a war that went from words to blows and the breaking of chairs. From the lower level of the former bank building, Ramón showed Lionia the third-floor window from which one of his compatriots was thrown.

"They say he fell there, in the middle of the street. Everyone thought he had been killed, because he wasn't moving, but suddenly he stood up, spit, scratched his head, and went back upstairs to continue handing out blows."

"And then they say *we're* savages." Eitingon smiled as they resumed their walk. They made a stop at the Sardinka beer hall, where Spanish refugees tended to satiate their alcoholic thirst, because of the wise prohibition of serving any of that flammable substance within the confines of the Casa.

The war of blows between the Spanish Communists ended with the arrival of the militia, who emptied the place, Ramón went on. At the same time, the reasons for its foreseeable continuation disappeared that same night, when a KGB unit took away the files full of the fratricidal revelations for safekeeping.

An hour later, when they came out at Dzerzhinsky Square, Ramón looked at the statue of the founder of the Cheka out of the corner of his eye and at the most feared building in the Soviet Union, behind the bronze man.

"Did I tell you I was also down there?" Leonid said, again in French, pointing at the Lubyanka's basement with his nose. "I don't know how long, but it was the worst time of my life . . . *Yob tvoyu mat!*" he exclaimed with an anger from deep inside, and Ramón didn't know if he was cursing the building or the bronze idol.

"Ever since I got to Moscow, it has always seemed odd to me that that statue survived the reforms."

"They had enough work with the statues and busts of Stalin. There were millions throughout the country. In Georgia, where Stalin was bloodier, since it was where they knew him best, there were mobs when they tried to take down the largest ones. The people were already so used to living under Stalin, to playing by his rules, that they were afraid that somebody could think they had approved of the demolition of those statues! Do you realize what fear can do when it turns into a way of life? To fill the millions of holes left by the removed statues of Stalin, they had to produce hundreds of statues and busts of Lenin."

They crossed the square, and when they got to Kirov Street, Eitingon entered a liquor store and came out with two bottles of vodka. On Petrovsky Boulevard, they looked for an empty bench. Before sitting down, Leonid slapped his limping leg three times while he called it *suka* and took his first drink. He put two fingers to the base of his neck, asking for company, but Ramón rejected the invitation. The sun was starting to set and the afternoon was becoming cool. When he saw Eitingon lounging comfortably, he wondered if a drink wouldn't do him some good, although he preferred to wait.

"What happened with the Casa de España files and the power disputes among the Spaniards reminded me of something that you surely don't know," Eitingon said, and had a second drink. "When Stalin died, a lot of things happened in very little time. Beria, Khrushchev, Bulganin, and Malenkov went right into action and practically the first thing they did was send a special group from the Ministry of the Interior to gather all of Stalin's belongings and files that were in the Kuntsevo dacha and in his offices at the Kremlin. Svetlana, Stalin's daughter, had the pass taken away from her with which she could enter her father's offices, and until last year, when she finally managed to flee from the Soviet Union, she always said that Khrushchev and Beria had stolen Stalin's treasures."

"What treasures was she talking about?"

"There were no treasures. What need for money or jewels does a man have who is the lord and master of an enormous country and all it contains? And when I say everything, it's *everything*: the mountains, the lakes, the snow, the airplanes, the petroleum, even its people—the life of its people . . . It's true that there were many silver objects, especially busts and plaques he had been given, but all of those were sent to a foundation. The furniture, the china, the rugs, and those things were distributed to different places. It was decided that the History Institute's Section for the Family conserve his marshal's uniform and some samples of the gifts workers gave him every day. But the majority of his clothing wasn't worth anything, some was fairly worn-out, and what didn't get thrown out was donated to centers for handicapped veterans."

"So there was no money?"

"There was. Those in charge of the operation were overwhelmed by the amount of envelopes with bills that were everywhere. Stalin earned a salary for each one of his ten posts, but as he didn't have to buy anything, not even to give gifts or host parties . . . But that money didn't make anyone rich, and what my companions were looking for were documents. Those seeking power, without telling each other, were afraid that a testament like Lenin's would appear, which would complicate things for some of them and benefit others. That was why they decided, like knights, to take all of Stalin's papers out and burn them so that none of them would have the advantage or disadvantage of having been selected or rejected by Stalin."

"And how do you know all of this?"

Leonid took another swig and Ramón held out his hand to take the bottle. He needed a drink.

"When I recovered a little, after getting out of jail, I began to work with Beria. They made me part of that team and I was one of the ones who, after the burning of the papers, found, in a drawer of a table in the office of the Kremlin, some letters that had been hidden under newspaper. There were five—just five letters—and it appears that Stalin read them from time to time. One was the one dictated by Lenin on March 5, 1923—I can't forget the date—in which he demanded an apology from Stalin for having insulted his wife, Krupskaya. Another one was from Bukharin, written shortly before he was executed, in which he told Stalin how much he loved him . . . And there was one, very short, written by Marshal Tito, dated 1950, I believe, but I remember perfectly well what it said: 'Stalin, stop sending assassins to liquidate me. We've already caught five. If you don't stop, I personally will send a man to Moscow and there will be no need to send another' . . ."

"So did anyone ever find out that Stalin's papers had disappeared?"

"Nothing has ever been said officially, of course. But besides the personal documents, there were what were called 'special files,' a supersecret record where laminated documents were kept and which could only be viewed if Stalin himself authorized it. These were kept and I imagine that within them there must be some reports that are too uncomfortable, because nobody yet knows where they are, if they still exist. Hopefully, one day they will be able to be read, because on that day we're going to discover that the earth is not round . . ."

"For example?"

"Stalin's pacts with Hitler and later with Roosevelt and Churchill. Or do you think that the partition of Europe was done just like that, à la 'I got here first and this is mine'–style? How can you explain that the Communists didn't come to power in Italy or Greece when they were the strongest party after the war? Or the Poles—do you think that the Poles are Communists and love us like brothers?"

Eitingon lifted the bottle, but something stopped him. He was serious, silent, until he said:

"Do you think they'll ever knock down Lenin's statues as well?"

Ramón looked at the river, where the sun was setting, and asked:

"Was our thing in those files?"

Eitingon at last took his drink and rolled down a little bit more on the bench. Suddenly he seemed relaxed.

"No, our thing never appeared. First of all, because almost nothing was written, and what was written went directly to Stalin's personal files. Beria told me that, at regular intervals, the Undefeated Leader sat down in front of the stove to burn what he had in Kuntsevo and turned the papers he thought should never be read into smoke. That's what I call having a good sense of history. We, like many other parts of history, went to the clouds, Ramón, sent there by our dear Comrade Stalin."

Ramón suspected that he could be exceeding the limits of what was allowed when he accepted the invitation. His game of "How far can I go?" seemed similar to the one the Czechoslovaks had played throughout the first month of that year of 1968, and he presumed that, if he reached the limit, perhaps then his defenses might be invaded with infantry, tanks, and planes willing to reestablish order. But he decided to try their tempers once again.

In his conversations with Leonid Eitingon over the last two months, Ramón had received so many confirmations and revelations about his fate and of the fates of so many millions of believers that he had become addicted to those dialogues, which shed light on the actions of his life, on the very idea for which he had fought, killed, endured prison and torture, to end up living an amorphous, disappointed, aimless life. Both knew uncomfortable pieces of the past and they comforted themselves with those painful plunges into the dark depths through which their lost souls wandered. Eitingon, from the vantage point of his cynicism and with the penetrating influence he had always exercised over his pupil, had forced him to see himself from other angles and, above all, to notice the shadowy side of the utopia for which Ramón had gone, pure and full of fervor (Leonid *dixit*), to the sacrificial altar. He discovered or confirmed that, among the many who were defrauded, he had a certain right of priority, like in the lines at the stores: his act stood out in that infinite circus ring where the whips have so often cracked and the clowns so often danced with their frozen smiles.

Luis had assured him that he knew Moscow like the back of his hand and that they wouldn't have any problems finding apartment 18-A, stairway F, of building 26-C, block 7, of Karl Marx Street, in the neighborhood of Golianovo. Eitingon had given them the statue of Lenin with his arm extended toward the future as a reference: from there, they would go as far as the Friends of the Militia kindergarten and, after turning to the left—always to the left, he repeated—they would find the street, the block and the building just next to the Ernst Thälmann kindergarten.

From the very day that, for his services to the Soviet homeland, he was assigned that nationally manufactured car—that, fresh from the factory, already needed a shove for its doors to close—Ramón had handed it over to his brother, since, despite his position as an engineer and university professor, a militant in the party and a veteran of the Great Patriotic War, Luis Mercader had still not managed to climb the ladder and obtain his own vehicle. That night, Luis went to pick him up a little bit before seven and, since Roquelia preferred to stay at home, Galina, Luis's wife, chose to leave her children with Ramón's so to better enjoy the adventure.

Golianovo reeked of Stalin. The housing blocks, square and gray, with tiny windows where the residents hung their clothing to dry, were separated by flattened dirt paths plagued with trees fighting for space. The monotony of that rushed architecture, insistent on demonstrating that a few square feet of ceiling were enough for a person to live socialistically, caused vertigo with its uniformity and depersonalization. The numbers that ought to identify blocks, buildings, and stairways had been erased long ago by the snow and the rain. The street signs had disappeared and, over each recycled pedestal (they counted four), rose one of the statues of a frowning and watchful Lenin forged in series by voluntary labor. But none of those Lenins were pointing anywhere. When they asked the few passersby out defying the cold about the address—it was Galina's mission, since she was a native—it always ended up being familiar, but did they mean Marx Street, Marx and Engels Street or Karl Marx Avenue? And yes, of course, they had heard of the Friends of the Militia kindergarten, and invariably they told them to turn to the left—always to the left—and ask around there, pointing at an unspecific point in the labyrinth of buildings copied from the template with the most terrifying faithfulness.

Since Leonid Eitingon was not one of the few privileged ones to whom the regional council had granted a private telephone, when Luis found himself lost in a corner of the satellite city, after searching for almost an hour, Ramón proposed they give up. He regretted that his former mentor would have invested time and savings in preparing them a worthy meal, and that they would not be able to give him the bottles of vodka that clinked next to Galina every time Luis went over a pothole, but they had to admit that they were hopelessly lost in the middle of the proletarian metropolis. At that moment Luis discovered the miracle of a taxi right in the middle of Golianovo and, after he gave the driver a bottle of vodka, he led them, in two minutes, to building 26-C of block 7. Galina then left the car and went to knock on the door of the closest apartment. A woman who still had traces of the countryside came out to the street with her and pointed at the second-to-last staircase of the large building and, with her hands, counted the floors they had to climb to reach the apartment they were looking for.

Eitingon received them with a big smile and they all had to submit to his bear hug and his alcohol-flavored kisses. While he thanked them for the vodka, he introduced his wife, Yevgenia Purizova, fifteen, perhaps twenty years younger than her husband, although she seemed even more wrinkled than him. According to what Ramón had managed to find out, when he left jail, Eitingon had resumed his relationship with his first wife, Olga Nahumova, who died shortly after, and he had been living with Yenia, who became his fifth wife, for two years.

The host and his visitors settled around the table in the center of a room

543

that was sometimes a living room and that, as they would later find out, also served as the bedroom for Yenia's two daughters, who lived with them. On the table, covered with an oilcloth sheet, there were already plates with copious appetizers of extreme flavors with which Russians padded their stomachs in order to drink more vodka: sliced ham, pickles, tomato and apple, strips of herring and salmon, a little bit of red caviar, scallions, Russian salad and fresh salad, sausage links, little squares of lard, and black bread.

"I don't know what you have to complain about," Ramón said as he cut one of the sour pickles, of which he had, curiously, become a fan.

Leonid served vodka in glasses almost to the brim and asked his wife to bring the pitcher of orange juice, specially prepared for Ramón, as he rarely drank alcohol. From the small kitchen came the pungent smell of boiled cabbage, and Ramón begged that the *pelmenis* serving as the main course not be loaded with the spicy pepper capable of making him cry.

"I didn't expect you so early," Lionia said as he handed Galina and Luis their glasses.

"But we've been driving around for an hour . . . !" Ramón began, giving free rein to his annoyance.

"It's normal. What do you think of my neighborhood?"

"It's horrible," Ramón admitted, and took a bite of caviar on black bread.

"That's the word, 'horrible.' Beauty and socialism seem to play on opposite teams. But you get used to everything. Do you see how lucky you are to live overlooking the Frunze and to have three bedrooms and even a balcony? . . . *Da dna?*" he challenged Galina and Luis, and the three raised their glasses and hurried their vodka in one gulp, until they saw the bottoms of their glasses as their host requested.

"I didn't always live like that. When Roquelia arrived, they gave us an apartment a little bit bigger than this one, in Sokol . . ."

"That can't be compared to this. Sokol is the waiting room to paradise, Ramón. You walk a little bit and you're in Utopia."

Ramón recalled his wanderings through Utopia, as Eitingon called it. In the 1930s, when the repression and the scarcity were at their highest, a group of artists, mostly painters, had obtained the Leader's permission to create an ideal commune in Sokol, and even received materials to make single-family houses with backyards and gardens. Many built izbas and Nordic cabins, but also, here and there, you could see a small Moorish palace or a house with a Mediterranean air. With full intent, they made sinuous streets with parks on the corners, on which they built beautiful pigeon houses in a variety of designs. The private areas and the communal ones were planted with a variety of trees not found anywhere else in the city, like rhododendrons, almond trees, and quince trees distributed in such a way that in autumn their leaves offered a spectacular chromatic show. From the rushed uniformity of the buildings built by Khrushchev where he had been confined, Ramón only needed to cross two streets to enter that singular space in Moscow, where the free will of its inhabitants had determined the kinds of houses in which they wanted to live and the trees they wished to plant. That part of Sokol was like a museum of the never-achieved socialist dream of beauty, a paradoxical individualized and human wart on the body designed in iron molds of the strict Soviet city planned by Stalin ever since he set out to "perform a cesarean section on old Moscow," too chaotic and stately for his tastes as the Supreme Urbanist.

"Stalin ordered Golianovo built after the war. As always, he gave a deadline to finish the buildings, without it mattering too much how they turned out," Eitingon said as he made space for his wife to place a casserole on the table with *kholodets*, pig's-foot gelatin, for which she brought a bottle of mustard and a plate with rounds of strongly flavored wild radish as accompaniments. "But if the apartments are small and ugly, the fault, of course, is of imperialism, which is also responsible for Soviet shoes being so hard and for there being no deodorant and for the toothpaste irritating your gums."

Luis smiled, denying something with his head, as he served himself the *kholodets* with the spicy radishes that Ramón detested.

"You're such a funny man, Kotov . . . Man, I remember when I met you in Barcelona. I was practically a boy and look, I'm already bald."

Lionia looked quickly at the kitchen, to where his wife had returned, and warned in a low voice, making use of Catalan:

"It's forbidden to mention Caridad."

"Does Yenia understand Catalan?"

"No. But just in case. Don't we have the most educated people in the world here?"

It was now Ramón who smiled.

"Stop fucking around and speak in Russian," Galina demanded in Spanish. "Besides, Caridad is an ugly old woman full of wrinkles."

"The devil doesn't get wrinkly inside," Eitingon said, and the rest agreed.

"I remember when Kotov talked to me about the Soviet Union," Luis recalled, and took his wife's hand. "I dreamed of this, and the day I arrived was one of the happiest in my life. I had arrived at the future."

"And you got to the future . . . ," Eitingon said through some pieces of lard in his mouth, and rinsed his mouth with a glass of vodka. "According to our leaders, *this* is the future. The West is the decadent past. And the most fucked-up thing is that it's true. Capitalism already gave everything it could. But it's also true that if the future is like Golianovo, people are going to prefer the decadence with deodorant and real cars for a long time. The world is at the bottom of a trap and the terrible thing is that we squandered the opportunity to save it. Do you know what the only solution is?"

"You're joking that you have a solution!" Luis was surprised, and Eitingon smiled, satisfied.

"Close this shop and open another one, two streets down. But start the business without deceiving anyone, without fucking anyone over because he thinks differently from you, without looking for reasons to shut you up and without telling you that when they give it to you up the ass, it's for your own good and for the good of humanity, and that you don't even have the right to protest or say it hurts, because you shouldn't give ammunition to the enemy and all of those justifications. Without blackmail . . . The problem is that the ones who decide for us decided that a little bit of democracy was okay but not too much . . . and in the end, they even forgot about the little bit we were due, and that whole thing that was so beautiful turned into a police station dedicated to protecting power."

"So you're no longer a Communist?" Luis asked, lowering his voice.

"They're different things. I'm still a Communist, I will be until I die. The ones who became the masters of everything and prostituted it all, are they Communists? The ones who deceived me and deceived Ramón, were those Communists? Please, Luis . . ."

Galina drank her vodka and spoke into the bottom of the glass.

"Was Trotsky a Communist? Khrushchev invited Natalia Sedova to visit Moscow. She refused, but the fact that they invited her shows something."

"Khrushchev was always a clown," Eitingon pronounced, and filled his glass.

Without making a comment, Ramón touched his hand where the half-moon scar showed. It was pathetic to him that his former boss was playing the victim. Eitingon, for his part, seemed upset. He picked a little bit from each plate, as if he were anxious, and at that moment Ramón remembered the lavish dinners, with delicate wines, that they allowed themselves in Paris, New York, and Mexico in their days as agents with expenses paid by the coffers of the Soviet state. How much of that money, he wondered, came from Spanish treasures?

"The country of the future. Stalin ordered the killing of millions of people," Eitingon railed. "But what they ordered us to do was excessive. We should have left the old man to die of loneliness or to mess things up in his desperation, leaving only himself covered in shit. We saved him from oblivion and made him a martyr—"

"That's enough," Ramón cut him off, refusing to listen to that reasoning. "Do we have to talk about this?" And he dropped a stream of vodka into his orange juice.

"What else can we the shipwrecked talk about but the sea, Ramón Pavlovich? Let's toast—to the shipwrecked of the world! To the bottom!" And he drank the vodka.

Following his cry, silence fell over the small room, but from the kitchen came Yevgenia Purizova's voice announcing that the *pelmenis* were ready. Leonid, Luis, and Galina focused on finishing their appetizers, and did so meticulously, something that always frightened Ramón. Wiping his mouth with the back of his hand, Eitingon stood up, and while the visitors cleared the table of empty bottles and plates, the host placed another basket of black bread, the tray with pickled cabbage and lard, a plate with meats and boiled potatoes, oil, and vinegar, and finally handed out clean plates, from different sets. Yenia entered with a slightly dented casserole and placed it in the center of the table; Ramón found that the sight of the *pelmenis* brought back his appetite.

"The girls ate already. They're watching television at a neighbor's house. Serve yourselves as much as you like."

She sprinkled the *pelmenis* with vinegar and Ramón tasted how Eitingon's wife's *pelmenis*, full of lamb meat, were much better than the ones Galina usually cooked.

"Lionia told me that your wife travels to Mexico every year," Yenia commented, trying to sound casual in the middle of the din of silverware, the clinking of glasses, and the noise of chewing jaws.

"She's getting ready for the trip right now. As soon as winter comes, she goes running."

547

Yenia smiled as if it were a joke.

"How nice to be able to travel . . . ," she said, pricked a *pelmeni*, held it in the air, and dared to ask, "Could you ask her to bring us some pretty clothing for the girls? I would pay her, of course," she rushed to clarify.

Ramón finished chewing and nodded.

"Tell me their sizes. I'll take care of it."

"Lionia says you have a very pretty apartment," Yevgenia Purizova continued, satisfied at having gotten her point across so expeditiously. Surely, in her mind, she could already see the pants, blouses, shoes, and hair barrettes that her daughters could show off, and the distinction that those different objects could give them: it would be that wind from the West, so demonized but so desired by each one of the Soviets.

"We bought the furniture and a lot of the decorative objects with the money we get from the things Roquelia sells . . ." Ramón smiled and poured a little more vinegar over his *pelmeni*s before attacking the potatoes and the roast meat.

While Yenia prepared tea and coffee, Ramón tasted one of the apple pastries Galina brought and got ready to face the most arduous part of those Russian banquets. Eitingon would try to liven up the night with his songs and toasts. Muttering under his breath, the host searched for music on the radio, but on almost all of the stations the announcers were talking without any intention of stopping, and when he found one transmitting a piece no one could identify, he left the receiver's volume on low.

"I've been meaning to ask you for a few days now, kid . . . Have you found out through your current friends if they know anything about África?"

Ramón looked him in the eye. The sharp blue of his former mentor's pupils had dissolved in alcohol, but continued to be sharp.

"Why are you asking me that?"

"Because I lost her trail ever since they took me out of the game . . . I know that during the war she worked as a radio operator with the guerrillas who infiltrated the rear guard and won several medals of courage . . . I imagine she wasn't one of the ones who were affected by Stalin's gratitude."

" 'Stalin's gratitude'?" Galina asked, attracted by such strange words.

"Stalin was very generous with the ones who served him, right? . . ." Eitingon's laugh was painfully forced. Not even the vodka he had drunk eased his bitterness. "In reality, the best that could happen to you was that he forgot about you. He didn't forget about me . . . After the war, the witch hunt began again, inside and outside the Soviet Union. But after the horrors of the Nazis and two atomic bombs, who could criticize him for killing a hundred or two hundred or a thousand former collaborators accused of treason? One of the ones who paid dearly for Stalin's gratitude was Otto Katz, one of the best agents we ever had. He was the one who pointed out Sylvia Ageloff and prepared the ground for us in New York."

Sylvia's name stirred Ramón's memory more forcefully than África's or Trotsky's. He could not forget how, every time the police had them face each other in numerous confrontations, the woman turned into a spitting demon, and when he thought of her, he still felt the warmth of her saliva running down his face.

"No one worked as much or as dirtily as Willi Münzenberg and Otto Katz did to consolidate Stalin's image in Europe. Willi was killed in France, during the German invasion. I still don't know if it was the Nazis or us who did it . . . But Otto kept working, and after the war he thought the time had come for his reward. Stalin considered him and others of his kind to be troublemakers and decided the time had come to show his gratitude . . ." Leonid worked himself up and continued. "Otto Katz was locked up in Prague and forced to confess to any number of crimes. The day of his public confession, they had to make him a set of dentures from the teeth of an executed man, since he had lost all of his own teeth during the interrogations. Otto and several others were executed and thrown in a common grave on the outskirts of Prague . . ." And turning toward Ramón, he added: "That's why I asked you if you've heard anything about África."

Ramón drank the coffee Yevgenia Purizova served him and lit a cigarette.

"She was working in South America until she retired with honors . . . Since I arrived, I've only seen her once. Now she gives conferences and belongs to the KGB aristocracy . . . In 1956 she wrote me a letter in prison."

Ramón would have preferred not to talk about that story that he had buried with so much effort. Because of that, he only told them that, in her letter, África de las Heras told him she was still working and that she was committing a serious infraction by writing to him, even risking her life, but she wanted to tell him that she congratulated him on the integrity—a communist integrity—with which Ramón had faced his years in prison. Ramón did not tell them that what África wrote to him almost amused him—it seemed like a caricature of the harangues the young woman launched in the meetings in Barcelona—if the news that followed had not moved him to the point of tears: Lenina had died two years before, having just turned twenty. His happiness on receiving that letter, signed by María Luisa Yero, but whose handwriting he recognized like the scar etched on his right hand, turned into a death pain from which he would never be able to free himself. Lenina had joined an anti-Franco guerrilla unit and died in a skirmish. Her parents could be proud of her, África said, with unnatural coldness, like someone issuing a war report. Ramón, who had already perfected his strategy of imagining a life parallel to his real one, tried to fit into his impossible existence the daughter he had never met, whom he had never kissed, and tried to conceive of how that girl's days would have been spent with parents capable of raising her, protecting her, and giving her love. The fact that he had never had even the remotest possibility of influencing the life of a person he created did not alleviate the strange pain caused by the death of a being who, since the beginning, had only been a name. The cause or family? Ramón had felt the weight in his chest of the fundamentalism to which he had submitted and that had prevented him from even weighing the possibility that it was not necessary to abandon his ideas in order to go looking for his daughter. Then he thought he would never forgive África for her sick orthodoxy and for having excluded him from a decision that was also his. But at the same time he had to recognize his own faults and weaknesses. Hadn't he accepted and considered África's will as logical, historically and ideologically correct? He had only the small consolation of telling himself that, like Lenina, he would also have fought against Franco and that perhaps having died as she did was preferable to living as he did with an unyielding scream in his ears and the certainty of having been a puppet.

Galina broke the silence and took his hand. "What's wrong, Ramón?" Eitingon's snores brought him back to reality.

"Nothing, just a bad memory . . . Lionia isn't going to sing. Shall we leave?"

The solitude prompted by Roquelia's trips and the forced confinement brought about by the devastating Muscovite winter allowed Ramón to recover one of his oldest passions: cooking.

In the years he spent in prison—following that initial period of interrogations, blows, and solitary confinement and ending with his sentence for homicide—he had felt an urgent need to focus his intellectual energies and asked his lawyer to buy him books to study electricity and learn languages. The mysteries of electric flows and the inner lives of languages had always attracted him, and at that moment, with seventeen years of prison ahead of him (he was starting to lose hope that his conspirators could organize his escape) and threatened by the claws of madness, he felt that he could and should satisfy his intellectual curiosities. Thanks to this, his stay in prison was more pleasant. Studying, his mind escaped the creaking Lecumberri, an authentic circle of hell, and his knowledge allowed him freedoms and privileges denied to the illiterate and coarse criminals crowded together in the compound. By 1944, inmate Jacques Mornard, known as Jac by his fellow prisoners, was acting as the person responsible for Lecumberri's electrical workshop and would soon take over the leadership of carpentry as well as the sound system for the prison's stage and movie theaters. His rapid rise, supported by certain directors of the prison in contact with emissaries from Moscow, gave rise to more than a little envy, and forced him to remind more than one prisoner that if he had driven an ice axe into the head of a man who had led an army, it mattered very little to him to cut the arm off a fucking nobody. His prestige among his fellow inmates increased notably when, in the middle of his studies of Russian and Italian, he found out about the governmental program through which he could reduce his sentence by one year if he taught fifty of his companions to read. Jac went to work and, with the help of Roquelia, who brought the printed cards, and with that of her cousin Isidro Cortés, imprisoned with him, they managed to teach almost five hundred prisoners how to read, the highest number ever achieved in the entire Mexican penal system. The prison authorities gave him a diploma but communicated to him that they could not apply the stipulated bonus to him unless he recognized his identity and the true motives for his crime. Ramón, as always, repeated that his name was Jacques Mornard and remained satisfied that the inmates who benefited from his work—besides teaching them literacy, he turned many of them into electricians—expressed their gratitude with the most coveted prison currencies: respect and peace.

But Ramón was always a special prisoner, not only because he enjoyed a certain protection, but also because things worked a different way for him. He wasn't granted the reduction in his sentence nor was he allowed to marry Roquelia, since if he married her, he could remain in Mexico and Mexico didn't want him—though they helped Siqueiros get out of the country. Pablo Neruda, the Chilean consul at that time, took him with him. And Diego Rivera, when he wanted to return to the party, began to say publicly that he had housed Trotsky so it would be easier to kill him and everyone laughed along with him. Ramón was sickened by those things. But he was the rejected one: the hypocrites of the world said they were disgusted by him, even as they laughed at the jokes of the cuckold Rivera and the coward Siqueiros (who had even dared to send him a painting as a gift).

Once he was settled in Moscow, his knowledge of various languages served to give some meaning to his time and, at the same time, to earn some extra money with his translations. Meanwhile, his love of cooking, also cultivated in prison, besides filling his hours, allowed him to hand himself over to the nostalgia of his Catalan youth and give flight to his dreams.

For four or five years, Ramón prepared a great dinner to send off Roquelia, who, at the first threat of snow, stepped on the plane taking her to Mexico. On that occasion, in addition to the usual guests he was allowed contact with (Luis and Galina, Conchita Brufau and her Russian husband, a couple of friends from the Casa de España, and Elena Feerchstein, the Soviet Jew with whom he worked on his translations), Leonid Eitingon and his wife Yenia would be there.

That morning, as soon as Ramón began to work in the kitchen, Roquelia, who hated any change in her routine, shut herself up in her room under the pretext of preparing her suitcases. Since Arturo and Jorge were at school, it was young Laura, seated on a stool, and Dax and Ix the wolfhounds, who were the privileged witnesses of the preparation of the meal and of the chef's commentaries on the ingredients, proportions, and cooking times. In reality, Ramón had begun to prepare that Catalan meal a week before. The difficulty of finding certain ingredients in Moscow limited Ramón's gastronomic possibilities, and after running (medals at the ready) to various markets and gathering everything that seemed usable, he had opted for an *arroz a banda* as his artillery appetizer and some pigs' feet (he lamented not having found the thyme called for by the traditional recipe) for the big offensive. There would be *pan con tomate*, and crêpes with orange marmalade would bring the agape to a close.

Conchita Brufau would bring some wines from Penedès, while Luis brought two bottles of cava for the toasts the Soviets were such fans of.

Those gastronomic journeys to their Catalan origins, which he usually shared with Luis and occasionally with his brother Jorge, a professional chef, hid Ramón Mercader's warmest and most longed-for hope for a return to Spain. During the months Roquelia spent in Mexico, Ramón and Luis multiplied their meetings in the apartment's kitchen. Besieged by snow, they tended to use meals to bring back memories and voice hopes. Luis, who was already past forty, dreamt that, with the death of El Caudillo (the bastard had to die someday), Spain's doors could open again to the thousands of refugees still wandering the world. The youngest Mercader still had hope of obtaining an exit visa from the USSR, so complicated for him despite his origins, and very difficult for Galina and his children because of their Soviet nationality. Ramón, in contrast, knew he would never be allowed to leave Soviet territory and that, in addition, no country in the world, starting with Spain, would deign to receive him. But in the dreams he voiced, Ramón usually told Luis about his plans to open a restaurant on the Empordà coast, specifically on the beach of Sant Feliu de Guíxols. There, in the pleasant months of spring and fall, and in the warm ones of summer, he could earn his living preparing dishes that would improve in taste, consistency, and appearance with every effort. Living in front of the sea, free of fear and the feeling of isolation, and without having to hide his own name, would be the happy culmination of his strange and miserable life.

A few months before, Ramón had made the mistake of discussing that yearning with Santiago Carrillo, the leader of the Spanish Communists. Carrillo had told him, as Ramón expected, that his case was, at the very least, special, and that it wouldn't be easy to free himself of the chains tying him to Moscow. Didn't anyone remember that, according to very well-covered-up memories, Carrillo must have been stained by the blood of the regrettable executions of prisoners in Paracuellos? . . . For now, like the rest of the refugees, every night before going to sleep Ramón should pray, communistically, for Franco's death, and then they would see. But the dream, the beach, the heat, kept beating in him, like an unreachable desire that was not possible to give up.

That late October dinner was a success. Even Roquelia was in a good mood (the proximity of her departure had that effect), and everyone praised Ramón's culinary skills. Leonid Eitingon, in addition to devouring an impressive quantity of pigs' feet, drank wine, cava, vodka, and even Cuban rum from a bottle brought by Elena Feerchstein, and seemed to be the happiest of men. After taking the lead with the toasts, he was the first one to start singing the old words to Republican anthems. With cigars between their lips, they posed for a photo, and Conchita Brufau told half a dozen jokes that revolved around the supposed resurrection of Lenin or Stalin. But the most successful one was about the best way to hunt a lion:

"It's very easy: you grab a rabbit and begin to beat him and tell him you're going to kill his whole family . . . Until he confesses that he's actually a lion dressed as a rabbit."

"I like seeing all of you like this," Eitingon said. "Happy and relaxed . . . Perhaps you don't know that these buildings are made of micro-concrete?"

"Micro-concrete?" Elena Feerchstein asked.

"Twenty percent microphones and the rest is concrete . . ."

That night, impelled by the alcohol he allowed himself on this occasion, Ramón thought that, despite the confinements, silences, deceptions, and even the fear and the obsession with real and imagined microphones, life was worth living. Eitingon was the exultant proof of that. His cynicism, resistant to blows and years in prison, was protective and exemplary. And wasn't he as cynical as his mentor? He thought that having believed and fought for the greatest utopia ever conceived of required a necessary dose of sacrifice. He, Ramón Mercader, had been one of those dragged along by the subterranean rivers of that battle, and it wasn't worth evading responsibility or trying to blame his faults on deception and manipulation; he was one of the rotten fruits cultivated in even the best of harvests, and while it was true that others had opened the doors, he had gladly crossed the threshold of hell, convinced that a life in the shadows was necessary for a world of light.

Past midnight, when the goodbyes were imminent, Luis asked Ramón to accompany him to the kitchen. With his nearly finished cigar at the corner of his mouth, Luis leaned against the small table where the crockery that Ramón (as part of his arrangement with Roquelia) had to wash before going to bed was piled.

"What's going on? Do you need something?" Ramón served himself a little coffee and lit a cigarette. He felt the alcoholic euphoria of a little earlier morphing into a diffuse but absorbing sadness.

"I didn't want to ruin your party, but . . ."

Ramón looked at his brother and remained silent. Experience had taught him that there was no need to push bad news, as its weight always propels it forward.

"Caridad is coming in two days. She called me this afternoon."

Ramón looked outside. The sky was reddish, announcing the coming snow. Luis dropped his extinguished tobacco in the wastebasket.

"She asked me if she could stay with you. Since Roquelia is leaving . . ."

"No. Tell her no," Ramón said, almost without thinking about it, and returned to the living room, where the visitors were putting on their coats to leave. Ramón bid them farewell with promises of speedy reunions, and when Leonid Eitingon went to kiss him, he moved his face and pressed it against the adviser's ear.

"Caridad is coming," he told him, and kissed him.

Ramón could see how Eitingon's blue eyes regained the brilliance dulled by the alcohol. The mere mention of that name seemed to reveal in him intricate chemical reactions that had to be beyond an already worn sexual empathy. He and Caridad were definitively kindred souls, united in their capacity to hate and destroy.

"I'll call you tomorrow, kid." He smiled and, with his gloved hand, patted Ramón's face.

"No, it would be better if you didn't call me again . . . I'm sick of rolling around in shit."

As he washed the dishes, Ramón put a record of Greek songs he had grown fond of on the record player at a very low volume. His mother's imminent visit was disquieting, and when he was drying the plates, he stopped to observe the arc-shaped scar on his right hand. Those marks on his skin, the scream in his ears, and the shadow of Caridad were like the chains tying him to his past, and the three could be terribly heavy if he tried to move them together. The scar and the scream were indelible, but at least he could keep his mother far away. In prison, accompanied by the scream and the scar, he had continued hating Caridad, blaming her for the failure of his escape plans. But he remembered that during the infinite psychological exams he had been subjected to in Mexico, the specialists thought they saw, in the midst of that hate, the presence of an obsession for the maternal figure that some classified as Oedipal. When he learned of such opinions, he chose to laugh in the psychologists' faces, but he knew that something lost in his subconscious must have freed itself through an unforeseen channel, alerting the specialists. The memory of Caridad's kisses, whose warm and aniseed-flavored saliva caused ambiguous feelings in him; the unease it always caused him to see her in the company of other men; and the uncontrollable power his mother had exercised over him had an unhealthy component from which he had tried to free himself through distance and hostility. The psychologists' opinion had made him meditate on her attitude toward him and on his weakness before her, and he began to rescue from his memory caresses, words, gestures, closeness, and palpitations that seemed painfully perverse to him.

Despite the exhaustion of an entire day of work and of having drunk more than he usually did, Ramón tossed and turned in his bed, pursued by the idea of a reunion with his mother, until dawn became visible in the sky and he watched the first snowfall of that autumn. Contemplating the snow, Ramón recalled the train trip he had taken at the end of 1960 to the limits of Soviet Asia, in the company of Roquelia, two young KGB officers, their guides and custodians. After twenty years of confinement, that trip was supposed to be a liberation, the enjoyment of moving for days and days, crossing such diverse worlds, crossing time zones and the logic of time (a few feet from where it is now today, you can return to yesterday or jump to tomorrow). With his own eyes, he discovered the country's economic strength, the schools built across its immense territory, the dignity of the poverty of its Uzbek, Kyrgyz, and Siberian children, a new world that made him feel rewarded—made him think that his personal sacrifice had been for something. But the return trip caused a contradictory feeling. It was not due to the fact that, in the two days the train was stopped due to a freeze, the restaurant car had turned into a kind of combination bar and latrine when a group of soldiers took it over and spent each hour of the delay drinking vodka, urinating, and vomiting in corners. What happened was that remaining immobile, surrounded by the infinite and impenetrable whiteness of the frozen steppe, returned to him an overwhelming feeling of powerlessness, more crushing than what he had felt in the many cells in which he had lived. Something in that January Siberian landscape paralyzed and oppressed him. And that oppression, he thought, was the exact opposite of confinement: it was the result of immeasurableness, of the oceanic immensity of the white landscape that could only be seen for a few hours each day. It suffocated him, and he understood that the infinite whiteness could overwhelm him to the point of madness.

Ramón wasn't aware of the exact moment he had fallen asleep. When he awoke, close to eight, he saw Ix's and Dax's anxious faces next to the bed, long after the time for their morning evacuations had already passed. The brief sleep, nonetheless, had not freed him from the growing unease that plagued him throughout the night.

As he got dressed, he placed the coffee on the stove. He saw on the balcony thermometer that the temperature was minus eight degrees and observed Gorky Park, on the other side of the river, completely covered by clean snow. When he withdrew the coffee pot, he placed the wide blade of a knife very similar to the one he had used in Malakhovka over the gas flame. He drank the coffee, lit a cigarette, and smoked until he saw the color of the steel go red. He put out his cigarette, wetting it in the sink, looked for the dishrag he had used the night before to dry the plates, and folded it twice, biting down forcefully on it. With his left hand, he took the knife's handle, which had turned from red to white, and, with his eyes closed, placed the tip over the scar on his right hand. The pain made his knees buckle and prompted tears and some smothered cries. He threw the knife into the sink, where he heard it sizzle in the water. When he opened his eyes, he saw wisps of grayish smoke and spit out the rag. The smell of burned flesh was sweet and nauseating. He opened the faucet and stuck his hand under the freezing water as he wet his face with his left hand. Relief came when the cold made his hand fall asleep. He took a handkerchief out of his pocket and, after drying his face, covered the seared skin, under which, he supposed, the scar had disappeared. He felt, despite the pain, that his soul weighed less. He took another clean handkerchief, wrapped his hand again, and went out.

Ix and Dax's anxiety made them bark a couple of times as they went down in the elevator. The building's watchman made a comment about the weather and the preparations for the parade for the anniversary of the revolution that Ramón, wounded by pain, barely heard. Awkwardly, with his left hand he wrapped his scarf around himself twice and went out to the path, where his borzois were already running with their snouts stuck to the ground. Ix and Dax started to run through the snow, like two children stepping on it for the first time. Snowflakes were still falling here and there and Ramón raised the hood of his jacket. With the dogs' leashes in his left hand and a cigarette between his lips, he crossed the Frunze Quay and descended the stairs that went down from the sidewalk to a platform that was almost level with the river.

Leaning against the metal railing, with his dogs seated next to him, his jacket sprinkled with snow, and his hand wrapped in a black-polka-dotted handkerchief, Ramón began to smoke with his eyes fixed on the flowing river, on whose banks a layer of glitter had formed. Instead of that dirty and frozen river, would he ever again see the resplendent beach of Sant Feliu de Guíxols? The pain and bitterness painted a frown on his lips, when he said out loud:

"Jo sóc un fantasma."

Breathing in the frozen air, feeling the burning pain rising up through his arm, again that specter who had once been called Ramón Mercader del Río imagined how his life would have been if on that remote early morning, on the side of the Sierra de Guadarrama, he had said no. Surely, he thought, as he liked to do, he would have died in the war, like so many of his friends and comrades. But above all, he told himself—and that was why he liked to get caught up in that game—that other fate would not have been the worst, because in those days the true Ramón Mercader, young and full of faith, was not afraid of death: he had opened all the windows of his spirit to the collective mind, to the struggle for a world of justice and equality, and if he had died fighting for that better world, he would have earned himself an eternal spot in the paradise of pure heroes. At that moment Ramón thought how much he would have liked to have seen that other Ramón come to his side, the true one, the hero, the pure one, and to be able to tell the story of the man that he himself had been all those years in which he had lived the longest and most sordid of nightmares.

30

Requiem

Thirty-one years ago, Iván confessed to me that for a long time he had dreamed of going to Italy. In the Italy of his yearning, Iván could not have gone without doing several things: visiting the Castel Sant'Angelo; going, as if on a pilgrimage, to Florence and contemplating the Tuscan landscapes that Leonardo had once seen; standing amazed before the city's Duomo and its green marble; wandering around Pompeii like someone reading an eternal book about the eternity of life, passion, and death; eating a pizza and real spaghetti, preferably in Naples; and, to guarantee his return, throwing a coin in the Trevi Fountain. Until the arrival of the great moment, Iván had fed his dream by studying the works of Leonardo (although it was Caravaggio whom he was really crazy about), seeing Visconti's and De Sica's movies, reading Calvino's and Sciascia's Sicilian novels, and swallowing the spongy pizzas and bland pastas that became widespread on the island in the seventies and assuaged so much of our hunger for so many years. His was a desire so persistent, so well designed, that I have come to wonder whether in reality Iván had studied journalism with the hope of someday being able to travel (to Italy) in those times when almost no one traveled and no one did so unless it was an official mission.

The first time my friend spoke to me of the existence and later fading of that dream so Cuban and so insular, of escaping from the island, was on the terrace of his house, two or three months after we met. Around that time, I was the worst-read student in the literature department, and that day Iván, after talking to me about his lost hope, put in my hands a novel by Pavese and another one by Calvino, while I asked myself how it was possible that a guy like him could give up and, at just twenty-some years of age, talk about dead dreams when we all knew that we still had a future ahead of us that announced itself as luminous and better.

The last time I saw Iván alive was three days after Ana's death. That night at the end of September 2004, while we engaged in the strangest conversation, at a given moment I found the story of Iván's Italian dream in the bottomless bowl of lost desires. I will perhaps never know if the recuperation of that thirty-one-year-old memory was the unconscious manifestation of a premonition or if it was my brain's preemptive answer to the question of the origins of the disaster.

After that night, I would live for several weeks trapped in the swamp of contradictions, feeling myself sinking in the mud of my egotism. In any event, since Iván didn't come by my house again, I took refuge in his demand not to see him again, since that's what he had asked upon saying goodbye to me, and I acted in a petty and puerile way, refusing to give in and go in search of him once more, although I knew it was my duty. Nonetheless, every time I ran into friends like black Frank or Anselmo, I asked them if they had seen Iván, and it didn't surprise me, or rather it calmed me down to always hear that they hadn't seen him, that he didn't want to see anyone, that he was writing something. And, like a good mediocre writer (and to top it off, without inspiration), I took refuge behind that excuse and didn't try to seek him out.

I know that my distance was also due, more than to any envious feelings, to the fear of a responsibility that Iván had thrown at me and that I didn't know how to manage: what was I going to do with what Iván was writing? Keep it in a drawer, as he did? Try to publish it, as he could also do but didn't want to? That absurd decision of my friend to hand over his work and his obsession of years to me, cutting all ties with that story and with his own life, seemed to me sick and, above all, cowardly. They were his problem, his book, his story and not mine, I thought.

It goes without saying, at this point, that Ana's death was a greater blow for Iván than all of us, including Iván himself, could have imagined.

Although in his final months, tormented by the impotence and pain caused by seeing her suffer—more than once he had confessed that it was preferable that she finally rest—Ana's irreversible absence submerged him in a melancholy from which my friend had no power or desire to emerge.

On that last visit I made to the small apartment in Lawton, the first thing I confirmed was how urgently Iván had to pull himself away from those testimonies of pain amid which he had lived for I don't know how many years. The activity that had unfolded in the days leading up to the burial had to have been frenetic, since, when I entered his house, the first thing I noticed was the disappearance of all hospital-related objects, which had overtaken that space. Along with the reclining bed and the wheelchair, the support for the IVs, the bedpans, the needles and the medicine bottles and even the color television with remote control (lent by a neighbor, so that Ana could entertain herself with something easier to see than the blinking black-and-white TV set that a client from the clinic had given to Iván before leaving Cuba a few years before). The floors smelled of cheap disinfectant and the walls, as always, of mildew, not alcohol and liniments. Even Iván had thrown himself into a metamorphosis. He had shaved his head and was exhibiting a skull plagued with hills and crossed by the river of the scar that, many years before, had been given to him by his adversaries in the bar fight that landed him in the trauma center of Calixto García Hospital.

The change in the atmosphere and his appearance—which was like that of someone recently released from a concentration camp—made the physical devastation my friend had suffered in recent months more palpable (at some point the idea had crossed my mind that Iván was going to disappear and go to heaven), and better prepared me to hear, at the end of that night, the word, the feeling capable of paralyzing him that he had hidden for ten years, ashamed by the significance enclosed in an inappropriate reaction: *compassion*. Because at the end it wasn't so much fear as that cunning noun, from which he tried to free himself, the brick that maintains the building of delays, mysteries, concealment, behind which Iván had been lost.

"Why in the hell did you do that to your head? Do you know what you look like?" I said to him as soon as I saw him, but my friend didn't answer and accepted, with a sad smile, the container full to the brim with food my wife had prepared for him. In silence, Iván began to serve himself and, before sitting down to eat, went to the room and came back with an envelope in his hands.

"A long time ago you wanted to read this . . ."

As soon as I heard him, I guessed what it was about. They had to be, and in fact they were, the pages written more than twenty-five years before by Jaime López, the papers whose existence I had known about for ten years and that, every time the subject came up, I asked Iván to let me read, since I considered that, by reading them, I would touch with my own hands the elusive soul of the man who loved dogs.

As he ate, I delved into that story, the reflections and letters about the years in Moscow of a Ramón Mercader who, in a sick way, insisted on clinging to the embarrassing mediation through the ventriloquist Jaime López and in presenting himself as a person who could be viewed with a certain distance. Or was it that he felt so stripped of his own self, so removed from the original Ramón Mercader that he preferred, to the end, to continue being one of his disguises? The essential man, the primary one, the one who had been in the Sierra de Guadarrama—had he been devoured by the mission, the dogma, and the ruthlessness of history until turning into a character who could only be seen in the distance? What was written gave off the bad flavor of a confession barely capable of hiding the request for forgiveness and the frustration of a man who, from the perspective given to him by years and experienced events, at last confronted himself and what he had signified in a sordid intrigue destined to devour him to the last cell.

But the most alarming thing, at least for me, was discovering the commentaries and questions that, in tiny letters, Iván had added in the margins of the pages, with different-colored inks and a variety of nuances—signs of an excessive and obsessive return to those words over the course of the years. I asked myself whether Iván, more than interrogating the author of the confession, had not been looking for an answer lost within himself. The papers, in addition, were greasy, as if they had been through many hands, when I knew that Iván and the tall, thin black man who brought them to him (and Ana?) were the only ones who had laid eyes on them. I was alarmed by the relationship my friend could have established with that confidence and with the intangible being living behind it.

"I'm left with a desire to know what happened once Caridad arrived in Moscow and how Ramón managed to get them to allow him to leave . . . ," I told him when I finished reading, without daring to comment that my real concern had to do with him. Then Iván handed me a cup of recently made coffee and turned around, as if my curiosity did not interest him.

On the small table, Iván began to serve Truco's food. Since I'm not especially fond of dogs, that night I had forgotten about the animal, and it was only at that moment that I realized he had not come out to greet me. I looked for him and found him under an armchair, his eyes wide open, lying on a piece of fabric. Iván brought him the plastic plate; Truco smelled the food, but didn't muster any enthusiasm to taste it.

"Come on, boy, eat," Iván said to him, kneeling next to the animal, and added tenderly, as if he were surprised: "Come on, look, it's meat!"

"Is he sick?"

"He's sad," Iván assured me while he ran his hand over Truco's head. I noticed the dog's eyes, and although I'm not the type to believe those things, I seemed to detect a certain pain in his damp and disconsolate gaze. Iván showed him some food, but the dog turned his head. "He knows what happened. He hasn't eaten for three days. Poor Truco."

Iván's voice sounded regretful. He moved away from Truco, washed his hands, and drank his coffee. Seated at the table, he lit a cigarette while looking at his dog, and I remember that I thought: Iván is going to cry.

"What Truco has is called melancholy, and it's an illness that cures itself or it can kill him . . . ," he said, nearly dragging out the words. He took a few drags from his cigarette and finally looked at me. "Take those papers with you. I don't want them near me."

"What's wrong, Iván?" His attitude, more than surprising me, was starting to worry me. In his eyes there was a damp sadness identical to the one floating in his dog's look.

"Meeting that man was the worst thing that happened to me in my life. And quite a few fucked-up things have happened to me . . . I'm going to finish writing about how I met him and why I didn't dare to tell his story from the beginning. I don't want to do it, but I have to write it. When I finish, I'm going to give you all of my papers so you can do whatever you want with them . . . I am not a writer nor was I ever, and I'm not interested in publishing it or in having anyone reading it . . ."

Iván left his cigarette in the ashtray on the table. He seemed very tired, as if nothing mattered to him, and it even seemed to me that he was breathing with difficulty, like an asthmatic. When I was about to reproach him for his last words, he got ahead of me.

"I am also a ghost . . ."

At that moment I understood what Iván was trying to say to me a little bit better. And I thought the worst: he's going to kill himself.

"Why are you going to give me everything you've written? What does that mean?" I dared to ask him, fearing the worst, and I wanted to make things less dramatic. "Look, you're not Kafka . . ."

"I'm not going to kill myself," he said to me, after letting me suffer for a few seconds. "I'm not crazy, either. It's just that I don't want to see those papers anymore. It's better for you to have them, since you are still a writer . . . But if you want, you can burn them; it's all the same to me . . ."

"I don't understand, Iván. Doesn't the truth matter to you? That man was a son of a bitch and there's no excuse nor . . ."

"What truth? What is the truth? And he wasn't the only son of a bitch who did inexcusable things."

"Of course not. But he was one of the ones who helped Stalin turn twenty million people to ash in the name of communism . . . And he didn't kill just anyone . . . He killed another son of a bitch who, when he was in power, ripped the heads off of who knows how many people . . . All of this is too heavy, Iván. Note that the Russians, after having taken the lid off things, closed it all up again, nice and tight . . . You have to do a lot of terrible things to kill so many people . . ."

"Mercader was a victim, like most of them," he protested, less vehemently, as he looked at the lighter the man who loved dogs had left him as an inheritance.

"He was more than a victim, and that's why he couldn't live in peace. Do you know why he told you his story and then wrote this letter? So that you would write about it and publish it . . ."

Iván rubbed his shaved head forcefully, as if he wanted to erase something inside it. And he was saying he wasn't crazy?

"Sometimes I think like you do. But other times I believe it was the need of a dying man. It has to be really fucked-up to live your entire life as if you were someone else, saying you're someone else, and knowing it's better to hide behind the other name because you feel ashamed of yourself."

"What kind of shitty shame are you talking about? None of them had any shame or anything like it."

"Don't you think he paid for all his faults? Do you know that another prisoner from Lecumberri said that Ramón had been raped in prison?"

"He had to know what the risks were, and even then he accepted it . . . And it seems fine to me that his ass was ripped open in jail."

"He wasn't running around killing people . . . He was a soldier who followed orders. He did what they asked of him out of obedience and conviction . . ."

Iván stood up, served more coffee in the cups, but neither of us drank. He was looking at his dog again when he said to me:

"Do you know how I was sure that López was Mercader, before reading those papers—before seeing the photo?"

"I don't know . . . Because of what he said to you about Trotsky's scream, right?" I guessed, willing to give him a break: at the end of the day, Iván hadn't killed anybody or helped anyone else get fucked over. He was definitely a victim, after all.

"No, no, the key was the way he treated his dogs and how he looked at the sea. He was Mercader in search of the happiness he felt in Sant Feliu de Guíxols. His paradise lost . . . Cuba was a placebo."

"So how could you keep talking to him after being sure that he was Mercader?"

Iván looked into my eyes and I stared back. He mechanically drank his coffee, grabbed the cigarette packet, and removed another cigarette. How many was he going to smoke?

"I think I was never sure that he was Mercader. When López told me about Mercader's life, it seemed that he was talking about a man from long ago, I don't know, from the nineteenth century . . . And although it sounds morose, I wanted to know how that story ended. But above all, I felt he needed me to listen to him." He paused and lit a cigarette. "Do you know what bothers me most about this whole story?"

"The lies?"

"Besides the lies."

"That Stalin perverted it all? That likely his same comrades killed Mercader, poisoning him with radioactivity?"

"More than that."

I stayed silent. When you looked at it all, everything in that story bothered me. Iván smoked without taking his eyes off of me.

"What he stuck in here," he said, and pointed at his shaved head. "When I read those papers and had a clear idea of what Ramón Mercader had done, I felt disgust. But I also felt compassion for him, for the way in which he had been used, for the shame it caused him to be himself. I know: he was a murderer and doesn't deserve compassion; but I can't help it, dammit! Maybe it's true that his own people released radioactivity into his blood to kill him, as Eitingon says, but it wasn't necessary, because they had already killed him many times. They had taken everything away from him: his name, his past, his will, his dignity. And in the end, for what? Ever since he said yes to Caridad, Ramón lived in a jail that followed him until the very day of his death. Not even by burning his entire body or by believing he was someone else could he get rid of his history . . . But, despite it all, I felt bad knowing how he had ended up, because he had always been a soldier, like so many people . . . And if they killed him, you can't feel anything but compassion for him. And that compassion makes me feel dirty, contaminated by the faith of a man who should not deserve any compassion, any pity. That's why I refuse to believe that his own people killed him, because, in a way, that would make him a martyr . . . And I don't want to publish anything, because just to think that this story could move someone to feel a little bit of compassion makes me want to vomit . . ."

I looked at my friend and felt that I was finally beginning to understand something. His life (if you've come this far, you already know) had been a series of disgraces and unwarranted but unavoidable frustrations—so many and at the same time so common that it seemed incredible that the weight of his times and his circumstances could fall on one man alone. It was as if he personally was chosen to receive each one of the blows meant for an entire generation of people forced to be gullible. To top it off, he had lived with that damned story inside him for almost thirty years and had the disgrace that Ana, the purest thing in his life, should reproduce with her death Ramón Mercader's final torture and that he should see himself forced to watch, day after day, an agony that couldn't cease to remind him of a despicable and despised murderer. Even so, along with indignation, Iván felt compassion for that man and his fate, and that feeling provoked an intense rancor toward himself.

"Iván, he was one of them and they treated him ruthlessly, as they taught him from the beginning that others should be treated. But he doesn't deserve your compassion for any of that."

Iván thought for a few seconds. He must have been weighing the consequences of what he wanted to tell me, and just by looking at him I sensed that it wasn't going to be anything pleasant. It was at that moment that I remembered, I'm not sure through what association of ideas, the story of Iván's desire to travel to Italy.

"It's just that I can't go on : . ." he said at last. "I've spent my entire damned life with the feeling of trying to escape from something that always grabs me, and I'm tired of running . . . Now, take those papers and leave. Go on, I want to lie down."

Almost relieved, I stood up, but I did not grab the papers. When I went to leave, I turned around and saw him smoking again. Iván had his eyes fixed on Truco, who was sleeping in the corner. I felt pity for my friend and for his dog, real and justified pity, but also an enormous desire to tell it all to go to hell, to curse the entire world, to disappear. Of course, I didn't need to ask Iván what he had been trying to escape from throughout his life; I knew that he was fleeing from fear, but as he himself said, no matter how much you run and hide, fear always gets you. I know all too well.

"We're fucked. All of us," I said. I don't know if I said it out loud.

How is it possible that I let so much time go by? It's true that I was—am—also afraid, but Iván deserved more from me.

It wasn't until December 22 that I finally went out to search for Iván. My wife gave me the excuse, although it wasn't very good, that she wanted to invite him over to eat with us the night of the twenty-fourth. The problem was that Iván and I both had always hated the holidays and viewed the festive spirit that people assumed around that time as an obligation.

When I got to his apartment, I found the door and the window shut. I knocked several times, without any response. Something about the house seemed strange to me, although at that moment I didn't notice what could be out of the ordinary, besides the inscrutability and the silence.

Since it was barely three in the afternoon, I went to the veterinary clinic where Iván worked and also found it closed, with the chain and the lock he tended to put between the door and the doorframe. I asked a woman who lived across the street and she told me that Iván had not come for two or three days, and that had her worried: he was never away for so long.

I returned to Iván's block and knocked on the house of the neighbor who had lent the color television during Ana's illness. The man recognized me and invited me in, but I told him I was in a rush and just wanted to know if he had seen Iván.

"Three days . . . No, I haven't seen him in about three days."

I thanked him and, out of basic courtesy, I wished him a Merry Christmas, and the man responded with two words full of meaning:

"*Lo propio.*"

When I was walking toward the Pontiac, asking myself where in the hell Iván could have gone, I remembered that the Christmastime formula his neighbor had offered me was the same one that, according to my friend, he had said by way of farewell to the man who loved dogs, on the very day they met for the last time, exactly twenty-seven years ago. And at that moment, a light went off in my head. How was it possible that Truco didn't bark when I knocked at the door of the apartment? Iván and Ana's dog was a compulsive barker, and he would have stopped making noise for only a few reasons: if he was very sick, or if he wasn't at home, or— the most probable—because he had died, perhaps of melancholy over Ana's absence.

Overcome by a bad feeling, I switched course and went in search of the only public telephone working in the neighborhood, at the newspaper and magazine stand that doesn't sell newspapers or magazines. From there I managed to call Frank's and Anselmo's houses, and both of them confirmed that Iván hadn't been by in a long time. Then I called Raquelita and she said she hadn't seen Iván in ages and it would be better if she never again saw that "miserable *comemierda*." Sitting in the Pontiac, I started to think and saw very few alternatives. I didn't have the least idea of where to look for him, although I knew I should look for him. In this country, people don't tend to disappear: when someone gets lost it's because the sea swallowed them up or because they still don't have enough coins to make a phone call from the first telephone they find in Miami. But that wouldn't be Iván. Not at this point, not after everything he had lived through inside the island's four walls.

Suddenly I was inspired. I started the car and went to the cemetery. That place was deserted after the last burial of the afternoon. I looked for Ana's grave, in her family's section, and found everything in the horrifying state of neglect that the dead are always left in. A long time before, the floral wreaths had given way to the dust and dirt that had again taken over a place that didn't seem to have been visited by anyone for several weeks.

Outside the cemetery, I found another working telephone and called Gisela, Ana's sister. She didn't know anything about Iván, either; he hadn't even called her again after the burial. More and more alarmed, I remembered his family in Antilla, out in the east, with whom he had gone to live for a few weeks after leaving the ward for drug addicts at Calixto García Hospital. Since I was in the neighborhood of El Vedado, I drove to Raquelita's house (the spectacular mansion that her second husband, a fat jeweler and trafficker whom most of Havana knew as Alcides "the magician," one of socialism's winners, had "managed" to get for her) and I managed to get his ex to find, in an old notebook, a telephone number for Serafín and María, the cousins of Iván's mother, out in Antilla. Raquelita, despite herself, had become infected with my concern and made the call herself, receiving the same response: that the relatives in Antilla didn't even know about Ana's death. When I left Raquelita's mansion, I was weighed down by an additional pain in my chest, since it was obvious that Francesca wasn't too interested in what could have happened to her father, although it didn't surprise me to know that she was also trying to figure out how to leave the island—a decision that her brother Paolo and my children, typical representatives of their generation, had already beaten her to.

At night, as I pushed around, rather than ate, what my wife had served, I noticed how the worry had turned into a feeling of guilt, since I was convinced that something very serious had happened. I told my wife about the afternoon's search and she gave me the idea, which I hadn't thought of, of going to the police. It seemed ridiculous and excessive to me, but I started to consider the possibility. Something could have happened to him: perhaps he was in the hospital after having been in an accident, or having a heart attack; I don't know what the hell I thought. And what if he had really gotten on a balsa raft and still hadn't arrived anywhere or had drowned like his brother, William? . . . Almost at midnight I got dressed again, resolved to file a report at the station on Acosta Avenue, and when I was just two blocks away from the police building, I felt a flash of certainty. I went off course and went down to Lawton. I still didn't know (nor do I know now) why I was convinced of what I would find.

I entered the apartment through the dark and slippery hallway. In my hand I had the sledgehammer that I always keep in the Pontiac's trunk. In front of the door, I was surrounded by a stench I hadn't noticed that afternoon, giving proof to my bad feeling. Nonetheless, I knocked several times, yelled Iván's name and Truco's. Only silence answered. I didn't wait any longer. With just one blow of the sledgehammer, I busted open the door, so rotten it almost fell off the frame. The stench intensified immediately, and I felt for the light switch, taking care not to run into the wooden stanchions holding up the structure. When the apartment lit up, I saw what I never wanted to see: in the other room was the bed, sunk in, its legs broken by the weight on top of it. On top of the mattress, also sunk in by the weight, I managed to make out the shape of some legs, an arm, part of a human head, and also something of the yellow fur of a dog below the pieces of wood, concrete, and plaster. I raised my sight and saw that from the ceiling were hanging a few pins of steel, rotted and gnawed away, and beyond that, a flat and remote sky, without stars.

I grabbed one of the steel chairs and dropped into it. Before me was a disaster with apocalyptic resonance, the ruins of a house and a whole city, but above all, of dreams and lives. That murderous pile of rubble was a mausoleum that was apt for the death of my friend Iván Cárdenas Maturell, a good man whom fate, life, and history had destroyed. His cracked world had at last come undone and devoured him in that absurd and terrible way. The worst thing was knowing that in some way—in many ways—Iván's disappearance was also the disappearance of my world and the world of so many people who shared our space and our time. Iván had at last escaped, and left me as a legacy his cosmic frustrations, the malignant weight of a compassion that I didn't want to feel and a cardboard box, marked with my name, with all of those papers written by him and by Ramón Mercader, which were the best picture of his soul and his time . . . What was Iván thinking of when he heard the wooden beams creaking and saw death coming down on him from the sky, dragged by inertia and gravity, the only forces still capable of moving us? It's possible he wasn't thinking about anything: he had finished writing what he needed to write, only to fulfill a physiological need, and his life had turned into the most desolate of all voids. This is what we come to after so much walking, with our eyes blindfolded. And at that moment I remembered Iván telling me about his dog's melancholy, of the infinite freedom and the open windows to the collective mentality . . . And again the vague image came to mind of the Trevi Fountain, where neither Iván nor I were ever able to throw a coin.

At last, I've been able to read all of Iván's papers. More than five hundred typed pages, full of cross-outs and additions, but carefully ordered in three manila envelopes that he had also marked with my full name, Daniel Fonseca Ledesma, so as to avoid any confusion.

As I was reading, I felt how Iván ceased to be a person who was writing and turned into a character within what was written. In his story, my friend emerges as a representative of our times, like a figure who is sometimes exaggeratedly tragic, although with an indisputable breath of reality. Because Iván's role is to represent the masses, the multitude condemned to anonymity, and his character also functions as a metaphor for his generation and as the prosaic result of a historic defeat.

Although I tried to avoid it, and I twisted and turned and denied it to myself, as I read I started to feel compassion rise within me. But only for Iván, only for my friend, because he does deserve it, and a lot of it: he deserves it like all victims, like all the tragic creatures whose fates were decreed by forces greater than they were, that overwhelmed them and manipulated them until they were turned into shit. This has been our collective destiny, and to hell with Trotsky with his obstinate fanaticism and his belief that personal tragedies don't exist, only changes in social and superhuman stages. So what about people? Did any of them ever think about people? Did they ask me, did they ask Iván, if we agreed to postpone our dreams, lives, and everything else until they disappeared (dreams, life, and even the Holy Spirit) in historical fatigue and the perverted utopia?

I won't think about it too much, because I might regret it. I'll do the only thing I can do if I don't want to condemn myself to forever dragging around the deadweight of a story of crimes and deceptions, if I don't want to inherit every ounce of the fear that pursued Iván, if I don't want to feel guilty for having obeyed or disobeyed my friend's will. I am returning what belongs to him.

I am arranging these papers in a small cardboard box. I am beginning to seal it with tape until the entire surface is covered with the steel-colored strips. This morning I buried Truco next to the wall of the backyard of my house, and inside the death shroud I made for him I placed a copy of Iván's long-ago book of short stories, Mercader's lighter, and Ana's Bible. This afternoon, when they close my friend's casket, the shipwrecked cross (of all of our shipwrecks) and this cardboard box, full of shit, of hate, and of tons of frustration and a lot of fear will go with him—to heaven or to the materialist putrefaction of death. Perhaps to a planet where truth still matters. Or to a star where there is no fear and where we can even be happy that we feel compassion. To a galaxy where perhaps Iván knows what to do with a sea-worn cross and with this story, which isn't his story but in reality is, and which is also mine and that of so many other people who didn't ask to be in it but who couldn't escape it. They will perhaps go to a utopian place where my friend knows, without any doubt, what the hell to do with truth, trust, and compassion.

Mantilla, May 2006–June 2009

ACKNOWLEDGMENTS

The writing of this novel may have begun during the month of October 1989, when, though many did not yet suspect it, the Berlin Wall was perilously close to falling over and collapsing, which it did just a few weeks later.

At the time, I had just turned thirty-four and was making what would be my first trip to Mexico. Since I was convinced that Coyoacán was a very different place from the rest of the city, I managed to get Ramón Arencibia, a Cuban-Mexican friend and the owner of Mexico City's ugliest car, to take me to visit the house where Leon Trotsky lived and died. Despite my almost absolute ignorance of the ins and outs of that former Bolshevik leader's life and ideas (like any Cuban of my generation), and, as such, of not being even remotely Trotskyist, I think the fact that I was so moved as I wandered around that place—converted into a museum several years before and into a real monument to the anxiety, fear, and triumph of hate during the time the Trotskys lived there—provided the seeds from which, after a long incubation period, sprouted the idea of writing this novel.

When I faced developing the idea, more than fifteen years later and in the twenty-first century, with the USSR already dead and buried, I wanted to use the story of Trotsky's murder to reflect on how the twentieth century's great utopia was corrupted, that process in which so many invested their hopes and in which so many of us lost dreams, years, and even blood and lives. That is why I followed the episodes and chronology of Trotsky's life, in the years during which he was deported, harassed, and finally killed, with as much accuracy as possible (remember that we're talking about a novel, despite the overwhelming presence of history on each of its pages), and I tried to rescue what is known with certainty—in reality, very little—about the life or lives of Ramón Mercader, built in large part on speculation rooted in what could be verified and what was historically and contextually possible. The exercise that falls somewhere between verifiable history and fiction is as valid in the case of Mercader as it is for the many other real characters that appear in this novelistic tale—I repeat novelistic—and as such is organized according to the freedoms and demands of fiction.

Between the proposal of writing this novel and the exercise of actually writing it came years of thinking, reading, researching, discussion, and, above all, delving with shock and horror into at least a part of the truth of one of the twentieth century's exemplary stories and of the biographies of those shadowy but real characters who appear in the book. In this drawn-out process, the cooperation, knowledge, experience, and previous research of many people were essential to me. In some cases, they shared with me their experiences and even their doubts about a story that was often buried or twisted by leaders who, for seventy years, were the owners of power and, of course, history.

As always, between writing and the publication of what I had written, I would need the help that various friends extended in looking for information and, above all, in reading the many versions through which I shaped the novel, and in discussing its content and literary answers, an exchange which little by little allowed me to make adjustments regarding everything from the punctuation and the narrative viewpoints all the way to the historical and philosophical visions that I handle in the more than five hundred pages of this book.

That is why I want to express my enormous gratitude to all who, in one way or another, at one stage or other, with their patience, knowledge, or common sense, or simply behind the wheel of a car (like my friend Ramón Arencibia), helped me to conceive, outline, write, and rewrite this novel many times. In Spain, Javier Rioyo; José Luis López Linares; Jaime Botella; Felipe Hernández Cava; Luis Plantier; Xabier Eizaguirre; Emilia Anglada; and my old friend, who is of course Cuban, Lourdes Gómez, gave me their invaluable support. Moscow would never have revealed itself to me without the generosity and willing collaboration of Victor Andresco, Miguel Bas, Alexander Kazachkov (Shura), Tatiana Pigariova, Jorge Martí, and Mirta Karcick. In France, Elisa Rabelo and François Crozade, and my dear editor, Anne Marie Métailié, were my pillars. My good friend Johnny Andersen was my guide to Trotsky's Danish footsteps. I appreciate the reading by, the very valuable biographic contributions of, and the intelligence of my Mexican friends Miguel Díaz Reynoso and Gerardo Arreola, perhaps the most enthusiastic supporters of this project, and of the Peruvian researcher Gabriel García Higueras and of my Argentine friend Darío Alessandro. From Canada and England came the support of my professor-friends John Kirk and Steve Wilkinson. And among my many Cuban collaborators (or almost Cuban in some cases), I can't leave out the bookseller Barbarito, Dalia Acosta, Helena Núñez, Stanislav Verbov, Alex Fleites, Fernando Rodríguez, Estela Navarro, Juan Manuel Tabío, José Luis Ferrer (on the other side of the pond), Leonel Maza, Harold Gratmages, Doctor Fermín and Doctor Azcue, Lourdes Torres, Arturo Arango, and Rafael Acosta.

As is the case with my latest books, I'd like to note my special gratitude, for their work, passion, trust, and patience, to my Spanish editors Beatriz de Moura, Antonio López Lamadrid, and, above all, Juan Cerezo, who reviewed the book word by word with an intelligence, dedication, and love that few editors have anymore and that even fewer employ. My gratitude goes as well to Ana Estevan, who took care of editing the text. I have not forgotten, either, the enthusiastic and sharp reading by Madame Anne Marie Métailié . . .

Finally, I think I will never be able to completely appreciate the "Stakhanovist" work of my most loyal and persistent readers, Elena Zayas, in Paris, and Vivian Lechuga, here in Havana, who practically wrote the novel with me.

And, it couldn't be any other way, I must leave written testament of my deepest and most constant gratitude to my Lucía, who plunged into the story and helped me like no one else, and gave me the best ideas, but who, above all, put up with me during these five years of sadness, joy, doubts, and fears (remember Iván?), in which I devoted mornings, afternoons, evenings, and late nights to developing, shaping, and wresting from within me this exemplary story of love, madness, and death that, I hope, adds something to the history of how and why the utopia was corrupted and, perhaps, provokes compassion.

Leonardo Padura Fuentes
Always in Mantilla, Havana, summer 2009